KNOCKED *Up*

A SECRET BABY ROMANCE COLLECTION

Coralee June

Kaylie Ryan

Lacey Black

Rebecca Jenshak

Kelsey Clayton

Nikki Ash

Thank you for donating to a great cause!

Knocked Up: a Secret Baby Collection
© 2021 All rights reserved

Nicole Blanchard, Kaylee Ryan, K Webster, Nikki Ash, Lacey Black, Jacob Chance, Kelsey Clayton, J.D. Hollyfield, Rebecca Jenshak, CoraLee June, Heidi McLaughlin, Lauren Runow, Micalea Smeltzer, Jenika Snow, Marley Valentine, and Misty Walker.

Cover design: Nicole Blanchard
Cover photograph: Shutter Stock

ALL RIGHTS RESERVED. This collection of books contains material protected under International and Federal Copyright Laws and Treaties. Any unauthorized reprint or use of this material is prohibited. No part of this book may be reproduced or transmitted in any form or by any means, electronic or mechanical, including photocopying, recording, or by an information and retrieval system without express written permission from the Author/Publisher.

This is a work of fiction. Names, characters, places, and incidents either are the product of the author's imagination or are used fictitiously, and any resemblance to actual persons, living or dead, business establishments, events, or locales is entirely coincidental.

Authors Note

Settle in and get your fill of sixteen NEW secret baby stories where hidden secrets are revealed and couples that were once separated are reunited. Each story guarantees cuteness, sexiness, lots of love, and of course a HEA.

This collection includes stories from USA Today bestselling authors Nicole Blanchard, Kaylee Ryan, Jenika Snow, Marley Valentine, and K Webster. Nikki Ash, Lacey Black, Jacob Chance, Kelsey Clayton, J.D. Hollyfield, Rebecca Jenshak, CoraLee June, Heidi McLaughlin, Lauren Runow, Micalea Smeltzer, and Misty Walker.

FINDING PRINCE CHARMING
BY NIKKI ASH

Fairytales don't start out with a happily ever after. Neither does real life. Sometimes you have to struggle first before you find your Prince Charming.
- Unknown

CHAPTER ONE

NATALIE
EIGHT YEARS OLD

"ONCE UPON A TIME THERE LIVED A LITTLE..." MY MOM STOPS SPEAKING TO cough and I wait patiently for her to continue. Her coughing lately has gotten worse. I've asked her to go to the doctor, but she tells me she's fine.

I reach over across my bed and grab a tissue for her. When she wipes her mouth, blood smears the tissue. "Mom, are you okay?" I ask nervously. Something has to be wrong. Coughing up blood can't be good.

"I'm fine, baby," she says, a fake smile spreading across her lips. "Now, where were we?" She opens the book back up and starts over again. "Once upon a time there lived a little girl named Natalie."

I grin every time she says my name. One day, when I was little, we were walking through the mall to buy me some new shoes, when I came across a little store that sells books with names in them. The nice lady selling them found my name and, surprisingly, my mom bought it for me.

It took a lot of begging, but when we got home, I got her to read it to me—because at the time I wasn't old enough to read. It's about a little girl who sets off on a journey through the magical but evil woods to find her Prince Charming. She escapes all of the scary and bad obstacles standing in her way and makes it to the beautiful, enchanted castle, where she finds Prince Charming waiting for her. He scoops her up into his arms and tells her he loves her and they live happily ever after. From the first time I heard the story, it became my favorite.

"Why doesn't the prince leave his castle to look for the girl?" I ask Mom. "She has to go through all the bad stuff alone. Why didn't he just ride into the woods on his horse and save her?"

She sets the book down and glances over at me. I could easily read the story myself now, but she insists she reads it to me every time she's not high and there are no men in her bedroom—which seems to be a lot lately. The truth is, I'm too old for this book now, but I love my mom reading to me, and I love how the story makes me feel like a princess who'll one day escape these horrible, evil woods.

"Because the prince didn't know she was coming," she says. "And she didn't know the prince was waiting. He was her surprise after the long, scary journey."

"I want a prince," I admit out loud. A man who is kind and sweet, who will hug me and kiss me and give me a beautiful castle to live in. And if I found him, I would tell him my mom has to live with us too.

"One day you'll find your Prince Charming," Mom says, "and when you do, you'll live happily ever after."

"What if I don't find him?" My stomach drops. Or what if the man I find is like the gross, mean men who are always sleeping in my mom's room?

"Then you will find your own happily ever after."

CHAPTER TWO
NATALIE
NINETEEN YEARS OLD

"YEAH, BABY, JUST LIKE THAT. YOU'RE SO FUCKING GOOD TO ME." WESTON thrusts his dick down my throat. I choke and gag, saliva dripping down the sides of my mouth. It hurts, especially with the belt tight around my neck, but I don't stop him because I know it's what he likes. He likes to be rough, and I like him. I like the way he looks at me like he needs me. I like that when he comes here, he always picks me. He tells me he loves me and that I'm good to him.

"Fuck," he roars, coming down my throat. "I love you so fucking much." I take it all, then lick him clean, waiting for what he wants me to do next. It's hard to breathe, and I can feel the belt chafing against my throat and neck, but I don't complain. When I do, he gets upset.

"That was so good, baby," he croons, granting me a smile. "One day I'm going to steal you from here and you'll be all mine." He runs a finger down my cheek, and I smile the best I can. I shouldn't want him, shouldn't want this. But I crave the attention he gives me… even if it hurts.

"Turn over on your hands and knees," he demands, his grin morphing into something darker, more sinister.

I do as he says, but when I turn over, the belt tightens along my windpipe. Black dots appear in place of my vision. "I can't breathe," I rasp out before I can stop myself. Immediately, I regret it, because Weston doesn't like when I talk back.

The next second the belt tightens to the point I can't breathe at all, at the same time something hard enters my body. I try to scream for him to stop, scared that I'm going to die, but he doesn't. At some point, my body gives out, but before it does, my last thought is, I don't think Weston Hightower is my Prince Charming.

I WAKE UP IN A SOFT BED. MY ENTIRE BODY HURTS. BUT I'M STILL ALIVE. SO, there's that. I glance over and see Dr. Fox sitting next to me. "Good, you're awake." She grants me a soft, sad smile.

"How are you feeling?" another feminine voice asks. I look over at Cecilia. She's the madam of the bordello I work at.

"I'm okay," I tell them both, not wanting to complain. After my mom died when I was eight years old, I was bounced around from shitty foster home to shitty foster home, until I ran away at sixteen, where I spent the next two years selling my body on the streets of Las Vegas to earn barely enough money to feed myself.

One night while I was looking for a man to fuck—and pay for my dinner—I met Giovanni Valentino. He didn't fuck me, but he did pay for my dinner, and then he offered me a job at La Stella Gentleman's Club. It's a high-end bordello. Only the beyond wealthy and influential can even be considered for a membership here. We're given a room and clothes and are fed the best food. We're also paid really well. I love it. It's like living in my very own castle—even if there's no Prince Charming in sight.

"Did he force you?" Cecilia asks. I can see it in her eyes, even though she sounds like she cares, I know she doesn't. She's fake as hell and, if given the opportunity, will fire me in a heartbeat. She's obsessed with Giovanni, even though he's made it clear he can barely stand her, and if it were up to her, this bordello would be shut down so all the attention could be on her.

Yes, I think to myself, but I need this job… "No," I choke out, shaking my head. "I agreed to it." Cecilia looks at me like she doesn't believe me, and Dr. Fox sighs, but neither of them argues.

As Dr. Fox is going over the damage Weston inflicted on me, Giovanni saunters in, concern and anger etched in his features. He asks how I'm doing, and the doctor explains to him all my injuries.

It's bad… really bad. Apparently after I blacked out, Weston didn't stop. And now I'm out of commission for the next several days. I hold my breath, waiting for Giovanni to tell me I'm fired, but I'm shocked when he looks me in the eyes and says, "I made sure he was punished, and he'll never be back here again. Take a few days off and get some rest, okay?"

Tears fill my eyes. I'm thankful he sent away Weston, but with that, reality hits me. He wasn't my Prince Charming. He won't be taking me away to his castle, and we won't be living happily ever after.

"I want you to speak with Dr. Simone before you go back to work," Giovanni adds. Dr. Simone is a therapist the women who work here are required to see. I'm not sure why he wants me to see a therapist, but I nod in agreement.

"NATALIE, HOW ARE YOU DOING?" DR. SIMONE ASKS. WE'RE SITTING IN THE living room in the east wing, where the escorts who work here stay.

"I'm okay."

She nods. "Now tell me the truth."

I laugh softly at her bluntness, then do as she asked. "My body has physically healed, but in a weird way I miss Weston. I know I shouldn't. I know it's unhealthy, but he was the first man to ever tell me he loves me. To see me as more than an escort…"

"Weston is the man who hurt you?" she asks.

"Yes."

"Do you believe a man who loves you would want you to be in pain?"

I think back to the years I watched my mom with all those men. They all told her they loved her and every one of them hurt her. Then, I think about the book she used to read me when I was little. The prince hugged her and kissed and told her he loved her, but he never hurt her. But that's just a story, right? Fiction. This is real life, and in my life, men aren't princes and they don't treat women like princesses.

"I don't know," I tell her truthfully.

"Then, it seems we have a lot of work to do."

CHAPTER THREE

NATALIE
TWENTY-THREE YEARS OLD

"NATALIE! THERE YOU ARE." NICO WALKS OVER TO ME. "WE'RE EXPECTING special guests tonight. When they arrive, they are to be treated like royalty."

"Are they famous?" I ask, clicking on my iPad, ready to take notes. Shortly after Weston Hightower attacked me, he went after his ex-stepdaughter, Aria, attempting to kidnap her. He convinced Cecilia to help him, and after Giovanni learned of her betrayal, he fired her and gave me a promotion—the new madam of the bordello. Shortly after, Giovanni moved to Italy to be with his now wife, Aria, and Nico, along with his wife, Amber, took over.

It took years of therapy with Dr. Simone, but I've learned that my mom was right all those years ago. I don't need a Prince Charming. I'm working my way to making my own happily ever after and I don't need a man to do that—especially not one like Weston, who used my vulnerability as an in to hurt me. He never loved me, and those three words he spoke were only used as a weapon to manipulate me. Thankfully that asshole is dead now, thanks to Giovanni, and can never hurt another soul.

"I'm not sure," Nico admits. "Dad knows someone who knows someone who…" He waves his hand through the air. "You get the point. They've paid enough money for me to not ask any questions, and I expect you to do the same. They're looking for a discreet good time, and I told them they can find it here. They'll be here all weekend, leaving Sunday evening."

"So, no background checks? How will we know they're not bad people, or that they won't hurt one of the women?" There's a process here and it's done to protect the women. To ensure their safety. And I take that seriously. Senator Hightower's background check checked out and he was still able to hurt me before Giovanni kicked him out. "I'm not exactly comfortable letting men, who have had no background checks done, just come in here and have free rein of my girls."

Nico sighs. "You've been around here long enough to know that not everything is done by the book. Dad requested this favor and I agreed. They've shown proof that they're clean, and I promise you, I will have security watching their every move in the rooms."

"Okay," I concede.

"Thank you. There's more. They've requested their photos not be taken, so I need you to confirm with the women who are willing to go in blind."

I groan. "So, in other words, they're all ugly."

Nico laughs. "I don't know. I haven't seen them, but they're offering to pay each woman triple their rate for their discretion. She'll have to sign an NDA stating she won't mention to anyone who she was with and she won't talk about their time together."

"Wow, they must be big time. That's a lot of money."

Nico smirks. "Does it make you want to add your name to the roster?"

I know he's only joking, but my stomach knots at his words. It's been four years since

I've had sex. Weston Hightower was the last man I was with. After that, I changed my profile to add sex as a hard limit, and once I was promoted to madam of the mansion, I stopped seeing men altogether. My friends and roommates, Jessica and Nadine, both escorts here, bug me all the time that I need to get out and meet a man, but honestly, I'm not sure I'm ready.

"When they arrive, please see them to the main office and text me so I can meet you there," Nico adds, without waiting for me to answer him. He knows I have no desire to ever escort again. I've come too far to go backward.

"Will do."

A couple hours later, after I've finished speaking to the women—and have had those who are interested sign an NDA—Edgardo, one of the bouncers here, texts to let me know the special guests are arriving. I step outside to greet them and see several men exiting a blacked-out Cadillac SUV.

"Damn," Edgardo says in awe. "Bullet proof windows."

I try to see if I recognize any of them, but I don't. Three of them are younger, most likely in their early, maybe mid-twenties, dressed in expensive suits. The three others who are following behind them are older, with gray hair and receding hairlines. They're also in suits, but they're all black, and they're wearing earpieces. They must be their bodyguards.

The three younger ones saunter over to Edgardo and me, and I note that they're all similar looking: brown hair, tanned skin, all clearly toned beneath their suits. Two of them are clean-shaven, but one is sporting a few days old scruff. That guy, the one with the scruff, catches my attention. His eyes are different from the other two—cornflower blue, reminding me of Prince Charming from my childhood book. Bright and carefree, as if he has the entire world at his fingertips and he knows it.

His gaze meets mine, and he slowly rakes his eyes down my body. Usually when men do this, I feel objectified, but with this guy, it feels different. I don't know why. Maybe it's because it doesn't feel like he's checking me out as if I'm a piece of meat, but instead drinking me in, like he's thirsty and is dying for a sip.

His eyes finally land back on mine, and they twinkle like he appreciates what he sees. A small, boyish grin curls up on one side of his mouth and my belly does some weird flip-flop thing. I take in a deep breath and break eye contact. I don't know what's wrong with me.

"Good afternoon," he says, speaking up first. "My name is Liam, and this is my brother, Nate, and my cousin Jack." He speaks with a sexy accent. His words are clear, but it's obvious he's not from here.

"Welcome to La Stella's," I say to him, extending my hand to shake his. "My name is Natalie and I'll be helping you find your perfect companion."

He takes my hand in his, but instead of shaking it, he brings it up to his lips and lightly kisses my knuckles. Butterflies attack my chest, making it hard to breathe, and I release a harsh breath.

Edgardo clears his throat and it's then I realize everyone is waiting for me to continue. Liam smirks, knowing damn well what he's doing to me. He releases my hand and I shake my head slightly to get ahold of myself. "I'll escort you to the office and we'll go from there," I tell the three of them, before turning on my heel and entering the mansion.

The three gentleman follow me with their guards trailing behind. I assume they'll leave them at the office door, but they all walk through. They stand in the back of the room, while Liam, Nate, and Jack have a seat on the couch across from me. Edgardo stays with me the entire time as well, standing behind me. The whole thing feels way too serious... official... like we're signing an act of congress as opposed to finding them a woman to spend the weekend with.

Nico walks in and introduces himself. They make small talk for a few minutes, before Nico assures them I'll make sure they're taken care of and if they need anything to let one of us know.

"Here are the catalogues." I hand them each an iPad. "You fill out the questionnaire with your likes and dislikes. What you're looking for in a lover. Once you hit submit, the women who meet your criteria will pop up. They have all signed an NDA as requested and are aware they're going in blind and will have zero details about you. You will have the entire weekend with them, if you so choose. You may select a private room or to leave the mansion, but if you opt to leave, a guard will accompany her. There are three indoor pools and two outdoor ones on the grounds. There are three Jacuzzis, a restaurant, and a theatre room. The woman you select is familiar with the mansion and the surrounding area, so you can ask her and she'll accompany you anywhere you wish to go."

The purpose of this gentleman's club is for them to be able to feel comfortable. Many men come here several times a week, and not just for the sex, but for the companionship. Some are single, widowed, and others are in a marriage they wish they weren't in. I've learned a long time ago not to judge. I don't know their backgrounds, just like they don't know mine.

"We want your stay here to be perfect, so if you need anything, please ask."

The three men nod, but Liam is the one who speaks. "Thank you. This is our first time in the States and La Stella's was recommended for their high-class service and discretion. I can now see why."

While they spend the next several minutes filling out their questionnaires, I take the time to assess them. They're all good-looking, and I doubt they would have trouble finding someone to have sex with, so them coming here must be because of the discretion, as Liam mentioned. They aren't able to just go out and pick up a woman at a bar and bring her back to their hotel rooms. It would be a little awkward asking her to sign an NDA before sliding into her.

Jack is the first one to complete his questionnaire and it notifies me on my iPad who he's selected. I let Edgardo know, and he sees him out to private room two to meet with Anastasia.

Nate is next, and since Edgardo isn't back yet, I offer to escort him. I show him to private room three and wait for Jessica to arrive. All private rooms have a bed, a bathroom, and a living room area complete with a television—like a small loft apartment. And inside the drawer of the dresser are various toys, depending on what they've requested, as well as condoms and lube. All members are required to show proof of them being clean as well as use protection, and all escorts are on birth control.

After introducing Nate to Jessica, I head back to the office. Edgar is back to standing behind the desk, and Liam is still perusing the catalogue.

"Is there something in particular you're looking for?" I ask after a few minutes of him still not selecting someone.

He glances up and his eyes meet mine. "No matter which likes or dislikes I select, your name doesn't come up."

My chest tightens. "That's because I'm not an option." And I'll never be again.

He tilts his head slightly in thought. "Are you married?"

"No."

"In a relationship?"

"No," I repeat.

"Lesbian?" he jokes.

"No," I say, allowing a small laugh to escape me. I might not be a lesbian, but my body probably thinks, after four years of not seeing a single dick, that I am.

"I want you," he says bluntly.

"Like I said, I'm not—"

"Just dinner," he says, cutting me off.

"I'm not an escort…" *Anymore*, I think but leave out.

"Then I won't pay you."

"I'll have to ask Nico," I tell him, shocked at myself for even considering this.

"I'll wait." He smiles wide and a tiny dimple pops out of his left cheek.

I shoot Nico a text and he tells me I'm more than welcome to go, but to make sure Edgardo goes as well if he takes me off the property.

"I'll need a few minutes to get ready," I tell him as I put away my phone. I'm dressed in a black pencil skirt, a silky cream-colored top, and a matching black blazer.

"You look perfect, but maybe you could change into something more… comfortable," he suggests. "I'm planning to change as well."

After changing into a cute flowy maroon top, dark skinny jeans, and a pair of Christian Louboutin ankle boots, I quickly brush my teeth and then fluff my hair. I glance in the mirror, taking myself in—brown hair down in natural curls, brown eyes that look neither happy nor sad, and a tanned complexion. I put on a light coat of mascara, then head back out to the front entrance, where Edgardo texted me they're waiting.

"We're leaving?" I question when I see Edgardo, Liam, and Liam's bodyguard waiting by the door. I had assumed since his brother and cousin stayed on the property, we would be as well.

"I mentioned dinner," he says.

"Yes, but you also mentioned wanting to be discreet, and we have a restaurant here."

"Let me handle that."

"Edgardo will have to accompany me," I tell him, suddenly nervous. I haven't been alone with a man in years.

"I figured as much. He can ride up front with Harold." He juts his chin out toward his guard.

I follow Liam over to his SUV. Like a perfect gentleman, he opens the door for me and I slide in. He speaks to his guard for a moment and then joins me inside.

The ride to wherever we're going is quiet. The partition separating the front and back is closed, so I can't see Edgardo, but he texted me to let me know he's up front and if I need him to let him know. I feel better knowing he's here with me.

When we arrive at one of the hotels on the Strip, I notice we're parked in the back, where the delivery trucks go. Harold opens Liam's door and tells him all is clear. Taking my hand in his, he guides us along the back and through a door. There's nobody in sight and I briefly wonder if he's made sure of this. We arrive at a restaurant and a hostess greets us as if she already knew we were coming. It's then I notice we're the only ones here. The entire restaurant is empty. Did they shut down the place for us?

"I paid for us to have the place to ourselves," Liam says, as if hearing my silent thoughts. He squeezes my hand before he lets go and pulls out my chair for me.

"Since you weren't on the list, you didn't sign an NDA," Harold says. "I need you to sign one before you continue." My gaze volleys between him and Liam, who looks embarrassed at the request. I have no intention or desire to speak about Liam or our date, so I have no problem signing on the dotted line.

"Thank you," Liam says, once Harold takes the papers and excuses himself. I can see him and Edgardo both standing at a safe distance. Close enough to keep an eye on us, but far enough away they can't hear our conversation.

"I know it all seems a little bit much, but my family is rather… influential. My dad is sick and soon I'll have to take over the family… business." He clears his throat. "We came here to have one last hoorah before I have to get serious. My mom would have a fit is she knew what we were up to." He mock shivers, and I laugh at how adorably sexy he is.

"I'm sorry about your dad. Your secret is safe with me." I wink and his lips curl into a grin, that sexy dimple popping out.

The waitress comes over and Liam orders a bottle of white wine for the table. She brings it over, pops open the cork, and pours us each a glass.

"So, where are you from?" I ask when she walks away, curious to know where his accent is from.

He frowns but quickly schools it. "I'd tell you, but then I'd have to kill you."

Realizing his joke was meant to lighten the blow over the fact that he can't tell me, I nod once and take a sip of my wine.

"I'm sorry," he says, reaching across the table and threading his fingers through mine. "I want to tell you, I do, but I have to protect my family."

"I understand," I tell him, even though I don't. Not really. But only because I don't have a family. The women at the bordello are as close to family as I've ever had—aside from my mom—and I would do anything to protect them, but they're still not family. "I was just curious about your sexy accent."

He barks out a laugh that somehow sounds both melodic and masculine. "I'm from a small country in Central Europe. How about you?"

"I'm from here." I shrug. "Born and raised."

He nods, taking a sip of his wine. "How old are you?"

"Twenty-three. You?"

"Thirty-one," he admits. "I'm the older brother. Nate is my Irish twin, only ten months younger than me." He chuckles. "We used to drive our mom insane. We were in the same year growing up."

"I'm pretty sure you both still drive her insane, if your trip to Las Vegas is anything to go by."

He laughs. "Very true, but in our defense, we've been here for a week and haven't gotten into too much trouble."

The waitress returns, and after we both order, I ask, "How are you liking Las Vegas?"

"It's a lot dirtier than I imagined."

I laugh. "Yeah, it's not all glamorous."

We spend the next however long talking and laughing and drinking and eating. The more we talk, the more I drink and the tipsier I get. I can't remember the last time I allowed myself to let loose like this. I'm pretty sure we've drunk our way through multiple bottles of wine, but I'm refusing to keep track.

When one of my favorite songs comes on, I jump to my feet and extend my hand. "Dance with me." I blame it on the wine making me brave.

A grin spreads across Liam's face. "It would be my pleasure."

He pulls me into his arms and a chill races down my spine at his touch. I don't believe in love at first sight, but lust? Maybe. Because as Liam and I sway to the music, and I rest my cheek against his chest, I've never felt like I belong anywhere more than I belong right here in his arms.

I close my eyes and inhale his scent. It's woodsy and masculine. I run my hands along his muscled back and know he's the kind of man who could protect the woman he loves. My heart swells as I pretend for just this small moment in time Liam is mine and I'm his. I imagine the book my mom used to read to me as a child, and I pretend like everything I've been through has led me to this moment. To finding my Prince Charming.

Liam pulls back slightly and his eyes meet mine for a brief moment before his mouth presses against my own. I'm so used to the rough way all the men I've been with kiss, I'm shocked at how soft his lips are. Gently, he sucks on my bottom lip, then my top. Then, his tongue swipes across the seam of my lips, requesting access. I've never had a man ask… They always take… and take and take and take.

But Liam asks, and I part my lips, allowing him entry. His tongue swirls against mine, and he tastes sweet like the wine. His tongue is strong like he is, but he doesn't push, only accepting what I give him.

My hands ascend, wrapping around his nape, at the same time his land on my ass. I wait for him to grab it, but he doesn't. His fingers glide up to my lower back and he tugs me closer, so our bodies are flush against each other. We're still swaying to the music, our tongues dancing with each other as well.

My fingers thread through his short hair and I pull him down to me, deepening the kiss. Liam groans into my mouth and then pulls away.

"Stay with me tonight, Natalie."

"I'm not an escort."

"You already told me that," he murmurs against my lips. "Stay with me because I only have three nights here and I want to spend them with you. Stay with me because you feel the attraction, the chemistry I feel. And even though we both know we only have this weekend, what's happening between us is still worth exploring."

My heart picks up speed at his words. I've never *willingly* spent the night with a man, let alone all weekend. My thoughts go to my mom, all the weekends she spent with men in our home. The way they would drug her and then hurt her, and once she was passed out, they would come after me… into my room… under my sheets…

"Natalie," Liam says, cutting through the fog of my horrible flashback. "It's okay, sweetheart."

I search his eyes for the darkness I would see in the men's eyes my mom would bring around, in the eyes of Weston and many other men I was with at the club. But all I can find is warmth with a hint of lust. Can I do this? Can I go up to his room and spend the night with him? I think about what Dr. Simone and I have talked about over the years—finding a healthy relationship. People my age do this all the time. They meet and hook up, no strings attached. I'm not prostituting myself out. We're not so drunk we can't make decisions. We're two consenting adults, and even though Liam isn't my prince, maybe he can be my practice.

"I want to," I tell him. "I want to spend the night with you."

"You sure?"

"Yes." I want this. I want him. I want to explore my feelings for a normal guy I'm attracted to.

A soft smile tugs on the corners of his lips. "Okay, then let's get out of here."

CHAPTER FOUR
NATALIE

AFTER I LET EDGARDO KNOW I'M GOING TO SPEND THE NIGHT, AND HE TELLS me he'll be here until Johnny, another bouncer at the bordello, arrives to take his place, Liam and I take the private elevator up to the Presidential suite. There are three at his hotel and he tells me he, Nate, and Jack all booked them, so nobody will be taking the elevator or be on the floor.

When we step into his room, I expect him to attack me—not in a bad way but in a sexual way—but Liam doesn't seem to do anything I expect of him. Instead, he hands me a shirt and a pair of sweats of his.

"Do you mind if I rinse off?" I ask, trying to tamper down my nerves.

"Make yourself at home," he says before disappearing to change.

Once I've showered—the warm water effectively soothing my nerves—and changed into his clothes, which smell like him, I head out of his massive room to find him. The suite is more like an apartment than a hotel room. It has a full kitchen, living room, and dining room—and that's just from what I've seen as I walk through the place to find Liam.

When I get to the back of the suite, I find him sitting on the balcony, with an identical bottle of wine from earlier next to him. He also has a tray of chocolate covered strawberries and a piece of cheesecake on a plate. He must've requested for it all to be brought up.

"Keep it up and I'm going to think I'm in the movie *Pretty Woman*," I joke, pointing to the wine and desserts. When I was little, it was my mom's favorite movie. She would tell me that one day a man like Richard Gere would save her. I didn't understand it at the time, but once I grew up, I did. My mom was a prostitute, and the men in her room were paying clients. And I followed in her footsteps…

Liam doesn't laugh. "You're not a prostitute and I'm not paying you to be here."

"I was just joking," I tell him, having a seat in the lounge chair across from him. "Besides, you were willing to pay." I shrug and take a strawberry off the tray, biting into the fresh, juicy sweetness. I glance out at the twinkling lights that make up Las Vegas. From up here, it all looks so beautiful. Too bad it's an illusion.

"I was," he admits. "But that's only because it's the only way to have fun and have discretion. Everywhere we go where we live, people know us. Anyone I'm seen with, everyone assumes is the next Mrs.—" He cuts himself off before he reveals his last name. "We thought being in the States would make it easier to have a good time, but all week we've had to be careful. We haven't been able to really do anything fun because we might be seen and photographed. We just wanted one weekend to let loose, be ourselves."

My heart breaks for Liam, and in a weird yet completely different way, I understand him. I don't think I've ever been able to completely be myself. Hell, I don't even think I know who my real self is.

I climb over the chair and into his lap. I straddle his thighs and place the other half of the strawberry up to his lips. He opens slightly and takes a bite. When a bit of the juice drips down the corner of his mouth, I lean in to lick it up.

"I can't remember the last time I got to be myself," I tell him. His fingers grab ahold of my hips, and his eyes lock with mine. "Let's spend the weekend being ourselves. And come Monday, we'll go back to being who everyone else expects us to be."

Liam swallows thickly, his Adam's apple sliding up and down, and nods. Then his hand wraps around the back of my neck and he tugs me to him, his mouth crashing against mine. The strawberry falls from my fingers, and my hands grip his forearms as I get lost in our kiss.

When I feel the hardness between his thighs, I grind down on his erection. He moans against my mouth and then breaks our kiss. He trails kisses along my jaw toward my neck, and I tip my head slightly to give him better access. He places open-mouthed kisses across my heated flesh and I revel in his soft touches. I've never felt anything like this, and it feels good.

When his mouth gets to my collarbone, he stops, the material of my shirt blocking him from going any farther. His gaze connects with mine, silently asking if he can continue, and to answer him, I lift the shirt over my head and drop it to the ground. I took my bra off earlier when I showered and never put it back on, so my breasts are bared to him.

With a swipe of his tongue across his lips, he dips down and takes one of my breasts into his hand and mouth. He licks my nipple and then sucks on it. An electrical current zaps through my body, going straight to the area between my legs that's been dormant my entire life.

"Let's take this inside," he murmurs, lifting me by my ass and carrying me inside. He drops me onto the bed and then removes his shirt, exposing his hard chest and steel-cut abs. I knew he was fit underneath that suit, but I didn't know just how fit he is. He pushes his sweats down, leaving him in only his briefs, which are outlining his rock-hard dick.

I lie in his bed, waiting for him to tell me what he wants, but then it hits me... I'm not his escort. This is consensual, which means I can do as I please. Take what I want. Give how I see fit.

Excited to actually be able to participate instead of having to take orders, I sit up and tug his briefs down. His dick springs free and I take a moment to admire it. It's thick and long, the surrounding area neatly trimmed. My mouth waters at the thought of tasting him.

He glances down at me, as if he's waiting to see what I'll do next, so I take charge, fisting his shaft and pulling him toward me. He dips down and his mouth closes over mine. I stroke his dick up and down, using the bit of pre-cum from the tip of his head to create friction.

He pushes me back slightly, never breaking our kiss, and climbs over my body, separating my legs so they wrap around his torso. His strong arms cage me in, and he grinds his hard length against my center.

"I need you," I moan against his mouth, but he ignores me, continuing to kiss me. "Please," I beg, when his pelvis rubs against my own.

"Shhh," he murmurs. "We have all night."

He breaks our kiss and untangles my legs from around him. He pulls my sweats and panties down my thighs and legs and tosses them to the side. I'm completely naked and exposed to him, and yet I've never felt so comfortable.

He drags himself slowly down my body, placing random kisses all over my skin. His lips land on my hipbone, and he kisses the tiny quote that reads, "Still I rise."

"What is this for?" he asks.

"I got it the day after my virginity was taken from me," I admit.

His eyes widen slightly, but he doesn't comment on it. Instead, he kisses it again, his lips lingering on the words. Then he trails his lips across my belly until he gets to my other hipbone, where another quote lies.

"This doesn't define me," he reads, before he kisses the tattoo. When his lips softly press against my flesh, my throat clogs with emotion. Nobody has ever been close enough to read my words, my thoughts. They were for me, to remind myself that even when I felt weak, I was still strong. No man has ever paid enough attention to my body to notice them, to *care* to notice them.

As Liam peppers kisses along my inner thigh, I shouldn't feel as emotional as I do, but I can't help it. I've seen it in movies, listened to my friends Aria and Amber tell me about the way their men worship them, but I've never felt it myself. I know this is just a fling and it doesn't mean anything—isn't going anywhere—but it doesn't stop my heart from feeling like it's so full, it's about to spill over.

Liam spreads my legs farther and then licks up my center. My body shudders in pleasure and he chuckles against my flesh. "Fuck, woman, you taste so good."

I can't help the giggle that escapes at his accented words.

"What?" he asks, stopping what he's doing.

"I love your accent."

He snorts. "My accent? You're the one with the accent. Now hush up, while I eat my dessert."

I'm about to say something back, but am silenced by the flat of his tongue gliding upward and landing on my clit. His teeth bite down gently, and his lips wrap around the sensitive nub, sucking on it. My back bows off the bed at the insane amount of pleasure he's creating.

"Liam," I breathe. "I need…"

"I know," he replies, then goes back to licking me. With his teeth and tongue and lips, he devours my pussy, until my entire body is shaking from my orgasm and I'm screaming out his name.

Needing him closer, I pull him up and kiss him hard. I moan into his mouth when the tangy taste of myself on his tongue and lips assaults my taste buds.

My legs wrap around his back and I push him into me. It's been a long time and he's a tight fit, but holy Jesus does he feel good inside of me. He wastes no time filling me completely.

When he pulls back and then pushes in, it sparks something deep within me. "Again," I rasp, desperate to feel it again. He pulls out then fills me again, then again and again. Before long I'm panting unabashedly as our bodies connect in the most intimate way.

My orgasm rips through me like a tidal wave, and Liam's mouth connects with mine, swallowing down my moans of pleasure. Warmth fills my insides and I'm lost in everything that is Liam as he growls out his own release.

He pulls out of me and wraps me up in his strong, comforting arms from behind, throwing the blanket over us. "It's never felt like this before," I admit softly, nuzzling my face into the crook of his shoulder as my eyes flutter closed. Between the long day, the bottles of wine, and the multiple orgasms, I'm crashing fast.

But before sleep overtakes me, I swear I hear Liam say, "It's never felt this way for me either." I think he kisses the back of my head too, but I'm too far gone to be sure.

CHAPTER FIVE
NATALIE

I WAKE UP TO THE FEEL OF A HARD-ON PRESSING AGAINST MY BACKSIDE. I PRY my eyes open and it takes a second to remember where I am—in a hotel room, and not just any hotel room, but the Presidential suite—and who I'm with—Liam, the man I was supposed to set up with an escort at La Stella's, only I ended up with him instead. My temples throb, reminding me I drank way too much wine last night, and I close my eyes, the memories of our evening coming back to me. The eating. The drinking. The dancing. The sex. *The sex.* Even in my half-drunken state, I can still remember the way Liam worshipped every inch of my body. The way he coaxed the most delicious orgasm out of me and then did it all over again.

"Are you moaning in your sleep or are you remembering last night?" he murmurs into my ear. My eyes pop open, realizing I was remembering last night a little too well.

His hand glides down my bare hip and he turns me over so I'm on my back. I don't have time to worry about how I look or whether I have morning breath, before he reaches across my chest and pulls my breast into his mouth, licking on the rose-dusted nipple. His tongue is wet, and it sends chills of pleasure through my body.

I peer down and watch as he sucks on my nipple while massaging my other breast in his palm. I notice everything Liam does is with care, for not just his pleasure but also my own. He could teach men a thing or two about being selfless in bed.

He releases my breast and then his mouth brushes against mine. He tastes of mint, and I wonder when he got up and brushed his teeth, but the thought is pushed away when he deepens the kiss, his tongue exploring my own.

Without breaking our kiss, I climb on top of him, and he grips the curves of my hips to help steady me. I'm already wet, can feel it dripping between my legs, so I don't waste any time guiding Liam's hard dick into me. My hands grab ahold of the back of the headboard and I ride him. At first slowly, finding what feels good. I've ridden men many times in my life, but it was always about them. They wanted it hard and fast.

Liam watches my face, his features bleeding pleasure, but he doesn't tell me what to do. He doesn't rush me or demand I hurry up. He lets me explore. When the head of his dick hits a spot deep within me, I moan, loving how good it feels. I do it again and again. My body tightening in anticipation. As my orgasm overtakes me, Liam rakes his fingers through my hair and pulls me down to him, kissing me hard and passionately as the most exquisite orgasm rocks me to my core.

Before I've come down from my high, he flips us over and enters me in one fluid motion. My legs come up and his hands grip the backs of my thighs as he drills into me.

"Fuck, fuck, fuck," he growls, before pulling back and gripping his shaft. He strokes his dick a couple times and then ropes of cum spurt out, landing all over my belly and breasts.

And that's when it hits me. We haven't used any protection. Shit. Did he pull out last night?

"Jesus, woman," he breathes. "I could live inside you for the rest of my life and be content."

I know he's just joking, but the sound of that—of being with him for the rest of our lives—has those crazy butterflies attacking my belly.

He dips his head and kisses me one more time, then crawls off me. "Shower with me," he says, already scooping me up into his arms before I can answer.

We're quiet while we shower, but it's a comfortable silence. I've never showered with a man before, but as Liam massages the shampoo and then conditioner into my scalp, I decide that I highly recommend it and hope to do it again in the future, sooner rather than later.

And with that thought, my heart plummets into my stomach. After this weekend, Liam will be gone, and I'll be back to showering alone. But I refuse to dwell on what happens after he leaves, reminding myself that I knew what I was getting into when I agreed to this weekend.

"I ordered you some clothes," he tells me, planting a soft kiss on my lips. "I went off your sizes. I also ordered breakfast."

"Don't you just think of everything," I joke, kissing him back.

"I didn't want to risk you leaving."

"I'm not going anywhere," I assure him. Not until Monday morning anyway…

After we're done in the shower, dried and dressed, we plate up some of the delicious food he had brought up and take it out onto the balcony.

We spend the morning lounging around, eating and talking. It's crazy how comfortable I feel with Liam. I've only known him for less than a day, but it feels like it's been longer. I had clients I would see several times a week for weeks, sometimes even months, at a time, yet I never felt as close and comfortable with them as I do with him.

When lunch rolls around, he orders us a couple of mahi sandwiches and a bottle of that delicious wine from last night.

"I'm going to need to order a case of this," I tell him, reading the label on the bottle before pouring myself another glass. "It's from Napa Valley."

"I've heard they have beautiful vineyards over there. Have you ever been? They're not too far from here, right?"

"No, but I want to travel." I think about all the plans I've dreamed about over the years.

"Where to?" he asks, taking a bite of his sandwich and washing it down with a sip of wine.

"Everywhere. I would start in California, visit the vineyards and then maybe work my way across the US, hitting up every photographic place, or I would go big and fly overseas, travel the world. My dream is to start a blog. Travel from place to place, taking pictures and writing about what I've seen."

A grin spreads across Liam's face. "That sounds like the perfect way to live."

I nod in agreement.

"What made you want to do that?"

"When I was in college, I took a journalism class—"

"You attended college?" he asks, cutting me off, his voice filled with curiosity.

"Yes, I graduated last year with a degree in journalism."

"That's awesome. Congratulations."

"Thank you."

"Sorry, so you took a journalism class and…"

"The professor had us take pictures and then write about them. What did we see? How did they make us feel? Before we could show others what we saw, she had us share the images, so everyone else could write what they saw. It was so eye-opening to see how one image could ignite so many different opinions and emotions."

"Where have you traveled so far?" he asks, leaning in closer to me. We're sitting in a double lounger and my legs are wrapped up in his own. The hand he's not eating with is massaging circles along my thigh. Even though he had clothes brought in for me, I chose to go with only his shirt and a pair of panties he bought.

"Nowhere."

"Nowhere?" he parrots, his brows furrowing in confusion. "Why not? You're a young, single woman. You could go anywhere, see anything."

He's right. I could. But… "I'm scared," I admit for the first time out loud. When my friend Aria moved to Italy and then Giovanni shortly followed after, we stayed in touch. She's invited me to visit numerous times over the years, but I've never gotten the courage to go.

"Why?"

"The bordello is all I've ever known. It saved me when I was younger, and I guess it's where I feel safe." I shrug, hating that I probably sound stupid. I dip my face and take a sip of my wine, but Liam isn't having it, because he presses his thumb and forefinger against my chin and lifts my face, so I'm forced to look at him.

"You can't live in fear."

"I know…" But it's easier said than done. "One day I will." The fact is, because I've lived at the bordello for the last five years, and they pay for everything, I have a good amount of money in the bank. I could take off and travel the world for quite a few years before I would have to worry about money. But it would mean leaving the place I feel safe, and I don't know if I could do it on my own.

Liam pulls his phone out of his sweatpants pocket and types on it. "A nine-hour drive," he says a few seconds later. "Less than an hour by plane."

"Huh?"

"To Napa Valley." He types some more. "Let's go. We can be there in a couple hours. We can visit…" He glances at the label. "Napa Hills Estates."

"What?" Is he serious right now? "Are you crazy? We would have to book flights and a hotel… And what about you needing to stay under the radar?"

He types some more and then grins. "The pilot said we're good to go." He pats my leg, gesturing for me to get up, so I do. "Get dressed and then we'll head out."

"Liam," I croak out, in shock. "We can't just—"

He cuts me off. "We can and we are. We'll stop at the store on the way and I'll have Harold run in and buy you a camera." He says all of this nonchalantly, as if he didn't just suggest we hop on a plane and fly over to California.

"You're only here for a couple days," I remind him.

"And we'll be back tonight," he volleys.

"I don't think—"

"Don't think. Just do. We only have a couple days together and I want to be there when you visit your first place. You can take pictures and make your first blog post."

My heart beats erratically. There must be a million reasons why I should tell him this isn't a good idea, but at the moment, I can't think of a single one. As a matter of fact, the only thing I can think of is how much I want to visit Napa Valley with Liam by my side. He's the first guy I've been with of my own volition, the first guy I've connected with, and I would love nothing more than to make this crazy memory with him, so years from now when I'm looking back, I can remember our time together.

"Okay," I tell him. "Let's do this."

A COUPLE HOURS LATER, COURTESY OF LIAM'S PRIVATE PLANE, PILOT, RENTAL SUV, and Harold, we're driving past acres and acres of vineyards—just us. I texted Nico and told him where we're going and that I don't need the guard anymore. I trust Liam. Nico texted back, telling me he isn't thrilled about it, but he'll respect my wishes, and if I need anything, to call him. I'm using the camera Harold bought on the way to the airport and Liam charged on the plane to take picture after picture of the beautiful scenery.

When I see the sign for Napa Hills Estates, I snap one more photo, then turn the camera off. "This place is beautiful," I murmur, trying to look to the left and right at the same time—not wanting to miss anything.

Liam chuckles. "You're going to give yourself whiplash. Whatever you miss, we can see later. We have all afternoon."

We pull up to the front of the estate, but Harold doesn't stop, instead continuing around back. "Do you think we'll be able to look around?" I ask.

"Of course." He laughs. "Do you think we just came here to stare out the window?"

I playfully slap his arm. "I don't know! It's all so unexpected. I know you have to stay low…"

"I handled it," he says with a wink that has my insides turning into mush.

The SUV comes to a stop and Harold opens the door for me. I slide out and thank him, then meet Liam around the front.

An impeccably dressed woman with a big smile on her face comes bustling out. "Mr. and Mrs. Smith, it's so nice to meet you. My name is Patricia, the person you spoke with on the phone."

She shakes each of our hands, and I glance at Liam, confused. *Who the hell are the Smiths?*

Liam leans over and whispers, "You know, the Smiths, like in the movie." I laugh. It was the movie we watched on the plane ride over, although there wasn't much watching, since we couldn't keep our hands and mouths to ourselves.

"Thank you for accommodating us on such short notice," Liam tells her, quickly shaking her hand and then wrapping his arm around my waist. "My wife loved your 2018 Sauvignon Blanc, and when she suggested we buy a case, I figured what better way than to fly over and visit the estate ourselves."

He glances over at me and kisses my cheek, and I damn near turn into a puddle right here on the sidewalk. I know he's just playing up the whole Mr. and Mrs. Smith cover story to hide his true identity, but the idea of being his wife has me feeling giddy, which is probably not a good thing since we just met and have no future.

"How wonderful," she says, as another woman makes her appearance. She's a few years younger than Patricia and dressed the same. "This is my daughter, Suzanne. She will be your sommelier today. Any questions you have, she'll be able to answer."

"Thank you," Liam says.

After Suzanne gives us the history of the vineyard, we take off on a golf cart through the vineyards. She tells us how they grow the grapes, goes into detail about the different varietals and the blends they make, and walks us through the process. I'm so caught up in all of it, I almost forget to take pictures, until Liam reminds me.

"This is so cool," I tell him. "Thank you."

He leans over and kisses my lips. "You're very welcome."

After the tour is done, we head inside for the tasting, and it's then I realize nobody else is here but us. "Liam, did you rent this entire place out?"

He simply nods like it's no big deal. "I told you I would handle it," he murmurs, threading his fingers through mine.

We enter the tasting room and Suzanne presents us with several different wines to taste. They're all delicious, but for dinner we go with their estate reserve Syrah. Liam insists we purchase a case of their Chardonnay and Sauvignon Blanc to take home since I loved them both.

I assume we're heading to the dining room, so I'm confused when instead Suzanne takes us up a flight of steps and opens a door that leads to… a room?

"I thought we could have a private dinner," Liam explains, pulling me into the room and closing the door behind us. He backs me up against the wall and presses his body to mine. He tastes sweet and fruity like the wine we've been drinking.

I go to unbutton his shirt, but he pulls away, shaking his head. "Dinner first," he insists, guiding me over to a table and chairs situated on a large terrace overlooking the vineyard. There are two silver domes covering ceramic plates on the table, along with the bottle of wine we chose, and two glasses.

My heart swells inside my chest and for a brief moment I wonder how I'm going to go back to my normal life when Liam leaves. I've never been high-maintenance. I only started understanding and buying expensive clothes after working at the bordello and Cecilia insisted it was necessary. The bordello would cover the costs and over time I became accustomed to wearing nice clothes. But aside from that, I'm a simple woman. I enjoy writing and taking pictures. I work out every day to stay healthy and fit. On my days off, I hang out with some of the women who work at the bordello, lounging by the pool.

As I sit down, with Liam of course pulling my chair out for me, I come to the conclusion that it's not about the money he's spending, it's about the time we're spending together. Before him, I didn't realize just how lonely I've been—closed off from the rest of the world. I've been so focused on healing from my past and creating a healthy future, I forgot to actually enjoy myself.

"What's going on in that beautiful head of yours?" Liam asks, pouring us each a glass of wine.

"I'm having a really good time. You know how to treat a woman."

He chuckles softly. "Well, that's good to know, because I'm honestly winging it."

"Whatever." I scoff.

"I'm serious." He pulls the domes off the plates, revealing our dinner. "Because of my family's line of work, I haven't had a lot of opportunity to date. My family is kind of... umm... strict." He rubs the back of his neck, his cheeks tinting a slight pink like he's embarrassed. It's a side of him I haven't seen yet and it's adorably sexy.

"Usually you hear that about girls, not guys."

"One day I'll have to take over the business, so I have to be careful with whom I date."

"So, no escorts?" I half-joke, hating how different our lives are. I don't know anything about his family business, but I can tell by the way he speaks, carries himself, dresses... the money he has... he comes from a nice, high-class family—the complete opposite of my upbringing.

His bright blue eyes sear into mine. "That's not who you are."

I break eye contact and take a bite of my food, not bothering to argue with him. We both know that even though I no longer spread my legs for money, I'm not the kind of woman you take home to your family.

We eat in silence, and I try not to dwell on my negative thoughts. I knew what this weekend was going into this. They came to La Stella's to spend a weekend with escorts. Liam may not have hired me, and he's not paying me, but the intention is still the same.

"Hey," he says after his plate is clean. "My life..." He releases a harsh breath. "You could be Mother Theresa and probably still not fit in." He laughs, but it's devoid of all humor. "If my dad wasn't sick... if I didn't have these obligations to my family... I need you to know that this weekend would only be the beginning for us."

I nod stiffly. "I'm not under any illusions about what this weekend is."

He opens his mouth to say something else, but before he can, I plaster on a fake smile and stand. "I'm thinking, while we're here and have this room at our disposal, we take advantage of it." I waggle my brows playfully, determined to get the mood back up, before things get deep and awkward. This is my make-believe fairy tale and I'm not going to let it be ruined by reality.

Liam's brows furrow, and I hold my breath, hoping he'll let it go. When he pushes out a soft sigh and nods, I release a breath of relief.

"I'm thinking out here... on the balcony." I step over to the wrought iron railing and place my hands on it, jutting my jean-clad ass out. "From behind."

He smirks playfully. "I think I like your line of thinking."

After slowly removing each other's clothes, we spend the remainder of our time at the vineyard getting lost in each other.

"WAKE UP, SLEEPYHEAD," LIAM SAYS SOFTLY INTO MY EAR. I OPEN MY EYES AND realize I fell asleep on the plane ride back home.

"Sorry," I croak out.

"Don't be sorry," he murmurs, tucking a stray hair behind my ear. "I enjoyed watching you sleep."

When we get back to the hotel, he excuses himself to make a quick phone call and steps out onto the balcony. Still feeling groggy, I head into the bathroom to splash some water on my face. I only have a short time with Liam, so I don't want to spend it half-asleep. I notice the huge spa tub in the corner and decide on a bubble bath for the two of us.

After turning the water on and filling the tub with bubbles, I strip out of my clothes, then light a couple candles. I lower the dimmer for the lights and then step into the bathtub. The hot water feels so good, I'm almost positive it's going to put me to sleep instead of waking me up. I pull my hair up into a messy bun and lie back against the cushion headrest, enjoying the quiet moment.

"Is there room in there for one more?" Liam asks.

I open my eyes. "Definitely."

Once he's removed his clothes, he steps into the bathtub, and I move forward slightly, so he can sit behind me. He encircles his arms around me and then pulls me to his chest. I sigh in contentment, wishing I could freeze time and we could stay just as we are for a while.

Liam kisses my bare shoulder and massages circles over my flesh—my breasts, my arms, my sides—but he never takes it a step further. When I reach behind me to get things going, he catches my wrist and entwines our fingers. "I just want to sit like this," he says, "with you."

He kisses the sensitive spot behind my ear and I close my eyes, willing the tears that are filling not to fall. Why is it that the man who has me feeling all these emotions is the one man I can't have?

CHAPTER SIX
NATALIE

I HAVEN'T EVEN OPENED MY EYES, BUT I CAN ALREADY FEEL HIM GONE. IT'S crazy that only after two nights together I already know what his presence feels like, but I do. I peel my eyes open and glance around and, sure enough, his luggage is gone. His clothes, which were strewn all over, are missing.

I reach behind me and the sheets are cold. Wrapping the blanket around my naked body, I quickly search the place, but it's void of all things Liam. It's as if he never even existed. My heart feels as though it's being squeezed in my chest. We were supposed to have one more day together.

Monday. He was supposed to leave Monday morning. Today is Sunday... Yet he's gone.

I pad into the bathroom and, without bothering to shower, throw on the outfit I wore Friday night—he, of course, had it dry cleaned—grab my phone and the camera from the bedside table, and rush out of the suite, leaving the two cases of wine behind. As I run to the elevator, hot tears prick my lids. My chest is tight, and it's hard to breathe. I knew better than this. Knew better than to open my heart up.

It was less than two days. I kept telling myself I knew the score, but my heart apparently wasn't listening. When I get downstairs, I find my way through the lobby and step outside. The humid desert breeze hits my face and my tears stick to my cheeks as I wave down a cab.

The moment I get inside, my heart implodes in my chest and I choke out a sob. It shouldn't hurt this much. Not after such a short time.

But it does.

"Where to?" the driver asks.

I give him the address and he takes off. The entire drive, neither of us speaks. I'm lost in thought about everything that has happened over the last couple of days. How happy and carefree I felt. My heart felt full and complete, and not just because of Liam, but because I was finally experiencing what this world has to offer. The thought of going back to La Stella's and going back to my life has me feeling jittery, anxious. It's not that this club hasn't been good to me. It has. Giovanni, Aria, Nico, Amber... the women I've gotten to know. I will always be grateful to this place. It saved me from the streets, gave me a safe place to call home. But now, it's time I begin the next chapter of my life. I have money in the bank and like Liam pointed out, I'm a young, single woman.

I use my phone app to pay the driver and once I'm inside, I waste no time finding Nico. He's in his office with his wife. Even though the door is open, I knock.

"Hey! How was your weekend?" Amber asks.

"Okay," I choke out, swallowing down my emotions. "I, um, I need to talk to you guys."

My strained tone has Nico lifting his head. "Did something happen with that guy?"

"No. He was a perfect gentleman." And I somehow managed to fall in love with him in under two days like a damn fool.

Nico's shoulders relax. "Okay, good."

"He left early…" I mention nonchalantly.

He nods. "The girls told me. They left a little while ago but still paid in full." He shrugs. "I'm not going to complain."

"What did you need to talk to us about?" Amber asks, eyeing me curiously.

"I know it's really unprofessional to leave you hanging like this, but I've decided it's time for me to leave."

Her eyes go wide. "*Leave*, leave?"

"Yes, and I think it's best if I go now before I chicken out."

"Where are you going?" she asks, standing and walking over to me.

"I'm not sure, but I always wanted to travel, so I think I'm going to go to the airport, buy a ticket, and just go." The idea of having no actual plan is both invigorating and scary as hell.

"If you need me to stay…" I begin, feeling like shit for leaving them on short notice without a madam.

"No," Nico says, his eyes soft and affectionate. "You go. It's been a long time coming. I'm surprised we got to keep you for this long." He chuckles softly. "Go. Travel the world. We'll handle things."

"You sure?" I kind of expected them to ask me to stay and now that they're not, I'm totally getting cold feet.

"Yes," Amber says. "And please know you always have a home here. We can put the stuff you don't take in the attic, so it's here whenever you need it."

"Thank you." I hug her tightly, then glance back at Nico. "Thank you for everything." Nico might not have been running the bordello when Giovanni first found me and brought me here, but he's always been kind to me. Never treated me like an escort.

"I would ask if you need any money, but I know how much I pay you."

"Nico!" Amber chides, slapping her husband on the arm.

I laugh, sniffling back my tears. "I'm good. I'm just going to quickly pack a bag and then I'm going to take off."

After packing one luggage full of clothes, shoes, and my toiletries, since I'll have to drag it everywhere I go, I say goodbye to everyone. I cry several times as each girl tells me how much she'll miss me. And a couple times I almost consider not going. But I know deep down I need to do this. Being with Liam made me see there's a whole world beyond the La Stella gates and it's time I explore it.

On the way to the airport, I click through the photos I took this weekend. The plane, the vineyards, the estate. I stop when I get to a picture from last night. We had just gotten out of the tub. We were both naked and I made a joke about his shriveled-up dick. He attacked me from behind, throwing me down onto the bed and pinning me under him. He then proceeded to tickle the hell out of me, while demanding I take it back.

He grabbed the camera from the bedside table and started snapping pictures of me laughing as he continued to tickle me. I screamed and begged him to stop, but it wasn't until I warned him I was going to pee the bed did he stop. He dropped onto the mattress next me and turned the camera around, snapping a photo of the two of us.

I didn't think about it at the time, but he probably wasn't thinking when he did it, lost in the moment, because if I wanted to, I could leak the photo, and whoever knows who he is will recognize him. I wouldn't do that, though.

My finger glides across the small screen of the two of us. Our heads are close together. My cheeks are flushed, and I'm laughing, my eyes staring directly into the camera. Liam's gaze is on me, though, and if I didn't know better, I would think it was love shining in his eyes. And maybe it was… Maybe, even though he knew we didn't have a future, he allowed himself to fall for me the same way I allowed myself to fall for him.

A fresh sob escapes past my lips, and I close my eyes. I'm twenty-three and experiencing my first broken heart. I laugh out loud at that and the driver glances back.

I click to the right to bring the images back to the first one, knowing that was the last photo we took before Liam set the camera down and then wrapped me in his arms, telling me how much he loved the sound of my laughter. He told me whatever we did tomorrow he wanted it to be fun, so he could listen to me laugh all day.

I don't know why he made me believe he wasn't leaving until Monday, or why he left without saying goodbye, but maybe it was for the best because feeling the way my heart feels now, I can't imagine actually having to say goodbye to him. Maybe he knew how hard it would be and wanted to spare us both the hard goodbye.

I refuse to believe he left the way he did to hurt me. That he would do anything to hurt me. And when I look back at our time together, I'm going to remember the man who came into my life and showed me how a man is supposed to treat a woman. I'm going to remember the way he looked at me, not like I was an escort, but like I was a beautiful, special princess. He'll no doubt be the man I compare all future men to, and one day, when I meet my Prince Charming, I'll tell him all about the man, who in such a short time, changed my life for the better.

The car comes to a stop and I glance up, realizing we're at the airport. After paying and taking my luggage from the driver, I walk up to the airline counter.

"How may I help you?" the woman behind the counter asks.

"I'd like to purchase an international flight," I tell her, thankful that Amber convinced me to get my passport recently, in hope of convincing me to go visit Aria in Italy.

"Where to?"

"You pick. And make it good. It's the first of many places I plan to travel to."

CHAPTER SEVEN
NATALIE
EIGHT WEEKS LATER

"IT DOESN'T MATTER HOW MANY YOU TAKE, THE RESULTS ARE GOING TO BE the same," Aria says with a small laugh. She's leaning against the bathroom door, her arms crossed over her chest, and is smirking at me.

"This can't be happening." I groan, dropping the fourth pregnancy test into the box and tossing it into the trash.

A few weeks ago, while making my way through Croatia, I started feeling sick. I thought maybe it was the food or the water. I mean, I had visited several new countries in a short amount of time, so anything was possible. I could've picked up anything. But as the weeks went on, and I didn't get any better—instead getting worse—Aria insisted I make a pit stop in Florence, Italy. I listed my symptoms and then she asked me one question: Have you had unprotected sex? She took one look at my guilty expression and had Giovanni run to the drug store to pick up a box of pregnancy tests.

"It is," she tells me in her soothing mom voice, "but it will be okay." She crouches in front of me and takes my hands in hers. "Is the father around?" she asks, her voice free of judgement.

"No. It was a fling," I admit. "I wouldn't even know how to get ahold of him." I've thought about Liam a lot the last two months. He mentioned he's from a small country in Central Europe, and I have to admit, after the airline agent handed me a ticket to Greece, I pulled up a map to see how close it was. Not that I would ever have a chance of finding him, or that our paths would somehow cross, but I liked the idea of knowing I was maybe close to him.

"You're not alone," she tells me. "You can stay here for however long you want…"

"No." I'm already shaking my head. "I appreciate that. I really do. But I can't stay here." I swallow down the lump of emotion in my throat. "But maybe I could get a place nearby…"

Aria squeals. "Yes! You totally can. And Gio and I will be here for you every step of the way. And since you're not that far behind me, we'll have our babies close in age." She clasps her hands together and stands, and my nerves instantly calm.

"Let's go look for a place nearby." She grabs my hand and guides me out of the bathroom and into the living room where her husband and three-year-old daughter, Bea, are sitting on the floor playing with Barbie Legos.

"Momma," Bea says, "Look at my Barbie house!" She lifts the Lego house and toddles over to her mom.

"Wow!" Aria gushes, carefully taking it from her and setting it on the table. "It's so pretty."

"I want my house like this. All pink," Bea tells her, making Giovanni laugh.

He jumps to his feet and walks over to me. "Congratulations," he says, kissing my cheek, obviously having overheard Aria and me talking. "If you need anything…"

"Thank you."

"I need to go to the restaurant," he says. "I'll only be gone a little while. Want me to bring home dinner?" He owns his own restaurant downtown and from what Aria's told me, it's become a popular place and was even featured in several different foodie magazines. I'm proud of him… of them. The odds were against them, and life pulled them in opposite directions, but they still found their way back to each other. Giovanni was born and raised in the mob, but he got out and started a new life here with Aria, and from what I've seen since I arrived, they're happy. Really happy.

"Yes, please," she tells him.

"Yes, please," Bea mimics her mom, only her please comes out sounding like *peez*. My heartstrings tug in my chest. In less than seven months I'll have my own little one… and Liam won't be here to see him or her grow up.

After Giovanni's kissed them both goodbye, Aria brings up the father of my baby. When I tell her he was kind of a client, she insists we call Nico. Of course, because it was a favor from his father, and it was only a one-time thing, they weren't required to complete the proper paperwork—only show proof they were clean—so he has no contact information.

We hang up and Aria wraps her arms around me. "I'm so sorry, Natalie. I'm here for you and so is Gio, but I know it's not the same thing."

"It's okay," I tell her, wiping the tears from my eyes. "It sucks, but maybe it's for the best. He chose to leave early and without saying goodbye. I'll always remember the time we spent together and maybe this is how it was supposed to work out. I learned a lot about myself that weekend. That I'm worthy of love and deserve to live my best life. I learned how sweet and caring men can be. If I hadn't met him, I would still be working at La Stella's instead of traveling, doing what I've always dreamed of doing."

I drop my hands to my belly. It's still flat, but I know what's in there. A baby. A tiny, innocent baby who will one day call me Mom. It will be my job to love and protect him, encourage him and cheer him on. My mom wasn't the best mom, but she taught me one thing. I don't need a Prince Charming. I'm strong and capable of getting through those magical, evil woods on my own, and that's exactly what I did. I came out on the other side, and the only difference is, instead of my Prince Charming waiting for me, my son or daughter is there. I might not have Liam by my side, but he gave me this little miracle and I'm going to spend the rest of my life loving this baby enough for the both of us.

CHAPTER EIGHT

NATALIE
SIX YEARS LATER

"WOW! DO YOU THINK A REAL KING AND QUEEN LIVE HERE?" JASMINE, MY five-year-old daughter, asks, her blue eyes locked on the beautiful castle we're standing in front of. She asks this same question about every castle we visit. Ever since I read her my childhood fairy-tale book, she's become obsessed with royalty. Since she was old enough to walk, we've been traveling all over the globe. We visit different cities, monuments, castles, parks, museums, learning about the different cultures, the history. I started my blog shortly after she was born—my first post being my first trip—to Napa Valley—and take photos of everywhere we visit, writing, not only about what I see, but what my daughter sees.

"Yep," I tell her. "Unfortunately, the queen has recently stepped down and has given the throne to her son..." I glance at the tour guide. "William Arnold Thomas Lewis Christiansen the Fourth. So, for now, until he meets *his* queen, it's only a king."

Jasmine sighs. "It's so pretty. One day I want to live in a pretty castle like this one."

I laugh at her comment. She always says the same thing every time we see a castle. When we were in the UK a few months ago and visited the Windsor Castle, she begged me to meet a king and marry him so she could become a princess and live in a pretty castle. When we got home, Aria, Giovanni, and I took the girls to see Santa and she actually asked him if he could bring me a king so she could live in a castle.

"I know you love the pretty castles, but remember—"

"I know," she says, cutting me off. "It's not about the size of the castle, but the hearts that fill it." She playfully rolls her eyes, having heard this too many times over the years.

I scoop her up, peppering kisses all over her face. "That's right. Our home might not be as big as this castle, but it's filled with love."

"Maybe this castle is filled with love too," she says, when I set her back down. "Maybe they get a big castle *and* love." Her eyes go wide at the thought, and I chuckle at how smart and adorable she is.

"Maybe. You ready to go check it out?"

"Yep!" She takes my hand in hers and we head to the gate where several security officers are standing guard. After being searched and having our passports and tickets scanned, we go inside to the main room to wait for the tour to begin. Every tour is the same thing: they walk you through roped off areas of the castle that the residing family doesn't use, tell you all about the castle and the history, and at the end, you go through a gift shop where you can buy a souvenir. Jasmine insists we buy a magnet from each place we visit, and at home, we have a huge magnetic blackboard filled with mementos from our travels.

"Can I take a picture?" she asks, pulling her digital camera out of her small backpack.

I glance around and don't see anywhere stating photography isn't allowed. "Yeah, go ahead, but stay close, please."

She's already running to the front of the room, her camera in hand. She takes several pictures of the fireplace and furniture, commenting on what's pretty and what they should replace.

The tour guide begins speaking, explaining where she'll be taking us, and we start walking from the first room into the second.

"We have a special treat for you today," she says. "King William is here and has agreed to take pictures and answer a few of your questions."

"Mom! Did you hear that?" Jasmine shrieks. "We're going to get to meet a real king!"

"I heard."

Everyone crowds around the front of the room as the tour guide makes a show of welcoming the king and thanking him for stopping by. Because we're in the back, we can't see him. Jasmine tries to stand on her tiptoes, but it doesn't do anything.

"I can't see." She pouts.

"Patience," I tell her. "I'm sure the line will move soon and everyone will get a chance to meet him."

She huffs, crossing her arms over her chest like the impatient five-year-old she is, and I stifle my laugh.

I'm checking out the photos I've taken on my camera and not paying attention, so when the line moves and we reach the front, I don't notice, until Jasmine tugs at my arm. "It's our turn, Mom!"

I glance up and my eyes land on the most gorgeous man. His brown hair is flopping partly over his eyes and his face is sporting a little bit of scruff. He's dressed impeccably in a suit that's obviously tailor-made to fit him. But none of that is what has my attention. Not his strong nose or his chiseled jaw. Or the way he's smiling down at my daughter. No, it's his striking blue eyes. The same ones my daughter has. She's all mine: same olive skin, same chestnut hair, but her eyes, they belong to her father.

"Hello there," he says, bending slightly. "I'm William, and you are?"

He extends his hand and she meets him halfway, her tiny hand being swallowed up by his big one. "I'm Jasmine. You have a pretty castle. Are you looking for a queen? My mommy will make a good queen and I'll make a good princess. I think your castle needs more pink, though. I love pink…"

He chuckles, amused, as she continues to ramble on, and I would be embarrassed, except I'm too in shock by what I'm looking at. Over the years, I imagined running into him. I knew he was from a small country in Central Europe, but Central Europe has almost two hundred million people, so I never thought it would actually happen. Still, when I was alone at night, I would close my eyes and pretend. We were at a café, waiting in line, or riding the tube. I imagined him seeing Jasmine, and me finally getting to tell him she's his daughter. But not in a single one of those fake scenarios, did I imagine he was the king of Lexenburg and we were getting a tour of his castle… Holy shit, this is his home. He's the king!

"…Mommy. Her name is Natalie."

My fog-covered thoughts are cut through with her words. Her attention swings over to me and his gaze follows. Our eyes lock and Liam's smile disappears as he recognizes me. It's been six years, but based on the shocked expression, he remembers me.

His eyes bounce from me to her and his eyes widen, telling me he's putting the pieces together. It's not every day you see a Hispanic girl with bright blue eyes.

"Is she…" His words trail off, but I know what he's asking, so I simply nod.

"Mommy," Jasmine says, completely oblivious to the thick tension. "Can you take a picture of me and King… What's your name again?"

Dad, I want to say. To you, he's Dad.

CHAPTER NINE

LIAM

SIX YEARS. IT'S BEEN SIX DAMN YEARS SINCE I'VE SEEN NATALIE AND SHE STILL looks as gorgeous as she did back then. Actually, I take that back. She looks even more beautiful. Aside from her current expression of shock from running into me, she looks radiant and carefree… happy. And I have a feeling that the reason for that is standing next to her handing her a digital camera so she can take a picture with me—the King of Lexenburg.

Robotically, Natalie takes the camera from her daughter and nods. Jasmine, as she called herself, steps toward me and turns around for the picture, and it hits me that I'm about to take a picture with my daughter. My own flesh and blood, who I had no idea about. Suddenly a bitter taste infiltrates my mouth.

This woman kept my child from me.

I had no idea about her.

I've missed everything in her life.

After Natalie snaps the photo and Jasmine takes the camera from her to check it out, I call my assistant over, who's waiting for me. I only make an appearance a couple times a year and one of those days is on my dad's birthday. He loved this country and the people, and to honor him I spend the day meeting them and taking photos with them.

"Your Majesty," Stephanie says, slighting bowing in respect. We've been friends for years, our families close, and when I'm not working, she addresses me informally. But in front of everyone, we keep things formal, by the book.

"The woman in the cream-colored top and her daughter…"

"Yes?"

"I need you to escort them over to the Garden Estate."

Her brows scrunch up in confusion. The Garden Estate is where my home is located. Nobody but family goes there, especially not tourists.

"Yes, Your Majesty," she says after a moment.

"Good morning." She greets Natalie and Jasmine. "Can you two please come with me?"

Natalie's gaze volleys over to me and I nod slightly, asking her to do as she's being asked. The last thing I need is for a scene to be caused. Thankfully, they were the last tourists and everyone has begun to move on to the next room.

"Mommy, where are we going?" Jasmine asks, as Stephanie guides them away from everyone else.

Once I see they're in the clear, I approach my guards. "There's been a change of plans. I need to go to the Garden Estate. I can go on my own. Thank you."

The three men nod, even though I'm sure they're confused. Stephanie keeps my schedule organized and I almost never cancel my engagements. I pride myself on being reliable and punctual. It's the way my dad and mom both were as king and queen… My heart tightens in my chest.

My mom. She has a granddaughter. One she doesn't know about. One who was born out of wedlock. I groan on the inside, imagining the lecture I'm going to get. I push it aside quickly, though. I have a daughter. And right now that's all I care about.

When I get to the Garden Estate, I find Natalie, Stephanie, and Jasmine in the sitting room. Jasmine is talking a mile a minute about the room and Natalie is smiling tightly at her, trying to remain interested, but no doubt freaking the hell out on the inside.

"Stephanie." The three women swivel around to face me. "Can you take Jasmine to the kitchen for a few minutes?" Stephanie's eyes bug out.

I step over to Jasmine and bend slightly in front of her. "Chef Sandra makes the best pastries and desserts. How would you like to have a piece of cake while I speak to your mom?"

Jasmine's blue eyes—the ones identical to my own—light up, but then she looks at her mom for approval, and my stomach knots at the fact I'm a stranger to my daughter, a man she knows as nothing more than the King of Lexenburg. She needs her mom's approval because she's her parent.

"Someone will stay with her?" Natalie confirms.

"Stephanie won't leave her side."

Stephanie's eyes form small slits. She's a smart woman and is no doubt putting the pieces together. She might not know Jasmine is my daughter, but that's only because she hasn't looked into her eyes yet. I'm the only one in my family left with those blue eyes. My dad had them and his dad did as well. Everyone else has brown eyes, a few green. But not blue.

"Go ahead," she tells her daughter—*our* daughter. "I'll meet you in there in a few minutes." She winks and Jasmine grins. It's so big a tiny dimple pops out of her left cheek—just like mine.

"Okay," Jasmine tells her. Then she leans in close to her mom, as if she has an important secret to tell her. "I'll try to save you a piece," she whisper-yells, making me chuckle. She's so young and innocent… and mine.

Fuck, she's mine.

Stephanie takes her by her hand and escorts her out of the room, closing the door behind them. I walk over to the bar and make myself a scotch, neat. Then, remembering my manners, I hold up my glass. "Want one?" She shakes her head and I down the drink in one swallow.

"You left," she says before I can gather my thoughts to speak.

Her words bounce around in my head, and once they land, I sit in front of her and look her dead in the eyes. The same mesmerizing brown eyes I've thought about so many times over the years.

"You left."

She scoffs. "Excuse me?" She crosses her arms over her chest and my eyes descend to her ample cleavage, my mind—and dick—remembering the way her pretty pink nipples would peak at my touch. I slam the door on that thought. Now is not the time.

"At the hotel in Las Vegas… when I came back in from speaking with Harold, you were gone. The bed was empty and your clothes and camera were gone."

"I only left because you left," she argues. "I woke up and the room was barren of all your stuff. You were nowhere to be found."

I think back to that day, everything that happened, and it hits me… "You thought I left you."

"You *did* leave me."

SIX YEARS AGO

THE INCESSANT BUZZING WON'T STOP, SO I GRAB MY PHONE OFF THE BEDSIDE table and look to see who's calling this early in the morning. Then I remember it's only early here. Where I live, it's several hours later. The name on my screen flashes **Mom**. She wouldn't call unless it's important.

Glancing at Natalie, who's fast sleep, I climb out of bed and head out onto the balcony to return her call.

"Oh, William," my mom breathes, her voice cracking. "I've been trying to get a hold of you and your brother all morning." Without having to ask, I know something is terribly wrong. My mom is the most relaxed woman I know. She handles any situation that's thrown at her with patience. She's the calm to my dad's storm.

"What's the matter, Mom?"

"It's your dad," she says through a soft sob. "He's had a heart attack."

My world tilts on its axis at her words. We knew he was sick, but I never thought something would happen during our week away. "Is he…" I can't finish my sentence.

"He's in critical condition. You need to come home now." In other words, he may not make it.

"We're on our way. I love you."

"Love you too, Son."

We hang up and I go on autopilot, packing my luggage, getting dressed, and getting Harold up to speed. I call the pilot and he tells me because of the storm it will be a few hours before we can take off.

I glance over at Natalie, who's still blissfully asleep. I need to wake her up and tell her my trip is being cut short. But then I think about how hard it's going to be to say goodbye. We don't have any hope of a future. Her life is here and mine is thousands of miles away, across the pond, in Lexenburg.

I lean over her and place a soft kiss on her forehead, inhaling her sweet scent, and for a brief moment I wonder if maybe we could somehow make it work. I don't know how, but I don't think I can let her go. I've only known her for a short time, but in that time, she's managed to crawl under my skin and bury herself in the cavity of my chest.

My phone buzzes. This time it's my brother. Mom must've gotten a hold of him.

I walk out of the bedroom and softly close the door behind me. "Hey."

"Jack and I are on our way to the airport. Jessica ordered us a car." Jessica must be the woman he's been spending his time with. I didn't pay attention to who either of them picked—my only focus on Natalie.

"The pilot said because of the weather it will be a few hours."

"Fuck," he hisses. "Okay, we'll see you there."

As we're hanging up, there's a knock on the door. I already know it's Harold to grab my luggage. I open the door and roll it out into the hallway.

"The car is ready, sir."

I glance back at the now closed door, picturing Natalie asleep, cuddled up with the blanket. All I want to do is crawl back into bed with her and ignore the world around us.

"I'll, uh… Give me a moment, please. I'll meet you down there." I can't do this. I can't leave her. I'll take her with me.

"Yes, sir."

As I'm reaching for the handle to go back inside, the phone buzzes in my pocket. Again. Fuck. It's my mom *again*. This can't be good. "Mom?"

"He's gone," she cries. "His heart… it just wasn't strong enough."

My forehead drops against the wall and I close my eyes. "I'm so sorry we're not there."

"There's nothing either of you could've done."

I shake my head at her response and start walking down the hall. Even if there was something we could've done, she wouldn't tell us that. "We're on our way. The weather is bad, but the pilot thinks we can take off in a few hours." I step into the elevator and press the button for the lobby.

"Stay safe," she tells me. "I'll be here when you return. Love you." Her voice is so broken and sad, I want to reach through the phone and hug her.

"Love you too."

When I hang up, I step out of the elevator and find myself standing in front of the hotel Starbucks, making me think of Natalie. Yesterday morning when I had breakfast brought up, the first thing she went after was the coffee, telling me she can't live without caffeine. I chuckle at the thought of her in Lexenburg. We don't drink coffee. We drink tea. I'll have to buy her a coffee maker and coffee…

And with that thought, I know I've made my decision. I can't leave without her. Maybe she won't even want to go with me, but I have to try.

With a coffee and pastries in my hands, I head back upstairs to our room. I should probably be nervous. I mean, I'm about to ask a woman I've just met to fly back to my country with me. But for some reason, I'm not. And I know it's because it feels right. Being with Natalie feels right.

I open the door and the second I enter, I already know she's gone. I check the bathroom, the balcony, the other rooms… but she's not here. Her clothes and her phone and camera are gone as well. She left.

My phone buzzes for what feels like the millionth time this morning. "Hello."

"The system has shifted and we're clear to take off as soon as you arrive."

"Thank you."

I set the coffee and pastries down and then head out. I consider stopping at the bordello on our way, but decide against it. If she wanted to be with me, she wouldn't have left, but she did. And now I need to focus on my family. My mom and brother are going to need me to be strong for them.

Everything is about to change.

PRESENT DAY

"YOUR LUGGAGE WAS GONE," NATALIE SAYS. "HOW WAS I SUPPOSED TO KNOW you were downstairs buying me coffee?"

I sigh, knowing she's right. "I wasn't thinking. My dad had just died and my mom was across the pond. I was scrambling to get back home to her and I didn't think." Of course she would've assumed I left. Because I was planning to. Harold took my luggage and I was heading to the car. I had every intention of leaving her there sleeping.

"I came back because I didn't want to be without you."

A single tear leaks from her eye and I reach over to wipe it away with my thumb.

"I didn't know your number," she says. "Your last name… nothing. You knew where I worked but—"

"I called there." Her eyes go wide. "A few days later, after the funeral, I was lying in bed and missing you. I looked up the number and called, but the man told me you didn't work there and he refused to give me any information."

"They won't give out any information over the phone. Some guys get… attached." Her cheeks turn a light shade of pink.

"I was attached."

"I was too." The pink of her cheeks deepens.

"We have a daughter…"

"She's amazing," she gushes, her entire face lighting up. "She's so smart and sweet. She's obsessed with castles." She laughs, glancing around at the irony. "We've visited so many over the years. I can't believe here, of all places, is where we found you."

"Were you looking for me?" I was upset at first that she didn't tell me, but again, I wasn't thinking straight. She would've had no way to find me, and it's my fault. I didn't give her my full name or phone number. I didn't even tell her where I live. Because I had no intention of ever seeing her again. Until I did, and it was too late.

"I didn't think I would ever find you," she says with a slight frown. "But you said you live in a small country in Central Europe, so whenever we're walking down the streets or are on the tube, I always look around, just in case." She laughs. "Which is now kind of funny because you're the king, so I doubt you've ever just walked the streets or used public transportation."

She's not wrong. Unless it was at an event, we never would've crossed paths. "Do you live here?"

"No, we're traveling." She beams. "After you left, I took your advice and took off. I quit my job and packed a single suitcase and started traveling." Her grin widens. "I started in Greece and was working my way through Europe when I found out I was pregnant." Her hand absently goes to her belly. "My friends, Aria and Giovanni, live in Florence, so I stopped there to confirm it. I was so scared…"

She swallows thickly, and I find myself taking her hands in mine. Her skin is still so soft. "I didn't have anyone, so I placed roots in Florence near them. I bought a small flat and continued to travel until Jasmine was born. Once she turned a year old and could walk, I started traveling again with her."

"Do you have a blog?" I remember her telling me about wanting to start one.

"I do." She pulls out her phone and types something, then hands it to me. I scroll through picture after picture, post after post about her travels. In every photo is our daughter. The Windsor Castle in England, the Carreg Cennen Castle in Wales. They've been to the Predjama Castle in Slovenia. The photos continue on and my heart swells with pride at the life she's created for her and our daughter.

"This was our last stop," she says. "Jasmine starts school in the fall."

Her last stop… because she's not staying.

"You can't go," I blurt out. "Please."

Her brows go up, so I explain. "I need to get to know our daughter and I can't do that if you're in Italy." I edge closer, my hands landing on her hips. "And I'd really, *really* like to get to know you again."

She nibbles on the corner of her lip and a horrible thought occurs. "Is there a man…?"

"No," she says. "It's only Jasmine and me."

I breathe out a sigh of relief. I'm not sure what I would've done if she had told me there was a guy in her and our daughter's life, but I'm glad I don't have to find out.

"Then stay, please," I practically beg. "We have so much catching up to do. You can stay here." I wave my hand in the air. "There are more than enough rooms." *You can even share mine if you want,* I think but don't voice, not wanting to appear too pushy and maybe a tad creepy.

Her eyes rake over the room and I wait with bated breath for her to say something. I imagine she's overwhelmed by the luxury of the place, but in my defense, this place is centuries old. Every royal family has lived here. It's not my choice.

"She starts school in four weeks," she finally says. "Are you sure it's okay for us to stay here? We're staying at The Lexenburg Inn. I'm sure we can extend our stay…"

"Nonsense," I tell her, refusing to let them out of my sight. "I insist. It's hard for me to travel out, so you guys staying here would work out better." And hopefully before it's time for them to leave, I can convince them to stay.

"Okay," she agrees. "So, how do you want to do this?"

"Do what?"

She laughs, but it's strained. "Do we tell Jasmine you're her father… or…?"

"Yes," I answer immediately. "I've already missed, what? Five years of her life?"

"She turned five in June. June fourteenth."

"I would like for her to know I'm her dad. As long as you're okay with that."

"Of course. You should know she's probably going to freak out." Her face heats up. "I wasn't kidding about her being obsessed with castles. Did you hear what she asked you about finding a queen?" Her entire neck and face blush crimson, and I laugh at how adorable she is.

"If I recall, she was trying to play matchmaker." I wink and she shakes her head.

"I read her this old fairy-tale story. It was mine when I was little, and she fell in love with it. Eventually I bought her her own and she makes me read it to her every night, even though she could easily read it herself." She laughs. "It's about a princess who has to fight all of these magical battles and eventually gets to her prince so they can live happily ever after."

I snort at the irony. "When you met me, I was a prince."

She doesn't laugh, her expression turning serious. "I didn't know you were a real one, but my time with you… it changed everything for me. You're the reason I had the courage to leave the bordello, to travel… it felt like you were my white knight."

"No," I disagree. "You were your own savior. I was just along for the ride."

"Well, nonetheless, over the years Jasmine has asked about her father and I've been honest with her, telling her that you were someone I cared deeply about but lost contact with. She even has the picture of the two of us that you took our last night together in a picture frame by her bed. From reading her the book, she's gotten it into her head that one day I'm going to find my king and she'll, by default, be a princess, and we'll all live happily ever after."

"That sounds like the perfect ending to this story," I tell her, not even caring what I'm implying.

Her eyes briefly widen, but she doesn't comment. Instead she changes the subject. "Is there anyone you need to speak to about this new revelation?" Revelation meaning I have a daughter I didn't know about.

"Eventually I'll have to make an announcement. It's a big deal that there's a blood-related princess. She's my only heir, and if something were to happen to me, when she's old enough, she would step up as the queen. But for now, I'll just need to meet with my family. We'll keep it quiet, so we can spend time together in peace." Once everyone knows, questions will be asked, and answers will be demanded.

"Okay." She stands. "Why don't we go tell our daughter you're her daddy and then go from there."

CHAPTER TEN

LIAM

I'M THE KING OF LEXENBURG. I WAS BORN AND RAISED TO FILL THIS ROLE. Every day I have to make tough decisions that can potentially negatively or positively affect an entire country of nine hundred thousand people. Sure, I have several different advisors who help guide me, but ultimately, it's me they count on to steer their country right. To make sure it's economically prospering. We're one of the smallest countries in the world, but we're one of the wealthiest. The weight of every decision rests on my shoulders and mine alone, and I'm okay with that. I can handle the stress.

But as I walk toward the kitchen where I'm about to be formally introduced to my daughter, I find my heart is beating erratically out of my chest. My hands are sweating. I have never been as scared and nervous as I am right now.

We step through the door and find Stephanie and Jasmine sitting on a couple bar stools talking and… my mom is with them.

Ah hell.

They hear us come in and three sets of eyes swing over to Natalie and me. Stephanie's squint in confusion and, if I'm not mistaken, a tiny bit of anger—I'll deal with her later. My mom's are filled with confusion, but I can detect a hint of excitement as well. She's a smart woman and has no doubt figured it out. All it would take is Jasmine looking at you with her blue eyes for you to know she's mine. And if she smiles, with that dimple popping out, well, that might as well be the paternity test.

I'll have to speak to my mom. But right now my focus is on the little girl who's smiling at her mother and me. She has a bit of chocolate on the corners of her mouth and the most adorable milk mustache.

"You were taking so long," she tells her mom, "that I almost ate your cake." She slides it over to Natalie and hands her a glass of milk. "It's the best cake I've ever eaten!"

"Thank you," Natalie tells her. "I'm not hungry right now, so how about I save it for later."

Jasmine shrugs. "Okay. Are you ready to go now?" She hops off the stool. "We still have to go visit the bridge and the gardens… and the church." I find myself smiling that she knows several of the most popular tourist attractions here in Lexenburg. They've done their research.

Jasmine walks over to me. "Thank you for letting us visit your castle. It's very pretty."

My eyes flit between her and her mom. She's ready to leave… because she doesn't know who I am. She doesn't know this isn't just my castle. It's *our* castle. Because this is where she belongs. Where they both belong. Here with me.

"Actually, my love, there's something we need to talk to you about." Natalie glances up at me. "Maybe… we should go sit somewhere." She glances over at Stephanie and my mom, uncomfortable with having an audience. My mom raises her brows, silently demanding an introduction.

"Before we do, I'd like you both to meet my mom, Helena Christianson. This is

Jasmine and Natalie…" And then it hits me, I don't know their last name.

"Zapata," Natalie finishes for me.

"We already met," Jasmine says.

"We did," Mom agrees, standing, "but it's nice to meet you." She extends her hand and they shake. This is all very informal and nothing like what would be happening if they met in public. I have no idea at this point where I'm going and how to handle any of this.

"It's nice to meet you too," Natalie says with tightness in her voice. She's nervous. She's meeting royalty and the grandmother of her daughter at the same time. This can't be easy for her.

Stephanie clears her throat. "I'm Stephanie," she says, introducing herself. "William's assistant, advisor, and much more." When she emphasizes the much more, Natalie flinches but quickly schools her features.

"Much more meaning friends since we were in diapers," I explain, refusing to allow Stephanie to insinuate anything else. She might want there to be more between us, but I've never gone there and I have no intention of ever doing so.

I ignore the hard glare Stephanie is shooting my way. "Mom, Natalie and I need to speak to Jasmine, but once we're done, I would like to speak to you as well."

My mom nods in understanding, then excuses herself, dragging Stephanie along when she doesn't get the hint that we want to speak to Jasmine alone.

"Mommy, is everything okay?" Jasmine asks, her gaze bouncing between us.

"Everything is perfect," Natalie says, her voice upbeat.

"Let's go to the sitting room," I suggest. Once the three of us are inside, I close the door for privacy and then join them on the sofa.

"Remember what I've told you about your daddy?" Natalie says to Jasmine, who nods.

"Yes, that you loved him very much, but you didn't get his phone number, so you couldn't find him. But if he knew about me, he would love me."

My breath catches at her words. She loved me and spoke fondly of me even though she assumed I left her all those years ago without a goodbye.

"That's right," Natalie tells her. "Well, I have some good news. Liam…" She stops and looks at me and raises a single brow. "Liam or William?"

"To you, Liam… To everyone else, it's William." I can't imagine her calling me anything other than Liam. Liam is the carefree man in Las Vegas, the man who didn't have the weight of an entire country perched on his shoulders.

"Liam is your daddy," she says with a small smile.

Jasmine's eyes comically widen, and her attention turns to me. "You're my daddy?" She looks at her mom. "He's the one in the picture?"

"I am," I tell her, then hold my breath, waiting for her response.

She's quiet, her top teeth gnawing on her bottom lip, just like her mom does. I would give anything to know what she's thinking, but I wait, not so patiently, for her to wrap her head around what she's just learned. She's only five and needs time to process.

Finally, after several long moments, the most beautiful smile spreads across her face. "If you're my daddy and the king, that makes me…" Her eyes light up. "That makes me a princess!" She looks at her mom. "Right? I'm a princess."

Natalie snorts, and I release the breath I was holding. "Yes, that makes you a princess," Natalie tells her.

"Wow," Jasmine breathes. "My fairy-tale story came true." Then she frowns. "Does that make you a queen?"

Natalie shakes her head. "No, my love, it doesn't, but that's okay because we found your daddy."

I want to argue and tell her if I have it my way, she'll become my queen, but it's probably too soon to be making declarations like that. Right now, our attention needs to be on our daughter, but once things settle down, I have every intention of figuring out how to make Natalie my queen.

Jasmine jumps off the couch and pulls her backpack off her shoulders. She digs through it and pulls out a book. "Look," she says, walking over and situating herself next to me. "It's my fairy-tale book."

She reads the title then opens it, reading the first page. Page after page she reads me the story about the princess who has to fight her way through the magical forest to get to her Prince Charming. When she finally gets to him, he professes his love and asks her to marry him. On the last page, they're smiling and happy, having gotten their happily ever after.

"I found you like she found her Prince Charming," Jasmine says. "But you're my daddy not Prince Charming and you're the king." Jesus, my daughter is so smart. She hands the book to Natalie. "Here, Mommy, you can keep it now since your book was old and broken. I don't need it anymore. You can have mine and read it until you meet *your* Prince Charming."

Natalie smiles softly, her eyes turning glassy. "Thank you." She pulls Jasmine into a hug and kisses her forehead.

"Can I see my room?" Jasmine asks once they separate, shocking the hell out of both Natalie and me.

"Umm…" I don't quite know how to answer that, but luckily Natalie jumps in.

"Remember Liam didn't know about you? So he doesn't have a room for you yet."

"But there are plenty of rooms to choose from," I add. "And we can have it decorated however you want."

Jasmine grins. "I want a pink princess room. Does this mean I'll go to school here?" she asks, jumping from one subject to the next so fast, I damn near get whiplash.

"No," Natalie tells her. "We still live in Florence, but we're going to visit for a few weeks, so you can spend some time with your daddy before we go back and you start school."

Jasmine must not like that answer because her bottom lip juts out. "But I want to live here with my daddy in the castle." Her words, like a prickly vine, wrap around my heart and squeeze, and I know in this moment, I would do anything in my power to make sure she's always happy. I don't know anything about parenting, but I *know* I don't like to hear that sadness in her voice.

Natalie frowns. "We live too far," she explains. "But we can visit. How about we focus on this visit and then we can plan the next one?"

Jasmine's face falls, but she nods in agreement, and that vine that's wrapped around my heart tightens, creating puncture holes in the ventricles. With every sad look she gives, it feels as though my heart is slowly bleeding out. I want to tell her she can live here as long as she wants—both she and her mom can—but I doubt Natalie will be pleased with me saying that without speaking to her first. I know she's planning to go home after their visit is over, but if I have it my way, they won't be going anywhere.

"Come," I tell them. "Let's go pick out a room for you to sleep in and I'll show you around." I glance at Jasmine, hoping it will perk her up, and it does. A tiny smile spreads across her face.

"What about your mom?" Natalie asks. Shit, caught up in telling Jasmine I'm her dad, I forgot I still need to speak with my mom.

"Maybe it would be best if we go to our hotel to rest and pack our stuff, and after you speak to your mom, we can meet back up."

I hate the thought of either of them leaving, but it's probably for the best. I'm not sure how my mom is going to react to the news, and I would rather we be alone than take the chance of Jasmine and Natalie witnessing any unkind words she may have regarding the situation.

"Do you have a phone?" I ask, taking mine out.

"Yes."

I hand her my phone. "Put your number in and once you're ready to come back, my driver will be waiting for you."

She looks like she wants to argue but thankfully doesn't.

After speaking with Tomas, one of our security guards and drivers, explaining he is to bring them to their hotel and wait while they pack, however long that may take, and then bring them back, I go in search of my mom. I find her in the reading room, her favorite spot, reading a book and sipping her tea.

"Mom." She sets her book down and gives me her attention. "We need to talk."

"That we do," Stephanie says, waltzing into the room like she owns it. I was hoping to speak to my mom alone, but I might as well tell them both at the same time. Two birds, one stone...

My mom's gaze slides over to Stephanie, and for a brief second I can see the annoyance in her features. My mom rarely lets her true feelings show. Even though she formally stepped down from her duties shortly after my father passed away, she's still the Queen of Lexenburg and she takes her role seriously, always remaining poised and neutral.

"As I'm sure you've both guessed, Jasmine is my daughter."

"Alleged," Stephanie adds. "We'll need to schedule a paternity test. For all we know that woman is lying and—"

"That woman's name is Natalie and she wouldn't lie." I might've only known her for a short time, but I know she wouldn't lie. I can feel it in my gut.

"Yes, a paternity test will be required," Mom agrees. Then she adds, "But she's your daughter. I could see it in her face the second I laid eyes on her. How old is she?"

"Five," I admit. "She just turned five in June."

Mom frowns. "I'm assuming you didn't know about her..."

"No, of course not." Had I known, she and Natalie both would've been a part of my life. "I met Natalie during my trip to the States."

Mom's eyes widen knowingly.

"I left abruptly when Dad passed away. She didn't know who I was and had no way to contact me. I went back to ask her to go with me, but she thought I left and so she left and..." I sigh. "We just missed each other and because of that, I've missed out on five years of my daughter's life."

"This is absurd," Stephanie cuts in. "Many children have blue eyes and dimples. What do you even know about this woman? She could be setting you up. You met her in the U.S., for God's sake," she spits. "She could be anyone. You can't just trust her word."

"I can and I do," I tell her in a tone leaving no room for argument.

"A paternity test will still need to be performed," Mom says. "She was conceived out of wedlock."

"I know, but I don't need one to know she's mine."

Stephanie huffs. "This is going to be a PR nightmare."

"My daughter is never to be referred to as a nightmare. Understood?" I give her a pointed look. "She and Natalie will both be staying here in the Garden Estate with me for the next few weeks so we can get to know each other." I consider leaving it at that but decide to throw all my cards on the table. There's no point in hiding my hand. "My goal is to convince them to stay… for good."

Mom's brows hit her hairline and Stephanie gasps.

"Are you implying your goal is to marry this woman?" Mom asks.

"Yes," I tell her honestly. "Had Dad not had his heart attack, I would've asked her to join me here. I know we have a lot of catching up to do, but I believe she's the one."

Mom knows better than to take my words lightly. I've never mentioned any woman in this regard. And it's because of Natalie. Because of what I felt when I was with her. No woman ever measured up to the way she made me feel.

"You don't know her!" Stephanie hisses. "She could be anyone. A con artist, out for your money. We need to have a background check done. The people are going to want—"

"Enough," I say, cutting her off. "I do know her, and I have every intention to get to know her further. Right now, nobody is to know anything. This is a private matter and will remain private until I say otherwise." I'm going to have to find out how much of Natalie's past is public knowledge, so I can bury it. I won't allow her past to taint our present or future. I know she's more than a woman who worked at that bordello and I won't let anyone be blinded by that small part of her life.

"Now, I need you to get the estate decorator out here. Jasmine will be selecting her room and it'll need to be turned into a room fit for a princess. I'll also need to reschedule any of my commitments for the next few weeks. Unless it's vital, cancel or reschedule it." Stephanie gawks at me like I've grown two heads. "I'm going to need you to contact the Lexenburg Gardens to schedule a private tour, as well as Saint Philipp's church. My daughter wants to visit both, and I'll be accompanying her." The bridge is too public, so that'll have to wait, but the other two I can make happen.

"William, as your advisor…"

"As my *assistant*, those are the things I need you to do."

With a huff, she exits the room, leaving my mom and me alone.

"Now that she's gone, care to tell me the entire story?" Mom says.

I sigh, running my palms over my face. "Where to begin…"

"How about the beginning," Mom smarts. "That's always a good place to start."

CHAPTER ELEVEN

LIAM

AFTER TELLING MY MOM THE ENTIRE TRUTH ABOUT HOW I MET NATALIE, she was shocked to say the least. But after the shock wore off, she told me that she will support my decision and will give Natalie the benefit of the doubt. She could've easily fought me on this, insisted the risk of a scandal is too high, but just like she's done my entire life, she took my side and assured me it will all work out. My mom is a romantic. She and my father met when they were in their teens and fell in love. Within weeks, they were married, and they remained in love until the day he died. She could've remained the acting Queen of Lexenburg, but without him by her side, she said her heart wasn't in it. He was the other half of her. So, she formally stepped down and I became the acting king.

I'm the first King of Lexenburg to reign without a queen by my side, and because of that, the country loves to speculate and gossip. I can't speak to a woman without stories being circulated. Because of this, I have to be very careful until I find out what's public knowledge regarding Natalie's past. It's not that I'm ashamed of her. If anything, knowing her past makes me that much prouder of her because I know where she came from and how hard she worked to make a better life for herself. But not everyone will see it like that.

"Daddy!" Jasmine yells, running down the hallway. She's wearing a pretty pink dress now and her hair is in pigtails. Natalie must've had her change at the hotel. When she gets to me, she throws herself into my arms and I lift her, my heart full. I thought it would take time for her to warm up to me. I had mentally prepared myself for her to be shy and for our time together to be awkward, but based on the way she's hugging my neck, she's already accepted who I am and is embracing it, and for that I am thankful.

"Sorry," Natalie says, catching her breath. "I told her not to run." She mock glares at Jasmine, who remains with her arms wrapped around my neck.

"I wanted to get to my daddy faster," Jasmine explains. "Can we go pick my room now?"

"We sure can," I tell her. "And tomorrow you can help Mrs. Evelyn, the estate decorator, decorate it." Stephanie, despite not being thrilled about all of this, scheduled for Evelyn to come out tomorrow. She also scheduled the private tours like I asked and rescheduled any meetings or events that could be rescheduled.

I give Natalie and Jasmine a full tour of the Garden Estate, which is where our family resides. The rest of the castle is broken up into wings and towers—all named after various flowers. There is a place for everyone, but aside from the occasional event that takes place in the Rose Garden tower, neither of them will need to go anywhere else. Everything they need is here.

After Natalie and Jasmine pick out their rooms, which are located near mine, we spend the remainder of the afternoon together. We go for a walk through my private gardens while Jasmine tells me all about her travels, her family in Florence, and how excited she is to start school. In return, I tell her about her uncle Nate, who is in Hawaii with his new wife, Annabelle, on their honeymoon, and my cousin, Jack, who lives in town and has twin daughters a year younger than Jasmine. There are many more people in our family, but I don't want to overwhelm her.

The entire time we hang out, Natalie and I exchange silent looks and glances. At one point, I catch her staring at me, and I smirk knowingly, making her blush. It might've been six years since we were together, but the attraction is still there on her part, and that's good because it's definitely there on mine, and I have every intention of exploring it.

When evening rolls around, we join my mom for dinner. She spends the meal asking both Jasmine and Natalie questions, but I notice she stays clear of our past, and for that I'm grateful. At first, Natalie is nervous, guarded, answering vaguely, but once she realizes my mom is simply trying to get to know her, she opens up. By the end of dinner, both she and my daughter have won my mom over. And when Natalie takes Jasmine away to give her a bath, my mom tells me as such.

"ARE YOU SURE YOU DON'T WANT ME TO LIE WITH YOU?" NATALIE ASKS Jasmine for the third time. She's been bathed and is in her princess pajamas, lying in bed. She insisted I read her the fairy-tale story she gave to her mom because she doesn't have any other books. I told her we would buy her some new ones tomorrow and that seemed to excite her.

"I'm okay, Mommy," Jasmine insists. "I'm not a baby."

Her words hit me straight in the heart. I missed her being a baby. Her first word, her first steps… I missed everything. I have so much time to make up for.

"I know you're not," Natalie tells her. "But this is a strange place…"

"No, it's not," Jasmine argues. "It's Daddy's castle and I'm the princess."

Natalie nods. "I know. Okay, well, if you need anything, my room is right next door." She gives Jasmine a kiss on her forehead and then one to each of her cheeks. "I love you."

"Love you too," Jasmine says through a yawn. Then to me, with sleeping eyes that are barely open, she adds, "Love you, Daddy."

And with those three words, I'm pretty sure my heart just imploded inside my chest. How my daughter can be told I'm her dad and, just like that, accept me so completely, is scary on so many levels. It shows you how vulnerable and innocent children are.

"I love you too," I tell her, meaning it with every fiber of my being. "Get some rest because tomorrow we're going to see the gardens and church like you wanted." Her tiny sleepy face lights up for a quick second before her blue eyes droop in exhaustion.

After kissing her cheek and wishing her sweet dreams, Natalie and I leave her to get some sleep.

"She'll be out within seconds," Natalie says, once we're outside the door. "Today has been a big day for her."

We remain standing there, quietly, for a minute and then she peeks her head in. "Yep, already out," she confirms. I look inside and sure enough, Jasmine's eyes are closed and she's snoring softly, cuddled up with her stuffed puppy that her uncle Gio and aunt Aria bought her when she was a baby. She told me she wants a real one just like it, but before I could offer to buy her one, Natalie cut me off, saying maybe when she's older. I shrugged, mentally noting to contact the animal shelter.

After closing Jasmine's door, Natalie walks down the hall toward her room. She stops in front of her door and I scramble to think of a way to keep her with me. To keep her talking so I can spend some time with her. All afternoon it's been about Jasmine, and I'm okay with that, but now that she's asleep, I want some time with Natalie.

"You never ate your cake," I point out.

She snorts out a laugh. "Is that the best you can do, Liam?" She raises a single brow. "If you want to spend time with me, just say so." Fuck, I love how open and honest this woman is.

"I want to spend time with you." I push her against the wall until our bodies are flush against one another. "I want to spend time around you…" I run my nose along the length of her slim neck. "In you." I kiss the sensitive spot behind her ear that I know from experience makes her squirm. "I've thought about what I would do to you if I ever saw you again, so many times over the years…"

Her breath hitches. "I have too," she whispers. "So many dreams… fantasies."

"And now here we are."

"I want you," she murmurs. "It's too soon." She shakes her head. "We've only just reconnected but—"

I capture her mouth with my own, cutting her words off. I don't give a shit how soon it is. I knew she was the one for me back then and I know it now. I let her go once, accepted that she had disappeared and I couldn't find her. I should've scoured the earth for her. Demanded to know where she was. But I didn't and we lost so much time because of that. I'm not going to waste any more. She's here, in my arms, and I'm going to make damn sure she never disappears again.

I lift her up and her legs encircle my hips. I carry her into her room, closing the door behind us. The room is dark, only a bit of light from the grounds coming in through the slats of the blinds.

I lay her down in the center of the bed and her face and body are lit up by the glow of the lights enough that I can make out her features, see the lust in her eyes. She's so fucking beautiful.

I prowl up her body, kissing every inch of exposed skin I can get my mouth on. When I get to her lips, I crush my mouth against hers, tasting her sweet scent, memorizing the way her lips feel. I roll us over so she's on top, her bare thighs straddling my hips. When she returned, she was changed out of her jeans and shirt, instead in a pair of dress shorts that were just short enough to be sexy, but still long enough to be considered appropriate, and an off-the-shoulder top. Instead of the boots she was wearing, she was sporting heels that helped show off her tanned, toned calves.

"I've dreamed of this," I murmur against her lips. "And now you're here." I grab a handful of her ass and grind her against my hard length.

"I'm here," she moans, threading her fingers through my hair.

I reach up and remove her shirt, exposing her black, lacy bra. Her perky tits spill out and I kiss my way along her cleavage. "I missed these," I tell her, pulling her cups down and revealing those perfect pink nipples I spent the weekend all those years ago kissing and sucking. I wrap my lips around one, swirling my tongue around the tip.

Natalie groans softly. "I need to feel you," she begs, unbuttoning my dress shirt. We both scramble to undress each other, desperate for what's to come. It's been so fucking long, but it's as if we're right back in that hotel room.

When we're both naked, she slides down my body and, without any preamble, takes my dick into her mouth, almost swallowing down the entire thing. It pushes against the back of her throat, causing her to gag, and I damn near come on the spot. It's been too long, and her mouth feels too good.

Fisting her mane, I flip us over again, then spread her legs, needing to taste her. I push her thighs back, until they're up against her chest and then, starting at her tight asshole—that I fully plan to one day claim—I lick up her center, savoring the taste and scent of her sweet musk.

When I get to her clit, sucking on it hard, her palms smack the sheets. Her face whips from side to side as I bring her closer and closer to her orgasm. When she falls over the edge, a cry of pleasure escapes her lips, and I climb over her, connecting our mouths to silence her cries, unsure how soundproof the walls are.

With her legs spread, the head of my dick pushes against her entrance, and before I can stop myself, I'm plunging into her. Her back arches and her legs wrap around my torso. I thrust into her over and over again, lost in the way her warm pussy strangles my dick. Her hands grip the back of my neck, holding me close to her, and my own cage her in. We're as close as two people can be, yet it still doesn't feel like we're close enough.

As I damn near fuck her into the mattress, her moans get louder, and I swallow each one down, devouring her mouth with my own. I rise up slightly, hooking her thighs over my arms, so I can go deeper. The move sends her tumbling over the edge, her second orgasm racing through her. When her insides grip my dick, I let go, filling her up with my cum. In the back of my mind, I know I shouldn't do that, but the primal, caveman part of me, the part that would give anything to *see* her carrying my baby, pushes the thought aside. She's mine, and if I have it my way, I'm going to fill her with my babies over and over and over again.

"Oh my God," she breathes, sounding completely sated. Her eyes are hooded and her body, which is tucked under me, is now loose and limp.

"I came in you," I point out, planting a hard kiss to her lips.

Her eyes widen. "I'm not on birth control… I haven't been, umm…" Her cheeks turn a beautiful shade of pink. "I haven't been having sex."

"Good." I pull out of her and back up, keeping my palms against the insides of her knees. I watch as my cum leaks out of her pussy.

"Good?" she squeaks, trying to close her thighs.

"Yeah, good." I hold on to her knee with one hand and, with the other, push two fingers into her cum-filled hole. "This time when I knock you up, I'll get to see you carry my baby."

I look up at her, expecting her to argue, but instead she frowns and her eyes go glassy. "I know it's not the same, but I have pictures… I took them every week during my pregnancy. I also have thousands of Jasmine."

I crawl back up her body and wipe the tears that are leaking out of her lids. "I can't wait to see them."

Refusing to let her clean up, because I love the idea of her sleeping with my cum inside her, I pull her into my arms and tuck her head under my chin. She wraps her arms around my waist and snuggles into my side. "Do you think we're rushing things?" she whispers.

I tug her chin up, so she's forced to look at me. "We missed six fucking years together. I missed your pregnancy, the first five years of our daughter's life. We missed out on six years we could've been making memories. All because of miscommunication. I don't want to waste another second. You and that little girl in the room next to us are mine."

A slow smile spreads across Natalie's face as she nods. "I like the sound of that..." She lays her head in the crook of my neck. "Of being yours."

CHAPTER TWELVE
NATALIE

BEFORE I OPEN MY EYES, I ALREADY KNOW LIAM IS GONE. IT'S CRAZY HOW, even after all this time, and only knowing him for such a short time, I can feel him—or in this case, lack of him. My eyes land on a piece of paper on the pillow next to me and I lift it up to read it.

> Natalie, I didn't want our daughter to see me in your bed until we speak to her, so I slipped out. I have some work to do, so when she wakes up, I'll have breakfast with her so I can spend some time with her. Sleep in, take a bath, and join us when you're ready.
> -Liam

A cheesy grin spreads across my face as I read the note for the second time. My phone buzzes from the bedside table, and I set the note down to see who it is. The caller ID shows it's Aria calling, so I answer it.

"Hey!"

"Hey you," she says back. "Are you getting on the plane soon?" Yesterday was supposed to be Jasmine's and my last day of our trip.

"Actually," I say, sitting up. "There's been a change of plans."

"Okay..."

"Are you sitting? Because what I have to tell you, you might want to be."

Aria laughs. "I'm sitting."

"I found Liam."

There's silence and then, "Oh my God! *Liam*, Liam? Jasmine's father, Liam?"

"Yep."

"Where?"

"This is the part you need to be sitting for," I half-joke.

"You finding him wasn't the crazy part?"

"Nope."

"Well, tell me!" she demands.

"He's the King of Lexenburg. It's a small country in—"

"I know where Lexenburg is!" she squeals. "It's where you guys were visiting the... Holy shit! The castle!"

"Yep, we stepped up to take a picture with the king, who made an unexpected appearance, and there he was."

"Oh my God. So, he knows?"

I spend the next twenty minutes telling her everything that's happened in the last... well, damn, it's only been less than twenty-four hours, yet it feels like it's been days, maybe even weeks. Being with Liam does that to me—forces me to lose all track of time. When we're together, it's like the entire world disappears and time means nothing.

When I get done telling her everything, she asks, "Does this mean you guys are going to move there?" Her question is tinged with a hint of sadness and I know how she feels.

As happy as I am to have found Liam, being with him will mean leaving Florence and the small family we've created there.

"We haven't discussed it yet, but I don't think the king can move."

"No," she agrees. "Well, damn."

"We'll be back in a few weeks. Even if it's just to get our stuff... And we can visit, and you can visit us."

"Yeah, of course," she says. "It's just, I'm going to miss you..."

"Me too." We've spent the last six years practically joined at the hip. Our kids think they're cousins instead of merely friends. I'm going to miss living down the street from them, but this is Liam—Jasmine's father and the man I fell in love with all those years ago and never fell out. It's all happening so fast, but he was right about what he said last night. We missed out on a lot and have a lot of making up to do.

We talk for a few more minutes, and once we hang up, I jump in the shower. After blow-drying my hair and getting dressed, I head out to find Liam and Jasmine. The part of the estate he lives in is huge and has what feels like a million halls, so when I turn the corner, one I could've sworn I already turned, I realize I'm lost.

As I'm pulling out my phone to call him, I run into someone. "I'm so sorry..." I say, glancing up to see... What was her name?

"Stephanie," she finishes. "I'm glad I ran into you. I was looking for you. We need to talk."

Her cold tone doesn't sit well with me, but she's Liam's assistant. "Sure."

She leads me to an office and closes the door behind us. She steps behind a large oak desk and gestures for me to have a seat. When I do, she sits as well, steepling her fingers together.

"Did you know that for the last several decades Lexenburg was the fourth wealthiest country in the world?"

"Actually, it's the third." I did my research when planning our trip. I love teaching Jasmine about each place we visit.

"That's correct. It's wealthy because of how it's run. After William took over for his father, making the changes he saw fit, he jumped it up from the fourth to the third wealthiest country. Our unemployment rate is the lowest in the world. Our country is thriving and it's because of William."

"That's amazing," I tell her slowly, my stomach knotting. I'm not completely sure, but I have a sinking feeling about where she's going with her factoids.

"The people trust William because he's honest. He puts them first..."

I nod because I can't speak with the huge lump forming in my throat.

"Have you ever heard of Gaitos?" she asks. Before I can answer, she continues. "It was the third wealthiest country in the world. Until a scandal with the royal family hit and the country crumbled. Which is exactly what will happen here if you stay." Her gaze sears into mine. "I know all about you. How you met William..."

I swallow thickly. "That was a long time ago..."

"Doesn't matter. Did you see Britain's reaction to Meghan? And she's not even married to the king."

She pulls something out and sets it on the desk. A checkbook.

"Really?" I roll my eyes. "Kind of cliché, don't you think?" This is like a scene from every royal movie on the Lifetime channel.

"Call it whatever you want," she says. "But I'm merely trying to protect William and this country from you. He isn't thinking clearly because of his alleged daughter."

"There's nothing alleged about her," I snap. "She's his."

Stephanie shrugs. "If you stay and the people find out the mother of his child is a whore, you will taint this family. They will lose their trust in him. It will be the beginning of the end."

I stand, refusing to listen to another minute of this. "If Liam feels that way, he can tell me himself."

Stephanie stands as well. "He won't tell you because he doesn't want to lose his daughter. You don't belong here, and you will only disgrace his name and this family. You will ruin everything he's worked for, everything his family has worked for."

She steps around the desk and over to me. "If you care about him, you will leave before you destroy this country."

She extends her hand, which is holding a single check. "It's blank and signed. You can fill in the amount."

I back away from her and that check. "I'm not going away until Liam tells me to do so."

I turn on my heel and exit the room. It takes me several minutes, and a few wrong turns, but I finally find Liam and Jasmine in the kitchen. They're both eating a stack of pancakes and talking to each other like they've known each other forever. I stop in my place before they can see me and watch them for a couple minutes. Liam is telling Jasmine all about the country and the people. I can hear the pride in his voice, see it on his face. I try to push everything Stephanie said from my head, but one thing she mentioned bounces around like a ping pong ball. *"He won't tell you because he doesn't want to lose his daughter."*

Everything he's said to me since we reconnected tells me he wants me too—it's not just about Jasmine. But as a parent, I know I would do anything for my daughter. Even if it meant destroying everyone around me. Can I let him risk that?

"Are you going to stand there and watch us eat or join us for breakfast?" Liam asks, meeting my eyes.

"Good morning." I step fully into the kitchen.

"Morning." He looks like he's dying to come over and kiss me, but he refrains since our daughter is here and we haven't spoken to her about us yet.

"Morning, Mommy," Jasmine says around a mouthful of pancakes.

"Here." He hands me a plate of food. "For you."

"Thank you." I smother butter and syrup on them before cutting them up. I take a bite and they're delicious. Fluffy and flavorful. "So good."

"Daddy and I made them." Jasmine beams.

"You did a great job." I lean over and kiss her temple. "Did you sleep well?"

"Yes, and this morning Mrs. Evelyn and I picked out everything for my room. It's going to have a princess bed and a princess couch and a princess rug!"

"That sounds like a whole lot of princess," I joke. She nods in agreement.

"When we're done eating, we're going to head to the church," Liam mentions. "We have a private tour scheduled."

"Sounds good." I stab a piece of my pancake and pop it into my mouth. While we eat, Jasmine jabbers away. I stay quiet, my conversation with Stephanie running through my head. At some point, I need to tell Liam what she said. I don't want to keep it from him, and I need to know his thoughts. I can't change my past. I can't change that from the time I turned sixteen and became homeless, I sold my body to make ends meet, or that the only job I've ever had was in a bordello. I've changed my entire life around, but if anyone finds out what I did, that'll be the only thing they focus on.

When we're done eating, Liam shows us to *the tunnel*. It's a massive garage and driveway that's completely covered. It's how he and his family come and go without being seen. There's a town car waiting for us, and he introduces us to Marcus, his driver, and then I see Harold. It's been six years, so he's older, a few more grays, but his smile when he sees me approaching is as sweet as it was all those years ago.

"Miss Natalie," he says, taking my hand and kissing the top. "It's so good to see you again."

"You too."

"Mommy," Jasmine says. "Who's that?"

"This is my bodyguard and friend," Liam tells her, bending to her level. "And now he's yours."

My eyes bounce over to Herald, who nods in agreement.

"There's nobody I trust more with you and our daughter," Liam says. "Nobody knows who Jasmine is, but once they do, they will be relentless to take her picture and get close to her, especially the American reporters," he says with disgust. "You can never leave without Harold. Okay?" His eyes meet mine. "It's for your safety."

"Okay."

He smiles softly then looks at Jasmine. "You're a princess now. And every princess needs a bodyguard to keep her safe."

Jasmine, who doesn't quite get it, nods. "Okay, Daddy."

We get into the vehicle and Harold sits in the front with the driver. Liam explains there will be a car following in front of and another one behind us. It has to be this way every time he leaves.

"You didn't have all of this in Vegas," I mention once we're in the car.

"I had a few guards…" He looks at me sheepishly.

"What?" I ask, confused.

"They were around, but you didn't notice them. That's their job. To remain in the background."

I try to think back, but aside from the one who drove us around, I don't remember anyone else.

"I also wasn't the king back then," he adds. "We're a small country, but because we're one of the most prosperous, we have a lot of dealings with other countries, and sometimes they aren't happy with the outcome." His eyes go to Jasmine. "I will make sure you're both always protected and safe."

The morning is spent touring the church. Since Liam knows all of the history, he insists on telling us about them, keeping it just the three of us without a tour guide. We laugh and talk and take what feels like a million pictures. I've never been in a relationship before. It's always been just Jasmine and me. I was worried how we would all come together, but as the day progresses, it's as if we all just slide into place, clicking with one another.

"This is the church the royal family gets married in," he mentions. "Eighteen weddings have taken place here since it was constructed in 1415…" His gaze meets mine. "Including my parents'."

"That's amazing," I breathe. "Was your brother married here too?"

"He was." He grips the curves of my hips and pulls me close to him. "And it's also where I plan to one day marry you."

I suck in a shocked gasp. "Liam…"

"I'm not proposing… yet. When I do, it will be way more romantic than this." He hits me with a sexy, crooked grin. "But it will happen." He kisses the corner of my mouth and a shiver runs through me. "I have no doubt you are the woman I want to spend my life with, and since I have every intention of filling you with another baby as soon as possible, we should probably get married sooner rather than later." He winks and my insides turn to mush.

When we leave the church, we go straight to the gardens. Like the church, the place is empty, and Liam shows us around. It's beautiful, filled with all types of flowers. Liam explains these gardens were built several decades ago because Queen Athena—a previous queen—loved flowers. Her husband built her the gardens as an anniversary present. It's also why the castle is labeled with names of flowers.

We get to the end of a path and waiting for us is a large, spread out blanket and a basket. "Is this for us?" I ask dumbly.

Liam smiles. "It is. I figured what better way to spend the afternoon than having a picnic with my girls."

Jasmine cheers excitedly, dropping onto the blanket and opening the basket. She passes out the food and drinks, then quickly devours hers, clearly starving. Once she's done, she asks if she can feed the fish in the pond her leftover bread.

"Sure," Liam tells her.

She skips over to the water and it's then I notice Harold standing a little ways away. "Has he been here this whole time?"

"Of course," Liam tells me, pulling me between his legs. It's a gorgeous day outside—not too hot and there's a nice breeze. I lean back against Liam's hard chest and glance up at him. He dips his head and kisses me.

"This is nice," I murmur against his lips. It wasn't until I spent time with Aria and Giovanni that I saw how a real couple behaves. Although I spent time with Amber and Nico, it's different when they're at the mansion. But with Aria and Giovanni, in their home, I got my first glimpse of what love looks like. The way Giovanni always hugs and kisses her. The way they work together as parents. I even witnessed a few arguments between them and was shocked by the way they would eventually compromise. Whoever was wrong would apologize and the other would forgive. I used to imagine what it would be like to meet someone and spend my life with him. To love and be loved by him. And now, it feels like I might have it.

"What's going on in that gorgeous head of yours?" Liam asks, kissing my temple.

"This is my first relationship," I admit. "And I'm scared. And nervous. I don't want to mess it up."

Liam tips my chin, so I'm looking up at him. "There's nothing you can do to mess this up. We're in this together."

We spend the rest of the afternoon playing in the gardens. Liam and Jasmine play tag, and afterward, he shows us the rest of the grounds. When Jasmine gets cranky, obviously exhausted from the busy day, Liam scoops her up into his arms and carries her back to the car. He's patient with her while she whines and cries, until she falls asleep, and I fall even harder for him. It's one thing to create a child, but it's another to actually be a dad. The man who helped create me was great at making babies, but he sucked at being a father.

When we get home, Liam lays her down, while I grab us both a cup of tea. We meet on the balcony in Liam's room.

"She's out," he says with a laugh. "Harold will let us know when she wakes up."

I hand him his tea and he takes a sip then sets it down. He plucks my cup from my hand and sets it down as well, then pulls me into his arms. "Did you have a good day?" he asks, his blue eyes meeting mine.

"A wonderful day. You are the perfect tour guide." I give him a chaste kiss. "So, what's on the agenda for tomorrow? A tour of the vineyards? Or how about we visit the beach?" I joke.

Liam's face drops. "We could maybe visit the vineyards, but I would have to get it approved first, but the beach... I don't think..."

"Whoa, stop." I cradle his face in my hands. "It was just a joke. I know you can't just go anywhere on a whim... and especially not right now, since nobody knows about Jasmine and me..."

Liam exhales a breath of relief. "I'm sorry. I just know Jasmine thinks this place is like a fairy tale, and I love that she thinks that, but I need you to understand that because of my position... my family's position... we can't just come and go. It's like the President of the United States."

"I get it. It'll take some adjusting, but like you said, we're in this together."

Liam's eyes soften, and then he says three words nobody besides my mom, Jasmine, and Aria have ever spoken to me in truth. "I love you."

Before I can say anything back, he captures my mouth with his own. He reaches around and grabs my ass, lifting me into his arms. He carries me inside our room and sets me on the bed. Our clothes come off and then he enters me. His movements are slow, his kisses soft. The way he touches me is as if he's making love to me. I've had sex too many times to count, but nobody has ever made love to me. Nobody has ever made me feel the way Liam makes me feel.

Emotional tears prick my eyes, and when Liam notices, he places a soft kiss to each of my wet eyelids. We both come at nearly the same time, and when we do, he whispers again into my ear that he loves me, and I know without a shadow of a doubt, I'm done searching for my Prince Charming because I've found him.

CHAPTER THIRTEEN
NATALIE
ONE WEEK LATER

I STARE DOWN AT THE GIFT-WRAPPED BOX WITH A HUGE GRIN ON MY FACE. There's a note taped to the front that reads: OPEN ME. I laugh, wondering what Liam is up to. We just laid Jasmine down for the night and Liam told me there was a surprise waiting for me in the bedroom. I assumed he meant him, but apparently he has something up his sleeve.

This past week, getting to know Liam again, has been nothing short of amazing. During the day, we spend our time as a family, and at night, after our little girl is tucked into bed and fast asleep, we spend our time alone, getting to know each other on a more intimate level. I know things won't always be like this. Liam will eventually have to return to his duties as the king, but I'm thankful for him choosing to put us first and taking the time to get to know us. Jasmine has fallen head over heels for her father. We've needed this time with him to connect as a family.

I open the box and find the most exquisite crimson dress and black heels. Inside, there's another note: WEAR ME. I'm not sure what he's up to, but I'm excited to find out. After putting on the gorgeous dress and fixing up my hair and makeup, I step outside of the room, unsure where to go from here. Liam has said we can't leave the grounds, so I'm not sure what he has planned.

"This way, Miss," Samson, one of Liam's many guards, says with a smile. I follow him down the hall, passing Harold, who is on his laptop in the sitting room. He's never far from Jasmine, even when she's asleep.

We walk for what feels like miles down several hallways and up a spiraling staircase. When we get to the top, he motions for me to enter the door, then bids me a good night. When I step through the door, I find I'm outside. The night is black, and the stars are twinkling high in the sky. It's beautiful out here.

I glance around and find Liam standing next to a table dressed in a suit. "You look stunning." He walks over to me and places a soft kiss to the corner of my mouth.

"What are we doing out here?" I ask, curious.

"We're going on our first official date," he says with a smile. "We can't leave the grounds, so I had to improvise." He motions toward the table. "Join me?" he asks, as if it's even a question.

He pulls my chair out for me, reminding me of the weekend we spent together all those years ago, then has a seat. Moments later, a server comes over and pours us each a glass of wine. I take one sip and immediately recognize it. Just to be sure, I turn the bottle to view the label. Napa Hills Estates.

"How did you do this?"

"I had it shipped over," he says with a shrug.

My heart pounds against my chest at his thoughtfulness. "I haven't had this wine since our time together." I had run out of the hotel so upset I didn't take any of the wine he bought with me.

"Good," he tells me, taking a sip. "It's our wine."

The server comes back out, setting an appetizer on the table between us. "Is this *insalata caprese*?" It's one of my favorite things to eat in Italy. It's a combination of mozzarella, tomatoes, and sweet basil.

"It is. I thought, since you've spent the last week learning about Lexenburg, we could bring a little bit of your home here. I figured you might be feeling a little homesick."

Oh, this man...

"Thank you." I cut into the tomato and mozzarella and take a bite. It's delicious.

"I also have a little surprise for you at the end of the meal," Liam says with a flirty wink that has my insides melting.

We spend the rest of the meal talking and getting to know each other. We talk about trivial things like our favorite colors and go deeper about what we want our futures to look like. I never imagined living anywhere but in Florence, but now I can't imagine living anywhere without Liam.

"You ready for your surprise?" he asks, after the dinner plates are cleared.

"I'm a woman, we're always ready for a surprise," I joke.

Liam laughs and gives a slight head nod to the server, who a minute later, walks over carrying cups of... "Is that coffee?" I squeal as she sets them down and I immediately smell the caffeine.

"It is," he says with a chuckle. "Ordered you a coffee maker and espresso machine."

"Oh my God, I love you," I breathe, taking a sip of the coffee. It's been weeks since I've had a cup of coffee and I'm dying for one.

Liam's brows shoot to the top of his head, and it's then I realize what I said. The statement was said as a joke, but the words... I mean them.

Setting my coffee down, I stand and walk around the table over to Liam, who must know what I'm doing, because he pushes his chair back slightly, so I can climb into his lap. I lift my dress up and straddle his thighs. I cradle his face, and he looks at me, his azure eyes searing into mine.

"I..." The other two words are on the tip of my tongue. I want to say them, but for some reason I can't. Not yet. Maybe it's because I've never said them to a man before. Maybe it's because I know the power those words hold and once I say them, they're out there. I've never felt like this before and I would be lying if I said it didn't scare me. "I need you," I croak out.

Liam sighs, and I worry he's upset, that he's disappointed I wasn't able to say the words he's so easily able to voice, but then his mouth collides with mine. His tongue delves between my parted lips, deepening the kiss, and it's as if he's telling me with his actions it's okay. He knows what I want to say. He knows how I feel. And he'll wait for me.

We kiss like this for several minutes, getting lost in each other. His lips are strong and his tongue moves in perfect sync with my own. He tastes of coffee and sex, and I want to rip this suit off him and ride him right here... Then, I remember we're alone on this balcony and I can do just that.

Without breaking our kiss, I reach between us and tug at the button on his dress pants. Understanding what I'm doing, he lifts slightly so I can pull his pants down enough for his dick to spring free. Not even bothering to remove my dress, I lift it up, so it doesn't get caught and guide his hard length into me. I lower myself slowly, and we both groan when I'm completely seated around him.

"Fuck," he hisses against my lips. "You feel so damn good."

I glide my hands up his shoulders and around to the back of his head, threading my fingers through his short hair. His hands find my hips and he digs his fingers into my flesh. I might be on top, but when he lifts and then lowers me, making sure to hit that perfect spot that will have me coming in no time, it becomes clear he's fucking me—and I let him.

I find my release first, and he follows shortly after. When we break our kiss, my lips are swollen, and my body feels like Jell-O. I lay my head against his shoulder, completely content to stay like this.

"Move in with me," he whispers into my ear.

That has me lifting my head back up. "What?" I heard what he said, but I need him to repeat it.

"Move in with me," he repeats. "I don't care that it's only been a week… I'm in love with you and I don't want to be away from you." His face beams with love. "We can even visit—"

"Yes," I tell him, not needing to hear anything more. He's right. I love him and he loves me, and I don't care how long it's been. We've wasted enough time and all I want to do is spend my days with him and our daughter. We can figure it all out as we go.

"Yes?" he parrots.

"Yes," I say again. "We'll stay."

His grin widens, his dimple popping out. "You've just made me the happiest man on Earth."

CHAPTER FOURTEEN
LIAM
TWO WEEKS LATER

"DADDY, THROW ME AGAIN!" JASMINE YELLS, SWIMMING OVER TO ME LIKE A cute little fish. Since Natalie agreed to move in with me, we've taken steps to move them in. We've hired a moving company to pack up and ship all of their belongings here. Their furniture is being put in storage for now, and once things settle down, we'll visit and get it sorted. Stephanie isn't happy that I've put off all my duties the last few weeks, but like I told her, my family comes first. I'll have a lot to catch up on when I do return to work, but it will be worth it.

Every day with my girls has been better than the previous day. Even though we can't leave, that doesn't stop Jasmine from living her best life. She loves exploring the castle, and her favorite activity is playing hide and seek. Today is an exceptionally hot day, so when Jasmine asked if we could spend it in the pool, Natalie and I thought it would be the perfect way to spend the day.

Lifting her by her tiny waist, I throw her a couple feet. She plops into the water, then quickly swims back up, the top of her head, then the rest of her body, breaking through the surface of the water.

"Again!" she squeals, shaking the water off her face.

"Food first," Natalie calls out.

I glance over and find her in a tiny as fuck string bikini. Her body is as perfect as it was all those years ago, but now, from carrying our daughter, her hips are a bit wider and her breasts are fuller. I love the way I'm able to grip her hips when I'm fucking her.

Her hair is up in a tight ponytail, exposing her slim neck, and when she looks at me, with the most gorgeous smile splayed across her face, I make a mental note to sneak her out here one night so I can fuck her in this pool… or on the lounge chair, or hell, maybe the hot tub. *Or maybe all three…*

My dick perks up at the thought, and I have to think about something else to make it go down before I can get out of the pool.

"One more time!" Jasmine begs.

"Your mom said food first," I tell her. She pouts but doesn't argue, instead swimming over to the edge so she can get out and eat. The first time she argued with her mom and I let her have her way, Natalie explained we have to be a team and provide a united front or Jasmine would pin us against each other. I laughed and told her she sounded like some of the countries I deal with. I mean, she's only five, and we're the adults. The next time she did it, Natalie gave me a look, so I had her back. Jasmine cried, and the tears in her eyes damn near killed me. So I gave in. Natalie glared, and Jasmine cheered—and those tears… they magically disappeared, and I realized I'd been had.

So, the *third* time, I didn't give in. The tears came and went, but she got over it. And Natalie thanked me. I'm new to this whole dad thing, but Natalie is a wonderful mother and I have no doubt she'll be by my side every step of the way.

"Your Majesty," Lawrence, one of my advisors, says as I'm wrapping a towel around my waist and walking over to the spread Natalie whipped up. I told her the chef will make anything she wants, but she insisted she's capable.

"Lawrence, how may I help you?" He only comes out of his office when it's important. He's been with my family for over fifty years and is planning to retire this year. He's grouchy as hell, but he's always had our family's best interest at heart and has never steered us wrong.

"You're needed in the Lavender room, sir." The Lavender room is where all our meetings are held, and I don't recall a meeting being scheduled. "It's of the utmost importance, sir," he adds.

"Okay, I'll be right there."

With a quick nod, he bows and exits.

"Everything okay?" Natalie asks once he's gone.

"I'm not sure. He's called an emergency meeting." Her eyes go wide in fear. "It's okay." I kiss her cheek. "Eat and relax, and I'll be back soon."

"Can we swim some more?" Jasmine asks.

"Of course, princess." I kiss her cheek as well. "As soon as I get back, we'll have a race."

Her eyes light up. "Okay, bye, Daddy. I love you!"

I still at her words. The one and only time she's said those words to me was when she was half-asleep. I chalked it up to her saying them out of habit, since she had just told her mom she loved her. But right now, those three words are done with purpose. Meant for me. Because my little girl loves me. "I love you too," I choke out.

My eyes meet Natalie's and she smiles softly. She hasn't told me she loves me yet, but I know she does. She just needs time to come to terms with how fast everything between us is happening, and I'm okay giving her that time. We have the rest of our lives for her to tell me.

When I get to the Lavender room, my mom, Stephanie, Lawrence, and one of my other advisors are all there. They're arguing with each other, and since they're all speaking at once, I can't make out what it is exactly they're arguing about.

The second I clear my throat, everyone stops talking and gives me their attention. Before I can ask what's going on, Stephanie speaks up. "I warned you this would happen."

"What?" What the hell is going on?

"It somehow leaked," Mom says, sadness and sympathy in her tone. My blood freezes, my body going numb. She's not talking about…

"They know about Natalie and Jasmine," Mom adds. "Everything."

My instinct is to run to Natalie and Jasmine to shield them both, protect them from the shitstorm that is about to come down on us, but it's better if they're outside at the pool, oblivious to what's happening.

"Everything?" I ask, dropping onto a seat.

"Everything," Stephanie says, pushing an iPad toward me. I click on the article and read it. Pictures of Natalie and Jasmine are on the screen. Ones I've never seen before. Someone must've found some. I read the article, then read it again. They know everything about Natalie, from her time on the streets when she was a minor, to her job at La Stella's, to the possibility of her being the mother of my daughter.

"I warned you this would happen," Stephanie says again, her tone condescending.

"She is an embarrassment to this family and country."

"Enough," I snap.

"No," she argues back. "You need to hear it… see what her being here is going to do to this family, to your credibility. She needs to leave before she destroys everything. How are you going to explain to the entire country that the woman you had a baby with is a prostitute? Huh?" Stephanie taunts. "Prostitution is illegal here!"

"She wasn't a prostitute when I was with her," I point out, my mind racing. Not because of what they'll think or say, but because it will all be aimed at Natalie. She worked so hard to put her past behind her and now, this… I wasn't thinking about how this would affect her. How badly she could be hurt.

"It's okay," Mom says, placing a hand on my bicep. "We'll get through this together as a family." I relax slightly at her words, grateful to have my mom on my side.

"She needs to leave," Stephanie says. "Both she and that child need to go."

"Stephanie," Mom tuts.

"She's right," I tell her, making my mom's brows furrow. "Natalie and Jasmine need to leave. It's for the best."

Stephanie's chin lifts, and I glare at her. "Not for good," I add. "Just until all of this calms down." I look at my mom. "I don't want her to read or hear any of this." I point to the iPad. "It will hurt her."

"What are you going to do?" Mom asks. "Send them back to Florence?"

"No, there's no way I'm letting either of them out of my sight." I turn to Lawrence, who's been quiet. "What are your thoughts?"

"Sir, I think it would be best to spin it. Explain what happened to her as a child and focus on how rough her life was. Tell them you met and fell in love but lost touch and you found your way back to each other."

Mom smiles warmly. "Like a modern-day fairy tale."

"Only the prince didn't save her," I tell them, my thoughts going to Jasmine's book. "She saved herself."

"She saves herself…" Lawrence muses out loud. Then his face lights up. "We could start a charity, in honor of abandoned children, to help them go to University."

"I like it, and I bet Natalie will too."

"That's perfect," Mom agrees.

"Paul," I say to another one of my advisors, who deals with the media. "Schedule a news conference and invite everyone. After I type up what I plan to say, I'll email it to you to approve. I'm going to address the people, and then I'm going to take Natalie and Jasmine away while the fires are put out, so they're not here to see and hear it all, and hopefully while we're away, I'll convince her to marry me."

Mom grins at the same time Stephanie gasps. "You can't marry her! What are you thinking?" She shrieks. "After everything I did—" She quickly closes her mouth, and I'm about to ask her what she means by that, when Flynn, another one of my advisors walks in.

"Your Majesty," he says, addressing me.

"Flynn."

"There's something you need to see, sir." He hands me a file and I open it. Inside are grainy pictures, but still clear enough to make out what they're of. I glance up at him, not wanting to believe what I'm seeing. I flip through the pages of pictures and emails that were printed, everything becoming clearer by the second.

When I've had enough, I close the file and look at Stephanie. "Care to finish your statement from a moment ago?"

"Wh-What are you talking about?" she mutters.

"I'm talking about the fact that you had Natalie investigated and then sold the story to The Lexenburg Gossip!" I bark, tossing the file across the table at her.

My mom gasps. "No, Stephanie…"

"I can explain," she begins, as Harold enters.

"Miss Natalie and Miss Jasmine are gone, sir."

My blood runs cold. "What do you mean, they're gone?"

"Jasmine was tired and wanted to ask for a kiss before her nap. She came in here and Natalie followed. I went up to check on them and they were gone. Their luggage is gone too. I spoke to security and they said they walked right off the grounds."

I close my eyes and take a calming breath. They came up here… which means Natalie heard us talking about her. Who knows what part of the conversation she walked in on.

"They left?" Mom asks.

"Yes, Your Majesty."

"William," she says. "If they left, they had to have been bombarded by the paparazzi."

Damn it, I didn't even think about that. "I need to find them," I say, heading to the door. I stop before I exit, remembering something. "Stephanie, you're fired," I tell her, before turning my attention to Flynn. "Flynn, tell security she is to be escorted to gather her belongings and then removed from the premises."

I don't wait for a response before I rush out. Harold is waiting for me by the car with the door already open. "Any word?" I ask, jumping in.

"According to my friend with The Post, several reporters swarmed them," he says once he's inside and driving. "They verbally attacked them and Jasmine started crying…"

"Damn it." I can't believe this is happening. I should've paid more attention to what Stephanie was doing. I knew she's had a crush on me for years and that she was upset about Natalie and Jasmine. But I never thought she would sell Natalie's story to the biggest, sleaziest gossip rag in Lexenburg.

"The last he saw, they got into a car," he says, snapping me out of my thoughts.

"The airport."

"That's what I'm thinking."

The entire drive there I text and call Natalie, leaving her voicemails and messages to please call me, but she doesn't answer. I have to hope that the flight she's catching will be late enough I can get there before they take off. I text my other guards, letting them know where we're going, and they let me know they're already ahead of and behind us.

When we arrive, we go straight to the only airline that flies into Italy. My guards are on top of it, keeping everyone back as I jog through the airport, straight to the terminal. When I arrive, I stop and glance around, not seeing either of my girls. When I ask a woman to please check the women's restroom, she comes out a minute later and tells me nobody is in there.

"This doesn't make any sense," I tell Harold, out of breath and confused as hell.

"Maybe they—" His words are cut off at the sound of the sweetest voice I've ever heard.

"Daddy!" Jasmine yells, running over to me. Her arms open and I lift her into my own. I take a second to inhale her sweet scent, then shift her to my side, so I can see over her head.

Natalie is standing several feet away, holding both their luggage. Her eyes are glassy and her cheeks are stained from her tears. She's chewing on her bottom lip and staring at me.

"Baby," I breathe, stepping over to her.

"Why did you come after us?" she asks, her voice cold, devoid of all emotions.

"Why wouldn't I?"

"You told them we needed to leave." I was right. She heard a piece of the conversation, but not all of it.

"Did you also hear the part where I said, after I addressed the people, I would go away with both of you?"

Her eyes widen. "I-I heard you say that us leaving would be for the best, so I left…"

"I also said I wouldn't let either of you out of my sight. That we would go away together." There was also the mention of my plan to propose, but I don't bring that up.

"You don't want us to go?" she murmurs, fresh tears pricking her eyes. "But everyone knows… Stephanie warned me I would embarrass you and she was right."

Fucking Stephanie. I'm going to speak to my attorney and see about suing her. She can't get away with what she's done.

"No, baby. I don't want you to go anywhere. Stephanie is the one who leaked everything to the media, and I've fired her." I shift Jasmine slightly, so I can pull Natalie toward me with my hand that's not holding my daughter. "I'm so sorry for what she did."

I run my knuckles down her cheek. "Please don't go. We'll get through this together. My team has a plan. Trust me to handle this. And then I'll take you both anywhere you want to go, so we can spend some time together while it blows over."

A single tear slides down Natalie's cheek and Jasmine reaches over and wipes it. "Don't cry, Mommy," she says, her tiny, sad voice piercing my heart.

"I already lost you once," I tell her. "I can't lose you again. Please."

"Okay," she finally says. "We'll stay."

"Yay!" Jasmine cheers. "I get to go back to my princess room!"

"Thank you." I press my mouth to hers. "I love you."

"I love you too," she murmurs against my lips. "Let's go home."

EPILOGUE
NATALIE
FIVE MONTHS LATER

"MOMMY!" JASMINE EXCLAIMS, RUNNING OVER TO ME.

"Hey, sweet girl!" I bend at the waist and she flies into my arms. "Did you have a good day at school?" Unlike the other royal children, who were homeschooled for pre-primary and primary school and then sent away to boarding school for secondary, I insisted Jasmine be placed in school here. Because of who she is, she couldn't be sent to a state-funded school, but Liam agreed to send her to a private pre-primary school in town.

"I did! I painted the most beautiful picture." She pulls the paper out of her backpack and hands it to me. "Melissa said it's her favorite."

Melissa is Jasmine's best friend. I was worried after everything that went down Jasmine would have trouble making friends, but I was right to trust Liam. He and his team handled my story and spun it in a positive way. By the time Jasmine started school, the majority of the country was supportive of us being together. It probably helps that he opened a charity in my honor called The Fairy Tale Organization. Its purpose is to help mothers who don't have the means, receive an education. He donated a significant amount to it and while Jasmine is in school, I'm helping to run it. Had my mom had something like this, maybe she wouldn't have resorted to what she did… and maybe I wouldn't have ended up homeless and on the streets.

"It is beautiful," I agree, looking at the photo. It's of me and Liam in the church, standing before the priest, saying our vows. I know what it's of because she drew the colorful windows in front of us. We were married three months ago, and on that day, Liam also signed Jasmine's birth certificate, making him her father legally. It was a good thing we married when we did because a few weeks later, Liam got his way and the pregnancy test I took, after throwing up three days in a row, came out positive.

When we arrive at home, the first thing Jasmine does is run through the house to find her dad. He makes it a point not to schedule any meetings between one and two o'clock, so he can spend time with her. He pulls her into his arms and she spends the next thirty minutes, while Sandra brings them an afternoon snack, telling him all about her day.

After they're done, it's time for Jasmine's nap. School kicks her little butt and by the time two o'clock rolls around, she's wiped out and doesn't fight going to sleep.

Wanting to relax for a few minutes, I head into our en suite bathroom and run myself a nice, hot bubble bath. I peel off my clothes, which are now slightly too tight, noting to buy some maternity clothes online, and strip out of my bra and panties. I'm about to step inside the tub, when a strong pair of arms wrap around me from behind.

"Mmm," Liam says, "I love feeling you like this."

I laugh. "You're not even inside me."

He turns me around and backs me up against the wall. "I mean… like this." He drops to his knees and kisses the center of my belly. "Your belly swollen with my baby inside." He glances up at me and the love shining through his eyes sends a zap of electricity through my veins.

He peppers kisses along my flesh, planting a soft kiss to each of my hipbones, before he parts my legs and gently pushes two fingers inside me.

"Jesus, you're soaked."

"You're touching me."

He smiles, liking that answer, and stands, lifting me onto the edge of the sink. He spreads my legs apart and drops back down between my thighs. He sucks on my clit until I'm coming apart under his touch and then he's back up and sliding into me. His mouth, which now tastes like me, crashes against my own while he thrusts slow and deep in and out of me, coaxing another orgasm from me.

After we both climax, he kisses me hard, then whispers, "Thank you."

I giggle at his words. "No need to thank me." I wink. "You did most of the work."

He laughs. "I wasn't thanking you for the sex… although, I am thankful for that." He smirks playfully. "Thank you for agreeing to go out to dinner with me all those years ago."

"I should be the one thanking you. After all, it was you who saved me."

"No." He shakes his head. "That was all you. I might be your Prince Charming, but you never needed to be saved."

And they lived happily ever after.

THE END.

If you enjoyed Finding Prince Charming and want more from this world, you can check out Aria and Giovanni's story: Bordello.

QUARTERBACK KEEPER
BY LACEY BLACK

PROLOGUE

ASHTYN

"I GOT THE JOB!" I BELLOW THE MOMENT I'M THROUGH THE DOOR OF MY twin brother's condo. "Alex?" My bliss practically carries me into his living room on a cloud of excitement and anticipation, but the moment I'm through the doorway, it's not my brother's face I see. "Oh, sorry," I mumble the moment my eyes land on the sexy man sprawled out on my brother's couch.

"Hey, Ashtyn," he replies in that deep, intoxicating drawl that does dangerous things to panties all over the world. His arm is thrown over his head casually, displaying a large tattoo on the underside of his bicep, and his strong, muscular legs span the entire length of the couch. He's wearing a T-shirt that hugs his arms and chest and a pair of basketball shorts that seem to do nothing to hide an impressive bulge between his legs. His hazel eyes are darker than I remember and his hair a little messy, as if he just got out of bed. Not to mention the totally irresistible dimple in his chin. He's pure sex, and the problem is he knows it.

Tate Steele, quarterback for the St. Louis Fire professional football team and my brother's best friend.

Even if he's not my type at all, I can still appreciate the glory only created by God himself that is Tate freaking Steele.

But what's he doing at my brother's place?

That's when I notice the ice pack on his knee. "What happened?" I ask, instantly taking a few steps his way.

Big mistake. The moment I do, I catch a whiff of clean, earthy shampoo and pheromone-producing body wash. It makes my nipples prickle with delight.

"A linebacker got a little overzealous in practice the other day. I'm out for another week to rest my knee," he tells me, his eyes lazily roaming my body from head to toe.

I quickly glance down, realizing in my excitement, I didn't even change my clothes. I'm still in the pair of small cotton shorts and tank top I was wearing to clean my apartment before the phone call came that changed the course of my future. Well, at least I'm wearing a bra. My eyes meet his as I try to comprehend what he just said.

Tate chuckles, slow and gravelly, and things start to tingle between my legs. "Football, Sweetness. It happened at practice on Wednesday. Thank fuck it's still early in the preseason, though, I'm not too thrilled with being sidelined for the next week. Fucking second-string QB has had a hard-on for my spot since they signed his ass last year."

"Oh, uh, well, I'm sorry you're hurt," I tell him, glancing around for Alex.

"He's not here. Got called into work for some big client he's trying to sign. Said he'd probably be gone all evening, taking him and his family to dinner to grease the wheels."

My brother is a recruiter and coach and loves his job. He played football growing up and eventually went to Notre Dame, where he met Tate. They were roommates and shared a love for the game. When it was time to graduate, Alex left the game behind and with his bachelor's degree in sports management started working for Notre Dame as an assistant for the sports program, while Tate, a Heisman Trophy winner, signed a contract with the St. Louis Fire for an obscenely large amount of money. Alex has worked hard, clawing his way up the ranks from the lowest-paid position on the team to being their head recruiter and assistant coach in just six short years.

"Oh," I mumble, dropping down in the chair with a plop.

"What's this about a new job?" Tate asks, removing the ice from his knee and tossing it on the coffee table. He turns his large body to face me as if giving me his full attention.

"Um, well, I got a new job at a large library. It's kind of a big deal," I tell him, intentionally vague about the position. Tate Steele doesn't care about books, and I'm pretty sure the only time he ever set foot in a library was to make out in the back.

His hazel eyes hold my gaze for a few extra seconds and something that looks a lot like pride flashes through them. "Wow, congrats, Ash. When do you start?"

"Next month," I reply, leaving out the part that involves relocating to an entirely different state. With this job comes a lot of change, and I'm still trying to wrap my head around it.

"Alex will be excited for you," he insists, giving me a genuine smile. Not one of those cocky, conceited smirks he flashes on television that makes women everywhere take off their panties.

I've seen and heard the tabloid stories on Tate. He's a playboy, an arrogant bachelor with a black book list of phone numbers longer than the Chicagoland phonebook. He never goes anywhere without a piece of arm candy at his side and is photographed constantly with the most beautiful women in the world.

I, on the other hand, prefer quiet evenings in. I don't even have cable. Not Netflix or whatever streaming sites are available. My best friend is a teacher at the school district I work for, and as far as my social calendar goes, it's usually filled up with long nights of reading Jane Austen, Harper Lee, and the Bronte sisters.

We're so far apart on the social circle scale we might as well be on different planets.

"I have an idea," he says, clapping his hands together and getting up. Before he tells me what's on his mind, he bends and stretches his knee. "How about we celebrate? Since I'm supposed to be laying low for a few days, we can order food and have it delivered."

My heart literally can't decide if it wants to stop beating all together or pirouette in my chest. "Oh, that's not necessary," I insist, jumping up and backing toward the front door. Suddenly, I'm all too aware of the fact I'm alone with an incredibly sexy man and I look like I've been scrubbing baseboards and behind my kitchen appliances all day.

"No, I insist. Your brother would definitely want to celebrate, right? So, let's celebrate, Ashtyn." There's something in his warm hazel eyes that says I can trust him, which is crazy, considering I've really only met him a handful of times.

"Um, I'm not sure I'm celebration ready," I state, glancing back down at my way too casual, way too exposed outfit.

Tate's eyes drop to my chest before returning to meet mine. "You look great, Ash. And we're staying in, remember?"

"Oh, uh," I start but struggle to find another excuse as to why I need to go home.

"Come on, it'll be fun. We can get to know each other better. You're my friend's twin sister, and I barely know you," he insists.

That's because we have nothing in common, and his eyes were usually too focused on some cheerleader or blonde with double Ds to pay any attention to anyone else in the room.

"I guess we can call The Tap and order something," I reply as if the words fly from my mouth entirely on their own.

"Great." Tate pulls up the menu on his phone and starts tapping away. Suddenly, he's thrusting it at my face, an indication it's my turn to enter what I want.

I scan the menu for my favorite entrée and toss in an order of fried cheese curds for good measure. I mean, it's a celebration, right?

When I hand him back the phone, our fingers touch. A jolt of electricity bolts up my arm, causing me to jump back and put a little more separation between us. Tate doesn't seem to notice, which makes me feel like one of those silly football groupies who swoon whenever he walks into a room.

"We have forty minutes," he replies, finishing up our order and slipping his phone into his shorts before disappearing into my brother's kitchen. A few minutes later, he comes back with two glasses of wine. "I hope you like white. It was all your brother has besides a bottle of scotch, and you don't strike me as a scotch drinker."

"The wine is actually mine, so this is perfect," I reply, taking the offered glass.

Before I can take a sip, he holds up his glass. "To Ashtyn and her new job at the library. May your new position bring you happiness and continued passion," he states. There's a flash of something in his eyes when he speaks that one word.

Passion.

Suddenly, the room is entirely too small, and I'm desperate for a little liquid to cool and soothe my dry throat.

BY THE TIME TEN O'CLOCK ROLLS AROUND, I AM NURTURING A HEALTHY buzz and my side hurts from laughing. Who knew Tate Steele was so funny? Not me, but after spending the evening with him, eating, drinking, and talking, I'm pleasantly surprised by how laid-back and witty he truly is. Plus, I could be way off base, but there's something else there. An underlying desire I feel every time he looks at me. My body has been strung so tight the last hour, I'm afraid he can tell I'm practically crawling out of my skin with need.

"I think I'm going to bed," I mumble, getting up out of the chair and stumbling a little as the room sways.

Strong arms wrap around my shoulders. The swaying stops but only because I'm pressed firmly against a hard chest. A nice, warm chest. The rich scent of sandalwood fills my entire being, and before I even realize what I'm doing, I have my nose buried in the material stretched across his pecs.

My face burns with mortification.

I really just sniffed my brother's best friend.

Cheese and rice, I've had too much to drink.

"I'm going," I start, pointing a thumb over my shoulder toward the bedrooms.

But Tate doesn't let me go. He walks with me, even though I have my footing enough now. It's only when we reach the guest room I occasionally sleep in that I realize the problem. Tate's stuff is there. His suitcase thrown on the floor and a pile of clothes strewn on the chair.

"Oh, I'm sorry. I forgot you were staying here too. I'll just bunk with my brother. As long as he's not bringing home anyone, he won't mind if I'm there. Or he can just sleep on the couch. It's not that uncomfortable. I've crashed there before too. I just wouldn't recommend the chair because your neck will hurt and—"

I'm cut off by his hot mouth. It slams into mine with urgency, one I reciprocate willingly as if kissing him is a necessity. Like air. His tongue pressing into my mouth at the same time he lifts me and pushes my back against the wall. My legs wrap around his lean hips and his erection presses firmly against my core. Holy hell, this man is…wow.

I rip my lips from his and suck in a greedy breath of air. Tate's mouth trails along my jaw and moves to my earlobe. I gasp and rock my hips into him as he sucks on my lobe before sliding those amazing lips down the side of my neck. "Oh God," I groan, my panties so wet, I'm certain he can feel them through my shorts.

His hazy eyes meet mine. "Do you want me to stop?"

Well, if that isn't a loaded question. My brain says yes, definitely stop. This shouldn't go any further. Tate Steele is an egotistical bad boy, and even though I'm sure the sex will be great, that's all it will ever be. I'll be a notch on his infamous bedpost. Something I've never wanted to be. Plus, there's the fact he's linked to my brother, and the chances are I'll see him again at some point soon. This has bad idea written all over it with a big black Sharpie marker.

Yet, my gut—and maybe a little bit of white wine—is telling me to do it. Have fun. Enjoy what is sure to be a good time and then leave it all behind. Move on and forward, ready to start my new job with a smile on my face and the memory of a few orgasms. If there's one thing I'm sure of, a man like Tate is good for at least two, maybe three. So why not?

"No, don't stop," I whisper.

My response seems to take him by surprise. "You're sure?"

"Yes, I'm sure."

That's all it takes. Like a can of gas thrown on a smoldering fire, we ignite spectacularly. Clothes fly, hands are everywhere, and mouths taste and suck on every piece of exposed skin possible.

When I'm completely naked, his eyes greedily consume me from head to toe. "Fuck, you're beautiful," he whispers, his voice hoarse and gravelly.

Part of me wants to cover myself. I'm not one to completely undress in front of a man, especially one I'm not dating, but I hold fast. It allows me to take in the man before me once again. He's completely hard, from head to toe. There's not an ounce of fat on him. Dark hair is sprinkled across his chest, with a line below his belly button that leads to his erection. It's large—larger than I've ever seen in person—and frankly, I'm equal parts nervous and excited.

Tate goes over to his suitcase and digs a condom out of the pocket before returning to where I stand. I watch as he rolls it on and tosses the wrapper on the floor. Then, his eyes are set on me like I'm the prey he's about to devour.

He threads his fingers in my hair as he slowly kisses me. My hands glide up his chest and wrap around his neck. There's a major height difference between him and my mere five foot five frame, but the way our bodies line up, it's almost comfortable and natural.

Tate wraps his hands around my rear and lifts again, my legs instantly locking around his lower back. The position puts his erection right where I want it, where I *need* it. His eyes meet mine once more as if he's giving me one more chance to stop, but when I kiss him, I practically feel all his restraint and control melt away.

He presses forward, stretching and filling me completely in one thrust. I gasp and close my eyes, savoring the sweet burn that disappears as quickly as it started. Tate doesn't move, just holds still for a few long seconds. "Good?"

"God, yes. So good. Do it again," I beg.

He glides his lips along my neck and whispers, "Hold on, Sweetness. This is going to be one hell of a ride."

And it is.

He starts to move, his thrust hard and long and filling me so completely, I'm not sure where he ends and I begin. Each time he moves, it's pure ecstasy, and I feel myself climbing higher and higher. My body starts to tighten as he swivels his hips, touching that magical place deep inside of me. The result is like an explosion, and I cry out as blinding white lights fill my vision. I can feel his fingers grip my ass as he thrusts harder, chasing his own release. When he finally let's go, it triggers a second orgasm I didn't even know was brewing.

I'm pretty sure the result causes me to blackout a little.

Suddenly, we're moving. Tate lays me down on the guest bed and curls up around me. My body feels completely boneless and weightless as sleep threatens to pull me under. I feel him shift against me, his softening erection slipping from my body. He places a kiss against my shoulder and pulls a blanket over my body. "You're going?" I whisper, my eyes cracking open to take him in.

He's gloriously naked and gives me a small smile. "I figured since Alex will be home any time, it's probably best if I'm not in here."

The mention of my brother is like a cold shower. I start to move, but he crawls on the bed and kisses me soundly on the lips. "This is your room," I reply when I'm breathless once more.

Tate grins and pushes my hair over my shoulder. "I'll take the couch. Sleep."

My eyes close as he runs his hand down my arm. His touch is so soothing and helps lull me toward sleep. His hand moves, gliding over every inch of exposed skin. For someone with rough, calloused hands, his touch is pure magic.

I feel the bed shift and hear the squeak as the door starts to close. "Goodnight, Sweetness." It's the last thing I remember before the blackness finally pulls me under.

CHAPTER ONE
TATE
PRESENT DAY

"THAT'S PERFECT, TATE. GIVE ME MORE OF THAT SMILE," REGGIE SAYS, HIS camera shutter clicking in fast succession.

I'm shooting for a sports drink today, both television and print ads. My agent worked out a sweet two-year deal with the company, and all I have to do is be seen during practice and after the game drinking the product. Since training camp doesn't start for another month, they figured now is the perfect time to shoot a handful of ads for their fall and winter campaigns.

"Yeah, more of that smirk. Cocky. You've got women lined up for miles waiting to spend just a little time with the infamous Tate Steele," Reggie shouts, not taking a break from pressing the shutter button.

I give him what he wants, but inside, I'm rolling my eyes and groaning. But I know this is what's expected of me. It's the image I've spent a decade perfecting. From the moment I stepped onto the field at Notre Dame, I've been this guy. Arrogant, sure, but I can back that shit up. Both on the field and off.

We move through the shoot with two more outfit changes before I'm finally shirtless, wearing cleats and football pants. The makeup artist adds a little touch of dirt-like makeup to my face and chest, and I'm pretty sure she got off when she rubbed the cream across my abs. When she finally finishes, I throw her a smirk and wink and watch as she practically orgasms without me touching her.

Reggie puts me in front of a brick wall, and his assistant hands me a football. She giggles as she steps out of the frame, and I'm pretty sure I could have her against the wall in my dressing room if I asked. Hell, I probably wouldn't even need to take her to the private room. The way all these women are virtually drooling on themselves and fighting to get close to me, I could probably have them all in one big fucked-up orgy. Hell, Reggie would probably shoot the whole thing and tell me how great I did at the end.

As we move through the different poses and looks, I spy Todd, the man in charge of PR for my agent, standing in the back of the room. He's on the phone, like always, but keeps one eye on me. He's wearing a suit, even on a Friday afternoon, and looks like he's ready to crawl through the phone and strangle whoever's on the other end.

I've been a client of Professional Athlete Sports Management since the league came sniffing around my senior year of college. My agent, Richard Porter, signed me right before I entered the draft six years ago. We have a good working relationship and I trust him explicitly. Todd joined the team about two years ago, and I'll admit, he's had his hands full. His job is to fix any of the bullshit I find myself in, some of it seems like on a regular basis.

The moment the shoot is over, I make my way toward him. He clicks off his phone and smiles. "Tate, good job up there," he says, shaking my hand.

"Thanks, Todd. What brings you here today?" I ask, taking the towel offered to me by one of the guys who manages the lighting. I nod my head in appreciation and start to wipe off the dirt-like shit spread all over my chest.

"Well, we had another woman come forward, claiming she's carrying your love child," Todd states like he's reading a newspaper article.

I snort and shake my head. "Another one?"

"Third one this year," he confirms.

"Do I know her?" I ask, wondering where these women come from.

Todd raises an eyebrow and gives me a pointed look. "Do you ever really know any of them, Tate?"

His implication grates on my nerves.

"It's bullshit," I tell him, pissed to have yet another damn paternity suit to deal with.

These women are all the same. They reach out, claiming to be carrying my spawn, and threatening to go public with the details of how I refuse to take care of my child. A few of the pregnancy claims worried me, I'll admit, but most of the claims I know are bogus. Women I've never met. Crazy fangirls who think I'll fall in love with them.

The ones who did make it to my bed would usually just go for the payout for the details of our night together. Most tabloids in the country will pay big money for those specifics, even if they're not entirely accurate. It's not like they come and get my side of the story.

This new one is just another in a long list of fake accusations against me. Like the ones from earlier this year, I know it's pure bullshit. It can't be true, because I haven't been with anyone in nine months.

Not since Ashtyn.

Just thinking of the woman I left back in South Bend nearly a year ago has my blood traveling southbound. Long, thick brown hair and rich, dark eyes, topped with a hard-on-inducing smile that still wakes me up in the dead of night. The sexy librarian could very well have been the best thing to happen to me and my greatest mistake, all in one.

I push Ashtyn out of my mind and focus on the man in front of me. "Take care of it, Todd. Make it go away," I tell him, frustrated, yet I'm not sure if it's because of the pregnancy shit or because the woman I still dream about has popped into my head yet again.

"I will," he confirms, pulling out his phone and typing out a message. "Are you sure you've never met her?" he asks, flipping the screen in front of my face and showing me the picture of a stacked blonde in a string bikini. Her boobs are as fake as the collagen-filled lips on her face, and I'm pretty sure she's had some work done on her eyes too. Oh, don't get me wrong, she's hot, and maybe when I was a rookie in the league, I would definitely have fucked her, but now I can't even seem to sport some wood when I look at her photo.

"Definitely. I'm sure I'd remember her," I say honestly, just leaving out the part about my nine-month dry spell.

Todd snorts. "Oh, I'm sure you would. She looks…bendy." He types for a few more seconds before sending off whatever notes he was taking and slips his phone back into his trouser pants. "I'll let you go get changed and ready to go. Big plans this weekend?" he asks politely, though I can tell it's more of a fishing expedition. Like he's trying to find out how much work he's going to have tomorrow morning.

"Old college friend coming into town tonight for dinner. Hopefully something low-key."

He laughs. "Right, low-key. I've seen your low-key, friend. I'll have my phone on later. Call if you need me," he says before slapping me on the shoulder and taking off toward the exit.

I sigh and stand there long after Todd has left. The playboy image I've created and nurtured for the last handful of years has done wonders for my career, but it's also done plenty of damage. The paparazzi follow me around, all jonesing to get a photo, a video, or a comment about me. I've had a fake wife who went on national television with doctored photos of our supposed Las Vegas wedding. And if every false baby daddy claim was true, I'd have about two dozen kids by now.

Don't get me wrong, I've earned this persona. I partied when I could and was usually photographed doing it. I've dated starlets, models, and artists at the top of every chart in the world. The camera loves me and has this uncanny ability to find me anytime, anywhere, any place.

Except in the last nine months.

Sure, I've been giving them what they want, someone young and gorgeous on my arm at a movie premiere or courtside at a professional basketball game, but that's all it is. Smoke and mirrors. Truth be told, I haven't felt like myself, like partying and dating, since my visit to South Bend.

Guilt.

That's a big part of it. As much as I've tried to ignore what happened all those months ago with Ashtyn, I just haven't been able to forget it. No amount of scotch or clubbing has dimmed the memory of her, and believe me, I've fucking tried. A lot. But she's there, embedded in my brain so deep I worry she'll always be there, front and center.

Now, throw in a visit from her brother with very little warning.

I haven't seen Alex since the morning he woke up and found me in his kitchen with my packed bags sitting by the door. I was supposed to stay through Tuesday, but the moment he came home and found me on the couch, the guilt of what I'd done with his sister started to eat at my soul. I didn't tell him, of course. I'm not fucking stupid. He'd cut off my dick and probably kill me with it. All I said was she came over and drank too much, so I did the gentlemanly thing and let her crash in the guest room. It's not that far off from the truth, but I did leave out a pretty big detail.

Not that I'd ever tell him that.

So, I took off, making up some excuse about the trainers wanting me back early to start working on my knee. It was pure bullshit, but I needed out of there, and fast. Especially since Ashtyn was just on the opposite side of the guest bedroom door, naked. I know because when I slipped in to get my personal belongings, I could still see some of her soft, silky skin on full display. Her fair complexion was a stark contradiction against the brown sheet.

Now, Alex is in town. He reached out to me last night, and in a moment of weakness, I agreed to dinner. As long as he doesn't talk about my last visit or mention his sister, I'm sure it'll be fine. This will actually be our first time seeing each other or even physically talking since all of our communication has been by text message. It works better that way, truth be told. We're both busy as hell, and texts work better for both of us. Plus, I'm apparently a big fucking chicken and have been avoiding more communication. But, no dodging it now. He's here for three days, most likely for work, and staying at the Hilton Hotel not too far from the stadium.

I'm about to face my best friend for the first time since I slept with his twin sister.

Piece of cake.

I CHOSE A COZY STEAKHOUSE WITH QUIET, SPACIOUS BOOTHS WHERE WE can visit without being disturbed too much. This place is pretty low-key, which is what I'm counting on tonight. The last thing I want is fans and groupies bothering us while we're trying to catch up.

I give my name to the hostess, but I can tell by her knowing smile she recognizes me. "Your party has already arrived. Follow me," she coos, leading me through the restaurant with a little extra swing in her hips, most definitely for my benefit.

Alex is in one of the back booths, typing away on his phone. When we arrive at the table, he throws down his cell, gives me a wide grin, and slides out of the booth. "'Bout time you got here. I had to start without you," he says, slapping me on the back.

"I'm sure that was a hardship," I comment, returning his bro hug before slipping onto the booth bench.

"It's been a long fucking day," he says, holding up the beer in salute. "I earned this one. And the ones that'll follow."

"What can I get you?" the waiter asks, as he stops by our table.

"Same," I answer, nodding to the brand Alex is drinking. He scurries off to get my beer, so I start browsing the menu, even though I already know what I'm having.

"So, how've you been?" he asks, leaning back and getting comfortable in his seat.

"Good. Had to shoot a bunch of videos and photos today for Alive Sports Drinks. Barely had enough time to run home and shower before meeting you."

Alex shorts a laugh. "Had to shower her off you or she came home and helped?"

My closest friend knows me well. Only, this time, he's way off base. "Neither," I reply, as the waiter delivers my beer.

"Are you ready?" he asks, pulling out a pad of paper to take our orders.

"I'll have the ribeye, medium, with a baked potato and salad with Italian," Alex says, setting his menu down on the edge of the table.

"I'll have the same, with steamed vegetables instead of the potato," I add.

"I'll get those right in for you," the waiter says before disappearing to the kitchen.

"So, what's new?" I ask, taking a drink from my bottle.

"A job, hopefully."

His words give me pause. I lower my beer bottle and meet his eyes. I can tell he's serious. There's a hint of excitement there, along with a touch of nervousness. "Wow, really? I thought you loved it at Notre Dame."

Alex sighs. "I did. *Do*, really, but the truth is, I'm the only one there now. I want to be closer to family."

His confession doesn't shock me too much. He's always been close to his parents, who live in Naperville, Illinois, but even closer to his twin sister. Ashtyn. Even in college, he talked to her all the time by text or video chat. She went to Northern Illinois University and rarely visited her brother. I think in the four years we were in South Bend, she came to two football games and maybe a surprise visit for their birthday our senior year. Even though they're as different as night and day, they've always been tight.

"Well, where is this job? Here in St. Louis?" I ask, taking another drink of cold beer.

Alex gives me a cocky grin. "With the Fire."

A wide smile spreads across my face. "No shit? Who are you interviewing with?" I ask, super excited at the prospect of having him in town to stay.

"Cortland McDaniels. We meet tomorrow at nine," he boasts.

"Well, I'm pulling for you. The Fire would be lucky to have you," I tell him, holding up my bottle in a toast.

Alex taps his beer against mine. "Thanks, man. Appreciate it. I'm sure the competition is fierce, so I'm trying not to get my hopes up." Our food is delivered and two fresh beers follow. "It'd almost be too perfect to get this job, you know? You and Ashtyn are both here, and the idea of seeing you two a little more regularly again is appealing."

I cut into my steak, but suddenly my knife stops moving. Did he just say… "What?"

Alex looks up from cutting his steak. "I mean, I know you're busy with that huge social calendar, but surely you can squeeze me in now and again, right?" he asks, laughing.

"I'd love it if you lived here, but I was meaning the other part. About Ashtyn." Just saying her name has my cock half-hard and wanting to play. I focus on cutting my steak and taking a bite to mask the anticipation and shock that's surely written all over my face.

"Oh, that's one of the main reasons I started looking. She could use the help, even if she keeps saying she doesn't. But I'm sure it's hard, you know? Raising a baby on your own? In a new city with no family to boot. That's why I'm here for three days. I get to meet my nephew tomorrow after the interview."

My mind is spinning. "Wow, uh, a baby, huh?" Why does my throat feel like I swallowed glass? "I didn't realize she was seeing anyone," I say casually, moving my vegetables around with my fork. I'm suddenly not hungry at all.

Alex seems pissed as he stabs his steak. "She's not. At least not someone she's talking about. She dated this guy before she moved here, but I think they broke up a month or two before. I don't know who he is, but he better hope I don't fucking ever find out."

I'm suddenly pissed right along with him. Not only because some douchebag got Ashtyn pregnant and ditched her, but because she was apparently seeing someone when we slept together. I always thought she was this shy, meek woman with a gorgeous smile, but apparently, there's a little more vixen in her than anticipated.

"I was hoping to talk to her about it again while I'm here. She needs help, and if she won't force that no-dick asshole into anteing up, then I'll just do it."

Somehow, we make it through dinner, but I'm not sure how. I have no recollection of actually eating my food, but when I look down, my plate is empty. My mind, on the other hand, is spinning as I try to put together the info shared. Ashtyn had a baby? A boy, apparently. And to top it off, she's living in St. Louis. For the last however many months, she's been here, and I didn't even know it.

Wait…

Nine months?

I mentally do the math. My knee injury was last August. It's now early June. Nine and a half months ago…

"Holy shit," I gasp, my heart pounding like a jackhammer.

"I know," Alex agrees, not even noticing I'm a second away from a full-blown heart attack. "It's a mess, but look at this. This makes it better," he says, pulling his phone out, moving his fingers across the screen, and holds it out for me to see.

There, in the middle of the screen, is Ashtyn, looking a little frazzled and a whole lot of exhausted. But the smile on her face is one of pure elation and love. As if everything she just went through was completely worth it. His face is wrinkled and red, and a little blue and pink striped cap covers the top of his head. The baby has chubby cheeks, but it's his chin that catches my attention. There in the middle is a dimple.

Like mine.

"…born a little over two weeks ago. My parents came and stayed with her the first week, but then left," he says, taking the phone back and sliding it into his pocket.

"I'd like to go," I find myself saying. Alex looks surprised. "I mean, it would be good for her to know she has another friend here, right? I'm surprised she didn't reach out to me." Very surprised, actually. And if my suspicions are correct, I'm pissed as fuck about that. But I'm not going to assume a chin dimple means anything.

Even if the timeline is a little fishy.

"Okay, I'm sure she'd be fine with a visitor," he replies with a shrug.

When the waiter delivers our check and collects the empty plates, I'm quicker than Alex. "I got it."

"No way," he argues, reaching for the folder.

I slip my card inside and hand it over. "Consider it a good luck gift for tomorrow, but something tells me, you don't need luck. That job is as good as yours."

He grins. "Well, I appreciate it."

As we head out, a few patrons recognize me, but I keep my head down and make my way to the front door. The hostess thanks me for dining tonight, slipping something in my hand, which I'm a thousand percent certain is her phone number. I stick it in my pocket and push through the door, stopping outside the door. "So, tomorrow?"

"Oh, uh, do you want to meet me at my hotel and hop in with me, or—"

"Why don't I follow you there?" I interrupt. "This way, if you want to stay longer, you don't have to worry about taking me home."

"Makes sense," Alex agrees, stepping in and giving me a one-arm, back slap hug. "My interview is at nine. I was gonna head over around eleven, grabbing her some lunch on the way."

"I'll be there," I tell him, turning toward the parking lot where my car is.

I have way more questions than answers, and there's only one woman who can give me what I need. Hopefully tomorrow I'll know what the hell is going on, and if that baby is mine, why the hell she hasn't told me about it.

CHAPTER TWO
ASHTYN

QUIET.

I take my cup of coffee to my home library, gingerly sitting down in my favorite wingback chair. Rowan just went down with a full belly and a clean diaper, and now is the one time I allow myself to indulge in a single cup of black coffee. A shower can wait. Breakfast too. Nothing comes before this small cup of dark roast Moroccan coffee.

Except for Rowan.

And maybe sleep.

Since I was able to snatch a solid three hours of sleep before Rowan woke up again, just before five, it felt like the perfect time to get up and moving. Today's a big day. My brother is coming for a visit after his interview with the St. Louis Fire. I'm excited to see him and for him to meet his nephew for the first time. Video chats aren't the same as in-person visits, and this'll be the first one I've had with him since I went home for Christmas and shared my big news. It was great having my parents here last week, but there's this unmatchable bond I share with Alex. He's not only my brother but one of my best friends.

And he's going to be here in a few hours.

I sigh and glance out at the quiet neighborhood surrounding me. When I first moved here, I was in a two-bedroom apartment within walking distance of the library where I work. Just after the new year, one of the regular patrons at the library mentioned she was packing up and selling her parents' house. Even though the apartment would have been comfortable for me and a baby, I went ahead and took her up on the offer to check it out. It's an older three-bedroom and one-bath ranch-style home in need of a little TLC and updating, but when I saw it, I fell in love. A little paint on all the walls and some area rugs to cover the old marred hardwood floors, and it's the perfect starter home for us.

If only I could figure out how to keep the shower nozzle from falling off.

I take another sip of coffee and watch as the world starts to wake up. Speaking of waking up, my mind goes to Alex and his interview. Is it too early to shoot him off a good luck text? Just because I'm up and moving by six doesn't mean he is. If anything, he might be sleeping in, enjoying his downtime. Or he could be fretting above the interview over a pot of coffee and a bagel.

It could go either way.

I offered for him to stay with me when he arrived the night before, but he had plans. Dinner. With Tate. Just thinking his name brings back memories of the last time I saw him. We were both naked and panting from doing dirty things in my brother's guest bedroom. Things I've tried to forget but can't. Not when my eyes are open, and most definitely not when they're closed. If anything, nighttime makes the memories worse. They're more vivid and consuming when the room is dark, and I'm alone in my bed.

But those recollections are always pushed away to the back of my mind. They have to be.

When my one and only cup of Joe is finished, I return to the kitchen. Last night's soup bowl is still in the sink, along with a few other dirty dishes. I decide now is as good of a time as any to try to clean up the house. Mom was a huge help last week, but with her gone, I'll admit, some of those pesky day-to-day chores have fallen by the wayside.

Including laundry.

Do I even have clean underwear?

Sighing, I fill up the sink with hot water and start washing. When they're done, I make sure the counters and stovetop are wiped down, along with the microwave. After that, I head to the laundry room and throw in a load of baby clothes. Who knew babies went through so many onesies? Rowan has at least two diaper blowouts a day, resulting in scrubbing baby poop off his clothes, and often my own too.

When my chores are somewhat caught up and my eyelids start to droop, I make my way to the living room. I don't bother with turning on the television. If it weren't for my dad last week, that thing wouldn't have been on in months. I'm not a TV watcher. I've always loved books, even as a child. Alex never understood it but in no way treated me as if I were different than him, despite the fact we're about as night and day diverse as you can get.

Exhaustion takes hold, refusing to let go. There's no way I can fight it. I let it pull me under.

"WOW, THAT'S NASTY," I SAY, GAGGING JUST A LITTLE AS I OPEN THE DIAPER. Rowan's mouth opens as he gets ready to let out a very unhappy wail. Diaper changes aren't his thing. Dirty ones aren't much of his thing either, so he's a whole lot of cranky until his butt is clean and dry. Then, of course, comes food, which makes him even happier.

I make quick work at cleaning his bottom and making sure it's dry before I slip on the fresh diaper. "Okay, Little Man," I coo, picking him up off the changing station and snuggling him to my neck. I kiss his soft little cheek, but his cries only mildly let up. "Yeah, yeah, I know. You're hungry." I'm already starting to get a bit leaky, a sign it's definitely feeding time.

Grabbing a clean burp cloth off the shelf, I head over to the glider and get myself positioned. His mouth is already opened as he seeks me out, and I know it's only a matter of seconds before he voices his displeasure once more. I slip the nursing pillow beneath him and remove my top one-handed, like the professional breast feeder I've become in the last two weeks. I'm a pro at nursing at night, half asleep and dizzy from exhaustion.

Rowan latches on immediately and does his thing. I use the opportunity to watch him, taking in his features. I can't get enough of his little button nose and his dark hair. Even the dimple in his chin makes my heart burst with pride and love. It also makes it flutter as memories of a certain similar dimple flood my mind.

But now isn't the time to think about the past.

Only the future.

So, I spend the next thirty minutes nursing my son, planning out everything from his first birthday to what I'm going to do for his college savings. I make a decent salary at the library, but admittedly, a baby has certainly changed things, both on the personal and financial front.

I wonder how different it would be if his father were involved. Not only for financial help but to have someone to share the day-to-day load. Having my parents here last week was a huge relief, their assistance meant more to me than I could have possibly realized beforehand. Plus, they got to spend an entire week with their first grandson.

But do you know what? I tried. I reached out to him, numerous times, and when I finally connected with him, I got less than positive responses. First, it was denial. The baby wasn't his. Couldn't be. Because, you know, I got pregnant all on my own. Then, it was radio silence. My messages went unanswered for months, even though I knew he was seeing them until I was eventually blocked. But not before I got one final communication. A threat of lawyers and harassment charges.

That's when I was done.

Sure, I could have hired my own attorney and went after him for support, but do you know what? He didn't want to be involved. I gave him every opportunity to step up and take care of his child, even if it was through financial support, but he chose a different route. The threat of a lawsuit was enough for me to realize he wasn't who I thought he was when I met him.

I feel sadness sweep in as I picture Rowan's life as he starts to grow up without a father. It's done all the time by brave mothers, and in some cases, heroic fathers who step up and become the sole provider. I can do this too. I don't need him. I don't need his money. Fuck him and his lawyers.

Rowan finishes feeding and burps a second time. This is when he's all snuggly and curls up so perfectly on my chest. I should put him down in his bassinet to sleep, but I can't help it if I want to hold him just a little bit longer. Everyone says to enjoy these moments, they don't last long, so I'm trying to do just that. Even if my lack of sleep and constant state of tiredness seems to be never-ending, I know someday, I'll look back and wish he were still my tiny baby again.

When he seems to fall into a deep sleep, I gingerly get up from the glider and head to my bedroom. I did plenty of research while pregnant and decided the best option for me was to have him in my room for the first three months. Then, when he reaches that milestone, I'll move him to his crib. Having him this close makes nighttime feedings much easier, that's for sure. Plus, as a new parent, I'm still in the checking on him fourteen times a night phase.

A quick glance at the clock confirms my brother should be here soon. Probably wouldn't hurt to steal a shower while Rowan sleeps. Plus, I'm not sure when I had one. I don't think I did yesterday, did I? I don't know. The days all run into each other at this point.

I grab clean undergarments and head for the bathroom, cranking up the hot water as warm as I can. Knowing Rowan can sleep for five minutes or three hours, I make quick work of cleaning my body and hair. I'm still a little tender from delivery, but every day gets better.

At least I'm not sitting on a donut anymore.

After a shower, I dress quickly, brush my hair, check on my son, and head down to the kitchen. My stomach growls, reminding me I haven't eaten much yet today. It's almost lunchtime, but before I can find something to snack on, there's a knock on my door. I practically sprint to the living room, taking a quick peek through the peephole before throwing the lock and ripping the door open.

There he is.

Alex.

My smile is so wide it hurts, but I don't care. I haven't seen my brother in almost six months. He drops his bag just before I leap into his arms and squeeze with everything I have. He does the same. Warmth and comfort envelop me as tears prickle my eyes. "God, I've missed you," I whisper, a mix of happiness and relief settling in my chest.

"Missed you more, Ash." He sets me down and gives me a once-over. "You look great," he adds with a smile.

I snort, because I know he's just being polite. My hair is still wet and limp, I've got bags under my eyes big enough to carry luggage for a week's getaway, and I'm still sporting an extra five pounds in my gut. Okay, fine more like ten pounds, but who's counting really? "That's sweet, but you don't have to lie to me. I look like hell."

But at least I'm smiling.

He goes to reply, but whatever he says is lost on me. A movement behind him catches my eye, and for the first time, I realize we're not alone. I glance around his broad chest to see who's with him. My heart starts to hammer so loud, I'm sure they can hear it throughout the neighborhood. The mystery guest is impossibly tall and muscular, with a very familiar dimple in his chin. Even though he's wearing Aviator shades, I can feel his eyes on me like a caress. Or a dagger. I'm not sure which.

But I know who it is.

Tate.

What I don't know is why the hell he's here, on my doorstep, smiling like he doesn't have a care in the world. My world changed because of him.

Because of that one night.

The night that gave me Rowan.

CHAPTER THREE

TATE

SHE'S EVEN MORE BEAUTIFUL THAN IN MY DREAMS. HER HAIR IS STILL WET, probably from a shower, and she looks like she's barely slept all week. Yet, there's a light in her eye, a glimmer of enthusiasm and bliss that I've missed. Sure, all of it is aimed at her brother and not at me. What's aimed at me has a little more fire behind it. Anger, even, and I have no clue why. I'm not the one keeping a big fat secret from everyone around her.

"Ash, you remember Tate, right?" Alex asks, looking back over his shoulder and smiling at me.

His sister, on the other hand, does not smile. She glares, hard and intimidating. It's pretty fucking cute but telling her that is probably a bad idea. "Hey, Ash," I greet, a little singsong in my voice.

Her eyes narrow into little slits. "Tate, yeah. What are you doing here?" she asks, trying to keep her voice breezy, but it betrays her. Her tone is very frigid, icy.

Alex gives her a look. "He came with me," he says, giving me an apologetic look over his shoulder. "Is that okay?"

She opens her mouth, but nothing comes out right away. Ashtyn gives her brother her full attention and smiles softly. "Yes, of course. Why don't you come in? Both of you." There's a touch of irritation in that last part, and it makes me grin.

"This place is great," I hear Alex state as we step inside Ashtyn's house, and he's right. It's a decent little place with a spacious living room and big picture windows. The floors are old hardwood, with scratches and marks from probably years of moving furniture, and the couch is well-loved. It's nothing like the firm, black leather sofa in my penthouse. The crazy part is, I can see her curling up on that blue and brown couch with a blanket to read a book a hell of a lot easier than I can see her trying to get comfortable on my sofa.

"Thanks. It's a little messy, but I haven't had much time lately to clean," she replies through a yawn. Ashtyn is still completely ignoring my presence in her house, which baffles me.

Unless she's guilty of something…

I glance around again, taking in her space with new eyes, and barely see what she's talking about. Does she think this is messy? She should check out my place on Monday morning, after me and a few of my teammates watch old game films, eat pizza, and drink too much beer. I pay a pretty penny for someone to come in every Monday and Thursday and clean for me, but it's well worth it.

Ashtyn doesn't have a maid, I'm sure, but her place is still tidy and loved. Sure, there's a glass sitting on the end table with a little water in it and some rags are thrown on the coffee table that are probably used, but her house is still cheerful and organized. Even though I don't know her too well, it feels like her, and for some reason, that draws me in.

I take the bags of food I'm holding and set them down on the coffee table. Alex insisted on grabbing lunch for his sister, knowing she probably hasn't had time to eat yet.

"So, when do I get to meet my nephew?" Alex asks with a beaming smile.

The mention of the baby has my eyes darting from one side of the room to the other. The baby isn't in here but is here somewhere. Most likely sleeping in another room. I'm not sure why my heart is suddenly beating like a racehorse at the prospect of seeing Ashtyn's son, but there's something oddly exciting and comforting at the same time. All night I mulled over the details I knew, including the timeline. It's too close to ignore, which is why I'm here today.

To find out the truth about her son.

Ashtyn smiles easily when her brother asks about the baby. "He's sleeping, but I'll go get him," she says, finally glancing my way for the first time. There's something in her eyes I'm not expecting. It's more than anger. It's disgust and maybe a little resentment. I really wish I knew why she's so pissed off at me. I'm not the one keeping all the secrets.

She disappears down the hallway, her hips naturally swaying a bit in her cotton shorts. They're not pajamas, but definitely look comfortable and casual. I can picture her lying around and reading, the material hugging the globes of her ass. It's enough to make my cock jump with excitement in my shorts.

Traitorous appendage…

Ashtyn returns a few minutes later with a blanket bundle in her arms, the softest grin on her pretty face. Alex moves, meeting her halfway. My eyes are glued to the scene, at the moment shared between brother and sister. I've never been a sentimental or nostalgic man, but witnessing my best friend meeting his nephew for the first time does a little something in my chest.

"Damn, Ash, he's beautiful," Alex says, the awe very evident in his voice. I watch as he reaches with his big finger and gently slides it across the infant's face.

"Isn't he?" she whispers. She looks back up at her brother and adds, "Do you want to hold him?"

"Uhh, yeah," he replies, glancing around and spying a bottle of hand sanitizer. Alex quickly squirts some on his hands before returning to his sister. I hold my breath as she carefully transfers her son to her brother's arms.

"Jesus, he's so tiny." I realize when Ashtyn looks my way, I said that aloud.

She gives me the side-eye, a touch of defensiveness when she replies, "He is a perfectly healthy seven-pound, ten-ounce baby."

I hold up my hands in surrender. "I'm not saying he isn't, Ash. It was just an observation."

She continues to glare at me, which I return. She's so fucking hostile, and to be honest, it's turning me the fuck on. Bad.

"Can I sit down with him?" Alex asks, glancing around.

"Take the recliner. It's more comfortable, and you can prop your elbow on the armrest." Ashtyn helps get her brother settled in the chair before stroking her finger across the baby's forehead. "He should sleep for a little while longer."

"Why don't you go ahead and eat?" Alex instructs. "Tate, will you take that food in the kitchen?"

I reach for the bags and head for the kitchen. It's easy to find, just off the main living area. The counter has a small pile of drying dishes, a small stack of mail, and some fresh garden vegetables. I start to pull the food from the bags and can feel her presence behind me. I choose to ignore her, focusing on sorting lunch. I figure it best to let her sweat for just a little longer.

"What are you doing here?" Ashtyn whispers harshly.

"Grabbing sandwiches," I state politely, pulling two BLTs and a ham and cheese from the first bag and two orders of onion rings and a bowl of chicken and rice soup from the second.

"No, Tate, what the hell are you doing here?" she asks with venom. As she steps up beside me, her rich vanilla scent slaps me right upside the face, eliciting all sorts of dirty memories that are better left where they were.

I pull off the lid to her soup and hold it up in front of her nose. "Here, it's like a Snickers. Maybe you won't be so crabby." Yeah, I know I'm poking the bear, but dammit she so fucking sexy when she gets all pissed off.

Her heated eyes narrow before they drop to the bowl in my hand. "What kind is that?"

"Chicken and rice. Alex says you love soup," I start, but am cut off from saying anymore when she grabs the Styrofoam bowl directly from my hand. Her stomach growls loudly the moment she turns her back to me and grabs a spoon from the drawer.

I turn and watch, slightly mesmerized by her beauty, as she drops down on one of the chairs and takes a spoonful of creamy soup. "Oh God," she moans, closing her eyes as she swallows. My cock, however, is suddenly very enthralled by the innocent sounds she's making, which only reminds it of what she sounded like coming on said cock.

It's like heaven and hell all wrapped up in one.

With my hip propped against the counter, I watch in odd fascination as she devours her soup. She's not messy or gross about it, just takes big bites, as if she knows she'll be interrupted at any moment. Like warm soup is a luxury she's not accustomed to.

Realizing I'm staring, I grab the second BLT and take it to her, setting it on the table beside the almost-empty soup container. Ashtyn glances at the package before slowly opening it to reveal the sandwich inside. I pop an onion ring into my mouth and say, "Soup is an odd choice for summer, isn't it?"

Ashtyn takes a bite of her sandwich and chews. When she swallows, she replies, "I could eat soup year-round. It's my favorite." She doesn't even glance up as she's talking, but at least she doesn't seem as hostile.

I carefully open up my own sandwich and take a hearty bite of bacon, lettuce, and tomato on whole wheat. No, a BLT isn't my favorite, but when Alex ordered it for his sister, it sounded damn good. When was the last time I had one? Two, three years? Probably longer. My parents used to make them for lunch on Sundays when I was growing up, and it was always one of my preferred meals.

I spy the veggies on the counter once more. "Do you have a garden?" I ask between bites.

Ashtyn shakes her head. "No. One of my regulars at the library has a greenhouse and grows things year-round. He brought those over to me yesterday."

He.

Something prickles at the base of my neck. Annoyance, maybe? Who is this guy and why is he delivering food to her house? How does he know where she lives, and what about the baby? A weird sensation blooms in my chest. Something foreign. I haven't felt it since…well, ever, maybe.

Jealousy.

It burns deep and spreads like fire.

Before I can stop myself, I ask, "You have a male friend who delivers vegetables to your home? Do you regularly give out your address to random men?"

She glances up, her beautiful brown eyes wide from my insinuation. "Yes, actually, I do, not that it's any of your business. Gary is seventy-two and lost his wife a few months ago. She loved to garden, which is why he has a small greenhouse. He's trying to keep it going in her memory."

My heart starts to settle from its rapid beat, and I keep myself occupied with finishing my sandwich. The moment the wrapper is balled up and tossed in the trash, I turn my attention back to her. Her soup is gone, and only a few bites remain of her BLT. I make myself at home, grabbing three glasses from the cabinet, and filling them up with water. I set one down in front of her, and she eyes it warily as if it might jump up and bite her.

Finally, when I settle back against the counter, I ask one of the many burning questions bouncing around in my head. "What's his name?"

She glances up, confusion written all over her face. "Gary, I told you that."

A smile cracks across my lips. "Not Gary, Sweetness. Your son."

Her face freezes in horror as if she doesn't want to talk about it. It's a cross between irritation and disbelief, like before, when she saw me standing on her front lawn. Ashtyn clears her throat and swallows hard. "Rowan. Rowan Alexander Harris."

"He's named after your brother," I respond in observation.

She nods. "Yes."

Our eyes meet and we just stare at each other. There's so much to say, so many questions to ask and get answered, yet all I want to do is kiss those lips. Even if it's true, if Rowan is my son and she's kept it from me, I still want to take her in my arms and hold her.

Why?

I should be outraged. I should be pissed the fuck off she didn't tell me about him. I should grab my phone and call my lawyer. I always wondered what I'd do if one of these damn fake pregnancy claims actually turned out to be true. I've never seen myself as a father, at all, but right now, if Rowan is my son, I want to hold him too and learn how to care for him. I've gone to great lengths to make sure I'm protected from the very issue, yet here I am with the prospect of having a child, and suddenly, it's not as terrifying as I expected it to be.

Because of Ashtyn.

Even though I should have kept my paws off my oldest friend's twin sister, I'm wildly attracted to her and feel oddly settled when she's near. Crazy, right? I can probably count on one hand how many times I've been around her. We didn't go to the same college, and her school visits were usually short. She stayed with her parents at a hotel, saw a football game, and went to dinner with them after. I, on the other hand, went out after a game. There was always a party to attend, always a group of girls ready to spend a little time with the quarterback.

Now, all I want to do is sit beside her. She's tired and stressed, and I wonder what I can do to help her situation. A situation she doesn't want me to be involved in, but still. If Rowan is my son, I want to step up and do what's right.

Alex is going to be so fucking pissed.

"Ash," I whisper, taking a few steps over to the table where she sits. Her eyes widen as

I approach, but she doesn't say anything as I pull out the chair beside her and sit. I keep my voice low so her brother can't hear. "Who's Rowan's father?"

Fire shoots from her eyes. No, not literally, but if that could happen, I would have been burned by the flames. "Funny, you're still denying responsibility."

My heart stops beating. I open my mouth, but nothing comes out. Did she just…did she just say what I think she did?

She stands up, her chair scraping loudly on the floor as it slides backward. She pins me with a look that would make a weaker man tremble, but for some crazy reason, makes me excited. "Go to hell, Tate Steele."

CHAPTER FOUR
ASHTYN

UGH, I KNOW IT'S NOT APPROPRIATE TO PUNCH PEOPLE, BUT I COULD seriously deck this guy in the face. Who does he think he is? I told him who the father is—that *he* was the father—months ago. He denied it and basically told me to go away. That was after he ignored my first message.

Screw him.

Screw his blasé attitude.

He just waltzes in here with food, under the guise of being a concerned friend of my brother's, and accuses me of trying to pass off my son as his. Like I'm some Tate Steele groupie, who throws their panties on the field every time he tosses a ball. Or grins. Or waves.

Or just looks at you with that smoldering intensity.

Damn him.

I open my mouth to let everything that's built up inside me since the moment I peed on the stick—hell, probably since the second I woke up in my brother's guest bed with only the memories of what happened the night before—when we're interrupted.

"Uhh, Ash?" my brother hollers from the living room, a hint of nervousness in his voice that catches my attention right away.

I turn and head that way, Tate hot on my heels. "What? What's wrong?" I ask the second I cross the threshold.

My brother looks horrified, my son starting to squirm in his arms. I can tell by his mannerisms he's about to let a very unhappy cry fly. I realize instantly what's wrong when the unforgiving scent hits my nose.

Tate sniffs beside me and gasps in disgust. "Holy shit," he mumbles, bringing his arm up to cover his nose. "That smell is coming from that tiny human?"

"Dude, I think it's seeping through the blanket. My arm feels wet." Alex looks at me with pleading eyes, but I can't help it, I laugh. "Really? This is funny?" He gapes at me, trying to hide his gags.

I nod, feeling somewhat lighter as I giggle at my brother's disgust and discomfort. "Sorry," I reply, trying to push my giggles aside to help. I carefully lift my son from my brother's arms, noticing the wet, brown mark on the arm of his T-shirt.

Alex seems to notice at the same time. "God, that's disgusting."

"Your nephew shit on you," Tate states matter-of-factly, but there's no missing the humor dancing in his hazel eyes.

"It happens," I say with a shrug before turning and heading off to the nursery. Rowan starts to squirm, no doubt not happy to have poop seeping from the top and bottom of his diaper. In Rowan's two short weeks of life, I've been pooped on three times and peed on twice. That thing's like a jet hose the second it's exposed to air.

Carefully, I remove the swaddle blanket, setting it aside to wash, and start to work on his onesie. Yeah, there's greenish-brown sludge everywhere. "You're not going to like this,

Little Man, but a bath it is." The cord fell off his belly button a few days ago, so bathing is a little easier. He doesn't mind, as long as his body is submerged in the warm water, but he's not a fan of soaping up.

I grab wipes and start to clean him as much as possible while removing his clothes. He really starts to get upset the longer it takes, but there's nothing I can do about it. Worse, my boobs hear his cries and think it's time for a feeding. I can feel the wetness seeping through my bra, but sadly, it's going to have to wait. Taking care of Rowan comes first.

I move to the bathroom, grateful when I don't see my brother or Tate in the living room. I'm assuming they're in the kitchen, eating the rest of the lunch they brought. I push the door so it's only cracked open and crouch down by the shower. I grab the infant bathtub and set it down. I've become a pro at doing things one-handed. Rowan still voices his displeasure, but it's not as bad now, as I fill the small tub with warm water. I strip off the clean diaper and carefully lower him into the water.

Squatting beside the tub, I lather up his little body, mindful of his face and eyes. Using a little frog pitcher, I use fresh water from the spout to rinse away the suds. "You definitely smell a lot better now," I tell him, as the door creaks open behind me.

I assume it's my brother, so when another voice fills the room. "Much better now." When he notices my startle, he adds, "Sorry, didn't mean to sneak up on you."

Ignoring his presence, I finish giving Rowan his bath. When he's clean and rinsed, I reach for a hooded towel, which, of course, is just out of my reach. Tate moves silently and quickly, pulling the top towel off the stack and handing it to me. I'm already smiling as I spread the terry cloth across my legs, because it has bear ears on the top, making my little guy look like the cutest bear in the world.

The moment his naked body hits the cool air, Rowan lets out a very unhappy holler, drawing his legs up as I lie him down on my lap. I work quickly, drying him off and wrapping him in the towel, completely oblivious to the very wet marks in the centers of my bra. When Rowan is secure, I stand up and turn around, only to be stopped in my tracks by a six foot four inch brick wall.

My gaze locks with his for a second before his drops down. He's staring intently, and while I assume it's at Rowan, the moment I follow his scrutiny, I realize it's not on the baby. Not at all. Tate is openly staring at my chest. Specifically, at the wet circles around my nipples from leaking.

I gasp, my mouth falling open as my shocked eyes meet his. "Uhhh…"

I adjust Rowan, using him as a human shield. "Can we pretend you didn't see that?" I ask, mortification burning my face.

"Is that…"

"Yeah, milk. Sometimes, when he cries, my breasts think it's time to eat."

Tate glances back down to my face, and then over my shoulder. It's as if he doesn't quite know where to look. He clears his throat and opens his mouth, but nothing comes out.

I take the opportunity to slip around his huge body. "I need to get him dry and dressed," I state, heading straight for the nursery. I don't pay any attention to Tate, though I know he's there, lurking in the doorway. I can feel his presence. I'm still not sure why, but I plan to find out.

Just not now. Not with my brother nearby.

When Rowan is dressed in a clean diaper and outfit, I scoop up my son, prepared to feed him. The moment I rest him against my chest, I realize I'm still wearing my wet shirt. I hate the feel of damp material against my skin, and especially against Rowan and his fresh outfit. "I need to change my shirt," I mumble to no one.

A shadow falls over me, and I look way up to meet Tate's hazel eyes. They look greener right now in the dim light, and I hate how much I love that particular color and the way my heart skips around in my chest with excitement. "May I?" he asks, breaking through my thoughts and holding out his hands.

"What? Where's Alex?" I whisper, my voice is barely audible.

Tate clears his throat. "He's finishing his sandwich," he says, running his hand through his hair. "I, uh, thought I could help you. So you can change your shirt." Yeah, he absolutely sounds nervous. I'm not sure I've ever heard the great Tate Steele sound unsure of anything.

"Oh…" Now I'm the one nervous. I don't know why I still feel like everything's a game to this man.

"Just for a few minutes, right? You can change and then feed him. The way he's sucking on his hand like that must mean he's hungry."

I glance down and notice he's correct. Rowan is gnawing on his little fist, and it won't be long before he realizes he's not getting anything out of it. I could feed him first, but then I'm still sitting with a wet shirt and bra. The most logical option is to hand over Rowan so I can do a quick bra and shirt change.

Hand over my son.

To his biological father.

The one who told me to go away.

When I take in his appearance, his hair is a little wild from running his hands through it. There's something in his eyes that's both eager and nervous, but also sincere and hopeful. Why I'd even put myself in a situation requiring me to believe this man is beyond me. He's proven he's only out for himself and no one else.

Yet, for some reason, when he whispers, "I promise you can trust me with him," I find myself carefully handing Rowan over to him so I can change my shirt. Tate's stiff and tense as I help him adjust his hold. My son looks so tiny in his big arms and against his broad chest, but the sight does something to my heart. Unexpected tears burn my eyes, but I quickly blink them away. The last thing I need is to get emotionally caught up in this tangled web of uncertainty. It's all smoke and mirrors. A mirage. The image he just created isn't real.

I'll do good to remember that.

Clearing my throat, I state, "I'll be right back. I'm going to change quickly." Then I'm gone, seeking the security and isolation of my bedroom.

Trying not to dwell on the picture of father and son, I rip off my top and bra faster than I ever have before, taking a few extra seconds to dry the moisture on my chest. I redress in record speed, not even caring which shirt I grab. At this point, I just want to get back to the nursery, back to my son.

That's when another image of Tate and Rowan pops into my head. The chin dimple. I could see it on both father and son as he held him in his arms. How anyone wouldn't see the resemblance is beyond me, but so far, no one has seemed to notice. Of course, no one has seen the baby actually in his father's arms before like I have, which reminds me, I need to get to him before Alex goes in there.

Unfortunately, luck isn't on my side as I slip across the hall and find my brother leaning against the crib, the smallest smile on his face. He grins widely when I step inside and find Tate sitting in the glider, Rowan contently gazing up at him.

"I never thought I'd see the day," my brother whispers.

My shocked gaze flies to his. "What do you mean?" I ask, my throat suddenly thick and dry.

He nods to his best friend. "The day he actually holds a baby, for one, but also look slightly comfortable doing it."

"I've held a baby before, asshole," Tate mumbles, just loud enough so we can hear.

"Yeah? When?" Alex challenges, his grin growing wider by the second.

"Two years ago. I was at a restaurant when a woman who claimed her baby was mine came up and thrust him in my arms," Tate replies, never taking his eyes off the baby cradled in his arms.

"Not the same thing," Alex argues. "You held that kid for like four seconds, only long enough for the mom's friend to snap that picture of you. They already had bidders lined up for that image." There's something in my brother's tone I wasn't expecting. Sadness.

"Does that happen a lot? Random women claiming you're their baby's father?" I find myself asking, even though I'm not sure I want to hear the answer.

"All the time," Alex replies for his friend. "What are you up to this year? Two already?"

"Three," Tate mumbles.

"But that's only because he sleeps with everything with a vagina. He's an easy target," Alex says with a teasing laugh, though neither one of us returns the hilarity. In fact, it's not that funny at all.

Tate blanches before he looks up and meets my eyes. I wonder if he's recalling what got us into this predicament too. That one night that changed the course of our lives without us even knowing. "I don't sleep with all of them. Just the ones I want to," he says, his gaze locked intently on mine.

I swallow over the golf ball lodged in my throat.

Too bad he sleeps with them and refuses to take responsibility for his actions. Tate Steele might actually be a decent human being deep down, if only he weren't such a selfish jerk.

Rowan lets out a squeal, letting me know it's time to eat. Tate looks up, a slice of panic across his face, and asks, "What'd I do?"

I can't help but smile. "Nothing. He's ready to eat."

"Can I help?" he asks, glancing back down at the baby in his arms.

"Not unless you've started lactating," I shoot off at the mouth.

Realization settles in and his eyes dip to my chest. I don't think my brother caught it because he doesn't reprimand his friend for gawking at his sister's chest. Her very large, very hard chest, I might add. In the last week, I've developed the boobs of a porn star, and if the way Tate keeps glancing at them is any indication, I'd say he's noticed too.

"Come on, dude. We'll go in the living room. No way do I need to see my sister's boobs," Alex says, making a quick retreat from the nursery.

"I wouldn't mind," Tate mumbles, only loud enough for me to hear.

"I think you've done enough," I whisper, bending down to take my son.

Our eyes meet. His are soft and sincere, apologetic even, as he looks up at me. "We're going to talk, Ash. Not with Alex around, but you and I have things to discuss."

I swallow hard. "I'm not sure what about. You've said everything you needed to already."

He's already shaking his head in disagreement. "That's part of the problem, Sweetness. I haven't said anything yet."

His words leave me mystified as he slowly lifts his arms for me to take the baby. I slide my hands through his arms, brushing my chest against him. In true guy fashion, his eyes dance with mirth and a wicked grin spreads across his too-handsome face. "Oh, stop it. It was an accident," I chastise, as I grab Rowan and cradle him to my chest.

"Best accident I've experienced today," he replies, grinning widely as he gets up to allow me to sit in the glider.

Tate lingers close by as I get positioned for feeding. I'm ready to lift my shirt when it hits me I still have an audience. Looking up, I give him a questioning look. He takes a step closer and crouches in front of me. Rowan is starting to squirm, getting more unhappy with each passing second, but the moment Tate sets his hand on his forehead, it's as if a calmness washes over him. Rowan just stops and looks up, his attention given completely to the man right in front of him.

His father.

Then Tate does something I'm not expecting, nor is my emotionally fragile state prepared for. He bends down and kisses Rowan on the forehead. He looks up and meets my eyes, whispering, "I'm not going anywhere."

CHAPTER FIVE

TATE

I'M TORN BETWEEN WANTING TO STAY IN THAT ROOM AND KNOWING I NEED to give her privacy.

The thought of someone doing what she's about to do has always made me a little squeamish. Breasts, I like. Breasts with babies attached to them have never been my thing. Yet, the thought of Ashtyn feeding her son…

My son.

There's no doubt in my mind now. Not after seeing him in person. He looks a lot like Ashtyn, yet there are other similarities to me too. The chin dimple is a big giveaway, though not a unanimous verdict. The shape of his eyes is Ashtyn, but the color? There's more gold in those hazel eyes than brown or green. And there's the shape of his face, which is a little more like mine than his mother's. When I was holding him, scared I was going to break him somehow, he just sat there and stared back at me. He was wide awake, his attention riveted on me the same as mine was on him. That's when I felt it.

Pride.

It was way different than what I feel on the football field after throwing a perfect spiral into the hands of an awaiting receiver. Better than all those times the coach praised me in the locker room for a job well done. Even greater than every list I've topped or award I've received, including the Heisman. This comes from somewhere deeper, something with more meaning, and frankly, that shocks the shit out of me.

I'm a basic man. I love football and women.

But the look in that little boy's eyes made me feel something bigger, something greater than football and women, all rolled into one.

"Hey, everything okay?" Alex asks, propping his feet up on the coffee table, remote in hand.

"Fine," I tell him, as I sit in the rocker recliner where Alex sat earlier. I sniff and glance around. "It still smells like shit over."

Alex snorts. "You weren't the one covered in it. I just threw the shirt away. Thank God I still had my carry-on bag in the rental so I could change my shirt."

We sit in silence, watching television, though I'm not sure either of us is actually watching the program. My mind keeps racing back to holding Rowan, and then catapulting the other direction and wondering if Ash is okay in the nursery.

"She seems like she's doing okay," Alex finally says, like a general observation.

I glance around the small, yet cozy place she's got here. There's a basket of baby things in front of the television and a swing on the opposite side of the room. "She looks a little tired, but that's probably normal, right?" I ask.

Alex shrugs. "Probably. Mom said she napped a lot when they were here last week. I guess the first few nights were rough, but by the end of their trip, they settled into a routine."

The thought of Ashtyn being here by herself this past week bothers me more than I expected. I'm grateful her parents were here to help after the baby was born, but at the same time, I feel a little shorted in that regard. What if she needs something? Who will she call? Her parents and Alex are hours away, and even though they'd drop everything to help, it could be too late before they arrive.

"I asked again last night if they found out who his father is," Alex continues, catching my complete attention.

My throat feels dry as I carefully glance his way, schooling my features to not give anything away. "Did they find out anything?"

Alex shakes his head. "Nope. Dad said no one but a few co-workers from the library stopped by, and she never took any calls or texts from anyone other than friends. That's why I want this job, Tate. I want to be here to help her if she needs it."

I open my mouth, determined to tell him I'm here, that I'll help, but I quickly snap it shut. I'm not about to give too much away yet. Not until I've talked to Ashtyn. If and when the time comes to have this discussion with Alex, I'll man up and do it, but for now, I'd rather not wave red in front of the bull's face. Right now, all I'm guilty of is sleeping with his sister, which yes, is bad enough. When I finally get confirmation that it resulted in a child, then I'll do what's right and tell my oldest friend, but not until I speak with Ashtyn.

"I'm here too," I find myself telling him.

Alex gives me a small smile. "I know, and I'm grateful knowing you're this close. Although, I'm not sure you'd pick my sister over some hot blonde with big tits grinding on your cock at a club."

See, that's where he's wrong. Little does he know, I'd pick Ashtyn over anyone, anytime. I haven't been able to stop thinking about her, or our night together, since it happened. And believe me, I've tried. But the only fucking I've been doing is my hand, but try telling Alex that. He'd never believe me. Especially not after rooming with me in college. Different girl every night. Hell, a few times it was more than one, sometimes even together. Our place was a revolving door of hot women, and when it wasn't football season, lots of booze. I enjoyed my college experience, probably a little too much.

"If your sister needed help, I'd drop everything," I insist, trying to keep it casual, yet wondering if I'm failing miserably.

Alex stares at me, and I wish I knew what was going through his head. Back in the day, it was easy, but now, after long periods of absences, I admit, I can't read my friend as easily as I used to. "I appreciate it. I'm going to give her your number before I leave. This way, she'll have it if she ever needs it."

I nod, knowing it'll be programmed into her phone by the end of today, not days from now. "So, tell me about the interview," I say, looking for a redirect.

Alex instantly smiles. "It went well, I think. I met with Roger Aspen and Tyler Duff. The position is in recruiting and available immediately. I'd work with Coach Colson directly, along with Roger, on scouting. The position involves a lot of travel, but I'm fine with that. Actually, I think I'd enjoy it."

I shrug. "Living out of a suitcase and pizza box isn't all it's cracked up to be."

"Probably not, but I'd also get to watch and meet players from all over the country. All those pro team reps I had to hobnob at Notre Dame would now be me. This world is full of amazing, talented athletes, and I'd love to be the one who goes out and finds the cream of the crop for my team."

I completely understand where he's coming from. I've given some thought to *what if*. What if I stopped playing football today? What would I do tomorrow? I've made enough money off my endorsements and investments to set myself up pretty nicely for the rest of my life, but that doesn't mean I'll be able to just sit on my ass and watch television all damn day. I'm a worker, always have been. From my very first job at fifteen to now, I'm always busy doing something.

And now I might have someone else to consider. Two people, actually. If it turns out Rowan is my son, I'll take care of him. Him and Ashtyn both. They'll not want for anything and will have the best of everything. I'll make sure of it. Though, something tells me she's not the type to just sit back and let me swoop in and save the day like Superman. Especially since she's still a little hostile toward me.

"Sounds like a great gig," I tell my friend, pulling my mind away from his sister and back to our conversation. "And I'll admit, it'd be pretty sweet having you here."

Alex grins. "Agreed." He sighs and leans his head back on the couch. "I love working at Notre Dame, but I'm too far away. If I don't get this job, I think I'll keep looking. I want to be closer to Ash, and you. I've got friends in South Bend, but it's not the same. Hell, even my parents said they're considering selling their place and moving this way."

I glance over, noticing the stress lines around his eyes for the first time. He looks as tired as Ashtyn does. "How long have you been thinking about this?"

He closes his eyes and sighs. "A year or two. Even before she got pregnant by some fucking loser. He probably doesn't even have a decent job. Why else would he not be here, supporting his kid?"

I swallow hard. Yeah, this conversation is coming to a head and isn't going to be easy. Probably one of the hardest I've ever faced. Even when I told my mom to stop reading the tabloid stories on me. They're always based on perception, not fact, and the photos don't help either. The assholes who follow me around have an uncanny ability to catch me at the most inopportune time.

Like the time I was at a club, chatting with one woman. Her drunk friends came up and all fell in my lap at the exact moment the one I was talking to shoves her tongue down my throat. The image made it look like I was having a fivesome right there in the VIP lounge. The headline read "Playboy QB Took Group Home Last Night."

Or what about the time a woman with a questionable night job was leaving my building in the wee hours of the morning. Not from my penthouse, mind you. Yet, she stood on the sidewalk and talked about everything but my shoe size. My mom about died when she read the "Playboy QB Pays Top Dollar Call Girls" headline. There's nothing worse than your mom calling, begging you to stop paying for sex like Charlie Sheen.

"I don't know, man. I guess…maybe he has a reason?"

"What kind of reason keeps you away from your responsibilities? Did he move to Timbuktu?"

I can tell he's getting irritated, and the last thing I want to do is piss him off by defending…well, me. "I'm not saying you're wrong, Alex. I'm just saying maybe there's a reason, like, he doesn't know?"

There. I said it.

Alex blows out a big breath that comes out a snort. "So now it's Ashtyn's fault for not telling him?"

I hold my hands up in surrender. This is going wrong, fast. "I'm not saying it's her fault at all. I guess I'm just saying there's more to the story than what we know, and she isn't exactly talking. So, don't get all worked up if you don't know all the facts."

Oh, I can feel his eyes glaring at me. Alex is super protective of his family, especially his twin sister. Always has been. One time in college, someone kept commenting about her to get a rise out of him while we were drinking, and Alex ended up punching the guy. We all learned real quick not to talk about his sister, even if we were teasing.

He sighs. "I guess you're right." Even though he agrees, I can tell he doesn't exactly mean it. His face is hard and his eyes narrow, but the conversation is closed. He's just done talking about it. For now.

I catch movement in the hallway and see Ashtyn slipping across to her bedroom, baby in her arms. I almost jump up and rush to help, but that'll be too obvious to Alex. Instead, I sit in the chair and wait for her to join us. She's there a few minutes later, yawning.

"Why don't you take a nap?" I say the moment she steps into the room.

Ashtyn's eyes narrow. "I'm not going to be able to take naps during the day when I return to work."

"True, but that's still weeks away, right? You might as well crash now while Row does." I throw in a shrug, so she knows it's just a suggestion and not an order.

"I agree, Ash. Tate and I will listen for Little Man," Alex says, stretching out even more on the couch.

She yawns again. "But you're only here for a couple of days."

"Yeah, but I'm not leaving yet. Go take a nap. I'll plan dinner," her brother says.

"You don't have to do that," she argues.

"I do. Tate and I will grill something."

She looks my way, one eyebrow raised in question. "You're staying?"

"I have nowhere else to be," I tell her casually, crossing my ankles and leaning back in the chair.

"Great," she mumbles, just loud enough for me to hear. "I guess I could go lie down for a bit. *If* you're sure."

"I'm sure. Go, Ash," Alex insists, and I'm grateful. She needs some rest.

"Fine, but just for a little bit. I want to hear all about your interview," Ashtyn vows, as she gets up and shuffles back to her bedroom.

Alex and I are both quiet until we hear the door click shut. "You staying for dinner?" he asks, eyes on whatever is on television.

"Yep." My answer is immediate.

He looks my way but doesn't say anything else. I can't help but wonder what he's thinking.

We watch some car program for about thirty minutes before his phone rings. Alex pulls it from his pocket and sits up straight when he sees the screen. "It's Roger," he says, referring to the VP of Operations of the St. Louis Fire. "Hello?"

They talk for a few seconds before Alex starts to pace. "Tonight? Oh, uh, I'm not sure," he stammers, his eyes wide as he glances my way. Alex covers the phone and whispers, "Roger says the GM wants to meet with me tonight for dinner."

"Go!"

"But what about Ash?"

"I'll help," I insist, realizing instantly how much I mean it.

Alex gives me a look, almost as if he's not sure he believes me, and to be honest, a year or two ago, I probably wouldn't have believed me either. Unless it's about football, I've always been a little fluid when it comes to maintaining my commitments. There's always another party or restaurant to be seen at.

"Seriously. The fact the GM wants to meet with you is great news, Alex."

My words register as Alex goes back to his phone. "Yes, sir, I'm here, sorry. I'd love to meet you all for dinner. Six o'clock at O'Reilly's? Yes, I'll find it. Thank you, sir. I look forward to meeting everyone." Then he hangs up the phone.

"Holy shit, man. The GM wants to meet me for dinner. This is huge."

"It is," I confirm.

"And you don't mind hanging out here for a bit? I mean, I'm sure Ash would be fine, but I hate I just told her I'd make dinner, and now I'm going to bail."

"First off, you know she'd understand, but second, I don't mind at all." Actually, I'm looking forward to it, but I won't be telling him that.

"Well, if you don't mind. Damn, I should head back to the hotel and shower. After dinner, I'll come back here and relieve you. I'm sure you have plans later," he says, grabbing his keys off the table.

"Nope, no plans," I confirm. The look he gives me tells me he doesn't believe me at all.

"I'll text you when I'm done with dinner," he says, glancing down the hallway.

"Don't wake her. I'll tell here where you went when she gets up."

He nods in agreement. "All right, see you later then."

I throw him a wave as he heads out the front door, leaving me here with his sister. Alone. The last time I was alone with her, I did dirty things to that sexy little body of hers. Those things definitely won't be happening this time, but I'm looking forward to hanging out with her nonetheless.

And maybe finally getting the answers to some very burning questions.

CHAPTER SIX
ASHTYN

I DON'T KNOW WHAT STARTLES ME AWAKE, BUT IT TAKES ME A FEW MOMENTS to get my bearings. Apparently, I was sleeping hard enough to drool, if the wetness on my pillow is any indication. I stretch my legs and stare at the wall, taking in the quiet.

Only, it's not exactly quiet. I can hear a noise, like the floorboards beneath my carpeting is squeaking. And then I hear Rowan make a sucking noise on what sounds like skin. I turn over in my bed, only to come face-to-face with Tate. He's standing beside my bed, rocking back and forth, Rowan in his arms. "He's probably getting hungry," he whispers.

"What...why are you in here?" I ask, confused over why he's in my room, holding my son.

"Rowan started to cry. I came in to check on him after a few seconds."

That's odd. "He was crying?"

"Yeah, I was surprised you didn't hear him, but when I peeked in here, you were dead to the world."

I've been so tired lately. Could I have slept through my son's hungry cries? What if it happens again?

"Don't beat yourself up, Ash. You're exhausted taking care of him, but you're a good mom. Even I can see that," he says, offering me a small smile that meets his eyes. They seem to turn darker, a deep golden shade of sex on a stick.

Wait, what?

Stop that.

"Thank you for grabbing him," I reply, climbing off my bed. I was so tired, I didn't even get beneath the covers.

"I'm no expert, but his diaper feels a little on the heavy side," Tate adds, as I reach for the baby. My hands brush against his chest, which seems to do wonders for the libido I was sure dried up and died in the last ten months.

"I bet it is," I answer, kissing the top of his soft, fuzzy head.

I head across the hall to change his diaper, Tate hot on my heels. I can feel his presence like a warm embrace, even though he hangs back near the doorway. Trying to pretend he's not there is futile, especially when his aftershave makes its way across the room. It's a sexy woodsy scent that would turn the best of girls into bad ones.

With a fresh diaper on, I scoop Rowan up and turn to face Tate. He's leaning against the wall, watching my every move. A piece of hair hangs down on his forehead, my fingers itching to touch it. "Where's Alex?" I ask, lightly patting my son on the back to give my hands something to do other than touch Tate.

His smile is instant. "He got a call from the Fire's office. The GM wanted to meet him for dinner. He apologizes for not being here, but I told him I'd stay. I've got some chicken breasts I found in the fridge almost ready to go on the grill, if that's okay."

"Oh, uh, you don't have to do that."

Tate shrugs. "Alex and I were going to do it before he got the call, so no reason to change the plan. Besides, I don't mind cooking, especially grilling."

Rowan starts to fuss again, ready for another feeding.

"Do you always feed him in here?" Tate asks, pointing to the glider.

"Sometimes, yes. I've sat in the living room a few times just for a change of scenery," I confess.

He shoves his hands in his pockets. "Why don't you come out and do…your thing? You can keep me company while I'm in the kitchen," he says, and I swear I can see his cheeks flush.

"Oh, I don't have to. I don't want to make you uncomfortable."

"You won't," he insists, glancing down at Rowan, a soft smile on his full lips. My heart skips in my chest, and I still can't help but wonder what his game is. Why is he all of a sudden interested in my son?

I shouldn't, but I grab a burp cloth and the lightweight blanket off the glider and follow him out of the nursery. Tate grabs a throw pillow and sets it beside me on the chair. When I get comfy, I slide the pillow under my arm, much as I did for my brother earlier in the day. It only takes me a few seconds to finish getting situated before I slip the thin blanket over my shoulder. Rowan latches on right away.

Tate busies himself in the kitchen, preparing dinner. I don't know why it's so comforting to listen to him move about my space, especially since no one but my parents have been here since I moved in. I'm used to quiet, to doing things on my own. Yet here I am, enjoying the sound of someone helping in the kitchen.

Rowan feeds for about twenty minutes, and throughout that time, Tate has popped his head in to check on me. He brought me water and a few slices of Colby Jack cheese he found in the fridge. By the time I've burped my son and he's passed out again, I can hear Tate on the back deck, finishing up the grilling.

I decide to try the swing again. The first time we used it last week, Rowan wasn't a fan. But he also had bad gas that day, and I'm wondering if it had something to do with it. Carefully, I set him in the seat and buckle him in, making sure all of the safety features are engaged before I press the button for slow swinging. It moves from side to side, gently rocking him in a soothing manner. Rowan doesn't so much as make a peep, so I set the timer for twenty minutes and follow my nose to where the food is.

Tate is just returning to the kitchen, a platter of chicken in one hand and my grilling tongs in the other. "I wasn't sure what you liked on your chicken, so there are plain, barbecue, and spicy," he says.

"Oh, I should probably stick with plain, though the barbecue does sound good," I say, taking a seat at the table.

"Why should you stick with plain?"

"What I consume, the baby consumes. So I should avoid spicy and acidic things so he doesn't get heartburn or an upset stomach," I tell him, reaching for a napkin.

"Huh, I guess that makes sense. Looks like I'm eating the spicy ones, though no hardship there." He sets a chicken breast on my plate before placing one of the spicy ones on his own. "Oh, shit. The vegetables." Tate walks over the stove and grabs a pan. "I hope you don't mind I cut up some of the veggies you had in the fridge and on the counter. They looked good, and I thought they'd make a great grilled vegetable medley."

Tate brings the pan over and scoops a healthy mound of veggies onto my plate. There's squash, zucchini, carrots, and cherry tomatoes all together in a foil pan. "This looks amazing."

He shrugs. "I hope you like it." He takes a bite of vegetables before asking, "Where's Row?"

It's the second time he's called him that, and I can't figure out if I like it or not. Though, if my rapid heart rate and schoolgirl exhilaration is any indication, I'd it's the former. "He's sleeping in his swing in the living room."

We eat in silence, but I'm all too aware of his presence. I still have so many questions, so much I want to know about why he showed up today with my brother, and before I realize it, the words are flying out of my mouth. "Why are you here, Tate?"

He slowly chews a bite of chicken before taking a sip of water. "Feeding you."

I'm already shaking my head. "No, not that. Why did you come here today?" My eyes plead with his to just tell me what's going on.

Tate sets his fork down and gives me his full attention. "Because when I saw that photo of your son, something inside me felt like I was being strangled. It was confusing, yet comforting. I wanted to see him in person and find out if my suspicions were correct."

I drop my fork with a clatter. "Your suspicions?" I ask, irritated to no end.

"If he's my son or not."

I close my eyes and count to five. When I open then, they lock on the hazel ones across the table. "I've already told you he is," I whisper, pain lacerating my heart all over again.

When I found out I was pregnant, I knew whose baby it was. There was only one possibility. I couldn't ask my brother for his best friend's phone number without throwing up every red flag known to man, so I sought him out on social media. No, not the best place to contact someone, but I was desperate. It's not like I was gonna drop the baby bomb on Facebook, but I was at least looking for a way to contact him.

He told me to get lost.

It's like my words register suddenly, and he becomes a little pale. "When? When did you tell me?" he asks. It's not anger in his voice, but more confusion than anything.

"After I found out, Tate. I looked you up on social media. You told me it wasn't yours and to go away or you'd involve your lawyers," I state, recalling all those horrible feelings when I read his final message.

Tate suddenly stands up, the chair flying backward and falling with a crash. I sit, shocked, as he paces the kitchen floor and lets out a frustrated growl. His hands are in his hair, a sure sign of aggravation. "That wasn't me." His eyes are closed and his head hangs.

"What?"

He picks up the chair and settles back down, this time, directly beside me. "That wasn't me, Ash. I don't manage my social media. I have my PR team do it for me."

Realization sets in. Could it be true? Was the person responding to me from Tate's account really not him? I guess it would make sense as to why he was so cold. That or he's an exceptional liar, and he's covering his ass right now.

Tate reaches for my hand. I didn't even realize mine was shaking until he holds it in his much bigger, warmer one. "Start at the beginning, Ash. Please."

I tell him about moving to St. Louis and peeing on the stick. "I waited until after my first appointment before I reached out to you. You never replied to that message. After a few weeks, I tried again. This time, you responded, but with a simple denial. I reached out again, asking to meet with you face-to-face, but your response was a legal notification. You were going to sue me for defamation of character if I went public with my claim. You even offered me money to go away."

I'm not sure when the tear fell, but I knew the moment it was caught. The rough pad of Tate's thumb swipes across my cheek before threading into my hair. "I'm sorry, Ash. So fucking sorry," he mumbles, closing his eyes and resting his forehead against mine. "I didn't know."

"I didn't take the money. I didn't want it. I could have pursued child support after proving paternity, but if you didn't want your son, I wanted no part of you either."

Our eyes meet again. "So you did it all yourself. Alone."

I shrug. "It hasn't been so bad. Sure, I get a little tired sometimes, but he's worth it," I reply with a smile on my lips.

Tate grins in return. "He is. I just wish I would have been here for you. I can't believe Todd didn't tell me."

"I guess I should have tried harder to contact you, but I assumed it was you I was speaking to. I'm sorry."

He's already shaking his head. "No, please don't apologize."

"I should have just told my brother and gotten your number through him. I was prepared to do it after my first message didn't get answered, but then you replied, and I thought you wanted nothing to do with us."

He closes his eyes again. "Your brother would have killed me if he found out. Shit, it's probably still going to happen."

"I'm an adult," I state, and even though I know my twin wouldn't actually kill someone, this doesn't bode well for their friendship.

"He's always had a rule, and I broke it."

"I was a rule?"

"More like a guideline. Don't mess with you, plain and simple."

My breathing becomes thicker as I recall that night at my brother's place almost ten months ago. "But you did."

His eyes darken. They remind me of that night, so full of desire and lust. "Yeah, I did. Turns out, it was a pretty damn good decision."

I feel the blush heat my cheeks and glance down at my now-cold chicken. "So, where do we go from here?" I whisper.

Tate pushes my plate toward me. "Now, you eat, Sweetness. The rest, we'll figure out as we go. But one thing is certain, Ash. You're not alone anymore."

CHAPTER SEVEN
TATE

"YOU HAVE TO MOVE QUICKLY. THAT LITTLE THING IS LIKE A FIREHOSE, waiting to spray."

I turn and lock eyes with Ashtyn. Her words don't exactly boost my confidence here. It's my very first diaper change, and now I have to move quickly or risk getting peed on? I glance down at Rowan, who's staring up at us with wide, hazel eyes. "Go easy on me, Champ. This is my first time." Rowan doesn't seem impressed with my pleas for leniency.

"Just have the fresh diaper ready. This one won't be too bad. It's only urine, but that little thing will go off with no notice."

I halt, my hands poised on the little sticky tabs, and glance her way. "Stop calling it a *little thing*. He has my genes. No way is it *little*." Then I throw her a panty-melting grin that causes a blush to creep up her neck and spread across her face. One hundred bucks says her chest is just as pink as the rest of her.

Ashtyn tries to brush off my cock reference, ignoring it completely. "Anyway, I'm just warning you. Be quick."

I make sure the clean diaper and wipes are even closer and slowly pull the tabs. Little legs and arms move, which makes it harder yet, especially since the moment I pull down the soiled diaper, a water fountain of piss shoots out. "Shit!" I holler, replacing the diaper to stop the flow.

"I told you," Ashtyn says through her laughter. "The good news is, he's already peed. So you have a little more time to get him cleaned up and the new one in place now."

"Swell," I mumble, returning my focus on the task at hand. I use the wipes and clean his body. "See what I mean? My son," I state, pointing down.

I'm smacked on the shoulder and laugh when she shakes her hand. "Ouch."

"That's what you get for hitting me," I tell her, as I start to maneuver the clean diaper around his body.

"You're impossible."

"You might be right, but look what I did," I state proudly, pointing down to the fresh diaper.

Ashtyn snickers, closing the dirty diaper and throwing it at me. "The quarterback has quick hands."

"What if I would have dropped it? It could have hit Row."

She gives me a sassy look. "I was pretty sure you weren't going to let it hit the ground."

"Hell no, I wasn't. I always make my play," I reply, wiggling my eyebrows suggestively and making her laugh.

After tossing the dirty diaper in the bin thingy, I scoop up Rowan, inhaling his skin as I bring him to my chest. What is it about babies that makes them smell so good? I've always preferred Chanel or the sweet scent of a naked woman, but I admit, this little guy is quickly becoming a favorite too. Weird. Before today I wouldn't be caught dead sniffing a baby's head.

"He seems pretty content if you want to hold him for a few minutes before he eats," she suggests, just as we hear the front door open and close. A few seconds later, Alex comes around the corner, still wearing a navy blue suit and a wide smile.

"Hey," he says, his eyes softening as he takes in his nephew. When he looks back up at me, there's a hint of a question in those brown orbs. "You're still here?"

"Where else would I be? I said I'd stay," I reply, bouncing from side to side like I've seen Ashtyn do.

Alex shrugs, removing his suit jacket. "I just figured you'd have plans tonight. I'm sure this isn't your usual Saturday night."

He wouldn't be wrong. Nothing about tonight is my norm, except enjoying the company of a beautiful woman.

"So how did it go?" Ashtyn asks, excitement laced in her question.

Alex instantly grins. "I got the job. They want me to start ASAP. Like tomorrow."

"Holy shit, that's awesome!" I congratulate my friend. His news means he's going to be moving here, closer to his sister and nephew. And me.

Ashtyn throws her arms around his waist and hugs him tight. "What does this mean? You still work in South Bend."

Alex sighs. "I'm meeting with my boss tomorrow morning at eight. I was honest with him when I told him I was coming here. He knows I want to be closer to my family. It just sucks I can't give him any real notice."

"So you're quitting tomorrow morning? Wow," she says.

"Yeah, formally. As I said, he knows. I just refuse to actually do it over the phone or an email. They've been too good to me there to not give them the courtesy of quitting face-to-face."

"That means you're leaving tonight, if you're meeting tomorrow morning," I realize.

"Yeah, my plane leaves in two hours. I have to run back to the hotel and grab my stuff. They're putting me in an executive apartment for up to six months, so I'll have time to find my own place. There's just so much to do, you know? I have to arrange a packing company, move, and be here Monday morning," he says, shaking his head as if the thought is already stressing him out.

"I'll help," Ashtyn says, hugging him again. "I'm just so happy for you."

He squeezes her tight and smiles. "Thanks, Ash. Listen, I know I'm supposed to be here another day, but I have to go. I'll be back Monday though, okay? Maybe we can do dinner? I'll bring something over."

She waves him off. "It can wait a few days. You'll need to get settled," she insists, but her brother is already disagreeing.

"Nope. Monday night. I'll bring pizza." With another quick hug to his sister, Alex turns to me. He meets my eyes first before they drop to his nephew. Those all-knowing brown eyes seem to linger on the baby before he steps forward and kisses the top of his head. "Are you heading out too?"

Shit. As much as I'd rather stay, it would be very suspicious if I insisted on hanging back and leaving after him. "Yeah, that's probably best."

As I carefully hand Rowan over to Ashtyn, something in my chest tugs hard. Suddenly, I don't want to leave Ash or the baby.

My son.

I run my hand through my hair in agitation as we make our way to the front door. "Thank you for hanging out with me tonight for a bit. It was nice to have company," Ashtyn says politely.

Fuck that polite. I want to pull her into my arms and kiss the air out of her lungs. I want to watch as her body sways my way as if an invisible string were pulling her to me. I want to feel her soft skin under my hand and against my body. "You're welcome. I'll get your number from Alex and send you mine. He mentioned sharing it, in case you need to get a hold of me."

Her eyes widen. "Oh, uh…"

"I know you're moving here, but probably still a good idea, right?" I ask my friend.

"Yeah, definitely. I'll give it to him," Alex says, kissing his sister's cheek one last time before we exit the house.

I turn around and give her a look as if to say I'll call you later. Ashtyn averts her eyes, but I know she saw me. We still have a ton of shit to discuss, probably sooner rather than later.

I CAN'T SLEEP. I'VE LAIN IN BED FOR THE BETTER PART OF AN HOUR AND AM nowhere near close enough to falling asleep. Usually, when this happens, I either workout in my home gym or call a friend. And by friend, I mean someone who'll help work me out in the bedroom.

That thought nauseates me. There's only one woman I want to work out with in bed.

After I got the number I was hoping for and said goodbye to Alex outside of Ashtyn's place, he took off for his hotel and then the airport. He sent me a message a few minutes ago, just to let me know he landed. Ever since, I've stared at his sister's contact information in my phone, contemplating on whether or not it's a good idea to reach out. I've convinced myself it's late, she needs her sleep and I don't want to wake Rowan.

But here I am, retyping a message for the fourteenth time that doesn't make me sound too desperate or too clingy.

Me: I know we have a lot still to discuss, but I hope you know I'm not going anywhere.

I'm surprised when the bubbles appear a few seconds later.

Ashtyn: Thank you

Me: Why are you up? Is everything okay?

I glance at the alarm clock and see it's after midnight.

Ashtyn: Yeah, all is good. Rowan was hungry.

I instantly smile at seeing his name on the screen. I smile even more when a photo comes through a few seconds later. He's cradled in the crook of her arm, his mouth hanging open as he saws logs.

Ashtyn: He just burped, and we're getting ready to go back to bed.

I run my hand through my hair, wishing I were there. Fuck, I hate being here. Ever since I got home, I've felt like the walls have started to close in on me. Usually, silence is sweet, but tonight, it's suffocating.

Me: *I can let you go.*

She doesn't reply right away, and I wonder if she's already in bed. In a way, I hope she is. I hope she laid down and fell asleep right away, so she can get as much rest as possible before his next feeding and diaper change. I just set my phone down, when it pings with a text.

Ashtyn: What are you still doing up?

Me: Can't sleep. Wish I was there.

Ashtyn: There's nothing you can do here.

Me: I can help, Sweetness. That's better than pacing the floors here, wishing I were at your place. I should have never left.

Frustration fills my soul once more as I think about leaving them alone. There's no doubt in my mind Ashtyn can handle it, but she shouldn't have to, dammit. I should be there, do whatever needs to be done, whether it's a midnight diaper change or running a load of laundry. Admittedly, I'd probably need a refresher on the whole laundry bit, since mine is done by my housekeeper, but I'm a quick learner. I'll figure it out.

Ashtyn: It's late.

Me: I know.

I take a deep breath and let it out.

Me: Can I come over? I'll sleep on the couch or the floor, but I can't stay here, Ash. I feel helpless and I fucking hate it.

She doesn't respond right away, which starts to worry me. Maybe I stepped over some invisible line and am pushing too hard. I'm about to apologize when her reply comes through.

Ashtyn: Okay

That's it.
Okay.
One simple word that feels equivalent to winning the fucking lottery.

I'm already up and moving. I grab a duffel bag from my closet and throw in some clean shorts, tees, and boxers. I add my travel shaving bag, only because I know it'll have everything else I need, and grab my phone charger.

Me: I'll be there in thirty minutes.

Ashtyn: There's a code on the front door. It's 030422

Me: Get some sleep. I won't bother you when I get there.

Before I shove my phone in my pocket, I add:

Me: Thank you, Ash. For including me and allowing me into your home like this.

Ashtyn: I never wanted to exclude you, Tate. I've always wanted you to be a part of his life.

"And I am," I say aloud, slipping my phone into the pocket of my shorts.

Because as long as I live, I'm going to be the father that boy deserves. I may not have pictured my life going this way, but fuck am I glad it did. That night changed my life, in more ways than one. It opened my eyes to the beauty of one woman and connected me with her forever.

I drive a little too fast as I head over to her house. It's on the other side of St. Louis, in an older neighborhood filled with ranch-style homes, elementary schools, and churches. It wouldn't be my first choice to live, but it'd be at the top of my list for my son. Maybe not these older, smaller places, but one of the big ones with a huge yard. Plenty of room to throw a ball back and forth and maybe add a pool.

Slowing my car, I notice a single light on in her house. I pull my sports car into her driveway, all the way up to the small garage. My red Lamborghini Aventador stands out like a neon sign most places, but in suburbia, it's worse. Thankfully, she has a thick row of hedges between her place and her neighbor's, so it's a little easier to hide the car. Though, all you'd have to do is simply look up the driveway to see it, and considering there are only three in this part of the country, it's not very inconspicuous.

I should have brought the BMW SUV.

Mental note to switch vehicles tomorrow…

With my bag in hand, I lock the car and set the alarm before heading to her front door. I enter the code and quietly slip inside, making sure the door is locked behind me. There's not a sound anywhere, and I hope that means Ashtyn fell back asleep.

I drop my bag on the chair, kick off my shoes, and slip down the hall. I know Rowan's room will be empty since he's sleeping in one of those bassinet things beside Ash's bed. The door is wide open, so I go ahead and peek inside. What I wasn't expecting was a sight that will forever be ingrained in my memory. The most beautiful picture I've ever seen.

Ashtyn is sleeping on her side with Rowan beside her. He's swaddled in a blanket, his arms extended over his head. Her right hand is resting on his legs as if she needs constant contact with him. Her hair is wild on her pillow, which only adds to her beauty.

I retrieve my phone and turn on the camera app. I take two photos of mother and baby sleeping soundly before I retreat from the room. I'm guessing he woke up again after she fed him, and so she moved him to her bed, probably only meant for a few minutes, but then she fell asleep. I'm not sure if I should wake her, but my gut says to let them be.

Smiling, I find a pillow and sheet sitting on the couch. She must have put it here after our text exchange. I sit back and throw my legs up on the worn cushions. When I close my eyes, I see them on the bed. I see Rowan in her arms, his dark eyes gazing up at his mother with so much trust and innocence. I see Ashtyn smiling, her face so full of love and adoration for one tiny human.

And then I see me, right there in the middle of it.

For the first time in my life, I fall head over heels in love.

CHAPTER EIGHT
ASHTYN

IT'S BEEN TWO WEEKS SINCE I CONFIRMED TO TATE HE WAS ROWAN'S FATHER, and do you know what? He's been here every moment he can. Sure, his personal training schedule is starting to pick up now that we're approaching July, but when he's not at the facility's gym or team meetings, he's here.

Alex, on the other hand, has been crazy busy. When he returned to St. Louis, he was immediately shipped out to scout and negotiate for a new kicker. He was gone a week, meetings with agents and players, and since he's been back, he's had meetings almost nightly.

The plus side to that is I haven't had to have an awkward conversation with him about Rowan's father.

The downside is I haven't had that conversation, and I'm afraid he's going to show up at my house when Tate is here.

Tate and I decided last night we'd tell him this coming Saturday at dinner. Tate wanted to tell him alone, but I insisted I be there. I know my brother. He's most likely going to be upset, but if he sees I'm okay, it'll help soothe the rough waters when he finds out it's his best friend who fathered his sister's baby. No sister ever wants to talk about who she sleeps with to her brother.

Speaking of sleeping, Tate has been here most nights.

On my couch.

He gets up and does midnight diaper changes before handing Rowan over for his feeding. Who would have thought? The infamous Tate Steele, bad boy, playboy extraordinaire, a pro at changing diapers. He brings me water and snacks, and on several occasions, has rubbed my back while standing in the kitchen. In fact, he seems to do whatever he can to touch me. Not grabbing my ass, as I'd expected, but those little grazes of his shoulder along mine or the gentlest swipe of his thumb over the apple of my cheek. It's messing with my girl-brain. Mostly because I like it so much.

He's often gone though in the morning when I get up for the day, heading off to a team workout. However, the coffee pot is always on, a clean cup sitting right in front of it, ready to go.

It's weird, really. Never once has he left to go out. I'm accustomed to seeing his photo splashed across every tabloid in the country hanging out at a bar or club, but he hasn't seemed to miss it. Granted, it's only been two weeks, but I don't get the impression he has one foot out the door. At least, not yet.

We've had plenty of awkward conversations, and a few that just outright pissed me off. Like last week when he came over with Chinese food and insisted I move in with him. Talk about an explosion of epic proportions. When it didn't seem to go the way he thought, he offered to buy me a house. Something bigger, newer, and in a gated community. While I listened to his valid reasons for wanting us both safe and taken care of, it was my refusal that won in the end. I don't want a white knight to swoop in and buy me things. I want a partner, someone to help with those late-night feedings, or to tell me it's okay to cry at the thought of going back to work. We compromised with Tate promising not to overstep and just react with his wallet, and I'll make sure to listen to his concerns.

I don't know what the future holds, but I do know he's a great dad. Rowan is lucky to have him.

Today is a big day for our little man. His four-week checkup with his pediatrician, which means more shots. I'm terrified already, hating the prospect of seeing him cry. Tate volunteered to go with me, which is good and bad. I'm glad to have the support, but also know outings with someone like Tate can be a little dangerous. He's recognized easily as the starting quarterback of the local professional team. Plus, his face is on the cover of just about every magazine or tabloid on a monthly basis. No way will we go unnoticed.

At ten until two, his SUV pulls into the driveway. I already have Rowan in his car seat, recently fed and changed. I've got his diaper bag packed—probably overpacked, actually—with everything he could need for the next hour or two. I open the front door before he has a chance to enter the code, and he's all smiles.

He's also freshly showered and smells amazing. And he's sporting a ballcap on his head, which I've never seen before, but somehow seems to make him look even hotter.

"Hey," he says, kissing me on the cheek before going over to say hello to his son. His now-familiar aftershave hits my nose and my girly bits react, like usual. I haven't had sex in closing in on a year, and my lady parts aren't too happy about that. They've taken notice of everything Tate does, every cock of his eyebrow, each arrogant grin he sends my way. I've resorted to taking longer showers just to get me through the day.

"Hi," I reply, my voice coming out a little squeak.

"Ready?" he asks, grabbing the baby carrier and diaper bag.

"I can get that," I insist, but he just smiles.

"I got it, Sweetness."

I climb into the passenger seat of his fancy SUV. It has butter-soft leather seats and more gadgets than I've ever seen in a vehicle. Tate clicks the carrier into the base, the one he installed a week ago. We've only used it once before today, when we decided to go for a ride one evening to get out of the house.

It takes us about twenty-five minutes to get to the doctor's office. Originally, I had been looking for a doctor a little closer to home, but the recommendations to Healthy Beginnings Pediatrics couldn't be ignored. Dr. Townsend is amazing, and I'm so glad I chose her.

We enter the cheerful building, and I approach the front counter. "Can I help you?"

"Rowan Harris," I reply, but realize quickly the receptionist isn't paying any attention to me. I glance over my shoulder and see why. Tate is behind me, slightly bent over, and carefully slipping Rowan out of the carrier.

"Is that..." she asks, her words so full of excitement and wonder.

I clear my throat, refusing to confirm what she already knows. The receptionist with the name Kami on her nametag blushes as she glances back to her computer screen. "Yes, Rowan Harris," she says, her eyes quickly darting once more over my shoulder. I mean, I get it. He's hot but come on. Ogle my baby daddy *after* you check in my son for his appointment, please.

"Am I set?" I ask, unable to mask my annoyance.

"Oh, uh, please sign here, authorizing us to bill insurance," Kami says, doing her darndest to no look at Tate again. I sign it quickly. "You're all set. Have a seat and you'll be called back in a few moments."

I head over to where Tate sits. Immediately, I notice two other moms in the room staring at Tate. Sighing, I take a seat beside him.

"What's wrong?" he whispers, his smiling eyes locked on Rowan's.

"You're being recognized. This was a bad idea," I mumble, realizing we could be in big trouble. No one has a cell phone out—yet—but it's only a matter of time.

"It's not a bad idea, Ash. It'll be okay," he says, pulling his ballcap down even lower.

Fortunately, we don't have to wait long. A friendly nurse calls us back, and if she recognizes Tate, she doesn't say anything. We stop at a baby scale, and she turns to take Rowan from Tate. "Ready to go, little guy?" she asks, carefully placing him on the scale. She removes his onesie outfit before taking his official weight and measuring him from top to bottom. "Okay, Mom, you can grab him and follow me into the exam room."

We go through a series of questions, the nurse making notes on her tablet, before telling me to hang tight. "Dr. Townsend will be in shortly."

Tate sits down beside me and glances around nervously. "So, now what?"

"Well, now we wait for the doctor. She'll come in and do a quick exam to make sure he's where he needs to be, and then the nurse will come back in for immunizations."

"Shots."

I nod, my throat suddenly so dry it's hard to swallow.

Tate reaches over and takes my hand. He runs his rough thumb over my knuckles. "It'll be okay, Sweetness. He's tough like me," he says, giving me that cocky half-grin that feels like a bolt of lightning between my legs.

There's a knock on the door right before Dr. Townsend enters the room. "Good afternoon, Ashtyn. How's Rowan?"

"He's doing well. His nursing schedule has finally leveled out."

"Good," she says, checking over the tablet in her hand. "He's gaining weight perfectly. How many times is he getting up at night?"

"Three?"

"Actually, the last few nights, it's only been twice a night," Tate says, drawing the doctor's attention.

She gives him a polite smile. "I'm Dr. Townsend, and you are?"

"Tate Steele, Doctor. I'm Rowan's father."

She nods and makes notes on her tablet again. I've never said Tate's name in any of the paperwork here, or at the hospital. He's not listed on the birth certificate, since I thought he wanted nothing to do with Rowan. Now, here he is, making a declaration to our son's pediatrician. "Well, nice to meet you."

Dr. Townsend does Rowan's exam. He's not too happy to be uncovered, but the moment the exam is complete, Tate scoops him up and holds him against his chest. "Do you have any questions for me before we get to the dreaded part of today's appointment?"

"No, I don't think so," I reply.

"Actually, I do," Tate says, drawing both mine and the doctor's attention. "I would like to order a paternity test."

My eyes widen and my mouth drops to my knees. Tate quickly turns to me and adds,

"It's not what you think. I know he's my son, but I was talking to my attorney earlier and he said we have to confirm paternity before I can establish rights."

I can feel the doctor's eyes glancing back and forth. "If you're both interested in confirming paternity, I can submit an order to a hospital for testing. We'll have the results back by Friday. You'd then submit those results to the Family Support Division of the Department of Health. They'll take it from there." She pauses before adding, "I'll give you two a minute."

As soon as the door closes, Tate crouches in front of me, our son still in his arms. "I'm sorry I didn't mention this earlier. I started to do some research last night when I couldn't sleep. I know I'm his father, but I want to make sure everything is established as so. If something happens to me, God forbid, I want everything to go to Row. I want to immediately start paying you support too, and my attorney said this is the step we need to take."

I exhale slowly. "Okay, yeah, it makes sense."

"We're telling Alex Saturday night at dinner, and your parents are coming for another visit soon to house hunt, right? I want to call them and my parents this weekend too. I'd also like to do an addendum to his birth certificate, if you're okay with that. I want to be his father in every way possible, Ash. Including on paper."

I give him a small smile before my eyes drop to our son. "You seem to have thought a lot about this. He's a lucky little boy," I whisper, reaching out and running my finger across his dimpled chin.

"No, I'm the lucky one."

I glance up and our eyes meet. I always said it was only possible in cheesy romcom movies from the eighties, but time actually stands still. I'm not sure who moves first, but his palm caresses my cheek at the same moment our lips meet. His mouth is warm and oh so inviting, as he masterfully slides his lips against mine.

Unfortunately, we're interrupted by another knock. Dr. Townsend and the nurse enter the room, both with sheepish grins on their faces, as we pull apart. I turn to face the doctor and say, "Let's go ahead with the order for paternity."

She nods. "I'll send it in. They work on a walk-in basis, and all the details are on the back of this information sheet." I take the offered paper. "Now, shall we get to the hardest part of the appointment?"

CHAPTER NINE
TATE

PULLING OUT OF THE TEAM FACILITY, I GUN THE ENGINE, LOVING HOW IT goes from zero to too fast in seconds. I haven't driven my car much in the last few weeks, mostly because I was choosing to be a little more inconspicuous when I'm over at Ashtyn's and drive the SUV.

Today, I had a meeting with the front office regarding my contract. It's up for negotiations at the end of this season, and I'm anxious to sign for a few more years. I want to finish out my career with the Fire. It's not logical, really, but I'll do whatever I can to stay put. One thing I have going for me is I'm at the top of my game. Postseason appearances the last four seasons and a divisional championship last year. I'm one determined motherfucker to get my team to the big game this season.

I want that ring.

When I reach a stoplight, my phone pings with a text. I shot a message to Ash to let her know I was leaving and heading her way. I've got to stop by my penthouse, grab more clothes, and switch cars, but I'm anxious as hell to see her and Rowan. I didn't sleep for shit last night in my bed. The first night in more than a week I didn't stay, but with the early meetings and workouts, she thought I'd be better if I was rested and refreshed going into my day. Little does she know I didn't sleep well at all in my large, king-sized mattress with fancy Egyptian sheets. All I wanted to do was be on her couch, tossing and turning, and catching little naps all night long.

I pull up my screen and find a picture. It's of Row, little fist under his chin and his mouth hanging open as he sleeps. She captioned it "Milk drunk."

My grin is wide as I gaze down at the little guy.

My son.

A horn honks behind me, so I quickly deposit my phone back into the cup holder and drive. My heart is light and my smile wide as I head through the streets toward my place. A few miles from where I live, my phone rings. I glance at the dash to see my best friend's name. I quickly accept the call.

"Hey, buddy, what's up?" I ask.

"What the fuck are you doing with my sister?" His words are low, almost a growl, and stop my heart.

"What?"

"Don't play dumb with me, Steele. Is it true?"

I'm taken aback by his words. I have a pretty damn good idea what he's talking about, but my mind can't wrap around it. "Is what true?" I ask, my words filled with dread.

"Playboy QB a Dad. Steele Settling Down. Baby Makes Three for Fire QB. That's what the headlines say, Tate. So why don't you tell me why you're in all of these photos, with my sister and my nephew."

"Headlines?" I ask, pulling my car into the first parking lot I can find. When I grab my phone, I see incoming texts from Todd, but I ignore them. Instead, I pull up my internet search engine and type in my name. "Fuck," I mumble, as link after link pops up, all new within the last thirty minutes.

"Yeah, fuck. What the hell is going on?" Alex demands.

My mind is racing. "I need to get to Ashtyn's," I state, turning around in the lot and heading in her direction.

"I'm already on my way there."

"Please don't…just wait until I get there, Alex."

"Oh, you bet your fucking ass I'm gonna wait until you get there." Then the line goes dead.

"Fuck!" I yell, slamming my hand down on the steering wheel. I knew I should have just told him before now. Too many people saw us earlier in the week at Rowan's doctor's appointment. I should have insisted on talking to him way before tomorrow night. I messed up, and that's on me.

As I fly through the streets, I pull up my phone and call Todd. "Where have you been?"

"I just left the training facility," I tell him.

"This is a nightmare, Tate. It's everywhere," he says. I can hear him clicking away on his keyboard.

"How'd it get out? I don't even have the results yet, so how did the media get them?"

"I'm trying to pinpoint the source. My guess either the lab or the doctor's office, but my gut says it's the latter. Labs are pretty fucking airtight when it comes to test results."

"How do we control this?"

"We're already working on it, Tate. At this point, I don't see how we can contain it. It's already trending on social media and we're getting calls for comments from national news agencies."

I briefly close my eyes and take a deep breath. "Protecting Ashtyn and Rowan is my top priority, Todd."

"I hear ya. We're going to have to make a statement. I've got Jenn and Olivia coming in to help prep something. I'll fire it to your email as soon as it's ready," he answers, still clicking away on his computer.

"Thanks."

"We should have talked about this before now, Tate. We could have prepared something and been ahead of the news. It's always better coming from the source, but now we're behind and scrambling."

I sigh, finally turning onto Ashtyn's street and instantly noticing extra cars. "Shit, I gotta go. It looks like they've already found out where Ash lives."

"I'm working on it now. You'll have an email within the hour."

"Sounds good," I say, signing off.

The moment my car approaches her house, the people gathering on the sidewalk start to move my way. I pull into her driveway, careful not to hit anyone, yet not giving a shit if I do. Alex's car is already there, so I park beside him and get out.

"Tate, is this where your baby lives?"

"Tate Steele, are you hiding a secret family?"

"Tate, how many children do you have?"

"Tate, was the other man who just arrived, the husband? Are you having an affair?"

I ignore them all and run up the front steps. Alex opens the door and quickly shuts it the second I step over the threshold. My eyes adjust quickly to the darkened room and seek her out. Ashtyn is standing by the kitchen doorway, her eyes wide with shock. I go to her instantly, pulling her into my arms and kissing her forehead. "It's going to be okay," I whisper, not only to her but to myself. "Where's Row?"

"Sleeping in his bassinet," she says, her brown eyes full of uncertainty and worry.

"I'm gonna fix this," I state, placing another kiss on the crown of her head.

"What exactly are you *fixing*?" Alex asks.

I turn around and look him straight in the eye, prepared to have the hardest conversation, yet make the easiest declaration. "I'm Rowan's father."

A plethora of emotions cross his face as he just stares at me. Anger, agitation, worry, surprise, and even a flash of joy.

I decide not to let him speak yet. "I know this is probably not what you expected to hear," I start, but his fiery gaze cuts me off.

"Not what I expected to hear? That my best friend, one of the people I trust the most in this world, knocked up my sister and left her to fend for herself? Are you fucking kidding me right now, Tate?" his voice booms through the house.

"It's not what you think," Ashtyn says, taking a step forward.

"Stay out of this, Ash. This is between me and my so-called friend," he argues.

"Now, wait a minute. Don't talk to her like that, like her voice doesn't matter. Sit your ass down on the couch and listen, dammit."

Alex seems stunned by my words, taking a small step back before slowly dropping onto the couch behind him. "Okay, I'm listening." There's still an edge, a bite to his words.

"There was a miscommunication," Ashtyn says, walking over and sitting beside him on the sofa. "I reached out to Tate but didn't hear from him. Then when I did, it wasn't actually him I was talking to, but someone who manages his social media."

"She thought I didn't want anything to do with Rowan, but the truth was, I didn't know… period. My team gets weekly messages from some woman claiming to be carrying my child or some other bullshit, Alex. They didn't know she was legit."

He takes a moment to process what we've said. "So, you found out when?"

"When I saw that photo you showed me on your phone, I suspected something was up," I tell him, heading over and taking a seat in the chair.

"That's why you wanted to come with me to meet him," Alex says, recalling that conversation just over two weeks ago.

"Yeah. I wanted to find out what was going on. Turns out, Ash wasn't too happy to see me here, considering she thought I denied him months before."

"But we talked that night when you went to your meeting with the GM," Ashtyn adds.

"And you guys are…what, together?"

"No," she replies at the same time I answer, "Yes."

Alex looks at me, irritated. "What does that mean?"

"Well, we're not officially together, but I'm not going anywhere," I insist, glancing her way with a pointed look.

"He's here for Rowan," Ashtyn tells her brother.

I'm up and moving before she can say boo. Squatting in front of her, I wrap her small hand in my own and bring it to my lips. "I'm here for you too, Sweetness."

I'm rewarded with a small, yet breathtaking smile. "Yeah?"

"Definitely."

Just as I move forward, ready to capture her lips with my own, I'm reminded we're not alone in the room. "So, let me get this straight. You slept with my sister? When? I mean, I don't want details, because yuck, but when did this happen? You've been living here the whole time, and Ash, you were in South Bend."

I turn to Alex, Ashtyn's hand still nestled in mine, and answer his question. "Do you remember last August, when I stayed at your place after my knee?"

Alex closes his eyes and shakes his head. "I remember. I got home and was surprised when Ash was there. She was offered the job here in St. Louis."

"Anyway, I came back home, but you should know, I never stopped thinking about her," I say, deciding to throw all of my cards on the table.

Alex narrows his eyes. "What does that mean?"

"There hasn't been anyone else since her, man. I felt this...*connection* back then and even more so now. I want to spend more time with her and my son. I want to take them out and make them smile. I want to kiss them goodnight and good morning. I want the midnight feedings and even the explosive diapers, even though I'd be okay with less of those." I glance over at Ash, who's smiling softly, her brown eyes shining just a little bit brighter than earlier. "And I know I don't need your permission to date your sister, Alex, but it would make it a hell of a lot easier on all of us if you were okay with it, because I'm not going anywhere. They're my family now."

The wetness I saw reflecting in her eyes moments earlier now falls freely down her cheeks. I don't care that her brother is sitting directly beside her, I take Ashtyn in my arms and kiss her. I kiss her the way I should have kissed her every night since she's been back in my life. Hell, probably since that one and only night we spent together. I knew she was different. I felt it in my soul, yet I ignored it. I left.

Never again.

"Okay, I don't want to break up this little smoochfest, but what are we gonna do about the growing crowd outside?" Alex asks, kicking his legs up on the coffee table and relaxing back like he hasn't a care in the world.

"I'm waiting on PR to send me a press release to proof, but I don't think Ash should stay here tonight," I reply, earning a nod in agreement from my friend.

"Definitely not," he says.

"She can come to my place. I've been working on setting up a nursery, so we don't have to take as much stuff," I tell Alex. He seems surprised by this revelation, but what he doesn't know is I've been thinking about nothing *but* Rowan since the day I found out he was my son.

"Wow, no more bachelor pad penthouse? What will all the ladies think?" he teases.

I sit on the coffee table and face him. "There hasn't been anyone since the night I got your sister drunk and knocked her up," I reply with a wicked grin. Mostly because I know he's going to hate that visual.

"Fuck, man, don't say shit like that." Alex sobers for a second and adds, "We could always take them to my apartment. No one would think to look for her there. Your place will probably be swarmed with even more photographers."

"Good point," I concede, trying to figure out how to safely get her and Row out of the house and into Alex's.

"Umm, excuse me. Does anyone want to know what *I* think?" The look she gives us lets us know she's not too pleased with our decision-making. As I open my mouth to reply, she holds up her hand, cutting me off. "I'm staying here. This is my home, Tate. They're not running me off."

"I think you need to consider what he's saying," Alex jumps in.

"No, I'm not leaving, Alex." She turns those gorgeous eyes on me. "I understand our life will be a little different because of you. My son's father is a professional athlete, so I get that we'll have to be a little more careful with our safety, but I refuse to move or run away. They'll get bored soon. Someone else famous will draw their attention. I won't let them dictate how I live my life."

"It won't happen overnight. They're relentless," I argue.

She just smiles. "Your bad boy persona wasn't made overnight either. I don't expect it to go away just as quickly."

I return her grin with my own. "Okay, well, if we're staying, I'm going to need to run home and get some clothes. I assume I can use your couch again?"

Ashtyn just shrugs. "There's room in my bed."

"Gross," Alex mumbles, scrubbing his hands over his face and standing up.

My cell phone pings, signaling a text. When I pull it out, I announce, "Todd just emailed me the drafted press release." I switch over to my email app and spot the one from Todd, but there's also one below it that catches my attention. "The test results." I tap on the email as Ashtyn moves beside me. My eyes scan the document, which confirms what we already knew. "99.9 percent. It's official. He's my son."

"I told you he was," Ash says, elbowing me in the gut playfully.

"I know, Sweetness, but to actually see it in writing, it's an amazing feeling."

Ashtyn smiles, and I almost lean down and kiss her again. Her lips are too tasty, too tempting to pass up. However, she reminds me of the other email in my inbox. I read through the press release, making a few notes. I read it out loud and get Alex and Ashtyn's opinions, and only when they're both satisfied, do I send it back to Todd.

Just as I slip my phone back into my pocket, I hear a cry from the bedroom. Holding up my hand, I head off to where my son is. "Hey, Row," I whisper, as I scoop him up and cradle him to my chest. He's already grown so much in the short weeks he's been in my life.

Kissing his forehead, we walk to the nursery for a diaper change. I don't even complain when I unfasten the onesie and find the smelly surprise he left me. Instead, I tell him all about finding that email in my inbox and what it means to be his father. Rowan gazes up at me, hanging on my every word, as I clean him up and get him ready for food.

When I turn around, I find Ashtyn standing in the doorway, leaning against the doorjamb, wearing the slightest grin. "Where's your brother?"

"He ran to pick up some food. We figured since we're chilling here for the rest of the day, we might as well eat deep-dish pizza."

I kiss Rowan's head before handing him off to his mother. "You know what I still don't understand?" I ask, meeting her gorgeous brown eyes.

"What?"

"We used a condom."

"We did."

"That must mean I have super sperm or something," I boast, a cocky grin on my face.

Ashtyn snorts. "Or something is right," she teases, brushing by me and heading for the glider.

I help make sure she's comfy as she gets Rowan positioned in her arms. I try not to sneak a peek as she pulls up her top and releases her nursing bra. I try not to, but I don't succeed. I totally steal a glance, but not exactly for the reason you'd expect. It's quite interesting to watch her nurse our child. Rowan knows exactly what to do and latches on right away. His little cheeks work hard as he eats, and I can't seem to pull my eyes away from it.

"You know, this one here is my favorite play in the whole playbook," I tell her, running my finger against his arm.

"Which one?"

I take in the sight of my son and say, "The quarterback keeper."

CHAPTER TEN
ASHTYN

IT'S BEEN SIX WEEKS SINCE THE WORLD FOUND OUT THE PLAYBOY quarterback is a father. I wish I could say they've left us alone, but that'd be a lie. They still follow him and snap pictures of every aspect of his life, but they're just different now. We've been photographed taking walks through the neighborhood, grocery shopping, and enjoying dinner at a local restaurant. They've even come into the library a few times, lingering between stacks of books, just to see if Tate will make an appearance. So far they've lucked out, but since my numbers for library cards have increased, I'm not complaining too much.

A judge signed off this week on the addendum to Rowan's birth certificate. He's now officially Rowan Alexander Steele. As happy as I was to give this gift to both Rowan and Tate, it was the happiness reflecting in his eyes that made me the happiest. I know my son has the best father out there, someone who will forever put Rowan's needs before his own, and that gives me more joy than I ever could have expected.

Alex still comes over weekly and doesn't seem to be too upset to see his best friend practically living in my house. In fact, they get along better now than they did before, if that's possible. Of course, they had to work out a few issues, like why Tate didn't tell Alex before he found out through the tabloids. Alex was still upset we kept it from him but understood when we explained our reasoning a little more.

My parents are coming for another visit next week, since Tate and Alex will be gone at training camp. Tate's family has already made one long weekend trip to meet their grandson and are planning another one soon.

Preseason starts next week. Training camp is set, and Tate is more determined than ever to take his team to the top. He wants a championship ring so bad he can taste it and is ready to put in the hard work to make sure it happens. His workouts are intense and he's spending extra time combing over game films and playbooks. Yet, he's always here for Rowan, gives him nightly baths, and helps with the bedtime routine.

Which brings us to now. After spending much of the evening in the home library, shifting through information from the coaching staff, Tate is finally in the shower. Rowan is passed out in his crib, and I'm pacing the bedroom. I'm nervous. When I glance down at myself, I don't see the confident, sexy woman I once was. Instead, I see a mom, ten-weeks post-baby, and I worry this navy negligee isn't hiding the baby fat I'm still carrying in the midsection the way I had hoped it would.

Should I get on the bed, or just stand here and pose?

Doubt sweeps through me as I hear the water shut off in the bathroom. What am I doing? Seducing a man like Tate Steele? He's probably going to take one look at me and laugh. I'm a good ten pounds heavier than I was the last time he saw me naked, though a good portion of that's in my boobs. I'm just…different now, and it's freaking me out a little.

Besides, what if he's not interested? What if his kisses and gentle touches don't mean what I thought? I know I fall asleep in his arms every night and on those rare occasions he's still in bed in the morning when I get up, he's usually wrapped around me like a blanket. And yes, he has morning wood, but don't all men? That doesn't mean it's because he wants to have sex with me. It just means he's a guy.

Oh, God, I can't do this.

Just as I spin around to grab an old T-shirt to change into, I find Tate standing in the doorway. He's wearing a pair of nylon basketball shorts that hide nothing, if you know what I mean. "Ash?" he whispers, unable to take his eyes off my body. The negligee barely covers my ass, the lace hugging my abdomen like a second skin. The cups barely hold my girls, but that doesn't seem to bother him too much. In fact, if what's happening in his shorts is any indication, I'd say he likes it.

A lot.

"Oh, uh, hi."

Tate steps into the room, shutting the door behind him. His eyes roam my body once more before meeting mine. There's raw lust reflected in those hazel eyes as he joins me in the middle of the room. He reaches out but doesn't touch me. "What's this?"

I glance down before meeting his eyes. "Just a little something I picked up," I state with a shrug.

He takes another step closer, this time, placing his hand on my hip. "You're breathtaking, Sweetness."

"Huh," I chuckle awkwardly. "I don't know about that."

"I do," he replies, taking one final half-step forward so we're right in front of each other. His other hand goes to my lower back as he pulls me against his chest. "You're the most beautiful woman I've ever known."

I don't reply with words. The blush creeping up my neck takes care of it for me.

Tate's finger touches my chin before slowly sliding down my neck to the valley between my breasts, leaving goosebumps in its wake. His hand carefully cups my left breast, my nipples already hard and straining against the material. I gasp as he slips one large hand beneath the lace and lightly pinches my nipple.

"Are you sure?" he asks, searching my eyes.

I'm already nodding. "Yes, I'm sure."

He moves, lifting me into his arms and kissing me hard on the lips. My hands grip his shoulders, reveling in the feel of his warm, hard body beneath my fingertips. Together, we fall onto the bed, his hands moving over my abdomen, gliding effortlessly over the negligee. I forgot how big, how amazing his hands are. It's like zaps of electricity every time he touches me.

Suddenly, we're turning and I'm straddling his hips. I can feel the length of him pressed between me, and it takes every ounce of restraint I have not to grind against him. But it's been a long time for me, and the slightest friction will probably set me off right now. Sleeping next to him for the last several weeks has only made my desire for him grow.

"There," he says, moving his hands up my abdomen, cupping my overflowing breasts, his thumb sliding over my nipple. "That's better. Now I can see all of you."

"I'm not sure that's a good idea. Maybe we should turn off the light," I tease, though not really teasing at all. I should have turned off the nightstand lamp before he came into the room.

"Fuck no. I want to see how stunning you look in that outfit."

I glance down to see what he sees, but all I see are the imperfections. The blemishes. Even if they were brought on by the best reason possible—Rowan—I'm still more self-conscious than I ever expected to be. Maybe it's because it's him. Tate Steele. Starting quarterback for the St. Louis Fire. Men want to be him, women *with* him. And here I am, in a new negligee I picked up from Victoria's Secret that I'm praying covers up the extra weight I'm still carrying in the midsection.

"Don't," he says softly, his always wandering hands tracing the lace over my mounds of breasts.

"What?" I ask, that single word coming out a gasp.

"Don't second-guess how incredibly beautiful you are, Ashtyn. I've never seen anything more breathtaking," he says, the words seeming to choke him up a little.

Relaxing, I bend down, my hands poised on his chest, and kiss him. There's a hunger there, a raw desire neither of us can contain. So we don't even try.

I grind against his erection, seeking some relief from the burn between my legs. Tate's hands go to my hips as I rock back and forth. "Shit, angel, you're gonna have to stop doing that. It's been a really long time, and I'm liable to blow in my shorts like a teenager."

All I can do is smile. Even though women were throwing themselves at him—and still do, by the way—after our night together, he never took them up on their offers.

I reach over to the bedside table and pull out the brand-new box of condoms. Tate's eyebrows arch upward. "You knew I was a sure thing, huh?"

I shrug, pulling a strip of the protection from the box and ripping off one. "Well, I had hoped you would be."

His hands cradle my jaw as he says, "I'm always a sure thing for you, Sweetness. Always."

I move enough so Tate can slip his shorts down his legs. His erection is a thing of beauty. Large, straight, and dripping with precum. When he has the protection in place, I reach down to remove my negligee. His hands stop mine as he says, "I want to see you riding my cock wearing this sexy thing."

I swallow hard and nod. His eyes watch my every move as I shimmy out of the tiny thong panties hidden beneath the negligee. Once they're gone, I crawl back onto his broad body, straddling his hips. I can feel how soaking wet I am, and the moment he slides his cock against me, he groans. "Fuck, I can't wait to be inside you again."

I lean up and take his erection in my hand, squeezing it lightly for good measure, and position it at my opening. His eyes are pure fire as he gazes up at me. Slowly, I start to lower my body onto his. There's a stretch and a slight burn, but I adjust quickly to his size. When I'm fully seated, I finally take a deep breath, one I didn't realize I was holding.

Tate takes my hands, holding me up to take control. I carefully start to rock, lifting my hips and grinding back down. His face is tight as I wiggle, taking him as deep as I possibly can. "Jesus, you feel so fucking good," he groans, watching my every move.

My body starts to take control, my hips moving faster with each passing second. I can feel my orgasm building and know there's no way of stopping it. "Tate," I gasp, as the end inches closer and closer.

"Take what you need, Sweetness. Make yourself come on my cock."

His words are like a detonator. I explode spectacularly, white lights bursting behind my eyelids as wave after wave of pleasure burns through my veins like lava. My limbs start to weaken, as every ounce of energy I have is expelled from my body.

Suddenly, we move again. Tate flips us around so I'm flat on my back and he's positioned between my legs. "There's nothing better than watching you come, Ashtyn. It's all I thought of all those nights we were apart." I feel him nudge at my entrance, reaching to fill me once more. "Ash?" he whispers, pinning me with a deep gaze. "I love you. I know you're not supposed to make a declaration like this in the throes of passion, but it feels like I can't go a single second longer without saying it. I love you, so fucking much. I've been in love with you since the moment I first laid eyes on you."

I feel the wetness sliding down my cheek as my hand goes up to cup his scruffy jaw. "I love you too, Tate."

He smiles so big, it's like he won a prize. Then, his lips descend to mine as he presses forward, filling me. His thrusts are gentle but with purpose. My ankles hitch on his hips, changing the angle a bit, and suddenly, desire starts to swirl low in my belly again. I spread my legs farther and gasp when he grinds against my clit.

"Oh God," I pant, feeling the second orgasm on the brink.

"Let go, Sweetness."

My second one slams into me like a Mack truck, and Tate is quick to follow me over the edge. He grunts my name before claiming me with a kiss that leaves me breathless. When I'm finally able to catch my breath, he disposes of the condom then gets back in bed and draws me into his chest.

"Best night ever," he whispers, the smile on his lips evident in his voice.

"I don't know, I think the first time was pretty damn good too."

He turns and catches my eye. "The first time gave us our son. That'll forever be the greatest night of my life," he says, kissing my forehead. "But tonight was the night I finally told you what I've wanted to say for a few weeks now. I unofficially made you mine, Ash."

"Unofficially?"

He gives me that cocky, playboy grin that makes panties wet all over the world. "Someday, I'll make it official. Until then, we'll just have to settle for living together, raising our son, and more great sex."

I smile back. "I can handle that," I tell him, my eyelids starting to droop.

"Sleep tight, Sweetness. We have the rest of our lives ahead of us."

As I drift off to sleep in his arms, I try to picture what our future might look like. I'm not sure what's in store, but I do know one thing: Tate Steele is on his game—on and *off* the field.

EPILOGUE
TATE

DEEP BREATH.

"Hike," I holler, the ball snapped back into my awaiting hands. I step back and twist on my feet, running in the opposite direction than is expected. My line holds the defense, creating that perfect opening for me to slip through, but it's a battle. Both teams want this. Need it.

Time stands still.

My feet carry me as fast as they can toward the end zone.

Crossing the fifteen…

The ten…

The five…

Touchdown.

The stadium erupts around me, the noise at a deafening level, but all I can do is take it all in as I throw my hands in the air.

We did it.

Champions.

Cannons of confetti rain on the field as the final score is flashed on the big screen. Down by three, we were out of time to make a move. It all came down to this final play. My team surrounds me, wrapping me in hugs, and slapping me on the pads. Their screams of excitement are drowned out, but I can read it on their faces, see it in their tear-filled eyes.

Holy shit.

We make our way toward the fifty, cameras shoved in our faces the entire way. I spot Cole Danner, the QB for the Lightning. His face is solemn, his heartbreak visible in those dark blue eyes. "Great job, Tate."

I hug the man who was one play away from being a champion himself. "Hold your head up, Cole. You played a hell of a game, man. I'm proud of you," I tell the young, eager quarterback. He's good. His time is coming.

He gives me a sad smile before turning away.

I'm engulfed in more hugs from my teammates and coaches. Head coach Juaquin Carter pulls me into a hug that's tighter than any I've received thus far. The words he whispers in my ear are both in excitement and pride, as he taps me on the pads and hands me a T-shirt sporting our new title. My helmet is replaced with a championship ballcap featuring the Fire logo.

As we're shuffled to the stage suddenly erected in the middle of the field, I spy the two faces I've been most eager to see.

Ashtyn and Rowan.

She's wearing a number four jersey with my name on the back, with Rowan wearing a custom made one that says "My daddy's the QB" on the front. I reach them in a matter of seconds, pulling her into my arms, and spinning them around. My lips settle on hers next, our son eagerly pulling on my jersey for attention.

"Oh my God!" she bellows, her eyes sparkling with excitement and confetti in her hair.

"Can you believe this?" I ask, taking Rowan in my arms, who tries to eat the new T-shirt thrown over my shoulder. He's wearing small headphones to protect his ears from the noise, but they're still big on his little head.

"I knew you'd do it," she states matter-of-factly. And she did. She's been my biggest cheerleader throughout the entire season, not missing a single game, including the away ones.

Even when we went through the purchase of a new house last fall, she's been by my side every step of the way. We sold her house and my penthouse apartment and settled together in a large Tudor home in a gated community. My favorite part? The huge backyard with plenty of room to play catch.

"Where's everyone at?" I ask, looking around for my parents and Alex.

"Your parents stayed up in the suite until it clears out a little bit down here, and Alex is floating around here somewhere."

I gaze down at my son, whose eyes are wide with excitement and just taking it all in. "You ready to go up and get our trophy, Row?"

My son smiles in return.

Security helps move us to the stage, where the coaches and owners are waiting. It's a moment I always wanted, yet somehow always felt was just outside of my grasp. Today was my day, the day my teammates and I played our hardest, best football, and won. This is our moment.

I listen as they present the owners of our team with the championship trophy, who make speeches about bringing the hardware home to the great city of St. Louis. Then, they have me step forward.

"Tate Steele, congratulations to you and the Fire on a successful season. You've made the year exciting to watch, and I'm sure your fans couldn't be happier to win their third championship in the history of the franchise."

"This is a dream come true for everyone, Stan," I reply, earning a round of applause and cheers.

"Well, I'd like to make your night even better by presenting you with the league MVP trophy, as voted by the fans throughout tonight's game," Stan says, as another huge trophy is moved to the front of the podium. "Tate Steele, your MVP," he announces to the crowd.

My eyes instantly go to Ashtyn, who's crying off to the side, her bare hands held up to cover her mouth. That's also when I spot Alex moving through the crowd, making his way to the stairs.

I run my hand through my sweat-soaked hair and gaze down at my son. "Wow," I say, as I step back up to the mic. "First off, I want to thank the entire Fire organization and all the fans for believing in this team and standing by us."

The audience erupts into more cheers. When they quiet down a little, I continue. "I gotta thank my parents and family too." I stop and glance down at Rowan. "And this little guy. He has no idea, but I'll always be his biggest fan." Everyone cheers again as I speak of Rowan, who has become a staple around the field, and in the photographs they continue to snap of me.

"This entire weekend has been a dream come true, but I'm going to be honest with you, it's missing something." I ignore all of the confused faces until my eyes land on Alex. He's right next to Ashtyn, where he's supposed to be.

He places his hand beneath her elbow and guides her my way. She doesn't go easy though. Oh no. Ashtyn wants nothing to do with this kind of spotlight and is dragging her feet and trying to turn around.

When he has her standing directly beside me, an uncomfortable smile on her face, I say, "I have an MVP trophy."

Cheers.

"I have a championship ring."

Louder cheers.

"But there's one ring missing."

That's when Alex takes his nephew from my arms and slips the ring into my hand. I turn my gaze to the woman I love, the one who has stood beside me, and who hasn't left me even when I leave the toilet seat up.

"Ashtyn," I start, taking her hand. Her eyes are as round as hubcaps as she gazes up at me. "My love," I add, taking a knee in front of her.

The crowd goes wild.

When I look up at her, everything else just falls away. "This ring is the most important piece of jewelry in my life. This one symbolizes my love for you. It's endless. I thank God every day that you walked through your brother's door that day because my life has been nothing but good ever since. I want to marry you, give Rowan brothers and sisters, and grow old with you standing beside me."

Deep breath.

"Ashtyn Harris, will you marry me?"

She nods once. Then yells, "Yes!"

She's in my arms a moment later, the ring I spent weeks picking out on her finger. "I love you, Ash."

"I love you, Tate," she beams at me, tears gathering in her eyes.

"Wow, Tate Steele, I don't know how your night could get any better," Stan says. "Congratulations to you and Ashtyn on your engagement."

With her eyes locked on mine, Ashtyn smiles. "He's a keeper."

THE END

SPARK BY
NICOLE BLANCHARD

CHAPTER ONE

AVERY
WEDNESDAY—OCTOBER 10, 2018
8:00 P.M.

A BOOM SHAKES THE HOUSE AND A WHIPLASH OF PURE, PRIMAL FEAR INVADES the tiny spaces in my body. Sensing my unease, the little life in my arms lets out a disgruntled squeal as hot tears leak from her reddened, tired eyes—eyes a blue-gray, the same color of the stormy evening sky outside the window. Neither of us has gotten much sleep today. I expect we won't get any tonight either. As if to confirm my thoughts, lightning flashes, turning the living room from night to day in one quick instant.

"Shh, shh, it's okay. It's going to be okay. I promise. It's only a storm." I wasn't sure if she could hear me over the roaring wind and lashing of rain against the tin roof. "A really, really loud storm. We get them all the time."

This isn't any storm, but I can't tell her that. At a couple months old, my words are to soothe myself more than her. All she knows is her mom is terrified. No doubt she can sense the sour tang of my fear coming off me in waves.

"That baby needs a bottle. Sounds like she's starvin'."

I close my eyes for a moment, then turn to my grandmother. She sits in her customary rocking chair, a green so worn it's nearly gray. "She's not hungry. She's just scared, is all."

Her and me both.

Grandma Rosie purses her lips and rocks more vigorously in her chair. I hold my baby closer and ignore her. Nearly eighty and suffering from dementia, Grandma Rosie has a habit of repeating herself and calling me by my mother's name. She also has a tendency for bluntness—which most people would classify as straight meanness—but I know that's the disease talking. Grandma Rosie raised me and before her brain started failing her, she'd been the sweetest woman alive.

That's why I bite my tongue and turn away from the living room, moving deeper into the house. The baby wails so loud it almost drowns out the wind and rain. Almost.

Readjusting her little body against my shoulder, I cradle her head and pat her back as I rock her back to a sense of calm. Soothing her helps me, albeit only slightly. Once she settles a little, I reach for my phone in my back pocket to check the weather again. I'm praying for a miracle with every atom of my being, though the only miracle I've ever witnessed is finally sleeping in my arms.

Please, please shift. Shift away from here.

I close my eyes as the weather radar loads and my heart thuds like a hammer in my chest. The last thing I want is to condemn someone else to the horror of what's to come, but at the selfish, human center of me, I'd rather it'd go somewhere else, anywhere else.

Please.

If I'd been stronger, I would have convinced Grandma Rosie to evacuate this morning. Dammit, I should have carried her out kicking and screaming if I had to, but she wouldn't budge.

"I've lived here for fifty years and I'll die here," had been her litany all day despite my pleading. I couldn't leave her to die all alone and confused. She didn't have anyone else but me.

So I'd spent the entire day battening down the hatches. I'd boarded up the windows, done last-minute runs for emergency supplies. Grandpa Jim had kept an old weather radio that still worked if only by the grace of God alone, so I'd have something in case the power and cell service went out.

Most people thought the hurricane would weaken as it came closer to the gulf. Most hurricanes that hit our area of Northern Florida did—in fact it's a running joke that most Floridians have hurricane parties to celebrate their landfall. But according to the radar and the Facebook Live from our local weatherman, Hurricane Michael hasn't weakened. It's grown stronger. It's predicted to make landfall as a Category 5. One of the strongest to ever hit our area.

And it's supposed to be heading right for us.

My phone wobbles in my hands as the weatherman's words ring in my ears. A Category 5. You hear about them, sure, and we've gotten some bad storms throughout the years, but nothing like this. A storm like this could obliterate everything. We are far inland, thankfully, so we won't get the brunt of the storm surge or the worst of the winds. I try to take a seed of hope from that thought and immediately feel guilty. So many people on the coast like me haven't evacuated.

The baby lets out a mewl of protest and I realize I'm squeezing her too close. I let out a shuddering breath and move from the kitchen to the room we share. Carefully so as not to wake her, I tuck her into her bassinet while I finish last-minute preparations. Really, I'm not sure what else I can do to save us, but I have to try.

With every hour that passes, the storm moves inexorably closer. Despite my fervent prayers, or perhaps because God knows I've never prayed with any intention before, it doesn't shift away. All of the models predict it'll make landfall and move right over us.

"What the devil?" I hear Grandma Rosie shout sometime later. "My pictures done turned off."

Moving from the hall bathroom where I've been filling the tub with extra water and organizing our first aid supplies, go-bags of food and clothes for each of us, and Grandma Rosie's medical supplies, I join her in the living room. The ancient television she insists on keeping to watch local channels is filled with snow. The sight of the gray static sends a spear of fear straight into my gut.

I check my phone and note I still have service. "C'mon, I can put your shows on for you on my tablet, but we have to watch in the bathroom."

"In the bathroom?" she repeats, aghast. "What in the world for?"

"It's the only place it'll work in the storm," I improvise. "I'll call the cable company and see if I can get your regular shows fixed, but for now this will have to do."

She blusters and dillydallies, but I manage to get her to sit on the toilet while I roll the baby's bassinet inside with us. Luckily, she's still sound asleep, so at least I don't have to worry about her still being afraid. Grandma Rosie is oblivious, so she won't be scared either. As I close the door behind us, I thank my lucky stars for that blessing because I'm scared enough for all three of us.

It lasts forever.

It's over in an instant.

I'm not certain which is true, maybe both.

Grandma Rosie isn't even hollering anymore. She sits on the toilet, rocking herself back and forth and carries on a conversation with Grandpa Jim like he's sitting right next to her. The baby woke up a while ago and after nursing, she contented herself with a pacifier and went back to sleep. I keep her in a sling wrap, close to my chest, because it's the safest place I can think to have her. I can't bear to let her out of my sight.

Unwelcome and unhelpful tears trail down my cheeks no matter how much I try to swipe them away. They're part fear, but mostly frustration. Everything I've worked so hard to achieve over the past two years could be ripped from my grasp—literally. This house is old. Grandma Rosie and Grandpa Jim bought it new when they were first married, but it's fallen into disrepair since his death. I don't even know if it'll withstand the 100-mile-an-hour winds. All of my possessions, all of the baby's things I'd painstakingly collected, and everything Grandma Rosie holds dear, could be sucked away in a moment. The thought fills me with a black, sucking despair.

The roaring sound intensifies. My hands are shaking too hard to manage my phone, so I don't try. My last radar check told me the eye of the storm was about to pass overhead, so another look would be pointless. The weather radio works in fits and spurts. Artificial light from the electric lantern washes everything in an eerie orange glow.

"Oh, Jim," I hear Grandma Rosie wail. The sound cuts me deep.

If I'm scared, I can't imagine what it must be like for her to be here, not really knowing where or even when she is with the madness going on around her.

"It's all right, Grandma Rosie," I say, even though I'm not certain she can hear me over the noise. "It's Avery. I'm right here with you. It's going to be okay."

"Where's Jim? I want Jim."

I dry my tears. Rosie and the baby need me to be strong for both of them. There's no use in crying. "We'll find him when the storm is over, Grandma, I promise. I'll be here with you until it's over. It can't be much longer now."

If the eye of the storm is close, that means we'll hit the other wall and then it'll go on to terrorize someone else. I cling to these thoughts as the winds beat at the walls, as some of the tin roof over our heads begins to peel away and slap against the slats underneath. *SLAP SLAP SLAP.* The sound is so loud I feel it in the backs of my teeth. The baby jumps against my chest and then settles again, snuggling closer. Thank goodness for small mercies. I kiss her head and murmur, "I love you," against her sweet-smelling skin.

Because I do, more than I ever thought I could, more than I've ever loved anything in this world. I'd make it through this for her, for them. I have to.

There's a boom and a large, shuddering crash from outside. I jolt and hug the baby tighter to me, rocking when she frets a little. I'm afraid to imagine what the sound could have been. A branch falling. A car being thrown by a gust of wind. The last news reports I'd watched had been of two storm chasers nearly drowned in the storm surge in Mexico Beach. We're landlocked here, but with a storm this bad a car being thrown about wouldn't be outside the realm of possibilities.

You've seen too many movies, Avery-girl.

Great. Now I'm not the only one hearing Grandpa Jim.

All at once, the roaring sound stops and the quiet is almost as deafening for its absence.

The runaway hammering of my heartbeat replaces the wind, and it takes me a moment to realize we must be in the eye. I'm equal parts relieved and terrified because it means we have the other wall to go through before this nightmare is over.

The only thought that keeps me from going completely insane is the thought that it'll be over. There will be an end. It may not seem like it now, but it can't last forever. No matter how much it seems like it.

Water drip, drip, dripping reaches my ears through the stillness. I have enough presence of mind to give a passing thought to the damage it could cause. Then I have to laugh at myself. We'll be lucky if we still have a roof over our heads when this is over, let alone a little water damage.

Soon, there's no time to think. The roaring wind returns, and it begins again. A hand reaches out for me and I look up to find Grandma Rosie solemn and lucid—which is so rare it distracts me for a moment from the horrors outside.

"Grandma Rosie?" I croak out.

"Don't worry. It'll be okay. Just a little rain." Her smile is tremulous, but warm and so like the woman who raised me that I manage to smile back, despite everything.

Her words are nearly identical to the ones I said only a few hours before—a sentiment I'll have to revisit when I have a spare moment to think on it more.

The baby in my hands lets out a little sound in her sleep and Grandma Rosie says, "What a sweet baby. What's her name?"

"Rosalynn Grace. I named her after you." I don't know why it seems so important to tell her this now, of all times, but I force the words out in a rush over the din.

"A mouthful for a little girl." Grandma Rosie's eyes begin to cloud over. "You should call her Gracie."

"I will," I say, but she's already gone, her eyes glued to the tablet where I've downloaded her favorite shows for her. It hasn't gone dead yet, but it must be on its last legs. I don't have a generator, so Lord only knows what I'll do when the last dregs of juice drain away. I doubt there will be power anywhere if we make it out of this.

I doubt there will be much of anything for a long, long time.

CHAPTER TWO

AVERY

I SETTLE GRANDMA ROSIE INTO HER BED, THANKFUL SHE STILL HAS ONE. SHE has one bar of battery left on her tablet, but it should be enough to help her off to sleep. I leave the lantern in her room in case she wakes up in the middle of the night and tries to wander around, as she's prone to do. I'd done a thorough once-over of her room and found the only damage was a broken window from the porch swing I'd forgotten to take down.

It could have been worse.

So, so much worse.

A broken window, damaged roof, those were things I could come back from. The complete loss of the house, or someone I loved? There's no coming back from that.

I settle onto the couch in the living room after cleaning up the glass. One of the flashlights sits beside me, pointed up at the ceiling. It's a poor substitute for the lantern, but beggars can't be choosers. From what I can glean from the radio and the spotty cell reception I have, rescue efforts are underway, but it's an arduous, painstaking process. The sheer number of downed trees is incalculable, making it hard for rescue operations to commence.

Needless to say, there won't be anyone coming through tonight and I haven't even looked outside to see what shape my car is in. I'm afraid to. One catastrophe at a time is all I have the energy to face. I'll deal with figuring out our next steps and clearing away debris tomorrow.

Now that the adrenaline is fading, weariness settles over me. I arrange baby Rosie's bassinet next to the couch. While she nurses, I attempt to connect to the internet, but it's next to impossible and loads indefinitely. It's strange, being so disconnected. It's isolating and in a weird way freeing all at once.

It's then that I remember the battery pack I use to charge my phone on vacations—or when I used to take vacations. I'd plugged it in when I first realized the storm was coming and there was no way Grandma Rosie was leaving her house, meaning I'd be stuck here too unless I wanted to condemn her to a horrific fate. Once the baby is done nursing and is once again sound asleep—thank goodness—I tuck her into her bassinet and retrieve the battery pack and charger cord.

Thankfully, it has half a charge, which allows me to hook up both my phone and the tablet, which I retrieve from a snoring Grandma Rosie's room. I take a full water bottle on my way back to the couch and a granola bar to stave off the breastfeeding munchies that will inevitably come. Once I polish off the granola bar and half of the water, I finally—finally—allow myself to relax into the couch with the baby close beside me. Sleep finds me easier than I thought it would.

"I WANT EGGS AND BACON," GRANDMA ROSIE ANNOUNCES WAY TOO DAMN early the next morning.

I blink blearily up at her hovering over me at the couch. "What—what?"

"Look at you sleeping the day away. It's morning time. Time to wake up." She shuffles over to her rocking chair, freshly charged tablet in hand. "Up, up, up. Everybody up. If I can't sleep, nobody sleeps."

"I'm up, I'm up." With a quick look at the baby, who is blissfully still asleep, I push to sitting.

The first thing I notice is the heat.

Then, I remember the night before.

The storm.

"I don't think we have power for eggs, but I can make you some cereal." I'd packed some of the contents of our fridge in a cooler while I was prepping the day before. The milk should still be good for a while.

Grandma Rosie harrumphs, but doesn't argue. Good. Maybe today will be a good day for her, relatively.

The front door protests when I try to open it, swollen from the moisture and humidity. When it opens, it's to an alien world on the other side. My hand flies to my mouth as I gasp. The front yard looks like a jungle. Several trees had toppled over. One thick oak limb lies horizontally across most of our fence, obscuring the front walk. Another has fallen over the front porch, its limbs spiderwebbing inside like a corpse's fingers. Dozens, hundreds, of smaller branches litter everything.

Debris covers the roads in front of the house along with more fallen limbs. I don't even see how we'd get help even if we needed it. There won't be any trucks on the roads until they can get them cleared and that'll take a couple men and a half dozen chainsaws. A water main has busted across the street, flooding a neighbor's yard. Several limbs crush another's car and my eyes fly to my own busted up sedan. Aside from debris blown on top, it's relatively, shockingly, unscathed—not that it'll do us any good now.

All we can do for the time being is sit still and stay out of the way. I don't know how long it'll take, but I do know there will be crews out at some point to help clear the roads, fix the downed power lines, and check on residents to make sure no one is injured. God, I hope no one has been injured.

Once I feed Grandma Rosie and the baby, I'll take a more thorough look outside, make sure there's no one close by who needs help. Then…I don't know. One step at a time, I suppose. That's all any of us can do.

While I'm making bowls of cereal, I attempt to check online for any news. The loading symbol at the top of my phone keeps going round and round and the pages stay blank. I don't know if all the towers are down or if it's taking a long time because of general chaos or what. It's strange not being connected to anything at all. It makes me feel very alone.

By the time we sit down at the small dinette table, it's nearly ten or so in the morning and already sweltering. It was a warm October before the storm, but it has to be in the high eighties, if not higher. Our house stays cool, but it won't for long if the temperature keeps rising. Once I find a way out of here and make sure no one is injured, my first priority will be to find a generator. Perhaps I can plug a window unit into it and keep our small living room cool, at least. The nights won't be so bad, but a hot Florida afternoon can be killer.

Later, I leave Grandma Rosie watching her shows and baby Gracie napping deeply. With the baby monitor receiver clipped to my belt, I strap on a pair of old sneakers and head outside for the first time since the storm. By the time I make it through the front yard to the gate, my legs are scraped to all hell and I realize all the fallen trees have disturbed dozens and dozens of yellow jacket nests. I'm stung twice and am left cursing and sweating, already lathered up in a mood.

Hissing through my teeth, I work my way across the road to my closest neighbor. I'm almost to their steps when I hear their shouts from the other side of the closed door.

"Hello? Can you hear us? We're trapped inside!"

I speed up picking through the debris on their porch—including a large downed limb that's wedged in their doorway, completely blocking the majority of their front windows and their front door. Quickening my pace, I shout back, "Mary? Tom? It's Avery. I'm coming!"

"Avery, thank God," comes Mary's relieved voice. "We've been hollering all morning. There's another limb that damn near crashed through the back door. We'd jump out the windows if I didn't fret about Tom breaking a hip."

"Fool woman," I hear Tom mutter, which makes me smile despite everything.

"You guys say there. I'm going to find a way to get inside."

The limb is the size of a small tree. There's no way I'll be able to move the damn thing, but I try nonetheless, to no avail. The windows on either side of the house are over my head, so there'll be no climbing up unless I can find something to stand on. They weren't kidding about the back being caved in. Half a rotten tree collapsed on it.

I come back around to the front, hoping I can wiggle my way in between the tree and the front door to get it open. Above the sound of distant buzzing chainsaws and humming yellow Tomets, I begin to hear the sound of more voices, some raised over the din. More people must be up and moving around trying to clear out paths, discern the extent of damage.

The crunch of boots on leaves snapping twigs has me looking up as I near Tom and Mary's front steps. Maybe it's someone who can help.

I open my mouth to call out to them when the words die on my tongue.

The man hasn't noticed me yet. He carries a chainsaw with one hand like it doesn't weigh a thing. He scans the area, sharp and observant. I know that gaze. I've stared into it, dreamed of it. His eyes haunt me every day.

"Walker," I say, louder than I intend, because it's the only thing I know about him other than what it feels like to have him inside me.

He stops. Turns to me.

Those blue-gray eyes meet mine.

CHAPTER THREE
WALKER
PAST

"I DON'T NORMALLY DO THIS," IS ALL I REMEMBER HER SAYING BEFORE SHE tugs me to my Airbnb.

"Neither do I."

She pushes open the door and stumbles inside. "No, I mean it. That's not just a line. I don't go home with strange guys."

When I'm over the threshold, she pushes it shut behind me and presses me against its surface. My brain short-circuits like it had the moment I saw her in the bar. Sounds cliché, but they're clichés for a reason.

She'd been waiting tables at the restaurant I'd gone to for dinner. Not my waitress, but one a couple sections over. I'd lingered over a mediocre steak and over-dry baked potato that I'd washed down with cheap beer to watch her like some kind of creep. I'd stayed through dinner rush, then wandered over to the bar where she'd taken over serving drinks. She plied me with alcohol until I, with some stroke of luck or fate or both, convinced her to go to the bar next door when we couldn't stay at the restaurant any longer. Some hours later, with enough alcohol to make bad decisions sound like good ones, I'd convinced her to come back to my place where we could be alone.

"I'm not complaining," I say and let my hands wander wherever she'll allow them. "I wouldn't judge you even if you did."

She pauses her own explanation to peer up at me with fathomless brown eyes. "That's so sweet," she says, causing me to laugh. "What did you say your name was again?"

"Walker," I answer and brush back her loose brown curls from her face. God, I want to kiss her.

"I'm Avery."

"I remember."

She presses her eyes shut, sighs a little. "We should probably talk some more. Get to know each other better. I think I'm a little drunk."

I close my eyes and lean my head against the door, praying for some self-control. "Whatever you want. I just don't want to be alone."

Her fingers pause their exploration of my chest over the thin material of my T-shirt. I glance back down at her, watching her study me. Fuck, maybe she was right. I'd had way too much to drink.

"I don't want to be alone either," she confesses.

Wanting nothing more than to taste those confessions on her lips, I instead put my hands on her arms and put some much-needed distance between us. "Why don't you sit down? I'll make us some coffee. I think there's some in the kitchen."

At this, she chuckles and carefully sits on the small leather sofa in the living room. "You don't know if you have coffee in your own house?"

"It's not mine," I answer as I hunt through the cabinets searching for K-cups. "It's an Airbnb. I was only in town for a few months. Didn't seem like it would make much sense to rent a place for longer when I'd be leaving soon."

"Oh, so you aren't from Battleboro?" Was I imagining it or was there disappointment in her voice? I like the thought of her wanting to have me around. Not many people do these days.

"I am originally. Just back while I'm in between jobs." I find the K-cups, an off-brand, but they'll do, and load one up in the machine. While it gurgles to life, I lean against the countertop and grip its edge to keep my hands from reaching for her. "I'm a Wildland Firefighter."

She nods, then laughs. "I have no idea what that means."

"You know those big wildfires you hear of on the news out west?"

Avery's eyes widen. "You fight with those?"

"Nine months out of the year. I'm in between contracts right now, but I'm going back for another contract in a few days."

"So, what brings you back to Florida?" she asks. "Why not stay out west all year round?"

Good question. I consider my words while I make one cup and start another. "You want cream or sugar?" I ask.

"Both," she says.

I stir them in and finally answer, "Family, I guess."

She makes a noise of understanding in her throat as she sips her coffee. "That'll do it. That's why I've stayed here. I've never been out of the state. I imagine it's pretty different where you go, even without the firefighters."

"You'll have to go sometime. Nothing like it."

She takes the offered coffee cup and smiles sadly. "Thanks. Maybe one day."

"What about you? What do you do when you're not working at the restaurant or bartending?" I sit on the small recliner with my own cup of coffee and suck it back even though it's piping hot. I could use the mental clarity before I do something stupid. Like beg her to stay with me.

"Not much," Avery answers with a self-deprecating laugh. "I'd like to go back to school one day, but for now all I do is work. Nothing as exciting as fighting wildfires." She lets out a yawn, then an embarrassed laugh. "I'm sorry, it's been a long day. I worked a double shift. The coffee is sobering me up, but unfortunately, I'm still dog tired. Some company I am, huh?"

"Do you want to crash here?" I ask before I can stop myself. At her curious glance, I say, "Just sleep, I promise. Or I can call someone to take you home."

She's already shaking her head before I finish the suggestion. "No, that's okay. Um, if it's not weird, I can sleep here and walk back to my car in the morning. I mean, if you're okay with that."

Okay with it? It'd be a relief not to wake up all alone shrouded in nightmares. "I don't mind. As long as you don't care if I snore."

Avery giggles. "I'm so tired, I probably won't even notice."

"Let me get you some clothes." The skin-slick jeans and tight restaurant T-shirt don't leave anything to the imagination, but they also probably wouldn't be comfortable to sleep in. Plus, I like the thought of having her in my stuff, my scent on her skin. Like an indelible mark in some way.

"Thanks. I appreciate it."

I take her empty cup and my half-drunk mug to the sink and retrieve a loose T-shirt and a pair of sweatpants from my suitcase in the bedroom. When I turn, she's already standing at the door, watching me. I'd be lying if I said having her near me with a bed so close didn't make me think of her in it—without the clothes.

"I'll let you get changed."

While she undresses in the bedroom, I change into another pair of sweatpants in the attached bath. I do us both the courtesy of brushing my teeth and ignore the red-eyed reflection in the mirror. She's lying under the covers when I come out. Maybe I like seeing her there more than I should.

You're a lonely piece of shit, Walker.

But I get into bed with her anyway, sliding in between the sheets to soak up her warmth. Without any urging, she scoots to my side and wraps her arm around my waist like we'd been doing this for years. Maybe it hadn't been her looks that had stopped me from going home by myself. Maybe the lost parts in me had recognized something similar in her.

I mean to tell her I don't normally do this either, but for the first time in months, I fall asleep without wondering what nightmares are waiting for me.

CHAPTER FOUR
AVERY

MAYBE I DIDN'T MAKE IT THROUGH THE STORM.

Maybe this is all a dream.

I never thought I'd see him again after that night, though I'd done enough social media stalking to try and find him. Kind of hard to do when I didn't even know his last name.

Walker doesn't break stride, merely shifts his destination to my direction, his long, lean legs eating up the distance between us. My feet are glued to the earth beneath them and it's like going through the storm a second time to have him right in front of me. He hasn't changed a bit in months since I last saw him. If anything, he's even more devastatingly handsome.

Kitted out in a Battleboro Fire and Rescue uniform, he's not only handsome, he's heart-stopping. I'd forgotten how tall he is until he comes to a stop in front of me. Nearly six-two to my five-six, he may as well be a giant. I remember waking up that night after being wrapped up in him and I'd felt so safe and protected. I'd never felt like that before in my life. It's addicting—that feeling of being safe. A girl could learn to get used to having a man make her feel protected. Maybe that's why I'd run.

"Christ, Avery. Is that you? What's wrong? Are you hurt?"

I have to close my eyes hard and pull myself back to the present. "No, it's not me. I'm fine. It's my neighbors. They're trapped inside their house. Can you help?" I want to take the words back as soon as they come out of my mouth, but Mary and Tom need my help. That's all this is. That's all it can be.

"Sure. Lead the way."

I'm hyper aware of him right behind me and my mind is racing the whole walk up to the front door. All I can think is that I need to get away from him as quickly as possible.

"If you'll keep them calm, I'll see if I can get this tree out of their door. Have them stay back just in case."

Nodding, I go to the front window and get as close as I can. "Mary, there's a firefighter here to help. He wants you guys to stay away from the door while he tries to get the block out of the way. Okay?"

"Okay, Avery. You tell him thank you for us!" Mary shouts and then everything is drowned out by the buzzing of the chainsaw.

I back away a few feet, but still stay in view of the front window in case Mary or Tom need me. Naturally, my eyes are drawn to Walker as he attempts to cut the limb down and I can't seem to look away no matter how much I order myself to. His uniform is covered in a fine layer of dust. They must have been working with chainsaws all morning clearing out paths to houses. If the dark circles under his eyes are any indication, he's been at it a while already.

A dozen questions spring to mind. Namely, what the hell he's doing here of all places and why? Then I wonder how long he plans to stay. If he's going back for another contract, I'd prefer he did it sooner rather than later…before things get even more complicated than they already are.

I worry at a nail, biting it down to the quick, as he cuts another divot into the limb. Sweat beads on his forehead and a dark furrow is already soaked into the material of his uniform T-shirt at his back. My mind instantly goes to the identical one I stole from him that I secreted away in my underwear drawer. I take another step away from him to find a pocket of cool air to breathe, but there's none to be found.

The limb gives way with a furious *crack* and Walker heaves it to the side with a strength that has all the feminine parts of me clench up in appreciation. Yes. I definitely need to make a quick getaway. Clearly the months haven't been enough to dull the effect he has on me. Though I'm not sure a decade would be enough time to accomplish that.

Another few minutes and he has the door all clear. Despite my reservations, I really do care about Mary and Tom, so I follow close behind as he sets the chainsaw aside, then knocks and enters. Their living room is a mess of broken glass and debris that Walker and I carefully pick over to where the elderly couple is hovering in their bedroom. Seeing them, I'm reminded of Grandma Rosie and the baby and know I have to get home soon. Grandma Rosie may have moments of lucidity, but she can't be in care of the baby for long.

"Are you two all right?" Walker asks. "I'm with the fire department. Do you need any medical attention?"

He conducts an interview with both of them as I watch, and I'm struck by his competence and efficiency. I've imagined him as a firefighter plenty of times before, but there's something more vulnerable about this aspect of his job that I'd never considered. There's a humane kindness in his bandaging of a scrape on Mary's forehead and a respectful concern as he takes Tom's heart rate and blood pressure. The fluttering inside me is located decidedly north this time. My heart can't seem to handle watching him care for these people.

"You'll call our daughter for us?" Mary asks for the second time. "She'll come out to get us when the roads are clear enough."

"Yes, ma'am. And I'll come by in the morning with food and water for you. They're supposed to be delivering some from Red Cross, the food banks. Do you have enough to last until then?"

"We'll be fine. We appreciate all your help," Tom answers.

"Any time. I'll see you in the morning."

"You let me know if you need anything before then," I tell Mary.

"Thank you for coming to check on us," she says. "I don't think we ever would have gotten out of here if it wasn't for you."

"Don't you worry about it. That's what neighbors are for. I better go and check on Grandma Rosie."

"You give that baby of yours some sugar for me," Mary calls after me.

My heart leaps into my throat and I glance at the porch to make sure Walker didn't hear her. Thankfully, he's too busy clearing a path down the walk to the driveway to have paid any mind to us.

"I will," I answer Mary and close the door behind me before she can say anything else too revealing.

Walker is probably in town in between contracts again. Next season when it's time for him to leave, he'll be gone again and that's probably for the best. Or at least that's what I tell myself.

He's waiting for me at the end of their sidewalk, the chainsaw and his kit of supplies at his feet looking like some sort of badass cross between a doctor and a lumberjack. When I get close enough, I open my mouth to say the words that'll put enough distance between us to keep us both in check, but instead he reaches for me in one smooth movement, then crushes me to his body for a kiss as long and steamy as a Florida afternoon.

CHAPTER FIVE
WALKER
PAST

WHEN I WAKE UP IN THE MIDDLE OF THE NIGHT, IT'S TO THE PERFUME OF her pear-scented shampoo filling my nose. It blots out the usual acrid tang of embers and ash and it's so welcome, I press my nose into her hair and breathe deep. She's like the springtime after years of the worst, coldest kind of winter. A cold so deep it almost burns.

She's wrapped up in a little ball in front of me, her legs tucked up into her chest, her hands folded innocently in front of her face. Somehow, I'd wound up wrapped around her with my thighs pressed close against the backs of hers and my chest framing her back. It's been so long since I've had a woman in bed with me, let alone falling asleep with one. I'd forgotten how comforting it can be to simply hold one with all their softness and curves.

If I weren't such a fucked-up man, I'd put some room between us. Even though she'd come back to my place, she doesn't know me. We've never met before tonight and I don't have any claim to her. But that doesn't have any effect on my lizard brain. All it knows is she's sweet and smells good and feels like heaven in my arms.

Reluctantly, I regain control of myself and start to pull away. A hand on my forearm stops me. "No, don't," comes her sleepy voice. "It's nice."

"You don't mind?" I can't see her face to read her expression, but I don't pull away.

"I hope this doesn't sound as weird as I think it does, but I don't get to do this sort of thing a lot. Like, the affection sort of thing."

"I guess that's a good thing to know."

"Why do you say that?"

"That you won't have some angry boyfriend chasing me down."

She puffs out a little laugh. "No, definitely not. I don't really have time outside of work to find any boyfriends, so you're safe."

I relax back into her, tightening my hold around her waist and pressing more closely against her slender body. "I'm the same way. I work a lot, and I'm gone too much for any real kind of relationship. Gotta admit, though, I do miss this sort of thing."

"That's surprising. I would have thought you'd have dozens of women falling at your feet. The whole sexy hero thing you've got going on must be pretty irresistible to them."

With a snort, I say, "Sure, until they realize I'm gone for weeks at a time and can be called away at any second. When I am home, I'm asleep or training. Women don't normally want to stick around when you don't."

There's a moment of silence and then, "I'm sorry. That must be lonely."

I lift a shoulder, then remember we're in the dark. "It can be sometimes, but you stay busy enough to forget. What about you? What keeps you busy outside of work?"

"My grandma. She has Alzheimer's. She has a nurse during the day while I'm at work, but I take care of her pretty much the rest of the time."

"What about your parents? Siblings? They don't help out?"

"My parents passed away when I was younger. They didn't have any other children. My

Grandma Rosie and Grandpa Jim raised me. Before he died, I promised him I'd take care of her. It's the least I could do. They were wonderful grandparents to me."

"Your grandma is lucky to have you. I've worked with patients as a paramedic who have Alzheimer's. It's not an easy job."

"It's worth it," Avery says. "I couldn't let her be taken care of by strangers, all confused without anything familiar around. She's lived in the same place pretty much her whole life."

"What would you do if you didn't have to take care of her?"

"I'm not sure. I've never really thought about it. Grandpa Jim got sick right after I graduated. If I had to pick something, maybe teaching? I really like kids."

I smile in the darkness. "Yeah? I could see that. You certainly had more patience last night than I would have."

"You should come on Friday night all you can eat crab legs. It's a madhouse."

"I'll keep that in mind."

"What about you? Have you always wanted to be a firefighter?"

My answer sticks in my throat. Clearing it, I say, "Pretty much. My brother was killed in a fire when I was ten. I guess I've been trying to save him ever since."

"Oh my God, Walker. I'm so sorry."

"It's been a long time."

"Still. I know how it feels. It doesn't ever really go away."

"No, I guess it doesn't."

She turns then, fitting her head underneath my chin. Her free arm goes around my waist and I freeze for a second, unsure. Then, I realize she's giving me a hug and I relax, accepting her feminine strength. I nuzzle my nose back into her hair and let the scent of her shampoo comfort me as much as her arms around me.

I'm not sure who reaches for who first, or maybe we do it at the same time. But somehow our lips find each other in the dark and tangle. There's desperation there, on both our parts. A need to fill a mutual void. A craving for similarities. To know we're not alone with our struggles. She tastes like the vanilla from the coffee, almost too sweet to handle, but I can't stop going back for more. Her groan fills me up and all I want is to hear her do it again and again.

If we only have tonight, then I hope tonight lasts forever.

Avery sheds her clothes as fast as a fox and then makes quick work of mine, too. "Is this okay?" she asks when she reaches for my sweatpants and I choke out a hoarse, "Yes," in response.

I wish there were light so I could get a better look at her. I wish there were more time so I could sample and savor every inch of her. But I'm driven by a desperation to be inside her that's so acute, all I can do is jerk her against my chest and lift one leg over my hip. She reaches between us and positions me, then takes me inside in one smooth motion. Her gasp of pleasure fills the darkness around us as I drive into her obliterating heat.

This isn't how I'd planned for tonight to go. If I was lucky enough to get her into bed, I planned to make it last, make her come at least twice before we got down to business, but I'll be lucky if I don't go off embarrassingly early at this point.

I try to slow down, try to reach between us to get my hands on her so I don't completely ruin this before we've even started, but she pushes my hands away.

"No, don't. You feel so good."

"Baby, if I don't help you out, this is going to be over before it starts."

She writhes against me and her hands dig into my shoulders. "I don't need any help. You're doing just fine."

At that, I give up trying to rein in any sort of control. My fingers bite into her hips and we come together like crashes of thunder in the middle of a storm. Wild and beautiful and unpredictable. She presses close to me like she's trying to climb into my skin. I twist us both so she's on her back. Her arms come around my shoulders, not letting me put any distance between us.

And that's what does it for me, what sends me over the edge. I don't know much about her, but in this moment all I know is she needs me. I couldn't hold back even if I tried. She gasps at the sound of my release and I feel her clench around me a second later, like the physical act of bringing me to the brink is what she needed to get off. If I could come a second time, knowing that would have done it.

We're quiet as our heartbeats slow and our breathing goes back to normal. I don't want to get up, break the connection, but the orgasm has rendered me exhausted for the second time. She breathes deeply beneath me and I know she's close to falling asleep again, too.

While I'm still conscious, I get up to clean us both up. She murmurs as I wipe away the remnants between her legs and get back into bed. As though we've been doing it for years, she settles back with her ass against my hips and once again the scent of her shampoo lulls me back to a dreamless sleep.

In the morning, I reach for her, but she's gone.

CHAPTER SIX
AVERY

MY HANDS GO TO HIS BICEPS TO HOLD ON THE MOMENT HIS LIPS TOUCH mine. The world spins away. I forgot what it's like to feel wanted by him. So many things happened in the months since I've seen him it's easy to push away the memories. The only thing I haven't been able to push away is when he stars in my dreams at night.

Now there's no forgetting the pressure of his lips. There's no washing away his addictive taste. His kiss burns away all my good reason and common sense. If I wasn't hyper aware of every way he invades my senses, I would have said his kiss is another fevered dream.

When his tongue brushes mine it's like I've been stung all over. Nerves that had gone dormant buzz to life like the yellow jackets swarming around us. I make a needy noise in the back of my throat and it's that sound that brings me crashing back to rationality.

My hands are twin vices on his biceps, and I force myself to relax my grip, although very reluctantly. The heat we're generating between us rivals that of the steamy afternoon air. It's a good thing I won't have any hot water when we get home because a cold shower is exactly what I'll need.

"I've been thinking about doing that since the morning I woke up and you weren't there." His rough voice is like honey in my ears.

Hot guilt washes over me. "I'm sorry about that. My grandma was having a moment and I had to leave in a hurry. Besides, I thought it would be easier without the awkward goodbyes."

I make a move to put some space between us, but his hands on my waist tighten, keeping me close. "Would it be creepy of me to say I've thought about you probably more than is healthy while I was gone?"

It's not creepy, but it does hit me right in the heart. I clear my throat. "It's not creepy," I manage to say. In fact, no one has ever said anything of the kind to me before and if I weren't so panicked to have him here in the flesh after all this time, I'd think it was kind of sweet. In the past, what few short-lived relationships I'd cultivated had crashed and burned when they realized how much time I had to devote to Grandma Rosie.

"Why don't we—"

In the distance I hear the squeal of a protesting screen door, cutting off my focus from what Walker's saying. Then the sound of Grandma Rosie's frail voice penetrates my thoughts. "Avery, is that you?"

Before I can say anything, Walker turns and spots Grandma Rosie on the front porch. He twists back to me for a moment. "Is that your grandma? The one with Alzheimer's?"

My hands grow clammy and I wipe them on my thighs. "What—what? Oh, um, yes. Grandma Rosie. But she's okay. We didn't have any significant damage and I stocked up before." I'm rambling. I don't know if he can hear the straight panic in my voice, but it sounds brittle and desperate to my ears.

"I should give your place a look before I get back to the guys. It's the least I can do." He gives me one last kiss on the lips and even though it's only the barest touch I feel it down to my bones.

"No!" I nearly shout, but he's already stalking across the street to my house. His long legs make easy work of the distance and I'm simply no match. He's at the fence before I get halfway. The air simply evaporates from my lungs as he eats up the space between the gate and the front door where Grandma Rosie is waiting patiently, innocently. I don't know where the baby is, probably still asleep in the bassinet, but she isn't holding her. With my heart in my throat, I follow behind as quickly as possible.

"Good morning, ma'am, I'm Walker Bryant with the fire department. How are you doing?"

"Has there been a fire?" I hear Grandma Rosie ask.

"No, ma'am. I'm helping with the cleanup after the storm. You remember the storm from last night?"

"Storm?" Grandma Rosie's expression is guileless.

"Yes, ma'am, there was a bad hurricane last night. How are you feeling?"

"Oh, I'm all right. My granddaughter Avery takes good care of me."

Walker glances back over his shoulder at me as I climb the steps to the porch, out of breath. Both from the kiss and the short sprint across the street.

"I bet she does."

"Do you want some sweet tea?" I wince at Grandma Rosie's ingrained hospitality. The last thing I want is for Walker to go inside.

"No, Grandma, I'm sure he's—"

But Walker acts like he doesn't hear me. "That would be great, ma'am, thank you."

I nearly wince. "Are you sure you aren't busy? Don't you have a ton of people to check on or something?"

Walker merely grins over his shoulder as Grandma Rosie leads him inside the house. "I always have time for the company of beautiful women."

My heart is at my feet as we move inside. Rosie busies herself making us all glasses of sweet tea. I already know I won't be able to drink any around the knot in my throat. All I can see are the baby things everywhere. A man like Walker must notice everything, so they can't go outside his observation. Once she gives him the glass of tea, Grandma Rosie smiles and goes back to watching her shows on her tablet in the recliner.

His throat works as he drinks deeply. Despite my panic, my eyes are glued to him. "Have you been working all night?" I figure distracting him will be the next best thing. Maybe if I do, he won't notice the bottles on the counter or the breast pump on the kitchen table. My cheeks burn with embarrassment and I hope he thinks it's because of the heat. I don't know if it's my nerves or the lack of air conditioning, but it feels about 100 degrees inside now.

Walker finishes the glass and sets it inside the sink next to a bottle he doesn't seem to pay any mind to. "Well, I'm between contracts again and I came back to visit. When I heard about the storm, I volunteered with the fire department for their emergency response. When they saw how bad it could be, they knew they needed all the help they could get. It's a mess out there."

"If it's anything like around here, you'll have your work cut out for you." I hope that didn't sound as inhospitable as it does inside my head.

"You're not wrong." With a quick glance at Grandma Rosie, he says, "So would it be okay if I came back the next time I'm free? I'm not sure when that'll be, but I want to see you again. I wanted to see you again after you left, but I didn't have any way to contact you. I never did get your number."

This is either my dreams come true, or my worst nightmare. I'm not certain which.

"Um, I'm not sure—"

Once again, I'm interrupted.

This time, by the thin, high-pitched wail of a hungry baby girl.

CHAPTER SEVEN
WALKER

THE FIRST THING THAT COMES TO MIND IS THERE'S A BABY AT A NEIGHBOR'S. With most of the electricity out, it's easier to hear ambient noises around even with all of the chainsaws buzzing around. Then I see Avery's pained ghost-white expression. My brows furrow, because the dots don't connect.

She'd never mentioned a kid before and I would have noticed if she had. Without a word, Avery turns and disappears into a bedroom and I'm left in a pile of confusion until she returns with a swaddled, squirming bundle in her hands. Throughout the paramedic arm of my training, I've been around enough babies to know a newborn or thereabouts when I see one and that baby isn't more than a month or two old.

Avery doesn't meet my eyes as she retrieves a container of milk from a cooler. She prepares the bottle in the absolute quiet save for the fussing sounds from the infant. The baby quiets as she teases its mouth with the bottle and begins to eat.

I don't know what to think at first. My mind goes incredibly blank. After some quick mental calculations, I realize either she was pregnant when we were together or…

No.

There's no way.

She would have found a way to tell me.

I couldn't have spent nearly an entire year as a—I nearly choke on my own spit at the thought that follows—father and not known it.

"Is that a baby?" I ask when I can finally get my voice to work again.

Avery's eyes are still on the gurgling infant and she nods silently.

"Look at me," I demand, my heartbeat throbbing throughout my entire body. I swear I can almost hear it pounding in my head and ears. When she doesn't, I say, "Avery."

Her wide eyes meet mine reluctantly and there's fear and defiance there in equal measure. "This is Rosalynn Grace," she says. "My daughter. Gracie."

"When was she born?" My words come out as harsh and choppy as the ocean in the middle of a winter storm.

"A few months ago." Her words are so faint I damn near have to read her lips to know what she's saying.

It doesn't take a genius to realize a few months plus nine months gestation means the baby was conceived roughly the same time we were together. The sweet tea turns sour in my stomach and the sugar now seems like a terrible idea. I want to sit down, but I'm afraid if I try to move, my locked knees will give out from underneath me, completely betraying the level of shock I'm experiencing.

"Is she mine?" I ask, the words coming out harsh and cold unintentionally. Or maybe the tone is intentional. How could she have kept a secret like this from me for so long? What if something had happened to me and I didn't make it out of a fire alive and died not knowing I had a child out there in the world.

At my question, Avery's eyes go back to the now sleeping baby's face. Mine follow despite how much I try to keep from looking at them, feeling anything for them. The baby must sense some of the unease in the room, because she shifts restlessly, her sleepy eyes cracking open just long enough for me to see how identical they are to my own.

"Yes," is all Avery says.

At her answer, I collapse into the chair at the table next to her, my thoughts racing. I have a daughter. The words repeat over and over until they have no real meaning. *I have a daughter.*

I'd never given much thought to children. I never had much time. If I wasn't training or fighting fires, I was traveling back and forth to Battleboro to make sure what was left of my family didn't splinter off and fall to ruin. There was never any room for starting a family.

"Why didn't you tell me?" I demand.

Her hand fiddles with the baby's blanket and a little chubby arm breaks free of its restraints and a pudgy hand finds her fingers and holds on tight. I can't say why the image makes my chest tighten, but it does.

"You were already gone. I tried to find you, but I barely knew you. I only found out your last name today because you told Mary and Tom."

"You knew I was from Battleboro. It's not a small town, but you could have asked around if you wanted to and someone would have pointed you in the right direction."

She bites her lip and I notice how red it is, nearly raw to the touch, from her constant gnawing. "I could have tried harder," she admits, faltering. "I take full blame for that. I was scared."

It's her breathless vulnerability that stops me from berating her further. Striving for calm, I say, "I've had a daughter for damn near a year and you couldn't tell me because you were scared? Do I seem like that much of a jerk to you?"

Her eyes widen. "No!" Her raised voice jolts a cry out of the baby. As Avery tries to soothe her, she says, "No, of course not. I just—I could hear how much you loved what you do. I could never take that from you. I knew you'd be back eventually and each day I didn't tell you I rationalized that maybe it was better this way if you didn't know."

"That wasn't your decision to make. I had a right to know."

Who knows what the hell I would have done with the knowledge, but now I'll never get the chance to find out.

"You did. I know you did. It was wrong of me and I'm sorry. I was scared."

"Of what? Of me?"

"No, of course not. Of a lot of things. She means everything to me. I thought I was doing what was best for her." The words sound torn from her very soul and I have to fight not to reach for her, bite back the words of consolation.

My first instinct is to soothe, but anger overrides it. "Do you have a police scanner?"

She glances up, confusion written on her face. "A—what?"

"A police scanner. Do you have one?"

"Um, I think so. My grandpa used to volunteer at the fire department. He liked to listen to it sometimes and I kept it around because listening to it reminds me of him." Her expression turns wary. "Why do you ask?"

I get to my feet, suddenly needing some space. "Because that's how we're communicating. You can listen to them for the most up to date information and to find out when they're organizing distribution of resources or whatever. Where's your phone?"

She blows out a breath, her brows still knitted with confusion. Pulling the phone out of her pocket, she says, "It doesn't really work."

I program my number into hers, then send myself a text from her phone so I have it stored in mine. "Texts do, but they take a little longer. If you three run into an emergency, you can shoot me a text and I'll be here as soon as I can. Do you have access to a generator? It's gonna get hot soon and that baby and your grandma will need cool air."

"No, not yet, but I—"

"If you don't have one by tomorrow, I'll have one delivered here. Is there anything else you need?"

"No, I think we're okay. But you don't have to go to the trouble. I planned to get one as soon as I could."

"I'll take care of it. Keep your phone and the police scanner nearby. I put in the numbers for the station if you need to get ahold of me and can't get to me with my cell."

"You don't have to go to all this trouble."

I shoulder my kit and head back through the house without answering. I'm not sure I can without spewing a ton of nasty thoughts and I'm not the sort to pop off without considering my words. Her footsteps follow close behind and I can feel the anxious waves of energy emanating off of her at my back.

"I'm sorry," she says when I reach the door.

I jerk my head in answer. I have nothing else left in me to say. Nothing nice anyway.

CHAPTER EIGHT
AVERY

TRUE TO HIS WORD, A GENERATOR MAGICALLY APPEARS ON MY PORCH THE following day. The only note with it are instructions on how to set it up safely. Apparently several people have already been killed by having the exhaust blow into their homes and causing them to slowly asphyxiate. The generator also runs on gas so there were an additional five cans of gas lined up like neat little soldiers.

I didn't plan to run the generator constantly, mostly through the hottest part of the afternoon because there was no telling how long the electricity would be down. From what reports I'd heard over the police scanner and the spotty connections I'd made on my phone I'd gleaned power lines were down from Mexico Beach to Tallahassee. It would take months of repairs and thousands of linemen from all over the country to repair the catastrophic damage.

You know your shit has gone sideways when the aftermath of a hurricane is easier to deal with than the wreck of your personal life.

In the long days that follow, I spend most of my time trying to get the front yard in some semblance of order. I learn through the patchwork communication grapevine that there will be debris pickups on certain days of the week if the community puts the debris on the side of the road. When I'm not taking care of Grandma Rosie or tending to the baby, I'm hauling limbs and logs to the ever-growing pile by the road. I borrow a spare chainsaw from Tom and after a quick lesson, get to work cutting down some of the more manageable felled limbs. There are a few monsters I don't know what I'll do with, probably pay someone to remove at some point, but that'll have to be put off until later.

It's a lot of work, but it keeps my mind off of Walker and gives me something to do since most roads are still closed unless you're getting food from the various distribution locations or getting gas for your generator. There's even a curfew for our town to discourage looters. Someone had tried to open our front door a few days after the storm, but our automatic porch flood lights scared them away. It's the only time I've ever wished I had a gun in the house, but thankfully I haven't had to resort to that.

All in all, it could be so much worse. The only tree that fell on the house was an immature magnolia and it didn't cause any structural damage. I was able to get it cut down for the most part. There's still the base of it sticking out at an angle across the yard, but at least it's not on the roof. The others that were blown down were in the back yard and out of the way. Most of the damage to the house was the window that was broken and some of the tin that was pulled up by the wind. Truthfully, we got lucky.

So, so lucky.

I've seen pictures of homes in our area that were completely wiped away. Roofs ripped completely off. Trees spearing through living rooms, through cars. That's not to mention the homes on the coast where the hurricane made landfall. The whole community of Mexico Beach…there aren't words to describe the devastation. My family and I have spent many summers swimming at Mexico and Panama City Beach. To many Floridians in the

Panhandle, they're as ingrained in your blood as choosing a side in the Florida / Florida State rivalry. Seeing the pictures of entire tracts of homes simply wiped away…there's no way to explain the hole it leaves. I can't imagine how that would feel to the people who live there. Lived there.

It's hard enough seeing images from my own town. Entire forests wiped out. Whole landscapes marred for the foreseeable future. The world I grew up in has forever been changed. My daughter will never know the Florida I grew up in and there's a bracing somberness to accepting that.

About two weeks after the storm, when I'm certain Walker has completely written me off, I wake up to the sound of a chainsaw close by. It's not an uncommon occurrence at this point—the chorus of chainsaws is almost comforting now—but this one sounds like it's right outside my door. It wakes the baby, too, so I nurse her back to a contented state and entertain her with a few toys clipped to a bouncer. She's more awake these days, so I try to tire her out a bit before I put her back to sleep.

While she's distracted, I take care of Grandma Rosie, getting her fed and making sure she takes all of her medication. Once that's done, I can finally investigate the source of the sound, which has now moved to the backyard. Hesitantly, I open the door and find a shirtless, sweaty Walker cutting down the fallen trees crisscrossing the property.

Stunned, a little confused, and a whole lot turned on, all I can do is watch as he works. The strong patchwork of muscles covering his back flex and contract with every movement. The sheen of sweat emphasizes each curve and bulge. He pauses to drink from a water bottle and uses the remnants to spray over his body, making him look like a real-life Chippendale's commercial. The sight of the water makes me realize my throat has gone dry and if it weren't for that, I'd be drooling.

Turning, he spots me standing on the back porch ogling him. The chainsaw cuts off, leaving a deafening silence in its wake. I swallow back my apprehension and put a damper on the raging hormones that had roared to life the moment they saw him.

"What are you doing?" I ask in a neutral tone, my voice raised to cover the distance.

He lifts the chainsaw in a gesture toward the tree. "Cutting down this tree for you."

I lift a brow. "I can see that. I guess the more appropriate question would be *why* are you cutting it down?"

"Because I had the time and the ability. Are you complaining about it?" There's a hard twist to his mouth I haven't seen before. So he hasn't forgiven me yet, not that I thought he would. He has a right to be bitter, mad, disappointed or maybe all of the above.

"No, I'm just wondering why. You don't have to do these things for us."

"What things?"

I wave a hand to our surroundings. "You don't have to get us a generator and gas or clear out my backyard. Those things aren't your responsibility."

"Like you didn't think a baby was my responsibility."

"That's not fair."

"I think in this circumstance, I'll get to decide what's fair." He props the chainsaw on the tree stump and moves closer to me. "I've had a lot of time to think over the past few weeks and I think what pisses me off the most is that you made the decision for me about one of the most important things that can happen in a man's life. That wasn't fair. You don't get to make that choice for someone else."

I don't know if it's the hormones, the heat, or the sting of righteous condemnation in his eyes, but I find my own temper rising. "That's what being a parent is all about. You think I didn't agonize about not trying harder to find you and let you know? It's all I thought about since I found out I was pregnant. But it wasn't about me and it wasn't about you. I had to do what I thought was best for my daughter. I've been through the loss of a parent. I didn't want to do that to her."

His eyes flash. "And what makes you think she'd have to lose me?"

"Look at your job! You jump into fires for a living, Walker. You're gone most of the time and there could be a day when you don't come back. What kind of life is that for a child? Would you want that for her?" When he doesn't answer, I push on. "It was that indecision that kept me from trying harder. That and we didn't know each other! We only spent one night together. How was I supposed to know the right thing to do? I made a mistake. I'm human. I promise I'm going to make more of them. Becoming a parent will surely teach you that." Striving for calm, I continue, "But I want to make things right. I want you to meet her. To figure out what you want your place in her life to be. Whatever that is, we'll deal with it and I promise as long as you're in our lives, I won't ever keep anything from you again."

When he says, "Are you done?" I nearly impale him with the chainsaw.

Instead, I gesture for him to speak before I commit a felony.

"I don't know where you and I go from here." I can't hide my wince at that, but it's what I was expecting. "But I do know I want the chance to figure this out. I never planned on having a family, for the reasons you listed and more, but she's here and she's mine. I owe it to her and to me to see exactly what that means."

I know if I don't say the words then I never will, so I blurt, "And us?"

His gaze meets mine. The spark I felt when we first met blazes to life between us. Sensing it, he takes a step back and I can't deny that hurts. "I don't know about us. I think we should take this slow and focus on one thing at a time. The baby—what did you say her name was?"

"Rosalynn, for my grandma. Rosalynn Grace. I mostly call her Gracie, though."

"Gracie," he murmurs, his eyes a little misty. "Well, Gracie deserves our attention now."

I know this is progress, I know I should be happy, but I can't help but feel like I've lost something that could have been amazing.

CHAPTER NINE
WALKER

"I'M NOT SURE IF I EVER REALLY THANKED YOU FOR THE GENERATOR. IT WAS really a lifesaver. I think Grandma Rosie would have melted without it." Her shy little smile throws me back to the night we met. How I thought I'd do anything just to see her aim that smile in my direction. "So thank you, really. I appreciate it more than you know."

"You're welcome, but I bet you're happy to have electricity back on." I pass Gracie from one arm to another. For a baby, she certainly has some chunk on her. She grins toothlessly at me and I find myself smiling back down at her. My family and I aren't close anymore. I come back to Battleboro to check on them because I imagine it's what my brother would want me to do so the feelings of love and connection I feel so quickly for this little girl simply astound me. "Aren't you Gracie-girl?"

"More than you know. Do they have power restored where you're at?" Avery asks.

"Last week. I have to tell you, it was nice taking a hot shower again." I don't say that I'm almost sad about it. Restoring utilities, getting most of the roads cleared for the most part, it means I won't be as needed here. The fire department is already scaling back hours for the volunteers. I never thought I'd say it, but I almost like the small crew of down-to-earth guys there. A far cry from the egos I'm used to.

"Agreed. Cold ones are fun when it's ninety degrees outside, but I missed bubble baths. Now if only we could get internet back up and running."

I try not to think about Avery naked and covered in bubbles. I try and fail. "They still haven't gotten yours fixed?"

Avery smiles sadly. "No, and they said it could be months, but I guess that's to be expected. Data is working faster on our phones and tablets, but they throttle it in the evenings, so everything runs as slow as a turtle."

"You know you can always come to my place. Mine is back up." And maybe I like the thought of her, the baby and even Grandma Rosie with me doing things like the dishes and watching her grandma's trash T.V.

At this, she pauses gathering the dishes from lunch. "Thank you. That's nice of you to offer."

"It's no problem. I'm hardly ever there anyway."

"Is the fire department still going door to door?"

That's not the reason I'm never there. It's because I can't stand the quiet. It's why I'm always here when I'm not working or training. "Not so much anymore." Gracie coos and gnaws on a teether in my lap. Avery says I'm crazy, but I'm almost positive she's going to be popping out some teeth soon. "We're mostly working on a volunteer basis to get more roads cleared out. When do you go back to work?"

"Monday, unfortunately. I've been enjoying the time off to spend with Gracie and Grandma Rosie, but with the restaurant opening back up—finally—I can't put it off anymore. They won't hold off on demanding payment on bills forever. I just hate that I have to send Gracie girl back to daycare."

Studying the baby in my arms, I find myself saying, "Why don't you let me watch her?"

Avery pauses in drying a plate. "Really? You want to do that?"

"If you don't mind. I think it'd probably be a good idea for us to spend some more time together. You work the evenings, right?" At her nod, I say, "That's perfect. I can switch around for the day shift and watch Gracie at night when you work."

At her look, I say, "What?"

"Are you sure? I can't imagine you dealing with diapers and bottles all day."

"And you know me so well," I say and she pauses for a minute before realizing I'm teasing.

"Ha, ha, very funny," she says and flings a handful of soap bubbles at me. "I mean you do know infant CPR, so that's a plus."

"Then what is it?" I ask.

"I guess I'm realizing that you were serious when you said you wanted to make this work. I figured you'd get bored after a while and need some action." At my lifted brow, she says, "Not that kind of action. I mean like a burning building or a pileup or something."

"You make me out to be more of a daredevil than I am."

"Right so jumping out of planes isn't because you like the adrenaline. Then why do you do it?"

I lift a shoulder. "Why do people do anything? I guess it started with a morbid fascination after my brother was killed in a fire and grew from there. Fighting fires is something I can control, believe it or not. It's the rest of the world that goes a little mad sometimes."

"You don't miss it?"

"You mean to imply that a category five hurricane isn't enough action for me?"

She leans against the counter, all hips and dark hair that tumbles down her shoulders. "Touché I guess. What time works for you?"

BABIES AREN'T AS EASY AS THEY LOOK. SURE, THEY SLEEP MOST OF THE TIME, but they spend a good portion of the rest of it crying. Give me a fire any day and I can take charge and get it put out, but a crying baby? May as well be the world's most complicated Sudoku.

"C'mon, girl. What's wrong?" I check her diaper. Still clean and dry. She just had a bottle not five minutes ago and I've bounced and rocked her so much my arms ache—and I'm used to carrying rucksacks that weigh upward of fifty pounds on a light day. "You can't be hungry. You aren't sick, are you?"

That would go over well with Avery, I'm sure. The first day back at work and I tap out because the baby has a cold. I press my hand against Gracie's forehead. She's warm, but not hot. She drools on my hand and I wipe it away.

"Don't worry, girl. I won't take offense."

Her gummy smile reminds me of my thought about her teething. I grab a piece of ice and put it in a clean rag for her to suck on. It's like magic. In an instant, she stops crying and goes to town gnawing on the cold rag. Avery is going to flip her shit. *Babies aren't supposed to get teeth this early* my ass.

"See there? We can do this. It'll just take some learning for the both of us. What do you think, Gracie-girl? You think you'd like to have me as a dad?"

At my question, she looks up from her chewing to smile at me again. I'm filled with twin shards of delight and guilt. Her smile is a carbon copy of Avery's, but her eyes? They're all mine. I don't need the DNA test we'd taken to confirm paternity to know she's mine. I knew the moment I saw her. To have her smiling at me? It's the world's best Christmas present and winning the lottery all in one.

But there's guilt there, too. Guilt because a part of me knows Avery wasn't far off the mark when she said I needed the thrill, that my job is dangerous. I won't deny both of those reasons are why I love being a Wildland Firefighter so much. If I do decide to stick around, could I give those things up? Much as I want to think I'd be the selfless parent that Avery is, I'm not sure I could.

CHAPTER TEN

AVERY

I'LL BE THE FIRST TO ADMIT, I HAD MY DOUBTS ABOUT WALKER.

Clearly.

But when the first night of babysitting—or rather I should say parenting—didn't end in absolute disaster, I have to admit, I was wrong. Gracie was happy and healthy when I went to pick her up after my shift and Walker didn't even seem frazzled. I guess when you compare it to a wildfire, watching after one baby can't really be that intimidating.

We continue with this routine for the next couple of weeks. He spends more and more of his free time cleaning up the rest of the larger debris in my yard. In no time he has the large fallen trees hacked to pieces and burned. He even climbs up on top of my roof and replaces the tin that had gotten torn up when I told him it was leaking inside the house during the next rainstorm.

The be-all and end-all, though, is when he's with Gracie. If I had no feelings for him after our night together, seeing him with our daughter would have done it for me. He was awkward at first, a little unsure, but the two of them have a rapport I don't think I'll ever be able to attain. He's lighthearted and daring, letting her grab onto his fingers to practice her wobbly legs and cheering her on while I bite my nails off. He lights up when he sees her and the more time I spend with him, the harder it is for me to remember why I shouldn't want anything more than a father for my daughter.

Before we can blink, it's nearly Christmas time. I insisted he spend the night so he could be there for Gracie's first Christmas morning. How could I not? Seeing him watching her would be the best Christmas gift I've ever received.

If I thought he was good-looking in a pair of cut-offs and a T-shirt, it was only because I hadn't seen him in a flannel and jeans. Or even worse, a Christmas onesie that matches the drooling giggling baby girl in his arms. "You're sure you don't mind?"

I give myself a mental shake. Must stop picturing him stripping for me. That's not exactly the platonic coparenting relationship we agreed on. "I'm sure."

"I can just drive over in the morning."

He has Gracie in his lap. He's staring down at her as she coos and waves her arms. The look on his face is indescribable as he babbles at her like they're having a full-blown conversation. It's like I don't even exist. I've never been so happy to be ignored in my life. I can't believe I thought it would hurt her to have him in her life. If anyone knows what it's like to be without a parent, it's me.

After clearing my throat, I say, "I said I was sure. Geez, Walker, are you going deaf already? You can borrow some of Grandma Rosie's hearing aids."

"Fine," he replies with an exaggerated expression which causes Gracie to giggle up at him. Be still my heart. He places her in her bouncer to kick and play with the toys hanging over her. "I'll stay, but I'm sleeping on the couch."

I nearly roll my eyes. "Really, like we haven't shared a bed before."

At this, his gaze turns molten and the air between us heats like we're creating our own personal wildfire. "Right. And remember what happened the last time?"

My cheeks burn. We'd been dancing around each other for weeks. The sexual tension hadn't gone away because we'd decided to be mommy and daddy. It had only gotten worse, at least for me, because I knew making a move would be a huge mistake. "Fine. Stay on the couch."

But my words come out way more breathless than I'd like. Instead of joking back with me, Walker says nothing. His eyes drop to my lips and I can feel his gaze like he's kissing me again—something he hadn't done since the first day. Something I'd been thinking about damn near every second since.

Grandma Rosie is napping and Gracie is happily kicking away in her bouncer, but it feels like Walker and I are the only two people in the world. It's the same way he'd made me feel the first night I met him at the restaurant. It had been crowded then with the dinner rush, but the second we locked eyes, everything else faded away. I used to make fun of women who talked about love at first sight. Okay, maybe it was lust at first sight and love the moment I saw Gracie smiling up at him.

I'd been hit on at work before, but it didn't feel that way with Walker. He hadn't hit on me, not really. At the end of my shift, he'd asked me to a nearby bar, no pretense, no phony coaxing, and I'd said yes without hesitation. I've asked myself a thousand times why? What made him feel so safe?

Now I know.

It had been his eyes. They'd been so achingly sad and lonely. Not in a pitiful, I'll be your female knight-in-shining-armor kind of way. More in an I've found my likeness in another sort of way. In his eyes, I saw my own loneliness reflected and for a moment, maybe I thought...it's silly now, but maybe I thought he'd understand how that felt.

I wonder if he can read how much I want him in my eyes just as easily. The air between us seems to crackle with potential. Potential for heat. For more. Potential for heartbreak. The tension sizzles along my skin, taking with it what little self-control I'd cultivated.

Giving in, I lift my hand to his chest and nearly shiver at the mere feeling of his warmth underneath my palm. I've spent so many nights since he kissed me after the storm reliving the moment and wishing I'd let myself enjoy it more that my knees nearly buckle at the contact. Underneath my palm, his heart beats in an unsteady gallop and I wonder if he's thought about touching me as much as I have him.

I look up and his blue-gray eyes have gone stormy dark. His lips are slightly parted and his chest lifts rapidly with each inhalation. My stomach clenches with the knowledge that I'm not the only one who has been tortured by the distance. I'm not the only one who has been suffering with needs long repressed.

"We should put the baby down for bed," he says in a rough voice. "So she gets enough sleep for tomorrow."

"She's fine," I say with a shake of my head.

"Avery," he warns.

But for the first time in my life, I don't heed the warnings. Don't follow the rules. I lift up to the tips of my toes to reach his lips and kiss him like I've been wanting to kiss him since I first saw him. His hands come to my hips, but they don't push me away. Instead, they grip and hold as though he's afraid to let me go, too.

A bud of hope takes place in my chest as his lips part for me and his tongue flits out to caress my own. The hands at my hips tighten almost to the point of pain, but I don't care. All I want is to drown in him for a little while longer. He retreats, but only to rub his lips over mine, to tease and tempt. I push myself up higher, riddled with need, which makes him laugh.

"Don't laugh," I say indignantly. "Just kiss me."

"So impatient," he teases and pleases us both by bringing his mouth back to mine.

This kiss is deeper and longer. It brings to mind tangled sheets and slick skin. If kissing him was a mistake, it's one I want to make over and over and over again.

I don't know who made the first move, but the next thing I know I'm beneath him on the threadbare couch. He feels so good on top of me it almost makes me want to climb out of my own skin because the wanting him is so intense. His hands are all over me, restless with his own urgency. My thighs part to bring him closer and I hiss my pleasure at the contact. All I can think about is that I want more.

The baby chooses that moment to start crying.

Walker freezes above me, his head popping up in disbelief. My body goes limp with frustration and I press my hands to my face to fight for some semblance of self-control. With careful movements, he gets to his feet.

"I'll get her," he says.

I'm grateful for the moment to myself to put the needy parts of me back together again. I'd been close, so close, to the edge and he'd barely even touched me. If I thought it would be easy to do this co-parenting thing without making it complicated, I knew now I was dead wrong.

CHAPTER ELEVEN
WALKER

"WE NEED TO TALK."

No one likes to hear those words, but I'd been expecting them ever since we kissed the night before Christmas. We'd been able to toe around the tension between us while we focused on Gracie, but her kissing me changed everything. "I know. Did Gracie go down?" I ask.

"For the count." Avery settles on the couch next to me. It's two days past Christmas, but I couldn't seem to make myself leave. Opening presents with Gracie, Rosie, and Avery had been the kind of holidays I'd never gotten as a child after my brother died. Maybe I wanted to soak up as much of it as possible, not that Avery seemed to mind.

Until now.

She didn't object when I suggested I stay the night—on the couch—to help with Grandma Rosie once she caught a nasty cold after the holiday. In fact, part of her seemed relieved. Maybe she thought I'd run at the first opportunity. Maybe she wanted me to stick around. At this point, I didn't know which option I preferred. Both equally scare the shit out of me.

"What did you need to talk about?"

"You've been avoiding me," Avery says directly.

I've learned since I've been around her that keeping things to herself is an aberration. She must have been truly scared to withhold the truth about Gracie for so long—not that that's an excuse. In her day-to-day life Avery tackles her responsibilities head on which includes any confrontations. I won't ever forget that she lied by omission, but I can understand her reasoning more. Or at least her state of mind when she did what she did.

"I've been less than twenty feet away from you for nearly a week."

Avery rolls her eyes. "Don't play dumb. It was the kiss, wasn't it? Did it make it too weird? Look, I'm sorry for coming on to you if that's not what you wanted. The last thing I want to do is to make this harder on anyone. Gracie is the only one who matters here and if you meant it about putting our parenting relationship first, then I'll respect that from this point forward. I know you may not have forgiven me for what I did, I mean I understand—"

I press my fingers over her lips and bite back a smile. God, she loves to ramble when she gets all worked up. I didn't know that about her. There are so many things I don't know about her. So many things I wish I could learn about her. "I've forgiven you."

She deflates a little, then says, "You have?"

Nodding, I drop my fingers and say, "I've seen how hard it is for you to work, take care of your grandma and take care of Gracie. You're a good mom, Ave, and I can accept that you were scared of how I'd react. We never really knew each other, and it was a crazy situation to be put in. I can't say how I'd react if something similar happened to me, so I have no right to judge you. I'm not going to lie and say it doesn't hurt having missed everything, but I'm willing to work with you to move forward."

"Wow, that's not what I was expecting you to say," she says with a laugh. "Thank you. I hope you know I mean that. You've done so much for us already and—"

"Stop, you don't have to keep thanking me. I do those things because I want to."

She gestures over her lips with a zipping motion.

"There's something I need to talk to you about, too."

I wasn't sure how I was going to bring this up. I'd spent the past few days since I learned about it to decide what I wanted to do, and I figure I'd better get it over with before I lose my nerve.

Her smile falls. "What is it?"

"I got offered a job."

She brightens a little. "At the fire department?"

Well, I had, but I couldn't tell her that. Shaking my head, I say, "No, another contract. This one for nearly double what I usually work and what's basically a promotion. It's something I've been working for my whole life."

"You did? A promotion, wow. You must be really hot stuff, huh?" Her expression is a mixture of surprise, pain, and false happiness.

Somehow, it's worse that she's trying so hard to be happy for me. Indecision chokes my words, but I say, "Yeah, I apply for them every year. The listings normally don't go up for a few months, but I wasn't sure how we, this, everything was going to work out, so when I saw it, I applied as a contingency."

Her smile is kind and understanding, which shouldn't feel like a knife to the heart, but it does. "You don't have to explain yourself. I know I was emotional about your job in the beginning, but I can't be mad at you for doing something you love. I saw you after the storm. I could never be so calm and brave like you were. If this is what you want to do, it would be wrong of me not to support you. You're a great firefighter, Walker. A good person. Gracie will always be proud to call you her dad."

I slump back against the couch. "What made you change your mind?"

"Well, I've seen you with Gracie and I can't deny you're so good with her. Even though you may not be the type of dad who's there every day, you're a man she can be proud to call her father and that matters more than anything to me. I was wrong. I had no right to dictate what your relationship would be. If you want to fight wildfires every year, I'm sure we can figure out a way to make your relationship with Gracie when you're here the best it can be."

"Do you really mean that?" I can't tell from her expression or her voice what she's feeling. No doubt she's drawing from that well of inner strength—or maybe that's my vanity talking. And then I feel like shit. I shouldn't want her to be upset that I'm leaving.

"I wouldn't say it if I didn't."

"What about us?"

At this, she pulls away and I feel the distance settle between us like a rock. "I think you were right. What's most important is that you and Gracie have a positive relationship. I don't ever want to come between you two or you following your dreams."

"What if I said I wanted to make it work? All of it?"

"How would we do that?" she asks.

"Well, we could start by going out on an actual date."

To my relief, she laughs, but her eyes are somber. "If we did that eventually you would feel obligated to stay and you would start to resent me. Or I'd get insecure about you being away so much. I don't want that to sour anything and affect your wanting to be with Gracie."

"Nothing would ever affect my wanting to be with Gracie. I'll admit, at first my instinct was to bolt. I've run from being tied down like this my whole life. My father never got over being married and not chasing his dreams. When we lost my brother, it damn near broke him and I swore I'd never fall into that trap."

"Exactly," Avery says. "I don't want you to try and stay for me. Whatever you do, we'll make sure Gracie gets time with you. When you're off season or on vacation when she's older, she can visit or stay with you when she's in town."

There's a glint in her eye and for the first time I don't think I'm going to be able to convince her otherwise when she has her mind set. "Is this really what you want?"

"I only want you to be happy. If this contract makes you happy, I think you should take it. I won't ever stand in your way of doing what you love, Walker."

The hardest thing I've ever done was walk away from the two of them the next morning knowing I wouldn't be seeing them again for a long, long time.

Then realizing if shit went sideways, it could be the last time I ever saw them.

CHAPTER TWELVE
AVERY

IF I HAD ANY DOUBTS ABOUT HOW THE SHORT TIME WITH WALKER HAD affected Gracie, they're extinguished by how cranky she is in the days following his departure. She may only be a baby, but she can certainly tell when her world is not as it should be.

I rock her back and forth, jiggling her in my arms and shh-ing with all my might, but nothing helps. Like me, she'd gotten used to having him around and now she doesn't like it when he's gone. Her face is flushed red and angry tears leak from the corners of her eyes. Nothing has ever made me feel as helpless, not even being in the middle of a hurricane, as not being able to comfort my baby.

Kissing her forehead, I murmur, "I understand, honeybee, but Daddy had to go fight fires. He'll be back in a few months to see you. He promised."

I'd come to the realization after we kissed that if I truly cared for Walker like I thought I did, then that meant I had to give him the space to come to terms with being a father on his own. I couldn't force a happy relationship with Gracie—or with me—not after I'd stolen it from him in the first place. I would do my best to facilitate, but it would be up to him.

"It's the right decision," I tell the fussing baby. "You'll understand when you're older. God, what a total mom thing to say."

Eventually, she settles down into a fitful sleep on my chest. I park myself on the couch to give us both some rest before my next shift at work. Gracie will be going back to the evening daycare, which I'm already dreading, but it is what it is. Life goes on. As evidenced by the healing community around me every day, life goes on, but only if you put in the effort.

Gracie fights me at drop-off, and I arrive at the restaurant already ready to go home. I'm not in the mood for the rude, entitled customers or the grabby hands, but I have a baby to raise and Grandma Rosie's night nurse isn't cheap, even after her insurance pays their portion.

Life goes on.

The thought rolls around in my brain over and over.

Life goes on.

Before Walker, I was passing through the days and weeks and years, just trying to keep my head above water. That one night with him had been like a buoy, reminding me I didn't always have to struggle through it alone. Even through the trials of pregnancy and birth, I'd held on to the feeling of having his arms around me, protecting me. Sheltering me. It's the safest I've ever felt.

I shake my head and try to clear it of thoughts of him. My eyes catch on a customer and I nearly do a double take until I realize I'm not seeing things. Either Walker has a twin or he's sitting at the same table he'd been at the night we first met.

Still thinking I'm dreaming, I walk toward him in a daze. "Walker?"

His mouth lifts in a half grin, no doubt at my dumbfounded expression. "You look surprised to see me."

Surprised doesn't cover half of it. I'm still not certain I'm not hallucinating. Gracie has been teething, so sleep has become a thing of the past. Hallucinations wouldn't be outside the realm of possibility. "W-what are you doing here? You're supposed to be halfway to Colorado by now. Is everything okay?"

"Everything's fine." He pulls me down into the chair next to him. Well, I felt his hands on mine. They felt real enough. So he's not a sleep-deprived hallucination, but still, I'm left with more questions than answers.

"Then what are you doing here?" My brain can't quite catch up with reality. Much like the day after the storm when he'd appeared out of nowhere, my thoughts seem to keep misfiring. "Was your flight canceled?"

At this he smiles again, which doesn't help my cognition one bit. "No, it wasn't canceled. I didn't get on it."

"You're not making any sense. Explain it to me in small words because I'm afraid I may be having comprehension issues. I thought it was what you wanted. Why wouldn't you get on the plane? You said yourself you worked for it your whole life. It's everything you ever wanted." I don't know why I'm arguing—having him back is all I've been thinking about since he left. After what I put him through, though, I can't fathom the thought of being the reason he walks away from something he loves so much.

"It's just a job. If it was everything I ever wanted, it wouldn't have felt so wrong taking it. Besides, before I left the fire department here offered me a position. Hell, they're hurting for bodies now they practically begged me to take it."

"I don't understand," I admit with a shake of my head. "Working at a small-town fire department isn't the same as jumping out of planes into wildfires. Would that even make you happy?"

He lifts a hand to cup my nape and warmth spreads all over me. I didn't think I'd ever feel that safe, protective warmth again. When I can meet his eyes again it's through a haze of tears in mine. "It took the time without you to realize I don't want to be anywhere if you and Gracie aren't there."

I can't help the smile that spreads over my lips. Then I frown, demanding through a voice laced thick with tears, "Don't play with me unless you mean it."

"I'm not messing with you. I mean it. Following my dreams doesn't mean anything if I do it alone. It's just going through the motions. I'm staying here in Battleboro. I want to be with you and Gracie."

"Wait. Wait. You don't have to do this because you think you have to. I told you I'd make your relationship with Gracie work. You don't have to give up everything for me."

"I'm not giving up anything. Having a life with you and Gracie—that's everything. That means more to me than any job."

"Are you sure?"

He leans forward, kisses my objections away. "I've never been surer of anything in my life."

LATER AFTER THE LONGEST SHIFT OF MY LIFE, WALKER PULLS ME INTO THE house and shuts the front door behind me. Grandma Rosie is long since asleep and Gracie is knocked out after the ride back from daycare, so they aren't disturbed when I giggle as he pushes me against the door and takes my mouth in a hot, sweet kiss.

"This is what I was hoping you'd do the night we met," he says against my lips as fire burns me up from the inside out. "It was killing me not getting to taste you."

His lips travel down my throat, making my reply breathless and desperate. "I wanted to so bad, but I chickened out." His mouth finds mine again and I pant when he breaks free. "What else did you want to do?" I ask, wanting to torture us both a little. It's been a long time…too long, but I want to make it last.

Walker grins wickedly. "Why don't I show you instead?"

My throat goes bone dry. All I can do is nod my assent.

He leads me back to my room on the back side of the house where he patiently, competently strips me of my clothes. Spreading me out before him, he crouches between my legs like a man at a feast. My fingers fist in the comforter as his mouth explores the delicate flesh. My thighs begin to shake at his careful ministrations. When I attempt to vise his head with my legs, his strong fingers clamp down on the trembling muscles and hold me wide for his attention.

"Please," I beg.

But if he hears me, he pays no mind. Clearly, he also wants to torture us both a little… or a lot.

I toss and turn as he brings me to the edge and back again several times. It's the most exquisite kind of torture. When I'm coated in a fine sheen of sweat, he finally pulls away to yank off his shirt and tug off his pants. Gloriously naked and hard, he climbs on top of me, fitting between my legs like he was made to be there.

When he slides inside me, it feels like coming home, like I'd been waiting for this moment since the morning when I'd left him asleep in that bed.

His fingers comb through my hair to grip my scalp and he says, "Look at me. I want you to look at me for this." I think he means to look at him when I come, because *God* I'm close, but then he says, "I love you, Avery. I think I have since the night I met you."

My heart stumbles and I grip him closer to me. "You what?"

"You want to hear it again?" he says, his mouth teasing my ear. "Greedy."

"It wouldn't hurt," I admit.

His smile strikes me in all the soft, tender places inside me. "You tell me first and I will."

"You've already said it!" He slides deep and I groan. "Okay. You're right. I love you, too. I think that's why I ran the first time. You scared the shit out of me." Then he kisses me hard and when I have a moment to breathe, I gasp. "We'll talk later."

And then he smiles and it's blinding, and I realize we'll have forever now for I love yous. For our family. For us.

Forever with him sounds like the best sort of beginning I could imagine.

Like a rainbow after a hurricane.

THE END.

MY RUIN
BY JACOB CHANCE

PROLOGUE

EMMETT

HAVE YOU EVER WONDERED WHERE YOU WENT WRONG? WHAT WAS THE ONE moment that changed the course of your carefully planned future?

Which simple decision set you on a path of self-destruction you never imagined you'd be going down?

For me it was a day four years ago. I can't forget, no matter how hard I've tried. And believe me, I've fucking tried. I still remember every moment as if it happened only yesterday…

FOUR YEARS AGO

THERE WAS A CHANGE IN THE AIR THAT MORNING WHEN MY EYES LAZILY fluttered open. Blinking repeatedly, the dark blue constellation-covered ceiling came into sharper focus as my sleep-filled vision cleared. Lying still, a low thrum of excitement coursed through my veins, and though I sensed the noticeable shift in the energy surrounding me, I didn't think anything of it.

Casting the premonition aside like any teenager would, I turned my thoughts to more important things, like my best friend Liz and the fast approaching end of high school.

Little did I know what I perceived as a small intangible ripple of something new and exciting, was actually foreboding of what was to come. Fate had set in motion events that would almost cost me my future.

I'd heard more times than I could remember how your life can change in a split second, but I never gave it any thought. I was an eighteen-year-old boy. I lived for the here and now and didn't deal with what ifs or worry about consequences. I submerged myself in a sea of narcissism and I contentedly floated there. The world revolved around me alone and I never had any plans for that to change.

Until I met her.

In a single moment, my whole world was thrown off its axis and I fell hard—head over fucking heels.

One glance in her clear, green eyes set me on a path I'd never intended to travel.

There was no way I could've known all the heartache that would stem from our gazes connecting for the first time.

I wish I would've realized the simple act of our palms meeting in an innocent handshake would be the catalyst for so much devastation.

Now, I have to live with the fallout our actions set in motion.

Lives were ruined from one innocent touch.

PART ONE

CHAPTER ONE

EMMETT

THE SCRATCHING AND SCUFFING OF THE RAKE DRAGGING ACROSS THE ground is a familiar sound at my house this time of year. Massachusetts winters are cold and, for the most part, snowy. We might luck out every few years with a milder one, but this winter, that wasn't the case.

We'd been buried under blankets of white for months, and now that it's Memorial Day weekend, it's my job to do a spring cleanup on our yard. It's usually done the first week of May, but I had finals to study for and senior activities to attend. My parents cut me some slack, but now that I just graduated, I can't put it off any longer—no matter how much I wish I could. I've only been out here for two hours and I'm already sick of yard work.

Why can't my parents hire someone to do this shit like all the other people in our neighborhood do?

Tugging the ball cap down, sheltering my eyes from the blazing sun, I continue working to clear away any leaves leftover from fall. I'm almost finished with the section along the side of our property when a moving truck reverses into the driveway next to ours. The high-pitched beeping of the backup warning breaks through the silence of the afternoon.

Keeping my focus on the task at hand, I work to knock the rest of this out as soon as possible. I need to get online with my friends. We have a big match planned tonight on one of our favorite gaming sites and it's against some other kids who went to school with us. The winning team only gets bragging rights, but it doesn't take much to make us happy.

Hearing the sharp slam of a truck door, I notice a guy who looks like he's in his early twenties—possibly a college student. His dark blond hair is long, falling just shy of his broad shoulders. He's tall and lanky like a basketball player. Looking over, he catches me staring. Shoving his hands in the front pockets of his jeans, he raises his chin in acknowledgement. I do the same, pausing to take a break and check out the happenings going on.

The house next to ours is a cape style with dark blue shutters and a two-car garage. It recently sold, and there's been a lot of speculation about who might be moving into this close-knit neighborhood. A shiny silver sedan pulls in beside the truck, and I wait to see who our new neighbor might be.

The driver-side door opens and a woman steps out. The first thing I notice is how long and lean her legs look wrapped in tight-fitting jeans with brown ankle boots. When she faces the car and bends at the waist to reach inside, I'm pleasantly surprised by the sight of her generously curved ass. Damn. It's the definition of heart-shaped.

She straightens up, slings a purse over her shoulder, and shuts the car door.

Returning to the job at hand, I resume raking the lawn, but like any teenage boy, I'm still picturing her ass.

"Hi there." A husky voice breaks into my lust-filled thoughts and clears my head of the inappropriate older woman fantasy I'm currently indulging in. My stomach muscles clench in reaction to her sexy tone. Tentatively flicking my eyes in her direction, all conscious thought of anything else flees when they meet her curious gaze. I lose my ability to speak for a moment. The rest of the world disappears around me while I'm submerged in a tropical sea of green that I'd happily drown in. She's beautiful beyond belief with her shoulder-length sandy brown hair and deep pink, kissable lips.

"Hi, I'm Emmett," I break the silence, my eyes remaining on hers. I couldn't move them if I tried. I'm locked in place, held captive by this energy buzzing between us.

"I'm Juliet Thatcher. It's nice to meet you." She extends her graceful hand for me to shake. Holding my left arm around the rake, I extend my right hand. Our palms meet, my large one swallows the cool, pale delicacy of hers. My ears ring when our skin touches for the first time—or maybe I'm imagining the high-pitched whine. Her hand in mine feels right, like I've been waiting for this moment all my life.

Her thickly lashed eyes flicker with surprise. *She feels it too.*

"It's nice meeting you, Mrs. Thatcher." My voice is a hoarse croak. Releasing her hand, I grip the rake's handle like a lifeline. I'm not comfortable with what just happened. She's our new neighbor and a grown woman. I have enough to deal with already. I tick items off my fast growing mental checklist of why I need to stay away from Mrs. Thatcher. I'm sure I can come up with many more when she's not within sight and I'm able to think clearly once again.

Why am I so attracted to her?
Because she's gorgeous.
I shouldn't be.
When have I ever done things the easy way?

"Please, call me Juliet." I give her a stiff nod, knowing I won't be calling her anything other than her full name. It can serve as a reminder of the vast differences between us.

Turning back to the task at hand, I ignore her presence while she remains quiet, observing my every move. There are leaves trapped between some shrubs that I focus on clearing out. Thick and wet from the rainy weather we've been having, it's not as easy as it normally is. Add in the fact that Juliet—I mean, Mrs. Thatcher—is watching, and I'm all thumbs. My tired muscles tingle from her heavy gaze.

"It was nice meeting you." Juliet's words break through the sound of my harsh breathing that's caused by a combination of physical exertion and her nearness.

"Yeah, you too." My eyes stay focused on the ground. *Do not glance at her.*

"I look forward to getting to know you better, Emmett." Mrs. Thatcher's soft voice is as sexy as she is. I squeeze my eyes shut and tell my dick to relax. It's only a voice and one I won't be hearing very often if I can help it.

"Bye," I mumble. Staying focused on clearing the yard for the next hour or so is my priority. Using every bit of restraint I can muster, I never once allow myself to look over at the house next door. Instead, I think about the future I've got planned out. I'll be at Ohio State for the next four years on a full athletic scholarship and then I'll be drafted to the NFL. I find myself grinning as I think about what's to come. The future sure looks bright.

CHAPTER TWO

EMMETT

"ARE YOU READY?"

Liz thoughtfully chews on the left corner of her lower lip before exhaling with a large sigh. "Yeah, as ready as I'll ever be."

I wink at her encouragingly. "Let's do this." Opening the door, I gesture for her to precede me inside The Bean Hub. The bright fluorescent lighting is harsh on our eyes at first and we both squint. "I might need glasses after working here." She giggles. She's not wrong. I'm still seeing spots everywhere I look.

We move forward until we reach the back of the long line of people waiting to order. I maneuver Liz in front of me and my hands land on her shoulders. Resting my chin on her head, I say, "I'm gonna grab a table and stay here for a little bit."

She nods and smiles over her shoulder. "You're such a great friend. How did I get so lucky?"

"We both know I'm lucky that you put up with me."

She spins in my arms and rises on her toes to hug me. Tugging her closer, I wrap my arms around her. We've always been affectionate with each other and we've never once crossed the line. I can't speak for Liz, but I've never been tempted to. I value our friendship too much to jeopardize it in any way. I can't picture my future without her by my side. We're going to different colleges in the fall, which will be a big adjustment for both of us. But ultimately, the distance will make us appreciate each other more.

A throat clears behind us and we break apart to find the line has moved on without us. Liz's cheeks flush pink with embarrassment as we shuffle forward to catch up. "I'll see you in a bit. I'm gonna go clock in and talk to the manager." She rubs her lips together and anxiously rocks back and forth on her feet.

"Liz, relax. It's just a job. If it doesn't work out, there are a hundred other places looking for help."

She smiles. "You always know just what to say to me."

I shrug my broad shoulders. "I'm a smart guy."

"And a humble one," she quips, stepping out of line and heading toward the back of the shop.

Once it's my turn, I place my order and take a seat at one of the tables. With my back to the wall, I have an unobstructed view of the entire space and I immediately notice Liz when she steps behind the counter. She looks so cute in the red apron her hands busily tie behind her back. Glancing up, she catches my eye, and we share a smile.

Sitting quietly, I drink my hot chocolate along with keeping an eye on Liz. She seems like she's perfectly comfortable behind the counter. If I didn't know her, I'd assume she'd been here for months, and judging by the lingering glances some of the male customers are giving her, she might be a little too proficient at this job.

The bell on the door jingles as it opens, catching my attention. My stomach sinks when I see Mrs. Thatcher entering.

Shit.

Our eyes meet before I can look away, and she smiles. "Emmett, it's nice to see you again."

"Hi, Mrs. Thatcher." My voice remains steady despite being shook by her sudden appearance. My leg bounces nonstop under the table like a jackhammer.

"Please, call me Juliet. Mrs. Thatcher sounds like an old lady."

"Sure, Juliet." What choice do I have when she's mentioned it to me twice?

She comes to stand at the edge of the table, and my heart thumps so forcefully, I'm sure she can hear it. "So, I have a proposition for you."

"Okay." I have no idea where she's going with this.

"I have a lot of yard work that needs to be done and also a pool that needs to be opened. I'd like to hire you to help me out." She shifts from one foot to the other, and I wonder if she's nervous about asking me. "I mean, if that's something you'd be interested in, and I'd pay you for your time," she adds.

"You don't have to pay me." Being around you would be payment enough.

"Oh, I insist. What I need done is hard work and I won't let you help me for free."

I smile. "If you insist."

"Excellent. We can schedule at a later time."

I want to ask when and what time. But it's not like I won't make sure my whole day is wide open for her.

"Sounds good."

"I'll see you then." Her toothy smile is happiness personified, and I want to see it as often as possible.

I nod.

She gives me a small wave and gets in line. My eyes leave her to search for Liz and I find her studying Juliet. I'm sure she's wondering who she is and will ask me later. I gulp down the rest of my hot chocolate before Juliet ends up sitting near me. Being around her was just as exciting, if not more so, as yesterday.

Rising to my feet, I pause and wait for Liz to look my way. When our gazes connect, I smile and wave. She returns the gesture as I back out the door. I try not to seek out Juliet with my eyes, but the draw is too powerful and I give in. She's at the counter waiting for her order. And her ass looks even better than I remember.

AFTER I LEFT LIZ'S WORK, I MET THE GUYS AT THE GYM. WE ALL WORKED OUT together and then played some basketball. Now, I'm chowing down on some pizza at my favorite restaurant with Tom, a friend from school.

"Where's Liz working again?" he asks.

"Today's her first day at The Bean Hub. I hope she likes it. She was wicked nervous."

"What's she got to be nervous about? It's not brain surgery, and she's making money. It beats school," he says.

I nod. "Yeah, if we got paid to go to school, it would sweeten the pot for sure. I can't wait to be done with school forever."

"Dude, what's the rush?" Tom questions. "We have the whole summer and it's sure to be sick. It's our last hurrah together before we all go our separate ways for college. We better make the most of it."

"We will," I say. I have no doubt that this summer will be the best one of my life.

"Dude, my parents told me we can use their Cape house for a week in August. They're not gonna be there. We can have a mad party and check out all the babes," Tom tells me.

"That's awesome," I say, rising. "I've gotta get home. I want to get up earlier than I have been and go for a run."

"You can run any time of the day."

"Yeah, but I have other stuff I need to do later on."

Tom holds his fist out for me to bump and then I head out the door.

The drive home takes only five minutes. When I park my SUV in our driveway and scoop my workout bag from the seat, I notice Mrs. Thatcher struggling with grocery bags. "Fuck," I mutter under my breath, dropping my backpack in the driver's seat, before closing the door. After my weird reaction yesterday, I don't want to be within five feet of her, but I can't ignore that she needs help.

I cross over the patch of grass separating the two driveways. "Let me help you with those," I call out as I approach.

She peeks her head out from behind the trunk and smiles. "Talk about a lifesaver. I was dreading having to carry all these by myself."

"No problem, I'm happy to help." I string four bags on each arm and grab a twenty-four pack of water. "Where do you want me... I mean these?" I clench my teeth to keep myself from blurting out a four-letter word at my slip of the tongue.

"Follow me," she replies without hesitation. Falling in behind as she moves, I order myself not to stare at her ass wrapped in faded, tight, blue jeans like a gift I can't wait to open.

We enter the house through the garage, which is still jammed full of boxes. "One of these days, I'll finish unpacking and be able to park my car in here."

My eyes take in the organized mudroom separating the garage from her kitchen. Looks like she's gotten some boxes emptied. "Unpacking sucks. I was young when my grandparents moved into their house, but I still remember my mother was miserable for weeks," I say. "Every day we'd head over to help them. That's time I'll never get back," I joke.

She laughs. "Yeah, I don't think anyone enjoys having to pack or unpack. Both are equally horrible."

"I think packing is worse," I state.

"Really? Why's that?" she inquires, setting the bags she's carrying on the granite counter.

"Because once you unpack you're done. When you pack, you still have more work to do on the other end."

"Good point." She winks, and my stomach lurches. "You can just drop everything on the floor and I'll take care of the rest."

Gently setting the water down, I place the bags on the counter along with the others. "I'll go grab the rest."

"Thank you, Emmett, You're such a big help."

"Anytime," I call over my shoulder as I head back outside. Picking up the remaining bags, I close her trunk and retrace my steps back to the kitchen. Mrs. Thatcher is busy putting all the groceries away, so I set the remainder down on the floor. I watch as she reaches to place things on the top shelf of the pantry before bending over to stack cans on the bottom shelf. I could watch her put groceries away all night. But I can't. I need to go home. "Do you need help with this stuff?" I gesture to the remaining bags to be polite.

"No, Emmett, that's really sweet of you to offer, but you've done more than enough." Straightening from her bent over position, she rubs her hands along the thighs of her jeans, calling attention to her legs. "Let me give you something for your time," she offers, reaching for her purse.

"No," I bark out louder than I intend. "Absolutely not." I shake my head and scowl. "I won't take your money just for being neighborly. Yard work is one thing, but five minutes of doing the right thing is completely different."

"I guess I'll have to figure out another way to pay you." I breathe in her smooth, sexy voice like a hit of my favorite weed. I'd be lying if I didn't admit I'm more than a little curious about what she has in mind.

"That's not necessary. I'm happy to help you with whatever you need."

"Do you like baked goods?"

"Yes, ma'am. Especially if they're homemade."

She scrunches her slightly turned up nose. "Ma'am? I'm only twenty-eight."

She's ten years older than me.

"I didn't mean to insult you. I'm just using my manners."

"I know you didn't. I'm teasing. You're such a polite young man. Your parents must be very proud of you." I'm at a loss for what to say because I'm not so sure they are. I can't remember them ever complimenting me like that. I jerk my shoulders in a quick shrug.

"You don't have to be so humble with me. I'd like to think we're already fast friends." Her full, berry-red lips tip up at the edges, tempting me.

"My parents aren't really the type to dole out praise. I imagine they're proud, but they expect a lot from me," I answer candidly.

"How old are you, Emmett?" she questions. Her green eyes appraise me, slowly moving up and down my body like a familiar caress.

How old do you want me to be?

"How old do you think I am?"

Her pink tongue peeks out to sweep the fullness of her bottom lip as she continues to study me. My dick twitches in reaction, and I quickly glance away. I can't be getting excited by the thought of her tongue and what it could do to me. *Fuck.*

"I have a feeling you look older than you are."

"I'm eighteen."

The sound of her boot heels clicking against the hardwood floor has my head turning to watch as she glides smoothly toward me. Stopping when there's only a foot of distance between us, she taps the tip of her index finger to her lips and hums while her eyes study me.

I can't remember ever being so sexually attracted to someone I just met. Her spicy scent and the sexy little sound she made have me clenching both fists at my sides. I remind myself of the age difference, but it doesn't help. *At all.*

My gaze locks on Mrs. Thatcher's shiny mouth and visions of what she could do with those plump lips assault my mind. Fuck. I'm an asshole. Here she is trying to have a polite conversation and I'm lusting after her.

"I have to go," I blurt out. Spinning on the rubber soles of my sneakers, I rush from her house as if I'm being chased. Grabbing my backpack from the front seat of my car, I hurry along the driveway to the side entrance. My fingers fumble as I insert the key into the lock. Once inside, my bag falls to the hardwood floor as I slam the door. My heart jumping like it's skipping rope, I lean both hands flat against the steel, barricading it with my body. The absurdity of the situation crashes into me like an unexpected wave. Only, instead of getting doused with water, I'm awash with shame.

"That was a close fucking call, Hawkins," I mumble, shaking my head in equal parts relief and disgust.

CHAPTER THREE
EMMETT

MY FINGERS DIG INTO HER HIPS, ROCKING HER AGAINST THE HARD LENGTH of my cock. She moans as I suck on the delicate skin below her ear. Her nails dig into the top of my shoulders when I add my teeth, biting her neck. "Oh… Emmett." Her head drops back. "Don't… mmm… stop."

"No fucking way," I growl, gripping the back of her head with one hand. My mouth trails down the length of her ivory neck, placing hot, wet kisses. She grinds on my lap, and my eyes squeeze shut at the exquisite pleasure. "God, I want inside you, baby."

"Me too," she whispers.

Capturing her lips with mine, I swallow her sighs of pleasure with a kiss. Our tongues tangle as I rock her back and forth on my dick, driving us both insane. She clings to me, and the twinge in my chest grows into a full-blown ache.

Tearing our mouths apart, I watch as she rides me, driving us both closer to release. I'm about to come in my pants and I don't care. I want nothing more than to be buried inside her, but my parents are due to come home any moment now. We definitely don't have time for all I want to do to her.

Juliet's cheeks are flushed pink and her lips are swollen from my kisses. She's the hottest thing I've ever seen with her passion-glazed eyes and tousled hair. I want to capture this moment like a snapshot in my mind forever.

The loud chime of the doorbell breaks through the sound of our harsh breathing. Juliet doesn't stop rocking her pussy into my cock. "Go away, I'm so close," she groans.

The bell rings again and I snap awake on the couch. "Fuck," I grit out, pissed that someone woke me from my dream. I roll to my feet and growl, muttering, "This better be fucking important." Stalking toward the door, I press down on my dick. I don't even look through the peephole as I turn the knob, ready to bite off whoever's head is unlucky enough to be standing on the other side.

My expression is murderous, but the moment I see Mrs. Thatcher's captivating eyes go wide with surprise, my scowl melts away.

"I'm sorry to bother you. I'm sure you must be busy," she apologizes.

I smile and shake my head. "No, it's okay. Do you want to come in?" I step back as Mrs. Thatcher moves past the threshold. *Shit. Why did I just ask her inside?*

"I wanted to thank you again for your help earlier. I made you some cookies." She smiles and hands me a plastic container.

Opening the cover, I peek inside. "Chocolate chip are my favorite." I swipe one and take a bite. They're still warm from the oven, and the chocolate melts on my tongue. "This is delicious." Snapping the cover back on, I set the container down on the bench near the door. "I can't believe you made me cookies. No one's ever done that for me before."

She arches one eyebrow. "Really?"

"Yeah. My mom works a lot. She doesn't have time for much else."

"I'm happy to make you cookies, or whatever else you'd like, anytime. I find it relaxing, so don't be afraid to ask." She places her warm hand on my arm, and blood pulses directly to my cock. Swallowing over the lump in my throat, I can only hope she doesn't notice the growing bulge in my pants.

"Thank you," I reply, my voice a ragged husk. Guilt and disgust consume me. She's merely trying to be nice to her new neighbor, and I'm getting turned on like a prepubescent teenager with no control over his dick. I'm beginning to despise the way my body reacts to Mrs. Thatcher. I've never had this happen to me before and I'm hoping it will stop soon.

I flick a glance toward Mrs. Thatcher and find a thoughtful expression on her face. "Well, I just wanted to drop the cookies off while they're fresh. I'm sure you have things to do. Have a good night, and thanks again, Emmett." She turns toward the door.

Don't look at her ass. Don't look at her ass. I chant to myself as I follow behind her, but it's no use. Of course my gaze locks on her curvaceous rear—I'm eighteen and she's wearing yoga pants for fuck's sake.

Who could resist?

"Let me get that." She pauses when I reach past her for the doorknob, placing the front of my body against the back of hers. The floral scent of her hair wafts up, teasing my nose, and the cushion of her ass bumps into my still semi-hard dick. My teeth dig into my bottom lip, suppressing a groan. It takes all my willpower not to slam her face-first into the door and rub my cock between her ass cheeks.

Tugging the door open, I step back and usher her out with a hand between her shoulder blades, needing some distance between us immediately. Of course, touching her isn't the best idea, but she needs to leave my house, stat.

The spotlight mounted to the side of the door isn't on and her face is cast in shadows. Her eyes appear dark and mysterious, instead of their usual calming, green color, but I can see them locked on mine.

"You better hurry home before the mosquitoes get you. Thanks again for the cookies."

"No need to thank me." She flutters her fingers in a graceful wave, and I find myself watching until she's safely home. Stepping back inside, I close the door and breathe a sigh of relief.

Pivoting around, I pick up the cookie container and head to my room. There's no way I'm sharing these with my parents. Sinking onto my bed, I let my thoughts drift into dangerous territory. *Maybe she made the cookies because she's interested in me.*

No way. I can't even indulge that line of thinking. Why would she be interested in me? *Good question.*

FLAMES AND SPARKS SHOOT UP FROM THE FIRE PIT WITH EACH POP AND crackle of burning wood. Watching the glowing flames is mesmerizing. They pulse and flair with ever-changing energy, and having Liz next to me adds to the rightness of this moment. This is the most relaxed I've felt since Mrs. Thatcher moved in last week. The night she dropped off the cookies was the last time I've seen her. With each new day, I think I blew the whole situation out of proportion in my mind. She's a beautiful, older woman. What eighteen-year-old wouldn't find her attractive? What I felt for her was nothing more than a normal hormonal reaction.

Liz leans into my side, like a kitten who always wants to cuddle. I don't mind. She's always there when I need a sounding board. If she needs a pillow, or anything else, I'm her guy.

"How's work been?" I ask.

Her head remains on my shoulder, but I feel her quick shrug. "It's okay. I don't love it, but I also don't hate it, so I guess it's not too bad." I laugh. "What?" she asks.

"Your logic is crazy."

She snorts. "This from the guy who screwed Mindi Allan."

"What? She's hot."

"Typical guy, thinking with his dick," she scoffs.

And I'm still doing it two years later.

"Are you going to come visit me at school?" I ask to change the subject.

"I could ask you the same question," she retorts.

"Yes, of course, I'll come visit you. What a dumb question."

"You asked it first," she points out.

Only to get my mind off Mrs. Thatcher.

"Right. We'll see each other on holidays and vacations. But I don't want you to miss me too much," I tease.

"Please. We both know who's going to miss whom. I might be able to sneak off to Ohio for a few weekends. My grandmother gave me some money and told me to use it for something fun. I can't think of anything better to spend it on than visiting you." She smiles.

"We also know who's the sappy friend, and it's not me." I wink.

"EMMETT, HOW HAVE YOU BEEN?" JULIET CALLS OUT AS SHE CLOSES THE door to her car. Slinging her purse over her shoulder, she walks from her driveway, across the strip of grass, and over to where I'm standing.

"Hi." I smile. I don't mean to encourage her in any way, but I can't say I'm sorry to see her. I like Juliet. She's a nice woman. "I'm good, thanks. How about you?"

"I'm well, but it's tough being here alone. I'm dying for some conversation besides the one-sided ones I have with myself."

Leaning down, I dunk the large sponge in the bucket of soapy water and resume washing the hood of my SUV. "You should get out more or introduce yourself to more of the neighbors."

"The other homeowners in the neighborhood haven't been as welcoming as you."

"Really? There are a lot of older people in this particular area of town who've been here for decades. My parents have been here for twenty years. Maybe they're feeling territorial because the family who used to live in your house had been here for fifty years."

"I guess that makes sense," she replies.

"Once they get used to you being here, they'll probably feel more comfortable with the change." Dipping the sponge into the bucket, I bend over and put some muscle into scrubbing a dead bug off the headlight.

"Do you have sunscreen on?"

"No." I shake my head. "I brought it out with me and forgot to put some on."

"Well, your shoulders are looking pretty red. Want me to apply some for you?"

I glance down at one shoulder and then the other and they do appear to be getting burnt. "Fuck." I drop the sponge in the bucket and walk over to grab the sunscreen off the deck stairs where I left it.

"Here, let me." Juliet walks toward me with her palm outstretched. I find myself handing off the bottle without a word as I rub my wet hands on my shorts. She squirts the white lotion into her palm and passes the bottle back to me. Rubbing her hands together, she moves directly in front of me and deliberately slides her hands up my pecs and over my shoulders. Her captivating eyes reverently trace over my skin and her red tongue darts out to lick her bottom lip. Fuck. Having her hands on me is temptation personified. My jaw is clenched, teeth gritting together as I fight off the urge to kiss her.

Juliet reverses direction, sliding back down to my pecs before spreading the sunscreen over the remainder of my chest and along the tops of my shoulders. Her hands massage up the sides of my neck, her palms dragging over the thick, dark stubble as they run along the sides of my jawline. Can she feel how taught my muscles are? I'm strung so tight, I'm sure to snap like a guitar string.

Our eyes meet, her irises shimmering beneath the sunlight, and every logical thought leaves my head. My gaze skims down to her bow-shaped lips, the bottom one plump and biteable. I'm gripped with a crushing need to taste them. I lean forward, and Juliet takes a step back, eyes darting in every direction but mine.

"I should get inside. I have… uh, stuff to do." She's flustered.

"Yeah, I need to finish up before the soap dries."

"See you later." She whirls around and races to her house.

What a dumbass. I curse myself for my rash behavior. Now things are sure to be awkward between us.

CHAPTER FOUR

EMMETT

"HEY, THERE. I WAS HOPING I'D BUMP INTO YOU," MRS. THATCHER CALLS OUT as she walks over to stand on the strip of lawn separating the two yards.

My head swivels around and my eyes bulge when I notice the red bikini adorning her lithe frame. I've seen plenty of bikini clad bodies, but none as alluring as hers. The triangles of the top and the strings on each side of her bottoms are a tease. My fingers are already itching to slide the triangles apart and pull on the ends of each tie and watch them unravel. If it wasn't for the mirrored shades I have on, she'd notice my gawking stare.

Hell, if she glances down at my groin, she'll know how much being around her affects me. My cock automatically responds to the sight of her. I can't seem to control my body's impulses when she's around. Which is why I've been trying to avoid her as much as possible. But here we are…

"Hi, what's up?" I keep my tone flat. I haven't seen her in a few days. Not since the "almost kiss".

"I saw you vacuuming your pool and I was wondering if you could help me with something?"

Inwardly, I groan. I don't want to spend any time alone with her. It's too hard—in every way you can imagine. But I can't be an asshole. It's not her fault that I'm so attracted to her. And at this point, it goes beyond physical attraction. She's intelligent and kind. I like talking with her and being in her company. "Sure, what do you need?"

"I can't seem to get the vacuum to work. It's not sucking properly."

I bet you know how to suck properly.

Shit. Stop. I scold myself. I can't seem to rein in the unbidden thoughts. They come as they please, usually whenever she opens her mouth.

I'd like to see her open her mouth around my… fuck. I sigh and rake a hand through my hair in frustration.

"Let me take a look and see if something's blocking the hose." Walking beside her, we head toward her backyard. "I used to swim in this pool all the time when I was younger. The former owners had a grandson my age."

"Well, you're welcome to come over and swim anytime you want. I could use the company."

Glancing her way, I take in the gentle curve of her smiling lips. Pink and shiny, they remind me of the inside of a watermelon—my favorite fruit. I wonder if they taste as good. Are her nipples the same color? What about her—.

"I'm sorry. I didn't mean to make things weird," Mrs. Thatcher yanks me back to the present.

"Huh?" I question, snapping out of my lust-infused fog. "I'm sorry, I missed what you said."

"I said, I didn't mean to make things awkward by inviting you over."

Shit. Now she feels bad and she has no reason to. I'm the one who made things awkward between us. I'm the one who can't keep my feelings for her reined in. I smile to ease her concern. "No, it's all good. In fact, how about we take a swim once I get your vacuum straightened out?"

"I think that's a great idea." She peers over her shoulder at me as she opens the gate on the fence surrounding her back yard. Her eyes sparkle, hinting at how lonely she truly must be if the thought of swimming with me makes her so happy.

I like Mrs. Thatcher and her mild manner. She's so easy to be around. If it weren't for my attraction to her, I'd want to spend more time in her company.

We continue across her expansive patio to where the hose is stretched out on the ground.

"I'm really not sure what the problem could be. I used it last week with no issues." She tucks one side of her hair behind an ear.

"First, I'm going to run some water through and see if it's clear." I turn on the outdoor faucet. Grabbing the garden hose, I place it on the end of the unconnected vacuum hose. The water should run through to the other end, but it's not. Shutting the water off, I wipe my hands on my board shorts. "Do you have a broom handle? Or a plumber's snake? Either one could work."

"You know, there was a broom handle left in the pool shed from the former owner. I wondered why, but I guess now I know." She giggles. "I'll go grab it."

I watch her walk off toward the shed, bikini bottoms revealing the bottom of her ass cheeks. *Damn.* She's got the perfect amount of jiggle going on.

Is there any part of her body that isn't banging? I force myself to look away until she's handing me the broom handle.

"Hopefully this works, because if it doesn't, I'm not sure what the problem is." Inserting the handle, I push it through as far as it will go, before repeating the same steps from the other end of the hose. "Let's try the water test again and see if we have better luck now." Turning on the faucet, I direct the stream of water into the end of the vacuum hose and this time it runs out the other end, along with the clump of leaves that must've been what was clogging it up.

"Yay," she shouts, jumping up and down. My eyes zoom in another direction like my pupils are in danger of getting burned by the sight of her. "This calls for a celebration," she announces. "How about a sandwich? Are you hungry?"

I rub a hand over my stomach and smile. "I'm always hungry."

"Excellent. Make yourself at home and I'll be right back." Winking, she hurries off. I settle myself on a comfortable lounger, clasping my hands behind my head. I close my eyes and let the beautiful early June afternoon envelop me. Birds are chirping happily, a slight breeze is wafting over me, and I'm feeling content.

"Here, I thought you might like some lemonade." She hands me the cold glass, and our fingertips brush. "I made these cookies this morning, they're chocolate chip." She winks, placing the plate down on the small table next to the chaise I'm kicked back on. "I figured I'd cover all bases."

If she made these this morning, then she must have been planning to see me. Unless she eats an ungodly amount of cookies by herself. My heart races at the thought of this amazing woman seeking out my company.

"Thank you, Mrs. Thatcher," I manage to reply, despite my racing thoughts. Grabbing a cookie, I raise it to my lips, biting off a large chunk. Cookies never tasted so good. "Mmm, this is delicious."

"I thought I told you to call me Juliet? Mrs. Thatcher is my mother-in-law."

She's married?

I cough, choking on cookie crumbs. I take a sip of my lemonade and clear my throat. "You're married?"

She shakes her head, her expression turning serious. "No, I was. My husband was in the army. He was killed in the line of duty two years ago."

Oh, damn. Not what I was expecting to hear.

"I'm sorry. That must be hard for you." And I really am. It's heartbreaking to think of someone as sweet as Juliet is having something so horrible happen to her.

She sits down on the edge of the chaise next to mine and remains facing me. "It hasn't been easy, but it's getting less painful every day. The first year was surreal. I felt lost. I went from happily married, to widowed at twenty-six."

I shake my head. "I can't imagine what you went through."

"When Chris passed, I not only lost him but the military life I'd grown to love and all the friends we'd made."

"That's a lot for someone so young to deal with," I tell her.

"It was. In the blink of an eye, my world flipped over. I lost my own identity and struggled to figure out who I was without my husband—without my military family."

"Did your own family help you?"

"I went to live with my parents in Maine. I stayed with them until I moved here."

"What made you choose this area?"

"I wanted a fresh start and I've always loved Boston."

"It might've been easier to move somewhere near your family."

"Maybe, but I need to learn to stand on my own two feet."

"From what I've seen, it seems like you're doing well."

"I get so lonely. I don't have any friends or family in this area."

"Do you work?" I ask. I've never seen her keep a regular schedule.

"I'm a painter, so I work from home."

"Like an artist?"

She smiles. "Yes, exactly. I'm an artist. Which is another reason I chose Boston. I have some connections here at a couple of art galleries."

"Can I see your work sometime?" I question. I don't want to be pushy, but I'm impressed by her job. Hell, I'm impressed by everything about her, and I'd like to see what she paints.

"Sure. I have some of my paintings displayed inside, and my studio is almost set up."

"How did you end up buying a house here in this neighborhood?"

Her eyes wander over her backyard. "This place felt right when I saw it online, but once I saw it in person, I knew I was home." Mouth gently curving contentedly, she leans back with her palms on the cushion, supporting her upper body. "I like the close proximity to the city without sacrificing the backyard." Her eyes settle on me. "And the next-door neighbor's not too bad." She smiles, and I bark out a laugh. Tingles erupt from the top of my head and move down through me when I notice the way her gaze leisurely traces over each part of my body. "You work out a lot." It's an observation, not a question, said in a breathy voice. "What else do you like to do with your free time?"

"I play football, hang with my friends, do whatever my parents need me to around the house. Gotta earn my keep." I shrug my shoulders.

"What about your girlfriend?" she asks.

"What girlfriend?"

"The girl I've seen you with. The one who works at the coffee shop."

"That's Liz. We're just friends."

"Really? I assumed there was more going on there."

I shake my head. "We've never crossed that line and we never will. She's like my sister. She's family to me."

"That's sweet. I never had a male friend… until now."

"I'm glad we're friends," I reply.

"Oh, I meant Mr. Vine and me. But you're okay too," she deadpans before giggling. Mr. Vine is our ninety-year-old neighbor who doesn't speak to anyone. She's adorable, and her laughter is contagious. Before I know it, I find myself joining in.

CHAPTER FIVE
EMMETT

I BRUSH THE CRUMBS FROM MY HANDS. "THANK YOU FOR LUNCH. THE sandwich was delicious. How about a swim?" I need to cool off in more ways than one, and it would be nice to get to a comfortable place with Juliet. Maybe the more time we spend together, the less attracted to her I'll be.

"Sure." She rises to her feet and walks to the edge of the pool to dip her toe in. "It might be a little cold at first, but I find it refreshing."

As I stand, I shove one more bite of cookie into my mouth and walk across the patio. I stop next to her and look down into the inviting crystal-clear water. "I haven't been for a swim yet this year."

"Well then, I guess it's time." Juliet uses both her hands to shove the middle of my back. She takes me by surprise, knocking me into the pool. The cold water feels icy against my sunbaked skin and surprisingly pleasant. I come up for air, laughing, and wipe the water from my face.

"I see how it's going to be." I grin like a shark. "Are you coming in or am I coming to get you?"

Juliet giggles and stretches her arms out in front of her, warding me away. "I'm coming in."

"Not fast enough." Pushing my hands through the waves, I send a curtain of water splashing her way.

"Aargh. Stop." She closes her eyes and turns her head to the side until I stop. Beads of water dot her bikini and drip down her golden skin. When she opens her eyes, I motion like I'm about to splash her again. She shrieks, jumping into the pool, and lands with a splash right in front of me. Immediately, we both begin propelling water at each other. Eyes squeezed shut, Juliet does her best to keep up with the onslaught I'm sending her way, but she's no match for my longer, stronger arms. She spins around, and a squeak escapes her lips while I continue forward, drenching her back.

"Okay, I give up. I give up," she yells, raising her arms over her head in surrender.

"Are you sure about that?" My arms slip around her waist from behind as I snatch her up in my grasp. Her back to my chest, I can feel the vibration as she giggles. "Or is this a ruse to get me closer so you can surprise me?"

"Let me go and find out," she dares.

"Hell no." I dive to the side, still holding on to her, and we go under together. A flurry of bubbles escapes both of our mouths as we laugh underwater. Releasing my hold, we both rise to the surface. As soon as my shoulders clear the water, Juliet is on me, doing her best to push me back under. She puts up a good fight, but her small frame is no match for my more muscular one. We end up laughing more than battling.

In an instant, we become cognizant of the close proximity of our two bodies, our laughter fading. Tits smashed to my chest, thighs clutching my hips, arms clasped around my neck, she's wrapped around me like a koala clinging to a tree branch.

My palms press flat to her back as I resist the urge for them to explore. Green desire-filled eyes framed with dark, wet, spiked lashes stare into mine. I'm frozen in place, trapped between my desire to connect our lips and my conscience telling me to break away. Juliet shifts her weight, and her taut nipples sear into my chest through the wet triangles of her top. Her legs clutch my hips tighter, pressing her pussy to my hard cock.

Clenching my teeth, I tell the voice screaming in my head to shut up as it urges me to kiss her. Though my will has never been challenged so much before, I somehow resist the temptation she presents. Gripping under her arms, I break our connection and set her down on her feet, a safe distance between us.

Raking a hand through my wet hair, I nervously struggle for what to say before settling on, "I'm sorry." She's been through so much already. She doesn't need me adding to it.

"Emmett." She shakes her head, stepping forward.

"No," I shout. "Don't. I'm gonna go now." I nod my head, repeating, "Yeah, I'm gonna go now," as if I'm convincing myself I'm doing the right thing.

"What if I don't want you to?"

"I think it's for the best."

"Says who?"

My conscience. "Me."

"I'm sorry. I didn't mean to pressure you in any way." Shoulders dropping, she turns around, wading through the water to the stairs. "Thank you for your help," she calls over her shoulder.

"Juliet, wait." Hoisting myself out the side of the pool, I leave a trail of water behind me on the patio as I hurry her way. I place a hand on her arm, my thumb caressing her damp skin. "You have nothing to apologize for. I can't think of anything I want more than to know what your lips taste like."

"I want that too."

"You've been through so much. I'm not sure we should cross that line."

"Waiting longer isn't going to change my past, Emmett."

"I know that. I want you to think about this and make sure you're ready for what will happen if we kiss."

"What do you think will happen?"

"I think you'll be my ruin."

"How so?"

"You'll be the woman who no one else will ever measure up to."

"You flatter me. There's only one way to find out for sure."

"You're right about that." I nod slowly. Should I step forward and slam our mouths together, consequences be damned? Or should I press pause and give us both time to make sure we're ready for what's to come?

"You never had that sandwich I promised." Juliet points out, making the decision for me.

I smile, the thick tension between us easing.

"HERE, I MADE YOU SOME SANDWICHES," MRS. THATCHER REACHES ACROSS the table to set the plate down in front of me. My eyes land on the tiny red bikini top barely covering her tits. She moves closer until she's behind my chair, the scent of her shampoo and chlorine teasing my nose. "I thought you might want to wash it down with an ice-cold beer. It will cool you off from all this heat." She leans forward, the front of her body making contact with my back as she places the green bottle down on the glass top. The touch is brief, and I imagine the sensation of her taut nipples grazing my skin.

"Thank you, Mrs. Thatcher," I reply with a raspy husk, my throat unusually dry. Grabbing the bottle, I take a deep pull and then another until half the liquid is gone.

"Emmett, I told you to call me Juliet. And this will be our little secret. You look old enough to drink." Her hand caresses from the nape of my neck to the top of my head in one smooth motion. "Your hair is so thick and soft." She combs her fingers through my dark strands. Her nails scrape my scalp, sending a shiver down my spine and blood rushing to my cock. *Fuck.* I can't react to her like this. Nothing can happen between us. At least not yet.

Pulling out the chair next to me, she sinks onto the seat and observes as I continue to eat the sandwiches. "I love a man with a healthy appetite." She winks.

"Would you like some?" I offer.

"Sure, I'll take a bite of whatever you're willing to give me."

Is she talking about the sandwich?

"You can have as much as you'd like," I reply, not sure what to say. I'm an eighteen-year-old boy, not used to dealing with grown women speaking in possible code.

I move to place the sandwich down on my plate, but Juliet catches my wrist and steers my hand to her mouth. I watch, transfixed, as she sinks her teeth into the turkey and cheese on rye. She moans as she draws back, and the carnal sound has me imagining she's moaning around my cock. Next, she directs the sandwich to my mouth. I bite around the same area she did.

Juliet smiles and nods. "Good boy."

I'm not sure why, but hearing her say those two words has my dick responding. This makes no sense—I'm not a boy—I'm a man. But when it comes to Juliet, I want to please her.

She picks up my beer, staring over the top as she raises the bottle. I watch in fascination as her tongue slinks out and licks her lips just before they close around the same spot I drank from. As the glass leaves her mouth, her tongue circles the edge, and I imagine her licking the head of my cock.

Oh, fuck. Fuck. Fuck.

I capture Juliet's hand, fingers closing on top of hers, directing the beer to my mouth. When my lips close around the rim, I pretend we're sharing a kiss. I imagine her taste as I swallow down the remainder. Together, we place the empty bottle on the table, and my hand is slow to end the contact with hers.

She leans in closer and places her palm on my bare leg, just above my knee. "Are you a virgin, Emmett?"

Wait. "What?"

"Are you a virgin? It's okay if you are." Her palm leisurely rubs my thigh, creeping under the edge of my shorts. "I'm a good teacher."

"N-no, I'm not."

"Oh, a boy with experience, huh?"

"Yes, and I'm not a boy." My words come out stronger now that I'm beyond the initial shock of her question.

"But you can be my boy toy." Her fingernails drag along the bare skin of my thigh, and I gasp. The slight sting combined with her words has my cock painfully hard. She notices. There's no way for her to miss the tented material.

"Has anyone ever given you head?"

Head? Yes, please. I swallow noticeably past the lump in my throat. "N-no." I stutter, shaking my head. "Never."

"Good." Juliet rises, stepping between my legs, before lowering to her knees. "I want to be your first." Her fingernail teases my stomach above the waistband of my board shorts. "Can I be the first person to taste your come, Emmett?"

My nostrils flare as I do my best not to blow just from the thought of her sucking me off. "Yes," I croak.

Her smile is pure sin as she undoes the tie on my bathing suit. I raise my hips from the seat, and she tugs them down until I kick them off.

"Wow, you are a man," she purrs, wrapping her hand around my shaft, stroking up and down. Her head drops forward, and I inhale raggedly with anticipation. She rubs one cheek along the length and then turns to repeat the motion with the other.

My fingers clutch her head, burying in her hair. "Please. Suck me," I practically beg, but I don't care. I'm past reason—lost in a haze of lust.

"Let go," she orders, raising her head. "Hold on to the chair arms and don't move." Releasing my grip on her hair, I do as she says. At this point, I'm so on edge, I'll do anything she wants. "Good boys get rewarded. You listened so well, and I'm going to make you come so hard."

"Please," I groan, my hands clenched around the metal. Every muscle in my body is taut, as if I'm prepared for battle.

Juliet's head drops to my lap, her light brown strands teasing my skin. I feel her warm breath wafting over me and then her hot, wet tongue licks from the base of my cock all the way up until she swallows the tip with her plump lips. Her tongue swirls around the head and then she slides all the way down.

"Oh fuck." She grips my cock, squeezing it tight in her fist and begins to bob up and down. "Yes, don't stop." My knuckles must be white, I'm gripping the chair so hard, but I can't take my eyes off Juliet. This is the hottest thing I've ever experienced—ever seen. Watching her devour my cock has me ready to explode. I'm so close.

Beep, beep, beep. My eyes shoot open at the racket of my alarm going off. I smash my hand down on the device to silence it and exhale long and slowly. I want to throw it across the room for ruining the best dream I've ever had.

Damn. I rake my sweat-dampened hair back from my forehead and groan with frustration. It was only a dream. Fisting my aching cock, I close my eyes and imagine the rest of the dream.

Juliet moves faster, bobbing up and down my length, her hand working me over too. Knuckles white, I clutch the chair arms and drop my head back. I'm so close. I'm so fucking close.

"Give it to me," she urges and then suctions her mouth over my cock once more. My hips raise as she takes me all the way in. My orgasm slams into me and jets from my cock, with Juliet swallowing every pulse of come down. She gives a long, final lick up my shaft and over the head before releasing me.

Chest heaving, my eyes open and reality hits. Not even the explosive orgasm I had can take away the disappointment that I'm in my bed alone.

CHAPTER SIX
EMMETT

"GOOD MORNING," MY MOM CALLS OUT AS I ENTER THE KITCHEN.

"Morning," I mumble. Even after my shower, I'm still not fully awake.

"Have a seat. I've got pancakes and bacon. They should help wake you up."

"Mom, you're a lifesaver. I need to go for a run this morning and I wasn't sure if I'd have the energy."

"Well, now you will." She sets a plate of fluffy pancakes down in front of me. The edges are perfectly crisped and the puddle of melted butter in the center makes me eager to dive in.

Pouring syrup over the stack, I ask, "Where's Dad?"

"He had to leave early for work." She sets a glass of milk in front of me.

"Thanks, Mom." I take a sip.

"Don't forget, your dad and I will be gone tonight through the weekend," she reminds me.

"Good thing you said that because I'd forgotten. I'd probably be wondering where you guys were." I laugh.

She shakes her head. "This is the third time I've told you. Are you sure you'll remember?"

"Yeah. Third time's the charm." I smile at her.

"Where are you going?" I ask.

"Pennsylvania to visit Auntie Mary and Uncle Bobby."

"I'm not invited?" I ask, pretending I care. When in reality, I'm looking forward to having the house to myself.

"Not this time."

I send her a skeptical glare. "Don't worry, I don't want to come. But you can't pretend that I'm some third wheel who you guys drag around with you. I've stayed home every time you've gone away since I turned sixteen. And I'm pretty sure seventeen is the legal age to leave a kid home."

"Like you wanted to come." My mom arches one eyebrow.

"I never said I did. I was merely pointing out a fact."

"That we're bad parents?" she retorts.

"That's impossible. I'm the perfect son," I jest.

"Speaking of being perfect, no parties while we're gone," she tells me.

"When have I had a party when you've been out of town?"

"Last year," she reminds me.

"Oh, yeah. How did I forget about that?"

"Don't do it again."

"Mom, no worries. I'm looking forward to peace and quiet. You and Dad make so much noise."

Mom snorts. "We're hardly home as it is."

"You work too much," I tell her.

"Your father and I need to put as much money away for retirement as we can."

"If you work yourself to death, it won't do you any good," I droll.

"Hopefully, that's not the case."

Rising, I take my dishes to the sink, rinsing them before placing them in the dishwasher. "I'm gonna go digest and then take a run."

"Okay."

"It's been nice talking with you, Mom. I've missed your pancakes."

"It has. I've missed your handsome face. I know your dad and I aren't the most affectionate parents." *That's an understatement.* "But we love you and we're proud of you."

"I love you too."

PIZZA BOXES IN HAND, I RING JULIET'S DOORBELL. I HEAR HER APPROACH and try to calm my already racing heart. Opening the door, she beams when she sees me. Talk about making me feel fantastic. It's a powerful feeling knowing I'm the reason she's happy right now.

"Hey, I didn't expect to see you," she says.

"Is this a bad time?" I ask.

"No. Is that pizza for me?" She rubs her hands together.

"That depends on whether you invite me in or not."

"Would you like to enter my humble abode?" She sweeps her arm out, gesturing for me to come inside.

"Don't mind if I do." I haven't been in here since she first moved in. My eyes scan everything I can as I follow Juliet. "This place looks great."

"Thank you." She smiles over her shoulder at me. "Here, we can eat in the dining room, since I haven't had a reason to use this space yet."

I set the two large boxes on the table while she wanders into the kitchen. I call out, "I hope you like extra cheese and pepperoni. I got one of each."

She ambles back in with plates, napkins, and a bottle of wine. Placing everything on the table, she removes two wine glasses from a built-in corner hutch. "I hope you like wine. My realtor gave it to me as a housewarming gift and I'll never drink it by myself."

"Sure," I answer. Wine's not really my thing, but spending time with Juliet is something I enjoy. If she told me I had to drink the entire bottle myself or go back home, I'd drink the fuck up.

She removes the cork like a pro and pours us each a generous portion of red wine. Handing over a glass to me, she raises hers. "To new friends getting to know each other." Tapping my glass gently to hers, I repeat the toast before taking a sip while she watches. "Do you like how it tastes?"

I lick my lips and savor the dry, fruity taste in my mouth. "It's not bad."

"Good. Let's sit and eat. I didn't realize how hungry I was until I smelled this."

"If you haven't had Pizzeria Ramona's, you've been missing out."

"Well, I haven't. I've been cooking a lot and haven't tried any of the local places aside from the coffee shop." She takes a bite of an extra cheese slice and moans exaggeratedly.

"Good Lord, where has this pizza been all my life?"

"Right? I don't know how I'll survive four years in Ohio without being able to order this."

"They'll have someplace to get good pizza," she says with confidence. "Even bad pizza is still decent."

"Not this good," I say.

"No, probably not."

We continue making small talk as we devour most of the pizza. Juliet refills our glasses each time they get low and it's not long until the bottle is empty.

"Well, that went quick." She giggles.

"After the first glass, it tasted much better." I wink.

"How did you manage to come over tonight? Don't your parents care that you're spending time with the new mystery woman?"

"My parents are out of town through the weekend. I've got four more days of peace and solitude."

"Nice. You can keep me company then." She lays her palm on my forearm, and my skin tingles as my nerve endings jump to life.

"I can spend as much or as little time with you as you'd like."

"Are you sure you want to do that?"

"Why wouldn't I?"

"We might give in to our urges and kiss."

I rake my teeth over my bottom lip and nod. "It's possible."

"What if we come to some kind of agreement?" she asks.

"Such as?" She's piqued my curiosity.

"We'd have to decide the details. But you're leaving for school soon and you don't need romantic baggage back here."

"You're not baggage," I correct.

"You know what I mean. You should start college free of any romantic entanglements. And as much as I enjoy your company and find you extremely attractive, I'm not in a position to be romantically tied to you."

"What are you thinking?"

"I miss sex, badly. My husband was the only man I've been with."

"You haven't had sex in how long?" I ask.

"Over two years."

"That's a long time."

"It is. Which is why I was wondering if you'd like to have sex with me?"

Allefuckinglujah.

"Hell yeah. Right now?" Rising, I press on the table. "It's time for dessert."

She laughs. "Not on the table, silly. I want the comfort of a bed beneath me."

"A bed works fine too," I agree.

"Okay, we need to work out the rest of our agreement."

"Do we need to sign a contract? Am I going to need a safe word, Mrs. Thatcher?" I jest.

She peers at me from under her thick lashes. "Maybe."

A groan expels from my lips. I'm already hard as stone.

"There's two possible ways this can go," she says. "We can do this tonight and satisfy our mutual curiosity. Or, we can take advantage of your parents being away and for the next four nights, you can spend the time with me."

"And we screw our brains out," I add.

"Exactly. What'll it be? One night or more?"

CHAPTER SEVEN

EMMETT

LIPS JOINED, WE SLAM INTO THE WALL OUTSIDE HER BEDROOM. WHEN SHE asked me what it was going to be, I almost laughed. What kind of question is that? One night with her or four to fuck my fill of her is a no brainer.

Caging her in, my hands cup her tits, squeezing their fullness. Oh, Jesus. She's not wearing a bra. I brush my thumbs over her taut nipples, and she whimpers into my mouth.

Gripping the hem of her shirt, I peel the material over her sleek stomach, continuing upward and revealing her breasts. Parting our mouths, I draw her shirt over her head so I can watch my hands cup her naked tits for the first time. Her hard nipples tease my palms as I knead the round flesh. My large hands appear dark against the pale, blemish-free skin.

Leaning forward, I close my lips around one rosy peak, sucking and teasing the flesh with my tongue. Her fingers sink into my hair, urging me to continue. I glide over to pay attention to her other nipple.

"Yes, Emmett," she sighs my name with pleasure. Sliding my hands down, I cup her ass and pick her up. She wraps her legs around me, heels digging into my ass, as she grinds into my cock. Carrying her, I get us to her bed as quickly as possible and topple us both down onto the mattress. Not wasting any time, I remove her shorts and panties, pausing to look her over. "You're so beautiful."

"You're not touching me," she reminds me, and I chuckle. "Sorry, ma'am. I got distracted."

Her fingers tug at my shirt, and I rip it over my head. Then her hands move down to hook inside the waistband of my shorts and boxers. Licking her lips, she drags them over my hips, and I smile. "I knew you wanted to get me out of my clothes since we met," I tease.

"Hell yeah. That's not all I want."

"Oh yeah? What else do you desire?"

Using her body weight, she flips me to my back, taking me by surprise. Straddling my thighs, she peers down at me, sandy hair cascading between us. "I'd rather show you." She grips my cock in her fist, and I clench my teeth. I've wanted her touch for what feels like forever—I've even dreamt about it. But nothing prepared me for the exquisite feeling when she guided me to her entrance and slowly slid down my length. I almost pulled a "Jim" from the movie *American Pie*.

I clutch her hips, guiding her movements as she rocks on me. Oh, Christ. While I have had sex, I've never had my cock ridden before. Watching her tits bounce and her pussy swallowing my cock is the hottest thing ever. I tenaciously hang on to the last thread of my resolve. This has to be as phenomenal for her as it is for me. I've never felt anything comparable to the ecstasy of being wrapped in her hot, wet channel.

I may have barely had a taste of what's to come for the next four days, but I already know it'll be damn near impossible to end the physical aspect of our relationship. But I'll think about it when it happens. Between now and then there's a lot of fucking to be done.

Sliding one of my hands from her hip, I lick my thumb and press it to her clit. Finding it swollen and needy for my touch, I rub circles on the bundle of nerves. Juliet moans her approval as she continues riding my cock, her hips rippling like waves on the sea.

"I'm close," she whispers, and I move my thumb faster. Her head drops back and her mouth parts as she unravels. Legs trembling and body shivering, I watch her orgasm travel through her with a series of tremors. When her pussy clenches my cock with every pulse of her release, my own orgasm can't be held back any longer. Exploding inside her with a hoarse shout, my orgasm feels like it's never going to stop. When it finally does, I close my eyes and go limp, stretched out on the bed.

"Are you alive?" Juliet asks, walking her fingers up my stomach to my chest.

"Not sure. Think I may have died and gone to Heaven."

She laughs. "As amazing as that was, it's only the beginning of what we're going to do."

"I look forward to finding out what surprises you have in store for me. All I ask is that you feed me periodically so I can keep my strength up."

IT'S FUNNY HOW FOUR DAYS DURING THE SCHOOL YEAR CAN SEEM ENDLESS and yet, my time with Juliet was over in the blink of an eye.

"I wish we had another day and night," I tell her.

"I know. Me too. But the extra time would only make it harder for us. We need to think of this like ripping off a bandage and do it in one strong yank."

"Okay." I lean forward and press my lips to hers for a final kiss. I keep it brief and as chaste as possible, even though it's a struggle to do so. Cupping her cheek in my palm, I stare at her striking features, memorizing them. "I'm glad you chose to buy this house, Juliet. You've made my summer way more interesting than it was shaping up to be." I know I'm not leaving for school yet, but I'm not going to spend much time with her before I do. Not if I can help it, anyway. Especially now that I know what I'll be missing out on. I'd only be torturing myself.

"Thank you for being my second-first lover." She smiles. "I wouldn't have wanted it to be anyone else. Everything was perfect."

"It was," I agree. "I'll see you around, Mrs. Thatcher." I wink.

"See you around."

"CALL WHEN YOU GET THERE SO WE DON'T WORRY," MY MOM CALLS OUT AS I back out of our driveway.

"I will. Bye, Mom. Bye, Dad."

My mom blows me a kiss and my dad yells, "Safe travels, son."

I drive off with a final wave and glance at Juliet's house as I pass by. She's not home. She hasn't been for three weeks.

"You haven't seen her at all?" Liz asks. She's along to keep me company for the almost twelve-hour drive that'll take us to Ohio State University. She'll fly home in two days and start school at a university in Maine.

"Nope. We haven't spoken since we said goodbye on our final morning together. She's been out of town." I only know this because one of the neighbors told my mom. I guess they're finally warming up to her if she shared her plans with them.

"I'm sorry. That sucks," Liz offers, trying to console me.

"It is what it is, right? I think we handled it the best way possible. We didn't drag it out and get all emotional."

"How are you feeling about everything? Answer honestly. Don't sugar coat things for me."

I shrug. "Juliet is amazing. If I was four years older and had graduated from college, it would be a different scenario."

"Are you in love with her?" Liz questions.

"We never shared our feelings."

"I asked if you're in love with her, but I already know the answer."

My grip tightens on the steering wheel. "Fuck. Yeah, I am."

PART TWO

CHAPTER EIGHT

EMMETT
FOUR YEARS LATER

"OH, HONEY, IT'S SO WONDERFUL TO HAVE YOU BACK HOME." MY MOTHER pats my cheek.

"Don't get too used to seeing me. It's not like I'm living at home again. Just because I'm back in Boston doesn't mean I have an excess amount of time on my hands."

"I never said you did. Don't get touchy. As your mother, I have a right to be excited to have my only child back in the same state. You barely came home during college."

I didn't want to be reminded of Juliet.

"That's how college is, Mom. It's a lot of work, but it's also the last hurrah before adulting really starts. I packed as much fun into those years as I could." I grin.

I did whatever I had to in order to get over Juliet.

"Do you ever hear from Juliet, that nice neighbor we used to have?"

Is she a freaking mind reader or what?

"No, why would I?"

"I don't know. You guys seemed to be friends."

"Mom, I don't really think helping someone with yard work or unclogging a pool hose classifies someone as a friend."

And apparently fucking them for four days straight doesn't either.

"She was very nice. After you left for college, I got to know her a little bit. It's too bad she moved a few months later."

"Yeah, I remember you telling me."

I've always wondered why she moved so quickly. I hope she's doing well. I wrote her one letter from school when I first arrived. Part of me hoped we'd find a way to remain in contact, but I didn't hear from her for a few months. And when I did, she sent me a painting of my hand on her thigh. Done in muted tones, it was sexy and so lifelike, I could practically feel her skin beneath my palm. There was no note included and at that time, I was a few months into my plan to forget her.

Instead of appreciating the painting and the work that went into it, I was resentful. There I was doing my best to move on with my life and she sent me a reminder of the one thing I couldn't have. I was tempted to throw it away, but when I spoke to Liz about it, she convinced me to hang on to it for the time being. I placed it in a storage bin and never looked at it again until two weeks ago when I moved into my new apartment.

With the passing of time, I have a new appreciation for the work that went into painting those parts of us so accurately. The careful brush strokes and meticulous details make it incredibly realistic. In my heart, I know she wasn't trying to hurt me. Maybe it was her way of telling me she wasn't over us yet either.

"Last week, I saw an ad on TV for the Metropolis Art Gallery and they mentioned Juliet's art being on display," Mom informs me.

"Really? Good for her."

"I guess she's the new big thing in the art world."

I'm not surprised. She was always immensely talented.

"You should attend her show. She'd probably get a kick out of seeing how much you've grown up."

Outwardly, my face is void of any reaction, but inwardly, I'm grimacing at my mom's choice of words. Pretty sure Juliet thought I was plenty "grown up" before. "Yeah, maybe."

My mom waves her hand like I'm an annoying fly. "I know that when you say maybe, it means no."

I smile. "Where do you think I got that from? You and Dad were famous for your maybe/nos."

"Before I forget, I made you some brownies to bring home."

Stepping over to her, I feel her head, checking for a fever. "Are you sick?"

She raises both brows in question. "Why would I be?"

"I don't know how to tell you this, but you've never really been the mom who bakes their kid treats."

"Can't I be that now? Do we have to stay in one lane our entire adulthood?"

"I didn't say that."

"Did it ever occur to you that your father and I might have regrets about our parenting?"

"You having them, I can believe. But Dad?" I shake my head. "No way. He's the definition of a hardass father. I can't see him regretting anything he's done. That would mean admitting to himself that he might've been wrong about something. That'll never happen."

"Don't be so hard on him." My mom's reply falls on deaf ears.

"How can you say that to me with a straight face?"

"I love you both," she says by way of explanation. For the sake of not upsetting her, I'm going to drop all discussion of my dad. His parenting skills might need improving, but he loves my mom and is loyal to her.

"I know you do. I love you too, Mom. You don't need to bake me treats to earn my love. You already have it. But if you want to try, then make me some chocolate chip cookies. Those are my favorite." I wink.

"WHY DID I LET YOU TALK ME INTO GOING TO HER SHOW?" I SAY TO LIZ.

"Because you know I'm right. And deep down, you want to see Juliet."

"I'm not so sure about wanting to see her. It's more of a need than a want. I'm always going to have fond memories of her, and I'm curious if the attraction is still there."

"What if it is? Would you want to pick right up where you left off?"

"I can't say until I see her."

"What if she's married?"

"That'll put an abrupt end to any thoughts I have about her. I'm not wrecking a marriage."

"What if she doesn't remember you?" Liz giggles.

"Come on. Like that's gonna happen. I may have been eighteen, but I rocked her world for four days and nights. I lost track of how many times we had sex." Just thinking about it gives me a semi. I discreetly adjust myself and focus on the road. I play our relationship off as just sex, but it was more than that for me. We spoke about our hopes and dreams for the future. I'm glad she's achieving hers, and while I'm unsure attending her show is the right thing to do, I'll be happy to personally witness her success.

I luck out when a Porsche pulls away from a curbside space and I'm able to back right in. This is no small feat on Newbury Street—maybe it's a sign that tonight will go well.

"Are you ready?" Liz asks once we're standing on the sidewalk in front of the large brownstone that houses the famous Metropolis Art Gallery.

"As ready as I'll be, I guess." Heart galloping behind my rib cage, we step inside the well lit gallery. Eyes sorting through the crowd of people, I search for a sign of Juliet.

"Any sign of her?" Liz asks.

"Not yet. But this place is five floors of exhibits, so she could be anywhere. Let's check out the artwork and eventually we'll find her."

She nods. "Sounds good to me. Her paintings are beautiful."

"They are," I agree.

We wander through the first floor, which consists of cityscapes, and then move to the second floor. Here we find images of a pregnant woman, but her face doesn't show. It's a view of her rounded, naked stomach with two hands resting on either side. It's painted as if the mother is looking down at her own stomach. As my gaze glides over the details, I wonder if she painted this from experience.

The next image is the back view of a little blond boy and a woman staring out at a harbor. The woman's hair falls to mid-back in slight waves. While the color is similar, Juliet's hair was shoulder length and pin straight, which makes me think this isn't a self-portrait.

"Uh… Emmett. You might want to see this," Liz says urgently.

Moving over to the next image displayed, I gasp. There's no question this time that Juliet painted herself. She's there in full color, every part of her face as accurate as if I were looking at a live version. But that's not what caused my surprised reaction. It's the little toddler posed next to her that caught my attention. He appears to be around three years old, and his blond hair sweeps across his forehead. But the most astonishing part is that my face smiles back at me from the canvas—make that a miniature version of my face.

What the fuck is going on?

My brain feels sluggish as I try to muddle through what I'm seeing.

"Jesus. Does this mean you have a kid you didn't know about? Or is she crazy and imagined one?"

I rub a shaking hand over my brow. "I don't know. I don't know anything right now." I'm shook.

Liz hooks her arm through mine, and I appreciate the strength she's offering. "Let's look around some more and see if we can find any clues." Her clear thinking is welcome. I'm still numb and don't know if I'm coming or going.

Do I have a son I didn't know about?

And if I do, why would Juliet keep him from me?

What could be her motivation?

"Breathe, Emmett." She pats my arm. "You look as white as one of these statues.

People might mistake you for part of the show," she jokes, and her humor is appreciated. If it wasn't for her, I'd probably have flipped the fuck out by now and demanded to see Juliet.

Moving to the next painting doesn't offer any clarity. If anything, it makes things more confusing when I see the same boy stretching his arms upward as if he wants to be lifted from his feet.

"This gets weirder and weirder," Liz mumbles under her breath.

"Emmett?" I hear my name called in a hoarse whisper.

Slowly, I turn and find Juliet standing before me. I feel disconnected. Like I'm broken apart and none of my parts are functioning at full capacity. My brain feels foggy and my limbs won't work. I'm frozen in place.

Her green eyes that reminded me of a tropical escape are so large in her petite face. Liz pinches the inside of my arm where her hand rests, snapping me out of my daze.

"Juliet," I husk her name.

"How are you?" she asks.

"Good. And you?"

"I'm well." She gestures at her paintings on the wall. "I wasn't sure this day would ever come."

"I was sure you'd have all the success." I smile.

"Excuse me for butting in, but don't you think it's time to talk about why you're painting pictures of a mini-Emmett?" Liz jumps in. And thank God for her because one glance at Juliet and I turned stupid.

"How about we go somewhere a little more private for that discussion?" Juliet suggests.

Fuck me. This can't be a good sign.

"Sure," I reply. My eyes meet Liz's. She looks as nervous as I feel.

"Right this way." Juliet walks in front of us and we follow. My eyes trail over her frame from head to toe and back up again. The navy blue short sleeved dress flows to her knees, leaving her shapely calves exposed. Her sandy colored hair, longer than before, is full of waves and curls. The view from the back is as stunning as the one from the front. If anything, she's more beautiful than when we said our goodbyes.

Leading us into an office, she closes the door behind us. "Please sit." Liz chooses to sit on the small couch to the side of the room, leaving Juliet and I facing one another.

"I think I'm going to stand for now," I say.

She nods. "You're wondering about the boy in the paintings."

"Is he mine?"

"No, he's ours," she replies.

I bark out a harsh laugh. "Oh, he's ours. Which is strange because this is the first I've heard that I have a son. Did I miss a phone call? A letter?" Sarcasm drips from my questions.

"No. I didn't try to contact you."

"Why didn't you?"

"You were so young. I didn't want you to throw away your future. I knew you'd leave school and come home, and that wouldn't have been fair to you."

"No. You know what's not fair?" My voice raises. "Being denied the right to know I fathered a son. Being denied the right to be a part of his life. You made choices for me that you had no right to." Bending over, I place my hands on my knees and drag in a few labored breaths.

"I'm sorry, Emmett. I panicked and tried to do the right thing."

I straighten up. "By keeping my son from me? My own flesh and blood doesn't even know I'm his father."

CHAPTER NINE
EMMETT

"ARE YOU MARRIED?" LIZ CUTS IN.

"No, I'm not. Are you guys?" Her eyes bounce between the two of us. She thinks we're a couple?

"No, I'm Liz, his best friend," she's quick to reply.

"I remember you, now. You look different, more mature."

"Yeah, four years will do that." Liz smiles.

"Now that you guys are besties, can we get back to discussing our son?" My anger is clear.

"What do you want to know?"

"Everything. But let's start with his name."

"Emmett. I named him after you," she says.

"Why would you do that?"

"I wanted him to have something of yours."

What? How can she say this with a straight face?

"That makes zero sense to me. If you wanted him to have something of me, then you would've let me be his father in more ways than contributing sperm." I hate that I'm the reason her brow is furrowed with hurt, but what she did is unacceptable. She dropped a bombshell on me, and I need to find a way to accept it. How's that for a fucked-up situation?

"I'm going to step outside and let you guys have some privacy. Take your time. I've got plenty of art to check out," Liz says, hurrying toward the door. She slips out before I can object, and Juliet doesn't look pleased she left either. Does she think I'll lose control without Liz to calm me?

"You were about to tell me why you gave our son my name."

"When I found out I was pregnant, you were already at college and I was alone. At first, I thought it must be a mistake. My husband and I had tried to have a baby and we were never able to conceive. After I'd taken enough tests to convince myself the results weren't wrong, I went to the doctor and they confirmed I was pregnant. I want you to know there was never a question of whether I was keeping the baby or not. I fell in love with him the moment I knew he existed."

"Why didn't you contact me?" I grit out.

"I did. I sent you the painting."

"You're right, you did. With no letter included, I figured it was your final goodbye gift to me."

Her fingers pluck nervously at the beads on her bracelet. "It was my way of starting up a line of communication."

"You could've just called me. You had my number," I remind her. "By the way, it's still the same."

"I did, but I second guessed myself so many times about having that conversation that

I couldn't follow through. You had plans to play for the NFL and I didn't want to crush your dream."

"I don't know if you're familiar with my football career, but junior year, I wrecked my knee. That was the end of my football career."

"I bet that was a difficult time for you," she offers sympathetically.

"It was. If I'd have had a son to focus on, I dare say it would've put things in the proper perspective much sooner."

"I'm sorry, Emmett. I really am."

"Those are empty words, Juliet. It seems like you're only sorry you got caught."

"I can't make you understand. But I've been doing a lot of thinking lately, and I was planning on reaching out to you as soon as I felt ready."

"How long would that have taken? Another four years?" I droll.

"I honestly can't say."

"You and I can go round and round about what you did wrong, but what I'd like to know is how do you plan to remedy the situation?"

"I… uh… I guess we can figure out how to introduce you to him."

I narrow my eyes at her. "You guess?"

"I'm doing the best I can, Emmett. Seeing you tonight was unexpected. I don't have all the answers."

"Save it, Juliet. Finding out I have a son was fucking earth shattering. I don't think you can compare it to seeing me."

"I'm not comparing them. I wasn't prepared to figure all the answers out now. I'd like it if you and I could hash out some of the details together. I've screwed up so much already. I don't want to mess this up too."

"There's no time like the present," I say.

"I'm in the middle of my show. Could we please get together tomorrow and come up with a plan for moving forward?"

"I'm sorry this came out during your very important show, but that's not on me."

"I realize that, but this show could be life-changing for me and Emmett."

I study her face before answering. "Okay. I'll be over for dinner tomorrow night. I want to meet my son. He better be there."

"Thank you. He will be. Give me your phone," she orders, holding out her hand. She sends me her address. "Emmett goes to bed at seven. Can you come over at five?"

"Yeah, I'll be there."

She smiles at me. "Despite the shitty circumstances, I'm happy you're here. It's a little disconcerting to see you so grown up. I've been remembering you as you were. But you look great."

"I'm glad you're well, Juliet. And you look beautiful, as always." It's painful for me to look at her. Not only because of her deceit, but it also stirs up so many happy memories.

We leave the office and she closes the door behind me. Walking side by side down the hallway, I watch our shadows on the white tile floor. Even with her heels, I tower over her. It's surreal that I'm here right now. How many times have I dreamed of seeing her again?

How many times my first year of school did I pick up my phone to call her and chickened out?

And now the universe has forced our hand by bringing us together. As scared as I am for what this could mean, in one sense I'm relieved. I know about my son and I'll be stepping in to help raise him. Things may become increasingly complicated until we sort out all the finer details, but we'll work through them for our son.

When we reach the gallery area, she pauses and touches my arm. "I'm glad you came tonight."

"Me too."

"I'll see you tomorrow. Say goodbye to Liz for me."

I nod. "Will do. Good luck with the rest of your show."

"Thank you." She presses her lips together in a small smile before walking off. I've barely made it across the room when Liz finds me.

"I thought it was best that I left," she says. "I hope you're not mad."

"No. Why would I be? I'm a big boy and need to deal with this on my own. It's not your responsibility."

"I know, but I want to be here for you."

I press a kiss to her temple. "You're always there for me."

"How did the rest of your conversation go?"

"We didn't kill each other." I smirk.

Liz hugs my arm. "Don't hate me for saying this, but I feel bad for her."

"I know. I do too. She's been through a lot. I can't help but feel like I made a horrible mistake by not telling her how deeply I loved her. That could've changed everything and there's nothing I can do to go back and fix things."

"Well, introducing you to your son is a good start. The rest will take care of itself." She squeezes my arm.

"I hope you're right."

THE DOORBELL CHIMES AND A WAVE OF NAUSEA ASSAILS ME. I RUB A HAND over my stomach. If anyone had told me two days ago that I'd be standing here, I'd have thought they were crazy. I hear Juliet pause on the other side of the door. Her shoes clicking on the floor give her away. When I hear the knob turn, I'm tempted to retreat, but I force myself to inhale and exhale slowly.

Tugging open the door, Juliet smiles and I force a matching one on my face. "Hi."

"Hi," she repeats, looking as uncomfortable as I am.

"Come on in." Stepping inside, my eyes make a quick scan of the foyer while she closes the door. "Emmett is in the living room. I wanted to talk for a minute before the two of you meet."

"Does he know who I am?"

"Not yet. I told him an old friend of mine was coming to visit," she explains.

"How long do you plan to wait until you share that I'm really his father?" I can hear the tension in my voice, even though I'm trying my hardest to remain calm.

"I don't have a particular amount of time in mind. I thought we could see how it goes and decide when it's right. I thought you might like to be here when I do have the talk with him."

"I would, thank you."

"Are you ready?" she asks.

I give her the first genuine smile in four years. "Hell yeah."

She angles her head toward the living room and then walks with me. The sound of Emmett giggling greets us, and I chuckle.

"Emmett, I want you to meet a very special friend of mine." He turns, looking away from the TV, and I gasp when I get a clear glance at him. He rises from the couch and hurries our way.

"He looks like me," I whisper. Overcome with emotion, my voice cracks.

"He does," she agrees. "Aside from the lighter hair he got from me, he's a shrunken version of you."

"Emmett, this is Emmett."

"We have the same name," he exclaims.

I nod, beaming. "We do. I'm so happy to meet you." I bend down, extending the wrapped box in my hands. "I brought you a present."

He takes it from me. "Thank you."

"Nice manners, Emmett," I tell him.

"Can I open it, Mommy?" His eyes sparkle with excitement.

"Sure." Juliet glances at me. "You look just as excited as," she pauses, "Emmett." Was she going to say *our son*? It's going to take some time for both of us to get used to my new role.

"Mommy, look." Emmett holds up a box with a t-ball set. "Can we play now?"

"Why don't we save it for tomorrow," she suggests.

"Please, Mommy."

"I need to finish making dinner."

"I can play with him," I offer. "If that's okay."

"Can he, Mommy?" Emmett bounces up and down. He's so adorable, I bet it's tough to refuse him. Besides, I've been deprived of enough time with my son. No matter how much of an adjustment this is for her, it's harder for me.

"Go for it. I'll be busy cooking dinner. I'll let you know when it's done."

"Come on." Emmett takes my hand like it's the most natural thing in the world, and my heart climbs to my throat, forming a giant emotion-clogged lump. My fingers close around his tiny hand and I never want to let go. My vision blurs with tears and I quickly swipe them away, but I feel Juliet watching me.

"I've got a roast cooking in the oven and I baked chocolate chip cookies for you. Not that I expect cookies to fix anything, but they used to be your favorite… and when have homemade cookies ever hurt?"

CHAPTER TEN
EMMETT

I CAN'T BELIEVE THIS LITTLE, PERFECT HUMAN IS MINE, THAT HE'S PART OF me. His tiny hand wrapped in mine is the thing I was missing most and didn't even realize. He points to the back door. "Open this."

"Say, please open this," I correct.

"Please open this." He does as I instructed, and I grin.

"Good boy." I'm so proud of him.

A beautiful blue-sky day, the weather couldn't be better for us to be outside. I set up the blue base and add the red T. "Emmett, grab a ball." He picks up two, bringing them to me. I set one on the base where there's a space allocated specifically for that and place the other on the T. I hand the oversized bat to my son and position him the correct distance away. "Bend your knees and choke up on the bat." He bends lower but doesn't move his hands, and I realize he's too young to know what I mean. I take his hands and move them up a little before assisting him through a slow-motion swing. He giggles when the bat connects with the ball and it falls to the ground. "Now, you try it without me."

"Okay," he shouts with eagerness. Getting into position, he swings the bat like we practiced, making contact with the ball and sending it off the T. It rolls about six feet before stopping. He jumps up and down. "I did it."

I tousle his fair hair. "You sure did. Try again."

He places a ball on the T twice and it falls to the ground before he gets it settled on the right place. His tongue sticking out of his mouth as he concentrates, he swings harder this time. The bat makes contact with the ball with a cracking sound, and this time it gets some air under it and lands about ten feet away. He spins to face me, wide eyes taking up a sizable portion of his tiny face. "It flew."

I hold my hand up for a high five and he slaps his palm against mine. At least Juliet taught him the importance of high fiving. "That was awesome, little man. You're going to be hitting the ball out of this yard before you know it." He nods emphatically. "Do you want to keep practicing?" I ask.

"Yep. I want to hit it out of the yard."

Like father, like son. He's already competitive with himself, like I am. Sports are in my blood and I have a feeling he'll be no different.

We spend the next hour "practicing" before we head inside to wash up for dinner. I've had a total of eighty minutes in my son's company and I'm already head over heels in love with him. If anyone doubts love at first sight, all they need to do is look at their child for the first time to experience it. I'm a full believer now.

How could I not be?

I fell for Juliet the first time I saw her, but this is a different feeling. It's my heart wrapped in warmth and radiating outward through every cell I'm made of. It's happiness filling me from head to toe like the stuffing inside a teddy bear, leaving room for nothing else.

How can I ever be angry again?

All the disappointment I experienced last night when I first found out about Emmett is behind me. I should be upset with Juliet for her deceit, and though we still have so much to work out, it's taking the backseat to my love for our son. In a split second's time, he became the most important person to me, and he always will be.

"You guys looked like you were having a great time," Juliet tells me as I finish washing my hands at her kitchen sink.

I smile. "We did. He's an amazing kid, Juliet. You've done a great job raising him."

"That's kind of you to say, especially under the circumstances. You should be resentful toward me."

"While I'm not okay with how you've handled everything, I'm grateful he's such a happy, well-adjusted child. That's obviously because of you."

"Can you stay for a bit after dinner? Once Emmett goes to sleep, we can talk some more. Maybe we can iron out some of the things that are up in the air right now."

"Sure, I can do that."

She smiles at me, and it's like a punch to my gut. I'm eighteen all over again, wondering how I'm lucky enough to be standing in her kitchen. I've never been able to completely push her out of my mind, no matter how many miles were between us or how many years had passed. I always assumed it was because she was my first in a lot of ways—first blowjob, first older woman, first taboo relationship, and first woman to steal a piece of my heart. They say you never get over your first love, so I chalked my lingering feelings up to that. But now I'm beginning to wonder if we were always meant to get to this point.

"DINNER WAS AMAZING. THANK YOU FOR GOING THROUGH ALL THAT effort," I say, relaxing back against the cushion on her front porch swing.

"I'm glad you enjoyed everything." She stretches her bare legs out in front of her like she's on a high-flying swing. Of course my gaze skips right over to rake along the mile of golden flesh. Her legs are still fantastic.

"You still make the best chocolate chip cookies. My mom made me some last week and I'm not going to tell her this, but they couldn't compare to yours."

She laughs. "Your secret is safe with me. How are your parents?"

"They're doing well. In the few months I've been back in the area, my mom can't do enough for me. It's like she realized she could've done more for me when I was younger and is trying to make up for it now."

"That's kind of sweet when you think about it," Juliet replies.

"It is, but it's unnecessary. I'm a grown man, and I don't have regrets about my childhood. Could they have done more for me, spent more time with me? Yes. But they were busy working to provide everything I needed. And they made me capable of taking care of myself at a young age. Independence isn't a bad thing."

She turns sideways on the swing, her knee touching the side of my thigh. "Will you do things differently with Emmett?"

I meet her curious gaze. "I guess a lot of that will depend on you."

"Why me?" she questions.

"I'm assuming you want this to be his primary residence."

"I do."

I take a quick glance around the surrounding neighbors' front yards. Everything is well manicured and there isn't a lot of traffic since this is a cul-de-sac. "This is a great neighborhood for him to grow up in."

"That's why I chose this house. The yard's big enough to add a pool when he's older and there are other kids his age nearby."

"You made a great choice. Let me ask you, did you sell the other house because you didn't want my parents to see that you were pregnant?"

"That was part of the reason. The other being that I couldn't get you out of my mind and I didn't want reminders around."

I grin crookedly. "You have a permanent reminder for at least eighteen years. How's that working out for you?"

She half shrugs. "I didn't take that into consideration at the time," she admits, and I chuckle.

"This is a nicer place to raise a child. The old neighborhood was all older families. He wouldn't have any friends to play with."

"That's what I tell myself." She smiles.

"I know it's only been twenty-four hours, but have you given any more thought to how we're going to tell him I'm his father?"

"Yeah, I didn't sleep much last night."

"Me either. It felt like the night before Christmas to me. So much anticipation I could barely restrain myself from coming over here as soon as I woke up this morning. If it hadn't been for needing to go to work, I might have shown up on your doorstep."

"I would've made you coffee and breakfast if you had."

"Don't tell me that or I might."

"It's all good. I have a feeling you'll be spending a lot of time here."

"It's good that you're preparing yourself, because you're going to be sick of me soon."

"I never asked you what you're doing for work."

"We had other things to talk about. I'm currently working as a producer for a sports network. In another month, I'll have my own show on there."

"You'll talk about sports for the duration?"

"Yep. Every day, we'll talk about what's going on and people will call in to offer their opinions."

"That sounds like every guy's dream job, getting paid to talk about sports."

"It wasn't my original dream, but plans change. We adapt and make the most of what life doles out. I wanted to play football professionally, but if I hadn't injured my knee, I wouldn't be sitting here right now. I wouldn't know I had a son."

She grimaces. "I'm so sorry, Emmett. There's nothing adequate for me to say to excuse what I did. All I can say is I was in a bad headspace. I missed you, but I also knew I'd be judged for sleeping with you. I didn't want to be the Mrs. Robinson of the neighborhood."

"You didn't mind when you were sucking my cock or riding me."

"Ouch. You're right, I didn't."

I shake my head and pinch the bridge of my nose. "I'm sorry. That was a low blow."

"No, it's true. I loved everything we did together and I wasn't ready for us to end."

Christ. Four years too late she tells me, and my dick still gets hard. She's always held this power over me. I've never wanted anyone as much as her. She's the one who got away. Her eyes lower to my lap, noticing my problem. "Juliet, why did you insist we respect the four-day time limit? I didn't go away to school for a few more weeks. We could've had more time together."

Her eyes slowly climb to lock with mine. "I was in love with you."

CHAPTER ELEVEN
EMMETT

SHE WAS IN LOVE WITH ME? HOW COULD I NOT KNOW THIS?

I blow out a mouthful of air and confess, "I was in love with you too."

"You were?" She sounds as surprised as I was. I guess the two of us need to work on communicating our feelings. We're both clueless when it comes to love.

I nod. "Yes. I'm surprised you couldn't tell. I figured I was someone you wanted to dip your toes back into the sex pool with. I never imagined you'd have real feelings for me."

"Why wouldn't I?" she asks. "We had fun together and shared secrets I've never told anyone else. You became my best friend. All of those things are a great foundation for a relationship."

"You don't need to sell me on it. You wouldn't have needed to back then either. Had I known you were in love with me, I would've found a way to make us work out despite going to college."

"But I don't think we would've worked. I stand by my decision to let you go." She's being stubborn.

"Even though we've missed out on four years we can never have back?"

"Yes. There's no guarantee that if we'd stayed together it would've panned out for us," she justifies.

"You're right. But it could've. We would've had a chance to be a couple instead of having no possibility at all."

"Do you have a girlfriend?" She cringes, as if she didn't want to ask me.

I slide my arm along the back of the swing behind her. "No. Do you have a boyfriend?"

She shakes her head from side to side. "Nope. I haven't been with anyone since you." Her words floor me. "Does this really come as a surprise?" she questions. I guess the shock must be clear on my face.

"It's been over four years."

"When do you think I'd squeeze in a date—between diaper changes and work?"

"I didn't think about it that way. I was thinking more about four years as a whole. That's a long time to go without sex."

"Don't worry, I know you weren't lacking female companionship."

I scratch my chin. "Yeah, I… uh, I can't say I showed as much restraint as you. But I think you'd be surprised that I didn't sleep with anyone until sophomore year."

"Why not?" she prods.

"I was in love with you, and I wasn't ready to give up hope that you might reach out to me. And I don't mean with another painting. Although, I love your artwork."

"Where's the painting now?" she asks.

"It's hanging on the wall in my apartment."

She smiles. "That's not what I expected you to say."

"Hey, I knew that sucker would be worth big money someday," I tease.

"Ha, I don't know about big money. I'm at the mediocre stage, but it beats the shit-money stage."

"I think you're being overly humble. I know what a big deal you are now. Only extremely talented artists get to show their work at Metropolis."

"I'm not gonna lie, it was an incredible honor, but one of my friends is the manager there, so that helped."

"How long have you guys been friends for?" I ask.

"Three years. Why?"

My hand on the back of the swing shifts forward, catching a strand of her hair between my fingers. "You just made my point for me. If you got the show because of him, wouldn't it have happened much sooner?"

"Maybe."

"Jesus, stop disagreeing with me. I'm not wrong. You're just too stubborn to admit it. Like you were too stubborn to tell me about Emmett."

The smile leaves her eyes, a somber expression replacing the lightness. "I'm not too stubborn to tell you I'm sorry. I hope you know how much I mean that." She places her hand on my thigh, squeezing. "I don't know how I'll ever make it up to you, but I'll find a way or die trying."

"You carried our son alone for nine months. I can't imagine how scared and lonely you must've been."

"I kept him from you all this time. How can you be so understanding? You should hate me."

"Juliet, I could never hate you. I don't know what would've happened if I had found out I was going to be a dad at eighteen years old. I like to think I would've handled it, but there's no way to know that for certain. But I can tell you that at twenty-two I'm ready to be the best father I can be. I fell in love with our son the moment I set eyes on him."

※ ※ ※ ※

FOR THE PAST WEEK, I'VE BEEN SPENDING ALL MY FREE TIME WITH EMMETT and Juliet. Tonight's the big night—we're going to tell him I'm his dad. I've been anxious about it all day. What if he's disappointed? Or even worse, he cries? I think my heart would split in two.

"Emmett, push me," my son yells as he tries to get on the swing.

"Hey, little man, what's the magic word?"

"Pleeeease," he sings.

"Good job." Picking him up, I set him on the swing. "Hold on tightly to the chains," I instruct as I give him a little push.

"Faster, please," he calls out. I add a little more force to the next push. "I'm like a birdie, Emmett."

"Hold on tight," Juliet calls out.

"He's fine, aren't you?" I ask.

"Mommy, I'm flying like a birdie. Watch me."

She smiles. "I'm watching, sweetie. Don't worry."

Every moment the three of us spend together feels so natural. We're our own little family unit.

"What are you thinking about?" Juliet asks.

"How great my life is." I smile. "I love being with you guys. It feels so right in every way."

"I've noticed it too," she replies. "You fit with us like a piece we were missing and didn't realize."

"That's the nicest thing you've ever said to me." My chest squeezes with emotion.

"I thought it was when I said I loved you," she throws back.

"Nope. You said you *loved* me, meaning past tense," I explain.

"Tomato—tomahto," she retorts.

"You say that, but don't you want to hear how much you both mean to me? How I can't believe how empty my life was before last week? How when I'm not with you both, I want to be?"

"Oh, Emmett, you mean just as much to us. When you're not with us, Emmett asks for you."

"You didn't let me finish," I say, locking our gazes. "How I can't stop thinking about *you*."

"Really?" she questions, hope lighting her sea-colored eyes.

"Yes."

"Hey, push me, please," Emmett yells, showering us with a dose of reality, and we laugh.

"EMMETT, SWEETIE, COME HERE." JULIET PATS THE COUCH CUSHION between us. "We need to talk to you about something important." He scrambles over and I place him on the couch and give Juliet a nod of encouragement. "You know how I've always told you your daddy loves you very much and someday you'd get to meet him?"

Emmett nods. "You said he was away at school."

"He was, but now he's home."

"Can I meet him?" Emmett cuts in.

I step in. "You already have. I'm your daddy, Emmett, and I'm so happy you're my son."

Emmett's eyes open wider as the meaning of my words sinks in. "You're my daddy?"

I grin and ruffle his hair. "I am."

He turns to Juliet. "He's my daddy?"

She smiles. "He is. I promise." He squeals and jumps in my lap, throwing his arms around my neck. "Daddy," he whispers, tightening his arms around my neck. "I'm glad you're my Daddy."

"I am too, son. I am too."

Emmett remains in my arms and falls asleep against my chest. "Stay here. I'll put him to bed and be right back." Rising, I carry him to his room and tuck him into bed. Pausing at his bedside, I study every feature on his face and marvel for the millionth time that

Juliet and I made him. How did we create someone so curious and precious? If I didn't believe in miracles before, I do now.

When I return to the living room, I find Juliet pouring wine into two glasses. Sinking down next to her, I take the offered drink from her. "Are you trying to get me drunk?"

"No. But I might be trying to get me drunk," she replies.

"Why do you need wine tonight? What's going on?" Immediately, my mind goes to the worst possible scenario. I assume she's about to tell me we made a mistake by sharing that I'm Emmett's father.

"It's been a crazy week or so, and I felt like some wine."

"That's all?" I question.

"No. There's more, but I'm not sure I'm ready."

"Ready for what?" I ask.

"To tell you I love you," she blurts out.

"Why aren't you ready?" I question.

"I'm scared you'll change your mind about being with us so much. Or decide you can't handle being a father so young."

"Juliet, that's pretty insulting to me and you. Basically, you're saying I'm too immature to know what I want."

"That's not how I intended it to sound."

Placing my untouched wine down, I sink my fingers into her long tresses and stare down into her eyes. "I loved you when I was eighteen and I love you at twenty-two. I'll still love you at twenty-six and thirty too. Do you need me to continue?"

"Can you say it again, please?"

"I love you, Juliet."

"I never thought I'd hear you say those words. I love you so much, Emmett."

Leaning forward, I connect our lips. Starting out slow and tender, it soon shifts to hot and passionate. The long-awaited reunion was worth the time we spent apart. And we'll never be parted again.

THE END.

CALM THE STORM
BY KELSEY CLAYTON

CHAPTER ONE
EMERY

WALKING THROUGH THE FRONT DOOR OF MY BEST FRIEND'S HOUSE, ASHLYN grabs a drink, and I collapse onto one of the barstools at the island. She passes me a bottle of water with the special judgmental look she seems to reserve just for me.

"Em, you cannot wait until the last minute to pack," she deadpans. "I told you it's a bad idea."

I cock a single brow at her. "You mean if I go upstairs, your entire room will be packed already?"

Her lips quirk into a smirk that answers my question. *Exactly.* After graduating high school and spending the summer being legal adults, Ashlyn and I are finally going to college. We always said we were going to go to the same university and share a dorm, and that's exactly what we're doing. There's just one problem: we haven't packed.

Like at all.

And we leave in two days.

Granted, the university is only two hours away, so forgetting something isn't the complete end of the world, but we should probably have at least the basics for move-in. Otherwise, we're going to be sleeping on bare mattresses and living out of a suitcase.

"It's not my fault," she argues. "Life has been...distracting."

"Sleeping with your neighbor is not life, Ash."

A deep, familiar laughter echoes through the room, and I whip my head around to see Ashlyn's older brother Harland standing in the doorway. His arms are crossed over his chest, and he looks like something out of my wildest punk-rock fantasies. The band T-shirt he's wearing suits the bad-ass rocker look he has going. I could spend all day just staring at him.

"Mike?" he barks. "You've seriously been banging that troll?"

Ashlyn narrows her eyes at me, and I mouth an apology as Harland comes closer. He puts his hand on the top of her head and messes up her hair, treating her the same way he always has and the same way she's always hated—like she's a child.

"Aw, sis," he sighs dramatically. "I thought you had better taste than that."

"Fuck off, H." Ash elbows him in the side to get him away from her, but he dodges it.

Leaning his arms on the island across from me, his gaze locks with mine, and I nearly forget how to breathe. Harland Storm has been the object of my affection for as long as I can remember. He's three years older than us, the singer in his band Sound the Sirens, and drop-dead fucking gorgeous. Seriously, I've spent years around him and still can't seem to contain myself in his presence. Especially when he's looking at me like that.

"And what about you, Emery?" My name is like honey as it drips from his lips. "Who did you spend the summer fucking?"

I all but choke on my words as Ashlyn saves me from having to answer him.

"Don't be such a pervert," she snaps. "Just because Lindsey dumped your ass doesn't mean you can live vicariously through everyone else's sex life."

Wait, what?

Harland and Lindsey have been together since his freshman year of high school. It goes without saying that I was devastated when they started dating. In my eleven-year-old brain, we were going to grow up, fall in love, and get married. No one could tell me otherwise. So how dare he go out and find a girlfriend that wasn't me? But I was a kid, and the big, bad high schooler wanted nothing to do with little old me.

To hear they broke up is a shock to my system, but it doesn't look like I'm the only one. Even Harland winces at Ash's words. His eyes meet mine, and for a second, I think I see a hint of a smile forming, but as soon as his phone rings, he's snapped out of it.

"What's up?" he answers. "Are you fucking serious? Shit. I'll be right there!"

He hangs up the phone and yanks open the fridge to grab a drink before heading for the door. Ashlyn looks over at the full sink and rolls her eyes.

"Didn't mom tell you to do the dishes, lowlife?" she asks exasperatedly.

"I'll do them later!" he calls back. "This *lowlife* has a record label that wants to meet with Sound the Sirens."

Our jaws drop. They've been trying to get a record deal for years, and have had rotten luck. It's a shame, because their band is incredible. I've fallen asleep to the sound of the EP they recorded last summer more often than I'm willing to admit.

Just when we think he's gone, he pokes his head back in the room. "By the way, tell Mike that if I see him, I'm going to put his dick through a meat grinder for touching my baby sister." He looks over at me, and the smile on his face threatens to knock my world off its axis. "Bye, Em."

I'm not okay.

I repeat, I'm *not* okay.

I TOSS AND TURN IN ASH'S BED, FEELING LIKE I JUST CAN'T GET COMFORTABLE. You would think after packing three-quarters of her room I'd be exhausted, but I'm not. My brain just won't shut off, and my mouth is the tacky kind of dry that makes it hard to focus on anything else.

Ash is sound asleep next to me. Her mouth is open, and I can't help but laugh at the tiny spot of drool that's pooling on her pillow.

I stay as quiet as possible as I slip out of bed and tiptoe from the room. I just need something to drink, and then maybe I'll finally be able to get some sleep. However, as I get into the kitchen, a dark shadow sitting out by the pool catches my eye.

Harland.

As if I have absolutely no control over my body, I bypass the fridge and head straight for the door. The warm summer air encases me as I make my way toward him, and it seems to settle my nerves a little. He stares out at the night sky, not even looking my way as I sit down on the lounge chair next to his.

"I'm surprised you're up," he says. "Don't babies normally go to sleep at eight?"

I roll my eyes but can sense the playfulness in his tone. "You just love treating us like toddlers. I'm not a little girl anymore, Harland."

For the first time since I came out here, his head turns toward me and his gaze skims over my body. "Trust me, I know."

What the hell does that mean? The fact that I'm out here at all is almost more than I can handle, so instead of attempting to unwrap that statement, I move into safer territory.

"How'd the meeting go?" Judging by the way he's acting right now, I'm guessing not well.

He smiles and lets out a puff of air as he looks down at his lap. "We sign papers next week."

"Holy shit, H! That's amazing!"

"Thanks."

It's huge news. News that will most likely change his life. But still, he doesn't look as happy as I thought he would be. I dip my head down to look up at his face.

"So why the frown?" I ask carefully.

He looks at me like he can see straight through to my soul. I'd kill for the ability to read his mind… hear the thoughts going through that head of his. Find out if his body tingles like mine just from knowing that he and I are alone together.

Who am I kidding? Yeah, right. Like that would ever happen.

"H?" My voice seems to snap him out of whatever trance he was in.

He looks away from me and shakes his head. "I guess I just thought things would be different."

It hits me like a ton of bricks, and I'd be lying if I said it didn't sting a little. "Shit, right. The breakup."

"No, that's not—"

"Of course, you're upset about Lindsey. You two were together for so long. I'm such an idiot."

"I'm—" He tries to talk but I cut him off again, on a nervous prattle roll.

"Shit. Now I said her name and probably made it worse. I'm really insensitive." I run my fingers through my hair. "Maybe I should just go to bed before I make things worse for you."

Reaching down, he grabs his beer off the ground and hands it to me. "Drink this."

My brows furrow. "What? Why?"

"Because you need to chill the fuck out," he says with a chuckle.

I sigh heavily and take a sip, trying not to relish in the fact that my lips are now exactly where his were only moments ago. The cold liquid covers my tongue and slides down my throat, cooling every inch of me. After drinking a little more, I hand it back to him.

"Thanks."

The corner of his mouth raises as he takes his own sip, and my eyes are glued to the way his Adam's apple bobs as he swallows. Everything about this guy screams manly: The way he speaks. The way he carries himself. The way confidence radiates from him. It's intoxicating.

He starts picking at the calluses on his fingers from years of playing guitar—a nervous habit he's had for years. "I'm not upset about Lindsey."

My breath hitches at his confession. "Y-you're not?"

"No," he answers, shaking his head. "I mean, it sucked when it happened, but I'm not upset now." His gaze turns to me, and his pupils are blown. I can barely see the light green that always seems to suck me in. His tongue darts out to moisten his lips, and I'm fascinated, like a moth around a lightbulb. "How could I be when I'm sitting here with you?"

At first, I think I heard him wrong. He couldn't have possibly said what I just thought I heard. But then he keeps his sights locked on my lips, and his hand comes up to gently hold my chin in place, and I'm a fucking goner. He slowly starts to lean in.

"Harland," I whisper.

His lips ghost across mine. "Shh. I just..."

Whatever he was about to say is gone the moment our mouths meet in a heated kiss. His hand wraps around the back of my neck and pulls me closer as our tongues dance together. It's feverish, and rushed, and everything I've imagined over the years.

"Fuck, Em," he groans.

Before I know it, he's laying me down on the lounge chair and climbing on top of me. I grip at his T-shirt and mentally will it to vanish as he starts moving down to kiss my neck. Every inch of my body is on fucking fire with his touch, leaving a lingering burn.

"H, please."

He chuckles against my skin. "Relax, baby. I've got you."

His hand slides down slowly until it reaches the waistband of my shorts. My breath stutters for a second, but the second he slips his fingers underneath my panties, all I can feel is overwhelming need. He lightly rubs over my clit, and my hips immediately arch into his touch.

All those years of guitar lessons clearly made him skilled in more than just instruments, because the magic he's working on me nearly makes me black out. Don't get me wrong—I've done enough to myself to be ashamed of, especially with thoughts of him running through my head. But having his hands on me, and his mouth sucking on the side of my neck, nothing compares.

Feeling daring, I reach down and grab his hard cock through his sweatpants. He gasps for a second and then lets out a moan I wish I could set as my fucking ringtone. It's possessive. Raw. Needy.

A single finger slips inside of me as his lips meet mine again, and I immediately clench around him.

"You're so tight," he murmurs in my mouth. "And so fucking wet for me."

Instead of answering, I grab the bottom of his shirt and rip it over his head. Tossing it onto the ground, he looks at me with a glint in his eyes that I've never seen before.

"Are you sure?" The question doesn't even sound like it's coming from him—like he doesn't want to ask it, and fears my answer, but knows he needs to.

I swallow harshly and nod. "Yes."

Harland bites his lip as he pushes my shirt up, exposing my breasts. His eyes rake over my body as his fingertips glide down my stomach. He lightly grips my shorts and panties together and pulls them down my legs, his slow and careful movements making me squirm.

"You're gorgeous," he whispers.

"I am?"

His gaze meets mine, and he smirks. "As if you didn't know."

I mean, I've always known guys in school thought I was pretty. They made it obvious with their unskilled efforts at flirting. But I never thought I was pretty enough for the one I wanted. The one who's staring down at me like I'm good enough to eat. The one I've dreamed of for as long as I can remember.

He rids himself of his sweatpants, and his hard cock springs free. I damn near choke on air the second I see how big he really is.

For my seventeenth birthday, Ashlyn thought she was hilarious when she gifted me a dildo that is probably double the size of anything a virgin should be using. I mean, it was porn star level shit, and it's still in my closet—untouched and *definitely* unused.

But Harland—fuck. I think he might be bigger.

He pulls a condom out of his wallet and tosses the leather pouch onto the ground with his clothes. Looking down at me, he takes himself into his hand and slides the rubber on before jerking himself slowly and leaning down over me. He runs the head over my pussy, and I throw my head back as I try to keep in sounds that would most likely wake up the whole damn house.

"Look at me," he demands, and I have no chance of ever denying him, so I do. "I want to see you as I push inside."

He can't be more than an inch in before I wince, and he does exactly what I didn't want.

He fucking stops.

"Emery." My name sounds like a prayer and a threat all at once.

"Harland."

His eyes narrow, as if he's trying to figure it out, but never in a million years am I going to admit that I'm a virgin. I'm eighteen. He'll think I'm a loser. He'll stop. He'll never touch me again. So, instead of being honest like I probably should, I mask over my fear with determination.

"Are you going to fuck me, or should I go find someone else?" I question boldly.

He growls, and with two hands on my hips, he slams inside of me in one fluid motion. I feel like every part of me is going to explode. With pain. With pleasure. With everything.

Harland doesn't let up as he slams inside of me over and over, and I don't want him to. As soon as the sting wears off, I'm arching my hips up and meeting him thrust for thrust. His fingers lace into my hair and hold me steady as his tongue tangles with mine in every way that I need.

"You're so goddamn tight," he moans. "Fuck, baby. I need you to come."

He uses his free hand and presses his thumb against my clit, rubbing circles in a way that gives me no shot in hell at resisting.

"Give me it, Emery." His voice is like a growl as he moves his lips to my ear. "I want every fucking ounce of your pleasure. Cum on my cock, baby. Let me feel you."

My hips grind into his touch, and on one particularly hard thrust, I go over the edge. My orgasm rips through my body at a rate that threatens to tear me apart. I can't even stop myself from screaming out as Harland rushes to cover my mouth, which somehow just enhances the pleasure.

As I clench around him and he works me through my high, I watch as he bites his bottom lip hard and his movements halt, his dick pulsing inside of me. He collapses on top of me and pants heavily as we both catch our breath. It isn't until we both feel something warm start to leak out of me that our eyes widen.

"Fuck," he sighs. "Please tell me you're on the pill."

My brows raise as I look at him like he's lost his mind. "With my parents, who swear my soul will be damned to hell if I so much as kiss a boy before I'm married? Right."

He pulls out, and there it is, clear as day—the condom broke.

Harland runs his fingers through his hair as he tries to figure out what to do, when he suddenly picks me up and jumps into the pool. The water feels cold against my heated skin, and I swim to the surface and sputter.

"Harland! What the fuck?"

He swims closer and pulls me toward him. "Wash it out of you."

I cough on some of the water that made it into my mouth. "Excuse me?"

"You heard me." His movements are slow, but I flinch when my back hits the cold side of the pool. "You want me to do it for you?"

I don't think I could trust my voice, so all I do is nod. He smirks as two fingers meet my sore pussy and push inside. My head falls against the edge as the intense pleasure takes over again. It's like every part of me that was sensitive before is multiplied from my recent life-changing orgasm.

"Does this even work?" I question.

He shrugs and continues to work his magic on my clit. "I don't see why it wouldn't."

I smirk, tilting my head to the side. "It would probably work better if you fucked it out of me."

Throwing his head back, he chuckles. "Your confidence in me as a man is flattering, but I don't think I can get hard again right now."

Well, that sounds like a challenge.

"Want to bet?"

I wrap my legs around his waist, and it only takes a minute before I feel him start to thicken.

Fuck, yes. Round two.

I WAKE IN THE MORNING, THOROUGHLY EXHAUSTED AND COMPLETELY sexed out. The sun shining in my eyes makes me wince, and I roll over to find Ashlyn already awake and at her desk. My brows furrow as I look at her and sit up.

"What time is it?" I ask sleepily.

She glances over at me and chuckles. "Almost noon. You were sleeping like the fucking dead."

Noon? "Ugh, I have to pack today. Why'd you let me sleep this late?"

"I tried to wake you. You wouldn't budge."

"Fuck my life."

As I go to stand up, the sore feeling left from last night causes me to stumble and memories flow through my mind. The way he touched me on the lounge chair. The feeling of his lips on mine. How we couldn't get enough of each other in the pool.

I have to see him.

"I'm going to get a drink," I tell my best friend. "Do you want something?"

She shakes her head and holds up her Starbucks latte. "Your iced coffee is in the fridge."

The corners of my mouth raise. "You're a goddess."

"I know."

I go to the bathroom first, just to make sure I don't look like a total train wreck. The last thing I want to do is scare him away the second I finally have him. I run a brush through my hair and resist the urge to put a little makeup on then deem myself acceptable.

My feet pad down the stairs in search of my coffee, and hopefully Harland in the process, when the sight in front of me stops me in my tracks. Harland is sitting on the couch with a total blonde bombshell.

Lindsey.

I'm frozen in place as I watch this nightmare unfold. It looks like they're talking about something, but I'm too far away to hear what. I inch closer, unable to stop myself. It isn't until she sighs and pulls him in for a kiss that everything inside me shatters.

"I love you," she tells him.

As he wraps his arms around her and holds her close, his eyes meet mine. I can't stop the tears from falling, but I bat them away as soon as they hit my cheek, furious to show him this weakness.

I'm sorry, he mouths at me, and then his eyes focus on Lindsey's face as he responds.

"I love you, too."

THREE WEEKS LATER

I WALK INTO OUR DORM ROOM AND COLLAPSE ONTO MY BED. THE LAST FEW weeks have been exhausting, and my classes haven't made it any better. It's as if I can't seem to find the energy to stay awake, and no matter what I do, I can't focus.

"You look like shit," Ash tells me. "But still a little better than before."

After finding Harland with Lindsey and witnessing their reunion firsthand just hours after he took my virginity, I was a wreck. I managed to hide it from Ashlyn, telling her that I had some sort of stomach bug, but it sucked. I hid from the world as I let my tears soak the pillow, thankful that we were in our dorm instead of back in our hometown where I could do something I'd probably regret.

Suddenly, the urge to vomit rips through my stomach and sends me rushing to the garbage can. The contents of my lunch spew from my mouth as my best friend comes over to hold my hair back.

"Jesus, Em," she says, rubbing my back. "If I didn't know any better, I'd think you were pregnant."

Her words send a chill right through me, and I instantly heave into the can again, but this time for entirely different reasons.

Oh, fuck.

CHAPTER TWO

HARLAND
NEARLY FIVE YEARS LATER

PICKING UP MORE OF MY CLOTHES, I SHOVE THEM INTO THE BAG WITH A little more force than necessary. This is fucking bullshit. All of it.

I look around the tour bus I've spent the last few years in and admire the awards that line the walls. Platinum records. VMAs. Grammys. The thought that all of that could be done now pisses me off beyond belief.

The sound of Vance and Rhys laughing echoes through the bus as they climb on board, but the second they see me, their smiles drop off their faces.

"Packing?" Vance asks.

I nod and throw another thing into my bag. "It's fucking stupid."

Rhys snorts. "You don't need to tell us. We know."

Sitting down on the bunk, I run my hands over my face and groan. "I'm sorry, guys. I feel like I ruined everything."

Rhys goes to say something, but Vance throws a hand over his mouth. "It's not your fault, dude. So, you got engaged to a psycho. We all make mistakes."

"Psycho is an understatement," I tell him as I'm pulled back into the memory of what happened.

There's nothing better than the buzz that runs through me as we get done with a show. The screaming fans all shouting our songs back at us…It's unlike anything I've ever felt in my life.

The guys all head back to the bus, but I'm going to the hotel. Lindsey has been traveling with us and really doesn't like staying on the tour bus. She says it's too stuffy and crowded. I don't really understand it, but whatever makes her happy. I know she's been doing a lot with planning our wedding, and still managing to follow me around the world. The least I can do is give my girl what she wants.

I step into the elevator and wait for it to make its way up to the penthouse suite. All I want to do is drink a beer and climb into bed, but as I walk through the door, something feels off. There's a jacket thrown across the couch that I don't recognize, and a pair of shoes by the door that aren't the right size.

You've got to be fucking kidding me.

It doesn't take long for my mind to figure out what's going on. Hell, I've suspected it for a while, but I always told myself she would never. She's not that cruel. Stupid me for thinking better of her time and time again.

The second I open the bedroom door, I see exactly what I've been denying. Lindsey is on top of some guy, riding his dick while her tits bounce. Fucking bitch.

I throw the door open further with a force that threatens to break it. The sound of it slamming against the wall pulls both of their attention toward me. Lindsey's eyes widen, but the guy who I recognize from a band we beat out this year at the VMAs just smirks.

"Harland," my fiancée pleads.

I put a hand up to stop her and focus on him.

"Get the fuck out before I throw your ass off the goddamn balcony."

He doesn't need to be told twice as he jumps off the bed and scurries out of the room. Once I hear the door shut, I turn all my attention to Lindsey.

"We're done," I tell her. "The wedding is off. You can keep the ring, but I want you gone by morning."

She shakes her head as tears rush down her face. "No, baby. No. Don't do this."

I scoff and roll my eyes before making my way toward the exit, but she's hot on my heels.

"It didn't mean anything. I was just jealous of all the girls who throw themselves at you," she tries. "I thought you didn't want me anymore."

Bullshit. It's all fucking bullshit, and I have no interest in hearing it.

I continue my way toward the exit when she screams my name, and a slap echoes through the room. I stop in my tracks, thinking maybe she hit me, but no part of me feels anything. I turn around with brows furrowed and stare at her. She looks at me with a manic gleam in her eyes as she raises her hand again and punches herself straight across the face.

"What the fuck are you doing?"

She smirks, blood pooling at the corner of her mouth by her own doing. "You don't get to leave me."

Un-fucking-believable. "You're psychotic."

"I'm the love of your fucking life," she growls. "And the woman you're marrying next spring."

Laughter bubbles out of me as I call her bluff. "Not a chance in hell."

I turn around and walk out the door, flashing her the middle finger just before it closes.

Good fucking riddance.

THINKING BACK ON IT NOW, I SHOULD HAVE STAYED AND CALLED THE COPS. I should've filed some kind of protection order. But I was mad and went back to the tour bus to get drunk off any alcohol I could find. It wasn't until the next morning—when I woke to fifteen missed calls from my publicist—that I realized I fucked up.

Apparently, after I left, Lindsey proceeded to beat herself to the point where she looked like she was jumped by a gang. Both of her eyes were black and blue, her lip was split wide open, and she managed to break her own cheekbone.

And of course she blamed me.

Police rushed onto the tour bus and took me into custody before I even had time to take a piss. I was dragged down to the station and interrogated for hours. No one wanted to believe that she did it to herself. Who would? The story itself is outlandish. No one is that psychotic, right? Wrong. Apparently, the girl I've spent almost the last decade with is.

Lucky me.

It took a few hours before they came in and said that she dropped all the charges, but that doesn't change the fact that all the media outlets already had a story printed. She told them that I beat her when she tried to leave me. Now the whole world sees me as a woman-beating prick with abandonment issues.

The guys and I tried to rough it out, wait for it all to go away and continue to do our thing, until the night of our show at Madison Square Garden. A fight broke out between a bunch of girls—some saying I was an abusive prick, and some trying to defend me. It was then that we knew we needed to take a break.

Two platinum records.

Nine VMAs.

Three Grammys.

All thrown down the fucking drain because I decided to get engaged to the devil herself.

Our publicist said that the best course of action was to go on hiatus. Basically, to take a few months break, maybe even a year or so. At least until everything dies down. She even tried to use the whole Chris Brown and Rihanna situation to ease my worries, but it didn't, because I didn't do anything fucking wrong.

The only bright side to this is that I'm heading home for the first time in almost five years. Maybe it'll be nice to lay low for a bit, out of the eyes of paparazzi and fawning fans. Where everyone loves me because I'm H, and not because I'm Harland Storm of Sound the Sirens.

PULLING UP TO THE HOUSE, IT ALMOST MAKES ME LAUGH AT THE WAY IT looks exactly the same. No matter how much I tried to bribe my mom to move out to LA, she refused. And now that I'm back here, I can see why. This humble abode is our home. It's the place I learned to ride a bike. The place I got my first guitar. It's every memory of my childhood all inside beige walls.

I walk through the door and toss my bag down. "Anyone home?"

My mom's squeal from the living room brings a smile to my face as she comes running toward me. My mother has always been a tiny little thing, but I love that about her. My 6'4" towers over her, and she needs to arch onto her tiptoes to hug me.

"I've missed you so much," she tells me, kissing my cheek.

"I've missed you too, Mom. It's good to see you again."

"I wish it were under better circumstances," she answers.

I drop my head and nod. None of my family ever liked Lindsey. They all swore from the start that she was bad news, but I didn't listen. I really wish I had.

Looking around the house, I notice someone is missing. "Where's Ash?"

My little sister graduated college last summer and still ended up moving back home. It's no secret that she's been mad at me since I missed her graduation. I tried to be there, but it was rained out and changed to a day where I had a show. No matter how many pleas I made to change the date of the show, they couldn't. Tickets had been bought and people had already flown in for it. I was stuck.

"Oh, she'll be home soon," my mom tells me. "Come. Let's sit down and talk. It's been a while."

I follow her into the living room, but while she sits down, I can't help but look around at the small differences of this place. Framed pictures of me on the wall aren't from my childhood anymore, but from award shows. She even has the article of when we sold out MSG for the first time in a frame on the mantle, next to one of the VMAs I sent her to hold onto.

"So, other than everything with that wench, how have you been?" My mom questions.

I chuckle at her choice of words. "Can't complain. It's exhausting but exhilarating. I love it so much."

"I always knew you would. Ever since you first picked up a guitar at five years old."

Looking over at her, I smile. "The yellow Fender Strat. You bought it for me for Christmas."

She gleams back at me. "And you did nothing but play it for years until you got a new one for your ninth birthday."

That's one thing I've always loved about my mom—she's supportive to a fault. No matter what Ashlyn and I have ever wanted to do, she was always there, cheering us on and pushing us to be our very best at it. Being a single mother to two rambunctious kids couldn't have been easy, but she never faltered.

I go back to looking at the mantle when one picture catches my eye. It's a little boy I've never seen before, but something about him is oddly familiar. He can't be any older than two in this photo, but I think I would've known if my sister had a baby. Or at least I hope someone would have told me. I stare at it for a moment before finally asking.

"Who's this little guy?"

My mom gets up and comes to stand next to me. "Oh, that's Hollis, Emery's little boy."

I damn near choke on air at her words. "Emery has a kid?"

With her parents' strict religious rules, I can't believe it. I used to think there was actually a chastity belt under those jeans of hers, or that she would end up being a nun. Then again, I know differently, don't I?

"Yeah," my mom answers. "Poor thing ended up pregnant a few years ago, no father to be seen. Her parents dropped her like a hot potato."

"Fucking seriously?"

She nods. "Ashlyn and I have been there for her as much as we can. You know that girl is like family to us. But she ended up having to drop out of college to raise him. She's done an incredible job, though. I just wish she could have at least gotten through school. Dropping out only months into her freshman year was rough on her."

Everything freezes inside of me, and time stands still. My eyes meet the little boy in the photo, and all the familiar things about him stare back at me.

Oh my God.

CHAPTER THREE
EMERY

I THROW MYSELF DOWN ON THE COUCH WITH A GRUNT. AFTER GETTING OFF work, the last thing I want to do is chase around a three-year-old, but I have no choice.

"Mommy!" Hollis shouts as he climbs up and jumps on me.

"Hey baby," I say, kissing his forehead. "Have you been good for Aunt Ashlyn and Aunt Mila?"

My sister laughs. "No. That child is a menace. He takes after you."

Hollis pouts. "She's telling stories, Mommy. I good boy."

Ashlyn comes over and grabs him off me. "You're a very good boy, H," she tells him. "Aunt Mila doesn't know what she's talking about."

I smile as I watch her take over with my son. My best friend has been a godsend throughout his life. After finding out I was pregnant, I knew I had two options: I could either terminate and try to move on, forcing myself to forget it ever happened, or I could put the baby first. The answer was clear. And when my parents told me I was no longer their daughter because I was pregnant out of wedlock, I knew I made the right decision, because I would never do that to my son.

Despite the circumstances, I've done well. I have a small apartment for Hollis and me, but the neighborhood is safe and there's space for him to play outside. I have a job that allows me to work from home. Mila and Ashlyn take turns coming over and watching him for me while I get work done. Honestly, I don't know what I would do without either of them. They have been my saviors in all of this. But out of everyone, Hollis has been the most important. He's everything, and every day that I watch him grow amazes me even more. I never knew I could love someone as much as I love him.

"But I want to play with Mommy," Hollis tells Ashlyn as she carries him away.

She looks over at me and crinkles her nose. "It looks like Mommy needs a nap."

"Mommy just needs to get laid," Mila jokes, and Ashlyn and I cough to cover up her words.

Hollis giggles. "Mommy buys me toys when she gets laid!"

Oh God. "No, honey. It's *paid*. When Mommy gets *paid*."

"Paid. Paid. Paid!"

Ashlyn puts him down as he scurries away. "What happened to that one guy you were seeing?"

"Yeah, what was his name? Jon? Ron?" She snaps her fingers. "Rob!"

I chuckle and shrug. "He had a tiny..."

"Aw, he had a push-pop," Mila quips with a giggle.

"Push pops?" Hollis chimes in. "I love push pops!"

Ashlyn facepalms while I cringe. "Okay, maybe we should put him down for a nap before we have this conversation."

"I've got it," Ash says as she gets up and grabs him as he tries to run away. "Come on, little H. It's nap time for you."

He struggles in her hold. "But I don't want a nap! I'm not sleepy!"

"Sure you are, buddy," she tells him as he starts to yawn.

As my best friend puts my son down, Mila scrolls through her phone.

"Hey-la, your boyfriend's back," she singsongs.

I look over at her like she's talking nonsense. "What?"

She turns her phone around, and an article about Harland is on the screen.

Sound the Sirens' Harland Storm is Heading Home to Weather His Own Storm.

Okay, whoever wrote that could have been a little less obvious. Still, I knew about all the shit that went down with Lindsey, because I needed to convince Ashlyn that finding her and slitting her throat was a bad idea. I didn't know he was coming home, though. The last time I saw Harland was when I was running from his house, and that's not a memory I like to relive.

The one secret I've kept from my best friend. The only thing in my whole life that I've never told her. The sole thing that could make her hate me—the night I spent with her brother and the result of that night, my son. The only person I did tell is my sister, which is exactly why she's looking at me right now with mischief in her eyes.

"He was already falling asleep before I even made it out the door," Ash tells me as she comes back in the room.

My brows furrow. "I didn't know Harland was coming home."

She looks confused for a second, and then her eyes go wide. "Shit! That's today?" She grabs her phone off the coffee table. "I've got to go! Love you!"

"Love you, too," I call back to her as she runs out the door.

Meanwhile, Mila is bouncing her eyebrows at me suggestively as she shakes his picture in my face. I roll my eyes and throw my arm over my face.

I'm totally fucked.

THERE ARE CERTAIN TIMES WHEN BEING A MOM IS A LITTLE HARDER THAN normal. Take his birthday, for example. Trying to juggle working and taking care of Hollis is a lot, but add planning his fourth birthday party to the mix, and I'm a walking train wreck.

"What do you want at your party, H?" I ask him as he plays with his favorite toy dinosaur.

He looks up at me and smiles. "Presents!"

"Well, obviously."

"And cake! Lots of cake!"

My grin widens as I watch his joy at such simple things. "There will be plenty of cake, baby boy. But what do you want for you and your friends to do?"

Not that he has that many friends. I've tried to get him out and socialize at the park and such, but whenever someone looks at how young I am, you can see the judgment in their eyes. I can practically watch as they do the math in their head and their eyes go to my hand to look for a ring.

Seriously, this isn't the 50s.

"Bounce house!" he yells and then proceeds to get up and jump. "Bounce! Bounce! Bounce!"

I can always tell when Hollis is getting ready to take a nap, because he fights it hard. He becomes overactive to try to keep himself awake. The problem is, if I let it happen, he becomes a total nightmare to get to sleep at all. Overtired toddlers are the worst.

"Okay, we can get a bounce house, but you need to take a nap for Mommy while I plan your party. Can you do that?"

His bottom lip sticks out in a way that always turns me to mush. "But I don't want to, Mommy. I'm not tired."

"Even so, you need a nap."

I reach out and take his hand and lead him down the hallway toward his room.

AN HOUR AND A HALF LATER, I'VE GOT THE BOUNCE HOUSE BOOKED AS WELL as the cake ordered, and a face painter scheduled. My thought is that the more there is for him to do at his party, the less he will notice the lack of other kids there. I have a few people coming, like the two little girls who live downstairs and the boy from across the courtyard, but sometimes I wish I had the money to put him in daycare so he could make friends.

I'm scrolling through Amazon at different presents he wants, making his wish list, when there's a knock at the door. There are only two people it could be, but being as Mila is at her friend's house, getting ready for her bachelorette party, it has to be Ashlyn.

"Why are you knocking? Just come in!"

Nothing. No movement comes from the door. No sound of keys on the other side.

I sigh and toss my computer onto the couch and make my way toward the entrance.

"Ash, I've told you," I groan. "I gave you a key for a reason."

But as I open the door, the words are sucked right out of me. Harland leans in the doorway, looking like everything I remember, only hotter. The scruff that lines his face makes me want to run my fingers against it and feel it prick my skin, and the look in his eyes shows all he's been through the last few weeks.

Fuck. Stay calm, Em.

"Same genetics, but wrong Storm," he says with a wink. "Though I like to believe I'm the better of the two."

I look him up and down. "Maybe for everyone else, but you know no one holds a candle to your sister for me."

He hisses in feigned injury. "Ouch. Growing up made you cold."

Cold isn't the word I'd use, but having to raise my son has made me harder. It's given me a level of confidence I didn't know existed. It's made me strong. I let my eyes rake over Harland once more.

"What are you doing here?"

He gives me a boyish grin that five years ago would have flipped my insides. Hell, it still has an effect, just one I've learned to tame since then.

"I can't come see my favorite little sister?"

I damn near vomit in my mouth. "Ew. Don't call me that."

Chuckling, he cringes. "Yeah. I realized as soon as I said it."

The way he's standing there tells me he doesn't have any intentions of leaving, so instead of asking why he's here—a question I'm more than afraid to know the answer to—I step aside to let him in. He smiles charmingly as he walks past me and into my apartment.

"Cozy little place you've got here," he says.

Yeah, and it looks a hell of a lot better with you in it.

Fuck, focus Emery. It's been less than five minutes, and he's already getting under my skin. As if I haven't been looking at a miniature version of him for nearly four years. How Ashlyn hasn't noticed the resemblance yet is a mystery to me, but I'm not about to point it out. Not when she'd kill me for it. Hell, she'd kill me if she found him here right now, but thankfully that could be justified as him just wanting to catch up.

"So, how've you been?" I ask him, guiding us into safer territory than my thoughts.

He shrugs. "Been better. Ex is a psycho. You know, normal shit."

I take a seat on the couch across from him. "I heard. That sounds rough."

The corner of his mouth raises in a smirk. "Don't act like you didn't know she was crazy."

"I'm not saying that. I've always known she's a damn nutcase. But no one could tell you that back then."

He looks down at his lap and nods. "I was a stupid kid."

"You were young and in love," I reason.

"Something like that," he murmurs, but before I can question it, he changes the subject. "Tell me about you though. How's life been?"

We spend the next half-hour talking about random shit, and I honestly think it might be more than he's ever talked to me at once. I tell him about my job as a marketing executive for a small corporation, and he tells me what Australia is like, knowing I've always wanted to go there. With every second that passes, I start to calm, thinking maybe he's not here for what I thought after all.

"The spiders cannot be that big," I argue.

He raises his brows at me. "I'm telling you, it was the size of my head. I don't think I've ever heard Rhys scream so loud in my life."

I can't help but laugh at that thought. Rhys has always been a tough guy, except for the time he tried hitting on me when I was sixteen, and Harland looked like he was going to rip out his jugular.

Reaching over, he grabs a picture off the end table, and my heart starts to race.

Play it fucking cool.

"That's Hollis," I tell him calmly. "I'm sure your mom or Ash mentioned him."

He nods. "Your son, right?"

"Yeah."

A small smile makes its way to his face. "He's cute. Looks like you."

Don't blush.

Do not blush.

Shit.

"He's a total terror, but in the best ways."

He chuckles. "That's what Ash said, that being around him for more than an hour and you're ready for a nap."

"Pretty much," I giggle.

Everything goes quiet for a second, and I start to look around the room for something I can talk about that isn't the little boy who's half his. I never expected this conversation so soon. Though really, I should have.

"So, how long are you back for?" I question.

He looks up at me, and it's written all over his face. There's no denying it. And he doesn't even try to beat around the bush as I swallow hard. With our gazes locked together, I couldn't break it if I tried. Instead, I'm stuck, just staring at him helplessly. Finally, he speaks.

"He has my eyes, Em."

Fuck.

CHAPTER FOUR

HARLAND

FOR HOURS, I LAY IN BED, BUT I'M WIDE AWAKE. NO MATTER HOW MUCH I toss and turn, there aren't enough imaginary sheep to count that could help me fall asleep. I mean, how is anyone expected to sleep after they find out they have a son they knew nothing about?

It took me days before I got up the courage to go over to Emery's place, after doing some detective work and sneaking the address from my mom's address book. And once I was there, I bit my tongue for a half-hour before saying something about him.

I guess I had hoped she would tell me first. Then again, if she had any intentions of telling me, she would have when she found out she was pregnant. And judging by the way Ashlyn never said anything, I'm guessing she doesn't know either.

"Ugh," I groan into the darkness.

Rolling over, I grab my phone off the nightstand and scroll to the one person I've always told everything.

"Hello?" Vance answers, thankfully wide awake.

"Hey, man."

"H," he sighs. "What's wrong?"

I sit up and run my fingers through my hair. "Every time I think shit is going to calm down, I swear something else knocks me the fuck over."

"Put him on speaker," Rhys says in the background.

Of course they're together.

"What the hell happened now?" Vance asks.

The words feel foreign in my mind, and now that I'm about to say them out loud, it's a shock to my system. "I have a kid."

"You what?" they say in unison.

Vance groans. "Please don't tell me you knocked up Lindsey."

"No," I answer rapidly. "God, no. Not Lindsey." I pause for a minute, knowing the reaction I'm going to get for this. "It's Emery. We have a son together. He's almost four years old."

"You fucked Emery?" Rhys squawks. "After you damn near decapitated me for even looking at her a certain way?"

Vance already knew. I had told him a few days after it happened. But Rhys has wanted in Emery's pants since she grew a set of tits and stopped looking like my little sister's sidekick.

"Focus, Rhys," Vance tells him. "How do you know it's yours?"

I snort. "Well, for one, he could be my twin. I have no idea how she's kept it a secret this long, but it's fucking obvious. And two, she told me."

She didn't exactly want to, but when I confronted her on it, there wasn't any room for her to deny it. And the second she started to tear up, I knew. Hollis is my son. I have a fucking son.

"That's shit, man," Rhys says. "She seriously never told you?"

"Do you really think I would have abandoned my son by choice?"

"No," Vance answers for him, and I can only imagine what face Rhys is making right now.

Prick.

"So, what are you going to do?" my best friend asks.

I sigh heavily. "I don't know, but I need to figure it out."

THE WHOLE NIGHT, I BARELY GET A WINK OF SLEEP. I CAN'T HELP BUT remember the look on Emery's face when I all but told her I know Hollis is mine. The way she couldn't look me in the eyes as she nodded, and the feelings that rushed through me when it was confirmed.

I have a son.

A little boy who's walking and talking and keeping everyone on their toes.

And then comes the realization that I missed out on so many milestones. His first steps. His first words. His damn birth, for fuck's sake. They're all things I can't get back. Things she took from me.

The more I think about it, the angrier I get. I mean, I knew there was a chance after the condom broke that night. Especially since we fucked bare in the pool. But I thought that she would tell me if she got pregnant.

Surprise. I was wrong. Again.

Just like I was wrong about Lindsey.

As I lay in my bed, staring at the ceiling while the sun comes up, I start to wonder what my life would've been like if I hadn't gotten back with Lindsey at all. That night with Emery—fuck, it was everything I wanted for so long. She was always there, with her perfect body and innocent doe eyes. I wanted her, but she was off limits.

My sister was my other half growing up, and as much as I may have picked on her, I never wanted to do anything to betray her. Even now, she's too important to me. So, dating her best friend, and indirectly taking her away from Ashlyn, was something forbidden. I don't know if that made me want it even more, but I told myself I'd never let it happen.

Until it did.

After finding out we were getting a record deal, I knew I'd be leaving. I was going to be on tour, and everything in my life was about to change. I sat out by the pool and thought about it all, let it play through my mind, and then she showed up. Emery came out looking every bit like what I needed in that moment.

And I was weak.

She's always made me weak.

I gave in.

And I loved it.

But the next morning came with the shame and regret I should have felt the night before, when she was staring back at me like I hung the damn moon. So, when Lindsey came over to apologize, I convinced myself that she was who I wanted. And I took her back despite the heartbroken look in Emery's eyes.

I PULL UP TO THE PARK WHERE EMERY IS THROWING HOLLIS'S BIRTHDAY party. It's got a huge field where she has an obnoxiously large bounce house set up. There are blue balloons with the number 4 tied in every possible place, and a face painter table is set up by the playground.

A few little kids run around, and it only takes me a second to point him out.

Hollis.

He's adorable, with Emery's light brown hair and my green eyes. He even has her smile. He's perfect, but she kept him from me.

I go to the back of my truck and pull out the massive ride-on Jeep I got him, throwing it over my shoulder as I walk toward the party. Don't get me wrong, it's fucking heavy, but it's not a bad thing to let her see my muscles flex.

"Ugh," Ashlyn groans when she sees me. "You're always such a showoff."

Emery walks up next to her as I place the Jeep down. I haven't seen her since I walked out of her apartment that day, saying I needed some time to think. Think on what exactly, I'm not sure. But in that moment, that apartment was way too small. I needed to breathe, and I knew the mood I was in right then was not the mood I want to be in when I meet my son.

"You didn't have to do that," she tells me.

I arch a brow at her in a silent message she clearly understands, but my sister is here and I'm not trying to throw her under the bus. "It's no problem."

"Whoa!" a little voice says in awe. "Is that for me?"

Turning my head, I see Hollis standing here with wide eyes as he stares at the Jeep. I squat down until I'm his height.

"It is, little man," I tell him. "Happy Birthday."

He lights up like a goddamn Christmas tree, and my chest aches at the sight. Hollis walks up slowly and carefully looks it over, running his hand across the custom paint job I had a friend of mine do on it. It says his name on the side in graffiti letters, and a teal paint job Ashlyn said is his favorite color.

"What do you say, Hollis?" Emery asks him.

Looking at his mom for a second, he rushes over and gives me a big hug. "Thank you!"

I close my eyes and try to hide the fact that I'm breaking under the surface as I hug my son for the first time. "You're welcome, buddy."

It only lasts a minute before he runs off to drive it around with his friends, but my world is changed by that single minute. I stand up and look at Emery, who murmurs a quiet thank you. I nod in response, because I'm not sure I know what to say to her yet.

SITTING ON A PICNIC TABLE, I CAN'T SEEM TO TAKE MY EYES OFF HOLLIS, except for when it's to look at his mom. It's one thing to watch what an incredible little kid he is, but it's another to see her with him. He looks at his mom like she's the greatest thing in the world, and she treats him with a level of care I've only seen from one other person—my own mother.

Ashlyn comes over and climbs up next to me. "Don't even think about it."

I look over at her in confusion, and she laughs.

"I see the way you're looking at her. Don't do it."

"I don't know what you're talking about."

She chuckles. "Yeah, okay."

It's quiet for a second as we both watch Emery cut the birthday cake and hand it out to all the guests.

"She's been through a lot," my sister tells me. "With her parents abandoning her and her having to raise Hollis on her own. She plays it off well, and does an incredible job, but it's been hard on her."

Her words strike a nerve, because she didn't have to do this on her own. She chose to. She chose to raise him on her own. She kept me from my damn son.

"I'm just saying," she continues when I don't answer, "you've both been through a lot, and while you're older now, I don't think it's a good idea."

I swallow down the lump in my throat. "Still have no idea what you're talking about."

"If you say so."

Hollis finishes his cake in record timing and comes running this way with Emery in tow. "Aunt Ashlyn, Mommy won't push me on the swings!"

Ash giggles and pretends to be mad at Emery. "Mean Mommy!"

Em rolls her eyes. "I told you. Mommy needs to start cleaning up."

My sister jumps off the table and puts out her hand for him to hold. "Let's go swing."

"Thank you," Emery tells her as they walk off.

I try to leave it alone. Really, I do. This isn't the time or the place, but I'm so sick of the women in my life making choices that fuck me over. And this? This is a massive fuck you.

Emery goes back to clean up the tables, and I make my move, coming up behind her as she leans over a picnic table to grab some trash.

"Do either of them know how legitimate that name is?" I growl with my lips pressed to her ear. "*Aunt* Ashlyn."

She sighs. "Harland, please. Not now."

"Then when? Huh?" I'm trying to reign in my anger before people hear us, but it's so fucking hard. "When?"

"I don't know," she answers and runs her fingers through her hair. "I just need to figure this out. I need some time."

Time. "You mean the past four fucking years weren't enough?"

For a second, it looks like I hit my target, but it's quickly masked over with a hardness I've never seen in her.

"You don't get to talk to me like that," she hisses, shoving her finger into my chest. "You're the one who ruined this. You're the one who hurt me. You're the one who took my virginity like it was yours to have, and then got back with your ex while I was still in your house."

Wait, what? "Took your…"

She scoffs and rolls her eyes. "Don't act like you didn't know. And I may have made some shitty choices since then, but I did what I thought was right and worked with what I had. So, if you're going to stand here and yell at me, you can just leave."

Turning back, she resumes what she was doing like nothing happened, but my mind is spiraling. I had my suspicions that night, especially with how tight she was, but I assumed I was overthinking it. She was eighteen and seemed so sure of herself.

I'm such an asshole.

⁂

NO MATTER WHERE I DRIVE TO, I CAN'T SEEM TO GET MY MIND TO STOP reeling. So, I pull up to the lake I always used to come to, and dial Vance—hoping Rhys isn't with him this time. I don't need his fucking shit right now.

"I figured you'd call me as soon as you left," V tells me. "How was the party?"

I smile at the memory of Hollis. "He's incredible. He's so smart, and probably one of the happiest kids I've ever seen. And he's polite."

He snorts. "Spoken like a true father."

"Fuck, you're right. I didn't even realize."

"So, if it went well, why do you sound so messed up?"

I lean my head back against the headrest and sigh. "I really fucked up, V. Ashlyn made a comment about Em raising Hollis alone, and I saw red. I cornered Emery about it."

"Shit," he groans. "Did anyone hear you?"

"I don't think so, but she gave it right back to me." I run my fingers through my hair. "She was a virgin that night."

He goes quiet for a minute before answering. "Are we pretending you didn't know that?"

"I *didn't* know that."

Chuckling for a second, he takes a deep breath. "You did. You may not have wanted to believe it, but you did. I mean, you saw how her parents were. Who did you expect her to sleep with?"

"Well, Ashlyn was fucking the neighbor kid."

"Oh, so clearly if her best friend is having sex, that means she is, too."

Fuck. "Don't do that."

He huffs humorously. "Do what? Tell you you're being a dumbass? I'm your best friend, H, but I'm not going to beat around the bush here. Everyone could see that girl was in love with you. It doesn't surprise me at all that she gave it up to you without a second thought."

"And then I went and fucked her over."

"Yep." No sugar coating.

"Still, that doesn't make it right that she didn't tell me about Hollis," I argue.

"You're right," he agrees. "It doesn't. But imagine what your life would have been like if she had. Do you really think our band would have gone as far as it did? I mean, I'm not saying it wouldn't have been worth it to give up everything for your son. I'm sure it would have. But everything would be different if she had."

He's right. If she had told me she was pregnant, I would have done the right thing. I wouldn't have gone on tour, and I probably would have sold all my instruments just to help her pay for things for the baby. But now...now I'm in a place where I can take care of them. I can give them the life they deserve. I may not have been around for the beginning of his life, but that doesn't mean I can't be now. She never said I couldn't see him.

"I hate when you make me feel like an asshole," I tell Vance.

He snickers. "Someone's gotta do it."

As we get off the phone, one thing has never been clearer. Emery and I have both made mistakes in our past, and it's not a pissing war of who fucked up more. There's a little boy who needs us both.

Hollis matters most here.

CHAPTER FIVE
EMERY

I WATCH AS HOLLIS RIPS THROUGH ALL OF HIS PRESENTS. IT'S NORMALLY MY favorite part of his birthday—seeing the huge smile on his face as he sees all the cool new things he got. But today, I can't seem to get myself into it. Harland's words replay through my mind and every time I close my eyes, I see the way he looked at me.

Like I was selfish.

Like I was cruel.

Like I ruined his life.

Mila plops herself down next to me. "I'd say it's your party and you can cry if you want to, but it's not."

That manages to pull a small laugh out of me. Mila had to work and wasn't able to make it to Hollis's party, but she made sure to come over immediately after to see him open all his gifts. I was grateful for it, because carrying a whole SUV full of presents up two flights of stairs while watching a hyperactive four-year-old is nearly impossible.

"He was so mad," I murmur.

She takes a sip of her drink before sighing. "Maybe he wouldn't be if you just came clean about it."

I shake my head without giving it a second thought. "No. It wouldn't do any good."

"You don't know that."

"I do," I tell her as I stand up.

Ending the conversation there, I walk over to Hollis and sit on the floor—forcing myself into the moment. I won't get many years of this, so I want to enjoy every last one.

BY THE TIME HOLLAND HAS ALL OF HIS PRESENTS OPENED, AND I MANAGE TO get all the wrapping paper cleaned up, I'm exhausted. The party today was a lot to handle. Thankfully, there's only a few more hours until Hollis goes to bed and I can crash.

I'm in the middle of opening a set of action figures when there's a knock at the door. Mila and I share a look before I get up. It's not like I'm expecting anyone. Ashlyn is on a date with a guy she met at work, and my sister is already in my living room.

I open the door, and my chest tightens when I see Harland standing on the other side of it. He looks just as good as he did at the party today, in his black jeans and AC/DC T-shirt. The black sunglasses that hang from his collar only draw my attention away from his chiseled jaw and onto his sculpted chest.

A soft chuckle snaps me out of my stupor, and I straighten up, looking him in the eyes. "Did you come to yell at me some more?"

He winces slightly. "I guess I deserve that, but no. I came to talk."

"Talk?"

"Just talk." He looks past me and into the apartment. "Can I come in?"

For a second, I wonder if I could tell him no. After everything today, I don't think I can handle another argument with him. But when I really think about it, I realize that talking is probably exactly what we need to do right now. So, instead of shutting the door in his face, I open it further and let him step inside.

Harland follows me through the kitchen and into the living room, where Mila looks up and smirks.

"Well, if it isn't Harland Storm," she drawls.

He huffs out a small laugh. "Hey, Mila."

"She was just leaving," I tell him, hoping she'll get the hint.

Of course, being the brat that my sister is, she's not letting me off that easy.

"I don't know," she says as she comes toward us. "I might have to stay now." Running her hand down Harland's arm, she smiles. "You look good, H."

No part of me believes for a second that she's actually hitting on him. After all, she's been the only person who has known this whole time that Harland is Hollis's dad. No. She's just fucking with me. Trying to get under my skin. And I'd be lying if I said it wasn't working.

Harland looks over at me with a subtle plea for help, and I snicker. "Bye, Mila."

She scoffs. "You're no fun."

"I'm plenty fun," I argue. "I'll see you tomorrow."

"Yeah, yeah," she says and waves me off.

"It was good seeing you again," Harland tells her.

Mila snorts. "Better to see my sister, I'm sure."

He turns to me in surprise as Mila makes her way past him, but I'll deal with him later. Meanwhile, my sister is bouncing her brows at me and mouthing *tell him*. She can't leave soon enough. I roll my eyes and watch her head for the door.

"Love you."

"Love you, too!" she calls back.

The second the door shuts behind her, Harland tilts his head to the side. "Does she know about..."

Looking away, I nod. "She's the only one I told."

"Ah," he says. "That makes sense."

We both awkwardly make our way to the couch when Hollis looks up at Harland and his eyes widen. "You got me the car!"

Harland's smile stretches across his face. "I did, little man."

He grins proudly and goes back to playing, while Harland turns his attention to me. I run my fingers through my hair, waiting for him to say something, but nothing seems to be coming out of his mouth. I guess it's on me.

"So, you wanted to talk?" I push.

Nodding, he looks over at Hollis, and I realize his hesitation.

"Hey, Hollis?" I say. "Can you go set up your action figures in your room? I'm sure they'd love to meet all your other ones."

He beams, as if the idea is the most brilliant one he's ever heard. "Okay, Mommy."

Once we're alone, I focus back on Harland.

"Thanks," he breathes.

I lean back against the cushion. "No, thank *you*. Sometimes I forget how old he is and how much he understands at this age. I guess my mind is still locked on him being a baby."

"Kids are sponges. I remember when Ashlyn was four. She heard my dad say fuck, and that became the *only* thing she would say for a whole week."

Laughing at the thought of my best friend, I shake my head. "I doubt that had anything to do with her being a sponge. That's still her favorite word."

"Why am I not surprised?" he quips.

We settle into an awkward silence, but it's not as bad as I thought it would be. I'm not itching for him to leave or staring at the clock and watching the seconds tick by. We're just simply...here.

"Listen, I want to ap—"

His words are cut off as the sound of my phone ringing blasts through the room.

Great fucking timing.

I murmur an apology and grab my phone off the coffee table. When I see it's work, I throw my head back and groan. Harland watches me as I hit answer, bringing it to my ear.

"Hello?"

My boss's voice comes through the other line. "Emery. Thank God you answered. I know you took the day off today, but I need you to log in for a bit."

Fuck. "What? Why? Stephen, it's my son's birthday."

"I know, and I wouldn't be calling if it wasn't urgent, but Mr. Garrison moved his deadline, cutting two weeks off the end. We need to finish this project ASAP."

Mr. Garrison is our biggest client, and he's right. There is nothing we can do about it. The company could end up going under if we lose that contract.

Just my luck.

"Okay," I tell him. "Give me like ten minutes and I'll be on."

"Thanks, Em."

I hang up the phone and run my hands over my face, for a second forgetting Harland is here at all. He watches me intently as I sigh.

"I have to work for a bit." Then I realize my predicament. "Shit, Hollis! I have to call Mila. Maybe she's still close enough to come back and watch him for me."

Dialing her number, I bring the phone back to my ear, but Harland takes it away and presses end. My brows furrow as I watch him.

"What are you doing?"

He shrugs. "I can watch him."

Okay, what? "You don't have to do that. I'm sure Mila wouldn't mind coming back."

"Em, it's fine," he tells me honestly. "I think I can handle it."

Hollis comes running out with every single action figure he owns wrapped in his little arms, clearly not understanding the concept of playing in his room. He drops them on the floor in front of Harland. Instead of just watching from a distance, Harland gets down on the floor with him and picks Batman up.

"Is this one your favorite?" he asks him. Hollis nods, making Harland smile. "He's my favorite, too."

Hollis lights up like this is the best day of his life and goes about setting them all up in what looks like a battle. Meanwhile, Harland looks up at me and smirks.

"I've got this, Em. Go do what you need to do."

I don't know what's more surprising—the way he seems so sure of himself, or how comfortable I feel about it. I mean, I've known him for most of my life, so I guess there is no reason for me to feel any other way, but I guess I just never expected this from him. Hell, even when their cousins were toddlers, he never wanted anything to do with them.

Running my fingers through my hair, I look around for a second and exhale. "Okay. Okay, thanks. I'll just be in my room. I shouldn't be too long."

But neither one of them are listening. They're already off on their own conversation about which superheroes are the best and which ones are just okay.

Boy talk.

IT ENDS UP BEING WELL PAST HOLLIS'S BEDTIME WHEN I FINALLY FINISH UP what I needed to get done. I can only imagine how much of a nightmare getting him to sleep is going to be.

I look myself over in my bedroom mirror, realizing I look as tired as I feel, but there's not much I can do about it right now. Running my fingers through my hair, I throw a sweatshirt on and make my way back into the living room.

The sound of Harland and Hollis playing together echoes down the hallway, and when I reach the doorway, I can't help but stop and watch them for a couple minutes. Hollis is dressed up in one of his superhero capes with the foam sword Mila got him. Harland lays on the ground in front of him with his hands up in surrender.

"You're done, bad guy," Hollis growls adorably in his little voice.

He hits Harland with the foam sword, and Harland doesn't miss a beat. He pretends like it actually injured him, but when Hollis leaps onto his stomach, the groan that comes from Harland sounds a little more real. Still, he grabs his waist and flips them over carefully before tickling him. Hollis squirms around in a fit of giggles.

"Hawlan, stop it."

"What was that?" Harland laughs. "You want more? Okay, buddy. You asked for it!"

As he tickles him even more, Hollis's laughter gets louder. It isn't until Harland stops that they both calm down. Hollis lies on the floor, catching his breath, and I notice him yawn.

"H," I call his name, but realize my mistake the second they both answer me.

"What?" they say in unison.

Covering up the similarity with a smile, I look at Hollis. "It's time for bed, babe."

He immediately starts to pout. "Do I have to?"

"Yeah. It's been a long day, and it's already an hour past your bedtime."

"Okay," he sighs and gets up, but instead of coming toward me, he stops and looks at Harland. "Will you come back and play with me tomorrow?"

My heart nearly explodes when I see how much they've managed to bond in just a few hours. Harland glances over at me, and I nod once.

"Sure, buddy. I can do that."

Hollis grins broadly and runs into Harland's arms, catching us both off guard.

"Goodnight, Hawlan."

Harland wraps his arms around him and closes his eyes as he embraces his son. "Goodnight, little man."

When they let go, Hollis runs over to me. I pick him up in my arms, but before I head toward Hollis's room, I focus on Harland.

"Wait here," I tell him. "I'll be right out."

He nods, and I leave to tuck our son into bed.

AFTER THREE BEDTIME STORIES AND A PROMISE THAT WE CAN HAVE ICE cream for breakfast, I'm finally leaving his room and closing the door behind me. Overtired children are more difficult than third-world dictators, I swear.

"Sorry that took so long," I say as I walk into the living room, but the sight in front of me stops me in my tracks.

The mess that looked like a volcano of toys erupted in my living room is gone, and everything is neatly put away. There is a stack of toys organized in the corner, and all the cards in a pile on the coffee table. The one thing that's missing, though, is Harland.

The sound of glasses clinking pulls my attention to the kitchen, and I won't admit to how much relief floods through me when I see he's still here. He pours wine into each glass and then puts the bottle back in the fridge.

"You cleaned," I breathe.

He shrugs and grabs both glasses, handing one to me as he comes close. "I figure you've cleaned up after him for the last four years. It was the least I could do."

"Um, thanks." His words are the last thing I expected, especially after how he acted at Hollis's party. "I guess that was my choice, though."

He walks over to the couch and sits down, patting the seat next to him like this is his place and *I'm* the guest. Then again, Harland has always had so much more confidence than me. That's probably why he makes such a great rockstar.

I take a sip of my wine for a little liquid courage and then sit down next to him. He turns his whole body so he's facing me and places a hand on my knee. It takes everything in me to ignore the feelings that flood through me from the gesture.

"That's what I wanted to talk to you about," he says. "The things I said earlier today were uncalled for. I'll admit, I was angry, but I shouldn't have taken that out on you."

"You shouldn't have?"

He shakes his head. "No, because think about it—as much as I would have loved to be there while he was doing all those firsts, and trust me, I would have given up everything for it, I also know that what I *have* been doing the last four years has been incredible. You sacrificed everything for our son, and I think also for me. Christ, Em. You've done an amazing job with him."

I look down at my lap, watching the wine swirl in the glass. "I still should have told you."

"You should have," he confirms. "I agree. But what is being mad about that really going to get me? As long as I'm in his life now, I'm willing to let it go. Leave it in the past and all that."

Surprise etches across my face as my eyes meet his. "You are?"

Nodding slowly, he smiles. "I am. He's my number one priority. And if that means forgiving you, then so be it. I want to be there, Emery. I want to be his dad."

Tears spring to my eyes, because despite the fact that I kept it to myself, there's still that small part of me that has always yearned to hear those words come from his lips. "I want that, too."

He smiles wider, with that one dimple he has on his left side popping. "Good." Removing his hand from my knee, he gives me the ability to think a little clearer. "So, tell me about him. Start from the beginning. I want to know everything about Little H."

Little H. I like the sound of that.

CHAPTER SIX

HARLAND

THE HOT WATER POURS DOWN ON ME, COVERING MY SKIN IN THE KIND OF relief I need. My muscles ache from all the nights I've spent sleeping on Emery's couch. It's been a month since we agreed to leave the past behind us and start fresh, and while no one but Emery, Mila, and me know the truth, I've loved every second of it. Spending almost every day with my son has been the brightest light in what was a really dark tunnel.

We've been trying to figure out how to break the news to everyone—especially Hollis and Ashlyn. Thankfully, my sister has been distracted with the new guy she's seeing and hasn't been spending every waking moment at Emery's like she usually does. But with every day I spend with Hollis, the more I love him and the more desperate I am to claim him fully.

He is by far the best little kid I've ever met. And sure, I might be biased, but what dad wouldn't feel that way about their son? He's always so happy. He's friendly and polite to everyone. And genuinely, I've never seen a kid who shares as much as he does. We took him to the playground the other day, and he gave one of his favorite action figures to a little boy who cried when he saw it, because that was his favorite one and he lost his.

Needless to say, I went out and bought him another one before the sun went down.

A part of me wonders what his reaction will be when he finds out I'm his dad. Will he be angry? Glad? Curious? There are just so many ways it could go, and the possibility that it could go wrong weighs heavily on me every day.

We're going to need to tell him soon, because the longer we go without it, the worse it could be, but first, we need to tell Ashlyn. The last thing Emery needs is for her best friend to find out the truth through Hollis.

I step out of the shower and wrap a towel around my waist. The cold air cools my heated skin in an instant as I leave the bathroom. Today, Emery and I are taking Hollis to the zoo. He's been addicted to watching YouTube videos of all the different animals lately, so I figured what better thing to do on a Saturday afternoon than to take him to see them in person.

It's going to take a little bit of effort to remain hidden. A hat, sunglasses, and long sleeves to hide my tattoos, even though it is nearly eighty-five degrees outside. I'll deal with it though. The last thing I need is for someone to notice me and call the media. Gossip about the end of my engagement has died down a bit, but if they found out about Hollis, they'd have a field day. I haven't even told my publicist yet.

Still, the look on his face will be well worth the risk.

AFTER I'M DONE GETTING DRESSED, I HEAD DOWNSTAIRS AND INTO THE kitchen to get a drink. Ashlyn sits at the island and from the second I walk in the room, her eyes stay locked on me. She watches me carefully as I go to the fridge and grab an energy drink out of it. When I turn around and see her squinting, my brows raise.

"What are you staring at, weirdo?" I ask her.

She tilts her head to the side and pinches her bottom lip between her thumb and index finger. "I just can't figure it out."

"Figure what out?"

"Why you're so cheery all the time lately," she says. "I mean, your band is still on hiatus. You're living at home with Mom, which I still don't understand because you have enough money to buy the whole damn town. And you're not getting laid." She clamps her mouth shut and her eyes widen. "Wait. Please don't tell me you're back with Lindsey."

I throw my head back, laughing at the mere idea. "Not a chance in hell."

"Are you sure? It would explain a lot."

"Positive, Ash. I can't just be in a good mood?"

She shakes her head. "No. It's strange, and so not you."

I chuckle and make my way around the island until I'm next to her. "I guess I just started enjoying the break. I'm home, and for the first time in years, I don't have a million things I need to do at once. And"—I throw my arm around her—"I get to annoy my little sister and scare her new boyfriend away."

Looking up at me, she glares. "Don't you dare. I actually like this one."

"I know you do. That's exactly the problem," I growl.

She chuckles and rolls her eyes. "Lord help the woman who ends up with you and your caveman tendencies. She better be a saint."

As her words sink in, thoughts of Emery pass through my mind. You'd have to be blind to not see how painstakingly gorgeous she is. The way her brown hair flows down her back. How her eyes sparkle in the sunlight, and the way happiness radiates off her. You can't be around her and not be in a good mood. And then there's how she is with our son.

I don't think I've ever met someone so protective and yet so gentle. Even within the last month, I've seen her patience hanging by a thread with how hard she's been working, but still, she never takes any of it out on Hollis. She keeps her voice calm and loving with him, and maybe a little firm when needed, but never angry. It's mesmerizing.

A part of me wonders what it would be like if she and I got together. If we finally got our chance. The same one we should have had years ago but didn't.

Would we be happy?

Would we fail?

It's not like I have much faith in relationships at this point, given my track record, but this is Emery. I've known her, and wanted her, for as long as I can remember. It was always so hard to stay away, especially knowing how much she wanted me too. It was so obvious, and sometimes I had fun messing with her, but I don't think anyone really knew how much I felt the same way.

But still, she's my sister's best friend.

Mother of my son or not, she's off limits for the foreseeable future.

At least until Ashlyn knows the truth.

I PULL UP TO EMERY'S APARTMENT TO FIND HER AND HOLLIS ALREADY outside. He's running around in circles, and the second Em points out my car, he starts jumping up and down. She chuckles and shakes her head as I get out and open the back door.

"Hey, little man!" I greet him.

He smiles brightly. "We're going to the zoo!"

"I know!" I match his excitement. "Climb in so we can get going."

Emery gets in the passenger seat as I buckle Hollis into his seat. When I'm done, I get back in the car and put my seatbelt on. Em looks over at me, confused.

"Why does everyone keep looking at me like that today?"

She giggles. "I'm just wondering why you're dressed for snow."

Oh. "I'm incognito."

Her brows raise and she reaches over and grabs at my sweatshirt. "Is that why you're wearing a Sound the Sirens hoodie? Harland, you're practically a walking billboard."

"Am I really?" I look down. *Shit.* "Hold on. I have another in the back."

I get out of the car and go around to the back, where I have another hoodie. It's solid black, but I still check it over to make sure there is no band insignia on it or anything. As I was getting dressed this morning, I decided not to wear a shirt underneath the hoodie in an attempt to keep me from getting too hot, which means taking this off leaves me bare from the waist up. I'm about to pull on the new sweatshirt when I catch Emery watching me in the rearview mirror. Her cheeks pink when she notices she's caught, but she doesn't look away. I wink at her and close the back hatch, ending the moment long before I wanted to.

When I get back into the car, Emery rolls her eyes at me playfully, but the second Hollis starts talking about how excited he is, the moment is gone. Honestly, it's probably for the best. She and I are unfamiliar territory, and until we have the chance to explore it, I'd rather stay in the safe zone.

As I pull out onto the road, I take a cigarette out of the pack and put it between my lips, but before I can even light it, Em reaches over and rips it out of my mouth. She breaks it in half, and throws it out the window. My brows furrow as I glance over at her, but she's completely unfazed.

"The fuck?" I mutter.

Her eyes widen, but it's Hollis who speaks. "Potty word!"

"Yeah, Harland," she teases. "That's a potty word."

"You have to put a dollar in the swear jar when we get home!" Hollis yells excitedly.

I chuckle. "*You* have a swear jar?"

Knowing Em, she probably fills that thing up once a week. The girl has the mouth of a sailor, and zero apologies for it. She shrugs and puts her feet up on the dash.

"He uses the money to buy toys I probably would have bought for him anyway." She glances back at Hollis, who is now happily absorbed in playing with his iPad. "And if you think you're smoking in the car with him, I'll be making you say a hell of a lot more than fuck."

"Mommy!" Hollis chastises.

She lays her head back against the headrest. "I know, H. Potty word."

Emery hits a few buttons on the center console, and my most recent album comes through the speakers. I can't help but subtly watch as she sings along. I always knew she liked my music, but I had no idea she was an actual fan.

It's then that I realize two things.

One: there isn't a single inch of me that isn't fucking drawn to her, and it's getting hard to deny.

And two, I really liked the way it sounded when Hollis said, "when we get home."

Yeah, I'm fucked.

CHAPTER SEVEN
EMERY

"HOLLIS, WE HAVE TO GET READY," I TELL HIM FOR THE MILLIONTH TIME.

He throws himself on the ground. "I don't want to!"

Ugh. This is what happens when he misses his nap. I can only imagine how he's going to act at dinner. We're going over to Ashlyn's for her birthday dinner, and of course this is the one day he decided to successfully boycott nap time. Lucky me.

I lower myself down to his level and reach for his hand. "H, don't you want to see Aunt Ashlyn?" He nods. "Then we need to get you dressed so we can go."

Hollis has been used to seeing Ashlyn almost every day for most of his life, but since Harland came back, everything has been different. She started dating this guy named Brandon that she met at work, and I started using Mila as an excuse for why I didn't need her to watch Hollis for me. It's not that I like lying to her, but I also couldn't necessarily tell her the truth. Besides, she didn't ask many questions, because it gave her more time to spend with her new beau.

The reality that I need to tell her weighs on me more and more every day. And I've come close. There was one night we went out to dinner to catch up, and I almost came clean, but I couldn't. The words got stuck in my throat, and I just couldn't seem to get them out.

It's only a matter of time before Hollis mentions something to her about it. Harland has been here just about every day, only missing a couple due to things his publicist needed him to do. Hollis has gotten used to that, and honestly, he's not the only one. Harland being around all the time has been messing with my headspace, but in all the best ways. It's like we've been hidden away, playing house together in my tiny apartment and ignoring that the rest of the world exists. Like our problems don't matter. But that can't last forever.

Once I get through her birthday, I'm going to tell her. She deserves to know, and Harland deserves not having to hide the fact that Hollis is his son. I know for a fact she's going to be pissed. I mean, I've been best friends with her since the third grade. I just hope it doesn't make her hate me forever.

I turn around to see Hollis playing with toys instead of putting his clothes on like I asked. Throwing my head back, I groan and take my phone out of my pocket. I dial the familiar number without even thinking and put it to my ear.

"Hey, Em," Harland answers. "Everything okay?"

"Not exactly." I pinch the bridge of my nose between my thumb and index finger. "I can't seem to get Hollis to listen to me today. Can you talk to him?"

He chuckles into the phone. "Yeah. Put him on."

"H," I call. "Phone for you."

I put it on speaker and hand it to him, knowing he would never hold it to his ear the right way. He tilts his head to the side as he takes it from me.

"Hello?"

"Hey, little man," Harland greets him.

Hollis lights up instantly. "Hi, Hawlan."

"I hear you're not listening to your mom. That doesn't sound like you. Is everything okay?"

He shrugs, not realizing Harland can't see him. "I don't want to go. I want to play with my toys."

"Would it change your mind if I told you that I'll be there?"

"You will?" Hollis smiles. "Can I bring my toys?"

Harland chuckles. "You can bring two of your favorite toys. One for you and one for me. Okay, buddy?"

He nods happily. "Deal! Here's Mommy! I have to get ready!"

Handing the phone back to me, Hollis goes running down the hallway like he can't get dressed fast enough. I roll my eyes at how easy that was for him and take the phone off speaker.

"Thank you," I murmur.

"Hey, that's what I'm here for, isn't it?"

I don't answer, mainly because I'm not entirely sure what to say. I've been so used to doing this on my own for so long that I never imagined what it would be like to have someone else to lean on.

As if he can read my mind, he exhales, and I can practically hear his smile. "We're a team, Em."

"Yeah," I sigh happily. "We're a team."

GETTING TO HARLAND'S, I'M NOT GOING TO LIE, I'M NERVOUS. THIS IS THE first time that we're going to be around Ashlyn and Harland at the same time since Hollis's birthday party, and things were *very* different then. And to top it off, their mom will be there, too. I'm just hoping Ash is too distracted by the fact that her mom and Harland are meeting Brandon for the first time today.

He's a decent guy. I met him one night when he came to pick Ashlyn up from my place. Her car was in the shop and I had picked her up so she didn't have to wait there. Brandon was the one to bring her back to get it. I wasn't able to find any red flags, and he seems to make Ash really happy. To me, that's what matters most, but I can already tell Harland doesn't like him.

"Hawlan!" Hollis yells as he runs up the driveway.

Shit.

He bends down and scoops him up into his arms. "Little man! I got you something."

He takes him around to the passenger seat of his car and pulls out the Avengers set he's been asking for. Hollis's eyes widen in disbelief, and he wraps his little arms around Harland's neck and pulls him close.

"Thank you!"

"You're welcome, buddy."

Ashlyn's voice flows through the air. "I thought I heard my favorite little guy."

But as soon as she sees how him and Harland are being with each other, confusion etches across her face.

Play it off, Em.

"Oh, sure. What am I? Chopped liver?" I tease.

That manages to distract her a little. She comes over and gives me a hug, but then looks back at Hollis.

"Since when are they best buds?"

I shrug nonchalantly. "Since every time he sees him, Harland gives him a present."

She chuckles, but still watches her brother closely. I walk over and take Hollis into my arms, telling him we should go inside so we can open the box. As we head up the walkway, I can hear Ashlyn behind me.

"If you're using that kid to get to her, I will literally cut you."

Harland laughs, as if it's no big deal. "You've been watching too many Lifetime movies."

"Maybe, but that doesn't mean I can't find a sharp blade and some bleach."

Yeah, I need to tell her soon.

And maybe make sure she isn't around any knives at the time.

SITTER AT THE DINNER TABLE, I'VE GOT HOLLIS ON MY RIGHT, WITH ASHLYN on the other side of him. Harland, to avoid suspicion, is sitting across from his sister, but his eyes stay locked on Brandon. Since the second he got here, he's been fucking with the guy.

"So, Bryan," he says, making me roll my eyes.

"It's Brandon, Harland," Ashlyn corrects him again, this time with more frustration. "Knock it off."

He smirks at her. "Right. Brayden. What do you do for a living?"

"I work at Bay Ridge Legal with Ashlyn, but I'm hoping that's just a temporary thing," he explains. "I'm trying to get onto the police force. I want to be a cop."

Harland's brows raise in amusement. "A cop? So you want my sister to be worried sick every night, waiting for you to come home?"

"Harland!" Ash hisses.

He leans back and puts his hands on the back of his head. "What? I just want to make sure he's thinking of you while making all these major decisions."

Oh my God. He's acting like they're engaged, when they've been dating for only a couple of months. Even their mom is staring down at her plate like she doesn't know whether to intervene or stay out of it. Honestly, while I'd normally choose the latter, I can't seem to watch this poor guy squirm anymore. And besides, if Ashlyn is on one of her *my brother is an asshole* rants for the next week, she really won't take the news of him being Hollis's dad well.

I take my phone out and discreetly send a text to Harland.

Me: Can you go a little easier on him, please?

Thankfully, he reads it and answers without it being seen.

Harland: Why? The guy's a complete tool. He doesn't deserve her.

Me: Maybe so, but she really likes him. At least give him a chance.

I debate sending something else for a moment before finally saying fuck it. What can it really hurt?

Me: Please? For me?

Harland reads the text, and I watch as his eyes soften and he bites his lip. He subtly glances at me and sighs.

"I'm just messing around, Brandon," he says, finally getting his name right. "I'm protective of my sister. I'm sure you can understand that."

"Absolutely," Brandon answers. "I'd be a little concerned if you weren't."

His jaw locks like he's holding back from making another snide comment, and I know he's only doing it for me.

I'll take that as a win.

AFTER DINNER, WE'RE ALL SITTING IN THE LIVING ROOM WHEN ASHLYN comes back with a stack of photo albums. She's going on and on about how she's been meaning to look at these for ages and tells Brandon that she wants to show him the bed she had as a kid. It was a top bunk, with a playhouse underneath, and an actual slide to get down. I remember that bed. I was super jealous of it.

However, as she's flipping through all the pictures, my eyes are locked on Harland. He's sitting on the floor with Hollis, playing with the new toys he got him. They laugh like they've always been the best of friends, and if I was thinking clearly, I'd be worried someone would notice, but I'm mesmerized.

"Oh, look!" Ashlyn exclaims, bringing my attention back to her. "I was what—one—here?"

I glance over at the photo album and smile at my best friend's toothy baby grin. She's wearing a light pink tutu dress, and the next few pictures show how it was ruined by the cake she ate that day.

"I was the cutest baby," she says conceitedly, but she's not wrong.

She really was adorable.

As she turns the page, Brandon's eyes narrow in bewilderment. "Why is there a picture of Hollis in your baby album?"

Ashlyn looks at where he's pointing, and my heart rate starts to quicken. "Oh, that's Harland."

I can see the very moment it clicks in her head, because her breathing stops, and mine does, too.

"Wait," she whispers, looking between the picture and to where her brother is sitting on the floor with our son. "No."

She looks over at me, her eyes begging for the answers she's already figured out on her own, and I don't think anything could keep it from being written all over my face.

"Ash," I start, but she throws the album off her lap and stands up.

"Are you kidding me?" she roars. "Are you actually fucking kidding me right now?"

"Potty mouth, Aunt Ashlyn!" Hollis chimes in, and I cringe.

She looks over at him and then at Harland, who is frozen in place. "And you. You knew about this?"

He sighs. "Maybe this isn't exactly the time for this, A."

The nickname is one that only he's ever used with her. One that originated when they were kids and she was jealous of his *H* nickname. And I know he used it in an attempt to calm her down, but it's hopeless.

"You're right," she scoffs. "It's not the right time for this. You know what would have been the right time?" She narrows her eyes on me. "Almost five years ago, when you found out you were pregnant!"

Tears stream down my face faster than I can wipe them away, and I just hope that Hollis doesn't turn around and see me upset. He's incredibly empathetic and will stop everything to comfort me.

"Let me explain, please," I beg.

"It's too late to explain, Emery." Her shoulders sag in utter despair. "You ruined everything."

"Ashlyn," her mom tries, and I realize that not only is Ash learning the truth, but so is her mom.

My best friend closes her eyes for a second, and then shakes her head. "No. I'm sorry, but no. I can't do this."

She walks right out the front door, and I'm a fucking mess. I look back and forth from the door that just slammed shut and where my son is playing on the floor, and Harland's voice breaks through my inner turmoil.

"Go," he tells me. "Go ahead. I've got him. Go talk to her."

I sigh in relief and mouth a silent thank you to him before running after Ashlyn.

She's halfway to her car by the time I get out there, but I'm just glad she hasn't left yet.

"Ash," I call. "Ash, please."

She throws her head back and stops. "What, Emery?"

"Don't leave. Just stay here and talk to me. We can work this out."

"Work this out?" she sneers. "He's fucking *four* Em, and I'm just now finding out that the deadbeat I mentally cursed out for years is my fucking brother. I think we're well past talking."

She turns around and goes to walk away, but then stops again.

"And you know what?" She spins back to face me again. "I noticed the similarities. When he was born, the thought went through my mind, but I told myself no. Emery would never do that to me. She would tell me. But you never did, so I convinced myself that I was just crazy. That the similarities were all in my head. Because my best friend would never lie to me."

"I'm sorry," I sob. "I'm so sorry."

"Yeah," she breathes. "I am, too. I'm sorry I ever trusted you."

CHAPTER EIGHT
HARLAND

EVERYTHING GOES EERILY QUIET AS EMERY RUSHES OUT THE DOOR AFTER Ashlyn. Brandon, the dumbass who started all this by asking a stupid as shit question, is literally twiddling his thumbs while still planted on the couch. Hasn't he gotten the fucking hint? Ashlyn left. That's his cue to go.

As the yelling outside gets a little louder, I grab my phone and turn on one of Hollis's favorite YouTube videos to drown out the noise. I can feel the eyes burning into my skull, but I can't seem to look at them. My focus, right now and always, is Hollis.

"Is it true?" my mom asks quietly.

I'm thankful for the way she doesn't say the words, since we haven't told Hollis yet. I know lying to her isn't an option, not that I would want to. Hiding the fact that Hollis is mine was never something I wanted, but something I did for Emery. She needed to figure out how to do this in her own way, and instead that was ruined by Officer Dipshit over there.

I nod once, feeling the relief of finally being able to tell someone. "Yeah, it is."

She hums softly, but when I look up at her, I notice she isn't shocked. I always knew she wouldn't be angry. My mom just isn't the kind of person to get mad at her kids, and Emery is just as much her kid as Ashlyn and me, but what I wasn't expecting was to see a neutral expression on her face.

"You knew?" I ask.

Her one shoulder moves in a half shrug and she smiles subtly. "I had my suspicions. I mean, it's no surprise that a few old pictures made the pieces fall together. He's the spitting image of you."

I look over at my son with pride. "He's better."

"I take it you didn't know?" she asks hesitantly, trying to gauge my mood.

In an effort to avoid Hollis listening in, I get up and sit next to her. "No, but don't hold that against her. It's something we've talked about and we've both agreed to leave in the past."

A small smile graces her lips, and she pats my leg. "I would never do anything to make Emery uncomfortable. She's family. But I have to say, I'm proud of you, H. You've grown into a very mature and responsible young man."

Warmth fills me, but as I go to respond, Hollis turns around with a huge grin on his face. "Look Hawlan!" he yells. "Cocomelon!"

"I see, little man!" I say back just as excitedly.

"He's so silly," he coos.

"Just like you," I tell him.

He scrunches his nose and goes back to watching the video, only for me to find my mom looking at me with fondness and adoration.

"What?"

She smirks and shakes her head. "Nothing. You're just really good with him."

A car door shuts outside, and I can hear as tires screech. Clearly Ashlyn is pissed, which I don't think any of us are surprised about, but she better lay off the gas before she kills herself or someone else.

"I think that's my cue to leave," Brandon says as he stands up.

I grunt. "Ya think?"

As he opens the door to leave, Emery comes walking back inside with tears streaming down her face. I don't think I've ever seen her this distraught, and my heart aches for her. I'm on my feet in an instant and take her into my arms.

"Hey," I whisper. "Shh. It's going to be all right."

She shakes her head against my shoulder. "I don't think so. She hates me."

"She doesn't hate you. She's just mad."

Pulling away from me, she looks me in the eyes, and I can see how broken up she is over this. "You didn't hear what she said. She wants nothing to do with me, Harland. She's my best friend, and she hates me."

I sigh heavily, trying to figure out what I could say to make her feel better, but there's nothing. Even if it's just temporary, which I'm almost positive it is, she's lost a part of herself. A part she's never needed to live without. And she needs to grieve that loss.

"Okay, why don't you go home?" I suggest. "I'll bring Hollis back in a little while, but he doesn't need to see you like this, and I know you don't want him to. Go home. Drink a glass of wine. I'll be there in a bit."

She thinks about it for a moment before she exhales and nods. "Okay."

"It's going to be okay, Em," my mom tells her.

As if she just now realized Ashlyn isn't the only one who had the bomb dropped on them tonight, her eyes nearly double in size. "I'm sorry. I'm so, so sorry."

My mom gives her a warm smile. "You don't need to apologize to me, sweetheart. That boy has been and always will be my grandson. Being related by blood is just an added bonus."

"You should hate me, too," she says, so low it's almost a whisper.

"Now what good would that do anyone?" Mom asks. "So, you made a judgment call. Harland has made several over the years that I disagreed with. I still love him."

"Hey!" I whine.

She chuckles. "Are you going to tell me I'm wrong? Would you like me to pull up your most recent headline?"

I wince at the thought of it. "No. Definitely not."

Emery seems to relax a little at knowing my mom isn't angry with her, but I can tell the second she starts thinking about my sister because she starts tearing up again. I wrap my arms around her and pull her close again, pressing my lips to her forehead. It's supposed to be completely innocent, but I'd be lying if I said I felt nothing from it.

"Text me when you get home," I tell her.

She nods as she steps back. "I will. And thank you."

Winking at her, I smirk. "We're a team, remember?"

Em gives me the best smile she can manage, and with a quick kiss on the top of our son's head, she leaves, and I can't help but stare at where she just was.

"You know, Hollis isn't the only one you're good with," my mom says, piercing the silence.

I take a deep breath, feeling the intensity of my next words, but not looking away from the door. "I love her, Mom."

She hums. "Yeah, I had my suspicions about that too."

TWO HOURS IS ALL I CAN SEEM TO STAND TO BE AWAY FROM HER. I KNOCK ON the door and wait impatiently for her to answer it. When she does, her brows furrow as she looks up and down the hallway.

"Where's Hollis?"

I shrug and push my way inside, shutting the door behind me. "My mom's watching him for the night."

She looks surprised. "She is?"

Nodding, I take in her appearance. She must have taken a shower when she got back, because she's changed into sweatpants, and her hair is still damp. And yet she's never looked better. I love knowing I'm one of only a few who gets to see her like this.

"He was having such a good time with my mom, I told her he could sleep in my bed and that I'd pick him up in the morning."

She swallows. "Oh. Are you meeting up with Vance?"

My best friend moved back home a couple weeks ago while we try to figure out the future of Sound the Sirens. I've seen him a couple times while Emery has hung out with my sister, but that's definitely not the plan tonight.

"No. I'm staying here," I tell her, as if it's obvious.

"H-here?" she croaks.

"Mm-hm." I take a step closer and pull her into my arms.

"Why here?"

God, she's adorable. "Because you had a rough day, and while Hollis might be my number one priority, his mom is definitely a close second."

I should tell her the truth, that she's tied for first, but I'm really not trying to show all my cards while she's on the verge of a mental breakdown. Instead, I'll play it safe, like I always do, and make sure she knows I'm here for her. Because I am.

Day or night.

Whenever she needs me.

Instead of fighting it, she leans into my arms and allows me to comfort her.

IT TAKES A FEW GLASSES OF WINE, BUT EVENTUALLY EM ACTUALLY STARTS TO laugh. My mom sent me a video of Hollis eating a giant spoonful of icing. You can hear her in the background telling him that he's supposed to put it on the cake, not eat it, but he doesn't care. He happily shoves the spoon in his mouth and smiles at the camera with icing all around his lips.

"You do know he's never going to sleep tonight, right?" Em wincing.

I chuckle and toss my phone onto the coffee table. "Her fault. Who gives a four-year-old a tub of icing right before bedtime?"

"Fair point." She plays with the rim of her glass, staring at the wine like it's the most amazing thing she's ever seen. "Is it weird that I miss him already?"

"No," I answer immediately. "Not at all, because I do, too. But I'm also enjoying this."

Emery finally looks up at me and I can see the wonder dancing in her eyes. "You are?"

My brows furrow. "Aren't you?"

"I am," she assures me. "That's not what I meant. I just figured you were only hanging around all the time for Hollis."

"You mean, our son who goes to bed by seven every night?" I tease. "Sounds logical."

She throws her head back and giggles. "Harland."

"No, no," I press with a smile. "It makes total sense that I would spend the entire evening here because of a kid who goes to sleep before the sun goes down."

"Well, I don't know." She reaches over and puts her glass on the coffee table, but I'm stuck on the way she licks the excess wine off of her lips.

"Don't you, though?"

Our gazes lock, and it's like neither one of us can look away. I can see the way her chest rises and falls with every breath, but her attention stays on me. Reaching forward, I tuck a stray hair behind her ear and a blush coats her cheeks.

"H," she whispers.

My hand lingers there, on the side of her face. I know I should stop. I should pull my hand away and move to the other side of the damn room, but tell that to my body that won't seem to listen. We both lean in slowly, but before I let myself have what I've been craving for months, I press my forehead against hers. After everything that happened tonight, I worry she's too vulnerable right now to realize what she's doing.

"If we do this, if we cross this line, there's no going back for me. I need you to know that," I tell her. "I don't want secret hookups in the dark. I don't want to hide it from my family. If we do this, it's real. I can't handle it being anything less."

She stares back at me with both fear and clarity. "Good, because I can't either."

Her words are all I need to close the gap, pressing my lips to hers in a kiss that's nearly five years overdue. As her fingers lace into my hair and her tongue tangles with my own, I can't help but think about how this is what I should've been doing since the night Hollis was conceived. I never should have run scared. I never should have chosen Lindsey.

It's always been her.

I GROWL UNDER MY BREATH AS I TRY TO GET THROUGH THE CROWD. I WOKE up this morning with an extra pep in my step. After connecting with Em last night, I couldn't be in a better mood. Granted, I have what is probably the worst case of blue balls I've ever had, but it was worth it. We made out for hours and then fell asleep with her exactly where she belongs—wrapped in my arms.

When I left her apartment, she was still sound asleep. I left a note on the nightstand letting her know that I was going for coffee and to pick up Hollis and that I'd be back.

What I didn't expect, however, was for someone to notice me while inside the coffee shop. By the time I walked out, there was a whole mob of fans and photographers. A mob I'm still trying to get through.

"Harland!" a girl screams in my ear. "Oh my God! I love you so much. Can I get a picture?"

"Sure, love."

I pose for a few pictures, hoping it will make them happy enough to give me space to get through. Flashes from paparazzi cameras come from all directions while they shout questions at me.

How do you feel about your failed engagement?

When is the band going back on tour?

The fans want to know, is there any hope for you and Lindsey to get back together?

After what she did? No.

After the night I just spent with Emery? Fuck no.

I push through the crowd and finally make it to my car. Thankfully, they all have enough sense to move out of the way so I don't hit them, but I know I'm far from safe when I see a couple of the pushier photographers jump into their cars to follow me.

Great.

Reaching to pull my phone from my pocket, I try to call the police. Usually they'll pull them over for reckless driving. However, my phone is completely dead.

I'm on my own.

IT TAKES AN EXTRA HALF-HOUR FOR ME TO LOSE THEM, TURNING DOWN side streets and alleyways that only a local would know. I finally pull up to my house long after the time I had hoped. Emery is bound to be awake by now.

I climb out of my car and head for the door when a familiar voice meets my ears.

"Hey, H."

Stopping in my tracks, I throw my head back and groan. "Today is really not my fucking day."

I stand there for a second and hope she'll go away, but if I've learned anything about this girl over the last eleven years, it's that she's like a bad fucking rash. She'll stand there for as long as it takes, and if I don't talk to her, it'll be worse.

"What the hell are you doing here, Lindsey?" I ask as I turn around.

She looks down at the ground and then back up to me, trying to be flirty. "I've missed you."

I snort. "That's rich."

My eyes rake over her, and I genuinely wonder what I ever saw in her. Her makeup is caked on, as if she can hide the ugly inside. Her clothes cling to her body, seeming two sizes too small, and she has her shirt pulled down so low that her tits are almost spilling from it. If she thinks that's going to win me back, it's not. She doesn't hold a candle to the girl I woke up next to this morning.

"Go home, Linds."

She starts to scowl but quickly masks it over with a smirk. "I am home, Harland. *You're* my home."

I shake my head. "No. Your actual home, or whatever dude's bed you've been sleeping in the last couple months."

"Oh, come on. You don't mean that."

"I sure as shit do. I don't want you here."

She takes a step closer and runs her index finger down my torso. "I'm sure I can think of a part of you that does."

Stepping back, I cringe at the thought of sex with her. "Cut it out. It's not cute, it's desperate, and that isn't a good look on you."

That seems to strike a nerve, because she drops the innocent act. "When are you going to just forgive me? You and I both know we're going to spend the rest of our lives together. That guy didn't mean a thing to me."

"That's what you think this is about?" I all but shout. "You think I'm mad because you cheated?"

"Yeah. What else would you be mad about?"

Oh my God. "You are seriously deranged, you know that? You beat the fucking shit out of yourself and then had me arrested for it! There's no going back from that."

She rolls her eyes. "Please. You were locked up for a couple hours before I dropped the charges. Relax."

"I shouldn't have been locked up at all!"

I know I need to drop my voice down. It's well past ten in the morning, which means Hollis is wide awake inside the house. The last thing I want is for him to hear me yelling.

Taking a deep breath, I close the gap between us so she can hear me despite the low volume. She gets the wrong idea, though, because she smiles as I get closer.

"Let me make this as clear as possible, since you obviously have an issue with understanding," I tell her firmly. "There is no us. No you and me. No Harland and Lindsey. It's over."

She glances past me and rolls her eyes before running her hand through my hair. "I've always loved when you grow your hair out."

My brows furrow. "Are you even listening to me?"

"Yes, but it's hard to focus when you look this good."

I close my eyes for a second to contain my anger before I lose my ever-loving shit. I think about how Emery is waiting for me to come back, and how I finally have the ability to kiss her whenever I want. It's all working to calm me down, but when two lips meet my own, I'm jolted back into reality.

"The fuck?" I ask as I push her away, but a whimper behind me sends fear straight through my body.

No.

Lindsey grins deviously as I spin around to see Emery standing there. If I thought she was devastated yesterday, it doesn't compare to how hurt she looks right now.

"Em," I plead.

She swallows, as if she's willing herself not to cry. "You weren't answering your phone. I got worried."

Lindsey wraps her arm around mine. "Oops, sorry. Old habits and all that."

What the fuck? Her tone is sickeningly sweet, in an evil kind of way, and I watch as they hit their intended target because Emery winces.

"Wait, no. It's not...This isn't..."

But she doesn't care to hear anything I have to say. She shakes her head and runs into the house. As I go to follow her, Lindsey steps in front of me.

"Get out of my way."

She puts her hands on my chest. "No. Being with her is a bad idea."

"Bad idea?" I snarl. "Being with you for so long was the worst idea of my life. Get the fuck out of my way!"

Rolling her eyes, she steps to the side. "Fine."

I start to rush past her, but her next words stop me dead.

"But imagine how the press will eat you two alive when they find out she hid your son from you for years."

My whole body goes cold. "How the fuck do you know about my son?"

She opens and closes her mouth before coming up with an excuse. "Your sister told me."

"Bullshit!" I roar. "My sister fucking hates you."

"That's not true."

I'm not interested in any more of her lies. "How long have you known I have a son?" She sighs and reaches for me, but I dodge her. "How fucking long, Lindsey?"

"She would have ruined everything," she says, and the last bit of respect I had for her vanishes in an instant. "I was protecting you. Your career. Your fame. Your success. None of it would have happened if I didn't step in and do what I did."

"Un-fucking-believable." I feel like I'm going to vomit, or maybe commit murder if she doesn't get out of my face fast enough. "All you have *ever* done for me is ruin my life. Now fucking leave before I show you what it would really feel like if I abused you."

The door opens behind me, and I see Emery walking out with Hollis. He waves at me happily, but she doesn't let go of his hand, marching quickly back to her car.

"Em!" I call. "Emery, please. You have to listen to me. Nothing happened."

She doesn't answer and instead robotically puts Hollis in the car and buckles his seatbelt.

"Babe, I wouldn't do that to you."

Shutting the car door, she turns to glare at me. "Really? You wouldn't?" she growls, shoving her finger into the center of my chest. "Do you not remember the morning after our son was conceived? Because this is *that* all fucking over again."

I shake my head, feeling my chest tighten almost to the point where I can't breathe. "No. I swear this isn't like that. It's not the same."

She laughs, but there's not even a trace of humor in it. "Really? Because it looks exactly like that."

Taking her face in my hands, she tries to pull away, but I won't let her. I need her to listen to me.

"Emery, please," I beg. "I meant every word of what I said last night."

For a second, it looks like she's actually starting to calm down. I wipe the tears from her cheeks and feel relief flood through me as she grabs my wrists, but it's gone the second she pulls my hands away.

"I'm sorry. I just can't trust you."

I stand there, frozen in place as I watch her climb into her car and drive away—leaving me with my broken heart in my hands.

CHAPTER NINE
EMERY

SOBS WRACK THROUGH ME AS I DRIVE THROUGH TOWN. NO MATTER HOW hard I try, I can't seem to calm down. I only get a couple blocks away before tears blur my vision so bad, I need to pull over. If I were by myself, I might chance it, but with Hollis in the car, I won't.

I knew better. I knew how bad he broke my heart five years ago, and I still let him back in. I fucking knew better!

"Mommy?" Hollis asks. "You okay, Mommy?"

Using the backs of my hands, I quickly wipe away the tears and put my brave face on. "I'm fine, baby."

"Did Hawlan make you sad?"

It's adorable how sweet he is, but the last thing I want is for him to think negatively of his dad, even if I think he's a lying fucking pig.

I shake my head and look at him through the rearview mirror. "No, honey. Harland didn't make me sad. I'm okay."

By the grace of God, he takes the excuse and goes back to playing with his iPad. And me? I shove my emotions to the side. They'll have to wait until later, because my son needs me.

I SIT ON THE COUCH IN A MESS OF SELF-PITY AND HEARTACHE. IT'S PATHETIC, really. Even *I* would make fun of me. Thankfully, Hollis has been pretty into his toys, so he hasn't paid much attention to the way I keep tearing up.

Out of all of it, the part that sucks the most is that the one person I would talk to about it, doesn't want to hear a single word from me. I texted Ashlyn when I woke up this morning, but never heard anything back. Everything feels different without her. It's like she's been such a huge part of my life for so long that I don't know how to function without her. And this morning's drama just intensifies that feeling.

Keys jingle outside the door and it opens, letting me know that Mila is here. She called me a little while ago, and I was able to play it cool for a bit, until she made a joke about Harland and I lost it. Immediately she told me she would come over as soon as she got off work.

"Can you grab me a bottle of water on your way through the kitchen, Meel?" I call.

She doesn't answer, but I hear the sound of the fridge opening, and before I know it, a water bottle falls into my lap.

"Thanks."

I'm mid-sip when the voice that echoes through the room catches me off guard. "You look like shit."

My head whips over to see Ashlyn standing there. I'm not sure if the sight of her makes me want to cry in relief or vomit at the thought of her still being mad at me. I mean, it's been less than twenty-four hours. Of course, she's still mad. But as I take in the sight of her, I realize that's not all. She looks just as upset as I am, and I hate knowing I'm the cause of it.

"I feel like it, too."

She huffs out a small chuckle and walks around the couch to sit down. "Mila called me. She told me what happened."

Fluttering my eyes closed, I try to ignore the pain in my chest. "We don't have to do this."

"Do what?"

"Talk about him. It's your brother, and I get it if that's weird for you."

She looks down at her lap and nods. "It is, but what's even more weird is not having my best friend to talk to. I just don't know why you didn't tell me."

"I wanted to," I admit. "So many times, I wanted to."

"But?"

"But I was afraid you'd hate me." The irony isn't lost on me as I start to tear up again. "A lot of good that did me. Now you hate me even more."

Ashlyn sighs and moves next to me, wrapping her arms around my body and pulling me close. "Em, I don't hate you. I'm really mad at you, yes—but I don't hate you. I could never. You're my best friend."

"You're my best friend, too," I sob. "I thought I was doing the right thing. She said—" I stop myself. "I just thought I was doing the right thing."

"Rewind," she orders. "Who said what?"

I shake my head. "Nothing. It's nothing."

"Emery." Her voice tells me it isn't up for debate as she forces me to look at her. "No more lies. *Who said what?*"

Taking a deep breath, I know she's going to lose her mind when I tell her. "Lindsey."

I feel like I'm going to throw up as I jump out of my car and run into Ashlyn's childhood home. Her mom's car isn't in the driveway, but Harland's is, so he must be here.

Good. He hasn't left yet.

I clutch the positive pregnancy test in my hand as I quickly make my way up the stairs and down the hall toward his room.

"Harland, I need to talk to y—"

My words are cut off as I find not Harland in his room, but Lindsey. She looks at me with pure disgust, the same way she always has. Her platinum blonde hair is perfectly straightened, and even with a scowl, she's gorgeous. It's no wonder Harland picked her. She's exactly his type.

"Can I help you?" she sneers.

I wrap my arms around myself, trying to hide how upset I am. Even a two-hour car ride wasn't enough to get my emotions under control. Not after finding out that I'm pregnant. Not even two months into university, and I'm fucking pregnant.

"I was just looking for Harland."

She gets up from the bed and comes toward me. "What do you want with Harland?"

Ugh. Of course, she's not going to tell me where he is.

"Nothing," I lie. "Forget it. I'll just talk to him later."

As I go to leave, she grabs my arm. "What's this?"

She yanks the pregnancy test from my hand, and her brows raise when she sees the two lines. "He slept with you," she breathes exasperatedly. "Of course he did."

I take the test back, finally gaining some confidence. "It's none of your business."

Her expression turns evil as she smirks. "Oh, honey. That's where you're wrong. Everything involving Harland is my business." She looks down at the test in my hands and back up. "Especially things that are going to ruin his dreams."

"What? I'm not trying to—"

"Well obviously you're not trying to, but you will." She looks at my stomach like the devil himself resides inside of it. "That baby will. I mean, you don't honestly think he could have it all, do you? His record label will drop the band the second they realize their lead singer knocked up some girl he's not even dating."

I shake my head like it's going to prove her wrong. "No. They wouldn't do that."

"Of course they would. That's just the music business, hun." She pauses. "Unless...never mind. You're not selfless enough for that."

"For what?"

She shrugs. "You could just keep it to yourself. I mean, he doesn't have to know."

She can't be serious. "That's fucked up."

"You're right, you're right," she says with a nod and waves off the suggestion. "He deserves to know about the baby. I just hope he doesn't end up resenting you both for ruining the chance he had at the life he's always wanted."

My stomach churns as I realize she might have a point. He's going to hate me. He might even hate our baby. Harland has everything he's ever wanted in the palm of his hand right now, and this? This would take that all away from him.

Lindsey purses her lips and goes back over to sit on the bed. "Your choice, babe."

Suddenly, the room feels like it's five sizes too small, and it's getting hard to breathe. I put a hand on my chest to try to ease the pain, but it doesn't work. Nothing works.

He's going to hate me.

I squeeze my eyes shut to keep the tears from forming, but they come anyway. In a split-second decision, I turn around and run from the room. As I book it down the steps, I run right past Harland himself.

"Emery?" he asks, confused.

But I don't stop.

I can't.

Telling him would ruin his life.

It would ruin everything.

I love him too much to do that to him.

"That stupid fucking bitch," Ashlyn fumes. "I'm going to kill her."

She goes to get up but I grab her wrist, pulling her back onto the couch. "Don't. Please? I just...I need you here."

Thankfully, she gives in and holds me again. I lean my head against her, feeling relieved that everything is finally out in the open, but still hating the emptiness in my chest that yearns for Harland.

"He's probably with her right now anyway."

Her brows furrow. "Who?"

"Harland," I say as if it's obvious. "I mean, he's not here trying to pound down my door. Where else would he be?"

She shakes her head. "I don't know, but it's definitely not with Lindsey."

"How do you know that?"

"Because." She shrugs. "I've seen him over the last couple months. He looked happier than he's been in a really long time, and after yesterday, I realized why. I take it he's been spending all his time here?"

I nod. "He wanted to spend time with Hollis."

"And you," she adds.

"No. I mean, I want to believe that. I do. But it's a losing game." I swallow down the lump forming in my throat. "He chose her over me back then, and he'll choose her over me now. I can't put myself through that again. A future between him and me just isn't in the cards for us."

Ashlyn hisses and slips away from me. "About that…"

My expression goes blank. "What?"

She cringes, like what she's about to say may unleash the beast. "I may have told him you were off limits."

I roll my eyes. "And since when has Harland ever listened to you?"

"Since I pulled the Bar Harbor card."

My jaw drops. "Ashlyn!"

When they were younger, during a trip to Bar Harbor before their parents' divorce, Harland broke his dad's computer. He was at an age where he was acting out a lot and constantly getting in trouble, and his dad had said that one more fuck-up and he was sending him to boarding school. Knowing the computer would be the last straw, Ashlyn took the fall for him and said she broke it. In return, he promised that he would do something to make it up to her. It could be anything, no questions asked. And now I know what she used it on.

She holds her hands up in surrender. "I'm sorry! I just—I saw the way he looked at you, and I could tell he was crazy about you, but he was such a jerk all the time. I didn't want him to take you from me."

"Ash." I frown. "You could never lose me. It's not possible."

"You say that, but what if he were to hurt you?"

I cuddle into her side. "Then it's a good thing I have a bad-ass best friend to get my revenge."

She snickers. "I would, too. I don't even care."

I'm sure she would, except she won't have to.

"Well, it won't come to that because he doesn't want me. Maybe he did at one point, who knows, but he doesn't now."

"You don't know that," she counters.

But I do, and I'm done getting my hopes up by letting myself think otherwise.

CHAPTER TEN
HARLAND

MY FIST POUNDS AGAINST VANCE'S DOOR HARSHLY. AFTER A FEW MOMENTS it opens, and Vance stands there in nothing but a pair of sweatpants and bedhead. He looks at me like I've lost my mind, but instead of forming a logical answer for my being here, I hold up the bottle in my hand that's wrapped in a brown bag.

"I brought whiskey."

He grunts and looks at his nonexistent watch. "It's like eight in the morning."

I push my way inside. "It's noon, but close."

"You couldn't have called? Given me the heads-up?"

Taking my phone out of my pocket, I show him the black screen. "It's dead, like my soul."

I throw the device behind me and onto the couch before unscrewing the cap off of the bottle. However, just before I take a sip, Vance grabs it from me.

"Okay, drama queen," he sighs. "How about you tell me what happened, and I'll decide if it's whiskey worthy, all right?"

Groaning, I plop down onto the couch. "What happened is I started dating a psycho nearly a decade ago, and she's made it her mission to destroy every bit of happiness in my life."

He sighs and pours a single shot before passing it to me. "Lindsey's back."

"Oh, she's back all right." I swallow the shot down and wince at the taste. "She's not only back, but she managed to get rid of Emery in all of like ten minutes."

"That doesn't sound like Em."

"And after Emery and I finally hooked up last night, by the way." I snort at how shitty my luck is. "But wait, it gets better."

Pouring another shot, he slides it over to me. I tilt my head back as I let it slide down my throat. And then, I drop the same bomb on him that was dropped on me no more than a couple hours ago.

"She knew about Hollis. Like, from the beginning."

Shock fills his face. "She didn't."

I motion for another shot, thankful when he doesn't refuse. "Oh, she did."

"And she never said anything?" He pauses. "Wait, how did she know but Ashlyn didn't?"

I shrug. "I don't know, and I can't even ask Emery because she won't talk to me."

"Have you *tried* asking her?"

"She didn't give me a chance," I answer. "I begged her to talk to me, but she wouldn't, and I don't blame her. I hurt her when I made the biggest mistake of my life and chose Lindsey. Then to see us together today, even if she doesn't know the full story, I can see why she hates me. Shit, *I* hate me."

Vance sighs. "So, what are you going to do?"

"There's nothing I can do but give her time to cool off and then see if we can come to an agreement about Hollis." I signal for another shot, but he doesn't give me one.

Instead, he just sits there staring at me.

"I need another."

He shakes his head. "You can't honestly be that stupid, can you?"

My bottom lip sticks out. "I didn't come here for insults. I just want whiskey."

"No," he says. "Fuck no. That is *not* how this is fucking going down."

"Dude, what the hell is wrong with you?" I ask, bemused at his tone.

"You're what's wrong with me right now, H!" he roars. "Are you forgetting that I was there all those years you used to stare at her from across the damn room? You should have made a move then, but you babbled some bullshit about a promise to your sister, so I left it alone. But Lindsey? You're really going to let *Lindsey* ruin this for you? You don't think she's ruined enough?"

I throw my hands in the air. "What else do you expect me to do? You didn't see how broken she looked! I can't keep doing that to her. I won't. She deserves better."

"Don't act all noble," he growls. "I don't know who the fuck you're trying to fool, but it sure as hell ain't me. Stop pretending like you're not taking the easy way out of this because you're scared."

"I'm scared?" I question sarcastically.

"You're fucking terrified," he replies. "Because while Lindsey might be a nutcase, a part of you loved her, and she screwed you over seven ways to Sunday. I'm sure seeing her today brought all of that back for you. And Emery? You feel something a million times stronger for her than you ever felt for Lindsey. So yeah, you're afraid. Afraid of letting your guard down. Afraid of letting her in. Afraid of giving her the ability to hurt you, because you don't know if you'd make it through that."

I look down at my lap, knowing he's right, except for one thing. "I know I wouldn't."

"What?"

"Make it through that. I wouldn't. I know that."

He exhales and finally passes me another shot but doesn't take his hand off it until I look at him. "And how does the alternative feel? Knowing you'll just have to live without her entirely— knowing that one day you'll have to watch her move on with someone else. How's that going to go?"

I move my hand away from the shot glass, leaving the amber liquid inside. Even the thought of seeing Emery with someone else makes me feel sick to my stomach. Growing up, I was so glad she never brought a guy around. I might have snapped his neck in a jealous rage just for hugging her. And now? It might only take a handshake.

She's my childhood obsession.

The mother of my son.

The love of my fucking life.

I flop back on the couch, utterly defeated. "What do I do?" I mentally beg for him to have the answer.

He leans back, looking utterly pleased with himself. "I don't know. Stand outside her window with a boombox over your head like one of those cheesy movies. Or sing her one of the dozen songs you've written about her that you submitted under my name so Lindsey wouldn't figure it out. Whatever the fuck it is, you're not going to find it at the bottom of a shot glass."

Knowing he's right, I stand up and head toward the door. When I notice Vance is behind me, I stop and look at him, confused.

"You just took a bunch of shots of straight whiskey," he deadpans. "You don't honestly expect me to let you drive right now, do you?"

"Good point."

PULLING UP TO EMERY'S APARTMENT BUILDING, I DON'T THINK I'VE EVER been so nervous. Even with all the liquid courage flowing through me, I genuinely think I might vomit. Let's just hope I can manage to keep it in until after I get her to talk to me.

If I get her to talk to me.

I thank Vance and climb out of the car, stubbing out the cigarette I smoked on the way over to calm my nerves. It didn't do as much as I had hoped, but at least it's something. With one last puff, I head for the door when I see Ashlyn step out of it.

The second she sees me, she throws her head back and chuckles. "Thank fuck you grew a pair. I was afraid I was going to have to hurt you."

"How is she?"

She tilts her head from side to side. "Upset, but I think us talking helped a little."

Silence encases both of us as I try to figure out what to say, but my sister speaks again before anything comes to mind.

"She loves you, H."

To hear that coming from the girl who knows her best gives me an overwhelming sense of hope.

"I love her, too. And I'm sorry that I couldn't manage to keep my hands to myself. And I'm sorry that I broke the promise I made, but I can't stay away from her, Ash. I can't. Please don't ask me to."

A smile spreads across her face. "It's fine. I never should've had you make that stupid promise in the first place."

"You were looking out for her. You've *always* looked out for her."

She snickers. "Yeah. Keep that in the front of your mind. Just because you're my brother doesn't mean I won't cut you if you hurt her."

"You don't have to worry about that," I tell her honestly.

"I know." She glances back at the apartment for a second. "You better get up there. Hollis is down for a nap, but I'm sure he'll be awake soon."

I nod and give her a quick hug, but as I go to walk away, she stops me.

"Wait." She takes a key off of her key ring and hands it to me. "This way she can't just refuse to let you in."

The corners of my mouth raise. "Thanks, Ash."

As I go inside and head up the stairs, I start to wonder what things will be like after this. If she takes me back. If she doesn't. Will I go back on tour? Would she and Hollis come with me? Would she be able to handle the pressures of dating one of Hollywood's favorite rockstars? Honestly, if I had to choose between the fame and the family, I'd pick her and Hollis without a second thought.

I slip the key into the lock and open the door. Emery's back is to me as she looks down at her phone, but she still looks incredible.

"What'd you forget?" she asks, but I don't say anything. "Ashl—"

Her words are cut off as she turns around and sees me standing there.

"I forgot to tell you that I'm in love with you." I take a few steps toward her. "I forgot to make sure you knew how much you mean to me without a fraction of a doubt. And I forgot to tell you that getting back with Lindsey when I could have had you was the biggest mistake of my life."

I reach my hand up and run the back of my knuckle down her cheek.

"But I won't forget any of it anymore."

"Harland," she breathes.

I shake my head. "It's you, Em. It was you when we were little kids building pillow forts in the living room. It was you when we started getting a little older and you would prance around the backyard in a bikini, totally oblivious to what it was doing to me. And it was you the night I finally let myself have what I had been wanting for as long as I could remember. It's always been you and it's always *going* to be you."

"But Lindsey—"

Putting a finger over her lips, I stop her. "Lindsey doesn't matter. She never has. Not like you."

I wrap an arm around her waist and move my other hand to her cheek before bending down and pressing my forehead to hers.

"I love you, Em."

She takes a deep breath and finally leans into my touch. "I love you, too."

Ashlyn telling me it's true and hearing those words come straight from her mouth are two different kinds of bliss, but neither of them are something I will ever take for granted.

In an instant, I pull her close and cover her lips with my own. The kiss is wet, made slippery by the tears that stream down her face, but perfect all the same. I reach down and grab her ass, lifting her up and sitting her on the counter to get a better angle.

As I slot myself between her legs, she grips at my back and deepens the kiss. I don't think I could control myself right now if I tried. The need I have for her is too primal to resist. I grip her hair and pull her head to the side as I start kissing down the side of her neck. The moan she lets out goes straight to my dick, and all I can think about is getting her in bed.

"Mommy!" Hollis calls, and I drop my head and groan into her shoulder as Emery laughs.

"Did my son really just cock block me?" I whine.

She moves me out of the way and jumps off the counter. "He did, but you'll get used to it. It'll happen a lot."

"I'm hiring a fucking nanny."

"That's fine, Casanova," she teases and puts her hand out. "But first, we have to do something else."

My brows furrow. "What?"

She stares at me with a raised brow and it's like I can read her mind. *Hollis*.

The excitement that runs through me is paired with an utter fear of rejection. I'm just not sure which one is stronger.

"What if he hates me?" I ask, but still putting my hand in hers.

She shakes her head. "Are you kidding? He could never hate you."

"I mean, he could."

Pulling me down the hallway, she stops outside his room. "He won't. But regardless, we'd get through it. We're a team, remember?"

She opens the door and goes to our son, and I'm left thinking about how right she is. With her on my side, I feel like I could take on the world.

"Hey, H," Em says softly as she sits down on Hollis's bed. "Harland and I have something we have to tell you."

He rubs his eyes with his little fist and then looks at his mom expectantly, still half asleep from the nap he just woke from. I calm my emotions as much as I can manage and step into the room. The second I sit beside Emery, she interlaces her fingers with mine just out of Hollis's view.

"Do you remember the time you asked me about your dad?" she questions.

Hollis thinks for a moment then nods. "You said he's a big rockstar and that I never got to meet him. But you lied, Mommy."

Her brows furrow. "I lied?"

He nods again. "Aunt Mila told me that my daddy was taken by the Wicked Witch of the West, like the dog in *The Wizard of Oz*."

I snort as Emery pinches the bridge of her nose. "Of course, she did."

"I mean, she wasn't wrong, per say," I counter.

Em chuckles and rolls her eyes playfully before composing herself and focusing back on Hollis. "H, did I ever tell you that Harland is in a band?"

He shakes his head, but I can practically see the gears turning. "He is?"

She nods and Hollis turns his attention to me. He crawls into my lap and I release Emery's hand to hold my son. Neither one of us say a word as his fingers reach up and graze my cheek. He stares into my eyes and I can practically feel the moment it clicks.

"Hawlan, are you my dad?"

A wave of emotion clogs my throat and I almost can't get the words out, but I do. "Yeah, little man. I am."

He gasps for a second before wrapping his arms around my neck and hugging me tightly. Tears fill not only my eyes, but Em's too. I don't think I've ever felt so content as I hold Hollis close.

"Are we going to be a family now?" he asks as he pulls away.

My gaze meets Emery's and she lets out a wet laugh, swatting away stray tears.

"Yeah, H," she answers, using our mutual nickname. "We're a family now."

Hollis scrambles from my lap to start jumping on his bed and cheering happily. Em and I watch him with warm smiles on our faces, until he stops suddenly and narrows his eyes at me.

"Wait," he says warily. "Does that mean you're going to be kissing mommy?"

I chuckle and look over at his mom. "That depends on if she'll let me."

Emery scrunches her nose, mocking disgust. I grab her by the arm and pull her close. She giggles just before I cover her mouth with my own and kiss her in front of Hollis for the first time, but certainly not the last.

"Oh, gross!" H groans and collapses on the bed with hands covering his eyes.

We both can't help but laugh at his dramatics and Em pulls away to pepper kisses all over Hollis's cheeks. He thrashes around on the bed in a fit of giggles before stopping and pressing a kiss to his mom's cheek in return.

The happiness that fills the room unlike anything I've ever felt before and I know that nothing will ever be able to drag me down. Not when I have them.

They give me strength.

They hold me together.

They calm the storm.

THE END.

TRUTH AND LIES
BY J.D. HOLLYFIELD

CHAPTER ONE

THE SUN BEATS DOWN, FORCING ME TO SHIELD MY EYES AS I TAKE IN THE perfect view before me.

Jake DuPont.

My neighbor.

The person who has owned my heart since the moment I understood what love was.

The water spreads like waves with each rhythmic stroke as he swims across his Olympic-size pool. The side of his face breaks the surface, and he inhales a quick breath, the sun's rays illuminating his plump lips. He glides through the water like a magical sea creature, and I imagine myself fighting against the current to get to him, escaping the reality that exists above the surface

My stomach twists at the thought of summer ending. Of what tomorrow will bring. I have to prepare for the emptiness that surfaces every time he leaves me—the ache inside my chest when he's away.

The wind picks up, and the chimes hanging from the trees sing. Leaves fall to the ground—another cruel reminder that summer is over. My legs hang over the edge of the pool, kicking back and forth, needing the water to cool my overheated skin. I inhale the breeze, memorizing the smell of the summer air, locking it deep inside my chest to reminisce on during the days and nights I struggle the most.

It's foolish, I know. Two kids, forbidden to be together, secretly in love. But he's all I've ever known. He defines love for me. He always has. The one who fills the loneliness inside me. The only one who feels like home.

Jake and I may come from the same world—a society built on stature and prestige—but we might as well be from different planets with the way our parents try to keep us apart.

We're what people called aristocrats. Well…our parents are. Jake and I are just chess pieces, puppets on strings. With us, they plan to gain access into superior circles. We will blossom into leaders of high society where the wealthy mingle with the wealthier in hopes of becoming the wealthiest.

Jake DuPont is four years older than me, top of his class at university. Dominating anything he touched, he was captain of the Rugby team, head of the debate team … and breathtakingly beautiful. I know, what eighteen-year-old calls a guy beautiful? But he is. He's every word that describes perfection.

Like everyone else in his family, he's always been destined to attend an Ivy League school and become a doctor like his father. His parents even had his wife chosen for him by the age of twelve. Rebecca, the daughter of a judge, will help merge two elite families into a fortress of power.

I had my own destiny. Not as high achieving as Jake's, but that's because I'm not the perfect, well-mannered, flawless daughter my mother so desperately wished for. The older I got, the more disappointed in me she became until I turned into a lost hope, and their plans for me shifted. My path turned out to be simpler: attend an Ivy League school and marry someone in politics—steal the hearts of Congress while carrying the name of a high society electoral official. The smile on my mother's face when she imagines herself having tea at the White House is ridiculous.

It's absolutely atrocious. But it's our world. We don't get to choose our path. Jake doesn't get to be a firefighter like he's talked about since he was seven, I don't get to become a ballerina or movie star, and we don't get to marry for actual love. Those silly dreams stay like that: dreams.

Jake is heading off for med school, and I'm finally starting college. The time has come to walk our separate paths, and I've never hated anything more. With both our futures unknown, there are no holiday promises or summer plans to hold on to. My heart squeezes as tears prick my eyes.

We've always been each other's safe place—and now our safe place is getting ripped out from under us.

I remember the first time I felt the flutter. I hadn't been sure what was happening to me. Jake, being older and more experienced, I think, knew the exact moment my feelings changed. He became more tender, patient. Being young and emotionally confused, he would take the verbal lashings when I became too confused to explain why it hurt to see him with another girl. He would ignore my whining and hug me, force us to the guest house at the back of his family's mansion, and make me hang out with him, listening to song after song until my walls broke down and we were back to being us: Jake and Willa.

As time passed, our feelings grew like wildflowers- uncontrollable and taking root in every crevice of our hearts. He owned me. I owned him.

The day he turned eighteen and left for college, it broke me.

His parents threw him a lavish going away party. I was stuffed into yet another floral gown with my hair wrapped tightly in a headache-inducing bun and had to watch across the pool as he mingled with guests, saying his goodbyes and feeding them lies about being so thrilled to start this journey. When he gazed across the pool at me, his smile so saccharine I tasted it on my lips, my heart crumbled at the thought of him being gone. I ran to the guest house—our special place—hid my face in my hands, and cried. When he found me sometime later, he did what he always did.

"Please don't cry." *He bends down, wiping away my tears.*

"I wish you weren't leaving. I can't do this without you. There's so much I want to say, but how do I? How do I confess that—"

Cupping my face, he presses his lips against mine, cutting off my rant. It's not long or ravishing. It's soft and kind. When he pulls away, his eyes lock on mine. "I'm going to miss you too. You have no idea. One day, our words will have meaning and won't be forced into the shadows. Stay safe for me, Willa. I'll be back soon."

I was fifteen the first time he kissed me, and we haven't spoken of it since. For years, we've danced around each other. He never made another move on me but showed in other ways that he was right there with me—the way he held me when we went swimming or how he gripped my hand when we walked together into parties. How he pulled me close after I suffered the abuse of my mother… and how my heart would break any time he had to make appearances with Rebecca…every ounce of him has always shown me he's felt the same.

I squeal as water shoots up, and Jake splashes me as he breaks the surface, his strong arms reaching forward to grab at my legs.

"You gonna come in?"

"And get my hair wet before family photos? Mother would have an aneurysm." Jake laughs, knowing I'm right. I wasn't blessed with pretty and manageable silk-blonde hair—more like curls with a mind of their own and a private stylist so no one tells my stuck-up mother her daughter resembles a low-class vagrant.

"I like it when your hair is all wild." Jake's lips curl upward into a smile that visits me every night in my dreams. His perfect white teeth and mischievous grin always have a way of turning any bad situation into something good.

Another reason why tomorrow is going to suck.

Jake glowers at the sadness in my gaze and tries to deflect away from what's truly upsetting me. "You know you can always tell her it was my fault. I pushed you in."

I roll my eyes. Like my mother would believe that. It was always one of our go-tos when we were kids and found ourselves looking like soaked rats at Sunday brunch because a simple game of tag turned into us jumping into his pool. "Yeah, then maybe I can tell her you made me roll in dirt so I don't have to wear the ugly flower dress she has laid out for me."

Jake scrunches his nose. I swear, my mother would have been over the moon with a dress-up doll instead of a daughter. We continue to stare at one another, holding onto a moment that doesn't belong to us. A silent stare that speaks volumes but can only exist in our hearts. Something burns like wildfire between us, but if we ever dared acknowledge it, it would turn us to ash.

"How about if I promise to blow dry your hair when we're done? Just a quick race. Three-lap parlay. Whoever wins has to go streaking down the street."

I laugh and slap his thick bicep. "You want me to get disowned? No respectable congressman's wife would be caught doing that, now would they?"

His lips thin, but he quickly masks his expression by waggling his brows. "Maybe I just want to see you naked." His eyes glimmer with truth, but he disguises his honesty with a wink. "It's my last day here. You're not going to leave me hanging by myself, are you? You know my parents have another huge going away party tonight. You can't ditch me. Please…" He puckers his lips, gripping tighter to my thighs.

"You have a girlfriend. Have *her* be your date."

His brows scrunch, and he scowls. "You know she's not my girlfriend. Rebecca is only a tool in my parents' plan to unite riches with riches—that's all she'll ever be."

I shake my head and laugh. "Well, you haven't looked like it was much of a hardship, smiling and carrying her on your arm all summer." A summer that has ripped my heart to shreds.

Jake's mood dies—and so does mine. Pushing up against the edge of the pool, he spreads my legs apart. "The same reason your mother's made you prance around with that Walter geek. Unless you two are actually hitting it off, and you find his nerdy bifocals and flood pants attractive—ouch!" I slap him.

"God, no. And he smells musty. It's horrible."

We stay quiet for a moment, the weight of our circumstances settling into that heavy place in our chests. "I don't want you to leave," I confess, feeling like a broken record. How many more times can we wallow in this moment?

His shoulders slump as sadness seeps into his gaze, matching mine. "You can come visit. Your university isn't far from the hospital. Even though I'm sure those aristocrats will flock to you the second you land on campus. You'll be engaged and forget about me in no time."

The mere thought creates panic inside me. How could he ever think I would forget him? He's embedded in my heart, and his imprint marks my soul. I'd die a thousand times, and his steely gaze would still give me life. But what if that's what he wants? For me to go to college and forget about him? Grow up and put a stop to this silly fantasy? Stop the harping and the tearful nights? Maybe he's grown up so much that his bond has faded.

"Whatever. Maybe you're right. Mother *was* talking ring sizes with Walt—"

He captures my waist and pulls me in. I have a split second to inhale before he brings me under the pool's surface. Just like the other times we've found ourselves in this situation, our eyes open, adjusting to the water, and we share a silent embrace where time stands still, where the loud noises of our parents' demands aren't suffocating us. Down here, we're just Jake and Willa, wanting to be free of the society we've been raised in. A girl and a boy who have possibly fallen into a forbidden love.

I beg him not to leave me again. And he screams he has to go. It never goes any further than this—a forbidden glimpse into each other's soul. There's no telling the destruction if we let ourselves bask in the touch of each other's lips. But in these stolen moments, I pretend. His lips, the taste of cherry Chapstick and mint. His hands, which stay innocent, but become rough and demanding. His body consumes mine. In my dreams, there's only one path, and we get to take it together. But after tomorrow, I'll be alone again, and he'll be off on another journey forced upon him.

CHAPTER TWO

THE DUPONTS DON'T MISS A BEAT WHEN IT COMES TO THROWING AN extravagant party—especially one where they can show off. The violinist in the corner of the backyard plays beautifully as the glimmering lights hang in perfect waves along the branches, illuminating the entire yard. Waiters walk around the pool with trays of champagne as friends and family chatter amongst themselves.

My mother's eyes meet mine as the mayor continues to speak to her, her face stern and unyielding. I ruined the family portrait. My hair rivaled a rat's nest, and there hadn't been any way for them to fix it in time. I explained I'd fallen in the pool by mistake, but she was past my silly lies when it came to Jake and me—and she was making it known.

"It was an accident. Jake and I—"

"Oh, for heaven's sake, Willa. There's no way that respectable young man would spend his day peddling around with a nuisance like you. You should be ashamed of yourself for trying to tarnish his good name."

"How would me being with Jake tarnish his name? We're friends. A perfect match, actually. And last I checked, we're both rich and powerful."

My mother's sharp laugh wounds me. "That we are, my daughter, but you have yet to prove you are anything but a disgrace to our family name. And trust me, someone with such a bright future would never attach themselves with such a disappointment."

My head still aches from being dragged up the flight of stairs, thrown into my room, and instructed not to dare leave until a new stylist arrived. God forbid someone got a look at me. My anger came in the form of heavy tears. Her hateful words couldn't have been farther from the truth. Our love was real.

I took a shower, washing away the chlorine and the feel of Jake's hands. Down the drain went the regret when he finally let me go and the anger that he could so easily switch roles and go back to playing the mischievous best friend and not the man I've been so madly in love with since my heart found its other half.

Mother tears her eyes away, slipping into her practiced and fake smile as they continue their conversation. I snag a glass of champagne, toss it back before getting caught, and ditch the crystal glass on a tall, lace-covered pub table.

Goosebumps spread over my arms, and I lift my eyes to the other side of the pool. Jake is standing with some of his father's business associates, his eyes locked on me. Everything around us seems to freeze. The chimes no longer ring, and the wind no longer blows- the universe belongs only to us. Two hearts beating in unison. His eyes never leave mine as we stare into each other's souls. He licks his lips and my legs quiver.

They open, and he mouths, "*Hi.*"

"*Hi,*" I mouth back.

"*You're late.*"

I laugh, gesturing to my attire and hair. His infectious smile appears, and I ache to tear away the space between us and claim those lips as my own. We can do this forever. Block out the world around us. Pretend. My heart rate quickens as he excuses himself, and we both make a move to get to each other. A man steps in front of him, and our bubble pops. The windchimes chatter. Annoying social laughter pains my ears. His pleading eyes find mine, and he mouths, "*Sorry*."

I force a sympathetic smile as he pulls his attention away from me, his own fake smile in place as he converses with the gentleman.

THE NIGHT DRAGS ON LIKE MOLASSES. I FIND MYSELF TRAPPED IN DULL conversations, my eyes constantly seeking out Jake. My mind keeps replaying how handsome he looked in his dark slacks and fitted dress shirt that accentuated his toned body. That was the last time I saw him, and it was hours ago. A waiter passes by, and I grab a glass of champagne and slam it back, wanting to numb the pain tonight is causing. "At least the champagne is—"

"Willa, darling." I jump, bumping into the pub table, and turn to Meredith, Jake's mother.

"Hello, Mrs. DuPont. Great party. The swans are beautiful," I rush out, throwing the glass behind my back into her rose bushes.

She waves me off, as if she doesn't already know and expects every guest to compliment them. "Just a little touch. You haven't seen my Jakey, have you? He's been missing for some time, and there are so many people who want to wish him well."

"No, sorry, Mrs. DuPont, I haven't. Maybe I'll go look for him."

She waves me off again. "No, dear. Let me find Rebecca. She should be the one to find him. Enjoy." She saunters away into the crowd.

"Rebecca should find him," I mimic, my tone dripping with sarcasm. Rebecca and I couldn't be any more different. For starters, she's tall and has nice hair. I'm pretty sure her boobs are fake, but Jake says he wouldn't know because he's never touched them. I'm not sure if that tidbit of information makes me happy that he hasn't or mad because he's feeding me lies.

Knowing his mother won't find him, I walk toward the guest house at the back of the yard. If he's hiding anywhere, it's there. I take a peek inside, finding him pacing. Walking in, I shut the door behind me and say, "Hey, what are you doing out here? Your mother's looking for—"

"Fuck my mother," he snaps. Picking up an antique off the desk, he throws it into the lit fire, shattering it.

I jolt back, startled by his sudden anger. "Jake, wh—what happened?" I eliminate the space between us. His eyes are bloodshot. He smells like booze. I don't stop until I wrap my arms around his waist and press myself firmly against him. "What happened?"

He captures me in his tight hold, his head dipping down, inhaling the scent of my hair. "Life fucking happened." His lips press against the side of my head, his breath skating along my earlobe. "This fucking life. These fucking fake people. Everything is about a deal. It's not about happiness or allowing us to *be* happy. It's about money. It's always been about money."

"I thought you were excited to start med school. What's changed?"

Jake pulls away to capture my cheeks. "Excited?" He laughs, but it's dark and cynical. "Why would I be excited to live someone else's life? This isn't my plan, Willa. It's theirs. I've played along. I've sacrificed. I've given up love—" He squeezes his eyes shut for a moment as his voice trails off. "No matter how far I go, I'll always feel caged. The chains from my family will always strangle me. The rules suffocate me. The expectations of who I'm supposed to be instead of who I am and what I want…" He releases a harsh sigh, his eyes dropping to my lips. "What do you want, Willa? What do *you* truly want?"

"That's not up to me. You know that—"

"If it was. If we got to decide—what do you want?"

His eyes plead for my words. My truth. My tongue feels too thick for my mouth as I struggle to answer him. I want to be free. I ache to live my own life and be loved. "I—I want to be loved by a person who doesn't belong to me. And I want to be free of the life we're both trapped in—free of the thorns that make us bleed. I want to finally admit I love—"

Jake crushes his lips to mine, and I tense, startled, then quickly melt into him. Having him this close, touching me, sharing this connection, feels like a dream. The warmth of his touch seeps into my skin as he grips my face harder and separates my lips, his tongue mingling with mine. He tastes like cherries, just as I remembered, with a hint of scotch. "I hate myself for waiting so long to do this. And now it's too late. Our time has run out and I can no longer show you what you truly are to me."

I latch onto his shirt, clutching it tightly, and deepen our kiss, frantic for more. "Why do you say that?" I plead. Just as frenzied, he reaches for the hem of my dress and pushes me up against the desk. "This isn't goodbye. It's just med school. Once I leave for college, we'll be closer. Our parents won't be able to stop us. We can finally—"

"We can't." He nips at my lower lip, feathering wet kisses down my chin. Tiny prickles of desire explode throughout my body as his tongue meets the dip in my neck and he bites at my shoulder. "God, I always knew you would taste sweet. I've thought about how sugary sweet your skin would be. Like silk against my tongue."

"Jake," I moan, allowing my head to arch back and my eyes to fall closed.

"I shouldn't be doing this. I should let you go and do what I have to do."

My fingers disappear into his hair and I tighten my hold, keeping him from pulling away. "Please. Please, don't stop," I beg. I may crumble into a million devastated pieces if he does.

"This is not okay. I shouldn't be doing this. You don't belong to me—"

"I've always belonged to you. Just because the words haven't been said doesn't mean they don't exist. I've loved you my whole life, Jake DuPont. Don't make me start hating you because you stopped."

His mouth covers mine. "Oh, Willa, if there were words to make you understand, to show you what I feel inside. All these years, I've spent so much time wanting and wishing, all while knowing it was wrong. I've tried to stay away, but I hate knowing you're going to be someone else's."

My chest constricts. I tug at his hair, try to kiss him harder, steal his breath, but nothing lessens the pain. My body starts to quake in his hold, and he pulls back, worry in his eyes. "What's wrong? Are you okay? Fuck, I shouldn't have kissed you—"

"You should have done this years ago. I want you with every thread of my being. I want to be the girl on your arm, the one who makes you smile, the one you wake up to day after day. It tears me apart knowing I can't—but my love is so strong, no matter how this ends, I'd spend eternity loving you from afar."

A scorching flame of passion lights behind his eyes, and he drops his lips back to mine. A lifetime of pent-up need explodes between us, threatening to burst into flames. He lifts me, placing me on top of the desk, his hands sliding up my bare thighs. "I want you, Willa. I know that makes me a bastard, but God, I want you."

"You have me. You always have."

He shakes his head. "But I can't. It's fucking wrong. I'm drunk. And what kind of man would I be to take everything I've ever wished for then leave? I'd never be able to forgive—"

"It makes you just as desperate as I am. If you don't want to spare my virtue…well, it's always been you who takes it in my dreams. My heart…that's yours too. Please stop acting like this is our ending. This is us beginning. A life we've secretly ached for can finally come true."

"Fuck, Willa." He devours my lips, and I kiss him back just as fervently, as if we've been doing this our entire lives, melting together, our lips, our hands, our souls.

"Are you sure?"

I stare up at him, allowing him a view into the window of my soul. His eyes glass over with the same intensity and he silently confesses what I've always wanted to know. He loves me too. I fight back tears at the pain his pending absence will bring but focus on our future—one where we'll be far from the grasps of our parents' controlling demands.

For now, I focus on the present—on his touch—his gentle praises and sweet endearments.

"I always have been. Please. Love me like I love you."

He grabs me by the waist and pulls me close to his chest. A shiver ripples through me as his lips seal over mine. My heartrate accelerates, and I melt into his devastating kiss. With a gentle finger, he brushes my hair away from my shoulder and presses his thumb against the pulse in my neck. "Dammit, Willa, you're shaking." He pulls back, his hand cupping my cheek to hold my gaze. "We don't have to."

Passion resonates in his steely gaze, magnifying the spark igniting inside me. I can't bear another second of not being with him. "Please. I love you. I want this."

He lifts me in his arms and carries me over to the bed we've laid on countless times. He gently lays me down, his warm body covering mine. The intensity of his gaze creates an inferno of desire in my belly. Anticipation for what's to come puts my mind into a frenzy, and I tremble.

"I've thought about this moment. About you like this…" His hand drops to my leg, latching a finger under the hem of my dress and sliding it up my thigh. His simple touch causes an unfamiliar wave of sensation to shoot to my core. I rock my head backwards, allowing him to push my dress up and over my head, leaving me bare aside from my underwear and bra. "Jesus, Willa, you're beautiful." His mouth dips to the exposed flesh above my breast, his wet mouth spreading kisses up my breastbone. Each touch overwhelms my senses and steals away my worries. The past, the future.

"I've wanted this for so long," I murmur as he kisses the corner of my mouth. His fingers work to unclasp my bra. He's gentle as he discards my panties, and his eyes stop to admire my bare flesh. My breathing hitches when his hands graze down my ribcage, his knee spreading my thighs.

"Tell me if you want me to stop—"

"I won't," I rush out. "Please." My voice shakes, exposing my nerves. I worry he won't continue. I reach up and capture the back of his neck and demand his mouth return to mine. I become acutely aware of the hardness against my belly as he kisses me back. His hand presses against the apex of my thighs, and a sudden moan breaks our kiss. A seed of desire blooms in my belly, and my eyes widen at the boldness of his touch.

He captures my gaze, allowing me to hold on to the trust that seeps from his eyes as he breaches my entrance with a single finger. I fight to hold his gaze, but with each stroke, I become lost. "Jake," I moan. My hips begin to move on their own accord, riding his finger. His eyes darken with desire, and his lips fuse to mine. He swallows each moan and pumps into me faster, more aggressively, until my legs begin to quiver as I gasp for air.

"That's it. Come for me." My eyes close as blinding pleasure explodes from my core. He rides out my orgasm until suddenly I feel the absence of his finger. I reopen my eyes to find Jake now standing in front of me. He's working the buttons of his shirt exposing every inch of his tanned skin. Toned chest. Not a flaw to be found. Once he's naked, he climbs on top of me, his knee pushing my still trembling legs apart. His lips find mine, and he's slow and gentle as he breaches my entrance. "This is going to hurt, but I promise, I'll make it feel good."

I nod, trusting him. I close my eyes and wait for the pain, but he captures my chin. "Open your eyes, Willa." I do as he asks, and his handsome face steals my breath. "We do this together, okay?" The passion in his eyes gives me strength. I lock my vision onto him as he slides into me. My lips part. A sharpness radiates in my core, but he kisses away my pain until it morphs into pleasure. His slow grunts collide with my whimpered moans as we create a melody of love, desire, and promise. The fullness of him has my body in a state of euphoria. My nails scrape down his back with each thrust, and I can't seem to get enough. My legs wrap around his lean waist, and I hold on to him, fearing he'll vanish at any second.

"I love you, Jake," I moan, and my head falls back as he thrusts deep into my sex. I never imagined it would be like this. Feel like this. I've surrendered my entire being to him, and with each stroke of his cock, I lose myself to him even more. "Oh god, Jake, I'm—I can't—I'm going to—" My walls clench around him, and I dig my nails deep into his flesh as my orgasm blasts through me. I climax, holding him close, and he whispers his love for me just before his own release. His brows tight, his hands grip my hips as he powers into me until he's groaning out my name.

He falls on top of me, our hearts beating rapidly against one another. I'm still riding the highs of what we shared, enjoying the simple touch of his fingers grazing up and down my sides. When his breathing labors out, he slowly lifts his head to assess my mood.

"You okay?" He tucks a piece of hair away from my face.

My lips curl into an upward smile. "I'm perfect." His muffled laugh vibrates against my neck as he presses wet kisses along my skin. "*You* are perfect. And that was perfect. I can't tell you how many times I've fantasized about having you this way. It was better than any fantasy."

I lift up and capture his lips, savoring this moment. The taste of his mouth. The feel of him wrapped around me. I fight the reality of what awaits us and focus on the rhythmic beating of his heart, the long strokes of his tongue against mine, but eventually, my mind wins over.

Jake senses the change in me and pulls away as the first tear falls. "Why the tears?" he asks, and I turn my head away, needing them to stop. He pulls me back. "What's wrong. Do you regret—?"

"Oh, God no. That was just…it was everything. I've wanted you since I knew how to love. When you left me the first time—"

"Willa, I didn't leave you."

"I know. But it didn't hurt any less. I'd never felt so alone, and my heart broke every time I had to watch you go. But now, after this…I can't fathom being apart. We'll see each. Once I'm at school and you're doing your residency, we'll be close enough to—"

"Willa—"

"We can be to—"

"Jakey? Jakey, dear, are you out here?" We both freeze at the sound of his mother's voice.

"Shit." He climbs off me, and we quickly dress. "Hide inside the closet. I'll go out first and get rid of her. You follow a few minutes later." There's no time for a goodbye. A kiss. A second to remember this moment. He's out the door, greeting his mother. A second voice sounds, and my heart burns as it cracks in two.

Rebecca.

"There you are, honey. They're ready to give a speech and serve cake. We need the guest of honor." Their voices fade, and I slide down the wall, holding my knees to my chest, fighting back tears. I hate how cruel life can be. How unfair this world is. I grip my knees, inhaling a slow breath to gather myself, holding on to the fact that soon, our destiny will fall into place. We will be together, and they will no longer stand in our way. Finally, we will have our happily ever after.

CHAPTER THREE
THREE WEEKS LATER

THIS CAN'T BE HAPPENING. I TAKE A DEEP BREATH, INHALING THROUGH MY nose, and exhaling through my mouth. *I can do this. I can do this.* Or not. Running back to my bathroom, I vomit for the third time today. As I brush my teeth, banging sounds against my door—the knock of my furious mother. I was supposed to be downstairs thirty minutes ago. Today, we leave for school.

"What in heaven's name is taking you so long? My word, the world doesn't just wait for you—oh good lord, what are you doing on the bathroom floor in that dress? Have some respect for couture. Get up."

I try, but my stomach turns, and I hide my head in the toilet bowl and throw up again. "For goodness sake, what's wrong with you now? If this is another stunt to stall us leaving, I swear to it, Willa, I will dump you with a driver, and he can take you. Get up."

"I can't," I moan, a Tilt-a-Whirl ride happening in my stomach. "I don't feel well. Something I ate—" Another round of harsh vomit expels up my throat. Anger seeps off her in waves, and I decide right now is not the best time to confess I'm sick because I'm pregnant. When she turns away, I slide the test under my dress.

"You ate the same thing we did." The heat of her disappointing stare burns at my back. "You inconvenience us all. I'll let your father know to go on with his meetings. We'll send for a driver to take you tomorrow. By God, Willa, pull it together." And she walks away.

"Ughhh," I groan into the toilet as I flush, then wash out my mouth again and crawl back into bed. I take out my phone and dial Jake's number for the millionth time, but it goes straight to voicemail. "Hey, it's me. Where are you? Please call me. We need to talk." The same voicemail I've left every time. All have gone unanswered. My stomach turns again. Gripping my belly, I curl into the fetal position, hoping the sickness passes.

I need to talk to Jake.

He left the guest house without another glance my way, and it was the last I saw of him. He was gone when I returned to the party, and when I walked over to say goodbye in the morning, I was shooed away by his mother, who said he'd already left.

"What do you mean he already left?" I ask, my eyes wide with confusion. He wouldn't leave without saying—

"Oh dear, he left last night. So eager, my Jakey is. He and Rebecca just couldn't wait to get started on their new journey." Her sickly-sweet smile causes knots to form in my stomach.

"Rebecca? I...I don't understand."

"France, dear."

I sway to the right and grab onto the doorframe to keep steady. "France? I thought he was doing his residency in—"

Mrs. DuPont waves me off. "Honey, those were just the stepping stone plans. His father has made sure his future is even more promising."

We weren't going to be close to each other and away from our parents once I went to school. Because he was doing his residency in *France*. Along with Rebecca. I felt the wind being knocked out of me as she smiled once again, wished me well at school, then left for her yoga class. He left for France and never told me. With *her*. My tears shed in horrid waves down my face as I ran home, threw myself onto my bed, and sobbed. He made promises that night. He said we would still be together. *But did he? Or were those just the words that fell from your naive lips?* Everything I confessed, looking back, he had the chance to tell me. But he let me fall into this belief we had finally found our path to one another. All along, he knew…

It's been three weeks since that night—twenty-one days since I last heard from him. I try to bury the worry that he's avoiding me. I refuse to allow myself to believe he regrets what we shared. Maybe he had his reasons for keeping the truth from me. He was protecting me. But why hasn't he called? Returned any of my desperate pleas to speak to him? For three weeks, I've obsessed over it. Over him. Waited for him to call. A simple text. But nothing. He's become a ghost. I've pushed off leaving for school as long as I can. And seeing how angry my mother is, I know I've used my last excuse. It's now or never. It's time to confess a secret I've been harboring.

"MOTHER?" I CALL FROM THE LIVING ROOM.

"What is it, dear?" She barely acknowledges my presence as she skims through her magazine.

"Have you talked to Mrs. DuPont about Jake? Has she heard from him?"

Her eyes glimmer with admiration. "Oh, yes. That young man is going to be magnificent. He's truly excelling, and it's been less than a month."

The thorns around my heart squeeze tighter, and I inhale a staggered breath. "Oh… well, does she have a number where he can be reached? Because the one I have, I don't think it works internationally. I really need to—"

"Willa, my goodness, don't you think it's time to get over this little crush? It's become quite humiliating. He's practically engaged, not to mention too old for you."

I clench my jaw so hard; I wait for her to yell at me next for ruining my perfect teeth. "It's not a crush."

She throws her head back and laughs theatrically. "Oh, come on. Really, Willa?" She tsks me and goes back to reading her magazine. "Why don't you spend less time pining over someone way above your means and more time on someone more suitable like Walter? He may become an asset to this family one day. If no one fancies you at school, we'll have to work something out so he'll—"

"I'm pregnant."

Shoot.

Did I just say that out loud? Mother drops her magazine and slowly turns my way. Darn it, I did.

"Excuse me?"

It's now or never. Deep breaths. "I said I'm pregnant. And Jake is the father." She stares at me for so long, I worry I broke her. Then she throws her head back and lets out a boisterous laugh.

"Oh, goodness, Willa. Desperation does not look good on you. Nor do your pale cheeks. Go upstairs and change. I see wrinkles, and your hair is ungodly—"

"I'm pregnant!" I yell. "I'm pregnant, and it's Jake DuPont's!" I yell louder, so tired of being swept under her fancy Persian rug like I don't matter. I'm so sick of being me.

"You better knock it off this instant, Willa Brianne. That is not amusing or funny. These games you're playing—where are you going? Willa! Get back here! Where are you going?" she shouts at my back as I walk out the front door and storm next door. Pregnancy hormones are no joke. It's my explanation for losing my marbles and thinking banging on the DuPonts' door until someone answers, telling them they're going to be grandparents, and demanding Jake's goddamn number is a grand idea.

My fist bangs against the mahogany wood until Mrs. DuPont answers. Her tightly pinned eyes widen in surprise at my evident distress. "Oh heavens, are you all right?" she gasps.

I open my mouth to confess just how not all right I am when my mother latches into my hair, pulls me backward, and slaps her hand over my mouth. "Of course! My daughter isn't feeling well and seems to have a fever causing her to act a bit outlandish."

Fever my ass. "I'm pwgamt!" I scream behind the barrier.

"What was that?"

"Pwegmang!"

"Not well. Truly, her time of the month. Some young women just don't know how to handle the hormones."

Mrs. DuPont's brows perk up, confused, and most likely embarrassed for my mother. And since I'm not in my right mind, I take my elbow to her sternum, knocking her arm away. "I said I'm pregnant. With Jake's baby."

Poor Mrs. DuPont passes out.

I MESSED UP. MOTHER IS FURIOUS, AND MY FATHER WON'T EVEN LOOK AT ME. At a time when I could really use some affection and understanding, I've never felt so neglected.

"How could you do this to us?" my mother hisses as she paces the living room.

"I didn't plan this. It just happened."

"How? Did you seduce him? Force yourself? Was it even *him*?" I chew on the inside of my cheek. No one believes me. My parents claim it's a cry for help. The DuPonts refuse to acknowledge it. I told them just to let me talk to Jake, but they denied my request. My parents sent me up to bed, telling me to stay there until they decided what to do with me, like I was some old, worn piece of furniture they were debating on dumping.

I cry myself to sleep, dreaming of Jake and wishing he was here, then wake up to my mother tossing my bedsheets off me and slapping a sheet of paper on the bed.

"Read this. Then get dressed. We're leaving in thirty minutes." She walks out, slamming the door behind her. I wipe away the sleep from my eyes and unfold the piece of paper. It's an email…from Jake.

Willa,

I'm shocked to hear the news my parents presented me with and cannot claim personal responsibility. I hope you can get the help you need and make this go away. I'm days away from asking Rebecca to become my wife and need to focus on my residency and fiancée. Hope you understand. Be well. - Jake

My tears soak through the paper. My head shakes back and forth in denial, making me dizzy. Dropping the paper, I run to the bathroom to throw up. No, no, no… There's no way he would just brush me off. That night meant something. He loves…

I don't realize my mother's been standing in the doorway, observing me this whole time. When my eyes catch hers, a chill radiates between us. "We're done with your games, Willa. You've embarrassed us for the last time. When you leave here, you won't be coming back. I suggest you take what valuables you consider worthy." Then she disappears.

I DON'T KNOW WHY I THOUGHT MY MOTHER WOULD PULL ME INTO HER arms, comfort me, and tell me everything was going to be okay the second I confessed. I don't know why I'm shocked my parents choose to ship me away as the solution. As I gather my minimal things, I wonder about school. Will I still attend? Will they welcome me back once I have the baby? Am I *having* the baby? I grab at my stomach, worry overwhelming me. How far will my parents go to make this go away? Make my baby disappear? Our baby?

The drive is long. My parents opt to drive separately, as if I'll infect them with my disease. I'm scared and alone, except for my stuffy driver, who refuses to tell me where we're going. My phone was taken away so I can't Google my location. My only clues are the scenery outside my window. The busyness of the city disappears, and we spend hours driving into the country. Worry starts to eat away at me. My parents are ruthless, but they wouldn't force me to abort…

The car stops, and I prepare to run as soon as the door opens. When the door is ajar, two women dressed in black, silver crosses hanging from their necks, stand in my way of freedom.

"What's going on? What are we doing here?" I ask, my voice trembling. My eyes take in the nineteenth-century old brick castle. *A church. Nuns…* They're abandoning me at a nunnery? I stare past the two nuns, fighting for my mother's attention. My lower lip begins to tremble, and the first tear since this horrid journey began slides down my cheek. "Mother, what are you doing? Why are we here? You're not going to leave me here, are you? I'm your daughter. Daddy?" I beg my father to do something, but he refuses to look at me.

"Miss Mazaar, I'm Sister Helen. This is where you will be staying until you give birth. The monastery is a safe and private place. You have our utmost discretion during your stay. As soon as you're healthy enough, you can return home."

My eyes flash to my mother. "You're stowing me away at a *monastery*? Hiding me like this never happened? What about the baby? What will you say when I magically appear in nine months with an infant?"

"Willa, you're certainly not returning home with it."

It. That's what human life is to my heartless mother. My blood runs cold as I stare at the woman who gave birth to me; she's no mother to me. She has never been. "Then don't expect me to come home either. I'm done being your puppet. You can find another daughter to put on your shows." I climb out of the car, allowing the nun to take my bag.

"Stop being so foolish. This is your mistake. Be thankful you have this option and that no one will think twice about you taking a year off school to travel—"

"But I'm not traveling! I'm pregnant. I will have a baby. *Your* grandchild. And you're so cold and heartless, you don't even care!"

She tsks me away as she and my father walk back toward their town car. "Wait, where are you going? Don't leave me here!" I cry out. I run toward them, but I'm secured by each arm. "Mother!" My scream tears at my throat. "If you leave me here, I'll never forgive you!" My heart cracks as I watch my parents get into their vehicle and leave without a second glance. A chill casts over me, turning my heart to stone with hatred. I will never forgive them for this.

"Shhh now, dear. You're in good hands. We'll take care of you."

CHAPTER FOUR
TWO YEARS LATER

"GIVE HER TO ME." SISTER HELEN FUSSES, GRABBING BRIA BEFORE I CAN SAY no. Everyone seems to be more needy than usual today.

"This isn't goodbye. I'll come visit. I promise." Sister Helen and Sister Anne both look at me, tears welling in their eyes. "What! I promise!" I laugh and shake my head. These ladies. Bria starts to whine, and I hand them a sippy cup, knowing she's in good hands, and go to finish packing my things.

After two years of calling this place our home, my daughter and I are saying goodbye and heading off on our new journey. A small part of me aches not to be welcomed home by the family who raised me. But with the reminder of how cold and evil the two people I share blood with are, I know my new life will be better if I don't hold out any false hope of them ever coming around and loving me the way a mother and father should, let alone their grandchild.

The only time my mother made contact was shortly after I gave birth. She asked if I had learned my lesson and looked thin enough to return home. Her only concern. She didn't ask if I had a girl or a boy. If he or she was healthy. If *I* was healthy. She wanted to make sure I looked thin enough no one would suspect.

I held in my shame and anger, refused to give her my tears, and told her if I couldn't bring my *daughter* with me, I wasn't coming home. Her only response was if I disobey, they'd cut me off financially - strip me of my name and lineage.

Any thread of love I harbored at that moment snapped.

If mourning the loss of my family wasn't enough, I was still grieving the betrayal of someone I spent my entire life believing in. I fought the memories that haunted me at night. His smile. The taste of his lips. His hands as they bruised my skin while making love to me.

Eventually, those happier memories began to fade, and anger taking their place. A man who once filled me with so much purpose tainted me with so much pain. I gave birth to our daughter surrounded by wonderful women who blessed our baby girl and held my hand as I cried for her father. For my mother, when the pain became unbearable. But when I heard her little cries for the first time, it made me realize I couldn't be weak anymore. I couldn't allow anyone to make me feel like I was nothing. I had a child to take care of—to protect from the evil in the world—and I vowed to show her what true motherly love was, to be the person my mother wasn't.

Brianne Jake DuPont.

Since my family turned their back on me, I refused to give her my birthname. I gave her Jake's. One day, she'll want to meet him, and I'll have to explain. At least I can give her that.

The sisters allowed me to stay another year and some months after she was born to get back on my feet. I only had the shoes and clothes I brought with me. I worked long hours at grocery stores and libraries, cleaned houses, and tutored local kids—anything to bring in income for my daughter.

Last month, as if the gods were finally shining down on me, Sister Anne came to me with a job opening from a friend of hers. A local business was in dire need of an administrative assistant. Not only was it something I could learn to do, but it offered tuition reimbursement and housing assistance. It wasn't an Ivy League school, not that I cared about that in the first place, but it would cover the cost of a local college and an apartment.

"I'm proud of you, you know." I turn at Sister Helen's voice, finding her standing in the doorway of my room.

"How so? Because I gave up the chance to live a luxurious life and to possibly put my baby in harm's way if I fail or struggle?" I wipe away a tear. Darn it. I promised myself I was done giving them my tears.

Her smile is comforting. "You won't fail. And I think you know that. You're a resilient young woman. Since the day you came to us, I could see such potential in you. A fighter. One who lives off hope and love."

"Yeah, and look where that got me."

"It got you Bria. It gave you the freedom to live your own life and become whoever you want to be. It taught you how to be strong and fight for what you believe in."

My tears fall too fast for me to hide them. "I did fight, and here I am alone, raising my daughter. He doesn't even care."

"Life has a strange way of telling us that even though we don't believe in second chances, we all get them. Believe that God is guiding you to do what's best for you and your daughter. He doesn't give you more than you can handle. If your path crosses with Bria's father's again one day, believe there is hope in you to do right. And if not, that you're given the strength to fight for both of you. Bria is lucky to have you. Remember that."

Sister Helen opens her arms to me, and I wrap myself in her embrace as tears stream down my face. I cry for all she's done for me and all the days and nights I'll miss her. We say our goodbyes as everyone gushes and tears up over Bria and me, and with one last gaze at a place that's felt more like home than the one I lived in for eighteen years, I take my daughter and step out into the world and toward our new life.

CHAPTER FIVE
ONE MONTH LATER

"COME ON! NOT TODAY…" I BOUNCE BRIA ON MY HIP, NEEDING HER TO STOP crying so I can get her fed before the sitter arrives. I'm running on thin ice at work. If I'm late one more time, I worry they'll fire me. The job itself is horrible, and I cringe every time my slimy boss calls me into his office. I officially understand why he goes through so many assistants and why this position was open to anyone desperate enough to take it.

"Come on, sweet girl—Mommy's gotta go. If you're a good girl, we can watch TV. Yeah, you like TV. All the lights and pretty colors." She starts to settle and finally latches on to her pacifier. I think her back teeth are coming in, which kept us both up all night.

The doorbell rings, and I yell to Carrie, my babysitter, that it's unlocked and to come in. "Oh, thank god. I'm running late. She's super fussy, but just started eating." I hand her over, my eyes catching spit up over my right shoulder. "Shoot! Um…I'm going to go change real quick, then I gotta run." I dash into my room and swap out my white dress for a navy blue one. "Oh, don't forget, I have drinks with some coworkers after work, so I'll be a bit later tonight."

"Got it!" Carrie yells back as she sings to Bria.

I make it to work with a minute to spare. I toss my purse under my desk and log into my computer just as my boss enters the office. "Willa, you look extra lovely today. Anything you want to tell me?"

Yeah, I had spit up all over my regular work attire—oh, and you're a pervert and should be fired. "No, just felt like something a bit fancier."

"Okay, then. Meet me in my office in five. Looking forward to all your morning intel." I smile slightly as my insides curdle with disgust.

⁂

"I CAN'T BELIEVE YOU HAVEN'T GONE TO HR YET. HE'S DISGUSTING." TRACEY, my coworker and closest friend, groans as she takes a sip of her beer. The bar is crowded with businesspeople with the same idea: drink many drinks to erase away the day.

I sigh, enjoying the coolness of my vodka and soda as it slides down my throat. I can only allow myself one since I need to get home to Bria, but I'm going to savor every last sip. "I can't. I need this job."

"But you don't need the harassment. Sue his ass. You could live off the settlement money while you look for a better job."

"I wish it was that easy. So many places require a degree. This is one of the few that doesn't. I'm kind of stuck until I finish at least two years of school." Which I plan on starting soon. I spent all weekend filling out forms for the local college.

"Girl, you're like a machine. I wish I had your stamina."

"Stamina? More like having a screw loose. Not sure how I'm going to juggle work, a baby, and college—"

"*Willa?*"

Tracey and I laugh as someone grabs my attention. Smiling, I turn to my right. My eyes land on him, and the glass I'm holding slips from my grip and shatters at my feet as everything sways and goes black.

"WILLA, COME ON. HEY, THERE YOU ARE." I START TO COME TO. MY EYES flutter open. I'm not sure what happened, but I'm now sideways…on the floor.

"Is she okay?" I hear Tracey, and I blink away the confusion.

"What happened?" I grab for the back of my head and find a nice bump.

"You passed out." That voice brings me back. His face. Those lips. It can't be…

I struggle out of his hold and climb to my feet. A wave of dizziness washes over me, and I sway to the right. Jake grabs onto me and holds me steady, but I thrust my palms forward and push him off.

"Let go of me," I snap. My bitter tone comes as a surprise.

His eyes widen in shock. "Hey, sorry, I was just trying to help. I heard your voice… swore it couldn't be you, but then…I saw you… What are you doing here? I thought… you were traveling?" My world starts to spin and spin and spin. I can't grab onto reality. "Whoa, you okay—?"

"Stop! Don't touch me." I reach for the table to steady myself. How is he here? In front of me? He pulls back, his eyes filled with confusion. His lips thin, and his brow draws down. He opens his mouth to say something, but I can't hear it. I need to get out of here. I turn to run out of the bar.

Tracey is right on my heels. "Hey, Willa, wait. What just happened in there? Are you okay?" No, I'm far from it. My chest feels heavy. Each breath I take is like shards of glass cutting at my insides.

I turn to face her as the door to the bar opens again, and Jake steps out. "No, I need to go. I'll see you tomorrow." I turn to run, but two hands quickly grab at my waist, halting me. "Hold up, Willa, what the hell?"

I bite down on my lower lip, almost breaking the skin. I can't take the feeling of his hands touching me again. Too many memories flood my mind, and I whip around. "What the hell to *you*, Jake!" Two years of built-up anger and betrayal. I've always imagined how this day would happen. What I would say. What he would do. Would it be a beautiful reunion or an ugly showdown? Right now I'm putting my money on the showdown.

"Yeah, what the hell? I don't see or hear from you in two years, and I finally run into you, and you run away from me?" He looks hurt, like I'm the one who wounded him.

"And how *exactly* did you imagine I would react after you turned your back on me?" You broke my heart.

"I didn't turn my back—" But he did, and he knows it. "You know I didn't have a choice," he growls.

"You didn't have a choice to…what? Warn me? Tell me you were moving across the world with no way of contacting you? With *Rebecca,* no less? Or should I have been content with your cold and heartless letter—"

"What the hell are you talking about? Heartless? I practically poured my damn heart out in that letter. I explained. Told you how to reach me so we could talk as soon as I was settled. I left it with your mother the night I left."

His steely gaze takes hold of me, and my heart stops. Air escapes my lungs, and I gasp. I wish I could deny my mother would do such a hateful thing and hide it from me, but I can't. The only letter I received was him turning us away. "Well...that's not the version I got." The worst part is there's not a doubt in my mind she read it, which means she knew damn well our love was real and still chose to shame me. "What did the letter say?"

He studies me for a moment before shoving his hands through his hair. "It said I was sorry for how I was leaving. It was why I was so angry at the guest house. My father tricked me, no doubt my mother as well. There was no plan for me to do my residency upstate. It was to ship me away to France and do it under the nose of a man my father owed a favor to. And by sending Rebecca with me, it would push us to get engaged."

It brings back the pain of his letter and his request to let him and Rebecca have their happiness. "And how'd that go? Did I miss the wedding invite too?" I snap, so damn angry, my hands begin to shake.

His mouth opens, and a stunned gasp falls from his parted lips. "What? No! No. It never happened." He shoves his fingers through his hair. "Turns out, she wanted to be married to me about as much as I wanted to be with her. She was so desperate to get out of it, she leaked some photos of herself in a compromising position. It caused a huge scandal. She was in France for less than a week." I don't know whether to be thrilled or angrier.

He takes a step toward me, but I back up. I can't be this close to him. "Willa, I came home a few months later, but you were gone. Your mother said you decided to take a year off and travel."

I shake my head, squeezing my eyes tightly closed. "My mother, huh?"

"Yeah. Where have you been? Why haven't you called me? I thought after that night. I thought we—"

I start to crack at the seams. It feels like the proverbial rug is being ripped from under me. I need it all to stop. To freeze time so I can catch up to the confusion threatening to suck me into this abyss. Without thought or consequence, I raise my hand and smack him across his face, stopping any further words.

His eyes grow wide at my assault, and so do mine. I cover my mouth, holding back the devastating sob threatening to tear up my throat. What have I just done?

Before he's able to react, I turn and run.

※ ※ ※

"I LOVE YOU, WILLA. I'LL NEVER LEAVE YOU." HIS LIPS FIND MINE AS HE BREACHES my entrance, kissing away my pain until it morphs into pleasure. His grunts and my moans collide into a melody of love, desire, and promise. I climax, holding him close, and he whispers his love for me just before he—

I shoot up in bed, the dream all too real. I've soaked through my shirt, hot with the lingering feel of his touch. I run my fingers down my arms, my skin suddenly too sensitive. It's not real. But...it is. *He* is. And after two years, he's back.

I reach for my water and take a huge gulp. My throat is dry, and my eyes are swollen from the tears that refused to stop once I got home and put Bria in bed. Sister Helen's words resonate in my mind. *Life has a strange way of telling us that even though we don't believe in second chances, we all get them.* But how am I supposed to forget the last two years? The betrayal I felt? The anger and brokenness I couldn't hide from? How am I supposed to say, "*Oh, wow, what a huge misunderstanding. If you didn't write the letter I read, then my mother's the worst kind of bitch. By the way, you got me pregnant, and we have a baby girl. Wanna do lunch some time?*"

As soon as I've cried myself to sleep again, Bria wakes up. Seeing her little face and the same eyes and smile as her daddy sets off another round of sobs. Why is this happening to me? Is this my second chance, or is life trying to take me out for good?

It doesn't matter. This is a big town. Trying to find anyone is like finding a needle in a haystack. Even if I want to, it's probably impossible to locate him. Does he even live here? Is he visiting? Is he alone? Is he with someone? My mind turns and turns on a vicious wheel, unhinged and too fast. He's not with Rebecca, but he didn't say he isn't with anyone else. Why didn't I look at his finger? *Because you were too busy looking at his lips, emerald green eyes—what used to be your lifeline.*

In the silence of us catching our breath, my mind screamed out to him. I miss him, I love him, I want us to rewind time and never leave that damn guest house. I would have convinced him to run away. That life wasn't about what our parents had made us believe. If I had known money wasn't what made the world go round, I would have run away sooner—made it on my own and lived the way the normal human race did. Being free is a richer feeling than being captive.

Before I can get back to sleep, my alarm goes off. "Great," I grumble and slide out of bed. The shower barely wakes me, and Bria has no sympathy as she cries in my ear. Maybe it's because she knows I saw her daddy last night, slapped him, and basically gave up my chance to tell him about her and let them have a future. She deserves that, even if he doesn't want one with me.

As usual, Carrie saves me, and I'm running to work, praying my boss is late.

"Tsk, tsk, Willa. You know I don't like tardiness. Meet me in my office immediately." Mr. Anderson walks by me, his stomach protruding as always, the stench of stale coffee and cigar smoke following in his trail.

"Yes, sir." I nod and drop my purse under my desk.

"Hey!" I jump at the sound of another voice. "Oh, sorry. Someone's jumpy today."

I turn to Tracey. "No, yes…I don't know. I didn't sleep well last night. Bria was up…"

She smiles at me with sympathetic eyes. "Aw, sorry, honey. She's still so young. They grow out of it." I hope so. I never imagined how hard it would be to raise a baby on my own. I miss the sisters and their support. Sometimes I worry I'm in over my head. Am I really cut out to give Bria the life she deserves? "Hey, don't look so defeated. It will get better."

"Will it, though?" I shake my head, ashamed of my unmotherly thoughts. "I'm sorry. I know it will. I love my daughter, and I'm thankful for everything, it's just…"

"You're tired. I get it. I watched my older sister go through this. She was a total bitch for the first three years with her first child."

"Oh, wow. Thanks."

Tracey laughs. "Well, she's normally a bitch, so that doesn't really say much. Listen, you know I love kids. If you ever need a time out, I'm your girl. I'll watch her, and you can frolic around town. Meet a guy. Find her a daddy—wait, speaking of, *who* was the guy last night?"

"Funny you ask—"

"Willa! In my office now!"

"Ugh," I grunt. "Sorry, I have to—can we finish this later?"

"Sure thing. Lunch?"

Nodding, I take a huge breath and prepare to fight off my gross boss.

I NEED THIS JOB.

I need this job.

I need this job.

I chant it over and over as I gather my things and leave for the night. Mr. Anderson found any and every tedious task for me to do today after turning down his disgusting advances. I was forced to work through lunch, and now I'm running late to get home. I rush down the stairs, because the building is old and the elevator is slow, and hurry out into the busy street in hopes to flag down a cab since catching the subway will take too long. The evening air chills my face.

"Willa."

I jerk back and drop my bag, turning to my right. Jake leans against the building, his hands hidden in the pockets of his gray overcoat. Seeing the contents of my purse spilled over the sidewalk, he pushes off the wall. "Shit. Let me help you."

"No, it's fine. I've got it." I gather my bearings and quickly bend to collect my discarded belongings. He doesn't listen and kneels down to assist me. Panic courses through my veins. Why is he here? How did he find me? Snatching up my keys and gum, I shove them into my purse. I reach for my work badge at the same time he does, and our hands touch. The warmth of his skin sends a rush of memories to the front of my mind. *Us in the pool. Movie nights. The guest house.* My eyes drift up, afraid of what I'll see when I look at him. His tousled hair hangs in thick waves over his forehead, and I ache to reach for it, feel the silkiness between my fingers.

Shit. What am I doing?

I push back the ache to spill my truths and confess the secrets I've been harboring. But then I remember the secrets he's also kept from me. "I—I have to go." I forfeit the remainder of my things, pulling my hand back. My skin goes cold at the absence of his touch, and I frown. He nods and stands with me.

Once upon a time, I had basked in our silences—our safe place we built where words didn't need to exist because our body language spoke for us. But now, as we stand here, his hands shoved into his pockets and mine clutched into fists, I beg for those words. I turn around to once again run away when his voice stops me.

"Willa, wait. Please. Just…have dinner with me."

My eyes widen, and my mouth gapes. "What?"

That smile. "I said have dinner with me. One meal. If for some reason you can't bear to be in my presence, I'll leave you alone."

I bite the inside of my cheek, fighting a whirlwind of responses. It's not that I'm scared I won't be able to bear his company, it's that I won't be able to let him walk away. My heart is too weak. My memories of us are always too fresh. How do I pretend? "I'm not—"

"Please?" A simple plea. One word that always got me to cave.

Please? Just one lap.

Please? Just one movie.

Please? Just one truth.

Before I can conjure up an excuse, my reply falls off my tongue. "Okay, fine." Oh God, that wasn't the no I'd planned on saying. "But I can't stay too long. I have to get home." He nods, thankful for my reply. Pulling out my phone, I text Carrie to let her know I'm running late. Thankfully, she replies with, "No problem."

We walk together in silence down the busy sidewalk. Every so often, our hands brush against one another. Each connection is like a livewire, sparking up feelings I've fought so hard to bury deep down inside. When I can't take it anymore, I stop to tell him this was a bad idea at the same time he turns and points to a neon sign. "It's right here. A hidden Italian place. Best in town." I look up, never noticing it before. "After you." He allows me to go first and holds the door for me. Ashamed, I can't help but inhale his cologne as I pass. My eyes flutter closed, memorizing the scent.

A small pudgy man in an apron approaches us as we enter the quaint restaurant "Ahhh, Mr. DuPont, lovely to see you this evening. Pleasure to have you dining with us again. And who is your beautiful guest you've brought in this time?" He reaches out to take my hand. I'm hesitant, but comply, and he cups my palm, kissing the top of my hand.

"Francisco, this is Willa."

"A pleasure, Willa." He raises his eyes to Jake. "You sure do have a good eye for the ladies."

I jerk, pulling my hand away. He brings women here, and I'm no different. I back up, inhaling a sharp breath, but his hands are at my waist, his lips warming my earlobe. "Relax. I've only been here with a colleague. A platonic colleague."

"Come, come. Let me get you seated." He signals for us to follow, and my legs eventually unlock. One in front of the other, I train my feet to move and not concentrate too much on Jake's hand resting on my lower back. When he pulls my seat out, I practically fall into it.

Jake settles into the chair across from me, weighing my mood. "So…how are you? How have you been—good? Healthy?" he stops, fidgeting with the napkin.

I'm torn between truth and lies. Confession or deceit. My mouth becomes dry, and I stall by taking a sip of water. "I'm good." He exhales slowly, disheartened by my short answer. "And you? How are you?"

"Oh, well…good too…" Silence washes over us. My fingers begin to tap against the table as his tear at the napkin. "Okay, I don't know why this is so nerve wracking. This isn't us."

My eyes stop bouncing off everything in sight and focus on him. "What do you mean?"

"I mean this isn't *us*. We've never been uncomfortable or nervous around one another. I don't know what's changed. But it has. Did I do something? Was it that night? Did I force you—"

"No." I cut him off. I can't bear to hear him tell me it was a mistake.

"Then tell me what's wrong. Why did you disappear on me?"

"I didn't disappear. I—" I was forced away. I had our baby. "I just had to get away."

His face turns ashen at my reply. He opens and closes his mouth, wanting to say more, demand I tell him more, but he gives in. "Look, I'm sorry. For everything—"

I shoot up from the table, unable to hear it. "Wait, where are you going?" His voice is laced in confusion.

"I can't sit here and listen to you tell me that night was a mistake. I just can't."

He reaches for my hand, the warmth of his fingers entwining through mine. Life sparks through my veins as his eyes pierce into mine. "Willa, if there is one thing in my life I will never regret, it's that." I inhale and exhale, needing to remind myself to breathe. "I'm sorry for what came after. I shouldn't have left you alone that night. I should have told you right away. That night at the party…my father told me. I was furious. I was sick of being pulled left and right. Being my father's pawn. And then getting told I was being shipped off to France…do you even know what that did to me?"

I remember how furious he was. "Then you showed up. You've always been this bright light in our dark world. For so long, I watched you, wishing things were different while knowing it was wrong to harbor all these feelings that kept me up at night. Then you came to me, and I knew it was now or never. It was in that moment I knew I either allowed you to see the feelings that had been suffocating me or walk away for good."

His words spin too fast in my mind, and I latch onto the table for support. "Say something. Tell me you hate me or forgive me. Tell me you have a reason for cutting me out of your life so I can understand. Tell me you hate me for stealing your first time meant for someone else. But talk to me."

"That night meant everything to me." The first truth falls off my lips, along with a single tear. "You gave me so much. A memory that gave me strength. A moment that allowed me to fight the battles ahead of me—"

"What battles? Why'd you disappear?" I shake my head. Anger consumes my thoughts at my mother. At his. Two conniving witches consumed with societal expectations. "Where have you been? Why didn't you go to school like you planned—"

"Because you weren't going to be there. Because you made a promise and broke it, and I couldn't be in a place filled with deceit." I can't. I can't do this. I rip my hand away from his and run from the table. Pushing through the restaurant doors, I take off down the deserted sidewalk when two hands reach for me and whip me around, pulling me into the alley.

Jake's plush lips collide against mine, our unexpected connection bruising and demanding. He pushes me up against the cold brick building, and I fight him off, but not because I don't want him, because I'm too angry, too hurt. My fingers clutch around his dress shirt, and I suddenly find myself tugging him closer instead of shoving him away. My hands tremble as I slide them up and around his neck, deepening our kiss. "Fuck, Willa. Was I wrong? Did I read us wrong? Was it all in my head that you and I—"

"No, it was all real." I pull at his hair as his hands work up my dress. "I wanted you. I loved you." He nips at my lower lip.

"*Loved.* Past tense?" His lips work down my neck, his hands disappearing beneath the fabric of my panties. I moan at his touch, aching to feel him once again, replace my fantasies with reality. "Tell me…tell me what you're thinking. It's just us now. No one standing in our way."

His ignorant words are like a bucket of ice being dumped over my head. I rip out of his hold, his fiery gaze a mixture of desire and confusion. "It's not just us. And there are too many things standing in our way. There always have been. You're just too blind to see them."

His mouth parts in shock. He takes a step back, prepared to fight me, but I take off. This time, he doesn't follow me. I forgo the subway. My legs are on fire as I run, and my entire body shivers at the memory of tonight. My mind gets lost replaying the events. When I come back to reality, I'm walking up my apartment steps.

"Hey—whoa, are you okay?" Carrie pops up from the couch and sets down a magazine.

"Yeah, just couldn't catch a cab and didn't want to be any later than I am." I grab onto a kitchen chair to steady myself because my legs are about to give out. "Thanks for staying late." I exhale, worried I may just pass out at my kitchen table.

"Uh…yeah, you sure you're okay? I can stay. Bria is asleep, but—"

"No. I'm okay. Promise. A hot bath and bed is what I need." With uncertainty in her eyes, she nods and heads home. After a hot shower, I climb into bed and reach inside my nightstand for a small box. I hold it to my chest before removing the top. The day my mother said to grab anything of value because I wouldn't be returning, I only took two things: the clothes on my back and an old picture of Jake and me. It was taken at his graduation party and the night he first kissed me. We were smiling, his arm wrapped around my neck, our heads knocking together. We looked happy. And we were. Jake had asked his mother to take it, and shockingly, she did. The next day, I woke up and it had been slipped under my door with a note.

Willa,
Remember this happy. You're always the most beautiful this way.
-Jake

He didn't say goodbye in words, but this was his farewell to me. A piece of himself I could hold on to when he was away. I brush my fingers over our faces, remembering the way his heavy arm felt so comforting around me, the smell of his cologne that stained my pillows from the nights when he would sneak into my room and we would stay up for hours talking, my obnoxious dress he tried hard to convince me looked beautiful but couldn't mask his goofy grin at the gaudy pattern of tacky orange passion flowers and purple peonies.

Inhaling, I wipe away a tear, place that picture aside, and pick up a photo of Bria and I right after she was born. She was so tiny and frail. The birth wasn't easy since they didn't allow drugs inside the monastery. A smile is on my face, but there is so much sadness in it. My heart felt full of life, but so empty from his absence. He should have been there.

I pull out the stained piece of paper. His email to me. A letter I forced myself to read over and over as a reminder that I needed to leave my so-called fairytale life behind. It wasn't real. And I needed to see the facts in front of me. He chose to abandon me. But did he? Did my mother hate me so much, she would have conjured up a scheme to allow me such pain? For my heart to bleed with betrayal? Could he truly not know about Bria and all I've endured?

I shake my head and shove the items back in the box and cover it, slamming my nightstand drawer. His words slice at me. *"Tell me what's wrong. Why did you disappear on me?"* He wrote that letter. He had to have. If he didn't, I've spent the past two years bleeding for nothing. All the wreckage around my heart caused by manipulation and lies.

I punch my fists against my pillow, hating the way I soak the cloth with my tears. "Why are the people meant to love me most, the evilest?" My heart is being torn in two directions. Betrayal and forgiveness. And now I don't know which one is the harder pill to swallow. What does this mean for us? For Bria?

If Jake didn't truly abandon me…

CHAPTER SIX

NO AMOUNT OF COFFEE IS GOING TO HELP ME TODAY. MY EYES ARE bloodshot and swollen. I attempt to lather on more makeup than usual, but it only makes me look more tired. I give up and kiss Bria goodbye and head off to work. I refuse to allow last night back inside my mind. I need to move on and be strong for Bria. I made a promise to myself I would never again be deceived. I have to believe that as much as my mother despises me, she wouldn't go that far. I can't allow myself to think what I've been through was for nothing.

As Sister Helen would say on the nights I felt I couldn't go on, this too shall pass. I repeat those comforting words as I push through my workday. Mr. Anderson is unbearable. I'm not sure how much more I can take before I have to get HR involved. He's getting closer and closer to crossing lines I may not be able to stop.

I hurry out of his office, once again fending off his wandering hands, when Tracey pops by. "Hey, you…uh, have a visitor…"

My eyebrows raise. "I do?" Jake comes around the corner holding a giant bouquet of passion flowers and peonies, his eyes searching the layout until they land on me.

"Yeah. Kind of romantic, even though he has horrible taste in flowers."

I lock eyes with Jake as we share a smile. Purple peonies and orange passion flowers. The same gaudy pattern on the horrid dresses mother would stuff me in. "Yeah…horrible." I can't fight the smile that spreads as he gets closer.

"Hey," he says softly, weighing my reaction.

"Hey," I return his simple phrase.

We stare at one another until Tracey clears her throat. "Yeah, so I'm going to lunch. See you later." Behind his back, she winks at me before she disappears.

"I hope you don't mind me showing up here. I'm not stalking you…well, I guess I am…it's just…I remember seeing the name on your badge…well, I found out where you worked beforehand 'cause I Googled you…and, I mean, it's the only way I knew how to reach you." He takes a deep breath and extends his arm. "These are for you. Truce?"

I accept them, relishing in the way our fingers brush against one another. "Thank you. They're—"

"Beautiful," he replies for me, his eyes piercing into mine. "Willa, can we talk? For real talk? No more tap dancing?" Sincerity shines from his eyes, and I take in his aged features. It's been two years since I've gazed into the softness of his emerald eyes. He seems taller, more masculine. His lips are just as plump and smooth as I remember. His sandy blond hair is a bit longer, but it fits him. It's never been about his looks for me, though. It's his essence that always drew me in. His aura that wrapped around me and made me feel safe.

"Please…" His voice breaks me from my spell.

Sister Helen's words replay in my head. *If your path crosses with Bria's father's again one day, believe there is hope in you to do right.* Maybe this is what she was talking about. This is my chance. A slow smile spreads across my lips, and I nod. "Sure. I'd like that."

Jake closes his eyes, briefly bowing his head in relief. When he recaptures my gaze, a flutter of sensations trickles down my arms. "Just let me...um...just put these in water, and we can go, okay?"

"Yeah, sure, anything..." His nervousness creates another round of flutters. I hide my blushing cheeks and bend down to grab a vase from my desk. The door behind me opens, and Mr. Anderson stumbles out of his office, brushing crumbs off his belly. "Willa—who's this?" he snaps at Jake.

"Sorry, sir. This is...my friend. I was just leaving for lunch." Mr. Anderson eyes him with contempt, evidently not approving.

"This isn't a social gathering. We don't approve of non-employees loitering. Make sure to keep lunch to under an hour, and I'd like to see you in my office the minute you return." He licks his lips, eyes Jake up and down, then walks back into his office, slamming the door.

"What was that all about?" He frowns at the closed door. "He seems...very unprofessional."

"It's nothing. Let's just go."

WE'RE SEATED AT A SMALL CAFÉ CLOSE TO THE OFFICE. WE'RE BOTH FIDGETY, waiting on the other to speak.

"I'm sorry..."

"About last night..."

We both sputter at once.

"I—"

"You—"

"Sorry, you go first," he starts.

I nod, intertwining my fingers to help remain calm. "I have some questions."

"Okay. Anything," he rushes out.

"Did you know you were leaving for France that night? Before we..."

"I found out a couple hours before. I didn't find out I was leaving that night until I walked out of the guest house. I would have never left like that...left you like that if I knew."

I nod, feeling the pit of anger that's weighed me down for years start to dissipate. "Did you know Rebecca was going with you?"

Shame forms in his eyes. His chin dips. "Yes." The pit returns.

"Was what happened that night out of guilt? Was it for—?"

He grabs my hand. "Please stop thinking that. I know I probably left you so damn confused. Even *I* left not realizing the consequences until it was too late. But don't think for a second what happened was out of anything but love. If anything, I was wrong for taking advantage of you."

I pull my hand away. "How was it taking advantage?"

"You were only eighteen—"

"And in love with you. If age hadn't been a factor, it would have happened sooner." He stares at me, truth shining back at me. I become angry. "Or had I mistaken what we truly were? Maybe it was just me being naive and too *young*—"

"You want me to be truthful, then you have to be truthful too. Stop pretending what we had was just a childhood crush. I never acted on it because it was wrong. You were underage, and I wasn't. I should have known better. If we got caught, in the eyes of the law, it would have been assault. How would that have looked for either of us?"

"Well, it doesn't matter because no one found out. Our parents made sure of that."

"Of what? How would they—you're speaking in riddles. I'm too confused to understand. What did our parents do? Why did you not go to school? You couldn't wait to leave. And there's no way your mother would have let you gallivant around the world. What are you hiding? Did they do something to you?"

I slam my hands on the table. "No! Just stop. Stop making this about them. It's about you and how you abandoned me when I needed you most—when I needed you to be there for me."

"Then explain to me why? You seem so angry with me, and I don't know why. You're the one who was gone when I came home. The one who didn't return any of my calls or letters. But I'm the one in the wrong?"

"Your email! You told me in your email exactly how you felt, so don't go turning the tables on me!"

"What email?!" His voice booms, attracting attention to us.

A waiter walks up to our table. "Excuse me, but I need to ask you two to quiet down."

Ignoring the man, I rip myself out of my seat. "How could you?"

Jake is up just as fast. "How could I what? You act so hurt by me leaving, as if I had a choice. As if you didn't know my hands were tied. They've always been tied, so have yours."

"It's not about you leaving. It's about you not coming back!" Tears rush down my face. When he attempts to clear them away, I slap his hand away. "About what I had to endure on my own."

"Then tell me! Fucking tell me. I'm trying to understand, but I don't!"

"'*I cannot claim personal responsibility. I hope you can get the help you need and make this go away.*'" He jolts back as if I slapped him. "Sound familiar? That's the letter I got. Or does your guilt keep you from remembering?"

"I—I have no idea what you're talking about. I wrote nothing of the sort. What did you need to make go away?"

"Oh, stop! Just stop. This ignorance is tiring. I'm done. I survived. She survived, even after your pathetic, cowardly response. And I'll continue to survive after you return to wherever you came from—"

"Survived what, Willa? Who's she? What the hell are you talking about?"

He goes to grab at my shoulders when a stranger steps in. "Hey, man. I think you should step off. The lady said to leave her alone."

"Fuck off," he snaps, then returns his searing gaze to me. "Answer me, Willa." He's so angry. I shield my heart from his anger, haunted by a memory that suddenly feels like a nightmare. "Willa—"

"I can't...I've gotta go."

"Willa!" he yells for me, but I'm already out the café door.

CHAPTER SEVEN

I DON'T GO BACK TO WORK, TOO FRAZZLED AND AFRAID JAKE WILL FOLLOW me there. When I get home, Carrie is struggling to get Bria to stop crying.

"It's fine. I think she's teething," I tell her, then let her go home.

I hold my little girl in my arms and cry, begging her to calm down, praying for her forgiveness. She doesn't have her father in her life, and it may be my fault. Does he not know? Did he not send me that email?

I curse my mother. How could I have been so foolish? I didn't even second guess that it couldn't have been him. Anyone could have sent it. Anyone being my mother. Or his. Two desperate women blood-hungry to be on top. His words were so cold and held no meaning. As if I'd never meant anything to him. Those words hurt so much, I was too pained to see it then.

He didn't write it.

He doesn't even know.

Bria doesn't let up. I soothe her gums with medicine and frozen toys. I rock her and sing to her, but she doesn't stop. I give her a bath, but she's too restless and flails so bad, I give up and redress her. "Please, baby girl. It's okay. It's going to be okay."

I fear it's not. How could I think I could do this on my own? Helplessness weighs me down. She's in pain, and I don't know how to fix it. She finally cries herself to sleep, and I put her in her crib. I try to go to sleep, but I toss and turn, the guilt too much to handle. I get up and check on Bria. When I touch my palm to her tiny head, it's on fire. "Oh my god." Running to the bathroom, I grab a thermometer and take her temperature.

"No, no, no," I cry, watching the number rise to an unhealthy temperature. "Shit." I pick her up and bundle her up. I should have taken her at the first sign of distress. Her fever is in dangerous territory, and it's all my fault. I throw my shoes on, forgetting to put a jacket on myself.

It's dark outside, so I run to the nearest intersection to flag down a cab. "Emergency room. Please hurry!" I hold Bria close to my chest, praying. "I'm so sorry. I'm so sorry." She's too calm, and I start rocking her in my arms. "Please, baby girl, you're going to be okay. Hurry!" I yell at the driver, fear creeping into my lungs and stealing my breath. He pulls up, and I jump out, running through the large sliding glass doors.

"Help! I need help!" I scream to anyone. My pulse is erratic, blocking out the whispers and gasps of onlookers seated in the waiting room. "Please, someone help me!" A nurse hurries to my side.

"What's wrong?" She tries to pull Bria from my grip. "Honey, let me see."

"She's got a fever, she was crying, I thought it was teething, but now she's so still! Please!" Panic washes over me and I become hysterical as the nurse pries Bria from my grip. I don't want to let her go. I'm afraid if I do, she'll disappear on me.

"Miss, we have to take her to get examined, okay?"

"*Willa?*"

My name echoes from a few feet away, and I whip around to find Jake dressed in a lab coat. "What's wrong? Are you not well?" He rushes over to me, taking notice of the nurse holding a baby. His eyebrows raise, and shock fills his gaze. My heart clenches as his lips press tightly into a thin line. He blinks, refocusing, and reaches for her.

The nurse addresses me. "Willa, is that your name? Jake is our best resident on staff. He will get her the help she needs, okay?"

I dare a look back at Jake. His focus is on Bria. I nod frantically as Jake gently unfolds the blanket she's wrapped in and glances down at the baby in his arms. His eyes flash with confusion, then understanding, and the final knife to my heart: anger.

He glances at me, furious, then goes into medical mode. "I'm taking her into triage two."

"Jake," I call for him, but he doesn't turn back. He walks through the doors with our daughter.

The nurse has me fill out paperwork, then guides me back, where I find Jake and a team of nurses working on Bria. I stand behind the glass window like an outsider while my baby girl lays motionless and pale. My world spins, and I grab onto the ledge to steady myself. If anything happens to her…

My mind takes a dark turn. All the horrible things that can go wrong. Everything I should have done differently. After what feels like an eternity, Jake walks out of the room. I hurry toward him. "How is she? What's happening?"

Gone is the gentle man I'm used to. His eyes are cold as he grabs my bicep and drags me away from Bria. "Jake, tell me, is she okay?"

He stops abruptly, opens a door, and throws me inside a supply closet.

"Jake—"

"Is she mine?"

His voice is consumed with utter rage.

"Jake—"

"Answer me!" I startle at his tone.

"Yes." Turning, he punches his fist to the wall, then swipes a row of supplies off a shelf. "I tried to tell you—"

"You didn't try hard enough!" He whips around, his chest heaving. "Is this what you survived? Is this why you left?"

I refuse to take the blame for this. I'm the victim here. Not him. He's been jet-setting in France and living his life while I debated whether *mine* was truly worth living. While I suffered from so much loneliness, I couldn't bother to leave my bed for days. While I gave birth to a child, alone and scared. All because everyone in my life shoved me away and forgot about me.

"Don't you dare turn this around on me. You left me. I tried to reach you. I spent weeks struggling to contact you. I even went to your mother." He freezes as his eyes narrow. "Yeah, and she told me to get well and shooed me away. Not even a day later, I received an email from you telling me you didn't want *it*. That I was a mistake, you were proposing to Rebecca, and you wished me well."

With wide eyes, he flinches and steps back as if I just slapped him. "I never would have done that."

"But you did!" I lash out.

"You think that low of me? After everything, you think if you had told me I got you pregnant that night, I would have sent you an email saying to abort it?"

I choke on my own truth. Because I *don't* think he would do that. "Yes." The lie is sour in my mouth.

He comes at me, his grip bruising my shoulders. "I came back for you."

"And I wasn't there because I was shipped off to a nunnery to have a baby alone while my parents told everyone I was touring the world. When I was given an ultimatum that I could either return home without my child and stick to the lie, or not come home at all, I chose our child."

His jaw tightens, and he backs away, rubbing the back of his neck. A hurricane of emotions flashes through his eyes. It triggers the storm inside me, and I inhale a deep breath, hoping I'm able to weather it. "I made a choice. I refuse to be the one to blame in this."

He clenches his hands on top of his head and lets out an anguished breath. He comes at me, cupping my cheeks. "Jesus, Willa. You had a fucking baby. Our baby?" His forehead rests against mine, our heaving breaths mingling. "I'm so sorry I did this to you."

He's sorry he did this to me? Fury flows rapidly through my veins, and I rip out of his grip. "You're *sorry*? You're sorry you did this to me? You know what—I don't need your sympathy. I don't need you at all. I've done this on my own so far, and I can—"

"Jesus, shut up!" He shakes me, lost in his own anger. "Just shut up and stop degrading what we are—what we were. I've been trying to tell you since I found you again, and you keep shutting me down, turning my truths into lies. You've made me into this person I'm not. And I *am* sorry. I'm sorry for the shit our parents caused, but I didn't know. I didn't fucking know."

I shake my head. I can't stop. My mind has been warped into believing one truth for the past two years. If I truly believe he didn't write that letter, then this whole time… My chest cracks, and a rugged sob tears up my throat. "They gave me an email. I was so upset—I just—I tried to call you. I tried, but they wouldn't let me. They sent me away—"

I cover my face. My knees give way, and I collapse. Jake catches me and cradles me in his arms as I convulse with sobs.

"Shhh…Willa, please…"

I thrash my head back and forth against his chest. "I did this. I caused our pain. They deceived me, and I allowed it." I slam my fists against his chest. "Why? How could they do this?"

"Because this is what they do. They control us like puppets and force us to play along." He hugs me tightly to him. We stay embraced until my cries subside, and reality smacks me in the face. I tear out of his arms.

"Bria—"

"She's fine. We have her on fluids. Her temperature is already down drastically. She had a small urinary tract infection."

"Oh my god, how did I—?"

"Willa, this was nothing you caused. It's very common in babies. You brought her in. You did exactly what a good mother would do."

"Can I see her? I need to know she's okay."

"Of course." He helps me stand, then leads us out of the supply closet, earning a few curious glances from a group of nurses walking past. He pushes open the door to her room, and I stare at her tiny little body in the hospital crib. I run to her, reaching for her little hand so she knows I'm here.

"Hey, baby girl. Mommy's here. I didn't leave you. I love you. You're so brave." My teardrops fall, soaking her blanket. Jake comes behind me, his hands cupping my shoulders.

"She's beautiful. Just like her mommy."

"She has your eyes."

His chuckle vibrates against my neck. "First thing I noticed in the waiting room."

My shoulders tense. I turn around so he can see the honesty in my eyes. "Jake, I'm sorry. I thought—"

He reaches up to cup my cheek. "No more apologizing, okay? We were both deceived." A nurse comes in, and we quickly break apart.

"Sorry, I just need to take her vitals and brought her chart in for you to review." She and Jake speak in medical lingo as she takes care of Bria, and Jake looks over her chart. What if something else is wrong? The what-ifs rattle me. I can't take the wait much longer. Jake's eyes widen at something, and my stomach bottoms out.

"Oh God, please don't tell me something's wrong." My chest constricts, and I struggle to get air into my lungs. I can't lose her.

"Thank you, Janet. I'll finish up her vitals. You can go." The nurse nods and leaves us alone again.

"Jake, please, tell me she's going to—"

"You…gave her my name. My last name." His eyes gloss over with unshed tears. "Why? If you thought I hated you or didn't want this, why would you…?"

"Because Bria deserved to have something to hold on to. Even if…" I can't finish. Both our emotions are running so high right now. He steps up to me, cups my cheek, and kisses me.

"Thank you," he hums against my lips. "I don't deserve your forgiveness. I can't imagine what you've been through, but just looking at our baby girl, I'm so fucking thankful. I've known her less than two hours, and I'm already so in love." He kisses me again. "I've always imagined having kids, but I never knew it would feel like this. She owns my whole heart." He brushes the hair off my shoulder, his lips finding the dip between my neck and shoulder. "Just like you always have."

"Oh, Jake." My tears fall. "I'm so scared. What if she doesn't get better—"

"Baby, I told you, it's common. She'll get to go home today."

Hope flashes in my eyes. "Really?"

His lips curl upwards into a beautiful smile, and he nods. "Yeah."

Bria starts making noise, and we both whip around. Her eyes open, and she stares up at us. God, I wish I could stop crying, but the tears still come. Jake is behind me, reaching over into the crib, and I choke on my own emotions as she wraps her little fingers around his thumb.

"Hey, little peanut. I'm your daddy."

She stares at him, as if she already knows. Her tiny lips form into a little smile, and my heart sings as tears prick my eyes. "I think she knows," is all I can say. My heart fills with happiness and squeezes at the same time. This moment was once a dream, being together as a family. But this is a reality. A light is shining through the clouds, and we can finally bask in the warmth of a possible future.

This is us finally creating our own path—one where we choose how it ends and where we go.

Jake goes into medical mode and finishes taking her vitals. Her labs come back clean, and she gets the green light to be released. He leaves momentarily and returns wearing his overcoat.

"So, what happens now? Where are you going?" I ask. I have so many questions. So much has changed in the past couple of days. I'm not sure how to truly take it all in. Believe this is all real.

He approaches me, kissing the top of my head. "We take our baby girl home."

Home. A place I never thought we would share. "Where's that?"

"Let's start with your place. That's what's familiar to her. Then we make a plan."

"Plan?"

"Yeah, Willa. A plan. One where we make the decision. Together."

I nod, biting my bottom lip. "All right."

He takes off his jacket to cover me, and we wrap Bria in our arms and make the trek to my apartment. When I unlock the door, I'm suddenly nervous about what he'll think. My living situation is far from what we were used to growing up, and what I'm sure he's still accustomed to. He doesn't say much when we walk in, and I take Bria to settle her in her crib. When I come back out, I find him bent over, looking in my fridge.

"Hungry? I can make us something. I don't have much, but—"

"You don't have anything." He straightens out and turns toward me. "What do you eat? There's barely anything in your cabinets. Even less in your fridge."

Shame thumps against my ribcage at his disgust. I tear my eyes from him, tugging my arms out of his jacket. "I survive. It's not about me. It's about Bria. What money I have after rent and someone to watch her while I work, I use for food. If you're just going to judge how I live, maybe you should leave."

He slams my fridge and storms toward me. I take a step back, unsure where his intentions lie, but then he grabs my shoulders and brings me to his chest. "Willa, I'm not judging you. I'm gutted at how you have to live and how I haven't been here to help you."

"I've been fine."

"I'm sure you have. You've always been so strong and resilient. But you don't deserve this. How—how long have you been living like this?" More shame engulfs me. "Tell me, Willa."

"I've only been here a month. I was at the nunnery with Bria since she was born. They allowed me to stay until I was able to save some money."

He pulls away. "Your parents seriously left you with nothing?" I nod and close my eyes, unable to endure the pity in his. "This isn't right. They'll pay for this."

"Please no. I just want to be done with them. I'm okay with never seeing them again, and I'm sure they feel the same." Guilt weighs heavy on his shoulders as they slump—his forehead pressing against mine.

"I'm going to make this right. I promise you." He fuses his lips to mine. "I don't know how to make amends for the mistreatment that you suffered, but please let me try to fix it."

"Jake, it's not yours to need to fix. Our parents—"

I gasp in surprise when he picks me up and walks us down the hallway. "I own those mistakes, regardless. Just thinking about what you've gone through..." He pauses, needing my lips as strength to continue. "I'll do anything to right their wrongs. Anything."

He lays me on my bed, the warmth of his body blanketing mine. His fingers graze up my sides, and my skin trembles with each touch. I've dreamed of this for so long. The feel of his hands on me again, and his body flush against mine. Our hearts beating together with anticipation and need. "Tell me how I fix this—how I fix us."

"I think you know," I pant, and my eyes close when his palm cups my breast.

"Tell me what you want, Willa."

Visions rush through my brain. All the moments he could have been there. Holding my hand and crying with me at the news of my pregnancy, holding my hand during her birth, smiling with me, changing our first diaper together. Images of us as a family. But those moments were taken from him, and I can't give them back. So, I respond with what I truly do want. "You."

His lips crush against mine. "Jesus, Willa, you have me. You always have." His lips break from mine, and he feathers kisses down my neckline, working his way back up until he's sucking my ear lobe into his mouth. "Two years, I've fantasized about having you back in my arms." His hands are rough, gripping my waist as if he's worried I'll disappear. "There wasn't a single night I didn't lay restless in my bed wondering where you were, what you were doing. Were you thinking of me? Did you hurt as much as I did?"

His mouth works its way to my cheek, pressing gentle kisses to my chin, to my bottom lip. "Some nights, I would convince myself this was my punishment for leaving you. For taking the most beautiful thing you could ever offer me and never looking back. I replay that night in my head. The good, the bad, the way you smelled. The way you shivered in my arms. The way I kissed away every tear and swallowed your moans. I've missed you, Willa. I've missed you so damn much."

He deepens our kiss, and my fingernails graze up his back until they're tugging at his hair, holding him closer to me. This feels unreal. I tighten my grip, fearing if I let go, I won't get him back. Our hands become frantic. Primal need takes over, and we tear at each other's clothes until we're both naked.

"You're so beautiful. You've always been so damn beautiful." His head dips, and his mouth covers my breast, biting at my nipple. I wince at the sudden pain, but it morphs quickly into a breathless moan as he sucks my flesh into his mouth.

"Oh god," I whimper. "I've missed you too. I've wished for you to appear so many darn times in my dreams. There were times I swore I saw you. Tell me you're real. Please tell me you're real."

"Does this feel real?" His hands slide down between my thighs, finding my wet sex. He inserts a finger inside me, then pulls back to insert another. "Does this feel like you're dreaming, Willa?"

"God, no." My back arches as my head tilts and my lips part. He works himself in and out of me, coating his fingers in my arousal. It's been so long, and this simple touch is going to make me come.

"Jake," I moan.

"Fuck, I miss my name on your lips. So damn much." He starts working me faster, and my grip on him tightens as I begin to clench around his fingers.

"Oh, Jake," I groan out.

He pushes my legs open and replaces his fingers with his cock. He works himself in and out, every thrust becoming more aggressive and demanding. "Jesus, Willa, you feel too good. Just like I remember. Perfect."

Our need ignites inside us as we claw at one another to get closer. The rekindling of our souls creates a fire that threatens to burn the entire universe to ash. Jake has always been my lifeline. Suddenly, I feel my heart beating again. With every thrust, he heals me, fills me with his love, his desire. He's the antidote to all the poison I've consumed. He's the reason I can finally breathe again.

My head arches back, and my lips part as a guttural moan travels up my throat. Jake grunts and takes my mouth while powering into me. Each thrust brings him deeper, and I cry out in pleasure. He captures my hips and works me fast and hard until we're both flying over the edge of ecstasy.

"JAKE, CAN I ASK YOU SOMETHING?" I NESTLE ON TOP OF HIM, RESTING MY head on his chest.

"Anything." He threads his fingers through my hair.

"What would you have done if I were home? You said you came back for me. Why? What were your intentions?"

He doesn't answer at first, and it worries me. "To be honest...I wasn't sure. I didn't have a set plan. All I knew was I couldn't take it any longer, and every day you ignored me drove me mad. What we shared...it did something to me. It opened up this floodgate of shit I'd been holding back. I couldn't explain it, but everything else in my life started not to matter. I only cared about hearing from you. Having you tell me you felt the same way. And as time ticked on, so many negative things ran through my mind too. Did you think I took advantage of you? Did you hate me? Had you met someone, and this was your way of telling me goodbye?"

"Far from it."

He presses his lips to the top of my head and continues. "So, finally, I came home. It was the first holiday break. I only had a three-day break and spent almost two of those traveling, but I had to see you. Even if it was for you to tell me to fuck off. But you weren't there. Your mother went on and on about how you'd decided to spend the year traveling. I tried to pry, figure out where in hopes of tracking you down, but she was all over the place. I should have known then. It didn't sound like you. She changed the subject, and no matter how hard I pushed, she wouldn't go back to the topic. My mother showed up, and then it was all about my schooling, and a shame about Rebecca, and how I must have been heartbroken." I roll my eyes at that.

"If you were supposed to do your residency in France, why are you here?"

"I did. Spent the first year and a half busting my ass. It was all I could do to keep my mind on track. About six months ago, a colleague of my father's offered me a spot at Rush Central. I was already ahead in school and had been on track to finish my residency a year ahead of time."

"Wow. That's great, Jake."

"I took it because I thought you'd be at school by then. I had a plan: come home, track you down, and demand answers. By this time, I was super bitter. I'd spent that whole time obsessing over the whys and what-ifs. I hated myself for leaving that night, and I was starting to hate you for leaving me in a way too."

I go to open my mouth, but he stops me. "You don't owe me any more explanations. I hate myself for being so naive when it came to every single excuse my mother gave me. If I had just listened to my heart, I would have seen past her lies. I would have found you sooner."

"But you did find me. That's all that matters."

"I should have been there for you. For Bria's birth. You should have never had to struggle. But that's over now."

He kisses the top of my head again while I get lost in the questions swirling inside my head. Where do we go from here? What does this mean for his future—or mine? What will our parents do when they find out? I open my mouth, needing him to help calm some of my fears, when the sound of Bria's tiny cries filters into my room. I start to get up, but he stops me.

"Let me. I want to do this."

"Are you sure?"

"Absolutely. Get some rest. I have a lot of time to make up for." He bends down, kisses my forehead, and disappears. I feel like an intruder listening to him, but I can't help it. He sings and praises her with loving endearments. Her little giggles warm my heart, knowing she's just as in love with him. I close my eyes, and for the first time in so long, I fall asleep to the sound of pure happiness, feeling like I'm not alone.

CHAPTER EIGHT

I WAKE WITH A JOLT AND GAZE AROUND MY EMPTY ROOM. "BRIA." I JUMP OUT of bed and run into her room, finding it empty. The panic starts to choke me. Baby giggles filter in from the kitchen, and I blow out a breath as I make my way there. Finding Jake shirtless in a pair of scrub bottoms looking like a god, standing in my kitchen holding a smiling Bria, I almost trip over my own feet.

"Look who's awake. Morning, Mommy." Jake bounces her in his arms, creating another flutter of giggles.

"What time is it?"

"A little after ten—"

"Ten? Jesus, why did you let me sleep that late—shit! I'm sooo late for work. I'm going to get fired. Where's Carrie? Did she come—"

"Hey, relax. I took care of it."

"How? Shit. I gotta get ready—"

I turn to dart back into my room, but he calls out for me. "Willa, it's fine."

I pause and twist around. "It's not. I'm going to get fired, and I need this—"

"I know, and I took care of it." He buckles Bria into her highchair and slides his hands into his front pockets. "Your phone was going off. I didn't mean to be nosy, but I saw it was your friend. She was worried about you because you never went back to work yesterday. I didn't want to wake you, so I texted her back. Told her you were sick and would be out a few days. She took care of your boss. I hope I didn't overstep. I also sent Carrie home and paid her for the day."

I turn around. "You didn't have to pay her. I have money."

"I know. I didn't mean to step on any toes. But what you needed was sleep, and I needed to spoil this little girl."

I stand there and stare at him. "What about you? Aren't you needed at the hospital?"

"I'm taking some time off."

"You can't just take time off."

"When you're the best resident they have, you can. And I did. Nothing matters right now more than spending time with you two. Now, are you hungry? I made some breakfast."

I glance behind him at my small table filled with food. The scent of bacon and coffee teases my nostrils. My stomach growls, and I cover it, embarrassed. "How did you find bacon?"

"I had some groceries delivered. Don't give me that look. I know you don't want anyone taking care of you, but that's where things change. I would have done this from the beginning. Since I wasn't given the option, let me do it now."

"I don't need handouts."

"No, you need to find some peace, to breath lighter, and to know I've got you." We have a stare-off until it becomes too much, and I wave my white flag. His smile is damn infectious. I can't fight the laugh as I shake my head and situate myself at the table.

I can't remember the last time I've eaten so much. My stomach is full, and my cheeks are flushed as I take in the cleared table. It's been a while since we've had enough ingredients to make a full meal in my kitchen. We make small talk, avoiding the heavy topics. Jake can't get enough of Bria, playing airplane with each bite he tries to feed her. When it's time for her nap, he puts her down and is gently shutting her door when I walk out of the shower.

"Hey."

"Hey," I reply, feeling shy in my towel, even though he's seen, licked, and bitten every single part of me.

"She's zonked out." He comes up to me, pulling me into his arms. "I want to stand over her and watch her sleep until she wakes up. I can't get enough of her."

I chuckle. "Well, prepare to stand for a while. She normally takes a three-hour nap at this time."

His hand threads into my wet hair. "Then maybe I'll spend my time showing you how much I can't get enough of you." His head dips, and I take the kiss he's offering. I'm light on my feet when he finally pulls away, not realizing I released the grip on my towel, and it now lays at my feet. I go to pick it up, but he stops me. "No more hiding from me. No more barriers. No more games."

"I'm pretty sure there was no hiding or barriers last night," I joke, my cheeks flaming.

"Looks like I have three hours to make sure I didn't miss anything." Pulling me into his arms, he carries me back to my bedroom and leaves no inch of flesh untouched.

TWO DAYS LATER

"NO MORE..." I BREATHE, UNABLE TO MOVE MY LEGS.

"I can't stop. I'm obsessed with these legs…this ass…these tits…" I moan as his mouth covers my breast. My eyes flutter closed, and I give in. Again.

"The baby's gonna be up soon."

"I can be quick." His teeth graze my nipple just as subtle cries come from the other room. "Or not. Saved by my little princess. You're lucky. I had plans for you."

I chuckle and shake my head as we both climb out of bed and dress. The past two days have been like this: Jake fawning over Bria, and when she goes down, he takes me into the bedroom and fawns over me. We haven't left my apartment. Jake ordered in groceries and had clothes sent over from his place.

"What do my girls want to do today?" Jake kisses the top of Bria's head. I'm feeling a bit restless. Some fresh air sounds wonderful, but there's this nagging feeling inside that says the second we leave my apartment, this little bubble of perfect is going to pop. "Uh oh, why the face?"

"What face?"

"The *I have something on my mind* face."

"I don't—"

"You've made the same face since you were seven." He walks up to me, giving me the same sweet treatment as Bria, and lays a gentle kiss on my forehead. "What's on your mind? No more secrets, right?"

I sigh heavily. "I just...I'm worried about what happens once we leave my apartment. But I also know we can't hide in here forever."

"Can't we?" He waggles his brows.

"Jake, I'm serious. You need to go back to work. So do I. The last couple of days have been amazing, but what happens when we go back to reality? When you have to tell your parents about us? When they threaten to cut you off too if you continue seeing me?"

He can't hide the stress in his eyes.

"You know they won't approve. They'll give you the same ultimatum my parents did, and there is no way you'll give up—"

"Don't tell me what I won't do."

"I'm not. I'm just speaking the truth. I can't see you giving up everything you've worked so hard for—"

"For them. I've worked so hard for *them*. Because it's what they've wanted. Not me."

"And are you going to tell me you don't love it? You don't love making a difference? They may have forced you into the profession, but you can't stand here and tell me you don't love helping people. You've always wanted that."

"That may be true, but there's more to life than status. We've both always agreed on that."

"But they'll make you choose."

"And I'll choose you. The same decision I would have made two years ago if I had been given the option." He cups my cheek, and I lean into his warm caress. "This is our fight. Together. We will hit some hurdles, I can't deny that, but I want to be a family. Nothing matters more than that."

I fight to conceal my worry. His promises are comforting, but they're only a blanket to cover the truth of what happens when his family finds out. And I hate that for us all. I smile, knowing he sees the unease in my eyes. "All right."

Bria takes this moment to make explicit noises in her diaper. "Well then, it's settled. We're going to clean whatever bomb she just detonated, and then we're venturing out." He offers me a quick kiss and a reassuring smile and starts babbling to Bria as he battles the blowout.

LEAVING THE HOUSE ENDS UP BEING A GREAT IDEA. JAKE TAKES US TO LUNCH, and this time, I don't run away when he brings us back to the Italian place. Francisco is happy to see us and fawns all over Bria. When I swear Jake will have to roll me out if I eat another bite, we say our goodbyes and leave.

The sidewalk is crammed with the midday lunch crowds. Jake tucks me to his side as I push Bria in her stroller. He slows and stops suddenly in front of a huge department store. "What?" I ask, curious what's caught his attention.

"Now, hear me out. What would you say if we bought a few things for you and Bria to stay at my place? I know it's rushing," he spits out, "but I don't want to be apart any more than we have to, and my place is close to the hospital. We can maybe stay there when I have shifts and go back and forth until we find something…more permanent." He shoves his hands in his pockets, suddenly nervous.

"What do you mean by permanent? Like, live together?" I know exactly what he means, but I'm enjoying giving him a hard time.

"Well…yeah, ya know…live together. Like a family. Willa, I want to make this work. I'll fight. I'll do anything. I'll—"

"Jake."

"What?"

"I'm messing with you. I know what you're asking. And I'd like that. We both would." I can't help but smile wide at how nervous he looks. It's cute and—

"Ouch!" I half chuckle, half groan when he smacks my ass. An old couple walking by gawks at us, and Jake pulls me into his arms.

"I'm going to make you happy, Willa. I promise you." He kisses me without a care that we're in the middle of a busy sidewalk. When he pulls away, I'm extra light on my feet. "Now, let's go in and get a few things for my girls."

"JAKE, YOU SAID A FEW—"

"Necessities, babe."

My mouth falls to the ground when the cashier reads off the total. "*Jake*." He didn't buy necessities; he practically bought out the entire baby section. He hands her his gold card, and with one swipe, he's thanking the lady and shuffling out with a million bags.

"Why did you buy a car seat when neither of us owns a car?"

"When you go back and forth, I don't want you taking the subway. I'm going to hire a driver for you and Bria."

"Oh, that's just insane."

"No, it's protecting my family. If I can't be there with you, I want to know you're safe. Don't fight me on this one." His tone is pleading. I let it go because it does get unsafe on the subway—not that I've had to bring Bria out of the house since we've moved here.

"Fine, but I'm pretty sure all those stuffed animals are a bit much."

He shrugs. "I asked her if she wanted them. Said smile if it's a yes. She did."

I shake my head. "She smiled for almost thirty minutes straight. She needs a whole room just for these darn animals!" I shake my head on the way to the exit and find a car waiting for us.

"Mr. DuPont."

"Good evening. We're headed to my condo. If you could take these things, a driver will be by later with the rest."

"Yes, sir."

The gentleman takes the bags, barely able to grab them all, while Jake installs the car seat. He folds up the stroller, and I settle Bria in, then climb in, the smell of new leather assaulting my senses. The last time I was in a fancy town car was the drive to the nunnery. I squeeze my eyes shut, pushing out the memory.

"You okay?" Jake asks, sliding into the car. The driver pulls into traffic, and I sit back, taking long, deep breaths.

"Yeah. I'm fine. So, where exactly are you living? Or dare I ask?" He looks away as if embarrassed to admit. "Jake, I was cut off, not you. It doesn't change what I think."

"The Cornerstone." I almost choke on my saliva. Of course. "For what it's worth, I didn't pick it. The living situation was arranged for me."

We fall silent, listening to Bria babble in her seat. She becomes fascinated with the busy sidewalk outside and the bursting of streetlights going on as the sun goes down. Every so often, she claps her hands and bounces in glee.

We arrive at Jake's condo, and he carries a smiling Bria in his arms. We take the elevator to the top floor, and he guides me inside. His condo is impeccable. Sleek and modern. The best money can buy, but I didn't think it would be anything less. I stare off at the floor-to-ceiling glass windows, wondering how spectacular the skyline will look through the messy glass when Bria gets her tiny fingerprints all over them.

"Come on. Let's get you and Bria settled." Jake orders food, and we put together the crib while we eat. Bria falls asleep the second we lay her down. We quietly shut off the light, crack the door, and walk out into the hallway.

A squeal escapes my lips when I'm suddenly scooped into Jake's arms. He carries me halfway down the hall and pushes open the door to his lavish bedroom. An enormous bed made for a king greets us, and I yelp when he tosses me on top of his feathered comforter.

"I miss that sound," he says, unbuttoning his shirt.

My heart races at the beautiful sight of his toned chest. "What sound is that?"

"Your little squeals. When I used to toss you in the pool or chase you, you would always make these cute little squeals. Sometimes I had to hold off on catching you because I was worried about what I would do if I did."

I sit up on my elbows, continuing to admire his naked chest while he works off his pants. "And what exactly would you have done?" I ask, biting my lower lip.

"Oh, it depends. When you were twelve, I wanted to pull your hair. When you were fourteen, I wanted to see if your boobs were real or if you were stuffing. At sixteen, I wanted to drag you behind the guest house and kiss those pink lips. By seventeen...well, I wanted to do a lot of things to you. Very, very inappropriate things."

I can't help but snicker at his confession. I remember once when we were goofing around in the pool playing Marco Polo. I was seventeen.

"Don't forget, only three feet circumference."

"Yeah, yeah. But you have longer arms than me. You can reach out and snag me at any time."

"Sounds perfect. Fine, four feet. If I catch you, you have to watch the entire Nightmare on Elm Street marathon with me."

"Ew...no way," I groan.

"Yes, way. Deal or no game. I'll just go inside. I'm sure my needy mother would love for me to-"

"Fine."

"Whole thing. All seven movies."

Ugh. *"Whole thing."*

He closes his eyes and counts to five, allowing me time to disguise my location. My heart instantly races as I move behind him, trying to swim away as quietly as possible.

"Marco," he purrs, his deep voice affecting my ability to play.

"Polo," I retort, swallowing and swimming in circles around him. We play this cat and mouse game for what seems like forever, until he cheats, launching at me. He grabs for my waist and tucks me back into him. His laughter vibrates against my shoulder blades, and his lips press against my skin. He doesn't move, and I swear I feel the hardness of— His grip suddenly becomes too tight, and he quickly releases me.

"So, what time are you coming back over? I'll have the chef make us our favorite movie spread."

Jake has discarded his pants by the time my memory fades, and my throat begins to work again. "And what did you want to do to me at eighteen?"

He climbs on top of me. His fingers move under my shirt, pushing it up my waist. "I wanted to do this." He pulls my shirt up, exposing my breasts. My bra is pushed to the side, and his warm breath skates over my nipple as he takes it into his mouth. My eyes flutter closed, enjoying the way his tongue circles around my nipple as he palms my breast, getting a mouthful. My fingers slide into his hair.

"That's it? Feels like a sixteen-year-old fantasy to me."

His other hand skims down my ribcage, dipping into my pants.

"Oh no, I wanted to do more than that. I wanted to do this." His finger disappears between my thighs, and I release a soft moan as he finds my hot center and enters me. "Then, this." He pulls out and inserts a second, then third. His thrusts are slow yet forceful. "But I knew this wouldn't be enough. I knew I wanted all of you." He works me faster until my legs begin to quiver, and I bite down on my bottom lip. He pulls away, taking my pants with him, and his fingers are replaced with his mouth. My back arches off the bed as he devours me. His tongue becomes ruthless, and mere seconds later, my fingers are gripping too tightly around his hair as my orgasm takes flight.

My lungs struggle to inhale enough air when he comes back into full view. "I'm a fan of eighteen," I pant. "Shame we didn't play that one out back then."

Jake chuckles as he crawls up my still quaking body and places his lips on mine. "Oh, I think we did." He kisses me again. "And it was one of the best nights of my life."

It was the night we finally fought the barriers of our feelings. The night we created Bria. The night he left.

"Hey," he pulls me back from the darkness, "I know where you're going in your head. Let's make a pact. From this moment forward, we only focus on the present and future. No more dwelling over a past we had no control over or a time we can't take back or erase. I don't want anything to tarnish what we're creating here—our future—because, baby, that's something we have control over. Things are different now; we're not kids. They can't control us. From this point on, no more sad faces. Just happy ones. And post-sex worn-out ones."

I laugh, swiping at a tear. "Post-sex faces?"

"Yeah, 'cause we're going to do that a lot. You're so damn sexy when you have that glow."

"I am *not* glowing."

"Yes, you are."

"No, I'm not—"

His lips slam against mine, and he spreads my legs apart, finding my still pulsating sex.

"Then I better make you glow," he says as he slides inside.

CHAPTER NINE

"HEY, WILLA?" I TURN MY HEAD TO JAKE, HOPING HE DOESN'T SEE THE devastation lurking in my eyes. He leaves for college today, which means I won't see him 'til Christmas. Every day for as far back as I can remember, I've been with him, and now he'll be gone for months. I suck in a breath and turn around, hoping my smile looks genuine despite being a mess on the inside. "Catch." My hands reach out, capturing the bundled-up cloth he threw at me.

"Wh—What is this?" I unfold it to realize it's his favorite t-shirt—the one he wore the night he kissed me. "Why...why are you giving me this?"

"'Cause it's my favorite shirt. Reminds me why I'm going to miss home so much. I thought you could keep it safe for me. Make sure you don't forget to wear that smile I love while I'm gone. Maybe a little memory will help."

He smiles and waves, the same sadness lingering in his eyes. When I raise my hand to return the gesture, his mother is already shooing him inside the car.

The sun begins to peek through the shades as I'm nestled in bed wearing one of Jake's oversized t-shirts. Bria lays in my lap, giggling at the beam of light coming from the window. As she wiggles, I play with her tiny toes and graze my fingers up her belly until I'm tapping on her baby nose. "Do you like that?" I babble as she smiles back at me.

Jake walks into the room, fully dressed. "I'm so damn sorry about this. If I could get out of it, I would."

"No, it's fine. There are plenty of things to do. Go save some lives." Jake got a call early this morning needing him to come in. The hospital was understaffed, and a horrible accident filled up the ER.

"You sure? I'll try to be back as soon as I can. We can make some dinner. Or go out. Anything you like."

I smile back. "I'd love that."

He kisses me hard, then gently places his lips on Bria's cheek. "I'll miss you two. Behave. No R-rated for her." He turns to me. "You either. I know how scared you get." I slap his shoulder.

"I was sixteen. You made me watch the entire Nightmare on Elm Street marathon."

"Maybe I just wanted to get you to cuddle with me."

"I did cuddle with you! I was scared out of my mind."

He smiles and offers me another quick kiss. "Then my plan worked. Okay. Be back tonight. I'll call you when I can. It gets swamped, so it's hard—"

"Go!"

"Yes, ma'am." He laughs, then turns back before heading out the door. "Willa?"

"Yeah?"

"I love you."

A smile explodes across my face. I love hearing him say that. "Love you too."

He nods, his cheeky grin so darn sexy. "Okay. I really need to go now. Love you both. Call you. Order anything you want." Then he's gone.

I don't stop smiling. Hours go by, and I'm still on cloud nine. When Bria is changed and fed, I put her down for a nap. It's impossible not to shake my head at the mounds of clothes, toys, and knickknacks Jake bought. I pick up a pile of onesies that say *I'm Daddy's favorite* to try and organize and put in the closet. I build a play center and a bouncy, and I'm opening up a box of stuffed animals when the doorbell rings.

I check the time. Jake said he would be home closer to bedtime. I jump up, unsure if I should answer the door. It's not my place, so maybe I should just let them figure out he's not here and leave. Another ring and I find myself walking toward the front door so they don't wake Bria.

I check my clothing to make sure I look decent—he *does* live in a million-dollar apartment—and open the door. Meredith DuPont stares back at me, her lips thinned, though not surprised to see me.

"So, it is true."

"What are you—?"

She pushes past me as if I'm nothing more than the help. "Where's my son?"

"Um, he's at work. He should be home—"

"Good. This doesn't concern him anyhow." She pulls her silk gloves off her dainty hands and retrieves something out of her couture purse. "I was hoping my son would be smart enough to stay away from you." She turns back to me. "He has a successful future, as you know. While you were away *finding yourself*, my son was excelling, becoming the man he was born to be."

"He was becoming the product of what you *constructed* him to be."

She waves her hand at me. "Always a mouth on you. You know, your mother was right to send you away. To think you would have straightened out at college. No proper man would have attached himself to you. Shame. Your mother did have high hopes for her future—"

"I'm not sure what your point is," I cut her off, "but Jake's not here. So, if you're done insulting me, you can go. I'll let him know you came by."

She pulls an envelope out and hands it to me. "What's this?"

"It's your future, dear. Go ahead. Open it."

I hesitate. I don't trust her, and my gut tells me I'm not going to like whatever is on this paper. I unfold it and immediately take note of the itemized list. "You've got to be kidding me."

"Not at all, dear."

"You can't just buy me. Jake won't go for this—"

"Oh, Jake won't know. Because you won't tell him." She takes a step toward me, her fake smile dropping, her wicked glare frigid. "My Jakey will not jeopardize his future over a mistake *you* made."

"*I* made? I think it takes two to make a child if that's the *mistake* you're referring to."

She scrunches her nose at the mention of Bria. "She has no standing in our family. For all I know, you became pregnant and claimed my son was the father. You were so desperate to grab his attention."

I hiss at her accusations. "How dare you. If you cared enough, you would know she *is* your granddaughter. And good luck trying to trick Jake. He's done falling for your deceiving schemes."

Meredith throws her head back and laughs. "Oh, but he will. If you read at the bottom, it says, in fine print, if you don't take the offer I'm suggesting, we will request a paternity test. It *will* come back that my son is not the father, and we will sue you for fraud. Then you'll spend the remainder of whatever sad life you have behind bars."

"But Jake *is* the father. You can't lie about it."

She snickers, peering down at her perfectly manicured nails. "Willa, I don't think you're understanding. I know it's been some time since you were in a civilized atmosphere and it's clear the nuns weren't able to teach you any proper manners. I'm going to be straight with you. We will offer you a nice settlement. You and that child will disappear and not return. You will not make contact of any sort. You will not relay any information to that child about her father. My son no longer exists to you."

"And if I refuse?"

"Then you will lose everything. We will make sure of it. It's quite amazing what power allows you to accomplish. Strip you of your child. Of her name. My son will be rid of you after the foolish games you've played with him. And you will be left with nothing but a cold cell. It's up to you."

She can't do this. Jake won't believe her. Crumbling up the piece of paper, I toss it to the ground and take a menacing step toward her. "And I choose the latter. I won't bow down to you. Try your worst with me. It won't work. Jake is her father; it'll take a blind person to argue that. And I don't need, nor want, your money. You're just like my mother, more concerned with how this will reflect on you than the health and safety of your flesh and blood. Bria is your granddaughter."

"I don't have a granddaughter."

"She exists whether you choose to acknowledge her or not. So does the love between your son and me. You can't control us anymore. We're not kids, and we're cutting those strings. So, why don't you turn around and go back to wherever it is you came from. I will be telling Jake you stopped by and what a conniving bitch you are." I turn to walk away, giving her my back. I don't need to see her witch of a face when she leaves. I move toward the hallway when her next words latch around my neck like a noose.

"Then I'll cut him off. Take everything."

I spin back, my eyes narrowed. "Go ahead. He's an amazing man. He'll be just fine without your blood money."

Her cold smile tells me there's more. "Oh, you don't get it. You know better than to underestimate the power of who we keep in our company. I will strip Jake of everything he's ever accomplished. His degree, his residency. With a snap of a finger, it will be gone. He will be as homeless as you are."

"You wouldn't."

"Oh, I would. Just to get rid of you and that bastard child. Don't test me, dear. How would Jake react to losing everything he's worked so hard for? Would your love still be enough? Or would he resent you? You know my son was born with the proverbial silver spoon in his mouth and wouldn't be able to walk away without a penny. He may talk a good game, but in the end, he knows who he is. Can you say the same? Are you willing to risk it all on a childhood crush?"

I want to run at her and claw her eyes out. Scream and shout that her evil words don't hurt me. But there's this inkling starting to take root. He loves me. I'm not doubting that.

But does he love me enough to sacrifice everything he's worked for? And can I hold the weight of that guilt on my shoulders by taking it all away from him?

"You know I'm right. Do what's best for that child."

"I *am* doing what's best."

She tsks me. "Are you now? Living in a low housing apartment that's a cesspool for drugs and prostitution—"

"That's not—"

"A job you maintain by offering sexual favors to your very lecherous boss?"

I gasp. "That is *not* true. None of that is true."

She lifts her dainty shoulders. "It won't matter, darling. How will that affect my son, his reputation, when one scandal after another continues to follow you? It won't ever stop. True or false, you will stain his good name. Always running from another scandal. Is that how you want to live your life? Do you think that's how Jake will want to live his?"

I need to fight and stay strong, but that little seed of doubt has me contemplating her threats. How do I win here? No matter the direction I take, someone loses. And for each option, Jake has the most to lose. She's asking me to do the impossible—rip Bria from him just after learning he has a daughter—leave him after promising to trust one another and our future together. But her threats have power, and each one ends in tragedy.

"This will break Jake."

"He's a resilient young man. He'll survive."

"He won't believe I just left. He'll know you did something."

She shrugs, sliding her purse up her forearm. "And that's no concern for you."

My stomach turns, and my chest constricts. To stay would cause too much havoc, and no matter how hard we fight, we won't be able to repair it. But to leave means ripping my heart out and taking away a life Bria could have with her father.

I angrily wipe at the tear that falls down my cheek, her triumphant smile making me sick. She knows she won. Pulling out a pen from her clutch, she hands it to me.

"Smart girl. Now, sign, and we'll both be on our way." I wipe more tears, my shaky hands fighting not to rip her to shreds, and bend down to grab the piece of paper. Each detailed demand echoes in my brain. Am I doing the right thing? Will I survive losing him a second time? My entire body feels numb as I scribble my name on the paper and throw it at her. "Wonderful."

"How is this wonderful? How is ruining two lives *wonderful*? It's evil. And callous. You should be ashamed of yourself."

"The money will be deposited into your account within the hour. Enough time for you to gather your belongings, which I assume isn't much, and be on your way."

"I don't want a dime from you," I hiss, but she disregards me.

"A driver will wait for you and take you to the bus stop. I suggest picking someplace... off the map?" She waves her hand in the air, turns on her heel, and disappears out the door.

I collapse, banging my knees against the floor. I hold my hands over my heart as if that will stop the bleeding. The tears come in wretched waves, and I slam my fists into the marbled tile. How can life be so cruel? How can someone hold so much power over another? Panic severs my airways. I suddenly feel like I've made a huge mistake. I should have trusted in Jake. Had faith he would choose us no matter what. Instead, I panicked and signed our future away. But every which way I looked at it was an endless pile of destruction.

When I've exhausted myself, I begin to stand, realizing a man in a black suit is taking up space in the doorway.

"Can I help you?" I snap.

"I'll be taking you to where you need to go as soon as you get your things, Miss."

Right.

I pull myself up off the floor, gathering my bearings. I need to focus on the now. Bria. I have to grab her things. *Bria.* My lower lip begins to tremble. I bite down on it to keep myself from another breakdown. I pack her a bag, my cheeks still soaked when I grab the onesies Jake picked out. I pack enough food to last us a few days. No matter how hard it gets, homeless, hungry, I will never accept her money.

The man is still standing by the door when I carry out a sleeping Bria in my arms. "I need to stop by my apartment to grab some things. Unless the wicked witch forbade it."

He steps aside, showing some human in him, and grabs my bags and the car seat. "Where exactly are you supposed to take me?" He doesn't answer me. The car is waiting for us just outside the building. He adjusts the baby seat and allows me to settle Bria while he puts our bags in the trunk. I stop to take a look back, knowing Jake will be home soon and I won't be there to greet him. I'll be gone with no note or explanation. He will hate me for what I've done.

I rest in the seat, my mind sinking back into a childhood memory.

"Have you ever thought about running away?"

Jake pushes me on the swing behind the guest house. "Today or in general?" he laughs.

"Any day. Have you ever thought about running away from here—away from all the expectations?"

He pushes me two more times before answering. "Of course. Probably just as much as you, if not more."

Silence washes over us until I speak. "I want to run away. I don't want to be what they want me to be."

"And what do you want to be?"

"Free to be me." He stops my swing and twists me around to face him.

"You should never let anyone tell you to be anything but yourself. That person is perfect. And if you ever decide to run away, I'll come with you. Keep you safe. We'll disguise our identities and live in a small town that only eats pancakes and popcorn. We'll have a gigantic pool and build a fortress so none of them can ever get to us again."

"We can do that?" I ask, hopeful.

"I would do about anything if you asked."

I don't realize we're sitting outside my apartment until the man opens my door. "Please be timely, Miss." I climb out and unlatch Bria from her seat, but the man stops me. "She stays here. In case you try anything."

I snap my hand away. "I'm taking my daughter with me. If you think I would trust leaving her with you—"

"That is not an option. I have orders. Grab your things or don't, and we go straight to the bus station." My eyes scan him, then look to my sleeping daughter. It doesn't feel right leaving her with a stranger. The wind picks up, sending a chill down my spine. My stomach shifts uneasily, and I look back at the man.

"I'm not leaving her. She comes with me."

He takes a menacing step toward me. "Then I'm going to ask you to get back in the car."

I clasp and unclasp my fist, unsure of what to do. There's only one thing I want in that apartment: my box. I can be quick. Just grab it and be back down within minutes. I start chewing on the side of my cheek. Five minutes tops.

"Fine. I'll only be a few minutes." I run inside, taking the stairs two at a time. The heaviness in my chest gets heavier the farther I get from Bria. My breathing becomes rapid as I make it to the last floor. My pulse slams against my temples as I unlock my door and dash into my apartment. I'm trying to count the seconds in my head as I race into my bedroom. I open my nightstand and grab my box. Underneath should be her… "Shoot, where is it?" I dig under nameless items, searching for Bria's birth certificate. My hands shake with onset panic. "It was right here. It's always been right here."

A splintering boom comes from my front door, and I jump, twisting around. I grip my box to my chest, my eyes frantically searching for any type of weapon to defend myself. A large shadow slinks through the doorway, and I drop the box and grab for the lamp on my nightstand, ready to swing.

The intruder thrusts my bedroom door open, and I freeze. "Jake—"

"What do you think you're doing?" His broad chest heaves. His face is rigid with tension. His fists clench at his sides. I take a step to run to him, needing his comfort, needing him to tell me everything will be okay and wake me up from this nightmare. I take one step but stall. "Willa, answer me. What the hell is going on?"

"I…I'm leaving." The words are sour on my tongue. My heart pounds, and my palms sweat.

"What do you mean you're leaving?"

You can do this, Willa. Think of his future. "I'm leaving you. This isn't going to work." I stop to take a short breath. My tone holds no truth, and he knows it. "I want nothing to do with you. Leave me alone." Shit, I can't do this. My tears give me away. I fight to suck in air. "Go live your life. Because I can't be in it." My brain feels like static. I'm losing focus on what I need to do. "Please, just go."

"Willa." A million tiny needles prod at my heart. He moves toward me, and I throw my hand out. I won't be able to get through this if he touches me. "Willa, tell me what happened."

I shake my head. I can't. I made that decision when I failed us and signed that paper. "I can't. Please. This is for your own good."

He ignores my plea to stay away and comes at me, gripping me in his hold. "What happened?" he demands, his voice is tight. "I'm not an idiot, Willa. What did she do? What did they say to convince you running is the answer?" He shakes me. "Tell me!"

"I can't. I promised. They won't take away everything you've worked so hard for. You'll get to live your life without the burden of me holding you back—"

"Stop! Stop. If you think leaving will do anything but destroy me, you're crazy. I don't care what they do to me. They can take it. Everything. I only want you and Bria. Why can't you trust me? Let her do her worst. We will fight. I told you."

Let her…

"How do you know—"

"I came home, and you were gone. The scent of my mother's perfume tainted the place, and I came to one conclusion. I had the doorman play me the security footage to confirm it."

"She made so many threats. I couldn't bear to be the reason…how would you still love me—stand to look at me, knowing I'm the reason you lost it all? How would you still—?"

He cups my cheeks. "I would love you through anything. Do you think I care if they strip me of my name? I've never wanted it, just like you. Steal my hard work? It's been for them—not me. I can start over. Be anyone. But if I'm not with you, I'm nothing. Let them do their worst."

I can barely see him through the tears. "What about money?"

Jake laughs. "Willa, I've always been one step ahead of them. I always knew something like this could happen. Play with the snakes, and one day you'll get bitten. I've been putting money away since before I left for school. I have enough saved for us to live on a private island until we're old and gray. I told you to trust me."

"Oh, Jake, she said such horrible things. I was so scared. I didn't know what to do, and I panicked. The only thing I could do was think about your future and what I would be taking away from you if I stayed, then what I'd be taking away from you if I left. I would've never taken Bria from you. Not again. But I felt so trapped. She threatened me. She made me swear to stay away from you."

"Nothing would keep me away from you."

"What do we do now?"

"We do what we've always wanted to do. We break away. Cut the strings for good and leave. Give you that cute little cottage in the woods. A king-size pool. A swing. I'll do anything. I'll build you that fortress so no one can touch us ever again."

My lips quiver as he presses his to mine. "No more doubting. This is the start of us. We leave tonight. Us three. I love you, Willa."

"I love you too. I'm so sorry for doubting. I'll never do it again."

He kisses me deeply, filling my heart with promise. His love shines so brightly, pushing away the dark clouds that have overshadowed us for half a lifetime. The warmth of his embrace is the comfort I need to know we finally won. Just like our silly fantasies as kids, we're finally getting our happily ever after. Together.

Jake pulls away quickly. "Grab what you need here. We can buy all new things once we get settled."

Suddenly anxious, I bend down and grab my box, remembering the missing birth certificate. I turn around and make another attempt and sigh in relief when I find it. With the certificate securely in my hands, I breathe easier.

But my relief is short-lived when the memory of the contract Meredith made me sign comes to mind. The color drains from my face, and I slowly lift my frantic eyes to Jake. "Oh my God, Jake, I did something… your mother—she had this contact. These terms… she made me swear, and I started to panic and signed—"

"What do you mean signed? What did you sign?"

"I don't know! It was just a bunch of details making me swear I would stay away. If not, she would take Bria. She would rig the paternity results and claim you weren't her father and send me to jail for fraud."

Jake grips my shoulders. "Willa, calm down."

"I can't! What if she finds out? She's going to take Bria from me!" A storm of emotions erupts from my chest, and tears begin to soak my cheeks.

He brings me to his chest. "Willa, look at me." He coerces me to fight through my anguish. "Breathe. I told you. I've prepared for this."

"How? How can you have possibly prepared for *this*? Jake, they are going to take our daughter and strip you of everything."

He offers me the sweetest, gentlest grin, and I'm confused at how he can find such courage to smile at a time like this. "I never trusted my parents as far as I could throw them. I knew one day I would have had enough. And when that day came, I would have to have a plan. Something that would allow me my freedom, no matter the claws they had in the world around us."

I shake my head. "I don't understand?"

"Right now, you don't need to. Let's hurry and get our daughter." He grabs my hand, and we hurry out of my apartment and down the stairs, barreling through the exit door. The driver's eyes widen in surprise at Jake's presence. He reaches for his phone, contemplating his next move.

"Jeffries, I see you're still doing my parents' dirty work. Go on. Call my mother. I would love to have a word with her."

The driver nods and presses the number on his speed dial. We hear Meredith on the other line, and before Jeffries can get a word out, Jake grabs the phone.

"Jeff—"

"Hello, Mother."

"*Jakey*, this is a surprise. To what do I owe the—"

"Enough. Save all your games and bullshit." I hear her inhaled gasp through the line. "And the pleasure is all mine. Because I will finally break free of your lies and deceit."

"Jakey—"

"You've messed with my life for the last time. And now, it's time to repay the favor." My brows perk with interest. "After today, you will never attempt to make contact with me. You will never attempt to make contact with Willa. From this point forward, I'm dead to you—"

"Jake, this is nonsense—"

"Because you are dead to me. I don't care what you tell your country club friends. Tell them I was shipped off at sea, never to return. Shit, tell them the truth—that you're a conniving bitch who only cares about herself."

"Watch your tone, son. You will not talk to your mother like—"

"I am not your son. You should get used to repeating that. Now, to the good stuff. If you think to ever go against my wishes and try to find me, send your dogs to harm Willa, or if I even feel anything is wrong, I will not hesitate to make my move. You think you're high and mighty, but you're not. That perfect marriage you and Father pretend to flaunt around—I will broadcast to the entire world the decades of exploits Father has enjoyed. The women. The hookers. The gambling." His mother's strangled gasp matches my own. "I will ruin you. Do you understand?"

"Jake, you wouldn't."

"Without a second thought or glance back. Are we clear?"

"Jake—"

"Are. We. Clear?" he growls.

There's a moment of silence, and I wonder for a beat if his mother had a heart attack or is just in shock. But then her beady voice sounds over the line. "Yes."

Jake doesn't say another word and hangs up on her. He thrusts the phone at Jeffries, pulls the door open, and reaches for our daughter. Once she's secure in his arms, he turns to me, a smile so carefree, it steals my breath. "Ready for that life I promised you?"

It's almost strange to laugh at a time like this, but I nod, a laugh made from happiness and promise falling off my giddy lips.

"Good. About time I build you that house I promised you."

THE END.

AND ONE
BY REBECCA JENSHAK

CHAPTER ONE
RYLEE

OF ALL THE THINGS I DREAMED OF OVER THE PAST TWO YEARS WHILE putting off college, sitting in the stands at a basketball game wasn't even on the long list. I fantasized about living in a small dorm room with a shared bathroom, pledging a sorority, studying in the library, finding a perfect spot somewhere on campus to people watch and write, staying up late to cram for tests, and even eating cafeteria food.

It's amazing the things that sound glamorous to an eighteen-year-old on the brink of freedom. At twenty, I now have a less idealistic world view. Life more than the years have shown me what is really important.

Upbeat music pumps from speakers. The Valley student section is alive with cheers and chants led by cheerleaders in blue and yellow outfits that show off their tan legs and toned stomachs. All around Ray Fieldhouse, locals fill the seats dressed in Valley gear, ready to watch their beloved men's basketball team in tonight's exhibition game.

The Valley players haven't made their entrance yet, but a team from a local elementary school has everyone's attention as they run up and down the court. A little girl, only a few years older than my Indie, dribbles the ball. It's bigger than her head, but that doesn't stop her. She rushes past a boy a foot taller than her and takes a shot under the basket. She's ecstatic when the ball goes in the net and I can't help but think I'm probably enjoying this more than I will the team we came to watch.

Dragged to watch if I'm being completely accurate. My best friend Lindsey insisted and after two months of turning down invites, it seemed like a better first official college outing than a frat party. A trip to frat row my senior year of high school is the reason I had to put off college for two years.

"Wow, maybe I won't need the book I brought in my purse after all. That little girl is amazing." I have to raise my voice significantly to be heard over the pep band who starts up in front of us.

Lindsey eyes me to gauge my sincerity. "You didn't?"

"No, I didn't, but I do have my phone and there are lots of books on that. Don't judge, you never know when you're going to need to escape a social situation. You do it with texting and scrolling Instagram, I do it with books."

"You won't need to escape this. It's the best game of the season. You know me, I don't really get that excited about sports."

I do know her. Or I did. Since high school, though, we've been separated. Her at Valley like we always planned and me back in our hometown raising a baby.

"Besides," she says. "This is the perfect place to look around and see if you see *him*."

"At a basketball game?" I shake my head, but even the ridiculous notion sparks a flame of hope that I can't seem to snuff out. "No way. He was nerdy and goofy, and… no, he isn't here."

"Nerdy guys go to basketball games." She nods her head to the ones in front of us. They're playing video games on their phones, completely ignoring the court and everything else around them.

Point made. "Maybe, but he didn't strike me as a big sports guy. He was so laid back and fun. He knew more trivia than anyone I've ever met. We talked about books and even politics a little." I chuckle as I remember the random things we discussed. Hours and hours of conversation. I've never EVER had that type of connection with anyone. Everything that was important to us, but nothing personal enough to locate him as it turned out.

"Everyone comes to the exhibition game. It's a giant pep rally followed by the most epic party of the year at The White House." She does a little shimmy. I've already told her there's no way I'm going to a party at the basketball house, but I have a feeling my friend will end up there when I go home. Even in my previous, much cooler, life, I wasn't cool enough to hang out with the jocks. High school was spent with my nose in a book and a superpower of invisibility. Good girl Rylee blended right in with her surroundings, which was fine by me. I had Lindsey and she was all I needed. Seems my friend isn't quite the wallflower she used to be though.

"I've looked everywhere, Linds. He must have graduated already."

"Not everywhere. You've looked in the places you expected. It's time to go unconventional. He's here, somewhere. I know it. Maybe you don't know him as well as you think you did. It was just one night."

That hurts more than it should, but she's right.

"We're here anyway, you might as well use this opportunity. Maybe he's a section over, scanning the crowd looking for the girl he met three years ago because he can't stop thinking about her. And if he's not here, he'll definitely be at The White House. Come with me."

Bless her heart, I think she actually believes that's possible. I did too for the first six months of my pregnancy. I hoped, against all odds, that I'd find that great guy I met one stupid (but absolutely fabulous) night. He'd be so happy I found him and confess that he too had been searching.

A first name was all I had. If only my hookup had been named Atlas or Zeus, or anything less common than John. By the time Indie arrived, I'd given up on finding him, or being found, and accepted that it was going to be just the two of us.

"No, I'm not going to a party to have people shove me around and spill beer on me." That's not a part of college I feel like I missed out on.

"Think about it. If only for research. You can observe and write it all down, become the Hemingway of our time, penning books about the parties and socialites of Valley University." She nods enthusiastically.

The buzzer sounds and the tiny players jog off the court to enthusiastic applause and a stadium on their feet. The overhead lights dim, and everyone continues to stand.

"Oh, it's time." Lindsey bounces beside me.

The music starts low. The jumbotron lights up and a video begins. Clips of the team, their games, and media shots set to a peppy playlist.

I lean over to Lindsey. "I'm going to call my mom and check in on Indie before she goes to bed."

"Now? The team's just about to come out. It's the best part."

"I'll be quick. Promise." I hold the phone to my ear and use my free hand to plug my other ear as I hustle up the stairs to find a quieter spot.

"Hello?" my mother answers on the second ring.

"Hi, Mom. I'm just calling to say goodnight to Indie. How is she?"

"She's fine. Your dad is reading to her."

"The entire bookshelf?"

"Of course." My mom chuckles.

Some of the worry I've been feeling since I left my baby girl fades. I know my parents are taking good care of her, but it still feels weird leaving her. Ever since Indie was born, it's been the two of us. My parents helped a lot in the beginning; they let us stay with them rent free and they watched her while I went to classes at a local community college twice a week. Since I came to Valley two months ago, though, this is the first time I've gone anywhere beyond school without her.

The stadium gets louder, and I look up at the giant screen to see they're starting to announce the players.

"Can you give him the phone so I can say goodnight to her. The game is about to start."

I press the video chat button and then my dad's voice greets me and his face, as well as my daughter's, fills the screen.

"Hey," I say, smiling at the two of them.

Indie leans toward the phone reaching out as if she's trying to touch me.

"Are you having fun with Grandma and Grandpa?" I ask.

She grins back, her beautiful indigo eyes that make my chest ache in remembrance.

"We're reading about penguin and hippo," Dad says, adjusting my daughter on his lap. "How's the game?"

"It hasn't started yet. They're announcing the players."

"They're what?" my dad asks. The place gets louder still and there seems to be no escaping it.

"Announcing the players," I practically scream. "I just called to say goodnight."

He must catch at least part of my response because he instructs my daughter to say goodnight to Mommy. She doesn't, her words are still few and far between, but she waves her little chubby hand and I wish I was there to breathe her in and kiss her cheeks.

"I'll see you guys in just a little bit. I'm coming straight back as soon as the game is over."

"No need to rush." My mom steps into the frame beside my dad. "Enjoy a night out while you've got free daycare in town."

"Thanks, Mom. Love you guys."

I slip my phone into my pocket and start back to my seat. The players come out one at a time from behind the far side of the basketball court. The overhead lights are still dimmed, but there's a lighted archway they step through when their name is announced, as well as a spotlight that follows them as they run out to half court with the rest of the team.

The guys are having a good time with it. Strutting out, dancing, high fiving people leaning over the railings. One cheerleader does backflips down the court. Two guys lift another up high as she holds a sign that says Let's Go!

I'm nearly to my seat when another player is announced and runs out to booming screams. I have to check the screen for his name because the deafening shrieks make it impossible to hear.

John Datson

My pulse quickens at the face on the jumbotron. Dark hair, shorter than I remember, but the relaxed smile that tips up his lips in a friendly smirk and those indigo eyes framed by long, dark lashes, I could pick out anywhere. I glance back to the guy making his way to half court. He's filled out more since I last saw him. His chest is broader, biceps bigger, but the way he moves is so him. Easy, graceful, cocky. And a basketball player? Lindsey was right; I don't know him.

My best friend's arms are extended up toward the roof and she screams along with everyone else. When I get close, she throws those flailing arms around me. "You're back!" She pulls away when I don't share her enthusiasm. "What's wrong?"

"He's here." The words sound far away. My ears are ringing, and my head is fuzzy and light-headed.

"Who?" Her eyes widen. "Wait. *He's* here?! Where?"

I turn my gaze to half court where he dances around with his teammates. "Number thirty-one."

"*Datson* is your John?"

I shoot her a glare. "You know him?"

The lights come back up and the players divide up into teams of blue and white. John wears a blue jersey. He tucks the top into his shorts as he walks out and then gets in position for the tip-off.

"Yeah, of course." She shakes her head. "I mean, no. It's just, he's Datson, everyone knows him."

"You're just mentioning him now?" Two years I've combed through Johns on the Valley directory trying to find him and she knows him?

"I've only ever heard him called Datson. I'm not even sure I knew his first name until tonight. Are you sure it's him?"

"Positive." So positive my heart races with fond memories I thought I'd hidden away more carefully.

Everyone continues standing until the first basket is made. Staring out onto the basketball court, watching his athletic body move, I can't believe he never mentioned he was a jock. A popular jock. I let my head hang as I remember complaining to him about how I didn't think professional athletes should get paid so much or take all the great college scholarships just for being born with superior genetics. He told me he thought there was probably a lot more work involved than being born really tall or fast, and we'd laughed. I'd mostly been joking, but also maybe a little bitter that the scholarship I'd received for the following year was only going to cover half of my tuition. God, what an idiot I'd been.

John's team has possession. He jogs toward the guy with the ball and gets in the way of the defender, then rolls toward the basket. The ball is tossed up high to him, his long arms reach up, and he dunks it. The crowd goes nuts. My pulse jumps and dances, and my stomach is taken over by a million butterflies.

I finally found him. After all this time, I actually found him. I thought I'd be more excited, but reality shoves that excitement right out of the way and instead I'm so nervous

I might puke. Knowing where he is means I have to tell him. Every good thing I've held onto, about him and that night, will either be proven right or die a spectacularly awful death, right along with my belief in love and soulmates.

Lindsey squeals. Her happiness doesn't understand my anxiety. "Looks like you're coming to the party with me after all."

CHAPTER TWO
JOHN

BY THE TIME I GET BACK TO MY PLACE AFTER THE GAME, THE WHITE HOUSE is already packed. Two beers and a bottle of Jack are thrust in my hand as I make my way through the kitchen.

My buddy Shaw and his girlfriend Sydney are sharing a bar stool. "Nice job out there tonight," Shaw says, his arms wrapped around Sydney's waist as she perches on his lap.

She melts into him. Cartoon hearts hang above their heads and in Shaw's eyes. They got together over the summer after years of being just friends and it's still a little weird to see them like this. Weird, but fitting.

"Thanks." I twist off the top of one of the beers and take a long drink. I haven't yet decided if it's a beer or liquor kind of night.

"I think Conner's vying for a spot on the welcoming committee." Shaw nods his head toward the freshman. He's walking around with a stack of cups, offering one to anyone without a drink in hand.

"I'm happy to pass the torch," I say. Though, he's doing it all wrong. There's an art to approaching people and making them feel welcome and wanted in a party this size. I think about helping him for all of two seconds. He'll figure it out.

I can't be the sole member of the welcoming committee forever. This is my last year at Valley. It really hit me tonight as I was running out onto the court to a stadium packed with fans. Everything I do from here on out is the last time. Last exhibition game. Last party after the exhibition game.

College has been a blast and I've lived it – every second, enjoying and savoring it. Now everyone is making plans for the future and I'm coming to terms with the fact I have no idea what that looks like for me.

Another swig of beer followed by a pull of Jack. The latter jolts my system, pushes away the negative, and awakens a little of the fun guy everyone knows me to be. Liquor it is.

My gaze goes back to Conner in the entryway of the house. Two girls step through the front doors and he fumbles the cups, the entire stack clattering to the floor at their feet. The girls look like they're two seconds from bolting back out the door.

"Would you look at that?" I motion toward the disaster. "He's going to start scaring people away."

"Unlikely." Shaw shakes his head. "Look around. This place is as packed as usual."

"It's killing you. Admit it?" Sydney grins. Her brown eyes twinkle with humor at my expense.

"No. Whatever." Pushing to my feet, I slide the bottle of Jack and my beers toward Shaw. "I'll be back for those. I'm just going to see if Conner needs any help. Not because I can't handle letting someone else be the host but because it's his first time. Rookie needs guidance."

"Whatever makes you feel better, dude," Shaw calls after me.

I live for throwing parties at our place. Maybe it isn't exactly a noble mission, but I always set out to make sure our guests have a good time.

More people have arrived and they're picking their cups off the fucking floor like barbarians.

"Conner, my man." I pat him on the back and smile at the girls helping him collect the fallen cups. "Why don't you go grab another stack of cups from the pantry. We don't want our guests using cups that have been on the floor, do we?"

He honest to God looks like he might say yes. I pat him a little harder to encourage him.

"Right. I'll be back."

Once Conner has gone, I turn my attention to the girls. One of them is still squatting down picking up cups and I crouch down to help. "Sorry about the mess. I got these. Conner will get you two clean cups. There's a keg out back and some liquor and mixers in the kitchen. I think someone's got a tray of shots somewhere too if that's your thing, but word of warning—they taste delicious, but they are strooong. Don't have more than two. Trust me on that."

I finally get all the cups corralled and stand. The girl in front of me is wide-eyed, gaze flitting between me and her friend, who is still crouched down with a handful of cups. Neither has said a word. Conner must have really freaked them out. They're probably freshmen.

Offering the redhead gawking at me a smile, I lean down to her friend. "Here, let me help you."

I reach for the cups and when my fingers brush hers, she pulls back like I've slapped her. The cups fall to the floor for a second time. *What in the hell did Conner say to her?*

"I'm sorry," she mutters quietly as she hurriedly grabs for the cups. Long, thick brown hair hides her downturned face.

"I got it. Really. No worries at all."

I try again to take the cups from her. This time she lets me. Her face tilts up blessing me with a glimpse of her full mouth and green eyes that lock on mine. Dark lashes flutter around those stunning emerald eyes as heat from her fingertips seep into mine. I feel my throat work as I swallow a thousand different sentences. I'm entranced with a familiarity that I can't place. She stands quickly, leaving me kneeling at her feet.

She's dressed in jeans and a simple T-shirt, but her feet are bejeweled with toe rings – one on each foot, and strappy, gold sandals that wrap around her ankles. They're such a contradiction to the rest of her simple outfit that I find myself smiling at her feet.

I stand tall and look her over more closely. "Hey, don't I know you?"

Conner reappears. "Here we go, ladies. Sorry about that. I'm a klutz everywhere but on the court."

They take cups and murmur their thanks.

I'm still staring at the green-eyed girl and trying, and failing, to remember her name. It's stored somewhere in my thick skull with a million more details that I desperately attempt to recover.

She doesn't offer anything or respond at all. Okay, maybe I've never seen her before, and I just further creeped out some poor freshman who is definitely never coming back. I keep right on staring at her though, even as she clutches onto her friend's arm and drags her away. She glances back just as they're exiting toward the keg and I try like hell to read her face for any indication of who she is or how I might know her.

"Dude, this job is stressful," Conner says. "You make it look easy. Any tips?"

"Yeah, don't drop the cups."

His shoulders slump. "I'm sorry. I get nervous around hot girls. I thought having an excuse to talk to them would make it easier."

Shit. Now I feel like an ass. "It's all right. They're just cups."

He tries to hand them over.

"Nah, man. You got this." I give him a reassuring smile. "Only way to get better is to practice."

I've passed the torch, I guess. Another last.

After tossing the dirty cups in the recycling and reclaiming my drinks, I head out back. The back yard of The White House is packed tonight. Our parties always draw a big crowd. We're within walking distance of most campus housing, and unlike the other party houses, we have room for everyone, without cramming into a dingy basement or crowding around a yard half the size of ours.

We have a pool, too. Early October nights are still warm enough that people are stripping down to their suits and getting in the water. Scanning the crowd, a perk of being one of the tallest people here, I nod and smile as I weave through familiar faces.

Being the welcoming committee was something I did because I like people. Meeting new ones, talking to all different kinds—jocks, nerds, partiers, the shy, the reluctant, and the overeager. Growing up on a farm twenty miles outside of the city limits, my options for socializing were wrestling with my three brothers or hiding somewhere Dad wouldn't find me to play video games. School and basketball were my outlets and I took full advantage.

I finally spot the girl from earlier and the friend she came with back near the house. She's holding a drink and smiling at the circle of people around them. As I walk toward her, I catalog every feature. I'm not great with faces, but hers is a pretty spectacular one that I know I should remember. It's right on the edge of my memory, but I can't bring it to focus no matter how hard I try. When I'm within ten feet of her, she notices me approaching.

My legs keep moving ahead at a steady pace, but my pulse lurches forward.

The redheaded friend throws an arm around her shoulders. "This is my friend Rylee. She's a junior, but this is her first year at Valley."

Rylee.

Slowly the gears turn and one by one the memories I've stored away flash through my brain.

For a solid year, I looked around every corner on campus for her. Her hair was blonde then and she wore these adorable cat-eye glasses, but it's her. My Rylee.

Technically she was only mine for one night, but it was the craziest night of my life. Spring of my freshman year. The team had just won the national college basketball tournament; everywhere I went people knew who I was and wanted to shake my hand, life was good.

Then I met her. Rylee was shy and a little sassy. Adorable and sweet, unassuming. She had no clue who I was. It was nice to escape, to have someone tell me what they thought without any preconceived notions. Being a basketball player is such a small part of who I am. I'm not going to be a professional ball player and I don't have any desire to be one of those guys trying to capture the glory years like I'll never achieve anything greater.

I'm all for living in the moment, but there's a difference in relishing it and being stuck in place.

Rylee. I must say her name out loud this time because everyone turns to look at me. I feel their eyes on me, but I don't take mine off her.

Her back straightens and she meets my stare with a penetrating gaze that tells me she recognizes me too. "Hi John."

Well this night just took a turn for the better.

CHAPTER THREE
RYLEE

"IT'S REALLY YOU?" HIS FACE LIGHTS UP WITH CLEAR RECOGNITION.

"You remember me?"

"Rylee. Yes, of course." He envelopes me in his big arms. A friendly hug, one with no animosity or hostility of the past. And why would there be? He has no idea what I've been through these past two years.

"I can't believe it's you." He pulls back and then squeezes me again. His body is warm, and he smells like soap. Something clean and masculine. "Where have you been? *How* have you been?"

"Good." I settle for answering only the second question for now. I'm all too conscious that we have an audience. It's nothing like the first time we hung out. That had been just the two of us off in a corner of the Sig Nu basement. Here, he's a king, and everyone's hanging on his every word. "How have you been?"

A deep, light chuckle escapes his lips, and he keeps staring at me as if he expects me to disappear before his very eyes. "Good, yeah. Were you at the game tonight?"

"I was. Yeah, congratulations. You were amazing. I hear the team's done really well." My face warms and I want to sink into the patio pavers. *I hear the team's done really well?* All the things I planned and dreamed of saying to him if I ever saw him again, and here we are making small talk about basketball.

His face scrunches up in confusion. "That wasn't the first time you've seen us play, was it?"

I nod. "It was. First college basketball game period."

"I remember you said you weren't much of a sports fan."

"Did I say that?"

"Ahhh…" He trails off and glances up, as if he's trying to remember it exactly. "Pretty much. You basically gave me a dissertation on the unfair balance of athletic versus academic scholarships at Valley."

"Guess that explains why you didn't tell me that you were one." I wave in front of him. All six feet, five inches of him.

Lindsey coughs next to me. She's biting back a smile. "I'm sorry. My throat's a little dry. Datson, do you have any water inside?"

"Uhh… yeah." He glances between us. "Of course. Follow me."

John takes off inside, and I hang back, holding Lindsey's arm to give us a little privacy. "What are you doing?"

"You need to talk to him, and it was clear you weren't going to do that with a crowd around." She marches inside with a smile that is entirely too pleased with herself.

Fewer people are inside and it's only me, Lindsey, and John in the kitchen. He grabs a bottle of water and hands it to Lindsey, then holds another one up to me.

"No, thanks."

"I'm going to use the bathroom," Lindsey announces.

John doesn't pick up, or chooses to ignore, how weird my best friend is acting. "The one upstairs is probably less crowded. First door on the left."

He leans against the counter, smiling at me and still looking me over that same way I did him the entire basketball game.

"Your hair is different. It took me a minute to piece it together. What's it been? Three years?"

"Little less than that." I go to push my glasses up on my face before I remember I'm not wearing them. A nervous habit that really doesn't work so well with contacts.

"This is so crazy. Why haven't I seen you around before now?"

"I…" I play out a thousand different ways I could answer him. I could play it vague or straight up lie. But the truth is, I'm tired of carrying the weight alone. "I lied to you that night. I wasn't a Valley student. I was visiting for incoming freshmen orientation. My friend Lindsey and me." I nod in the direction Lindsey went. "Sorry."

Even years later my face heats with embarrassment.

"I guess that makes us even for me withholding the whole awesome jock thing."

A smile tugs at my lips and I laugh off some of the nerves I'm holding. "I'm sorry for that too. I was bitter about not receiving a full-ride scholarship."

"I looked for a while, asked around, typed in Rylee to the student directory more times than I'm willing to admit."

"You did?" My pulse quickens at that tiny bit of acknowledgment that our time together meant something to him, too.

"Hell, yeah. That night was awesome."

"It really was."

He shakes his head slowly. "I'm bummed that you've been here for the past two years and I didn't bump into you again until tonight. I ask this at the risk of sounding like an arrogant prick, but you never saw me around and thought of saying hey?"

My palms start to sweat, and my throat goes dry. "I didn't end up coming to Valley until this year, and until tonight, I assumed that you'd already graduated. Like you, I looked around. There are a lot of Johns at this school."

He steps forward and extends his hand. "John Datson. D-a-t-s-o-n. Easy to find now that you know my full-name name and where I live."

I slip my hand into his. Warm, calloused fingers squeeze mine and heat travels up my arm. "You live here?"

"Yeah."

Dread tosses icy water over my head as I try to picture what his life looks like day-to-day and how I'm about to upend it. Or, I guess maybe not, but I'm really hoping he's not that kind of guy.

"Where'd you go instead, or did you just hold off and do something cool like travel Europe for writing inspiration?"

"You remembered?"

"Yeah of course. I remember everything from that night. God, we talked for hours. My throat was sore the next day from talking so much."

The honesty and charm in his version of the story and the flicker of desire in his gaze shifts something in the air between us. It's a reminder of how easy and fun it was between us, but also an opportunity that I know I need to take advantage of before we skip too far down memory lane."

"I did go to college, sort of. I had a baby, so I took classes at a community college part-time for the first two years."

There's a slight change in his expression. It lasts only a fraction of a second, but I recognize it as disappointment. I've gotten this same look from other guys my age when they find out I have a kid. I used to get super offended, but I know it isn't personal. Most guys my age aren't ready for all of that, and honestly, it's better to know right away.

"Wow," he says. I can tell he's grappling for the right words. I usually let them flounder in this situation, but I desperately don't want this moment to be any more awkward than it has to be. "Her name is Indie and she's going to be two in December, and… she's yours."

"Mine? Like… mine?" He motions between us.

I can only nod. My voice is frozen in fear waiting for his reaction. While his jaw hangs open, I pull out my phone and swipe to a recent picture of our baby girl. I hold it out to him. He takes it and stares at it silently for a long moment.

The noise of the party around us heightens the craziness of the situation and I feel like the biggest buzzkill ever, until I remember the party ended for me several years ago. Crazy or not, it's a weight off my shoulders to have found him and told him about Indie. He can be a part of our lives or not, but now I've put it on him.

"Look, I know this is a lot and I'm sure you have a million questions, but yes, I'm sure she's yours. Just want to get that out of the way. If you still want a paternity test, we can do that," I ramble on.

"She looks just like me." His tone is deep and filled with wonder. His eyes lift slowly from the phone. "I'm so sorry. I thought we were careful. If I had known…And you've been doing this on your own ever since?"

"We were careful." I shrug. Seems like a bad time to remind him condoms aren't one hundred percent effective.

"Yo, Datson!" A guy carrying a tray of red and green shots approaches. "Pick your poison."

My phone is handed back to me and then he takes two of each color from the tray. "Thanks, man." He looks to me. "Want one?"

I shake my head.

Standing tall, he lets out a long breath that makes his cheeks puff out. "Is your friend coming back?"

"I'm pretty sure the bathroom was an excuse to give us privacy."

He nods his head. "Come with me?"

I stick close to him as he heads farther into the house and to the stairway. We go up one flight and Datson unlocks a door and holds it open to let me enter first.

The court is smaller than the one they played on tonight, but even a non-sports fan like me can appreciate how cool it is that he has a freaking basketball court in his house.

He flips on a light and then walks to the middle of the court and sits down. He sets the shots out in front of him in a line.

"Sorry, this is the only place I could think of where we could have privacy outside of my bedroom. Given the circumstances, figured that was a bad idea."

A giggle escapes me and I walk over and sit in front of him. "It's okay. We can talk as much or as little as you want. If you need some time, I get that. I had six months to adjust to it before she was born, and I think it took three of those for it to really sink in."

He's taking it better than I expected. Minus the strong shots he warned me against earlier that it now looks like he's about to consume.

"I want to know everything. I'm just figuring out what to ask first." His fingers wrap around the first shot glass and he tosses it back. "When was she born?"

"December twenty-third. I got to bring her home on Christmas day."

He mulls that over for a minute and then another shot is drained. "What's she like?"

"A little shy. She loves books and car rides. She doesn't talk much yet, but she likes when I read to her or sing along to the radio. Her favorite toy is this big stuffed cat unicorn. I bought a backup because I fear the day she loses it or it falls apart. She will seriously have a meltdown without it."

As I talk, John relaxes a little. He leans forward listening intently and smiling occasionally. Each time I get more than a slight upturn to his lips, he catches himself and his brows furrow as if he doesn't think smiling is acceptable in this moment.

His mannerisms are familiar, but he's changed too. He's not as quick to joke or laugh – whether that's because of the situation or just him, I'm not sure.

"Can I meet her?"

I take a steadying breath. "Of course, you can."

CHAPTER FOUR
JOHN

"A BABY?" SHAW ASKS, HIS EYEBROWS HAVE DISAPPEARED INTO HIS HAIRLINE and his eyes are bugged out of his head.

"Oh my gosh!" Sydney looks just as stunned, but her version is a much happier, optimistic expression. I focus on her. "You knocked someone up?"

Or maybe not.

"Can we not phrase it like that?" I rub at my temples. Between the booze and the restless sleep, I'm already on edge and these two are not helping. "What do I do? I'm supposed to be there in an hour, and I have no idea what to wear, or bring, or do, or say, or…"

"You're sure this chick isn't scamming you?"

"For what?" I shake my head. "Nah. The timeline adds up, and the kid looks just like me. She suggested we do a paternity test so that everyone is comfortable, but I don't need it to know it's mine."

"She," Sydney corrects me. "Don't call your baby an it."

"This is so wild." I run a hand through my damp hair. "I always wondered what happened to her. We had this crazy night together. One of those memories you pull up every so often and smile because it stands the time test."

"What's the time test?" Shaw asks.

"You know those moments where people or events seem great, but then in a day or a week or a year you realize it was the booze or your lack of experience or… a million other variables that alter your perception."

They both stare at me like they have no idea what I'm talking about.

"That's never happened to you guys."

Shaw grins. "Dude, I was in love with a girl for two years before I got her… of course I know what you're talking about. I'm just surprised to hear you talk like this. I didn't realize you were carrying a torch for this chick still."

"Still? You knew about her?" Sydney asks her boyfriend.

"Well, yeah. We were rooming together when he met her and then spent the next month trying to find her." He dodges a playful slap from Sydney. "What? I didn't know you freshman year."

"I can't believe I'm just finding this out. Some friends you guys are."

Shaw pulls her onto his lap and kisses Sydney's neck. "I'll tell you the entire story. Every detail I remember."

These two. I can't get over them finally acting on how they feel. We all knew they were in love with each other, but I really never thought I'd see the day they figured it out and did something about it.

"First, can you tell me what the hell I'm supposed to do in…" I check my watch. "Fifty-five minutes?"

"No idea, buddy." Shaw slaps me on the shoulder. "Congratulations, though."

"Syd?" I ask hopefully.

"This is beyond my expertise, but I'd love to meet both of them. And we'll be here for you every step of the way. Whatever you need."

"You mean except now when I'm asking you to tell me what to do?"

She nods. "Sorry."

"All right, well I have to go. Thanks for nothing," I grumble.

"Hey, wait," Shaw calls before I step out of the kitchen.

"Yeah?" I pause and hope like hell he's going to provide some guidance because I'm lost here and desperately want to choose my next step carefully.

"You found her and maybe it doesn't look like what you expected, but you have another chance. Take it. The rest will fall into place." There's a sincerity in his words and in his eyes. I don't know if it'll be as easy for me as it was him and Sydney, but he's right about one thing – this isn't going anything like I expected.

***

IT'S LATE AFTERNOON WHEN I PULL INTO THE PARKING LOT OF RYLEE'S apartment complex with two bags filled with baby stuff. I broke down in the middle of the store while trying to buy an outfit for Indie. I hope the unfortunate store employee that I melted down in front of, while trying to figure out the madness of eighteen month versus 2T clothes, works on commission because I bought out half the store to apologize.

I'm the oldest of four boys. My youngest brother is seven years younger than me, so I vaguely remember him being little. Mostly I remember that he got out of chores and people fawned over him a lot. Then, when he got old enough that my mother let him out of her sight, he followed me everywhere. Drove me crazy, little shithead. I'd have done anything to protect him though. Still would.

And it's that sense of family that has me trudging up the stairs to Rylee's apartment with determination to… I don't know what. Whatever she needs, I guess.

Nerves set in again when I knock on the door. Surreal is the only word I can think to describe everything about this situation. Any moment now I feel like I'm going to wake up from the weirdest dream ever.

Rylee opens the door and gives me a shaky smile. "Hey. Come in."

I follow her into the living room. She moves a rainbow-colored stuffed animal off the couch and motions for me to sit. "Indie is still napping, but she should be up any minute."

"I brought some stuff." I set the bags on the floor in front of her and then sit next to her on the couch.

"I see that." One of her dark brows quirks up above her glasses. I dig her in them but telling her so feels weird now. Are there rules for hitting on a chick you accidentally got pregnant?

"I didn't know what she might need or want. Also, I have some money. Not a lot, but I can help pay for whatever she needs. Daycare, food, rent—"

"Woah." She places a hand on my thigh, which I now realize was bouncing up and down. "We're okay. Part of why I waited two years to come to Valley was so that I could save up enough to keep us afloat while I finish my degree. I am not expecting you to do anything except meet her and be a part of her life if you want."

I sense that she doesn't like the idea of me coming in and trying to take over, not that I could even if I wanted to. I wouldn't even know where to start. "I want to be a part of her life, of course. I also want to help you anyway I can. Sorry feels like the wrong thing to say, but I am so sorry."

An uncomfortable silence hangs between us. My leg goes back to bouncing.

"She's usually up by now, but my parents were in town so she's a little off schedule."

Parents. Shit, I gotta tell my parents. "What did your parents say? Oh my god, they must think I'm the worst."

"They were surprised, of course, but I couldn't have done it without them."

Guilt punches me in the gut. I have no idea how my own parents are going to react, but they're the least of my concerns right now because a little girl cries in the next room and my heart stops as I hear my daughter for the first time.

Rylee stands. "I'll be right back."

I wipe my sweaty palms on my jeans, stand, then sit again, then stand. The living room isn't big enough to pace, so I settle back on the couch and grab the multi-colored stuffed animal. It's a cat, no, a unicorn. It's a caticorn or maybe a unicat?

I'm squeezing the marshmallow textured toy and watching it expand back to size when Rylee steps out of the bedroom with Indie in her arms.

I get to my feet, but she shakes her head and speaks softly, "It's probably better if I come to you."

My heart's beating so fast I worry I might have a heart attack and traumatize my kid on our first meeting. The cushion dips next to me. Her dark head of messy ringlets rests on Rylee's shoulder with her back to me. Her limp little body clings to her mother.

"Relax, John," Rylee says, a hint of a smile on her lips.

I do my best to uncoil the muscles that are strung up so tight I'm about to break a sweat.

Indie raises her head and looks back to me as if she's just realized there's someone else in the room. Those dark blue eyes lock onto mine and I stop breathing.

"Indie, this is my friend John."

I wave awkwardly while she looks me over and then hides back in her mother's shoulder. Rylee motions for the stuffed animal still in my hands.

"Is this yours?" I ask hesitantly. "I was trying to decide if it was a caticorn or a unicat."

Her little head slowly turns and I hold out the toy. Rylee situates Indie so that she's on her leg facing me and ever so carefully, my daughter reaches toward her stuffed animal and pulls it to her chest. It's nearly as big as she is.

"Does he, or she, have a name?"

Indie doesn't respond but talking makes me feel like I'm doing something productive, so I keep going. "I brought you a few new toys and some clothes. Do you want to see?"

I look to Rylee for approval and she nods. While I lean forward to get the bag, Indie scoots off her mother's lap so she's sitting between us. I pull out each item for her. She looks them over. Most end up tossed on her mother, but she holds onto the small rubber ball. I smirk over her head at Rylee.

"I also got some books. I wasn't sure which you already had. The receipt's buried at the bottom of the bag so you can return anything that isn't right."

Indie brings the ball to her shoulder and tosses it. She watches as it bounces across the floor and her little face lights up with happiness. Off the couch she goes running after it.

"Well, that seems appropriate." Rylee laughs lightly.

"She's beautiful."

Rylee seems taken aback by my words, but nods. Indie brings the ball back and sets it in my lap. "Is your mommy raising a jock?" I wink at Rylee who makes a face.

It goes like this for a while. Rylee and I watching Indie play with the basketball. Eventually, she tires of it and goes to a little bookshelf lined with books of all shapes and sizes in a rainbow of colors.

"Clearly, she has your love of books. What else does she like?"

"She likes going outside for walks or to the park. We do that quite a bit." Rylee feels her pockets and then checks the couch next to her.

"Lose something?"

"My phone. I was going to show you a picture from this morning."

"Uhh…" I point toward Indie. Her little fingers are wrapped around the device and she swipes at the screen.

Rylee laughs, goes and gets the phone from a grinning Indie, and then settles on the couch a little closer this time. "She also likes stealing my phone."

The first few pictures are of the ceiling and that makes me chuckle. "And taking pictures, apparently."

Rylee flips through photographic evidence of their outing this morning.

"Those your parents?" I ask, looking at a photo of Indie and an older couple.

"Yeah."

There must be fifty photos just from today. Some candid, some posed, one of Rylee and Indie with their faces smushed together in a selfie. That beautiful girl I dreamt about all these years grew up into this amazing woman and mother. It's sexy as hell. But the best part is that even without knowing the specifics of what's happened the last two years, I know my daughter has been loved. That helps me relax just a little.

"Thank you for this. For all of it. Taking care of her and loving her so hard, and for letting me in now even though I've been absent all this time."

"I'm glad you know and that you've met her. I didn't realize how much it was weighing on me. Guilt for not getting your name, for lying to you, for getting pregnant. I never meant to keep her from you. Although, I admit that I was worried about what would happen if I did find you. It was such a perfect night, and I was afraid I'd built you up in my mind, that you'd disappoint me and her."

Well, shit. That feels heavy. "And now?"

"I'm not disappointed."

CHAPTER FIVE
RYLEE

THE FOLLOWING NIGHT JOHN COMES OVER AFTER PRACTICE. "COME IN. SHE just got out of the bath. I need to find her some pajamas and then we've got about an hour before I usually put her to bed."

"Sorry, I came straight over, but practice ran a little late tonight. We've got our first game this weekend and–" He stops abruptly, looking a little frazzled, but still as hot as sin. "Doesn't matter. I'm sorry. Can I help somehow?"

"No. I got it. Sit. I'll be right back."

Indie's still in her room where I left her. She's naked except for her pull-up. She has the ball John got her in her lap as she flips the pages in a book on the floor in front of her.

"There's someone here to see you, pretty girl. Which pajamas do you want to wear?" I bring her two options and let her choose.

After I help her get dressed, we walk out to the living room. John is looking down at his phone with his brows furrowed. Indie halts when she sees him and takes off back toward her room and grabs her ball with a smile.

"Well, she likes the ball," I say with a teasing eye roll.

"It's in her genes," he pipes back and then goes quiet, eyes wide. "Sorry," he whispers.

I take a seat next to him on the couch. "It's okay. She doesn't know what genes are, and besides, I don't plan on keeping it from her. If you're going to be a part of her life, then she should know."

"If?" His dark brows pull together again. I know he's offended, but I've given him a lot to process.

"Let's just take it slowly, okay? This is a lot for all of us to get used to."

He nods. "I thought we could compare schedules and figure out times I could hang with you guys or help with Indie while you're at school or work, if you're comfortable with that." There go his furrowed eyebrows again.

My heart pinches at the thought of splitting my time with Indie. I already feel guilty for the hours I'm at school.

"I don't remember you being so grumpy," I say, deflecting.

"Yeah. I'm trying it on for size. It's kind of like wearing a medium shirt. I know I still look good, but it isn't very comfortable."

And there's the guy I remember. Funny and a little cocky.

"That you do. Look good, I mean." He gives me a lopsided grin that makes my stomach do somersaults. My flirting skills are rusty. Yikes. "I'll grab my laptop."

Turns out, John's schedule is as nuts as mine. Between workouts, classes, and then practices and games, there aren't a lot of hours for him to choose from.

He frowns. "I could pick her up from daycare on Wednesdays, but other than that I'm not a lot of help."

"No, that's great. That'll give me an extra hour or two on campus to study. It's been hard to fit everything in," I admit.

He scans my face. "I can come over in the evenings and hang with her while you study, if you want? Or she could come to my place and give you some time to yourself."

"You want to take her to The White House?"

His grin is sheepish. "It's much calmer on the weekdays, but I'll come here if you prefer."

"Thank you."

Indie brings a book to me. My girl might like her new ball, but she *loves* books. "Do you want us to read to you?"

She nods and climbs up between us. I spread the large picture book out onto her lap and John scoots closer to hold the other side. I sneak a glance at him and smile. The nervousness he's displaying is charming. I can tell he wants to do right by us. I just hope he doesn't get freaked out when he realizes just how hard it is to juggle everything. I'm barely managing right now with my classes. So much reading, which I love, but by the time I get Indie into bed at night, I'm so exhausted that it's hard to stay awake long enough to finish everything.

I read the words on the left page and, with a little prodding, John reads the right. Our little girl watches his face as he reads. She's totally enamored with him. Not that I can blame her.

His deep voice sends a shiver down my spine. And that easy smile he gives our daughter melts me into a pile of goo.

They both look to me expectantly.

"Your turn," John says.

Right. My face warms at being caught checking him out. I turn the page and keep reading.

After several more books, Indie's eyes start to droop, and her temperament goes from sweet and adorable to cranky.

"All right, baby girl. I think it's time for bed."

She shakes her head. Her mouth pulls into a thin line of disapproval.

"Book." She puts the book in John's hands, and he looks like he's about to cave.

"No. It's bedtime. Come on. Let's brush your teeth." I stand, but she stays put.

My stubborn daughter stays glued to the couch.

"How about, you brush your teeth and get in bed and then I'll read one more." He looks up to me. "If your mom says that's okay."

Two sets of dark blue eyes lock onto me, waiting for an answer. "Okay. *One* more."

She gets up and heads toward the bathroom, but then stops and looks back to John. "Brush?"

Some of her words are hard to understand for other people so I decipher it for him in case he missed the plea. "I think she wants you to go with her."

"Oh." He unfolds himself from the couch. He looks ridiculous standing at his full height in my small living room. I wonder if Indie will be tall. I never considered it before. I'm average height and so are my parents. My daughter will probably be taller than me if she got even half of his giant genetics.

I pick up the apartment while listening to them in the bathroom. She shows him every single bath toy before he gently encourages her to brush her teeth. He's good with her. His uneasiness is evident, but she's fascinated with everything he does and that seems to coax him to talk and interact with her more.

She comes out of the bathroom wiping her mouth, John on her heels.

"Ready for night night?" I ask.

The three of us go into her room. John takes it all in with a grin. "You like purple, huh?"

She nods, grabs his hand and tugs him toward her toy bin, which is purple just like half the other items. Purple sheets, purple blanket, purple letters on the wall that spell out her name. My gaze is stuck on her little chubby hand holding on so tight to his pinky and ring fingers.

"Bed, sweet girl," I say, before she can coax him into doing something else. Something tells me he's going to be a push over until he realizes that only causes more problems later.

I pick her up and place her into her crib. We keep a stack of books next to the bed and I grab the one on top. "Penguin?"

"Yeah!"

I kiss her. "Night. I love you."

Handing the book to John, I say, "*One* book."

He grins. "All right, *mom*."

I force myself to leave the room, even though listening to him read to our daughter sounds like just about the sexiest thing I can imagine.

At the dining room table, I settle in with my laptop and books. Every literature class has a weekly reading assignment and I'm taking four of them. Gothic literature, women's literature, Victorian prose, and topics in literary theory. I love all of them.

Reading and dissecting words is everything I hoped it would be, but I may have bitten off more than I can chew. And that's not even factoring in the hours I attempt to write my own words. I love reading, but it's writing that I want to do after graduation. The thought of my words being read and loved by others inspires me to keep going.

I could take fewer classes per semester, but that means more semesters and I don't know how long Indie and I can survive on my teaching assistant salary and savings.

John's low voice pulls at my attention and I realize I'm still listening in when he finishes the last page and Indie asks for more.

"Your mom said only one tonight, but maybe I could come back another time and read to you again?" He asks.

I can't make out her response, but I don't need to hear her to know she said yes. She's falling hard for him. I really hope he doesn't break both our hearts.

Faking like I'm deep into my reading, I glance up slowly when John closes her bedroom door.

"Did she beg for more?"

One side of his mouth lifts. "Yeah. Good thing you said only one. I have a feeling I would have easily been roped into reading every single book she owns."

"Probably more than once."

He takes a seat at the table and nods toward my books. "How are your classes going?"

"Good. There's just so much reading. By the time I get her to bed every night I'm so exhausted I have to pry my eyes open to finish."

Guilt etches into his features and I backtrack. "I'm exaggerating. Classes are great."

"You've done a really great job with her and I'm so thankful. I know I've apologized a bunch, but I feel awful. Let me help. I get that you want to make sure I'm going to stick around and not screw up too much, but I'm in this with you now." He reaches across the table and takes my hand. "You look good too."

"What?" I laugh.

"Earlier you said I look good. So do you. I really dig the glasses."

It's been so long since I've dated, but the warmth and desire that stirs inside of me from a simple touch has so much more to do with him than a lack of contact. His touch, his affection, is unlike any other. There's something reassuring about his impact on me after all these years. It makes me feel less guilty for sleeping with someone I just met. That wasn't something I'd done before, or since, but we just connected. And, sure, maybe I was feeling a little rebellious that night, too. I was about to be a college student and I'd spent my high school years being the good girl.

Some people live a life of rebellion and break rules without consequences. I was clearly not that person. Still, I wouldn't take it back or trade Indie for anything.

"Thank you." I squeeze his hand. And I don't let go even as I go back to reading.

CHAPTER SIX

JOHN

"WHAT TIME DID YOU GET IN LAST NIGHT?" SHAW ASKS AS WE WORK OUT with the team the next morning.

"Late. After midnight." I'm going to be dragging ass today. During the season, my day begins at six a.m. and doesn't end until seven or eight at night. It's never bothered me before, the hours I spend with the team. I love these guys. They've become family.

He smirks. "I guess that means things went well?"

"Yeah, I think so. We held hands for like an hour." Since I hadn't brought any of my own schoolwork, I read one of her parenting books while she studied for class and we just hung out silently. It was nice.

My buddy laughs. "How very junior high of you, but I meant between you and the kid."

"You studied while holding hands?" Cameron asks. He's lifting next to us and I thought he was minding his own business. Obviously not.

"It was nice," I say with a shrug. I don't expect these guys to understand, but it doesn't matter.

"You have a kid together. I think it's okay to go to second base," Cameron says.

"I want to do this right." Though I have no idea what right is, and these fools clearly aren't any help. "Like ask her on a date but I can't exactly do that."

"Let me get this straight," Shaw starts. "You want advice on asking out your baby momma?"

They bust up laughing.

"I hate both of you." Apparently, I'm on my own figuring this out. "Can we keep this between us for now? I need to talk with coach. I don't want him to hear it from someone else."

"Yeah, of course," Cameron says. They both nod their agreement.

"But, uh, did you want me to pass her a note to find out if she likes you? Maybe chaperone the two of you at the movies?" Cameron is a sophomore transfer. Funny guy and super talented ball player. Because of the transfer rules he has to sit out this year, but he's going to be a force next season.

"Actually, smart ass, that gives me an idea. Can you guys make yourselves invisible tomorrow night? I want to invite Rylee and Indie over to the house."

Cameron looks like he might make another crack, but Shaw claps him on the shoulder and squeezes. "Whatever you need, man."

* * *

"The place looks so much bigger when it isn't packed with people." Rylee tilts her head up and scans the entryway. I remember all too well what it was like walking into this place for the first time. I couldn't believe I was going to get to live here. Still can't.

"I thought we could let Indie run around in the court while we study."

Rylee smiles tentatively. "Admit it, you're trying to convert our daughter into a jock?"

Our daughter. My chest feels a little funny hearing those two words. Three nights of hanging out as a trio, and I can feel Rylee starting to trust me a tiny bit.

In the gym, I flip on the lights and Indie takes off running. She heads straight for the rack of balls. It's amazing, I thought this place was childproof, but within seconds I have a vision of her pulling the entire contraption down on top of herself.

I jog to beat her there, grab a ball, and put the rest in the small supply cabinet.

She holds the basketball in two hands. She's so small, but she clings to it with everything she has while eyeing the hoop. Lifting her, I say, "Show me what you got."

With a lot of lift and a little extra help getting the ball over the rim, she makes her first basket. More pride than I've ever felt making a shot fills my chest as she squeals with joy. Rylee claps from the sideline.

When I put her on the ground, Indie takes off for her mom. Rylee hugs her tight and twirls with her. I rebound the ball and dribble it over to them.

"What about you, Mom? Got any sweet moves?"

"On the court, no." Her lips twist into a teasing smile and blood rushes through my body with a million sexy thoughts of all the moves I'd like to see from her.

"Gonna want to see those later," I say, my voice gruff.

We sit together on the far side, backs resting against the wall and our books laid out in front of us. Indie eventually tires out and rummages through the bag of toys and books Rylee brought to keep her entertained.

I run interference as much as I can so that Rylee can get some studying done, knowing I'll have time later when they leave.

"I should get her home soon," Rylee says, as our little girl starts to cry for no reason. Or, well, I'm sure there's a reason but I haven't a clue what set her off. Indie doesn't talk a lot. Rylee had mentioned that the first night I found out I had a daughter, but I was too overwhelmed to be concerned at the time. Now, though, I wonder if it's something I should be worried about.

"I set up a crib in my room if you want to try it out. Maybe she can rest a while here and we can keep hanging out?"

"You bought a crib?" Rylee's head tilts to the side as she studies my face.

"Yeah. I wanted to be prepared in case…" I trail off. "I just wanted to be prepared."

"I hate the idea of her staying anywhere without me. I guess that isn't fair. I know you're trying, and I appreciate it."

"I don't want to take her away from you. You're an amazing mother, Rylee. Truly, I just want to help. Well, no, that isn't all I want. I want to be a dad to her and a partner to you. If that means she naps here while you study or I take her for an afternoon or a night, then we'll do it at a pace you're comfortable with."

Indie's meltdown pulls us away from the conversation before we've finished.

"Let's try out this crib then," Rylee says. I can tell she's uneasy, but she scoops up our daughter and I lead them down the hall to my room.

Indie goes straight for the purple corner of my bedroom. I take Rylee's hand. Her soft palm and slender fingers curl around mine.

It doesn't take a lot of coaxing to get Indie to lay down inside the crib. I take the baby monitor and tuck it into my back pocket, and Rylee and I leave.

With our backs against the hall wall, we wait and listen. After a few seconds of silence, my attention is taken by the woman next to me. Her dark hair falls past her shoulders. She's wearing her glasses again tonight. I'm choosing to believe it's because she knows I dig them. I'm also choosing to believe the faint scent of perfume was for me.

I'll be honest, I'm looking for any reason to convince myself she's into me. Maybe my memory of that night is better than hers. I don't know if she'd be here if it weren't for Indie, but I know that I've hoped to see her again a thousand times over.

"I think she's asleep," Rylee says. "I can't believe she didn't fuss."

I'm in a bit of a daze staring at her, relearning every detail from the light smattering of freckles on her cheekbones to the deep green of her eyes. Rylee's gaze drops to my mouth and then slowly moves up. The air around us is charged.

I stroke her cheek and then let my thumb slowly slide down to one side of her lips. My heart is hammering in my chest as I bring my lips down to hers. Tender and careful, I slant my mouth over hers. For several moments, neither of us moves. I lavish in the pleasure shooting through my body. Simple, uncomplicated, magic. All the things our situation is not. Our bodies say otherwise. Or, well, mine does.

I move my lips only a millimeter so I can speak. "I missed you."

Breathing her air, talking to her, kissing her, just being nearby. It was only one night, but it set the bar for every woman I've met since her.

And here she is trampling over the bar like it was nothing. So much more than I ever could have imagined.

"I'd normally invite you up to my room, but there's another girl occupying it currently."

She smiles. "I hope it isn't serious."

"Oh yeah, really serious, but I'm pretty confident I can juggle both of you."

Rylee giggles. The sound and the playful tilt of her lips make her look younger. Man, she's been through so much. Life is crazy. It's a wonder she doesn't hate me. Or at the very least resent the hell out of me.

I've been living it up at college like everyone else and she hasn't been able to.

"Come on. I have a backup plan."

Taking her hand, I lead Rylee downstairs. The house is quiet. I'm a little surprised that the guys heeded my request so easily and made themselves scarce. Shaw is probably at Sydney's apartment, and Benny and Cameron mentioned going to The Hideout with some other guys on the team. I'm not sad about having the place, and Rylee, all to myself.

Before we get to the theater room, I pause and kiss her again. "Wanna watch a movie?"

"Sure," she says, breathless.

Pulling her into the room, I come up short and Rylee walks into my back.

Shaw's bare ass blinds me.

"Dude," I say and cover my eyes.

"What?" Rylee asks, peering around me. She presumably gets the same eyeful I did. "Oh."

"Seriously guys?" I ask, still not uncovering my eyes. I can hear them moving around though, hopefully putting their clothes back on.

"You said to make ourselves invisible," Shaw says, like that's a good excuse for boning in our theater room. Though, that was exactly what I had in mind when I dragged Rylee down here.

"You can uncover your eyes," Sydney says. I wait a few seconds more just to be sure before I drop my hand.

She swats at Shaw. "I told you we should have went in the bathroom."

He's pulling his T-shirt over his head. "They were upstairs. This was safer."

"Clearly." Sydney smooths out her dress and steps forward. "Hi, I'm Sydney. You must be Rylee. I've heard so much about you."

"Nice to meet you," Rylee says. "Sorry we interrupted. We were going to watch a movie."

"A movie, huh?" Shaw snickers.

Behind Rylee's head, I flip him off. "Indie's asleep in my room."

"I'm bummed I didn't get to meet her too," Sydney says. "How old is she?"

"Twenty-two months," Rylee says. "She'll be two in December. Do you want to see a picture?"

"Absolutely."

While the girls huddle together and Rylee shows Sydney pictures, Shaw steps to me.

"I assume things are going well. Or it's going so bad that a movie is the only option where you can't put your foot in your mouth."

"Definitely not the latter," I say as I watch Rylee. She lights up as Sydney fawns over a photo of Indie.

Definitely not the latter.

CHAPTER SEVEN
RYLEE

WHEN SYDNEY AND SHAW LEAVE US IN THE THEATER ROOM, JOHN RUNS A hand through his hair and scans the room. "Well, this place probably needs to be sanitized."

He seems much more bothered about it than I am. How exciting. Getting naked in the theater room with your hot boyfriend, totally carefree and unworried about being caught. Silly things that I haven't given much thought to, but that I now think I might have missed out on.

I want a taste of all the fun and spontaneity John and I might have if things were different.

I walk fully into the room and turn in a circle. "Let's have sex in here."

Indigo eyes widen. "You want to…" He trails off as if he's afraid to finish that question.

"Yes." I nod. *Desperately.*

He still doesn't move so I lift my shirt over my head. Nerves make my fingers clumsy and I'm certain he can see my entire body shaking.

His fiery gaze rakes over me, heating my insides, but he's still frozen.

I drop my shirt on the closest leather chair. "It can't be any worse than the bathroom we had sex in last time."

He winces and the bubble of attraction we were living in for a few seconds pops.

"Oh, come on, I was teasing," I say and walk to him. "That night was amazing. I'm not some fragile thing now just because I had a kid."

"I know." His tone sounds like he's convincing himself as much as me.

"Did I misread this? Do you not want to…" Now it's my turn to trail off without finishing a question. Oh crap, maybe I'm reading desire for and interest in me when it's just our daughter he wants. Which, of course, is fine, but I'd rather not be standing here in my bra if that's the case.

"No, of course not. I'm stoked to have found you again and I want…" He motions to my naked upper body. "All that you're working with. Seriously, wow, my memory did not do you justice," he says, staring at my cleavage spilling out over the top of my bra. He doesn't remember because pregnancy increased their size by a full cup that never went away.

"But–" he starts.

I clap a hand over his lips. "Does that but include anything that would make our having sex tonight illegal, dangerous, or otherwise harmful in some way?"

He shakes his head slowly. I feel his lips pull up into a smile under my palm.

"Then I don't care. For the next thirty minutes or even an hour, however much time we have until Indie wakes up, I want to pretend I found that really awesome guy I met at a frat party and we're having a fun and crazy night like two normal college kids."

He leans down to take my mouth as his strong arms pick me up. John walks us toward the back row of leather chairs. Pulling his lips away from mine, he kisses my nose and then asks, "You're sure?"

I nod.

"And you're not going to disappear on me this time?"

"I'm not going anywhere," I promise as his mouth crashes back down on me.

We fall back onto the chair. John can't really lie down because he's so tall, until he raises the arm rest between two chairs. I spread out along both and he angles his body to cover me. He grins down at me. Placing kisses along my collarbone, he cups me over my bra. He takes his time dropping hungry kisses all over my heated skin.

One arm goes around my waist and his hand reaches up to unfasten my bra. I'm all too happy to help. I need more of his mouth and I need it immediately.

"Damn, Ry," he murmurs against my skin. His hands stay on my boobs, but his mouth travels south, licking and nipping my stomach.

I'm lost in sensation, enjoying the way he adores my body. One of his hands finds mine and intertwines our fingers, then lifts it over my head. It's only when I can't touch him that I realize how much I want to. It's been so long. Each caress, each response is magnified. Or maybe that's just being with John.

With my free hand, I reach under his shirt. His skin is warm, muscles corded and defined. John shifts so the bulge in his jeans brushes against my sensitive pussy. Even through my jeans, the jolt of pleasure it brings makes me call out, "John."

I drop my hand to undo his pants. With a little help, I manage to get his dick free. I stroke him as he pumps into my hand.

Abruptly, he stands. He pulls his shirt over his head and then works on removing his jeans and boxers completely, all while staring down at me with such desire that it makes my heart pound in my chest. He takes the baby monitor from his back pocket and sets it upright on the floor and then pulls a condom from his wallet and tosses it on the chair. I bite back a giggle. He'd done the exact same thing last time. Taken the condom out and then tossed it beside me on the bathroom vanity.

I've replayed that scene over in my head so many times. At first, I wanted to slap myself for being so impulsive. Why couldn't I have just given him a blowjob or let him feel me up? But after Indie was born, I stopped placing blame. I'd been given a gift. The way it impacted my life didn't always feel like one, but my daughter was the absolute light of my life.

I don't feel any of that hesitation now. In fact, I'm basically floating as he undresses me.

His cock twitches and leaks as I roll the latex over him. For a moment it's just us, naked, taking each other in and then it's as if someone fired the start gun. John pulls me onto his lap and carefully I sink down on top of him.

"Wow." It's not the most poetic sentence to come out of my mouth, but it perfectly sums up every thought in my head.

"Right?" John asks with a chuckle. "Two seconds inside of you and I don't know my own name. Fuck you feel so good."

I start to shift, and he grabs my waist. "Wait."

His sexy smile pulls into a wide grin. "As soon as you move, I'm not going to be able to take it slow and I want to revel in this for just a moment longer."

He stares into my eyes. He brings a big palm up to my cheek and I lean into his touch.

"This may be a weird time to mention this. You know, since my cock is buried inside of you and all, but, uh, I'm really looking forward to spending more time with you."

"Same." I rest my arms on his shoulders. "But there's a little girl upstairs that has a habit of waking up an hour after bedtime, so let's chat about that later."

He grins.

"Can I move now? Technically we're having sex, but I was so looking forward to being manhandled."

"Manhandled, huh?" His grip on my waist tightens.

"Yes. Please?" I am not beyond begging.

Instead of answering, he lifts his hips and thrusts into me.

"Something like that?" he asks.

"Yes." My eyes close. He takes over every part of me. Body, mind, heart, and soul. I'm not sure if I believe in love at first sight, but I believe in this all-consuming feeling anytime I'm near him. It was the same that night. An undeniable attraction and chemistry.

John moves us so that I'm sprawled on my back along the chairs. He takes both of my hands in one of his and pumps into me. His lips take mine, hard and controlling. Our kiss gets deeper and more frantic the closer we get.

As the orgasm slowly builds and then slams into me, I get absolutely everything I wanted. Hot sex in the theater room and, more importantly, him.

JOHN PLAYS WITH MY HAIR AS I LEAN AGAINST HIM IN A POST-SEX HAZE. "YOU know, you could stay. Indie's already asleep."

"I can't. I still need to read for classes tomorrow."

"Oh shit." He rakes a hand through his hair. "I'm sorry."

"No, don't be. Tonight was great. I need to figure out how to juggle things better. Indie and I have kept a really rigorous schedule and I'm still struggling to manage it all."

"I meant what I said the other night. I want to help. Let me. What can I do to make things easier on you?"

"Well. Thursday night there's this thing. The Creative Writing department puts it on once a year. Department professors set up this mock pitch fest."

"Like book pitches?"

"Yeah. And each professor chooses one student to work with on the book for the rest of the year. It's not likely I'll get selected, but just the pitch practice will be great. They announce their selections at the department Halloween party."

"The department has a Halloween party?"

"Oh yeah. Apparently, it's quite an event. My professors have been talking it up for months. I wasn't planning on entering because I can't really take Indie to something where I need her to sit still and be quiet, and if I get selected that means adding even more to my plate-"

"Done."

"Really? You don't even know the details."

"Doesn't matter. I'm there. What time?"

"The pitch fest starts at seven. Can you be at my place by six forty-five? It would probably be easier on Indie if you watch her there."

He hesitates but nods slowly. "Yeah."

"You're sure?"

"Yes." He squeezes me against him and kisses my neck. "I'll be there."

CHAPTER EIGHT
JOHN

WE'RE MESSING AROUND AFTER PRACTICE. TWO ON TWO. CAMERON AND I against Shaw and Benny. Shaw's a talented dude. He's a great offensive player, but his defense is killer. I've got the ball at the wing. With a cocky grin, he stands in front of me in position, trying to strip me of the ball. Not today, fucker. I feel too good to let him best me.

What a crazy week. Each day that's passed has just made me more thankful though. Spending time with Rylee and Indie is the best part of every day. All day long I walk around with a smile on my face, knowing I'll get to hang with them later. I head over every night after practice, hang with Indie for about an hour before she goes to bed. That gives Rylee some time to do school stuff so that when our daughter is asleep, we can spend time together.

I never pictured dating like this, but I can't say I hate it.

I fake left and then dribble behind my back and go right. Shaw curses under his breath. "You cocky bastard. Get that weak shit out of here," he says, as he hustles to stop me from getting around him.

Cameron is posting on Benny. I send a high pass to him and jog to the top of the key to give him some space to work.

Shaw moves down, ready to help Benny defend, if needed. Cameron drop-steps and tries to get a shot off, but Benny and Shaw have him trapped. He sends the ball back to me and I take it to the basket. I see Shaw coming toward me, but I manage to get the ball up and into the net before he gets a hand in my face. He clips me on the way down.

"With the foul," Cameron says and holds his wrist up for me to tap.

I take my shot from the free throw line. It sails up and in. I might not be as deadly on defense as Shaw, but I never miss a free shot.

"And one." I pause in the follow through with a smirk aimed right at my buddy. His defense cost him today. I always capitalize on the and one.

"That's game," Cameron says.

Shaw rebounds the ball and bounces it hard against the wood floor. "Time for another game?"

"No, I have to get to Rylee's. She's got an event tonight. I'm watching Indie on my own."

"Poor kid." He grins. "Things are going well then?"

"Yeah. Things are great."

"Told your parents?"

I wince. "No. I thought I should tell them in person. They're coming down for the game next weekend."

"Good plan. Catch them off guard and then toss the baby at them. Everyone loves babies."

"They'll be all right, I think." I hope.

I check my phone for the time. "Fuck. I'm late. See you guys later."

"I'll keep my phone nearby in case of emergency," Shaw calls after me.

After a quick shower and change, I head for Rylee's apartment.

She opens the door with Indie in her arms. "You're late. I wasn't sure you were going to make it."

"Sorry. I lost track of time."

Indie squeals when she sees me, which makes Rylee hurriedly handing her off to me less awkward.

"Hey, pretty girl," I say and kiss her soft, sticky cheek.

"I'll have my phone on silent, but I'll check between pitches. The event is in the English building on the second floor. I laid out pajamas for her. If she has trouble falling asleep, call me and I can try to sing to her or something."

"We'll be fine." I grab her wrist and pull her to me for a kiss. "So will you."

She takes a deep breath. "Thank you. I'm nervous."

"Go kill it. We've got it here." I take Indie's hand. "Don't we?"

Rylee smiles as she looks between us. "That's a good look for you."

"And that is a good look for you," I say. Her hair is down and curled. Her normal jeans and T-shirt have been replaced with black pants and a white button-down. She has on those sexy glasses and a touch more makeup than normal, I think. She looks sexy and smart.

She leans forward and kisses Indie. "Bye. Call if you need me."

She's still slow to leave, watching us as she opens the door and steps out.

When she's finally gone, I look at my daughter. "Looks like it's just us. What should we do first?"

I set her down and she walks to the bookshelf in the living room.

"You are your mother's daughter," I say, sprawling out to sit on the floor. I take up a good portion of it with my long legs. Indie hands me three books and then sits on my lap.

She babbles as I read. Some of the books are pretty entertaining and soon I realize I've read nine books instead of the three I intended.

"How about a bath?"

The b word turns out to be the word that sets off an hour-long struggle to get my daughter clean and in bed. All week she's effortlessly gone into the bathroom for her bath. I've seen her play in the bubbles and squeal with delight. I know the kid likes baths, but tonight it's as if I'm torturing her. She thrashes and climbs out every time I place her in the tub.

"Just have to get clean, sweet pea." I'm also trying every form of endearment I know in hopes it's the magic password that unlocks the sweet child I know is in there. Sweet pea isn't it.

I get soap in her eye trying to quickly wash her, which obviously doesn't help.

The bathroom is soaked, so am I, by the time I get her to her room. She's good and worked up now. I forego the pajamas but manage to get her in a diaper and rub some of the nighttime soothing lotion Rylee always puts on her before bed.

She's really wailing now. I refuse to call Rylee for help. I've got this. Probably.

There's absolutely no getting Indie into her crib. My heart breaks as she sobs into my shoulder. I pace and pat her back. I pull out my phone and bring up a picture of Rylee and Indie I took at The White House in the gym. Indie clutches onto the device and her sobs get a little quieter. She's got herself so upset she's hiccupping too.

"Mommy will be home soon, sweetheart." My voice mixed with the photo seems to be helping so I keep reassuring her as I pace.

Sweet little Indie is heavy. Forget lifting weights, this is the best workout I've had in a long while. My arms ache from holding up her limp body.

"I'm sorry," I apologize to my daughter. "I'm not as good at any of it as mommy is, but I'm trying. We'll be okay, right?"

She's quiet. I pull the phone from her hands, but I'm too afraid to move her to check to see if she's sleeping. I creep to the couch and slowly lower us onto it. It takes some weight off my arms and I let out a long breath. Man, if this kid isn't tired by now, there's no hope. I'm exhausted.

My arms are spent. I lay down with her on my chest and pull a blanket over the top of her. Her droopy eyes flutter open and then close. I shut mine. Maybe if I pretend to sleep, she'll take the hint.

That's my last thought. The next thing I know Rylee is standing over me with Indie in her arms, talking to her in a hushed tone.

"Hey," she says to me. I sit up and run a hand over my hair. My T-shirt clings to my body with sweat where Indie slept on top of me.

She disappears toward Indie's bedroom and I stand and stretch. I check the time surprised it's only ten. Man, no wonder Rylee struggles to get shit done. Three hours and I'm toast. And we probably slept one of those hours.

When she returns, she's barefoot and her hair is pulled up into a ponytail. "Are you okay?"

"Yeah." My voice is deep from sleep. "Is she okay? I might have just traumatized our child with my subpar bedtime skills."

"She's fine. Did she give you a rough time?"

"Everything was going great until I started getting her ready for bed. I am not as good at this as you." I rub at my chest. "Fuck, I'm exhausted. I have a new appreciation for what you've been managing on your own."

"She likes routine. She'll get used to you putting her to bed if you do it more."

I might have to psych myself up for that, but I don't admit that out loud. "How'd pitching go?"

"Good. I think." She takes a seat on the couch next to me and pulls her feet up under her. "The first couple of times I did it, I was really nervous, but it got easier."

"What were you pitching?"

"It's this young adult fantasy novel I've been working on for like three years. I've rewritten the first twenty pages so many times." She shakes her head.

"Fantasy, huh?"

"Mermaids and underwater adventures. An evil king and a swoony prince trying to redeem the family name."

"Sounds awesome."

"Yeah, well. It can only be awesome if I actually write it. Otherwise, it's just a really great idea. The world is full of those."

"Can I read what you have?"

"What if you hate it?"

"That seems unlikely."

"I don't know. Maybe."

"Did you have any professors interested in working on it with you?"

"A few seemed interested. They might have been faking or had others that they felt were a better match. I won't know until the Halloween party."

"Is it a costume party?"

"Oh yeah. The more elaborate, the better." Her chin tucks and her eyes fall to her lap. "I'm not sure I'll go."

"Why the hell not?"

"For starters, I don't have anyone to watch Indie. You have a game. Lindsey has other plans, I'm sure. Besides. I'm not sure it's a great idea to take on another project this semester. As I was talking to some of the professors, I realized just how much extra work this could be."

"I can help more."

She meets my gaze and smiles sadly. "I know you want to, but your schedule is as crazy as mine."

"We'll figure it out." I take her hands in mine and squeeze.

She climbs into my lap and kisses me. "I still need to do some reading tonight."

I slide my hands around her waist and pull her shirt out from the waistband of her pants so I can get my hands on her bare skin. "Guess I'll have to be quick."

Which is never a problem with Rylee. Every time I touch her, I feel like the luckiest guy in the world. She helps me get her out of her clothes and I lie her down on the couch. Hurriedly I strip myself and cover my dick with a condom.

"One of these days I want to spend hours worshipping you."

She pulls me down on top of her and her lips take mine, greedy and demanding. So fucking sexy.

I push into her and just like every other time it takes my breath for a moment.

"You smell like lavender and bubble bath."

"I'm pretty sure there's more on me than Indie."

She laughs and then moans when I thrust deeper.

She clings to my shoulders and moves under me. We're dashing to the finish line trying to beat the real world that threatens to burst the happy bubble we both want to live in.

Dating the mystery girl I dreamed about all these years is nothing like I expected. It's so much better.

"WHAT ARE YOU DOING THIS WEEKEND?" I ASK AS I FINISH GETTING DRESSED.

Rylee grabs her books and her laptop and takes them to the dining room table. "No plans. I usually take Indie to story time at the library on Saturdays. Do you want to come?"

She goes to the fridge and pulls out two iced coffee drinks. I realize then how tired she must really be. I feel it too, or at least a fraction of it. Pains me to leave. Not that I can be much help while Indie sleeps anyway.

"I don't think I can. We have a game Saturday."

"Oh." She stops short, brows knitted in concentration. "Right. I forgot. Home game this weekend, right?"

"Someone's been checking in on the jocks, huh?"

"Just on you. I'd offer to come, but I'm not sure Indie would last more than an hour."

"I don't know. She's a pretty big fan, I think."

"She's a fan of yours, mostly."

"It's fine if you don't feel up to coming, but I was hoping you'd come out to dinner with my parents after." I shove my hands in my pockets and attempt to look charming.

I don't think I succeed because her mouth gapes open.

"I haven't told them yet, but I know once I do, they're going to want to meet you."

"Wow. Yeah. I mean, of course." She wrings her hands together. "Holy crap. I'm already nervous."

I step to her and take her into my arms. "They're gonna love you two."

CHAPTER NINE
RYLEE

JOHN'S MOM PULLS ME INTO A HUG. IT'S THE THIRD OR FOURTH TIME SHE'S clutched me to her chest. She's tall and freaky strong. I'm struggling to breathe as she rocks us back and forth. "Oh, you're such a brave girl doing it on your own these past two years."

Indie is loving all the attention the Datson family gives her. John holds her as his dad, John Sr., tickles her stomach. The Datson brothers, all dark haired, tall, and varying shades of dark blue eyes, are something else. Jacob, the youngest at fourteen, is the most talkative of the group. Julian, seventeen, has a friendly smile but barely spoke all dinner. Jayden is sixteen and rounds out the brothers as the sullen one who spent most of the time looking at his phone.

I'm finally released, and I take a deep breath.

"You three have to come up to the farm some weekend," Mrs. Datson, or Jennifer as I've been instructed to call her, says.

"My schedule is nuts until the end of the season," John says.

She swats at him and then wraps her arms around him and Indie.

"Anything you need, you let me know," she instructs me. She points a finger at John. "Make sure my beautiful granddaughter has everything she needs."

She cups his cheek and looks to Indie so lovingly. I should have known that John's family would be as great as he is, but I breathe a little easier knowing my daughter has two parents, and two sets of grandparents to love her. Maybe we'll get through this yet.

The Datson family piles into their SUV outside of my apartment. Indie waves her little hand as they drive off.

"I hope you didn't give my mom your phone number," John says, handing over Indie to me.

"I did. She gave me hers, too. Why?"

His lips tug up and he gives me that charming smile. "I predict daily phone calls. Regret meeting me yet?"

I lean up on my toes to kiss him. "Not even a little."

OVER THE NEXT WEEK, JOHN STAYS AT MY PLACE MOST NIGHTS. INDIE IS loving it as much as I am. The team had an away game today, but they're headed back. I have a meeting with my advisor in thirty minutes.

Lindsey's playing with Indie in my room while I get ready. I check my phone to see if he's texted recently. He said he'd let me know as soon as they arrived. I expected to hear from him by now, but I'm hoping he's on the way over. It's less than a two-hour flight from California so adding a little extra time for baggage and driving to my place, I figure he should be here in the next five minutes. Which means I can make it to my meeting on time. I might even be a few minutes early. Imagine that.

"Did she say why she wanted to meet with you?"

"No. And I'm trying really hard not to think about it. If the department cuts my TA position, I'm sunk."

"I'm sure that isn't it." She picks up the book on my bed and flips through it. "Did you make this?"

"Yeah. It's a little photo journal of Indie. I made it for John. All the big moments in her life before they met."

"It's the cutest. You're so dang talented." She scoots off the bed. "All right, girls. I need to get to the library. You're sure Datson is going to be here before you need to leave?"

"Yeah." I add another coat of mascara to my lashes. My phone beeps. "That's probably him. They're…" My words trail off when I finish reading the text.

"Well?"

"They're delayed. The plane landed but they don't have a gate so they're waiting. It doesn't look like he's going to make it." Even if he stepped off the plane right now, it'd take him too long to get to my apartment. I toss my phone on the bed without responding and go to my laptop. "I'll email my advisor and see if I can reschedule."

"No, I've got this. I'll stay with her until you get back."

"What about your plans?"

"My study group will be fine without me for an hour. Seriously, go. I've got you."

"Thank you." I don't bother putting up a fight because I need the help.

Dr. Matthews is in her office sitting behind her desk when I get to the second floor of the English building.

"Come in." She waves me inside.

I take a seat in front of her desk. My nerves are frayed.

"Thank you for coming by."

"Of course. Is everything okay? I'm freaking out a little."

"Oh, I'm sorry. It's good news. I should have mentioned that in my email." She leans forward. "I've selected your fantasy novel from the pitch fest. I want to work with you on it."

My body relaxes, but my heart skips several beats. "You do?"

"Yes. It's a great concept and your characters are well thought out and interesting."

"Wow. I don't know what to say."

"Say that you're as eager as I am to get started. Formal announcements aren't until next Friday at the Halloween party, but I'd love to get started right away." She turns to stare at her computer monitor. "I've got your schedule pulled up. I could do four o'clock after you're done with classes."

"On which day?" I have to pick up Indie by five, but maybe I could figure something out one day a week.

"As many as you can."

"Oh. I didn't realize we would meet so often."

"Not forever, but for the first month or so, I think it would be good to have a time scheduled to touch base. This is a really hands-on process with the goal being that you have a finished manuscript next spring. I will give you everything I have, knowledge, resources… but you have to work hard too."

With a gulp, I nod. "Of course. I appreciate the offer. Can I think about it?"

She cocks her head to the side. I doubt anyone ever has to think about it. It's such a great opportunity, but how am I going to make it work? I can't expect Lindsey to be available to help when John and I are busy. I could hire a sitter, but I already feel guilty about the number of hours Indie is in daycare.

"It's just that I have a daughter. She's almost two and juggling it all is… taking more of a toll than I expected." It feels good to admit it out loud. I am struggling. School is taking more time than I expected. It's harder, too. And Indie is more active every day. I thought the baby years were hard but keeping up with her now is exhausting. I want to do it all, but maybe it's time to acknowledge it's more than I can handle on my own.

Her smile is warm and understanding. "Sure. Take as much time as you need."

My legs move slowly back to my car. Maybe if I went part-time. The thought of extending college for another three or four years, instead of two, makes my stomach cramp. Can I manage being a mom and a full-time student for that long?

I let myself into the apartment and force a smile for Indie as she runs toward me. "Hey, sweet girl."

John stands from the couch. He's still dressed in the team travel jacket. "Hey."

"Linds leave?"

"Yeah. About ten minutes ago."

I nod and set my purse on the dining room table.

He closes the distance between us and wraps me in his arms. "I missed my girls."

"Da-da."

We both freeze and look down at Indie.

"Did she just say dad?"

My heart squeezes. "Yes."

He scoops her up and kisses her face. "That's right, sweet cheeks. Daddy."

She tries it again.

"Traitorous thing." I smile. "She's only said mama once and I'm starting to believe I made it up in my head."

He carries her into the living room, and I follow. We sit on the couch and Indie grabs for his phone. I'm surprised when he hands it over so easily.

"She likes to look at my pictures," he says by way of explanation.

"She also likes to put things in the bathtub."

"I'll keep an eye on her." He sits back against the couch and pulls Indie onto his lap. "What did your advisor want to talk about?"

I pick at a piece of lint on my pants. "She selected my book from pitch fest. She wants to work together."

"That's amazing." He bounces Indie on his legs. "Yay, mommy."

She claps a couple of times and then goes back to swiping through pictures on his phone.

"Congratulations." He kisses me quick.

"Thanks. It's great, but I'm not sure it's the best idea right now."

"What? Why?"

"Because I'm already burning the candle at both ends, trying to get schoolwork done and take care of Indie."

"I can help more." His forehead wrinkles in concentration.

"I know that you mean well, but you don't have the extra time to give either. I have to focus on what's important right now. Taking care of Indie and finishing school. Everything else will have to wait. I think that needs to include us."

He looks completely crestfallen. "You don't want to be with me?"

"I do, of course I do, but I'm overwhelmed. I need to slow down a little."

"A little or a lot?"

"I'm not sure."

"What about Indie?"

"You can still see her, of course. She's absolutely in love with you." We both are if I'm being honest. I think I fell for him the first night and I don't think I ever really stood back up. "We'll work out a schedule that works for both of us."

"I don't want to lose you, Rylee. My life finally feels like it makes sense. Why I spent the last few years feeling off-balance and unsure of my future. I was waiting for you and Indie."

"You won't lose us. Ever." I plaster a big smile on my face even though my heart breaks. What if he finds someone else or decides that waiting for me isn't worth it?

We spend the next hour working out a schedule. It all feels so tragic. I want to spend every moment as a family of three, but the reality is that I need to make sure I have time for studying. And John needs time with Indie by himself. He's a great dad that just needs more practice doing it on his own.

"I guess I should go," he says. "It isn't technically my night, but do you want me to take her so you can work on stuff?"

"No. Thank you. I'll bring her by The White House tomorrow morning." I can't think of anything I want more than to cuddle my baby girl all night.

"Okay." He shoves his hands in his pockets.

"Wait." I leave him in the living room while I run to my bedroom and get the book I made. "This is for you. It's sort of like a memory book. I started it when she was a baby. Every month I wrote a little about something funny or amazing she'd done, then added in the pictures."

He takes it into his hands and stares down at the cover. It's a picture of Indie as a baby. Her first smile. "Thank you."

"Of course."

He gives me an awkward kiss on the cheek, and I walk him toward the door. "See you later, Rylee."

"See ya," I whisper.

And then he leaves.

CHAPTER TEN

JOHN

I'M LYING IN THE MIDDLE OF THE COURT, MY BACK AGAINST THE HARD wood, staring up at the ceiling. The ball rests on my stomach, one hand holding it in place. I love the feel of the worn leather against my palm. It's comforting. Uncomplicated. Everything this situation isn't.

"Thought I might find you in here." Shaw's voice echoes in the quiet gym.

I don't look up but feel him take a seat next to me. "Are you okay?" he asks. "Been a week and you've said less than two sentences. You didn't even scold Conner for sitting down as he handed out cups at the party last night."

"Doesn't matter. It's all bullshit."

"From the man who once told me that a good host was the hallmark of a baller party."

"That isn't what I was talking about."

"I know. It's just a pause. You two will find your way back to one another. Look at me and Sydney. We almost got together and then didn't. We still made our way back. You and Rylee will too. You guys have a lot going on right now."

"I could deal with not being with her if it meant it took a load off her, but it doesn't. Not really. Talk about a pause. She put off college for two years to raise Indie. And she's talking about going part-time after this semester. I wish I could give her back some of that time, help her out more. I was here goofing off, worrying about fucking cups."

"You didn't know."

"But I do now." I sit up. "There has to be something I can do."

He takes the ball from my lap. "We'll have to figure it out after practice. We need to leave in fifteen minutes. But after practice, let's go to The Hideout. You buy the drinks and I'll give you all my best ideas."

"Maybe invite Sydney. We all know she's the brains." I get to my feet. "I've gotta change. I'll meet you over there."

"I resent that," he calls after me. "But noted. She'll be there. We've got your back, man."

I climb the stairs feeling just the tiniest bit hopeful. I've sulked all week. Aside from the two nights I got to spend with Indie, and the brief encounters with Rylee, the week sucked. All the usual joys, basketball, friends, parties, lost their luster.

Hard to believe in such a short amount of time how much my life has changed, but it has. From the second I laid eyes on Indie.

I sit on my bed with my phone. We have a light practice tonight and then we leave early tomorrow for an away game. My clothes are strewn on the bed where I dumped them after doing laundry earlier. I pick through to find shorts and a T-shirt. My fingers brush against something hard and I uncover the book Rylee gave me.

At least three times I've started to flip through it. I know she meant it as a nice gesture, but that first photo of Indie as a baby gets me every time. I hate that I wasn't there.

I open it and steel myself for that pang of hurt. Little, sweet Indie. Eyes closed, face still swollen and red. She's got a pink and blue hat on her tiny head with a big bow and she's wrapped up in a white blanket.

Beneath the photo, it has the words *Chapter One* and then several paragraphs written about Indie as if she's the main character of a great novel. I guess she is.

Chapter after chapter, photo after photo, Rylee cataloged two years of our daughter's life. Big things like learning to walk and her first tooth, and little things like her preference for peas over green beans.

I don't want to miss any more of those. And, not only that, I want Rylee's take on it. I want to laugh with her over the tantrums and then celebrate the milestones together. I don't just want a daughter. I want a family.

RYLEE

"I AM DIGGING THIS WHOLE SEXY MERMAID PRINCESS THING YOU HAVE going on," Lindsey says as I tug on the green skirt. It's long and skintight. I added tulle at the bottom to cover my feet.

Tonight is the English department Halloween party. John has a game in Colorado, so Lindsey offered to watch Indie for a couple of hours.

"I hope I don't have to walk up any stairs because it will be a struggle."

"Worth it. You look hot. Has Datson seen this?"

"No. We haven't talked much this week."

"Ry."

"It's okay. He's here for Indie and that's what counts."

"But you guys are crazy about each other."

"It's too much right now, Linds. I have to focus on Indie and school." I turn toward them and hold out my arms. "It's okay? Really?"

Indie claps. "Da-da."

Yeah, sweet girl, I miss him too.

"You look great. I promise," Lindsey says with a reassuring nod.

"I will not be gone long. I just need to make an appearance and talk with Dr. Matthews."

"You're still going to turn it down?"

"Yeah. It isn't the right time." I've come to terms with my disappointment. There will be other opportunities. My time is coming. I just have to be patient a few more years.

I ignore my best friend's sad face. "Okay, I'm off. Call or text if you need me." I give my daughter a kiss and thank Lindsey again.

The party is being held in a banquet room in University Hall. *Monster Mash* plays over the speakers. Students and professors are dressed up. There are more literary characters than I can count. Inspirations ranging from Harry Potter to Shakespeare.

I spot Dr. Matthews on the other side of the room and start toward her. I get punch and slow my steps. Now that I'm here, it's much harder to walk up and turn down her mentoring than it was when I rehearsed it in my head.

As I approach, she looks up from the circle of students and professors around her and smiles at me. She steps out and I meet her halfway.

"I haven't heard from you all week," Dr. Matthews says. "Can I assume no news is good news?"

"I really appreciate the offer. I do." I swallow and glance around. My gaze snags on a tall, dark head entering the room. All around, people are turning to stare. The gorgeous man dressed as a prince, crown and all, holds onto the hand of a little girl – a mermaid. My mermaid. I made us matching outfits, never dreaming we'd get to wear them together here. "I'm sorry. Can you give me a minute?" I ask, but don't wait for her response.

John glances around the room, leading Indie through the crowd. When I step into his line of vision, a grin pulls at his lips.

It feels like a dream as I walk toward them.

"What are you doing here?"

"We came to cheer on mommy, didn't we?"

"Mama!"

I squat down and hug Indie. "You said it! You said mom."

"Da-da."

I chuckle and stand with her in my arms. "Did your game end early?"

'Nah." He shakes his head. "I didn't go with the team to Colorado. I quit."

"I don't understand." I search his face. "Why?"

"I've been living out all my college dreams for the past three years. It's your turn to live yours. You didn't turn down Dr. Matthews yet, did you?"

"No, but–"

"No buts. I've got you. Let me do this. It's one small thing."

"Small? This is huge, John. You've played your last college basketball game? Couldn't you wait until the end of the semester or something?"

"Nah, not really." He shrugs. "I'm not worrying about lasts anymore. This is just the beginning."

The head of the department speaks into the microphone. "If I can get everyone's attention, we are going to announce the winners from pitch fest."

"You don't need to do this. What if you regret it and resent me later?"

"I won't."

"You don't know that."

"But I do. I've been living my college dreams. It's your turn." He takes my hand and steps closer. "Nothing is more important to me than you two. And I'm not expecting anything. You want to focus on Indie and school, and I respect that. I'll be whatever you need. Friend and co-parent. Maybe more?" He grins. "I know you want to take it slow, but I'm here. I'm following your lead."

"You make a good prince charming." I rest my hand on his chest and tug him by the gold sash. I kiss him just as they call my name.

I feel his lips pull into a smile and he steps back. Reaching down, he picks up Indie and together, they clap for me as I clumsily make my way to the stage.

A MONTH LATER, THE THREE OF US HEAD TO RAY FIELDHOUSE TO WATCH the basketball team play. Indie's in the smallest, most adorable Valley University shirt and matching blue headband. She sits on John's lap and the two of them clap and cheer. They are far more entertaining than the game.

He catches me watching and winks. We've continued taking things slow. We still split time with Indie so that I can study, and I've gotten better about drawing limits for myself. It isn't easy, though. Not with the two of them always being so dang sweet.

"Do you miss being out there?"

"No way. I've got the best seat in the house." He leans over and kisses me. "Plus, they're getting their asses handed to them. Coach is going to be pissed at halftime. Tomorrow they'll be running suicides and I'll be snuggled up with my girls."

"I love you." The words I've held in tumble out at a time I hadn't planned.

He doesn't immediately speak, and I think maybe he hasn't heard me. Then ever so slowly, an easy grin spreads across his face. "I love you too, Rylee."

Indie looks between us and claps.

THE END.

HIDEAWAY
BY CORALEE JUNE

CHAPTER ONE

"THEY FORGOT THE ANGOSTURA BITTERS, AND THE LIME JUICE WASN'T fresh. If a club is going to pride themselves on having a Drunken Elephant as their signature drink in *every single one* of their press releases, the least they can do it get the recipe right," I complained.

My cousin, Dax, laughed on the other end of the line. "You are such a cocktail snob."

My scuffed, designer thrift store heels walked down the dimly lit sidewalk toward my apartment. It was late, the flickering streetlamps illuminating the walkway and casting a glow over my bright red hair. A chill made me shiver and wrap my Max Mara puffer jacket tighter around my body. My breath was visible in the winter night air. "It's kind of my job to be picky," I replied. This was a conversation Dax and I had numerous times.

"It's seriously not fair that you have such a dream job. I'm bartending five nights a week and barely getting by. Meanwhile, you have a waitlist of like five gazillion bars and mixologists waiting for you to visit them." I knew for a fact that my cousin wasn't *barely getting by* as he so eloquently claimed. The women who frequented his bar tipped him very generously. He just poured all his money into his classic truck. Typical.

I was a blogger and influencer. My job was to visit different clubs and write up reviews of their signature drink. I knew Dax was being playful, but I still worried about him. My mom raised us both, and when she died, he was all I had left. "Do you need me to send you some money?" I asked quietly.

"No. Don't you dare. I'm fine. I'm just saving up for a new transmission, so I'm living that ramen noodle life for the next few months." We both chuckled and he continued. "Aunt Deb would be so proud of you, you know."

I smiled to myself before turning the corner toward my apartment building. "She would have ripped my bartender a new one tonight. She used to make the best Drunken Elephant," I said softly. Mom passed away from cancer just last year. It was a loss I still felt daily. She was a famous mixologist in the city and worked with bars all over the country, helping them create unique and delicious drink menus for their clientele. She taught me everything I knew, and now, I used that knowledge to review local hot spots on my viral Instagram and YouTube accounts. I inherited her ability to analyze flavors and associate them to brands, emotions, and feelings. I could pick a signature drink for any person, club, or event. Dax got her mixology genes and loved concocting new beverages. Pretty soon one of these bars was going to swoop him up. He just hadn't had his big break yet.

"Are you almost home? I hate when you walk this late," Dax said, changing the subject.

"Just a couple more blocks. I could have taken a cab, but you know how I like stretching my legs."

"Why don't you stretch your legs during the day? When it's bright outside and when the creeps are asleep?"

I rolled my eyes. I was born and raised in Chicago. I knew every street corner like the back of my hand. The city could be dangerous, but I was more than capable of taking care of myself. "I'm fine. I'll be home soon."

"You better. Listen, my break is almost over and there's a cute girl here I'm trying to impress with my cocktail skills."

"Oh?" I asked with a smile. "Well, you better get going, Romeo."

"What drink should I make a girl who's cute, flirty, fun, but has this mystery about her? She's got deep chocolate eyes you just get lost in and a vibe that's both dark and playful. When she's with her friends, she's bubbly. When she talks to me, she's got this depth. She comes in every Friday and I'm trying to get the courage to ask her on a date."

I chewed on the inside of my cheek for a moment, thinking over this mystery woman and assigning her a drink. "Make her a Basilica."

"Ahh. Haven't made one of those in a while."

"Vodka, limoncello, simple syrup, lemon juice, and sweet basil leaves. Oh, and add a strawberry for garnish. It's a refreshing cocktail that showcases the basil. Although it seems to be sweet and playful, it's impressively balanced and has a depth about it you can't quite put your finger on. Just like your mystery girl."

"You're the best, Lydia. Seriously," Dax replied.

"Have fun. Don't do anything I wouldn't do," I replied playfully before hanging up the phone.

I kept walking, feeling a slight buzz from the drinks at the club and a happiness in my chest from talking to Dax. He moved to LA a few years ago and I loved getting to chat with him. I really needed to go visit him soon. I put my cell phone in my purse and kept marching on.

The Chicago night air was crisp and cold, biting at my cheeks as I walked. The wind was like a slap to the face, but I was used to it. I noticed a shadow walking behind me but didn't think anything of it. It wasn't until I turned down an alley—a shortcut to my apartment building—that the shadow approached.

"Lydia Love," a masculine voice called out. I spun around on my heels to face the man. He had greasy hair down to his shoulders and wore a thin jacket, despite the freezing weather. "It's really you!"

I took a step backward. "And you are?"

"Well, I'm your soul mate. I've been following your Instagram since your twenty-first birthday. I knew we were meant to be together when you wore a red dress. Red's my favorite color. You were speaking to me, weren't you? Trying to tell me that you love me, too."

My heart started to race at his words. What was wrong with this guy? "I'm sorry. I don't know you. Please leave me alone," I stammered.

"But you do know me. I message you every day. I comment on all your photos. I tried sending you flowers, but I couldn't find your address until now. When I saw that you were at the Broken Bulb for drinks tonight, I knew I had to take my chance. I drove all the way from Oklahoma to see you. Now we can be together. Now we can get *married*."

I had a few creeps on my Instagram over the years. Most of the time their messages were harmless. I typically avoided my DMs because it was a mess of weirdos or influencers wanting to collaborate. If this guy had been sending me messages, I didn't see them. And it was obvious that something was wrong with this dude. I needed to get away from him. Now.

"What's your name?" I asked.

"You don't know my name?" he asked, his tone angry.

"I'm so sorry. I'm just not feeling well," I lied. I didn't think such a question would make him so furious.

"It's Bradley, Lydia. My name is *Bradley*, and I am your future husband. I brought you a wedding ring. I want you to wear it."

I wondered if I screamed if anyone would come out and save me. In big cities like Chicago, everyone liked to mind their business. "Bradley. You're scaring me."

"I'm not scaring you!" he roared. "Just come here and let me love you."

A limousine drove past, and I quickly waved them down, praying they would see me. What was I going to do? How was I going to survive this? Bradly grabbed my upper arm and I tried jerking out of his grip, but he was surprisingly strong for being so scrawny. "I love you, Lydia. I've always loved you. I just want you to love me back."

I lifted my leg and kicked him in the shin, making him double over in pain. "Go away, you freak!" I screamed, not caring if it hurt his feelings. Bradley was delusional and I needed to get away from here. I quickly kicked off my heels and made a break to run for it, but Bradly grabbed me by the neck and pulled me close. His breath was rancid. His eyes wide and wild.

"You're lucky I love you so much. I don't normally let people talk to me that way."

I whimpered. What was I going to do?

"Back off." A low growl echoed around me. It was a demanding, protective sound. Bradley let go of me to see who was intruding and I, too, looked at my savior. Thank fuck. The limousine had stopped, and a man wearing a suit and black leather gloves stood in front of me. The shadow of night hid some of his features from me, but I saw the strong line of his jaw and the harsh angle of his sharp nose. "Are you all right?" he asked me with a slight nod, his tone gravely and clipped with an accent I couldn't place. He nodded at me, and for a moment, terror and confusion had my response stunted in my throat.

"Please get him away from me," I finally croaked out.

From the limo, two large men who looked well over six feet tall approached. They grabbed Bradley by the arms and dragged him toward their car.

"I'll be with you one day, Lydia. I'll have you!" he screamed while trying to jerk out of their hold. It felt surreal, watching him being carried away like a rag doll. One of the men got annoyed with his screeching and hit him on his temple with a closed fist. Bradley slumped over, knocked out from the hit.

It was almost humorous how easily they grabbed him—how easily they picked him up and placed him in the trunk of their car. "Thank you so much. I thought he was going to get me. I'll call the police—"

"That won't be necessary."

I balked at the man just as his goons slammed the trunk shut. "What?" I asked. "What are you going to do to him?"

My mystery savior walked up, and a soft glow from an apartment above us hit his face just right. He was beautiful. His face perfectly symmetrical yet rugged all the same. A light scar was on his cheek, and his eyes were fanned with thick, dark lashes. He had eyes black as night and plush lips I wanted to run my fingers over. Something about him *screamed* danger.

He was like Glenfiddich Grand Cru, twenty-three-year-old luxury scotch. Elegant.

Only the finest international flavors. Smooth with a sandalwood finish and slight afternote of pear sorbet. Heavy. Burned when it went down. A celebratory drink, something decadent you think about with fondness. It was the sort of drink men with money running through their veins indulged in.

"What do you want me to do with him? He was attacking you when I pulled up."

"I want you to call the cops. It's their job," I scoffed. "He's been stalking me. He said all sorts of crazy things. Said we're going to get married and even had a motherfucking ring. I just met him, and he was following me home. I just think he needs to talk to a doctor. The guy needs mental help."

The nameless man observed me, cocking his head to the side as he looked me up and down. Smooth. He was smooth. Calculative. "The police won't do a damn thing. You want to help a man who might have hurt you? Raped you? Murdered you? If I take him to jail, he'll just get right back out. Can't punish a man for what he plans to do, only for what he's already done. You'll live the rest of your life wondering when he'll come for you again. That's how the system works. I can make the problem go away if you'd like."

What was he suggesting? "What are you, the mafia?" I joked. "Don't hurt him. He's just…confused. Maybe we should take him to the hospital?"

He didn't respond. I watched him as the horror I felt grew tenfold. I itched to reach for my phone. "Don't worry about him. Do not call the police, or you will regret it. I'll make sure to take him somewhere he won't hurt anyone else. Remove it from your mind."

"That's easier said than done. Am I an accomplice to a crime?" My fingers twitched, aching to grab my phone and dial 911. It was like I left one monster and found another.

"You were about to be a victim of a crime. What's your name, beautiful?"

I swallowed. "Lydia. Lydia Love." My tone was rough.

"You live nearby, Lydia Love?" he asked.

I should have said no. I shouldn't have told this strange man where I lived. Maybe I had a bit of a hero complex because he saved me from Bradley. "Just around the corner."

"I'll walk you," he replied dangerously. "Make sure you get there safely, hmm?"

"Oh, you don't have to—"

"Walk with me."

I bent down to pick up my shoes and put them back on my feet. The strange man walked up to me and grabbed my arm, steading me as I slipped the heels back on. "What's your name?" I asked.

"You don't need my name," he whispered.

Okay. This man was definitely dangerous. "And you don't need to walk me home."

His hand remained wrapped around my arm and he nodded at the driver of his limo. "Come. Let's go."

CHAPTER TWO

"WHY ARE YOU OUT THIS LATE?" HE ASKED ME AS WE TURNED THE CORNER. He still hadn't let go of my arm, and the pressure of his grip was sending a thrill throughout me I couldn't explain. Up close, he smelled like green woods and citrus. I breathed him.

"I was working. I'm a cocktail blogger," I explained.

"A cocktail blogger? Do you work for a publication?"

I glanced up at him, noting the intense way he studied me as we walked. "I sometimes freelance for a few journals, but mostly I review on my own site and socials. My blog is called Arsenic Lace."

The corner of his lip twitched. "I'll have to look you up. What made you want to do that?"

"Aside from the obvious?" I asked with a light chuckle, the adrenaline and uncertainty of before wearing off. I could do this. I could talk about my job. Talking about my job was easy. "Having a job that only requires me to work one day a week and that workday is spent drinking cocktails, it's a pretty sweet gig."

"Sounds like it," he agreed. "How does one become a *cocktail blogger?*" He didn't say it sarcastically. The mystery man sounded genuinely curious about my job, but there was a sense of amusement in his tone. A lot of people looked down their noses at influencers and bloggers.

"You follow your mother around to different nightclubs and bars, taking sips of her cocktails and learning the different flavors. She loved it. I just sort of followed in her footsteps."

He let go of me to place a hand at my lower back, guiding me closer to him. "Sounds like an unconventional relationship. Was she an alcoholic?"

I laughed. A lot of people had that perception. Even though my mother wasn't your traditional parent, she was lovely. Positive. Loving. Protective. Perfect. "No. She was more of a connoisseur. Sometimes she'd bring buckets with her to spit out her drink. She just loved developing unique flavor pallets. I inherited her superpower."

"And what superpower is that?"

"I can figure out anyone's signature drink within minutes of meeting them."

The mystery man's lip twitched once more. "And what is mine?"

We walked up to my building and stopped underneath a streetlight. The harsh shadows made him look fierce. "Glenfiddich Grand Cru, twenty-three-year-old luxury scotch."

His eyebrows rose in surprise. "Oh? And why is that?"

"Try it. You'll like it," I replied. If he wasn't going to give me his name, then I wasn't about to give my assessment of him.

"I just bought a club. We had a soft opening last week and will fully open our doors in three weeks. I want you to review it. I have one of the best mixologists in the country working there, and we're tweaking the menu."

What were the odds? "What club?" I asked.

"Satin Sheets," he replied easily. My mouth dropped open.

"You own it? That club is extremely exclusive. There was a waitlist for opening night of like fifteen thousand people. Even influencers with crazy followings can't get in."

This time, he did smile, amusement at my awe bleeding through his expression. "I own it, and we've put a lot of work into making sure every inch of the club is opulent. I want your impression of our drink menu. Stop by tomorrow night." It wasn't a suggestion, but a demand.

I licked my lips and stared at him. "Tell me your name."

The limo he'd ridden in pulled up in front of my building and one of the large men in suits opened the door for him. "Nico," he answered while walking toward the car door. "Go inside, Lydia. See you tomorrow."

He shifted his jacket, and I saw the glaring outline of a large gun holstered to his hip. I watched the taillights as he drove off, then let myself inside.

"YOU'RE NOT GOING, ARE YOU?" DAX ASKED. I HAD HIM ON SPEAKERPHONE and was currently applying highlight to my cheeks. My red hair was curled in tight spirals and I applied blended smokey eyeshadow to my lids. I looked hot. My gold, sequined dress was tight in all the right places, and the heels I wore made my long legs look dangerously sexy.

"Of course I'm going. Satin Sheets is all the rage. I was on the waitlist, but now I get to see it before anyone else!" My followers were going to go apeshit. I'd spent all day researching the club, and even thought there was no mention of the *elusive owner,* there had been a significant amount of chatter about the luxury of it all. Marble imported from Italy. Fine crystal chandeliers from France. A signature scent pumped through the vents curated by one of the most famous noses in Germany. No expense was spared. Everyone who was anyone wanted in.

I'd had an entire day to process what happened to me. I'd debated multiple times on whether or not to report Bradley, and maybe it was naïve to hope that Nico had dropped the deranged man off at the local mental health hospital, but I didn't want to know.

Do not call the police, or you will regret it.

Nico had said it so easily, like spitting threats was something he did regularly. I didn't doubt him. I knew it would be dangerous to challenge him. I told myself Bradley was insane, but ultimately decided that whatever happened to him was probably not nearly as bad as what I was imagining.

"I'm not comfortable with you going," Dax replied. "He's obviously into some mafia shit. I've watched enough crime television to predict that this isn't going to end well. I know he rescued you, but—"

"It's just a night at the club. I'll go, have a drink, write a review, and come back home. Nothing is going to happen. This opportunity is too good to pass up." My gut twisted at my words. I wasn't being completely truthful. I wanted to see Nico again. There was something about him that intrigued me in ways I couldn't explain. Mysterious. Powerful. Dangerous.

"I'm just not sure," Dax replied.

"I promise to call you as soon as I get home. Okay? And I'll take a cab this time."

"Fine," my cousin replied. "I want regular updates. If I don't hear from you, I'll be on a plane to Chicago and you know I'm broke as hell, so take my threat seriously."

I smiled. "How did mystery girl like her drink?" I asked.

He cleared his throat and started speaking in a low voice. "She really liked it. Stopped by last night. Then stayed all day. She's in the shower. I'm taking her to dinner…"

I grinned. Dax didn't do things half assed. Once he found someone he liked, they were moving in with one another within a month—then breaking up a month after that. That man jumped in with both feet, then ran for his life once he got in too deep. I predicted that this relationship would last three months. "Get off the phone then!"

"Aye, aye, captain," he teased. "Be safe. I'll call you later."

Dax hung up and I let out a sigh while staring at my reflection in the mirror. It was almost nine, and I didn't want to show up early, but after last night, I was nervous about staying out too late, also. My buzzer rang and I got up from my vanity to answer the door.

"Hello?"

"Lydia Love?" a garbled voice answered.

"Yes? Can I help you?"

"I'm Mr. Mariano's car service. I've been instructed to take you to Satin Sheets," he replied. My cheeks flushed, and I stood there dumbfounded for a moment. "Ma'am? Are you still there?"

I pressed the call button and cleared my throat. "Nico Mariano?" I asked. "He sent you?"

"Yes," he replied, his tone annoyed. "Mr. Nicolo Mariano sent me. Please, ma'am. It's cold outside."

"Okay. I'll be right down," I answered before jumping up to grab my wristlet and coat. He'd sent a car. Maybe he'd seen my blog and just wanted to be courteous. My blog *would* build hype for his grand opening, after all.

Downstairs, a man wearing a suit and an earpiece opened the door and let me inside. "Thank you," I mumbled, feeling uncertain and awkward.

He simply nodded and slammed the door shut before joining the driver in the front seat. Well, damn. Nicolo Mariano didn't fuck around. The limo had a fully stocked bar, spacious leather seats, and a television. I'd been in a few limos over the years, but nothing like this.

As I rode to Satin Sheets, I couldn't help the erratic way my heart beat. I would see Nico again, and I couldn't wait.

CHAPTER THREE

I'D BEEN SITTING AT THE BAR FOR ABOUT THREE MINUTES WHEN I REALIZED I was completely out of my depth. Satin Sheets was unlike any club I had ever been to. It was opulent and extravagant yet surprisingly understated. Every single detail was curated to create a luxurious vibe. Even the bar top was made of only the best material. Golden accents, chandeliers that glistened in the soft light. It had that old money, timeless class about it that you couldn't fake or replicate. It was beautiful. Every cocktail waitress wore a perfectly tailored outfit, the bartenders wore tuxedos from Armani. Excess. Satin Sheets was an art exhibit, and its focus was the finer things in life.

The bartender immediately served me a drink without asking what I wanted. I was surprised by the gesture but assumed that Nico was behind it. I watched him mix my drink, smiling at the precious care he took with each ingredient. "Enjoy," the bartender said in a smooth voice before handing me the glass. I let it sit for a brief moment while taking in the ambiance.

It wasn't crowded, and you could still speak over the music without feeling like you had to scream. Usually, the moment I sat down at a bar some idiot would try to bother me. But it was like an invisible line circled around me, creating a four-foot perimeter around my seat. The only person near was my driver, and he stood like a personal bodyguard almost with his feet shoulder width apart and his hands clasped in front of him. His eyes, dark and menacing, scanned the crowd as he stood next to me. "Are you my bodyguard for the evening?" I asked while running my index finger over the embossed cocktail napkin in front of me with Satin Sheets' logo on it.

"Please pretend I'm not here, miss. Enjoy your drink. Mr. Mariano will be here with you soon."

I bit my lip and wrapped my fingers around the glass. "It's hard to pretend when there's a man looming over me while I'm trying to enjoy my drink. What's your name again?" I asked. I wasn't actually going to drink the mixture in front of me, but I was still trying to get the man to talk.

"It's safer if we don't speak, miss. Mr. Mariano was very clear of his expectations for the evening and I do not want to upset him." The man looked wildly uncomfortable and I stared at him for a moment.

"And why would speaking to me anger Mr. Mariano, exactly?" I asked.

Instead of answering me, the man simply pressed his lips into a thin line and took a step away from me, steeling his face into a hard line. Well, I suppose I wasn't going to be getting any information out of him today. After letting out a huff of frustration, I stared at the chilled glass in front of me and picked it up to inspect it. Because I watched the bartender mix the concoction, I knew what went into it, but I was still curious about the choice of drink. "What is this called?" I asked the bartender. He looked nervous yet eager to please.

"Vida Paloma," he answered.

I eyed him curiously. "It's a more contemporary drink than I expected. It doesn't seem to fit the theme for this establishment. I expected something more…luxurious."

I eyed my glass once more. The foundation of the drink was Mezcal, an earthier agave spirit. It also had fresh grapefruit and lime juices, simple syrup, and soda, which created a natural grapefruit soda; the dried chile-pepper-rimmed glass was meant to leave every sip with a spicy pop. The presentation was flawless and mixed well. I just couldn't figure out why I was being served this.

"Do you not like the drink I chose for you?" a warm voice said at my back. "You haven't taken a sip."

I smiled to myself, a nervous blush flooding my cheeks as I casually looked over my shoulder to greet my mysterious hero. Nico looked stunning. Naturally, he wore an expensive suit. The designer, expertly tailored number was a slate gray, understated yet powerful. His dark hair was slicked back. His lips had a waxy sheen to them, as if he'd applied Chapstick just before walking up to me. Dark eyes ran up and down my back.

"I was just taking in the ambiance," I replied with a grin before nodding at the stool next to me. Sauntering over, I watched the confident way he moved, as if the entire world was his for the taking. He was a conqueror. A claimer. A monster in a suit.

"Is this not Satin Sheets' signature drink?" I asked.

"You were pretty accurate when deciding my drink last night. I thought it might be fun to return the favor, instead of handing you whatever thousand-dollar concoction my usual clientele would prefer. You're spicy. Slightly bitter. Guarded. Sweet. Beautifully refreshing. Something a person savors."

My breathing deepened as I listened to Nico describe his impression of me. "You're surprisingly accurate," I replied with a grin.

Please with himself, Nico tossed me a flirty smile before continuing. "You have an interesting take on a person's tastes and how it reflects on their personality. It's a concept I'd like to bring to Satin Sheets."

His voice was warm like honey and I had to force myself not to sigh. "Oh?" I asked.

"Instead of offering one, singular Satin Sheets' specialty drink, my mixologists will give a personalized concoction. To every patron who asks for their signature drink. It'll always be different for every person. We'll offer a unique and diverse drinking experience, not just a quick vessel for getting drunk. Still intoxicating, but wildly personal." Wow. I loved the concept but wasn't sure how that would work for the masses.

"Aren't you worried you'll get it wrong?" I asked while pulling out my notepad and a pen. Since I had Nico here, I wanted to take notes for my blog.

"No. We're building a brand—a concept. Satin Sheets knows who you are even if you don't know yourself. My customers will go home and wonder why they're a glass of chilled *Grand Marnier Cuvée du Centenaire*. They'll obsess over what it means."

I blushed at the mention I coined for him last night. "And what about repeat customers?" I asked.

"We're an exclusive place. I'm having my bartenders create profiles for every customer. And tastes, personalities, preferences, and experiences change over time. Your signature drink a year ago might not be the same today."

I grinned. It truly was a cool concept. Everyone was always searching for themselves, trying to make sense of their lives.

But there was still one problem.

"I think the concept is very refreshing. It will bring a lot of new customers and generate buzz for Satin Sheets," I agreed.

"But..." Nico added, the corner of his lip ticking up. "You have yet to enjoy the drink I chose for you."

He was right. I hadn't. *Because I couldn't.* "I can't enjoy my signature drink, unfortunately."

Nico's cocky expression dipped, and his eyes darkened. "And why not?"

I leaned in to whisper in his ear, "I'm allergic to grapefruit. Seems you don't know me as well as you think." Feeling mischievous, I stood up from my seat and grabbed my jacket. "Thank you for inviting me here, Mr. Mariano. I truly enjoyed our conversation."

He gritted his teeth and stood up. "Might I convince you to stay? Perhaps we can find something that won't potentially kill you," he rushed out. Nico seemed like the kind of man to never waver. He was confident and poised. Was it me causing him to act frantic and unsure?

I bit my lip. "I really must get going—"

"I insist." Nico stepped closer and reached out to wrap his large hand around my forearm. "I would truly enjoy spending more time with you."

I looked up at Nico and let out a shaky breath. "I really must get going..."

"One night," he whispered. "I'm just asking for one night." He leaned over and brushed his lips against my neck, sending a shiver down my spine. He was so warm, so solid.

I sensed what he was insinuating and blushed. "One night?" I asked, grinning. I bit my lip and pressed my legs together as he straightened to get a good look at me.

He smiled like a champion just winning a race. The predator had me right where he wanted me. "One night."

CHAPTER FOUR

NICO HELD ME IN HIS ARMS AS WE DANCED TO THE SOFT MUSIC PLAYING. WE both enjoyed scotch on the rocks and an impersonal conversation for the last couple of hours. I had a buzz in my veins that was growing by the second, but I wasn't sure if it was brought on by the alcohol, or him. "Why do you have men in suits guarding you at all times?"

"My answer would tie you to me for longer than a night. Forgive me, but I need to keep my work life private for your safety."

I nodded and wrapped my arms around his neck while we swayed to the music. I knew Nico was into some dangerous mafia shit, and it was probably wise that I didn't go searching for more information. It wasn't like I'd ever see him again. But still, I ached to understand the mystery man who saved my life. "I'm just trying to get to know you," I whispered.

He ran his fingers down my arms and gripped my ribcage, teasing the sides of my breasts. "What would you like to know?"

"Who is most important to you?" I asked. You could tell a lot about a person by the way they loved others.

He gripped me tighter, as if my question pained him. "My brother. He's all I have. Our parents died a few years ago in an... accident. There is no one in the world I trust more. I would literally do anything for him. I've even jumped in front of a bullet or two," he said while chuckling to himself. I tried not to jump at the casual mention of his near-death experiences.

"What's his name?"

"Lorenzo. Enzo for short," he replied. "What about you? Who do you care most for in this world?"

I knew my answer immediately. "My cousin, Dax. He's kind of like my brother. It's just us, too. He moved to LA a couple of years ago and I miss him a lot."

We continued to dance, and he paused to pull his phone out of his pocket and curse. "Fuck," he growled before nodding at a suited man standing against the wall.

"Do you need to go?" I asked while pressing my cheek into his chest. I wasn't quite ready for this to end.

"I have an associate who will handle it."

I licked my lips and squeezed him tighter. Why was I so drawn to Nico? I should be running for the hills. "Do you not get many breaks?" I asked.

"I'm always working. It's rare that I get to enjoy an evening with a beautiful woman," he replied in a rasp. "And I'm going to be selfish tonight and let someone else handle the mess."

I pulled away and grabbed the lapels of his suit jacket. "So that's what you do?" I asked. "Clean up messes?"

He grinned and leaned over to hover his lips just above mine. "Something like that."

I closed the distance between us, boldly pressing my lips to his on a moan. He responded quickly, lavishing my mouth with passionate kisses, parting my lips so he could explore my tongue. Our teeth lightly clashed. His hands roamed my body, as if we weren't in a room surrounded by people. Arching my back to get closer, I lifted my leg ever so slightly, bending it at the knee so I could put my core closer to his hard cock.

"Lydia," he whispered. "Would you like to go somewhere private?" he asked.

I pressed my forehead to his and nodded slightly, my heaving breaths coated with lust and need. One night. Nico Mariano was too intoxicating to pass up.

He slammed his lips to mine once more in appreciation, then threaded his fingers through mine to guide me across the floor of his lavish club. I stared at him, my wobbly legs shaking with each step. Something deep within me felt rattled. It was like standing on the edge of a cliff. I'd slept with plenty of men. I'd snuck out the next morning like nothing had happened, too. But this didn't feel like just one night. This felt like something more. A contract signed in blood.

"Where are we going?" I whispered when he pulled me to a hallway.

"I have an apartment above the club," he replied huskily. "I stay there when I'm too tired to drive to the other side of the city where my penthouse is."

I ignored the way he casually mentioned his penthouse on the other side of the city and nodded. "Let's go."

Each step made the tension between us grow. Ignoring the men trailing at a distance behind us, we ascended a secret set of stairs, traveled down a long, low-lit hallway, and to a large set of wooden double doors, sealed with a stainless-steel padlock.

Nico spun around and addressed his guards. "No one is to bother me until tomorrow morning."

I chewed my lip.

"Yes, boss."

Once inside, I didn't have time to take in the decor of the room. I didn't look at the four-poster bed, the expensive comforter, or the oak desk piled with papers. I didn't notice the pistol sitting on his nightstand. Nico slammed into me and pushed me against the wall, stealing my attention for his own.

"I've wanted to do this since I saw you yesterday."

I shoved his suit jacket off and picked at the buttons of his shirt while he tossed his tie to the floor. I was pinned under his strong body, his leg thrust between mine and pressing against my core. He bit my lip, nearly drawing blood.

"You looked at me like I was a motherfucking hero." His palm slammed against the wall beside my head and I jumped. His other hand captured my chin, squeezing.

"Thank you for saving me," I whispered, a sliver of fear spiking up my spine and making me tremble.

"Don't thank the villain, baby. I'm going to ruin you."

Nico kissed me harder, his mouth open, swallowing me whole. He pawed at my dress, tearing the straps, ripping it off until it was nothing but a pile of fabric on the floor. I cried out when he grabbed my breasts with his strong, massive hands.

Soon, he was lifting me up and carrying me to the bed. Slipping off his Gucci belt, he looped the ends, creating leather makeshift handcuffs. After slipping them over my wrists, he pushed my hands over my head. "Stay just like this. Don't move until I say so," he demanded before standing up to undress the rest of the way and fully admire me. Slowly, he stepped out of his pants and underwear. Seeing his hard cock, jerking and solid made me swallow in anticipation. He fisted it, letting me appreciate the view, before stalking closer.

"These are in the way," he murmured before taking off my dusty rose lace panties and tossing them on the floor. "Look at you. So wet for a monster."

"You're not a monster," I whispered.

My legs were hanging off the side of the bed, and he dropped to his knees so that he was eye level with my pussy. He chuckled at my words, as if it was nothing more than a joke to him, before dragging his firm tongue up my slit. I jerked when he landed on my clit, the needy nub spasming at his attention.

Nico consumed me. He knew just the right tempo, the right amount of pressure. He fingered me while eating me out, his mouth wet and hot as I writhed, arched, and cried out. But I didn't dare move my arms from above my head. Something told me that Nico would punish me for disobeying him.

And when I came, he smiled triumphantly as I grinded against his face. Light stubble along his jaw added a tantric texture to the feel-good pain of coming so hard.

"When you leave here, Lydia, you're going to remember the way I felt." He wiped his lips on the inside of my thigh and started crawling up my body. "I don't get many nights to myself. I'm always on. Always working. Always thinking of the next chess piece I'm going to knock off the board." He wrapped his plush lips around my nipple and flicked his tongue over the needy nub before continuing. "But tonight? It's just you and me."

His lips found purchase on the sensitive skin of my neck. He sucked and poised his hard cock between my legs. I opened wider for him. "Can I touch you?" I asked. I wanted free of my restraints so I could roam my hands up and down his sculpted body.

"Wrap your arms around my neck, baby," he whispered, and I obeyed. Both of us lay there, waiting, panting. Another moment passed, and he plunged inside of me.

Fuck. He was so big that the invasion of his hard cock burned. I pulled him closer with my arms and bit my lip. He didn't ease in and out of me with sensual, slow movements. He was fast and desperate. We were being so irresponsible, but the tension between us was too much to ignore. I wanted him. Bare. Impossible to forget.

Hours seemed to pass. Every single position, surface, and second was filled with his desperate pumps, my frantic orgasms, and the sound of his filthy talk in my ear. We didn't stop until we were completely spent with his cum spilling out of my sore pussy and our heaving bodies languid on his mattress.

He wrapped his arms around my body and pulled me close, savoring the feel of our nakedness. I fell asleep in the arms of a stranger, feeling like I'd known him my entire life.

CHAPTER FIVE

I WOKE UP ALONE, NAKED, WITH THE SMELL OF NICO MARIANO ON MY SKIN. Someone was pounding on the door. I sat up, rubbed my eyes, and looked around the empty room for signs of the man who rocked my world. "Open up, miss."

I wrapped a satin sheet around my body and stumbled to the front door. With shaky hands, I opened it.

"Hello, Miss Love, the car is downstairs ready to take you back to your apartment." The man standing there was the same man from last night. He averted his eyes, taking great care not to look at me.

My heart panged. Though I had no right to feel disappointed, the fact that Nico couldn't at least see me off after the intense night we shared stung. "Oh," I replied "Is Nico—"

"Mr. Mariano is gone for the day. He instructed me to stop for coffee and bagels on the drive home should you wish."

"How thoughtful of Mr. Mariano," I replied before letting out a huff. "I won't be needing your services. I'll call a cab, thank you. Just give me a couple minutes to get dressed and I'll be out of your hair."

I knew what this was going into it, but it was still harsh. The man cleared his throat. "Mr. Mariano had strict instructions—"

"Nico isn't here. I'm a free woman. I'm allowed to do whatever I please. Excuse me. I need to get dressed so I can get the hell out of here."

I fumed as I got dressed, furious that I felt this way. I'd had plenty of one-night stands. I knew the drill. It was the fact that he had one of his employees to fetch me that pissed me off. I didn't bother looking in the mirror. I didn't need to see the evidence of my reflection to know I probably looked like shit. After grabbing my purse, I opened the door and paused when I saw the man standing there.

"Mr. Mariano insists that you use his car to go home," he stammered. I waltzed over to the stairs with him following behind. After pulling my phone from my purse and ignoring the various missed calls from Dax, I ordered a car and stomped down the stairs. "Please. We can bring you straight home. I would really prefer—"

I opened the front door to the club, wincing at the bright light outside. "Tell Nico thanks for the orgasms," I replied with a smile and a wink before slamming the door in his face.

During the car ride I silently fumed to myself, feeling insecure and foolish. Of course this didn't mean anything to him. What did I think was going to happen? We'd wake up, have breakfast, and end up getting married two years down the line? Ridiculous. This was what wealthy, mysterious men did. They fucked and then got the fuck out of there.

My phone started ringing and I answered it with a wince. "Heyyyy, Dax," I croaked while looking out the window and bracing myself for his anger.

"I was two seconds from hopping my ass on a plane. Are you okay? What happened last night?"

My chest tightened. "I ended up hooking up with a guy from the club last night. Stayed at his place and I'm headed home now. Sorry I didn't text you."

He let out a sigh. "Shit, Lydia. I was really freaked out. How was the club? And who is the guy?"

I wrinkled my nose. "The club was extravagant. The guy was like absinthe and champagne."

"*Death in the Afternoon,* one of my least favorite drinks," Dax agreed with a scowl.

"I'm headed home now to work on my blog post for Satin Sheets. No need to fly here. I'm good. Can I call you later?"

Dax went quiet for a moment, and I sensed that he wanted to ask me more questions. "Are you sure you're fine? You didn't hook up with the owner, did you?"

I clenched my teeth and steadied the embarrassment and strong emotions coursing through me. "I'm fine, Dax. Talk to you later?"

He huffed. "Fine. Call you later. But don't think I'm dropping this."

"Love you," I said softly.

"Love you, too."

CHAPTER SIX
SEVEN WEEKS LATER

THE ROOM SMELLED LIKE SWEAT AND SEX. I WRINKLED MY NOSE AND TRIED not to outwardly gag at the stench in this place. I was tired and not necessarily up for doing a review on this new club, but they promised to pay a premium for a good review, and since I hadn't really been maintaining my blog since Satin Sheets and my incredible night with Nico, I couldn't turn it down.

I was in a funk. I couldn't stop thinking about Nico and the passionate night we shared. I was tired and burnt out. Not to mention, I was still freaked out by the whole stalker situation. Every time I went to post on social media, I thought of Bradley's frantic face and the way Nico's men dragged him away and shoved him into the trunk of a car.

"Do you not like the drink, miss?" the bartender asked while staring at me. A group of men were in the corner, arms crossed over their chests and glaring at me. The club was called Dark Knight and for a Saturday night, there was no one here. They got new management and were desperately trying to save their establishment. I wasn't the only blogger or influencer here to enjoy a free drink on the failing business. I could tell that they were hoping to get more buzz, but by the looks of my drink, they needed to stop wasting money on influencers and hire a better bartender.

"What is this called again?" I asked. It was a sad day when I couldn't even tell what they were trying to accomplish. I lifted the glass up to my nose and took a sniff. Oh God. My stomach revolted. Bourbon.

Normally, I loved whiskey, but this smelled too potent. I felt like I was going to puke.

"It's a Smoked and Salted, miss. Two ounces of Four Roses Bourbon. Twenty-five ounces of maple syrup, slightly thinned out with hot water. Five dashes of Crude Smoke & Salt Bitters. It's our most requested cocktail."

I took another sniff and gagged. The men in the corner fumed. The maple syrup was sickly sweet. There was no way in hell I could drink this. I looked up at the bartender, who was pleading me with his frantic gaze to take a sip. I felt bad for the guy, but this sounded terrible right now. "Right," I replied. "I'll try it."

I lifted the drink up to my lips and took a small sip. The taste on my tongue made me shiver in disgust. It was awful. Absolutely awful. Nausea swirled in my gut and I couldn't hold back the rising vomit. Within minutes I was puking on the bartender, my sludgy lunch leftovers projected over the bar top and onto the poor man. Once it was out of my body, I clasped my sticky mouth with my hand and hopped off the stool. I felt dizzy and tired and so fucking embarrassed. What the hell was wrong with me? This was *so* not professional.

The bartender gagged and wiped at his shirt with his wet rag. I looked up to see some of the club owners marching my way. Yeah. This was bad for business. I grabbed my clutch and made a beeline for the door. Shit. Shit, shit, shit!

Outside, the cool air hit my cheeks, and my feet wobbled as I hailed a cab and pulled out my cell to call Dax. Something was seriously wrong with me. He answered the moment my ass landed on the stained cloth seats of the cab.

"Hello. How'd the club go? You headed home?" I could hear the sounds of the bar where he worked in the background. He probably couldn't talk for long, but for some reason, I just wanted to hear his voice.

I started to cry. My eyes watered and I felt stupid. What the hell was wrong with me? I didn't even cry when my stalker attacked me. "Dax?" I sniffled.

"Are you crying? Shit! What's going on?"

"I just puked on a bartender. I puked all over him. He was wearing my cobb salad!" My voice was shrill as I sobbed. The cab driver gave me a horrified look in the rearview mirror, and I had to force myself not to chuck my purse at his head. It wasn't his fault I was having a complete emotional breakdown.

"You puked?" Dax asked, trying to make sense of my emotional rambling.

"Yes. I'm just so tired. I hate going to these clubs. I just want to sleep and watch Netflix."

Dax went quiet. "Are you PMSing? I know you hate it when I ask because I have a penis and I'm not allowed to make comments about your emotional state and how it correlates to your Menzies, but I'm just trying to navigate this carefully."

I blinked twice. Wait. When was the last time I'd had my period? I did some mental calculations and nearly dropped my phone in horror. Oh shit. Ohhh shit.

"Lydia?" Dax asked. "I'm sorry. I didn't mean to make it worse. Maybe you should go home, have a glass of wine and just relax?"

"Dax?" whispered.

"Yeah?"

"I'm late. I'm fucking late."

Dax went silent on the other end of the line. "Go to a pharmacy right now and get a test."

"No. No, no, no. This isn't happening. I can't."

"Lydia! You just puked cobb salad on a bartender. You have to. Oh my God, I'm going to be an uncle!"

"You're my cousin. It doesn't work like that, Dax."

"I'm basically your brother," he snapped. "Wait. Who is the father?"

I swallowed; another wave of nausea laced with shame consuming me. Oh shit. There was only one person I'd slept with recently... "We don't even know if I'm pregnant or not," I hissed into the receiver.

"Oh man. This is epic," Dax said. Why did he sound so goddamn happy?

"I'll go take a test and let you know," I replied. "And stop sounding so excited."

"I'll stop when you tell me who the father is."

"Byeeeee."

TWO LINES. TWO FUCKING LINES.

Holy fucking shit balls goddamn motherfucking cock sucker.

Did we use a condom? Nope. I was drunk. I get bad migraines from birth control, so I wasn't on the pill. It was a careless night all around. Not only did I have unprotected sex, but I fucked someone who didn't even have the decency to pat me on the ass and say *good game*. It was irresponsible. Stupid. What the hell was I thinking?

I was pregnant. I was actually pregnant. Like legit pregnant.

I didn't call Dax, because I wasn't ready for his questions and accusations. I wasn't ready to be a mother. I wasn't ready to raise a child with a man I barely knew. I mean, who even *was* Nico Mariano? Did I want to tell him? Should I tell him?

Did I want to keep this baby?

I was sitting on my bathroom floor, staring at the test and pressing my palm to my flat stomach. I tried to imagine what it would be like to raise a whole ass human. A living, breathing soul with my eyes and Nico's intensity.

No. I couldn't do this. What about my job? I couldn't review drinks while pregnant.

I licked my lips and felt tears well up in my eyes. It was moments like this that I wished I had my mom here. She'd know the right thing to say. She'd rub my back, get me a glass of water, and help me pick myself up off the floor.

I just wished I knew what to do. I lived in a one-bedroom apartment and my baby daddy wanted nothing to do with me. What if he thought I did this on purpose? He was one of the wealthiest men in the city.

No. I refused to feel bad. It took two to tango, and he didn't even bother to wear a condom. We both got ourselves into this mess. And he had a right to know, didn't he? What happened next was my choice, but the least I could do was tell him.

I spent the next few hours Googling anything and everything about being pregnant and having a baby. I learned that my kid probably had a heartbeat. I learned that I couldn't have caffeine.

I also learned that I wanted to keep my baby.

I worked myself into a frenzy of anxiety. The thought of just sitting in my apartment and not talking to Nico was freaking me out. I had to tell him. Like now.

I impulsively got dressed into jeans and a sweatshirt at 3:00 a.m. and made my way to Satin Sheets, with plans to leave Nico a message and let him know we needed to talk. I was sure someone was bound to be at the club who could relay the information.

It was stupid, but I couldn't sleep. I couldn't think. I needed to do something. Tell someone. At least this way, I could put the ball in his court. If he wanted to call, he could. If he didn't, I'd take it as a sign that I would be on my own in this.

As I walked the dark streets searching for a late-night cab, I thought about Dax and LA. Maybe I'd move there so I'd have more support. I knew my cousin would help me any way he could. I could probably find work there if necessary. My blogging career would have to go on pause for a bit. I had residual income from my YouTube channel and enough savings for a move and a few months of figuring shit out. I could totally do this.

Right? Right. Yep. I could do this.

By the time I made it to Satin Sheets, it was empty of patrons. I let out a shaky breath and doubted what I was doing. Maybe I should have found an email address? Instagram? Sent a letter? Tried coming during the day? Holy shit, this was a mistake. What the hell was I thinking, coming here in the middle of the night?

I was about to knock on the front door and face the music, when the sound of crashing glass and a pained scream drew my attention. I was trembling when I circled the building.

I could feel the fear deep in my gut, my intuition pleading with me to turn around and stop this. But I couldn't stop. My feet dragged me toward the sound, toward the cries of anguish and the stark bark of an angry man—a man I knew.

Nico.

"You're pathetic," he cursed. I pressed my body against the brick and peered over the edge, looking down the dimly lit alley with wide eyes and a racing heart. There was a bloodied man slumped over on the ground. One of his fingers was bent at an awkward angle, likely broken. He coughed up blood, and Nico reared back his leg, then kicked him in the stomach. I pressed my fingers to my mouth to stifle a gasp.

Nico looked like the devil, wearing a black suit with his burning eyes on his target. The scowl on his perfect lips—lips I knew intimately—terrified me.

"You think you can take a bit off the top, old man? You think you can steal from me—from the Moreno name? You think you can hurt us? You hurt the wrong person. You're a dead man." Nico pulled out a gun that was holstered to his side and aimed it at the man.

I should have squeezed my eyes shut. I should have run the fuck away. But I watched. I stared as Nico pulled the trigger, lodging a bullet in the stranger's skull.

I'd expected a boom, but his death was silent and swift. My heart raced. Shock coursed through me. I didn't feel an instant sense of horror. It crept up on me as the disbelief slipped away.

Fuck. I just witnessed a murder. Holy shit. This was bad. So bad.

"Clean it up," Nico ordered to a suited man standing by, and I worked up the courage to leave my spot against the side of the building and walk back to my apartment.

I couldn't let Nico anywhere near my child. I was right to think he was into some criminal shit. He just killed a man. I wasn't a mafia wife. I wasn't prepared to raise a child with a monster. Even though Nico saved my life, I still didn't know him well enough to trust that we would be safe in his world.

And I wasn't all too familiar with criminal politics, but the mafia didn't like to leave any witnesses. What if someone saw me watching? I couldn't go to the police. They wouldn't protect me and my unborn child from Nico's wrath. What if—

"Hey, who are you?" a gruff voice asked as I passed the front door to Satin Sheets. I looked over my shoulder and nearly tripped over my feet when a bald man with bulging veins at his temples glared at me.

"Just going home..."

I picked up the pace and he took a step closer to me. I felt stuck. If I ran, he'd know I was suspicious. If I stayed...

I walked faster and he started following me.

"Stop. Let me talk to you for a minute."

I swallowed and started to run; thankful I'd worn tennis shoes. Nausea rolled within me, the adrenaline and shock at seeing someone murdered finally settling in. The blood. The silence. The slumped form of his body. I pressed my hand to my mouth and kept going, until a rogue taxi came into view. Flagging it down, I got into the passenger seat just before one of Nico's goons caught up to me.

I was shaking. My skin felt like ice.

"Where to, miss?" the driver asked as he drove.

Where to? *Where to?* I couldn't stay here. A man like Nico had connections. He'd find me. What if there was security footage outside the club? What if they saw me watching? What if?

I had to leave. I had to pack a bag and get the fuck out of town. Say goodbye to my apartment, my belongings, and everything I knew.

"Los Angeles," I whispered to myself before giving him the address of my apartment building. I was going to pack a back in ten minutes flat and head to the airport.

I was leaving the city and raising the baby far, far away from Nico Moreno.

CHAPTER SEVEN
TWO YEARS LATER

`"WHO IS YOUR FAVORITE UNCLE? HMM? WHO IS IT?" THE BRIGHTEST LITTLE giggle broke out and I rolled my eyes. Dax loved making Viviana laugh. My daughter had him wrapped around her little finger. "Are you going to be a good girl for the babysitter while Uncle Dax and Mommy go out, hmm? I know you are. I know you are! You're such a perfect little girl, right? You can do no wrong. I don't care what anyone says."

I was putting on my earring as I turned the corner to stare at my cousin as he cooed at my baby. She was a little over eighteen months now, and she could charm anyone into doing anything. She had dark hair, light brown eyes, and thick lashes that cast shadows on the plump little cheeks. She had her father's devastatingly good looks and my gentle heart. My cousin looked silly with all his tattoos and muscles falling at the feet of a one-year-old.

"You're going to give her an ego," I joked. Dax turned to see me and tossed me a friendly smile.

"I haven't seen her in six whole hours. I was just trying to remind her that she's perfect."

"Oh. She knows," I replied with a grin before walking over to my baby and picking her up out of her crib. She rested her head against my chest and mumbled something incoherent.

"I'm excited for tonight. Lydia Love is back in business, and now I get to go to all the hottest clubs in LA."

Dax knew all about Nico and what I'd witnessed. Two years ago, I showed up on his doorstep crying and carrying everything I owned in a suitcase. He got me a job as a cocktail waitress at the bar he worked at and when I had my daughter, he was sitting outside the room with his ear pressed to the door so he could hear her first cry. I had the best family in the world, and he stepped up to care for my daughter and me.

And Dax was now the reason I was going to start working with clubs again—this time as a consultant instead of a blogger. I missed my following and the platform I'd built from the ground up, but it was worth it to be safe for my daughter. Even though Nico or his men never chased me down, I couldn't risk getting on their radar. I wasn't sure if they knew I'd seen what happened that fateful night in the alley, and I refused to risk it. Being a single mom was difficult, but her safety was the most important thing to me.

"You ready?" I asked Dax. Our babysitter had just arrived.

"Ready," he replied.

I hugged my sweet baby and reluctantly set her back down. I felt off about leaving tonight but chalked it up to nerves about starting my consulting business. I could do this.

"I'm so proud of you," Dax said as we stepped outside my apartment building. "You're getting back to it, raising the cutest baby I've ever seen, and just thriving."

I stopped walking toward my car to wrap Dax up in a hug. I was so thankful for my cousin.

"I couldn't have done any of this without you," I replied.

Dax grinned and squeezed me tighter. "I'm really glad you came to LA. I couldn't imagine not being a part of Viviana's life and watching you become a mom. You're my best friend. I'm just...happy."

I pulled away and smiled, feeling emboldened about starting this new journey, a little of the old mixed in with my new life.

But a bullet piercing through the air stopped me in my tracks. Blood splattered out of a gaping wound in Dax's chest, littering my face with droplets. His face flashed with shock, then morphed into blank emptiness. "No!" I screamed as I wrapped my arms around his body and helped him to the ground. I looked in the direction of where the bullet came from but only saw scattering pedestrians running for their lives.

I wiped Dax's cheek. "Someone call an ambulance!" I screamed. He smiled a little, his eyes glossy as he looked at me. I sobbed and pressed my palm to the wound in his chest to try and stop the bleeding, but I didn't know what I was actually doing. "No. No. Dax. Stay with me."

His lips worked to say something, mouthing the word love.

"I love you. Please stay with me," I cried out. "I love you, Dax. You're my best friend. You have to stay to watch Viviana grow up."

My cousin died in my arms, and a part of me died along with him.

CHAPTER EIGHT

THE POLICE CALLED IT A RANDOM ACT OF VIOLENCE. THEY SAID HE WAS A victim of a faceless crime. They had no leads. No information about his shooter.

I became a hollow shell of the girl I once was. Always looking over my shoulder, having groceries delivered to my apartment because I was terrified to go outside of my apartment building. Every time I looked at the parking lot I wanted to vomit. What if Nico sent someone to kill me? I wasn't sure if we should leave or stay.

The loss of my cousin hit me hard. I could barely eat, and every time I closed my eyes to sleep, I saw his face. I saw his limp body on the concrete. I felt his life leave every single night. It was torturous. I tried to be strong for my daughter. I knew she could sense that something was wrong. And my heart broke every time she cried out for Dax. She didn't understand why he was gone, and I couldn't explain to a baby that he was never coming back.

It wasn't until a month after Dax's funeral that the weird things started happening. A rose on my doorstep was the first sign that something was wrong.

A few days later, a cracked, framed photo of me.

A week after that, a baby onesie ripped to shreds.

I called the police, but they didn't take it seriously. They claimed that someone was just trying to prank me, and since nothing had happened, I couldn't really do anything about it. I was convinced that this was related to Dax's murder, but no one wanted to believe me. I felt like I was losing my mind.

"Mama," Viviana said while nuzzling my neck. She was refusing to sleep, and I couldn't seem to turn my brain off either. I was terrified, unsure what to do and feeling more alone than I'd ever felt. The police weren't any help, and the items kept showing up.

A cut-up pacifier.

Rose petals.

A broken cocktail glass.

Hair that looked suspiciously like mine.

"Mama!" Viviana said again. I bounced her while walking over to the window. Looking outside in the dark night, I saw a figure standing there and looking straight up at me.

My heart dropped.

I stopped breathing.

I knew who it was.

He'd finally come for me. He killed my cousin. He was leaving things on my doorstep. I closed the blinds and started to shake.

There was only one way to get out of this. One way to survive. Once again, I had to do everything in my power to save my daughter.

I packed all of my daughter's belongings into a massive suitcase and grabbed a couple of outfits, my toiletries, and any necessary items for me.

I had to run. Again.

But this time, I was running back.

I CLENCHED MY FIST WHILE WALKING UP TO THE BOUNCER. I'D DRIVEN FOR the last four days, stopping only to stay at secluded motels and to feed and change Viviana. She was exhausted and fussy, screaming her head off as I marched up to the doors to Satin Sheets.

It seemed like ages ago that I was here, and standing on the doorstep with my daughter in my arms felt like a mistake, but I didn't know what else to do.

My stalker was alive, and he was after me. He killed my cousin and I worried what he was going to do to my daughter. The police weren't much help, and I was afraid to tell them about my stalker, and how my crime boss baby daddy handled the situation. Or at least I *thought* he handled it.

I'd been living my life fearing Nico, but maybe it was Bradley I should have been worried about all this time.

"Lady, you can't bring a screaming baby in here. You don't meet dress code, and I doubt you're on the list," the bouncer said while looking me up and down. Tears glistened in my eyes and I tried to be strong for my baby, who was now crying harder. I needed to find a hotel for the night.

"I need to see Nico Mariano," I said, trying to keep my voice steady.

The bouncer, with his beefy exterior and piercing blue eyes laughed, like I'd told him a joke. "You and everyone else. Next!"

I didn't move. "Please. My name is Lydia Love, and this is his daughter. I'm in danger." It took a good chunk out of my pride and self-preservation to say that, but I kept my spine straight.

"Mr. Mariano doesn't have any kids."

"Not any he knows about. Please just tell him Lydia Love is here," I begged.

The bouncer must have seen something in my expression because his demeanor softened a fraction. "Lydia Love?" he asked as I dug through my diaper bag for a juice box for Viviana.

"Yes. Please. If he doesn't want to see me, I'll leave. I promise. I know your boss is very busy. I just really need to speak to him. I wouldn't be here if it wasn't an emergency."

He clenched his jaw. "You do look like you haven't slept in a week and bringing a baby here is pretty drastic. Hold on just a minute," he said before pressing an index finger to his earpiece and talking to whoever was on the other side of his radio. I slumped my shoulders in relief and Viviana started sucking down the juice box like it was God's gift to man. I knew I'd regret the sugar later with her sleep schedule, but she was already completely off from our last-minute road trip.

The bouncer's brows lifted in shock. "Come inside, Miss Love. Mr. Mariano will speak with you immediately."

My chest tightened with anxiety, but it was too late to back out now. There was only one person who could save me, and it was Nico.

CHAPTER NINE

NICO MARIANO SAT AT HIS DESK, HANDS FOLDED IN FRONT OF HIM, EYES trained on me. He hadn't said a word since I was guided to his upstairs office. The time apart had changed him, hardened him. He looked deadlier than before, but he was still impossible to resist. His strong jaw, soft hair, and rough beard enticed me in ways that were inappropriate for the situation.

Viviana was sitting in my lap, hyper as hell and chewing on a toy. Slobber dripped down her chin as she happily played, unaware that we were in the lion's den. Despite the crazy few weeks we'd had, she seemed perfectly at ease. I knew in my gut that babies had a sixth sense about these things. If she wasn't screaming her head off, maybe there was hope.

"She's mine?" he asked after a long, pregnant pause. I let out a sigh and nodded. Nico snarled. I could tell he had more questions to ask, but this felt like an interrogation, one where he'd be silent until I spilled all my secrets. It was an exercise in control not to cower away from him.

"I found out I was pregnant seven weeks after our night together," I boldly explained. If I was going to ask for his help, I had to be honest. "I was a mess. I was scared and I knew I needed to tell you. I must have been crazy out of my mind because I marched here at 3:00 a.m., prepared to tell you. It's not like I had your number. You made it clear we were nothing more than a one-night stand when you disappeared the next morning."

I was surprised at the bitterness in my tone. What the fuck did it even matter now?

I shook my head, marching on with my story and forcing the resentment out of my tone. "I witnessed something," I said, my voice cracking at the admission. "I didn't mean to see it. But I saw you shoot a man in the back alley. I got scared and I ran."

Nico's face turned red, anger burning through his expression. "You claim to have seen me murder someone?" he said, carefully using his words. It was as if he expected me to be wearing a wire.

"One of your guys saw me hanging around and I ran. I was worried you'd kill me for what I saw. I realized I couldn't stay here. I didn't want to raise the baby alone, and I was worried you'd come after me."

"Which of my men saw you?" Nico asked, his voice cold.

"I don't know. He was bald. One of the two men standing out there with you," I explained, not sure why this mattered.

Nico causally picked up his phone, typed something, then set it down. I got a sinking feeling in my gut that whoever let me go was in big trouble.

"Are you here to blackmail me, Miss Love?" Nico asked, shocking me. "Are you here to ask for child support of some kind? Threaten to tell the feds what you saw in exchange for money? There is no guarantee that child is mine, and quite frankly, I don't appreciate being blackmailed."

My heart sank. I couldn't even blame Nico for assuming this. How could I possibly convince him that I didn't want or need any of that? Before my stalker resurfaced, we were doing fine. I had a life in LA. I had...Dax.

Tears started to form in my eyes and I furiously swiped at them. Viviana, noticing my distress, dropped her toy and grabbed my cheeks, saying "Mama," over and over again.

"I'm not here to blackmail you. I don't want or need your money," I whispered. "I need your protection."

If Nico was surprised by my words, he didn't show it.

"My stalker is back. He killed...he killed my cousin. He's been leaving stuff on my doorstep and I'm worried he'll kill my daughter. *Our* daughter. I'm so fucking scared, Nico. I haven't slept in weeks. I'm sick with worry, with grief." I stood up, still holding Viviana. "I know you don't trust me. I know I hid her from you. I am so sorry. I don't care what you do to me. You want to get rid of a witness? Fine. I just need to make sure Viviana is safe from that monster."

Nico watched with apprehension as I marched over to him and put Viviana in his lap. His spine was rigid with tension and he looked like he was worried she'd drool on his suit. "Look at her, Nico. She's yours. Look at her eyes. Her hair. Look at the shape of her nose and chin. I wouldn't lie to you."

Obeying my command, Nico stared at our daughter with softer eyes, taking in every inch of her expression. I stood and watched, forcing the warm feeling in my chest to go away. I wasn't disillusioned. Nico wouldn't be the father I wanted for our child, but he could be her hero, just like he was mine once upon a time.

"Where are you staying?" he finally asked, neither confirming nor denying my claim.

"We just drove here from LA. I was going to get a hotel—"

"You'll stay at my home."

I nearly collapsed from relief. "Thank you, Nico."

"When was the last time either of you ate? What does she even eat? How old is she?"

"Eighteen months," I choked out. "I have baby food, but she ate earlier. Honestly, she just needs a quiet place to sleep."

At my words, Viviana yawned and leaned on Nico's shoulder. She looked completely at ease, relaxed at Nico's embrace. The terrifying man softened more, holding her against his muscular chest like she was the most precious thing he'd ever seen. "And you? When was the last time you ate? Or slept? Or sat down, even?"

More tears filled my eyes. I hadn't relaxed since Dax died. Hell, I hadn't relaxed since I ran away from here. My life had been spent living in constant fear since seeing Nico kill that man.

Nico's nostrils flared, like my sadness greatly upset him. "Let's go home, Lydia."

CHAPTER TEN

I WOKE UP IN THE SOFTEST BED I'D EVER LAIN IN. THE LIGHT WAS CREEPING through the thick, drawn shades, and I felt more well-rested than I had in months. When Nico brought me to his penthouse last night, I was too tired to take in the extravagance of it all, but I remembered the open floor plan. The extensive security guarding his building. And after I got Viviana ready for bed, I passed out in one of his guest rooms, finally feeling safe, despite being at Nico's house.

Viviana. Shit.

I shot out of bed and padded out of the guest room. She wasn't in the pack-n-play Nico had delivered to his house at midnight last night. Oh my God, where was my daughter?

I traveled down the long hallway, listening for the sounds of voices or baby noises, and paused at the kitchen. There, my daughter was sitting in a highchair and Nico was feeding her breakfast. I grabbed my chest in relief at the sight of her but seeing her father smile so tenderly as he tried to get her to eat made my heart warm.

I waited to make my presence known, enjoying the view far too much. Around me was box after box of baby gear. Car seats. A jogger. An unassembled crib. Diapers—so many diapers. Nico had been busy all night.

"Mama!" Viviana yelled, splattering rice cereal everywhere. Nico chuckled and spun to look at me.

"You're up earlier than I expected. I was trying to let you sleep in," he noted casually before wiping at Viviana's face. I almost felt bad that I slept through him coming to get our daughter. Ever since Dax died, I hadn't had a support system when it came to taking care of my daughter. And truth be told, we were still virtual strangers. It was weird letting him into Vivian's life. I wasn't sure what had changed overnight, but Nico seemed to be taking his new role as her father very seriously. I would have to adapt and learn how to let go of the reins and trust him, even though I was still scared. I couldn't wipe the image of what I'd seen from my mind. I struggled to believe that we were safe here, but the alternative wasn't any better.

"Thanks for feeding her breakfast," I said with a genuine smile.

"Did you have help?" he asked.

"Help?"

"This whole time. Who helped you with her? Was anyone there in the delivery room? Did anyone help you with late night feedings? Hospital appointments? Milestones?" His tone was gruff, and I couldn't figure out if he was angry with me.

"My cousin," I whispered. "Dax. He was my best friend. I showed up with nothing but a suitcase. He helped me find a job. I got an apartment in his building and for the first three months he slept on my couch and helped with late night feedings and diaper changes. He called himself Uncle Dax. He always was more like a brother to me than anything else, so it fit that he was Viviana's uncle."

I felt tears stream down my cheeks and Nico carefully got up and walked over to me as our daughter played with her food. "I'm sorry for your loss. I remember you saying he was the most important person in your life," Nico said softly. He reached out and wrapped me in a hug that probably should have felt awkward, but instead calmed me in ways I couldn't articulate.

"I'm surprised you remember anything about that night," I said jokingly before pulling away and bravely swatting at the tears on my cheeks.

Nico's brow dipped. "I remember everything about that night, Lydia. I treasure those memories. I remember what you wore. The smell of perfume on your skin. The sound of your moans…"

My heart raced at his words, but more out of anger than lust. "Then why did you leave the next morning?" I snapped.

He let out a sigh. "Because I knew that if I allowed myself to spend any more time with you, I'd end up dragging you into my world. I'd completely own you, Lydia. And you've seen firsthand what my life is like. I don't date. I can't let anyone close to me." He turned to look at Viviana and cursed. "It's too risky to have people I care about. My empire is unforgiving, but I'm afraid it's too late now." He looked at me once more. "Coming here comes at a cost, Lydia. I'll protect you. I'll save you. But I'll drag you to hell while I do it. I can't let my daughter be out in the world without my protection. I have too many enemies. Word will get out and they'll make your stalker look like a playground bully in comparison."

I dipped my head and stared at the ground. I knew this. I knew that going to Nico could possibly change our lives forever, but I still felt in my gut that it was the right thing to do. "I know what being here means, Nico."

He wrapped his arms around my body and pulled me flush with his. "Do you, Lydia? Because I don't think you have the slightest clue what you're in for. You're the mother of my child. It was hard enough walking away from you the morning after we had sex. There's no way in hell I can leave you now. Are you prepared to be pursued by the devil, baby? 'Cause I'm not just into petty crimes. I'm a leader in the Mariano family. We're ruthless. Vicious. Evil. We deal drugs, guns, and counterfeit cash. You're all in now. You saw what I did to that man."

I bit my lip, a rush of lust hitting me full force. Why was what Nico was saying turning me on? "I don't believe you," I whispered.

"You don't? What more proof do you need?" he asked incredulously.

"I know you're involved in shady shit, Nico. But I don't think you're bad. I don't think you're evil. Why did you kill that man in the alley that day? I've always wanted to know."

Nico pulled away from me and popped his knuckles. "He stole from me," Nico gritted. "I didn't know that while I was ending his life, he had his men attacking my brother. Both of them died that night."

"I'm so sorry," I said softly. It seemed both Nico and I had lost people we cared about. My eyes drifted over to Viviana and I smiled. We were both gifted with someone, too. All we had was one another. And that had to be enough for now.

"It's business. It's what happens in my world. Kill or be killed, Lydia."

"Why didn't you kill my stalker?" I asked. "You obviously let him go. He wouldn't still be following me otherwise."

I didn't mean for my words to sound so accusatory, but Nico didn't seem fazed. "I didn't see him as a threat. Contrary to popular belief, we don't kill unless we have to. I don't want the feds breathing down my neck any more than the next guy. I guess I just thought he'd back off if my guys roughed him up a little. I never expected him to kill your cousin, Lydia. And if I had known he would threaten my daughter, I would have ripped every bone from his body and burned what was left of him."

A shiver traveled down my spine at his words. Nico clenched his fist.

He'd said his daughter. He truly had fully accepted that she was his.

"We'll find him," I whispered. "And we'll make him pay."

When I walked over to Viviana, she smiled and lifted her messy hands up in the air, indicating for me to pick her up.

"What's her full name?" Nico asked.

I chewed on the inside of my cheek and blushed.

"Viviana Nicole Mariano," I replied. I wasn't sure why I gave her his name. It just felt right in the moment. He was still her father. He still gave me the greatest gift of my life. He gave me a family. A purpose. He gave me my pride and joy.

I picked up my baby and turned to look at him. Nico had his eyes closed, the twitch of a smile gracing his lips. "I love her name," he whispered.

"Me too."

"Now we just need to change yours," he added before spinning on his heels and walking out of the kitchen.

CHAPTER ELEVEN

A FEW DAYS PASSED AND NICO GOT TO KNOW HIS DAUGHTER. I WAS SURPRISED when he canceled all his business for the week. Not a single person was allowed to disturb us, and aside from a couple of housekeepers and his round-the-clock guard, he spent every single day with us.

And oh, did she love the attention he gave her. She was giggling nonstop and spent every waking second laughing at him. Nico was surprisingly attentive and patient. He didn't get frustrated when she cried. He stared at her like she was a miracle, and he was lucky enough to look at her.

"She wears me out," Nico said while closing the guest room door. It took him four bedtime stories to get her to fall asleep. We were both working on a nursery for her, but it wouldn't be ready for a couple of weeks. I didn't mind. I liked sharing a room with her. Despite all the change, being with my daughter was still the same.

"You're good with her," I said with a smile while walking down the hallway and to the living room. I wanted a nice glass of wine and a relaxing evening. It had been so long since I relaxed. I knew that we were in our own little bubble, and this temporary reprieve from all the stress in my life wouldn't last forever. But still, I enjoyed it. I liked feeling like a family, even though Nico hadn't pressured me for anything other than parental partnership. I would catch him staring at me, though. His eyes followed me around the room. He was *always* watching me.

"Sir?" one of his guards said while entering the room. "I found this outside." I peered at what was in his hand and gasped. A baby blanket with blood on it. What the fuck?

"I'm going to get Viviana," I said quickly before running down the hallway to her crib. I opened the door and swallowed a scream when I saw a shadow standing over her.

"Don't say a word, or I'll hurt her," Bradley said. He had a knife in his hand and was staring at me.

I held my breath. How did Bradley get inside? What was he doing?

"I thought you were done with these games, Lydia. You ran from me. You let someone fuck what was mine. You made a baby with someone else, Lydia."

I itched to get closer and take Viviana far away from him, but I couldn't risk angering him. "I'm sorry, Bradley," I whispered, trying to appeal to his insanity. "You know I only love you."

His shoulders relaxed some, but he was still clutching a long knife, the threatening blade glaring at me in the dark room. Viviana stirred some and I winced. "I'm sorry I killed your cousin, Lydia. I didn't like him hugging you. Why did you let him into your life but not me? I'm the *only* person you need."

Bradley took a step closer to me, away from Viviana. I needed him to get as far away from her as possible. "I'm sorry," I croaked. Bradley stepped into the light, illuminating his terrifying face. He had a full beard now and scratches on his face. The whites of his eyes were large, and he cocked his head to the side while looking me up and down.

"He tried to take me away from you. But he can never take me away. We're meant to be, Lydia. God made us perfect for one another. I am yours."

Another step away from Viviana. *Fuck. Nico, come in here, please.*

My daughter stirred and let out a whimper. Bradley turned to look at her. *No, fuck. Look at me, Bradley.* "She'll always get in the way between us. You'll always love her more. I can't have that, Lydia."

No. No, no, no. "I'll leave with you right now. She can stay here, and we can go. How did you get in here? Why don't we leave?"

Bradley turned to look at me. "I can't have you loving someone more than me, Lydia," he said, his voice terrifying.

I knew what I had to do. I had to rush him while screaming and tackle him to the ground. I could only hope I could fight him until someone came to help. Nico was just down the hallway.

"Billy. Let's go. I love you so much. I don't want to be here anymore," I said, desperately trying to put more space between him and Viviana.

I heard movement down the hall. I prayed Nico was coming to save us, but I didn't dare look. Bradley raised the knife in his palm, and I took a step closer to him, prepared to save my baby at all costs. *I love you, Viviana.*

A loud bang pierced through the air. He collapsed on the ground. Viviana started sobbing uncontrollably, startled from being woken up with such a loud sound. Bradley jerked on the ground as I ran to my baby and pulled her out of the crib. In the doorway stood Nico, surrounded by his men. The gun in his hand was trained on Bradley.

"Thank you," I sobbed. I had been so scared, but it was finally over. I ran from the room, desperate to keep Viviana as far away from the scene as possible. How could this happen? How did he break in?

"Is she okay?" Nico asked while following after us. Viviana let out a wail.

"She's startled but will be okay," I whispered.

"Are you okay?" Nico asked.

"No," I cried out before spinning around and running into his open arms. The three of us held one another until Viviana calmed down. I was so thankful to Nico in that moment. We had truly made the right decision in coming here.

He rubbed my back. "You're safe. You're both safe. He'll never bother you again."

I let his words soothe me, and I spent the next few hours in the arms of my hero.

CHAPTER TWELVE

"SHE'S FINALLY ASLEEP," I SAID WHILE WALKING ONTO THE PATIO WHERE Nico was standing. His team had everything cleaned up so efficiently, that I wondered how often Nico Mariano had dead bodies in his home. The thought made me shiver. The sun was rising outside, and we looked out over the city. People were just now waking up, as if last night my entire world didn't almost end.

We moved into Nico's bedroom because I didn't want to be away from him. Even with Bradley dead and gone, I felt safer at Nico's side.

Nico was clutching a drink in his hand and I stared at the amber liquid.

"What's your poison?" I asked while nudging him.

He looked down at his drink and smiled at me. "Glenfiddich Grand Cru, twenty-three-year-old luxury scotch." I was suddenly drawn back to two years ago, with Nico saving me and me telling him what drink matched his personality. "I've had a glass of this every night since I met you, Lydia. I've sat on this porch, thinking about the girl I pushed away trying to save, and what this drink is supposed to mean."

I moved until I was poised at his back. Carefully, I rested my cheek against his spine and wrapped my arms around his middle. He used his free hand to pat my intertwined fingers at his stomach. "Now that Bradley is gone, are you going to run away from me again?"

"No," I whispered. "We still have a lot to learn about one another. But I want to try, Nico. I want to be a family."

He sighed in relief, then set down his glass on a nearby table, spun around, and wrapped me in a hug. "I'll always protect you and our daughter. Seeing you today with that maniac terrified me. I'd burn the world down to save you, Lydia."

I licked my lips, drawing his eyes to the movement. "You're my hero," I said.

He slammed his lips to mine. I melted. *Fucking melted* in his arms—in the safety of his embrace. Nico nipped at my lips with his teeth and roamed the expanse of my back with his strong fingers. It felt like finally coming home. All the pain, all the uncertainty and fear. It was washed away, and I knew with complete certainty that Nico would never hurt me. It might be difficult to navigate. We had so much to learn about one another, but I had a feeling the two of us were stubborn enough to make it work.

"I've been thinking about these lips for way too long," he murmured before lifting his thumb to drag it along my bottom lip. I closed my eyes. "I've dreamed about your skin. About your tight cunt. About feeling you again."

Heat pooled between my legs at his words and I lifted up on my toes to kiss him again. Moaning into his mouth, he pulled at my shirt as the sun started to rise. Like a God, he didn't care who was watching. He wanted me. Only me.

We stripped out of our clothes and he shredded my panties in a frantic effort to remove all the barriers between us. We collapsed onto his lounge chair on the patio and I straddled his hips. We were clawing at each other, moaning, frantically arching to be closer.

"Condom?" I asked. Unprotected sex was what got us into this mess.

"I want to feel you completely. If I have my way, I'll put ten babies in your belly. We can have an entire house full of adorable kids just like Viviana."

I bloomed at his words. The idea of another baby should have terrified me, but the fact that he was so thrilled by our family had me position myself over his hard cock and sliding until I was fully seated on him. It was crazy, but I just wanted him. All of him. "Fuck," I cried out while stretching to accommodate him. He was so big. I felt so fucking full.

I started riding him. Sunbeams illuminated us, casting a baptism of light on our sweaty skin as I fucked him. There were no secrets between us now. Everything had come to light. A car honked on the street below, and I moved faster. My legs burned. My body tensed with the impending orgasm.

"Mine," Nico murmured, sending me over the edge.

My mouth parted in ecstasy, his declaration an anthem to my pleasure.

Mine. Mine.

I had a family.

I had Nico Mariano.

EPILOGUE
ONE YEAR LATER

"MRS. MARIANO, WOULD YOU LIKE OUR SPECIALTY DRINK?" THE BARTENDER asked. I was visiting a new club, one that Nico was considering buying out.

"No, thank you," I murmured before patting my flat stomach. I found out just last night that we were expecting our second baby. I couldn't wait to tell Nico; I just didn't know how. With Viviana, he missed out on so much. I just wanted to make this special for my husband and the father of my children.

My husband was over in the corner, talking to the current owners of the club. Satin Sheets was doing so well that he wanted to expand. I supported him completely. I really wanted to handle the drink menu. I'd started my own consulting business and was building back up my brand.

My husband eyed me and excused himself before walking my way. "Do you not want a drink?" he asked, which was code for, *is this place a bad investment?* He knew that I could sniff out a bad club within the first five minutes of walking inside. It was why he brought me with him to all his investment opportunities.

That and it was hard to separate us.

I bit my bottom lip. "I'm taking a break from drinking," I replied with a sigh.

His brow furrowed. "A break?"

I waved down the bartender and asked for a water. "Yeah," I replied nonchalantly. "For the next nine months at least."

A hand wrapped around my wrist and I was gently pulled off my barstool. I smiled at Nico while realization settled in his expression.

"Nine months?" he asked.

"Viviana is going to be a big sister, Daddy," I said with a grin. He wrapped me in a hug and spun me around.

Nico was dangerous. Our life was unconventional. But we were a family.

And we were *happy*.

THE END

A PIECE OF US
BY HEIDI MCLAUGHLIN

CHAPTER ONE
JACK

MY HEAD FALLS FORWARD, STARTLING ME AWAKE. I LOOK AROUND AND readjust in my seat before looking out the plane window. It's then the flight attendant announces our descent into Logan International Airport. My friend Mitch sleeps next to me with his mouth open, inhaling the stale and stagnant air. I poke him with my elbow, enough to wake him. Once he's alert, he looks at me and smiles.

"We're in freaking Boston, man!" Within seconds, Mitch has gone from a sleeping, germ huffing passenger to a full-blown tourist. The only issue is, we aren't staying in Boston. Our destination is Montreal, Canada, for a friend's wedding, and then Mitch and I will return to base.

"I think we have time to drive around, but from what I remember, traffic is a pain in the ass, and we have to drive north for a bit."

"Still, we're in freaking Boston!"

I love his enthusiasm. Mitch is from the west coast, near Sacramento, California. We met in boot camp, somehow managed to stay in the same unit for the past ten years, and have been best friends this entire time. Right now, we're stationed in Tirrenia, Italy, at Camp Darby. We've been there for almost three years, and I still don't know a lick of Italian, although I'm rather fond of the food.

We're currently on leave for the week, and both up for re-enlistment. We have a month to decide whether to re-enlist, retire—although ten years doesn't give us crap for benefits—or join the Guard. I'm leaning toward re-enlistment. The work is stable, as is the housing, and it's not like I have family waiting for me to come home. On the other hand, Mitch has an on-again, off-again girl back in Cali, and his parents want him to come home. He's always talking about how they want him to settle down, get married, and have kids because they're not getting any younger. Mitch wants to party and play the field. Personally, I'm not sure he's ready to be an adult yet.

Mitch and I have also talked about what we'd do if we left the Army. We've tossed around the idea of opening a business, maybe a brewery or a winery. After living in Italy, we have both discovered the fine art of wine drinking and eating pasta.

The flight attendant announces our arrival. "Welcome," she says and then adds, *"benvenuta"* in Italian.

"I say we leave Montreal a day or so early and tour Boston. I want to see where they dumped the tea."

"I'm game," I tell Mitch as I unbuckle my seatbelt. I do this every time I fly commercial because it makes me feel like a rebel. This one time, the flight attendant came on over the intercom and said she could see who wasn't buckled in. You could hear the clicking of belts over the roar of the engine. Everyone feared some sort of wrath I have yet to see.

We reach the gate, the plane jerks to a stop, and everyone unclicks their buckles to stand and open the overhead compartment for their belongings. I grab mine and Mitch's bags. He slides over to my seat and stands, stretching and yawning. Jet lag will be a bitch tomorrow, but thankfully we'll be in Montreal with nowhere to go until later.

Once we deplane, we make it through the airport and outside, where we get on the shuttle for our car rental agency. We both packed light, mostly because we own minimal clothing. I never had much when I enlisted, and we wear the same thing to work every day. I think at last count I owned a pair of jeans, a couple of pairs of shorts, a nice pair of pants, and maybe five or six shirts. I'm not even trying to live the minimalist life, but I do not need a closet full of clothing I'll never wear. That's another reason to stay in the Army. I don't want to have to buy a houseful of items. I can't even imagine the cost of things these days.

As promised, instead of getting right on the Interstate, I drive through Boston and point out what I remember. It's been a long time since I took a high school field trip to the Revolutionary War sites, but there are a few things I haven't forgotten. Before we drive north, I make a stop at Dunkin Donuts, something Mitch has never experienced.

"Nope," he says after taking a sip. "It's bitter. Nothing like the stuff we have back home."

"Back home as in Tirreni or Sacramento? Because that shit in Cali is probably Starbucks."

Mitch laughs and continues drinking. Over the years, I've come to drink whatever caffeine source will keep me awake and functioning. I'm not picky, nor can I afford to be. Awake and alert keeps my team and me alive.

Not an hour into the drive, Mitch is itching to pull off for something to eat. I haven't paid attention to signs, but one town grabs my attention when I start looking at the upcoming exits. "Wow," I mutter.

"What's up?"

I shake my head and contemplate telling Mitch my thoughts. There are a few things I haven't told him, mostly because I don't want his pity. I don't need it. I've long accepted the fact I come from nowhere and my family doesn't exist. That, if I were to die, the service secretary takes care of my body. It's pretty sad when I think about it.

"There's a town coming up, Holyoak. I lived there for a bit, right before I enlisted."

Mitch leans forward and looks out the window. I catch his expression. He looks confused. "Is it a real town?"

His question sparks laughter from me. "As opposed to a fake one you build on *Sims*?"

"You don't really build towns on *Sims*," he replies. "Just houses."

"Same diff," I mutter. "And yes, it's a real town, with real people. Actually, one of the nicest places I lived." At the last moment, I signal to get off the Interstate. My heart races, for what or why, I'm unsure. It's not like I remember much. It was only six months with a woman I haven't spoken to since I turned eighteen and became free from the system. The lady I lived with was nice, but I was seventeen, the state placed me with her, and I had pretty much checked out on life.

"Are you going to turn right or left?" Mitch asks, pulling me from my thoughts. If I go straight, I get back on the highway, and we continue our trek north and can stop in the next town or any of the others we'll come across. Or, I turn right and head into Holyoak. There were a few places to eat that had something to offer everyone. It would be nice if I remembered the names, but I don't. Honestly, I didn't pay much attention to my surroundings, except for one of the girls in my history class, and to my grades. I needed them to be fair enough the Army would take me.

Mitch clears his throat, and my finger pushes up on the leveler to signal my intent to turn. I don't understand my hesitation and why I'm so reserved around returning. The town was fun and good to me. The kids I went to school with were nice for the most part, and I had a good time. I can recall a few stories about what the kids planned to do during the summer, and for a brief moment, I wish I could've stayed behind to spend those last few days sitting on the beach or water skiing, but I had other plans. Plans I set in motion on my seventeenth birthday, enlisting in the Army. Being a ward of the state—no one really cared if an adult signed for me or not.

The drive into Holyoak takes only a few minutes from the exit. The roadway into town is tree-lined, giving most people the impression there is nothing for miles. It's only after you come around the bend, does the lake, the houses, and finally the bustling town come into view.

There's a line of traffic, which makes me consider turning around and heading to the next town, but Mitch has put his window down and is taking in the sights. I swear, the simplest things make this guy smile. Honestly, it's sort of refreshing.

"This town is hopping."

"Yeah, seems so."

"And you lived here?"

"Yeah, not for long though."

We inch along Main Street until I find a parking spot along the curb. I feel sorry for the car behind me as I maneuver into place. There is nothing I hate worse than parallel parking when there is a line of traffic behind me. I somehow manage to get the rental parked without holding up the people behind me for too long or scratching the cars on either side.

Mitch and I take a few minutes to gather a couple of things from our bags before we get out of the car. I stretch and shake my legs out to wake them up. After an eight-hour flight and now stuck in the car for at least five hours, my legs are going to cramp. I'm hoping to prevent this with a few more stops. I motion for Mitch to follow me across the street and onto the sidewalk.

"You don't want to walk by the lake?" he asks, keeping pace with me.

"I do, but the crowd is smaller on this side. On the way back, we can." I don't remember Holyoak being much of a tourist town, at least not until summer. In the few months I spent here, I barely had a summer. I was gone by July, but those last couple of weeks, right after school let out for vacation, the town was lively.

We walk in silence until I stop dead in my tracks.

"What's wrong?" Mitch asks.

I swallow hard and look at the sign that definitely wasn't there when I left, *Lottie's*.

"Do we like Lottie's Pub?"

I nod slowly. "Yeah, I think so. Although I think the place had a different name."

"Restaurants change owners all the time," Mitch says as if he has some experience in the matter. His parents are everything you read about in books or see on television. Mitch's dad is a psychiatrist, and his mom is a kindergarten teacher. Our lieutenant teases Mitch that his family is like the Seavers from *Growing Pains*—only we really don't understand what he means since the show is way before our time. "Are we going to go in?"

"Yeah, we should."

Mitch is the first one to move toward the building. I can't explain why I hesitate. Maybe it's because I'm waiting for memories to surface. Nothing comes. I'm not surprised in the slightest. I've spent most of my years blocking out my past. There isn't much I want to remember, and it's not like I ever made any long-lasting friendships. My Army friends are the only family I have, and even they're not forever. Some of us move around a lot, going from station to station. Mitch and I have just been lucky to have stayed together this long.

He opens the door to Lottie's Pub. It's bright, airy, and lively. We stand there, looking around, and for some odd reason, I feel like a cowboy walking into a saloon. "Do we seat ourselves?" I wonder aloud.

"Is that a thing here?"

"From what I remember, sometimes."

Mitch points to a table, and we take a few steps toward it until the bartender hollers out. "Seat yourselves. I'll be over with a menu."

We sit, and Mitch says, "This place is busy. The food must be good."

"I didn't eat out a lot when I lived here, but from what I remember, the place this used to be was decent."

The bartender approaches us and sets two menus down. "First time in Lottie's?" he asks.

Mitch and I nod.

"Well, welcome. We recently remodeled and now have the longest bar in New England with over two hundred beers on tap and growing. Our seafood is fresh, and according to my niece, we have the best chicken tenders she has ever had." He laughs at his joke. "Our burgers are one pound locally grown beef, made to order, and our vegetables are grown here as well. Let's see what else am I supposed to tell you," he pauses and thinks.

"You've sold me on the burger, and I'll take whatever IPA you recommend. It's my first time here," Mitch says, although the bartender has already asked us.

"Welcome. Your first time, too?" the bartender asks me. Okay, so maybe he doesn't remember or wasn't paying attention to us when we nodded.

"Actually, no. I lived here for a few months about ten years ago."

"No shit," he says. We make eye contact for a brief moment. I search my memory, trying to place him, but I'm unsure. "Wait, are you, Jack?"

I'm surprised when he says my name, but surely there must be a million Jacks. It's a relatively common name. But I have nothing to lose, so I say, "I am. Do we know each other?"

"Yeah, man. You hung out with my family when you lived here. I'm Krew Scardino. If I remember correctly, you dated my cousin, Charlotte, for a bit until you left."

His words hit me like a Mac truck going one hundred down a steep incline. "Wow, I . . . uh . . ."

"How you been?" he asks, skipping over my lack of vocabulary.

"Good. You?"

"Not too bad. Charlotte owns this place now. How long are you in town for?"

"Just passing through on our way to Montreal for a wedding."

"Marines?" he asks.

"Hell no," Mitch blurts out. "Army. Huah!"

The battle cry is lost on Krew. He looks at me, smiles, and says, "You should call Lottie." He scribbles on his notepad and hands the piece of paper to me. "She would really love to hear from you, and I think you'd definitely like to see her."

"Okay, I will." Krew takes my order and then leaves us be.

"You never told me about this Lottie," Mitch says.

I stare down at the piece of paper with her name scrawled over a set of numbers. I never told anyone about her because there wasn't much to tell. We were young, she was hot, and paid attention to me. She never cared that I didn't have a family, and neither had her family. Which, if I remember correctly, is massive.

"I only knew her and her family for a few months."

"You gonna call her?"

Again, I look at her name. This time I smile. "Yeah, I have nothing to lose by saying hi."

CHAPTER TWO
CHARLOTTE

WHEN MOST PEOPLE HAVE A DAY OFF, THEY DO THEIR CLEANING OR RUN errands. Me, I go to my grandparents, Gentry and Arlyne Carmichael, to sit on their deck or curl up on their sofa. I could do both things at home, but there's something about being with my grandma that centers me. She's my best friend, my confidant. Right now, we're in her kitchen. It's her favorite place to be. I'm watching her prepare dinner for tonight—homemade buttermilk fried chicken—a recipe she learned from her grandmother. It's my grandpa's favorite. Mine too. And I'm listening to her rant about the women in her knitting club. Every week, she has something new to tell me, and I think deep down, this is one reason I come here on my days off.

"Anyway," she says, bringing my attention back to her. "Gertrude is dating Margaret's husband."

My mouth drops open. Not only at the fact that my grandma drops this bomb and somehow doesn't miss a beat when it comes to dipping the piece of chicken into the buttermilk, but also how Gertrude is openly having an affair with her friend's husband.

"Did Margaret stab Gertrude with her knitting needles?"

Grandma chuckles. "Elaine almost did. Trudy was so flippant about the whole thing. Honestly, I wasn't paying attention to their bickering until she blurted out that she and Todd have been sleeping together. I swear, it was like we were back in high school."

"You didn't go to high school with them," I say, fearful that her memory could be fading away. Ginger, my best friend, her grandfather has dementia, and the stories she tells me are heartbreaking.

Grandma pauses, and my heart drops. Did I just remind her of this fact? She turns and starts to place her milk and flour-covered hands on her hips but seems to think better of it. "Child, I'm aware I didn't go to school with anyone who lives here. I may be old, but I'm far from senile. These women act the same way the girls in high school did when the cute popular boy asked them out. They're all after one thing, this generation of mine, and that is security and comfort."

"I'm sorry, I didn't mean to imply—"

She cuts me off with a wave of her hand and turns her back toward me. I feel dumb for even saying what I said. I stand and go to her, standing hip to hip with her. "I love you the most," I tell her. It's the truth. She's always been my advocate, the one to stand up to my parents when they felt I brought shame to the family. The relationship I have with my grandma isn't like the one she has with my siblings or cousins. They've commented on this many times, how I'm the favorite. I tell them it's because I named my daughter after our grandmother. I've given her a namesake. But they don't believe me. It's fine. My grandfather favors my brother and my baby cousin, Birdie. Although, Birdie is far from a baby anymore.

"I love you too," she tells me. "And I appreciate you looking out for me, but my mind is as sharp as a tack." She brushes my hair away from my face and then cups my cheek.

"I promise."

Somehow, she knows how much I need her. We have a large, close-knit family, but even in a family like mine, there is always someone, or a few someones who won't always agree with a decision you make. My grandmother is the most objective one out of everyone and also the most vocal. That doesn't mean she doesn't have an opinion though, and isn't afraid to let you know what she thinks or how she feels.

I wash my hands and begin to help her finish preparing tonight's dinner. Arla, my nine-year-old daughter, and I will join my grandparents this evening. Arla spends most of her weekends here, at my parents, or brother Trey's house, so I can run Lottie's. Between the ski lodge and the marina, Holyoak barely has an off-season. The summertime lake goers turn into skiers, and the skiers turn into leaf peepers. For those of us in town who own businesses, we enjoy the constant tourism.

After we finish the chicken, my grandma takes out the ingredients to make her homemade cornbread and suggests I start working on dessert. "What is it?" I ask her.

She shrugs. "You tell me."

I turn away, so she doesn't see me smile. Everything I know about cooking and baking I've learned from her. At Lottie's, we strive to give our customers a homecooked meal. Of course, all the beer my cousins encouraged me to install isn't hurting. The people who come from all over seem to enjoy the-mile-long bar. The twins, Krew and Kiel, wanted the bar to wrap around the entire restaurant, which my grandfather vehemently objected to. My great-grandfather bought the building where Lottie's is many moons ago and turned it into a restaurant. My grandfather inherited it, and he handed the restaurant to me about five years ago. I don't own it outright, but it's mine, and I can do whatever I want with it. My grandpa's idea was to change the name to Lottie's, and my idea to completely renovate and change the menu. I like to think my changes allow us to thrive.

Above the stove, my Grandma keeps all of the cookbooks she's collected over the years. I finally find the one I'm looking for, a Betty Crocker cookbook from the 1950s. Inside, there is a tattered recipe for apple cinnamon strudel, my grandma's favorite. I pull the book from its spot and set it on the noodle board, adorned with my grandparent's last name—Carmichael. I flip through, looking at some of the recipes in there, hoping something will catch my eye until I get to the worn-out piece of paper that has been taped over and over again. Long ago, I asked my grandma why she doesn't just buy a new Betty Crocker cookbook, and she said the recipes aren't the same, that the essence of cooking has changed over the years. *"Everyone is always looking for a shortcut. No one wants to take the time to make a full meal anymore,"* is what she tells me when I bring it up. She's right. Quick meals are nice. Arla and I often practice the grab and go lifestyle. But I also appreciate a homecooked meal, especially if I've made it all from scratch. There is something satisfying about sitting down and seeing all your hard work pay off.

I head into my grandma's walk-in pantry. My grandfather had it built a couple of years back after grandma had seen something similar on one of those home makeover shows. Of course, this meant her entire kitchen had to be remodeled. The finished space is comforting, with its farm style family seating at the table, a vintage décor, and all brand new appliances. One of my favorite parts, aside from the pantry, is the deep countertops. My grandpa knew what he was doing when he had the contractor extend them. There is so much more workspace than before.

After pulling the ingredients I need from the pantry and four apples, I get to work. Normally, I would put my earbuds in and listen to a book or a podcast, which allows me to think about other things while working. With my grandma in the room, I'd much rather listen to her hum or sing her favorite song even though she can't sing worth a lick. I'll never have the heart to tell her she's tone-deaf and completely off-key.

Once my apples are sliced, and in the pan with raisins, cinnamon, sugar, and brandy, I set them aside to let the liquor soak into the slices. The dough is the tricky part. Most people will use a store-bought version, but not in this house. I mix the ingredients I need to make the paper-thin dough and roll it out until it's perfect. Even my grandma comes over to make sure it's thin enough. I don't mind that she's checking. I like reassurance. It's my brother Tripp who likes to tell me I'm doing something wrong. I know he means it jokingly, but after years of him teasing me, it gets a little old. You would think with him being younger than me, he'd know his place. Unfortunately for me and everyone who meets Tripp, his ego is immense, and he's not afraid to use it. As the head ski instructor at the lodge during the winter, and the "jack of all trades" at the marina, Tripp has a gaggle of women following him around town. Every time I hear a group of women giggle when they say his name, I puke a little in my mouth.

Grandma and I assess the rolled flour and determine it's perfect. Over at the stove, Grandma turns the burner on and sets my pan of soaking apples onto it. She stirs while humming a show tune. The song is familiar, but I can't place it. When I was growing up, she often took all the grandkids to her childhood home in New York City. My grandma never thought twice about taking eleven grandchildren to the city. Now with nineteen of us, along with four great-grandchildren, she would never think of it.

She brings the pan over and starts laying the apples out and drizzling the remaining sauce over the top of them. While I wait for the apples to cool, I make sure to coat my hands in flour so I can move the pastry around the fruit, folding as I go. Every so often, I look at my grandma, seeking her approval. Each time, she nods or smiles, and when I get to the last fold, she has a baking dish ready to go.

"It looks perfect," she tells me as she carries it to the oven. Grandma closes the door, turns the light on so we can keep our eyes on the pastry, and sets the timer. "Come," she says, motioning for me to follow her. I start to, but my phone rings. My grandma pauses in the doorway between the kitchen and the dining room and tells me to answer it.

I rush into the entryway where I left my belongings, and frantically search my coat pockets, and then my purse, until my hand brushes over the metal. I glance at the screen and send the unknown caller to voicemail. While I'm at it, I decide to check my text messages. There's one from my sister, Missy, who wants to tell me about one of her sorority sisters. One from my cousin, Frankie, asking me what time dinner is. And the last one is from my cousin Krew, who is working at Lottie's today.

Lottie, you're never going to believe who came in today.

Don't ignore me, Lottie. I gave someone your number today. He's going to call you. I hope.

Charlotte Carmichael, I need you to text or call me back!

If there is anything I know about Krew, it's that he's dramatic. He's a therapist, but likes to moonlight as a bartender because he says it helps him work on his pick-up game.

As much as I disagree with his theory, when he works, I get the freedom to not worry about the restaurant and come here and visit with my grandma. I'm curious about who Krew gave my number to and wonder if that was the unknown caller. In the process of texting Krew back, mostly to let him know that I don't need his help meeting people, the notification that I have a voicemail pops up. I click and bring my phone to my ear to listen.

"Ahem . . . Um, hi Charlotte, or Lottie. This is uh . . . well I'm not sure you remember me, but I used to live in Holyoak, Jack Hennewell. I don't even know why I'm calling, but your cousin said I should. Anyway, I hope things are well with you. I'm just passing through to Montreal for a wedding, but I have my phone if you want to call me back. Take care, Lottie."

I pull my phone away from my ear and look at it. There is no way I heard what I heard. I listen, again and again, barely registering his words over the sound of my rapidly beating heart.

"There's no way."

"For what, sweetie?"

I drop my phone to my side and turn to look at my grandma. "Arla's dad was in town," I say even though I don't believe my own words. "He ate lunch at Lottie's."

She deadpans, and her mouth drops open.

"Yeah," I say, answering her unasked question.

CHAPTER THREE
JACK

MITCH RAMBLES ON AS I DRIVE NORTH. I'M NOT ENTIRELY FOCUSED ON what he's saying, though. My mind is still in Holyoak, with what Krew said and the voicemail I left for Lottie. I'm tempted to go back, but to what—a girl, no now woman, who may or may not remember me? I can't. I can't do that to Mitch, who is excited to see the Northeast, and I definitely can't do that to our buddy who expects us to be at his wedding. I glance in my rearview mirror and grimace. Why? I think because deep down, I'm hoping Krew or Lottie is trying to chase me down. Again, I ask myself why I would want this or expect this—sadly, I don't have an answer. I'm surprised Krew even remembered who I was . . . or am. The brief time I spent here wasn't overly memorable. At least that's what I thought when I left.

We finally reach the Vermont border and Mitch hangs out the window to take a picture of the sign welcoming us. "Why's it in French?" he asks as he situates himself in his seat. He leaves the window down, which I don't mind. It's relatively warm out, and the fresh air feels good. It's also keeping my mind clear and focused on the road and not the urge I have to turn around and drive back to Holyoak.

"Back in the 1600s, a French explorer discovered the lake we're going to come across and named the state. Vermont translates to green mountains," I tell him.

"Did you have to learn all of this when you lived here?"

I shrug. "Sort of. This area is rich in history, and it's not uncommon for someone to talk about the Revolutionary War or Ethan Allen."

"There's a National Guard unit called the Green Mountain Boys, right?" Mitch asks.

I nod. "They were the patriot militia of the war. They defended property rights and fought to protect what is now considered Vermont. They were only around for about eight or nine years before they disbanded and all but faded away until Vermont joined the United States as the Vermont National Guard and used the nickname The Green Mountain Boys." I can feel Mitch looking at me, so I peek in his direction. "What?" I ask him.

"How the hell do you know all of this?"

I shake my head slowly. "I've researched the National Guard."

"Why?"

"For retirement," I say, shrugging. "I don't know, just looking to see what else is out there."

"I thought we were starting a brewery?"

"We are or can. I'm totally down for it, but we can still serve our country and keep our benefits if we join the Guard. It's one weekend a month and a few weeks out the summer or something like that. Just an option."

"Options are nice," Mitch says and turns his attention back to the passing scenery. "It's really green," he mumbles.

Leaning forward slightly, I peer out the window until the trees make me dizzy. After

I sit back and readjust, I chance a look at my phone. Deep down, I'm hoping there's a message or a phone call from Lottie, even though I doubt she'll call me back. She has no reason to, and the more I think about it, I should've never listened to Krew. I don't even understand why he was so insistent that I call his cousin. It's been ten years, and a lot can happen in those years.

"Any place to stop around here?"

He makes me laugh. "I've only been to Vermont once, but when I mapped our trip out, there wasn't much until we reached a few exits. I have a list of places on the back of our itinerary."

Mitch reaches into the backseat and struggles a bit until he pulls out all the pieces of paper I have folded together. "Geez," he says when he unfolds the stack. "You're freaking anal."

"I can't help it."

"You can. You choose not to." Mitch flips through the pages, muttering as he goes. "Shit, you even have the rest stops marked on here, and how long it should take us. What if I need to take a crap?"

I roll my eyes. "It's just . . ." well, now that I think about it, I'm not sure why I put so many details down. "I think I was bored when I started mapping this out."

Mitch shakes his head. "Says here that Burlington is the place to get food and where we will find a hotel."

"We don't need a hotel," I tell him. "We'll be fine to make it to Montreal."

"How long until we're there?"

I point to the GPS. "What does it say right there, spanky?"

Mitch backhands me. "Don't be an ass."

He's right. I shouldn't be. "Sorry, my mind."

Mitch turns slightly in his seat and folds his hands together, placing them in his lap. "Do you want to talk about it?"

He's genuine, even though he's a facetious jerk. I've never been one to share or show affection, whereas Mitch talks about everything. Because of how I grew up, I've learned to compartmentalize my thoughts, and I often forget there are people out there who care about me.

"I will," I tell him. "As long as you turn back to sitting normally."

Mitch does and even goes as far as to reclining his seat a bit. "There, now you'll be the therapist, and I'll be the patient since you're the one driving. We'll call it role reversal."

I inhale deeply and center myself. "You remember what I told you earlier, right? About living in that town?"

"Yeah, made a few friends."

I nod. "Well, Krew was one of them. His family is really nice, but also wealthy. They pretty much own the town. He has a twin brother but also has a bunch of cousins, most of who are around my age."

"I'm guessing one of these cousins is this woman he wanted you to call today?"

Nodding, I continue, "Lottie, although I prefer to call her Charlotte, was the nicest and prettiest girl in school. Beyond popular, every guy wanted to date her."

"But she wanted you, you devil."

I give Mitch a side-eye glance. "Let me finish."

"Roger that."

"Anyway," I sigh heavily. "I was definitely in the mix of boys who liked Charlotte but knew I never stood a chance. When I say wealthy, I mean the upper echelon of people. Each kid had brand-new cars, they all live on the lake, which I believe they own, run the only ski lodge in town, among other things. We're talking boats, jet skis, parties—every teenager's dream. I'm on the outside, looking in, and thinking *this* is what a family looks like.

"I'm in town maybe three weeks when Charlotte comes up to me in history class and asks if I need a partner. I'm fairly sure I bit my tongue and nodded, completely frightened to speak because I was afraid of saying something embarrassing. She gives me her address and tells me what time to come over. One of our other classmates sees the entire exchange and tells me I need to pack condoms because Charlotte Carmichael puts out if I want to get laid.

"I'm shaking like a leaf when I push the doorbell. The house is so damn big, the chime echoes, which makes matters worse for my nerves. Charlotte answers the door wearing sweatpants and an oversized sweatshirt, hair in some bun thing on top of her head, and in slippers. She will never know how much relief I felt in that moment because if a girl is trying to get some action, this was not the thing to wear," I point out. "Don't get me wrong, she's still a total knockout, but with no skin showing, teenage Jack can cope. She invites me in, introduces me to her parents, and then takes me into the kitchen, where I stumble over my feet at the view. Her house faces the lake, and her home has these floor to ceiling windows, which lets you see everything. For some reason, I think it's wise to go over and drool, and when Charlotte stands next to me, I expect her to tell me to leave because I'm gawking, but she hands me a bottle of water and starts pointing out who lives where. It's like a damn compound or some shit.

"I follow her to the kitchen table where her books are spread out. Charlotte tells me to sit, and I do. It takes me a long minute to figure out that she really wants to study and that she must've turned the dickwad in class down. Her parents invited me to stay for dinner and asked me a lot of questions about my life, where my parents were, and how I like living in Holyoak. After that night, I was in their group, with Charlotte, her brothers, and cousins.

"It wasn't until a week or so before I planned to leave that we hooked up. Most people in town thought we were dating. I guess we were, sort of, I was just too nervous to really make a move. Her parents went out of town, and she invited me over. I expected things to be normal until she answered the door in bra and panties and pulled me upstairs."

"Was she as easy as the dickwad said?"

I shake my head slowly. "Not at all. We were each other's first. Before we went through it, I tried to tell her that I was leaving, but hormones, man. Those things are a bitch when you're a teenager and haven't learned self-control. For the next week, we screwed as if our lives depended on it. In her car, the lake house, on the boat, in the lake. She unleashed a beast. I didn't want to stop, and I also didn't want to tell her I was leaving.

"When I finally found the nerve to tell her I had already enlisted before I moved to Holyoak, she cried. I cried. I had a good thing going but also knew, deep down, good things end. When I turned eighteen, I would have no place to live and needed to take care of myself. It was hard for her to understand because she had everything. Come fall, she would leave for college, and I'd be," I pause. "I'd be nowhere, with no one. It wasn't like I could go to college with her, and there was no way I had the money even to enroll.

"Charlotte drove me to the bus station. She never asked me to write or call, so I figured she intended to move on. I wasn't in any place where I could ask her to stay or wait for me, ya know. I climbed aboard, sat where I couldn't see her, and just pushed her out of my mind."

"I wonder what she wants," Mitch says. "Maybe she missed the D!" He laughs at his joke and jabs me a few times.

I slow the car down when I see the sign for the border. I was so lost in recalling my time with Charlotte I never stopped in Burlington to rest or refuel. I pull off on the last exit before the border and turn into the first gas station I see.

"Good, I gotta piss," Mitch says ever so eloquently. When the tank is full, I head into the store and use the restroom before deciding to stock up on some road snacks. It'll be late when we get to Montreal, and only bars will likely be open. Food options might be scarce until the morning.

Mitch is standing by the car when I come out. We both get in, grab our passports, and head back toward the interstate.

"Why do you think she wants to talk to you?"

I shrug. "I have no idea. I honestly haven't thought about her until I saw the exit," I pause and shake my head. "No, that's not true. I thought about her all through basic and at graduation when I saw all those girlfriends there. It made me wonder if she would've come if I had asked her."

CHAPTER FOUR
CHARLOTTE

THROUGHOUT DINNER, MY GRANDMA REACHES OVER AND SQUEEZES MY hand. Aside from Krew, she's the only one who knows Arla's dad is in town or was. However, she is the only one who supported me from the beginning when I told my family that I was pregnant. My parents wanted me to give Arla up for adoption, but my grandma was adamant I make the best decision for me.

I was barely eighteen and recently graduated from high school. I had big plans for my future. More so, my parents had plans for my life, and they definitely didn't want an unwanted and unplanned pregnancy with an absentee father. My dad was up for reelection as mayor, and he feared he would lose votes once people saw that his picture-perfect family wasn't so perfect. That's what the Carmichael's are—perfect. It's all my family knows.

Our roots are deep and generational. My great-great-grandfather worked his fingers to the bone to provide for his family. He bought his first piece of land in Holyoak and built a three-room shack in front of what everyone in town considered a swamp. When he wasn't fishing, he worked the land, and when he wasn't working, he dug around the swamp. Somehow, he knew the swamp would turn out to be his gem. He slowly bought the land next to him, and then another piece. By the time my great-grandfather started working, more land was purchased and then developed. Soon, the Carmichael's owned a bank and grocery store. Every year, their property grew. My great uncle would build houses, another would cut the lumber, and another would give a future homeowner the loan. In a nutshell, they created a monopoly.

And while all of this is going on, they're still digging in the swamp and turning it into a lake, which is now one of the most popular vacation spots in New England. It seems my great-great-grandfather saw more than a swamp.

We are the family people strive to be—the big happy, close-knit family who are always together, who are always smiling. We are the upper-class people read about in magazines, the high society, elitist. We are rich and expected to marry rich. My mother comes from a high-powered family from Boston. My aunt's father is one of the highest-ranking senators for New Hampshire. So, when I announced my pregnancy, there wasn't a single person happy for me. Not even my grandma, but she accepted it and told me she would support my decision. Whatever it was going to be.

I don't remember when I decided to keep Arla. I think it was after my first ultrasound. My doctor knew adoption was on the table and suggested that I look at the wall during my ultrasound. I couldn't. I wanted to see what this baby growing inside of me, the one making me sick at night, looked like. It's odd to say I fell in love with a blob, but I did.

Telling my parents was not easy. It was harder than telling them I was pregnant. Once I started showing, I moved to my grandparents and hid out. Not because I was embarrassed, but to keep the questions at bay. No one really suspected anything because I should've been in college. And then one day, I'm pushing a stroller down the street. People talked. They asked questions. Most of which weren't answered. I let people think whatever they wanted.

My plate disappears, startling me. I look up to find Arla and my grandma clearing the table. "I can do this," I tell them.

"Gramps said it's my turn to clean the table," Arla says as she stacks plates on top of each other.

"You're a good girl, Arla." My grandma kisses my daughter on top of her head and looks at me. I don't need to know what's going through her mind right now, she's already given me her two cents. She's a little upset with me right now because I didn't return Jack's call. By the time my shock and surprise wore off, I deduced he was halfway to Canada and didn't want to bother him or ask him to turn around. Plus, I need to think about what I'm going to say. How do you tell someone you haven't seen in ten years that they have a daughter? I would've told him earlier, but it seems you can't walk into a recruiter's and ask for someone's address. I asked my uncle, the senator, but he wouldn't help. Something about compromising his job. I think my parents told him to ignore my request. I don't have proof, just suspicion.

I finally rise from my seat and start helping with dinner clean-up. My grandfather has retired to the den to watch some sport program. He's a diehard anything New England fan and will watch whatever comes onto one of the many channels. Sundays, at my grandparents, are crazy. Their house is full of people, and the dining room table turns into a buffet. If you come over, you must bring a dish or something to share.

Once the table is clear, and all the dishes are in the dishwasher, I tell Arla it's time to head home. She groans and drags her feet toward the entryway. I used to be the same way when it was time to leave here. "Go, give Gramps a kiss."

She heads toward the living room and says, "Mom says I have to leave now, Gramps. I'll see you tomorrow."

"Bye, Bum."

Arla returns to the kitchen and dramatically throws her arms around my grandmother's waist. Arla does this every time she leaves here or my parents. She makes it seem like she's never going to see them again.

"I'll see you tomorrow," Grandma says as she kisses Arla the top of her head. Next, it's my turn. I pull my grandma into my arms and tell her that I love her.

"Please call him," she says softly into my ear. I nod against her.

It takes Arla and me less than five minutes to drive from my grandparents to our home. Our house, like many of my family members, faces the lake. And while I don't have lake frontage, I do have access and a dock. As soon as we get inside, Arla drops her backpack and heads to her room. She has a routine to follow, and I rarely need to get on her to take care of her stuff. I smile as soon as I hear the shower start. While she's showering, I putter around my living room. I go from sitting, to standing, to moving the pile of gossip magazines from their usual place next to the couch to the kitchen table and then back again. I decide to start the pellet stove, even though it's not cold out, and pull a bottle of red wine from my small rack. I definitely need some liquid courage to get through the rest of the night.

The shower stops, and Arla appears moments later dressed in her bathrobe and her hairbrush in her hand. She gives it to me and then sits down on the floor. Quietly, I brush her long blonde hair, working through a few snags and snarls.

"I think I want to cut my hair."

My heart seizes. I love her long hair and have only cut it once since she was born. "How come?" I ask, trying to remain calm.

She shrugs. "Pippa got her hair cut."

"Pippa got gum in her hair, and Aunt Caroline had no choice but to cut Pippa's hair."

"Oh."

"But if you still want a haircut, we can make an appointment."

Arla shrugs again. "Maybe. I'll think about it."

My hope is that this subject matter is now closed, and my heart can return to a somewhat regular beat, although this is likely to change when I find the courage to make a phone call tonight. Part of me hopes Jack doesn't answer, while the other half hopes he does so I can get the news out there and let him figure out what he wants to do. The question plaguing my mind right now is whether I tell him over the phone or not. There isn't some handbook on how to say to the father of your nine-year-old daughter that he, in fact, has a child. Believe me, if there was, I'd have pages dog-eared, tabbed, and highlighted.

Arla and I snuggle on the couch together and watch a show before I tuck her in for the night. We read her favorite story, *Rugby and Rosie*, which we've done every night since she was three. After I shut her light off, I head back to the kitchen and finally open the bottle of wine I pulled out earlier. I pour more than customary into the glass and take a sip while looking out my kitchen window.

My phone rings, and I jump, sloshing my drink. "Shit," I mutter as I rush back into the living room. My heart pounds rapidly, echoing in my ears until a wave of relief washes over me when I see my cousin Frankie's name on my screen. "Hello."

"Krew said I needed to call you." Frankie may be family, but also one of my best friends. We are only a few months apart in age and grew up together.

"I'm sure he did." I sit down with a heavy sigh and set my glass on the table next to the couch. "Jack came through town today. Krew served him at Lottie's and told him to call me. He did, but I didn't answer because it was an unknown number. He left a message and asked me to call him."

"Holy shit."

"My sentiments exactly. I'm nervous. What if he hates me?"

"How can he? He left, and you had no idea how to get a hold of him. It's not like you didn't try."

"I know, but I always wonder if I could've tried harder."

"Lottie, you can't second guess yourself. Even that lady he lived with had no idea how to get in touch with him. We tried everything we could think of."

I sigh and lean back into the cushion. "I know. Should I tell him I want to see him or just tell him over the phone about Arla?"

Frankie is quiet for a minute and then says, "As much as it's going to suck for him to hear this over the phone, I think you need to tell him. If you invite him back to Holyoak, he may decline or think you want to see him. I know you want to tell him in person about Arla, but if he's married or something or needs time to process this, he should be able to decide if he wants to come to Holyoak."

"What if he doesn't want to meet her?"

"That's a bridge we will cross after you tell him. If he doesn't, you go on telling Arla the same thing you've told her from the beginning. You haven't lied to her."

"I know," I say quietly. When Arla first started asking about her father, I didn't know what to say. Lying didn't seem right, so I told her the truth. She knows I have no idea where he is but has always known his name. I thought that was important. "I'm going to call him or at least try," I tell her. "I might need you to come over and actually dial the number."

Frankie laughs. "Just let me know. I can be there in ten minutes. And call me when you're done talking to him. I want to know everything!" Her excitement for my situation makes me smile.

"I'll let you know." I hang up, finish my glass of wine, and get a refill. There isn't anything I can do about my nerves, the tightness in my throat, or how I feel like my life will change when I tell Jack he has a daughter.

I replay Jack's voicemail and scribble his number down on the notepad I keep next to the couch. For a moment, it feels like I'm back in high school and inviting him over. Only we aren't in history class. We're adults with a massive bomb between us whose fuse is about to run out of space.

My thumb hovers over his number. I finally press it, close my eyes, and pray, I can do this. Jack answers on the second ring.

"Hey, Jack. It's Charlotte."

CHAPTER FIVE
JACK

THE VOICE ON THE OTHER END OF THE PHONE MAKES ME SPEECHLESS. Never in a million years did I think I'd ever speak to Charlotte again. As an eighteen-year-old leaving for basic training, I had zero expectations to carry on a relationship with her. Would it have been nice? Without a doubt. But I also wasn't hurt that we ended. This was and still is how my life works. Aside from the Army, Mitch is my longest-lasting relationship.

"Hi . . . Charlotte." It takes me a second to get her name out. I had zero expectations that she'd call me back, despite what Krew said, and I'm wholly unprepared to hear her voice. It's like I remembered, soft and quiet, and can still get my heart racing. I point to the door of the hotel room, signaling to Mitch that I'm stepping out.

"Sorry I missed seeing you," she says. "What dumb luck it is that you'd come in on the one day I'm not there."

"Yeah," I sigh. "I guess luck has never been on my side."

"No, I guess it hasn't." There's a long, awkward pause until she clears her throat. "Is this a good time to talk? I'm not interrupting anything, am I?"

"No, not at all. I'm happy to hear from you." I imagine she's smiling on the other end. Like she mentioned earlier, it seems luck has never been on our side.

"How have you been?" she asks.

"Good, I guess. I'm in the Army and currently stationed in Italy."

"Wow, Italy. I bet it's beautiful."

Not nearly as beautiful as I thought you were when we were together. "It has its moments, just like any other place. So, what about you? Are you married?" As soon as the question comes out of my mouth, I want to take it back. Of course, I want to know, but it shouldn't be the first question I ask her. "I'm sorry, that was a bit rude."

"It's fine," she says with a hint of laughter in her voice. "I'm not married. Are you?"

"No, I'm not either."

"Good . . . I mean, oh." There's another pause. "I'm sorry, this seems really awkward, doesn't it?"

"It does, but only because it's been ten years or so since we've spoken. I'm sure we have a lot to tell each other and probably some stuff we'd rather not say."

"You're probably right. To answer your other question, obviously, I still live in Holyoak, and like I said earlier, I work at Lottie's—well, run it mostly. My grandfather handed it over a few years back."

"Did you major in restaurant management or whatever the degree would be? If I remember correctly, you were headed off to Boston for college."

"Yeah, I never went. I stayed home instead."

"How come?"

Charlotte's deep inhale echoes in my ear. "Jack," she says my name tenderly, sending shivers down my spine. "I have something to tell you," she pauses.

My heart sinks as I wait for her to finish. "Go ahead."

"I have a daughter. Her name is Arla. She's nine-years-old. And she . . ." There's another pause and what I believe to be a sniffle. Is Charlotte crying? "She's yours. You're her father."

My mouth opens to say something, anything, but there are no words. It's like my brain has stopped working. The silence grows between us. Only the sound of us breathing can be heard. Surely, I didn't hear her right. There is no way Charlotte said the words I'm replaying over in my mind.

"Jack, this isn't how I wanted to tell you. When I found out—"

I interrupt her and ask, "Can you repeat what you said?"

"Which part?"

"The important part."

"We have a daughter. A beautiful, energetic, smart, and amazing daughter."

"Daughter," I mutter. "Are you sure—" I stop myself before I insult Charlotte further. "I'm sorry, I don't mean that the way it sounds. I just . . . I don't know what to say."

There's some movement on her end, and I definitely sense that she's crying, making me wish we were having this conversation in person. Damn it, why couldn't she have asked if I was coming back to town? I would've, for her.

"I know it's a lot to take in. I can send you a picture of her if you want. I think she looks like you. The only pictures I have of us together are from that summer before you left. We were both so young."

"I'd love to see her," I tell Charlotte. "What did you say her name was again?"

"Arla," she says. "Arla Mae Carmichael. I named her after my grandma."

"Arla," I say her name slowly. It's cute, different, and I find myself smiling when I think of her name. I bet she's the only Arla in her class.

"I just sent you a picture. It's from a few days ago. We were at the lake, feeding the ducks."

"Okay, let me look. I'm in Montreal, so the service is a bit spotty." I pull my phone away from my ear and open my text messages. It takes a minute, but Charlotte's name appears. I had added her name to my contact list as soon as Krew gave it to me, even though I was unsure whether I would call her not. Now that I know why Krew was so insistent that I do, it all makes sense.

I open her text and wait for the image to load before clicking to enlarge. Her face, with a toothy grin, fills the screen of my phone. Her hair color is the same shade mine was when I was younger. A dirty blond is what my foster mothers would say. Once I shaved it, my roots started to darken. Honestly, I can't remember the last time I let my hair grow enough to remember what it looked like. It's Arla's eyes though that catch my attention. Big and bright blue, full of life. She looks like a happy child, a loved child. Tears fall from my eyes, and I wipe them away. I'm not a crier. I'm not even emotional most of the time because I've learned not to care, but there's something about this little girl staring back at me that makes my knees weak.

"Charlotte, I'm so sorry," I say when I bring the phone back to my ear.

"For what?" she asks.

"For leaving you alone to deal with this, to raise a child by yourself."

"You didn't know, Jack. I tried to find a way to get word to you, but it was hard not knowing where you were."

"That's my fault. I could've written or called." I take a big shuddering breath to try and compose myself. "Fuck, I really messed things up for you."

"You didn't, and we're fine. I promise. I'm not telling you about her because I need or want anything from you. I'm telling you because you have a right to know. Krew was right to tell you to call me."

"Does she know about me?" I don't even know why I ask because I'm certain the answer is no. Who would tell a child about their missing father?

"She does. She knows your name and knows that we cared deeply for each other when you were here, and she knows that you joined the Army to protect our country and her."

"Jesus," I say as tears stream down my face. I've done nothing in my life to deserve this sort of care or love. Hell, I'm not sure how to return it.

"Can I meet her? I know I don't have the right to ask."

Charlotte lets out what I'd considered a chuckle or gasp for air. I can't be sure. "Of course, you can. I won't keep her from you unless it's what you want."

She's giving me an out, an escape. I've never had anything in my life that was mine. Even now, the Army owns me. They tell me where to go, what to do, and how to dress. Arla gives me something to live for, someone to love that could love me back, even though I have no idea how to make things work.

"I'd like to know her, Charlotte, as much as my job allows. As I said, I live in Italy. It's not like she can fly there for a weekend visit."

"We can figure all of this out later. Are you passing back through this area? I can arrange a meeting."

I get the sense that she doesn't plan to be there, and the truth is I'd like to see her as well. "What about you? Can I see you?"

Charlotte doesn't say anything. My phone vibrates with an incoming call—a video chat from Charlotte. I accept and wait for the screen to show me the girl I once knew. She smiles, and just like that, I'm transported back to the day when she invited me over to study. I was so foolish in thinking she just wanted to hook up, thanks to that kid in our class.

"Hey," I say to the most beautiful woman I've ever known. Her hair is darker than I remember, and small pieces frame her face. She looks tan, likely from the summer she spent on the lake.

"Hey," she says back. There are more awkward pauses, much like the rest of our conversation, but this time, we're staring at each other, and it feels good.

"It's really good to see you," I tell her.

"You too. I wish this were yesterday or even tomorrow when I'm at the restaurant."

"You know, I almost didn't stop, but my friend was hungry. I saw the sign for Holyoak and took the exit. I'm still in shock that Krew remembered me."

"I'm thankful he did," she says with a grin.

"Are you? This doesn't make your life complicated?" I've heard enough stories from my team about a weekend fling turning into a lifetime commitment. However, Charlotte and I had more than a weekend thing going on.

Charlotte nods. "This is a good thing for you and Arla. She's asleep now. Otherwise, I'd let you talk to her."

"Is it okay that I'm okay with her being asleep? I don't know what I'd say."

She chuckles. "Fair enough. I guess she has the upper hand since she knows your name."

"Yeah, I guess she does. Do you think she'll like me?"

Charlotte gets up from sitting and walks through the room. She keeps her phone focused on her face, making it hard for me to see where she's going. A light comes on, and she sits down again. "I want to show you something. We are in my office, and this is a picture she drew in school a few years back." She turns the camera around and zooms in. The drawing is of three people, two adults standing on either side of the child, holding hands. Above it, it reads "my family," which brings another wave of tears. I wipe them away before Charlotte can see them.

"She's going to love you, Jack. It may take her a bit to warm up, but I wouldn't worry about her feelings or her being scared."

"I'm worried she will have expectations that I can't meet."

"She's nine. She expects the moon and then some," Charlotte says, laughing. "Do you know when you can stop by, or we can meet you, someplace?"

"I have a wedding to go to tomorrow, and my buddy wants to tour Montreal, although I'm very tempted to get back into the car and drive back to Holyoak because I don't want to wait to meet our daughter," I pause and let the word "daughter" soak in. "Wow, that's powerful."

"I can imagine you're probably going through the same things I went through when I found out I was pregnant."

"I'm sorry I wasn't there," I tell her. "I would've been."

"I know you would've, Jack. That's why she knows about you . . . about us. It's never crossed my mind you would've abandoned her."

"Or you," I point out.

Charlotte smiles but says nothing.

"I'll be back in Holyoak in three days. I won't have much time because we have to be back on base, but at least a day and a half. I'll book a room."

"I'll take care of the room with my aunt, or you can stay with Arla and me. There's a couch in my office, and we have a guest bedroom."

"I don't want to impose."

She laughs again and shakes her head. "Your daughter is going to insist on it. Call me when you're on your way."

"I will."

"Good night, Jack. I'm really happy you're back in town."

The video ends before I can say anything. I don't know how long I stay out in the hall, an hour or longer, once we've hung up. I keep looking at the picture of Arla, trying to memorize her features. She looks like her mother, but maybe there's a hint of me in there as well. It's hard to say.

That night, I stare at the ceiling and wonder how different my life would be if I hadn't boarded the bus that day.

CHAPTER SIX

CHARLOTTE

ARLA STANDS IN FRONT OF HER MIRROR WITH HER HANDS HOLDING THE hem of her dress. She insisted on getting a new one for this occasion even though I told her the ones she has hanging in her closet would do. Her new one is pink, much like the others, but with a small petticoat underneath, making the dress poof. I think she likes it because it fans out when she spins, but what do I know?

"You're very pretty," I tell her as I come into the room. Gently, I brush my hand down her hair, trying to tame the curls she asked for. She moves away and sends me a glare through the mirror.

"You're going to mess my hair up."

"I'm sorry." I sit on the edge of her bed and continue to watch her. The morning after I spoke with Jack, I told Arla he was in town and asked if she wanted to meet him. In hindsight, I should've waited until after she was home from school because her teacher called two hours later, saying Arla was having trouble sitting still in class. I've since kept her home until after the meeting because she's far too excited, and I don't want her to get into trouble.

Arla turns and looks at me. "What if Jack doesn't like me?"

"He's going to love you." I try to assure her with a smile.

"But what if he doesn't?"

"Then it's his loss, and we go about our day like any other day."

She faces the mirror again. "Do I look like him?"

"I think so."

"But Gram says I look like you."

"It's hard because Gram sees us together every day. If Gram saw Jack, she would probably say you look like him as well."

"I suppose." She studies herself, tilting her head from right to left. "I'm going to give him the pictures I drew."

"I think he would like that. It gives him something to take back to his home."

As soon as I say the word, her mood turns sour. There's nothing like dangling a shiny new toy in front of them, only to take it back and say they can't play with it for a long time. Jack lives an entire world away in her mind. I haven't even discussed what a time zone means. That's a whole other conversation for a different day and a battle I expect to lose with her. She's nine, going on fifteen, and isn't afraid to let me know it at times.

"Can you do me a favor, sweetie?"

Arla nods and looks in my direction.

"Please remember that Jack just found out about you, and he might be nervous. You know about social cues and when to back off, so watch for his. Okay?"

She nods. "What if I scare him away?"

Even though she'll be mad because I might wrinkle her dress, I pull her toward me. I rub my nose against hers in a back-and-forth motion. "There is absolutely nothing scary about you, my sweet baby girl. You are kind, sweet, and perfect. Jack knows your name, what you look like, and he knows how much you care about him even though you've never met him. Just don't forget, he has to leave. He has a very important job."

"But he can come back, right?"

"He can visit you anytime he wants," I tell her.

The doorbell rings, and her eyes go wide as her mouth drops open. Before I can form a response, she bolts from my arms and her room, yelling, "I've got it." I'm hot on her trail even though my heart is pounding out of my chest. I feel sick to my stomach like I did the first time I invited Jack over when my parents were gone for the weekend.

Arla swings the door open and stands there with Jack on the other side. He looks better in person, rugged and handsome. He crouches down, focusing on Arla. She towers over him, but they're staring at each other. I do everything I can to fight back the tears, but it's impossible. I've pictured this moment a thousand times, but never like this. Never in the doorway of my home.

"Hi, I'm Jack," he says, breaking the silence between them. He holds his hand out to shake hers. Arla's head tilts downward, making me wonder what she's thinking. She answers my thoughts when she launches herself into his arms. Jack picks her up and wraps his arms around her waist. We make eye contact and hold it until he covers his face with his hand. Behind Jack, there's a shadow, and his friend comes into view. The last thing I want to do is interrupt Arla and Jack, so I motion for his friend to come into my house.

"I'm Charlotte," I tell him as we shake hands. "You can call me Lottie."

"Mitchell Lochlan. My friends call me Mitch," he says. "I've heard so much about you on this trip. I feel like I've known you most of my life."

"Oh boy, I can't imagine what Jack had to say. Come on, I'll show you to your room."

Mitch follows me down the hall. I show him into my office. I've opted to give Jack the guest room because it's closer to Arla's room, and I have a feeling he might want to be nearby. "You're away from all the noise in the morning," I say. "Arla can be a bit loud when she wakes up. She likes to sing and dance before school."

"Sounds like my sister. She hasn't met a song she doesn't like."

I laugh. "That's Arla. She knows none of the lyrics and still belts out the words like she wrote the song."

After Mitch sets his stuff down, I show him the bathroom and into the kitchen, where I have set out some sandwiches my grandma made, as well as lemonade and a plate of freshly baked cookies.

"You own the restaurant with all the beer, right?"

I nod. "I do." There is no need to explain that my grandparents are private partners or that someday I'll inherit the business entirely if I want it.

"The beer bar is amazing. Best thing I've seen in years."

"Really? I figured in Italy they must have something similar."

"Nah," he says with the shake of his head. "Wine everywhere. Craft beer is starting to become popular, but it'll never be as popular as wine."

"Well, I'll have to visit because I do love a nice wine."

"Jack would like that." Mitch's eyes go wide, and he closes his mouth. He likely just betrayed his friend, and I'm going to pretend he never said anything.

I suggest Mitch dig in and hand him a plate. Over the years, I've learned that people are unlikely to start eating until the host does, so I make myself a plate and set two more out—one for Jack and the other for Arla. As tempted as I am to check on them, I don't. They need their time together to navigate these thick waters created by absence and distance.

Mitch and I sit down across from each other. I ask him where he's from and about his life. He talks a mile a minute, telling me everything about his family and how his girlfriend from high school is still around, but he can't decide if he loves her the way he should or if he loves the idea of her. "Either way," he says, "with me being stationed in Italy, our relationship is sort of a moo point."

"Moot," I say automatically. I pause and shake my head. "I'm sorry I shouldn't have corrected you."

Mitch laughs. "I say moo because Joey from FRIENDS is my favorite character ever. He makes me laugh when I need it the most."

"Moo, it is."

Mitch's statement makes me wonder if he and Jack have been to war. It's not a question I should ask, even though it's on the tip of my tongue. Honestly, aside from Jack and Mitch, I've never spent much time with anyone from the service. Shockingly, none of my siblings or cousins have ever talked about enlisting. Although my cousins, Rhys and Oscar, could use the discipline. My uncle Dean lets those boys run wild.

We are halfway through our meal when Jack and Arla finally join us. They're holding hands, and I try not to get choked up, but my efforts fail me.

"Hey," he says when we make eye contact.

"Hey."

"Can I talk to you for a minute? Somewhere private?"

"Of course. Arla, sweetie, this is Mitch. Jack's friend. Be nice," I warn her even though she'll be a real peach to him.

"Sup," he says to her as I push my chair away from the table. I follow Jack but tap him on the shoulder to come with me down the hall. We step into my bedroom, probably not the best idea, but it's the most private, and Arla knows to knock and wait before she's allowed to enter.

I sit on one end of the bed and pat the other for Jack, but he's too focused on the photos I have around my room to pay attention. "I have duplicates of most of those if you want them."

He nods and says nothing.

I get up from my bed and go into the closet. I pull down the box marked "Jack" and take it to him. "Everything in here is yours."

His eyes are red-rimmed and full of unanswered questions. Jack takes the box from me and opens it carefully. "Why?"

"Why what, Jack?"

"Why does this box have my name on it?"

"Because I have held out hope we'd meet again someday. Or that when Arla turned eighteen, she could put her DNA into one of those search databases and find a match." I shrug.

He thumbs through the box and pulls out a photo. "She looks a lot like you."

"And you."

"Let's hope for her sake she takes after . . ." Jack pauses and smirks. "Never mind. She'll have to tell all the boys that come calling her—" he stops and looks at me.

"Do you want to be Jack to her? Dad? Father? It's your choice."

He guffaws. "She asked me the same thing and told me pointedly she intends to call me dad, so I should accept it."

I start to laugh. "I think I forgot to mention she's very opinionated, strong-willed, and quick on her feet. There isn't much that gets by her."

"I think she's amazing," he says as he sets the box down. He finally sits, the mattress sagging a bit. "I don't know how to proceed. Do you need money?" Jack asks. "I don't have much, but I can pay child support. I'll change my life insurance over to her name right away. I'll have the base call you so you can give them all her information if that's okay."

"That's fine, Jack. I don't need child support or anything." I reach for his hand and hold it in mine. "My door is always open for whatever you want or need when it comes to Arla. I'm not keeping her from you, hiding her, or demanding anything. She knows you live in Italy but doesn't quite understand that part other than you not being here every day. I fully expect her to text you non-stop, video chat, and she's already started a new book of drawings she wants to send. If you don't want any of this from her, just say so. I can deal with it. But, if you start a relationship with her, I ask that you keep it. I don't want to hear in six months, or a year this isn't working out for you."

Jack looks at me. There's so much emotion in his eyes, in his features. He's hurting, and I caused it even though that was never my intent. "I'm not going anywhere, Charlotte. I don't even know her and can already say she's the best thing to ever happened to me. Already, my life has meaning and purpose. I've never had something that belongs to me until now."

Without hesitation, I pull him into my arms. I know all about his childhood and going from home to home. He confided in me when we were teens how he'd often show up at a new home with nothing but the clothes on his back. Until he met my family and me, Jack never had anything new. One day, while we were shopping, my mom bought him a whole wardrobe of things without him knowing. When we arrived back at my house, and he was helping carry bags in, she pulled him aside and handed everything over. I know he cried in her arms that day, but he would never admit it.

"I'm so sorry it's taken me this long for you to find out."

"I'm sorry it's taken me this long to return."

We part, and both dab at our eyes. My heart aches for him. Jack clears his throat and reaches for my hand again. "Where do we go from here?" he asks.

"Well," I say after taking a deep breath. "We can go to eat lunch and let Arla tell us what to do."

Jack laughs. "I can already sense she's going to be the death of me."

"The perfect way to die if you ask me."

He looks up and smiles. He pulls the box of photos onto his lap. "I'm going to look at each picture until I have them all memorized."

I take the one in his hand and flip it over. "They're date stamped, with a little note of what we were doing or what milestone it's for."

"Wow, it'll be like I was there. What made you do this?"

"You," I tell him. "I figured if I ever found you or we crossed paths again, you'd want to know your child has had the best life possible."

He shed a tear and doesn't bother to wipe it away. Jack continues to go through the photos and finds one of us. "Blast from the past."

"I put that in there after Arla used it for a school project. I'm not sure why."

Jack chuckles. "It's so when I'm back on base and lonely, I can look at it and remember that summer. That one, unforgettable summer."

CHAPTER SEVEN

JACK

TODAY HAS BEEN A DAY OF FIRSTS. THE MOST IMPORTANT BEING THE meeting of my daughter. *My daughter.* The concept is so hard to grasp even though the evidence is right in front of me. Arla looks like me and even has a few of my mannerisms. Earlier, Arla laughed at something her mom did. Her laugh was infectious and brought a smile to my face. I wish I would've written down what exactly happened to make her laugh so I can remember it when I'm back in Italy or had my phone recording all day. I'm afraid I'm going to forget all of this.

Another first, I finally feel like I belong somewhere, almost as if I'm home on leave and my family is happy to have me here. There isn't anything awkward about being here, I don't feel uncomfortable, and when Arla has asked her mom to do something, Charlotte suggests she ask me, her dad. *Her dad.*

And then came bedtime. Arla asked me to read her favorite book to her. I jumped at the opportunity and sat near her head to read the words. She told me her mom has been reading this book for as long as she can remember, and though she's nine, she doesn't want her mom to stop. When we finished, I made a note of the title to have one sent to base. I want to read the story so Arla and I can talk about it when I'm back in Italy.

When I come out of Arla's room, I walk into the living room. There's a fire in the pellet stove, and it's relatively quiet. I lean against the doorjamb and watch Charlotte, who is curled up on the couch with a blanket over her legs and a book on her lap.

"Hey, how'd it go?" she asks, closing the book and setting it on the table next to the sofa.

"It was one of the most amazing experiences of my life. I can't even explain it."

"I know what you mean."

I push off the doorjamb and walk toward Charlotte. She moves the blanket away from the cushion next to her, which makes me pause. Does she want me to sit there even though the seat at the end is available? Maybe she does. I know I do. I sit down with a happy sigh, one of contentment and elation.

"What a day," I say.

"I'm glad you could shorten your sightseeing trip with Mitch to come here. It means a lot to Arla and to me as well."

Glancing at her, I smile. "After what you said on the phone, a hurricane wouldn't be able to keep me away. I'm just sorry I can't stay longer."

"We wish you could stay longer too."

"We?" I question.

She nods and reaches for my hand. I give it to her willingly. "We. I feel like we have a lot of lost time to make up for. I know Arla wants you to stay. She has a list of things she wants to show you."

"I want to stay," I tell her. "I haven't wanted something so desperately until now. In a matter of hours, you've given me the one thing I've never had—a family."

Charlotte smiles. I know we haven't seen each other in ten years, and I'm probably reading into things but damn it if I don't want to kiss her. My luck, she has a boyfriend. But if she does, would she hold my hand?

"Can I ask you a few questions?"

"Of course," she says.

"Some of them might be a bit personal."

"I'm a big girl, Jack. I can take it."

I chuckle and shake my head. Shy is never a word I would use with Charlotte. Inhaling deeply, I prepare for the questions lingering in my mind. "Okay, here goes nothing," I say as I look at her again. "Has Arla ever referred to another guy as dad?"

Charlotte's head shakes back and forth so fast her hair whips her in her face. "Absolutely not. From the day I found out I was pregnant, I knew you were her father. I said this when we were on the phone the other night, I tried to get a message to you, my attempts were futile. I asked my family to help, but . . ." Charlotte stops talking, making me wonder what her family thought.

"They weren't happy?"

She shakes her head. "My parents weren't thrilled. They talked about adoption, and at first, I went along with it because I was young. Then I saw Arla on the screen during my ultrasound and promised her I'd be the best mom possible."

"You did all of this by yourself?"

"No, I had my grandma. She was very supportive. My cousin Frankie—do you remember her?"

"I do, and Ginger, right?"

"Yeah, Ginger Ward. I had a good team, and my parents worship Arla. She is the light of their lives, as with my grandparents. She's the best thing to ever happen to me."

"It can't be easy dating."

Charlotte laughs. I don't know why, but it makes me smile. "If you want to know if I have a boyfriend, just ask. I'll save you the time—I don't. I haven't dated since you left. It's never felt right, and I've never wanted some random man coming around Arla. Too many horror stories, and she's far too important for some guy."

I'm thankful Charlotte can't hear my heart beating because right now, it's thumping loudly. I can't tell if it's because she hasn't dated anyone since I left or if it's because her love for our daughter outweighs her happiness.

Oh, who the hell am I kidding—my heart is going wild because I like her, and she's single. I sort of expected her to be when Krew told me to call her, but I didn't want to assume.

"If I had run into your brother, would he have told me to call you?"

"Yeah, anyone who knew you back then would've told you to call. You're not a dirty little secret. You're my daughter's father. You're family."

"I'm family." Those words bring a wave of tears forward. To some, it's just a word and doesn't mean anything. To me, it means I have a place to call home. It means people love me. I cover my face with my hand to hide my reaction. Within seconds, warm arms wrap around me.

"It's okay," Charlotte whispers. "Everything will be okay."

"How do you know?"

"Because you're here. This will be your home. Arla isn't going anywhere."

I move my hand and tilt my head to look at Charlotte. "What about you?"

"I'm here, Jack." Charlotte adjusts the way she's sitting and faces me. She's so beautiful. She always has been. Her dark blonde hair is in a low ponytail. Earlier, when we arrived, she had it down and curled. It took every part of me not to reach out and pull on one of the ringlets. It was something I had done in the past. Now, those curls are resting over the front of her shoulder, still tempting me.

"We haven't seen each other in ten years," I remind her. "We've changed. What if we're different?"

Charlotte chuckles. "I should hope we're different. We've grown up, we've changed. Life changes us. I'm a mom who runs a restaurant with a meddling family who has an opinion about everything. You're protecting our country, making us safe, and now a dad. The dad part is a huge pill to swallow. I'm just letting you know that I'm here if you want. There's a reason I told you to stay here."

"What's that?"

"Because selfishly, I wanted to spend time with you as well. I wanted to see if those feelings I remember from so many years ago are still there," she says with a shrug.

"Are they?"

Charlotte nods, and this is my cue. I lean toward her and cup the back of her neck to bring her closer to me. "I had no idea how much I missed you until I saw the sign for Holyoak. Living here was the only time in my life I felt like I had friends or any semblance of a family, and now . . . I can't put into words what all of this means to me, and it's because of you. You kept our daughter when you could've given her up, and now you've given me the best gift I have ever received. I feel like I should give you a thank you card or something. I don't even know."

"I know what you can give me, Jack."

"What's that, Charlotte?"

"A kiss. If you don't kiss me, I'm going to kiss you. I've thought about it since Krew texted that he saw you. I wondered for the rest of the day if you had a wife or a girlfriend and asked myself how I would react. The truth is, I've waited for you to come back. Deep down, I knew you'd return to Holyoak, and I'd be here, waiting. Right along with Arla."

Her words are enough to spur me into action. I close the distance between us and press my lips to hers. They're soft and familiar. Her mouth opens, welcoming me to deepen the affection I hope she feels coming from me. When we part, her forehead rests against mine.

"I'm so happy you're back but hate that you're leaving."

I pull away and hold her gaze with mine. "I have a lot of decisions to make. My enlistment is up for renewal. There are options for me, and they all have pros and cons, but I promise you, any decision I make, we'll make together because I'm not going anywhere, Charlotte."

"Neither are we."

I nod and fight back another wave of tears. "We can text and video chat every day, and I'll call on the weekends. With Arla being in school, the time zone sort of messes up when she and I can talk, but it'll work. There are times when I have trainings and such, but you'll always know. And I'll be back for Christmas. If you want me here."

"Jack," she says my name softly. "Stop asking if we want you. This is your home now, and if you need me to prove the point, I'll put your name on the mailbox and give you a key."

Charlotte makes me happy. I pull her back into my arms and kiss her again. "I think if you're going to do that, you'll have to give me some space in your closet."

Her head falls back in a giggle. "Now you're pushing it, but I think I can find some space."

"That's all I can ask for."

It may have taken my entire life, but I finally have a family. One that wants me, no matter what.

THE END.

MY FAVORITE MISTAKE
BY LAUREN RUNOW

CHAPTER ONE

AS I SPIN THE BOTTOM OF MY BOTTLE AROUND, MY MIND GOES BLANK, AND my sight stays glued to the reflection the glass is making on the table from the flickering candle next to me. It's been quite the day, and seeing the design helps me remember the beauty I know our world still has.

I need to find any sign of goodness I can right now.

I know I should be at a church or doing a good deed, so I might find better Karma coming my way, but somehow, I ended up here, at a corner bar in the middle of San Francisco.

The pressure was becoming too much, and I had to get out of my house before I snapped. Or at least, more than I already had.

I drop my head to my chest, close my eyes, and take a deep inhale.

"Everything okay?" a man asks.

When I raise my head, there's a handsome guy with the most piercing blue eyes I've ever seen. His hair is short, and his jaw is straight, but his expression is what makes me pause. Genuine concern laces every centimeter of his olive skin.

The kind of concern I wish I got from other people in my life.

When I don't respond, he tilts his head, leaning down a little closer when he says, "I'm sorry to bother you, but I couldn't help but stop to make sure you were all right."

I nod, trying to grin through the pain I'm feeling deep inside that I've had to hide for so long. "I'm fine. Thank you for asking." I blow him off and go back to tilting my bottle.

He doesn't buy my lies. "Want to talk?"

I glance around the mostly empty bar to see if he's with someone else.

He points to the door that's closing after someone apparently walked out. "My friends just left." He holds up his hands in declaration. "I swear I'm not the type of guy who comes to bars alone, looking to pick up distraught girls."

I chuckle under my breath. "So, you think I'm distraught?"

"Sorry, wrong word choice. Maybe not distraught. More like you might need a shoulder to cry on or an ear to talk to."

"I thought guys didn't like listening to other people's problems?" I say with my eyes still glued on the table.

He leans down further to catch my sight. "Tonight might be the exception if you're up for hanging out with a stranger."

Everything about him is caring and sincere. The way his eyes soften as he waits for my response makes me want to talk to him, and surprisingly, I feel comfortable with him.

I point to the chair in front of me. "Sure. Why not? Have a seat."

He does and holds out his hand to me. "I'm Travis."

I shake it. "Michelle."

"Well, Michelle, can I get you another beer?" He points to the empty bottle now sitting in front of me as I nervously run my hands down my pants. "Or do you want another shot?" He picks up the shot glass that I downed the second it was handed to me.

I purse my lips to the side, wondering which one I want more, and he laughs, picking up both.

"I'll get one of each. What was in the shot?"

"Whiskey."

"Nice." He raises his eyebrows. "Any particular kind?"

"Nope. As long as it's dark and it picks me up, it's all the same to me."

He points his finger at me acknowledging my request in a *sounds good* type of way and steps toward the bar. With no competition for the bartender's attention, he returns quickly, setting both drinks in front of me.

I pick up the tiny glass, pausing when I see I'm doing the shot alone. "Nothing for you?"

"Nah." He holds up his beer to cheers my shot glass. "I have an important day tomorrow. No hard stuff for me."

"What's so important?"

"Big test. I'm finishing my doctorate at USF."

"Well, Mr. Fancy-Pants Doctor-to-Be, I'll be here, drinking my whiskey alone then, if you don't mind." I tilt my head back and down the amber liquid, which burns all the way through my body.

"No, please, by all means." He pauses. "How was it?"

I chase it with a beer. "Horrible now, but it will be worth it here shortly."

"So …" He waits to make sure it's safe to ask and then goes for it. "What are we drinking to? A broken heart? A fight? A job? Family?"

"All of it. Every single one." I take another drink.

"Well then, now, I understand why it's a shot-and-beer kind of night. Want to talk about it?"

I shake my head while I inhale a breath. "Nah, I'd rather hear about you. Tell me, where are you from? Something tells me it's not here."

His grin proves I'm right. "And why would you say that?"

"Most guys would pass right by a girl who's alone and having trouble."

"Well, my mom raised me right, I guess." His smile grows as he takes another drink.

"And where is said mom?"

"In a very small town up in Humboldt County. Population: nothing."

My eyes widen. "And you came to USF for school?"

"Yeah, there's not really a ton of med school options up in the middle of nowhere."

"I'd love to live in a small town." I sigh at the notion. I never thought I'd be living in the city, yet here I am, hating every minute.

He laughs out loud. "No, you wouldn't. Everyone knows everyone, and don't even think about trying to keep a secret."

I grin at him, biting the inside of my lip as I try not to laugh.

"What?" he asks.

"Nothing." I pick up my bottle to take a drink, eyeing him over the rim.

"Don't lie to me. What?"

I shrug. "It's just funny. That's all."

"What is?"

"The fact that you said everyone knows your business. I think that trait rubbed off on you."

"How?" He sits back in his chair, waiting for me to make my point.

"Well, you're sitting here right now, aren't you? Wondering what my problems are? You won't go tell Sandy at the co-op if I tell you, will you?"

A sharp laugh escapes his lips and hits me deep in my chest. A bright smile grows across my face at the sound. It's been a while since I've made someone laugh or even felt they were happy to be in my presence.

"Touché," he says. "And no, I won't go tell Sandy. Now, Todd at the gas station though? He has a way of getting information out of anyone. So, if you don't show him you're upset, then he won't ask me if I know anything, and we'll be good."

I pick up my bottle to cheers him. "You've got a deal."

We both sip our drinks, not taking our eyes off of each other.

"So, what about you? Where are you from?" he asks.

"Originally about an hour from here. I've lived in the city for three years though."

"Do you like it here?"

"No." I take another sip, not even contemplating the question.

"Whoa, don't try to fight those feelings now. Tell me how you really feel."

I sigh as I set my drink down. "It's not the life I thought I'd have. That's for sure."

"Isn't that everyone's life?" he asks so nonchalantly that I'm intrigued.

"Do tell. What's different in your life than you expected?"

He crosses his arms as he thinks. "Multiple things. I'm about to graduate, and I have no job offers. And I've been single almost my entire time here in San Francisco."

"You mean, you haven't been the knight in shining armor who sweeps in to save the day of a woman drowning her sorrows in a beer and a shot?"

He lets out another deep laugh, and it lifts my spirits more than the last. "Nope. Definitely hasn't happened … until you."

I playfully raise my eyebrows and take another drink, letting that comment sit in the air for a second. "So, if you don't have any job offers, will you go back home?"

"I doubt it. Not much to go back to. My mom already said she'd move wherever I landed."

"Seriously? She'd pick up and move her life for you?"

"Yeah, she knows there's not much work there for me. Family is everything when it's just the two of us. I want her near me too."

"Just the two of you? Can I ask where your dad is?"

"He died before I was born. Killed in the Gulf War."

I suck in a sharp inhale, surprised to hear this so nonchalantly. "Oh my God, I'm so sorry."

"I mean, I never met him, so …" He shrugs and takes another drink. "My mom moved back home, where they both were from. I was raised with his parents, so I know a lot about him. Over the years though, they passed as well as my mom's mom, so now, it's just us."

"She never remarried?"

"Oh no." He vehemently shakes his head. "She says he was the love of her life. I'm hoping once I get her out of there, she'll find someone. It's kind of hard to date in a town of twelve hundred people."

My eyes widen. "Only twelve hundred people?"

"Yep. I told you, everyone knows everyone."

"I'm sorry you never got to meet your dad though. I'm sure he'd be proud to see you're becoming a doctor."

"Yeah, it's a weird catch-22 with that. I attend college for free because he passed in the war. Where all of my friends are in debt up to their eyeballs, I've only had to pay for books and my housing while I've been in school. I work part-time at the Lazy Bear in the Mission District, so that hasn't been too hard."

"That's a fancy place to work," I say, impressed he works at a restaurant like that.

"Yeah, pays well too. So, I guess it's nice that I get to let his legacy live on that way." He pauses and eyes me suspiciously. "Wait, why am I spilling my guts to you when I'm here to lend you a shoulder to lean on?"

I rest my elbow on the table, placing my chin on my hand, and move closer to him. "Because you're way more interesting than me, and you're helping by giving me a chance to forget my problems."

His grin covers his face ear to ear. "Well then, glad I can help." He raises his glass and takes another drink.

CHAPTER TWO

"THERE'S NO WAY YOU ACTUALLY DID THAT," I SAY, SLAPPING MY HAND ON the table.

Travis snorts as he laughs, and it's the cutest thing ever.

"I'm telling you, when you live in a small town, you have to get very creative when it comes to entertaining yourself. Tipping over the sheriff's tractor seemed like a good idea at the time."

"Were you ever caught?"

He shakes his head with a huge grin on his face. "Nope. It was a big ordeal too. The city was in an uproar for weeks. They finally blamed it on some weed growers who live in the hills, thinking the sheriff must have pissed them off."

"I can't believe none of your friends spilled the beans."

"Are you kidding me? We saw firsthand how much trouble we would be in. Hell no. We all stayed tight-lipped on that."

"So then, it is possible to keep secrets in your small town," I say with a grin, raising my eyebrows.

He flashes me a gorgeous smile. We stare at each other, and I feel that pull, that connection that's been happening between us.

"Tell me, Travis ... how have you been single the entire time you've been in San Francisco?"

He takes my hand that was playing with the Sierra Nevada coaster, which originally sat under our drinks. "I've never met someone like you." I blush, and he continues, "I'm serious. Look at the time. Did you realize we've been sitting here for four hours?"

My eyes open wide. "Seriously?" I search around the bar to see no one around us.

"I don't know about you, but I'm learning I'm not a city person. Everyone here is into big clubs or fancy dinners. Give me a barbeque and a backyard with just a few people, and that's my kind of night. Call me a small-town boy, but the big city doesn't really fit me, you know?"

I nod, pursing my lips. "Yes. I know exactly what you mean. I moved here three years ago, thinking it'd be exciting but it hasn't been. I'm over not being able to find parking and then walking three blocks in the freezing cold with the wind blowing like crazy every time I'm in between the buildings."

He laughs out loud, knowing exactly what I mean.

I grew up an hour away, where it's normal weather. Here, it's always cold and windy.

"So, no matter what, you're leaving the city after you graduate?" I ask. I'm not sure how his answer will affect me, but for some reason, it's making me nervous.

His lips tilt up in a slight grin. "If you had asked me that yesterday, I would have said absolutely. Now, I guess it all depends."

My face turns flush as my heart beats rapidly. I don't get to respond because the bartender walks over to our table, interrupting our moment.

"Sorry, guys, but we're about to close down."

He grabs the four beer bottles that cover our table. Besides my shots when he first got here, that's all we've had these past four hours.

Travis looks at me, and I sigh, pursing my lips together as I reach for my purse. Sadness rips through my body at the thought of leaving and going home. Tonight has been the best night I've had in a while, and I'm not ready for it to end.

Our conversation has flowed this entire time. I didn't even notice it'd been an hour since I finished my drink, and I never cared or needed another one. All the stress that had riddled my body as I entered this place is totally gone, and I feel like a completely different person, just being in his presence.

I stand, and Travis covers my hand with his.

"Don't leave yet," he says, and I see the sincerity in his eyes.

They click off the lights to a portion of the bar, and we both laugh as he stands. We walk together toward the door. The silence is painful. I'm not ready to say good-bye, but I fear this is it.

As we step outside, I turn to him, taking a deep inhale, readying myself to say goodbye. Before I do, he slips a hand around the nape of my neck and kisses me with so much passion that I melt.

As he pulls away, he holds me close, placing his forehead to mine. "Please don't leave. Come back to my place for the night."

With my brain still in a lust-filled haze, I nod and forget my entire life when he kisses me again. Then, he walks me back to his truck, which is parked on the street.

His place is only a few blocks away, but we both stay silent for the entire ride. The air is so thick, as we both know what's coming and are dying to get the opportunity to touch again.

When he parks, I try to make my mind go blank and think about nothing else but that kiss and the emotions I've been missing for so long.

I open the door, and when he meets me at the front of the truck, his fingers slip into mine. He leads me to a bottom-floor apartment. It's dark when we enter, but I breathe a sigh of relief that he doesn't have roommates—or at least, they aren't home if he does.

He clicks on the lights and wastes no time in walking me back to his room. After he kicks the door shut, I'm back in his arms, and his lips are pressed to mine.

All my inhibitions go out the window, and I reach down, pulling my shirt over my head, revealing the black lace bra I have on underneath. His hand runs over my breast as his other hand grips the back of my neck, bringing his lips back to mine.

There's this urgency between us but also this passion I've never felt before. With every breath, I breathe him in, and it opens my heart to things I've only read about.

Things I never thought I'd actually feel.

As his lips trail down my neck, I take a deep inhale, letting the emotions run through me like a drug, living in the moment.

I run my fingers under his shirt and slowly lift it until he pulls away from me briefly, so I can remove it completely. Once it's off, he yanks me closer to him, and the warmth of his body envelops my soul as he holds me tightly while making his way to his bed.

We simultaneously lie down together, him on top of me, and he kisses his way down my neck and over my breasts. He slides the bra strap down my arm, and when my nipple pops free, he sucks it into his mouth, sending sensations directly to my core, which only makes me want him—want this—more.

He unbuttons my skinny jeans, and I shimmy my hips, kicking off my shoes and helping him slide them down my legs until they're completely off. He stands to remove his own jeans and then his boxers.

When his cock springs free, I lick my lips as my chest tightens. I can barely breathe; I feel so much need to have him near me, inside me, claiming me.

As he lowers himself to me, he tucks his fingers under my panties, pulling them down until they're on the floor. He reaches for his drawer, and his face tightens when he doesn't find what he's searching for.

His eyes meet mine, and I know he's saying he doesn't have a condom. I rub my lips together and slowly shake my head side to side, telling him I don't have one either.

I watch as he closes his eyes and takes a deep inhale. My heart sinks when I realize this probably won't happen, as neither one of us has protection.

I sigh as I move to make my way up when he stops me and says, "Wait, I have one in my wallet."

He moves faster than a cheetah on the hunt and reaches for his wallet, where he does indeed produce a condom from the sleeve.

Relief floods my body as I bring my hand to his face and kiss his lips, just like he did with me before, hoping to revive the feelings I almost lost.

Within seconds, I'm breathing heavily as I wrap my fingers around his girth, tightening my chest for the second time in the short period I've been in his room.

I lie back on the bed while he wraps the condom on and positions himself against my entrance. When he pushes in, his lips crash to mine, and I moan from the pleasure ripping through me, finally getting what I wanted—what I needed—since his lips first touched mine.

As he moves in and out of me, my body glides with him in synchrony. We're in perfect alignment, and for this moment, I feel free, alive, and like I'm floating above my body.

My life has been nothing but stress and pain for the past year, and right now, none of that matters. I only exist to feel his strength glide through me and bring me the happiness I need now more than ever.

When his hands find mine, intertwining and gripping them tightly, he moves them above my head as he grinds into me. My entire life erases. I fully give it over to him. Handing him my heart and my soul.

He hurries his thrusts, and I feel the urge, the desire to fall climbing higher and higher. He grunts a manly sound, and I explode around him, clenching him with my body and letting that last bit of me go.

His hands hold mine tighter, and I feel his release. Once we both float down to earth, his lips find mine, and he kisses me so softly, so meaningfully that I almost want to cry.

I want this.

I want him.

But my life has already been given to someone else.

CHAPTER THREE
SEVEN WEEKS LATER

AS I STAND ON THE STREET, I CHECK MY WATCH FOR THE THIRD TIME, nervous he's not going to make it. Finally, I see Daniel turn the corner. One look at his face, and I know he's not in a good mood. I remind myself that at least he's here, and I try not to second-guess anything.

I head toward him, wrapping my arm around the elbow he offers me, not removing his hand from his pockets.

"Thank you for coming," I say nervously.

I've been sick for weeks, and I finally made a doctor's appointment that I was too afraid to come to alone. Having to beg my husband to attend an appointment with me is something I never thought I'd have to do.

We've been spending more time apart while he dives into his work as a criminal attorney as I try to be the doting wife, making dinners for him, only for him not to come home.

I try to remember the man I married, and I know he's still there somewhere inside. He has to be. People don't change into completely different human beings overnight, yet that's what I've been facing for the last few years.

We were happy in our small town. At least, I thought we were. After we got married and moved to the city, away from my family and friends, he did a one-eighty. The nice guy who had swept me off my feet seemingly couldn't care less about me—that is, unless he wants to tell me how horrible of a wife I am.

If I don't have the table set and house spotless when he gets home, I know I'll never hear the end of it. He's even gone as far as throwing all of our clean, folded clothes across the room because I was in the middle of putting them away when he walked in the door.

I'm starting to feel like his maid rather than his wife.

I keep trying to tell myself that this is just a rough patch in our marriage, but the more time that passes, the more I don't know what to do.

I believe in the sanctity of marriage. When I said, "Till death do us part," I meant it—even though more recently, I've been spending more days wondering about death rather than the marriage I'm in.

I think all the stress I'm under is what's causing my current issues. I'm so conflicted with my life that I'm literally making myself sick.

That's why I wanted Daniel here. I'm hoping it will open the conversation of our home life in the safety of my doctor's office. Maybe if Daniel hears how stressful situations are bad on people's well-being, he'll soften his demeanor with me.

I know it's wishful thinking, but I'm desperate at this point.

Daniel opens the door to the doctor's office for me. I sign in, letting the doctor know I'm here before we both take a seat in the waiting room. Daniel instantly takes out his phone, answering an email, so I pick up the *People* magazine sitting next to me.

The nurse calls us back and leads us into the room. Once she takes my temperature and vitals, she leaves us alone as we wait for the doctor. Daniel doesn't even spare me a glance and continues to type away on his phone, like he's at his desk and not at an appointment where there might be something horribly wrong with his wife.

Dr. Parker enters the room with a friendly smile on his face. "Michelle, Daniel." He reaches his hand out to me and then Daniel, who finally puts his phone away and places a fake smile on his face. "It's so good to see you. What brings you in?"

"Well"—I place my hand on my stomach—"I really haven't been feeling good. I feel nauseous all the time, I've had horrible headaches, and sometimes, I'm so tired that I feel like I can't get out of bed. I just feel weak and flush, no matter what time of day it is."

He sits down on the rolling stool and types his password into the computer. "The nurse said your vitals are good. When was your last period?"

"I'm due in about a week."

"And was your last period normal?"

I bite my lower lip. "It was really light, but I've had that before. My period has always been all over the place."

"Well"—Dr. Parker reaches in a cabinet, handing me a container—"why don't we have you take a pregnancy test? That way, we can rule that out before we do anything else. Just take this and go to the bathroom. While you're doing that, I'll look over your chart some more and see what our next plan might be."

My stomach instantly turns even more than it already was as my heart beats rapidly through my chest. I wasn't even thinking about pregnancy because we barely have sex. Hell, it's been weeks.

Ever since before that night with Travis.

I push the idea out of my head as I hop off the chair.

I grab the container from him as Daniel says, "Dr. Parker, is this even necessary?"

I turn to him, furrowing my brows. *What kind of question is that?* I was thinking a baby was exactly what we didn't need in our marriage right now, but I can't believe he would be so blunt about our lack of a sex life.

"It doesn't sound like that's what's going on, but let's just rule it out before we move on," the doctor says to Daniel and not me.

I head to the restroom, taking deep breaths so I don't throw up in the hallway. On top of feeling absolutely run-down, now, my nerves are shot. If I am pregnant, I'll have to make some big decisions. With the way my marriage is going, I would never want to put a child through my life. Marrying him was my fault that I must live through, but I don't want to ruin someone else's life with my poor choices.

When I enter the room, I set the container on the counter and take my seat back on the exam chair. Dr. Parker talks about the weather and how the fog has been pretty light, but honestly, all of his words are mush in my brain as I stare at the test, waiting to see what it says.

When Dr. Parker's shoulders fall forward, I breathe a sigh of relief, as no one would ever be sad about having to tell someone they're not pregnant, especially if they weren't even trying.

He is probably tired and was hoping this would be an easy answer, so he wouldn't have to run more tests and help me figure out what's going on.

"Congratulations," he says as he turns toward me, sitting up straighter.

I inhale a sharp breath.

"You're going to be a mother."

"I'm what?" I ask, my eyes feeling like they're going to bug out of my head.

"She's what?" Daniel asks, standing so fast that the chair he was on hits the wall behind him.

His eyes meet Dr. Parker's, who steps back with his head down. Confusion races over me until Daniel strides out of the room, leaving me.

Well, I guess that answers any questions I might have had about him wanting to be a father.

I blink away tears that make me even more upset. I hate the way he constantly makes me feel.

Frustration from the past few years races through me and fuels my fire as I jump off the chair. "Where are you going? Daniel?" I yell, grabbing my stuff.

I stop at the door and turn back to Dr. Parker. "I'm so sorry. I don't know why he did that. I should—"

"Go," Dr. Parker urges. "You two need to talk."

I turn and follow Daniel out of the office. When we get to the street, I yell to him, "Daniel! Please, stop. Why did you leave like that?"

I run after him, and he stops. He glares down at me, and I see anger I never thought I'd see from him. He might be rude to me on a constant basis, but the rage radiating off of him right now is new and frightens me to my core.

"How could you?"

I step back. "What do you mean?"

"You do realize that Dr. Parker now knows you're a whore who cheats on her husband?"

My eyes widen as visions of that night with Travis flash through my mind, but I quickly blink them away. There's no way. This baby is Daniel's. It has to be. Travis and I used protection.

But why would he say that, and how would he know?

"I don't know what you're talking about," I say not very convincingly, even to myself.

He lets out a huff, shaking his head, stuffing his hands deeper into his suit pockets. "Let me see if I can spell it out for you. You're pregnant, and I know for a fact that it's not mine."

I shake my head in disbelief. "No. No. That's not true. You have to be the father."

He shakes his own head. "Nope. I'm not, and you want to know how I know that?"

I take a deep breath, feeling like my life is collapsing around me.

"Because I had a vasectomy a year ago."

My fear turns to rage. "You what?" I yell, not holding back one bit.

He gets closer, his anger even more evident. "I decided I didn't want kids. So, I took measures into my own hands and solved the problem before you got pregnant without allowing me to be a part of the decision. Dr. Parker is who gave me the referral."

I cover my mouth with my hands, not sure whether to cry or scream. "And you didn't tell me?"

"No. It's my body." He gets closer to my face. "So, there you go. I. Can't. Have. Kids." He takes a step back and crosses his arms. "So, tell me, oh wife of mine, who knocked you up?"

I see red, nothing but flaming red, when I bring my hand up and slap him across his

face before turning and walking in the opposite direction.
The day I married this man has just turned into my worst nightmare.

CHAPTER FOUR

IN THE SUNSET DISTRICT IN SAN FRANCISCO, I STAND AT THE FRONT DOOR of my best friend, Liz's, house, carrying my bags with tears running down my face. I didn't bother to call before I came, so when she sees me for the first time, looking like a hot mess, her reaction is exactly what I expected.

"Oh my God, what happened? Come in. Michelle, sweetie." She wraps her arms around me.

I sob into her shoulder for a solid minute before she leads me inside. Thankfully, her husband is still at work, and I try to hide my face from her daughter, Sophie.

"Sophie"—she kneels down to her—"would you mind going to your room and turning on a movie, so I can talk to Michelle?"

"Sure, Mommy," she says as she skips down the hall with her blanket in tow.

Seeing her disappear around the corner just makes me cry harder. I've wanted a child for so long, but I thought it would never happen with the marriage I was in. Now that I'm pregnant, I don't know what to do.

When Liz sees me with my face in my hands, she rushes to my side and leads me to the couch, leaving my bags in the middle of her living room.

"Okay, please tell me what's going on. I'm really getting scared here," Liz says, rubbing her hand down my back.

I sit up, swallow the shame I feel, and admit, "I messed up."

Her eyes open wide. "You messed up? How?"

"I slept with someone else," I say through more tears.

Liz rubs her lips together as she takes a long inhale. "I know this isn't what you want to hear, but, girl, I've never been prouder of you."

I flip my head up to see her more clearly. "Excuse me?"

She sighs before she lets it all out. "None of us like Daniel, but we wanted to support you, hoping we would see what you did. It only seems like he's gotten worse instead of better. I've always felt like you deserved more."

I close my eyes as tears spill out. She wipes them away.

"Sweetie, don't cry." She reaches for a tissue from a box she has sitting on the end table.

I take it from her and wipe my cheeks. "You're right. It has gotten worse, but I still had hopes that the man I'd married would return somehow."

"So, did you tell him? Or I'm guessing he found out somehow?"

I stare right at her, my face frowning so much that I might look like I'm melting.

She grabs my hand. "Is there something else you want to tell me?"

I nod ever so slightly, taking in a shaky breath, and when she sees my face, everything sets in.

"Oh …"

"Yeah. Oh …"

"So, I take it, you don't know which one the father is then?"

I shake my head. "No, I know whose it is."

"Then ..." She leans down her head to try to see my face, waiting for me to speak.

"I thought for sure it was Daniel's. I mean, I was only with that guy once. It was a huge mistake, but Daniel and I had just gotten in a big fight, so I'd left and ended up at a bar. The guy was there, and he was so sweet. He made me feel alive for the first time in years. I'd thought, with age, that feeling just disappeared, and real life took over. I'd thought what I felt every day was normal."

She grabs another tissue and wipes my face. "No. You should never feel anything but happy. Why didn't you tell me it was that bad?"

I shrug. "Like I said, I thought it was normal."

"But wait, how do you know it's not Daniel's? Did you guys not have a sex life?"

My fists clench as I hear his words in my mind. I close my eyes, letting the anger, frustration, and hurt wash through me before I open them and say, "Because he told me he had a vasectomy a year ago."

She stands instantly. "He did what? And he never told you?"

I shake my head, placing my palms on my face as more sobs escape my lips. She races back to my side.

"Then you told him you were pregnant, and that's when he told you it couldn't be his?"

I nod. She pauses as the silence bounces between us.

"Can I ask who this guy is?" she asks cautiously.

I sit back and slump on her couch. "His name was Travis. I left in the middle of the night when everything sank in. I panicked. So, yeah, I never got his number."

"But you know where he lives then?"

I nod.

"Are you going to tell him? Or are you thinking of ..."

My eyes meet hers, and she knows my answer to the second question she didn't have to ask. I'm absolutely keeping this baby, no matter what. Just like my beliefs in marriage, I feel the same way about life. Since I already ruined one, the other isn't even a thought.

She grabs my hand again and smiles brightly. "Well, we're having a baby. Let's not let that asshole take that away from you. Maybe that's why you met this Travis guy. He gave you the one thing you couldn't get from Daniel."

A sharp laugh escapes my lips. "That's one way to look at it."

CHAPTER FIVE

THANKFULLY, LIZ IS LETTING ME STAY AT HER PLACE AS I FIGURE OUT WHAT I'm going to do. When her husband got home, he was quick to tell me how much he didn't like Daniel as well.

It's weird to learn how everyone has had the same feelings I was starting to experience with Daniel. Yes, they figured it out before I did, but I was blind by hope and empty promises. It's nice to know they still supported me even though they had certain feelings about him.

I've spent the last week in absolute despair, but I have finally faced the facts. I'm ready to pull my big-girl panties up and move on with my life, no matter how different I thought it was going to be only a few short days ago.

As I stare in the mirror, I take a moment to let the fact that I'm pregnant really sink in.

I place my hand on my stomach, closing my eyes as I say, "Hey there, little one. I know you're entering the world in a different way than I would have liked, but I need you to know that you will always be wanted by the only person who matters—me. I'll always be here for you, and I can't wait until we get to meet."

Tears fill my eyes, and I blink them away. I don't want to mess up my makeup that I just did. I have an important conversation to have, and I don't need to look a wreck when I have it.

I exit the room I'm staying in and see Liz in the kitchen, making breakfast. When our eyes meet, she puts down the spatula and heads toward me to give me a hug.

"Are you sure you don't want me to go with you?" she asks once she steps back and tends to her eggs again.

"No. I got myself in this mess, so I can do this," I say with all the confidence I can find deep inside because, honestly, I'm freaking out.

"Here." She steps around the counter to the fridge and opens it, handing me a glass from it. "I made you fresh juice. You have a baby to care for now. We'll get you one of these daily to make sure you get your fruits and veggies."

I take it from her and give her a hug. "Thank you for everything."

She smiles big. "Go knock 'em dead." Then, she laughs. "Okay, bad advice for what you're about to do." She pauses, searching for the right words. She finally shakes her head with a shrug. "I guess just *good luck* fits."

I hold up my glass in thanks again. "I'll take all the luck I can get."

I leave her place with my juice in hand and hop in my car, driving toward my destiny with no clue what's going to happen.

When I pull up to Travis's apartment, my stomach is in my throat, and I have to calm my breath, so I don't throw up. I've never had nerves like this.

As I approach his door, all the memories of that night and the way I felt alive when I was with him come rushing back. All I can think about is what Liz said when I first told her. I'm a huge believer of everything happening for a reason, and maybe she's right.

We used protection, yet something went wrong, and I still got pregnant. I was married for five years and never once had a scare—well, that is, before he had his vasectomy. Maybe this is God's way of trying to show me Daniel isn't the one I should be with and that I deserve to be happy.

I stand out front of Travis's door and take a deep breath, knowing this will change both of our lives forever. Before I can chicken out, I raise my hand and knock.

I hear a female's voice on the other side of the door and question if I should run and come back later. I don't have time to make up my mind because the door swings open, and a gorgeous blonde with long legs and big boobs smiles sweetly at me. She looks around eighteen, and when I glance down at my summer dress that I barely fill out, my chest tightens.

"Can I help you?" she finally asks when she sees me staring and not saying a word.

I swallow the lump in my throat and ask, "Is Travis here?" My voice cracks, so I cough and then repeat myself when she shows me she missed what I said, "I'm sorry. Is Travis here?"

"Who is it, babe?" a male voice asks from down the hall.

She turns and shouts back. "Someone asking for Travis."

The guy approaches, and to my dismay or delight—still trying to process things as I go along here—it's not Travis.

"I think I saw some mail with the name Travis on it," he says.

The girl turns back to me. "Sorry, we moved in a few weeks ago. You must be looking for the previous tenant." She takes in my expression, and I feel like I have a flashing neon light that says *I'm carrying his baby* by the way her face changes. She reaches her hand out to me, placing it on my wrist. "I'm really sorry we don't have more information. You might be able to ask a neighbor where he moved to."

I nod and take a deep breath, faking a smile. "Yeah. Um, it's okay. No worries. Thanks for your help."

I turn and leave before I make a bigger fool of myself. Once I get to my car, I turn and see she's following behind me. I stop, and she gives me a sweet smile.

"Hey, do you maybe know where he works? Or you could check social media."

"I don't know his last—" I stop myself short. How embarrassing to admit to the girl that I don't even know his last name. I quickly recover. "I don't know his last place he worked," I lie even though I know exactly where my next stop will be.

"Okay." She smiles again, and I know it's laced with sympathy.

I give her the same grin back and hop in my car, heading straight to the Mission District and the restaurant he said he worked at.

Of course they're closed due to it being so early so I walk around the back and, thankfully, people are there who must be prepping for the day. I knock on the back door and wait for a response.

A guy dressed in a white apron opens the door and stares at me with a questioning expression covering his face. "Can I help you?"

Instantly, I feel like a stalker when I realize just what I'm doing and how it must seem to them. I really should have thought this through and come back later today when the restaurant was open and I could enter through the front door.

I try to come off as normal as possible. "I'm sorry to bother you, but I'm looking for Travis. Do you know if he's working tonight? I'm from his hometown, and I wanted to surprise him," I lie and pat my back when I remember he's from a small town up north.

The guy shakes his head. "Travis quit a while back. He moved somewhere out of the city after he graduated."

I close my eyes, trying to fight back the tears, and then I open them and put on an act because, now, my lie isn't coming off so well. "Well, shoot. His mom didn't tell me that. You don't know where, do you?"

The guy shakes his head, narrowing his eyes, and I can tell he's starting to think I'm some crazy woman.

"Sorry. I got nothing," he says.

Before I can say anything else, he shuts the door, slamming out any hope I had of finding him without coming out and saying, *I'm a whore who cheated on my husband, and I got pregnant from a guy I barely know that used to work here.*

I step back, and with my head held low, I walk back to my car as Liz's words sing through my mind again. If everything happens for a reason, then there must be a reason he left as well. Maybe he did give me the one thing Daniel couldn't.

I place my hand on my stomach, not sure if I should try harder to find Travis or just enjoy the gift he gave me and be thankful for it.

CHAPTER SIX
SIX YEARS LATER

"LEIGHTON TRAVIS JOHNSON, IF YOU DON'T COME HERE RIGHT NOW, YOU will not get ice cream after your appointment," I yell as I stand at the front door, waiting to leave.

"I'm coming! I'm coming!" I hear my young boy say as the pitter-patter of his little feet come running toward me.

"Where are your shoes?" I place my hands on my hips in question.

He's definitely been testing my patience lately with his whole *no, I do it* mentality. I want to encourage his independence, but having things take ten more minutes than necessary is trying at times.

"They're in my room. I'll get them!"

He turns and runs away, and I have to take a deep breath to calm my frustration. After a minute, I head toward his room to find him playing with the new game I bought him.

"Leighton," I say as I pick up his shoes, walking toward him to put them on his feet, "we have to go."

Leighton has a doctor's appointment for a yearly checkup, and then we're going to enroll him in kindergarten. I can't believe my little boy is old enough to go to kindergarten. These past six years have been a whirlwind but one I wouldn't change for anything.

Raising my son by myself has been difficult, but we've figured things out together, and now, he's my best friend.

I know that's weird to say, that a five-year-old is my best friend, but he really is. He's my bud, and there's no one on earth I'd rather be with. We cook dinner together every night. Well, he sits and watches me cook dinner, but we dance to music while doing so. I love waking up to his snuggles, and his hugs good night are my everything.

He might not have come into this world like I had hoped, but God knew it wouldn't matter, and he was exactly what I needed.

He didn't give me Leighton though without a constant reminder to go with it. If I ever thought I'd forget what Travis looked like, he made sure that would never happen. Leighton is a spitting image of him. At least, what I remember of him.

He has curly blond hair, where mine is dark and straight. His eyes are crystal blue, like Travis's, and his skin tone matches his, whereas mine has a paler tone. There's not a day that goes by where Travis doesn't cross my mind, just by looking at Leighton. I only hope he has his personality as well and that I raise him to be just as kind as I thought Travis was.

I close the Velcro on his shoe and stand him up. "You ready?"

He reaches for my hand. "Let's go, Mommy."

We head out the door and face the next challenge—him wanting to buckle his own car seat. He's gotten faster, but I've learned how to guide him while still making him think he's doing it himself.

When we finally arrive at the doctor's office, we make our way to check in. "Hi, we have an appointment with Dr. Rivers."

"I take it, you're Leighton?" the kind woman behind the desk asks, coming around and leaning down to speak with him at his level.

"That's me!" he says proudly.

"You don't look like you're five years old," she says, playfully narrowing her eyes.

"It's because I'm almost six!" Leighton says.

I laugh. "Not for a few months still."

She smiles at him. "Well, I'm Sandy. Welcome to our office." She holds out her hand to shake his and then walks around the counter, back to where she was, gathering the forms for me.

I recently got better health insurance, so even though the community clinics were okay, I'm glad I was able to get in with Dr. Rivers. I've heard on the playground that he's the best around and he really knows how to work with the kids to ease their fears of going to the doctor.

After she copies my ID and insurance card, I make my way to a chair to finish the registration paperwork. Leighton heads to the corner, where a play area is set up. He's instantly in heaven when he sees the racetrack they offer with the bucket of Hot Wheels to go with it.

Once all of our paperwork is finalized, another woman opens the door and turns to Leighton. "You ready to see how big you are?"

Leighton hops up, running through the door.

I laugh as I follow. "You know how to get their attention, huh?"

"Yep, especially the boys. They always want to see how much they've grown." She shows me a growth chart they have in his paperwork, where they'll mark his height as he grows. It's super cute with his name written big across it.

She has him stand tall against the contraption that measures him and then marks it on the chart.

Leighton's face lights up. "Mom, look. It has my name on it!"

I rub my hand over his curls. "I know. Pretty cool, huh?"

The nurse shows us to the treatment room, where she takes his temperature and blood pressure, and then leaves after letting us know that Dr. Rivers will be in soon.

Only a minute later, the door opens, and my entire world stops. My heart freezes, and my mind goes blank. I glance to Leighton and back to the man standing in the doorway. When our eyes meet, I see exactly what I'm feeling.

He recognizes me.

I know it's him.

When he looks at Leighton, his face turns pale.

It should. He must feel like he's looking at a smaller version of himself.

CHAPTER SEVEN

WE SIT IN SILENCE AS I LET EVERYTHING SINK IN FOR THE BOTH OF US.

How is he here?

I went back to Travis's restaurant one more time and left my number for them to give to him. After a month went by without hearing from him, I gave up hope and decided if I was going to raise this child on my own, I would need the help of my parents. So, I moved back to my hometown of Rohnert Park, which is about an hour out of San Francisco.

No, my parents weren't too happy with my life choices, but we can all say without a doubt now that Leighton is the exact joy that we needed in our lives.

I watch as he stares at Leighton, who's playing with the shirt he's wearing. It has a sequin design that shows a cat smiling on one side, and when you swipe your hand up the design, it changes to the same cat sticking his tongue out.

He thinks it's hilarious, and it's been a distraction right when I've needed it a few times now.

Travis picks up the chart again and reads the form I filled out. He closes it, and my heart pounds when he looks at me and asks, "Michelle?"

I take a big inhale and nod. "How are you, Travis?"

"I'm … I'm fine. How have you been?" He's talking to me, but his eyes keep wandering to Leighton.

"I've been good." I raise my hand to Leighton. "Busy, as you can see. How are you in Rohnert Park?"

"I was about to ask you the same thing."

"I grew up here. I moved back home when I was pregnant with …" I let my words trail off, not ready to go there yet.

"You're from here?"

"Yeah. How did you end up here?"

"I was hired out of school to work for Kaiser up the road. I left and started my own practice last year."

"Yes, you're spoken of very highly on the playground. I was lucky to get an appointment with you."

"I'm glad you did." He inhales, trying to get back to business and not let the shock overtake our moment. He turns to Leighton. "So … tell me about this young man."

Leighton looks up and smiles brightly at Travis. "Hey, you have the same eyes as me!" Leighton says with excitement, and my heart sinks.

Travis turns to me with a questioning expression that he tries to wipe away. "Yes. Yes, I do." He holds up his hand for a high five. "Give me five for cool matching eyes."

Leighton slaps his hand hard, and Travis acts like it hurt him as he laughs.

Travis grabs a stool and sits down while removing the stethoscope from his neck and shows it to Leighton. "Do you know what this is?"

Leighton shakes his head.

"I hold this up to you, and I can listen to your heart. Can you tell me where your heart is?"

Leighton places his hand over his heart like he's saying the Pledge of Allegiance, which his preschool taught him when discussing going to kindergarten next year.

Travis smiles and nods his head. "Good job. Now, I'm going to hold this up, and what do you think I'm going to hear?"

"When I lay against my mom, I hear a thumping sound. Will it be like that?"

"Yes, it will." Travis holds it up to Leighton's chest and smiles when he hears the beat. He takes them out of his ears and holds them up to Leighton. "Do you want to hear?"

Leighton grabs it quickly and puts them in his little ears. When his face lights up, I can't help but smile, thankful for the distraction, no matter how small it is.

Travis continues his exam of Leighton, and when he opens the chart to make notes, I watch as he stares at the paper, at what I know is the smoking gun, revealed in my own handwriting.

Leighton's middle name is Travis.

Travis stops what he's writing and meets my eyes, and then he turns to Leighton and back to me. I close my lids, afraid of what his expression will be, and nod my head slightly. When I open them, Travis's eyes are filling with tears. He quickly blinks them away as he gives me a blank stare.

He takes a large inhale, closing the chart before placing his hands on his knees as he nods his head slowly. When he jumps up off the stool and opens the door without saying anything, my heart stops.

Did he really just walk out on us?

I turn to Leighton, who's still playing with the stethoscope Travis left in his hands.

I go to stand but am stopped short when the same nurse who brought us in here comes in and holds her hand out to Leighton. "Come here, sweetie. We have a toy box you get to go through when you've been good for an appointment."

Leighton's eyes light up. "That was it? I'm done?"

The nurse laughs. "That's it. You did really well, so let's go pick out the best toy we can find."

I help Leighton off the exam table, and he rushes to hold her hand. I walk behind them but see Travis standing at the door. He holds his palm up, making it very clear that I am to stay put.

He smiles at Leighton as he leaves, and then he enters the room and shuts the door behind us.

We sit in silence as we stare at each other. The air is so thick that I feel like I'm suffocating. I rub my lips and grip my purse tighter when he steps closer.

"I woke up, and you were gone," he says, surprising me by going straight for it.

I tilt my head down, ashamed, not sure what to say in response.

"He's …" He leaves the question hanging there.

I inhale a deep breath and take the leap that I know will change my life from here on out. "Yours."

He leans back on the counter and crosses his arms. His head is moving like he's nodding, but I get the feeling it's more of a shocked response than on purpose. I guess it's not every day you find out you have a five-year-old you knew nothing about.

"How come you never told me?"

My head snaps up. If there's one thing I will not feel guilty about, it's that. "My period is never normal. I spotted the first month, so I never questioned it. It wasn't until seven weeks later that I felt really sick and went to the doctor. When I knew I was pregnant, I went to your apartment, and you were gone."

"I moved a few weeks after I graduated," he says more to himself than to me.

I step toward him, making sure he knew I tried. "I even went to your work. I'm sure they thought I was a stalker."

"Did you tell them why you needed to reach me?" His expression is covered in pain, and my chest tightens at the sight.

I step back, shaking my head. "I was too ashamed. They said they would never give out your information, so I gave them mine to give to you."

"They never did."

I bite my inner lip. "I didn't know what to think. I wanted to keep the baby, so I figured this was what was meant to be. I moved back home and have been living here ever since."

"Do you have—" He stops himself and checks out my left hand.

I shake my head. "No. I'm not with anyone." I tilt my lip up to the side. "He's the only guy in my life."

He steps closer to me with hope gleaming in his eyes. "Can we talk? Tonight?"

I grin as I nod my head. "Sure. I'd like that. Let me get my mom to watch Leighton."

"Leighton …" he says under his breath.

"Do you like it?"

"I love it. It's unique."

"He's a pretty special kid."

The slight laugh of amazement, disbelief, and shock that escapes his lips makes me laugh. I bet neither of us had any idea how different our days would end versus how they started.

I guess that's life, constantly throwing you curveballs. If you decide to swing or not is up to you.

A knock on the door startles us both, and Travis turns toward it as it slowly opens.

"Dr. Rivers, sorry to bother you, but your next appointment just threw up all over the floor, and I need to get the bucket that's in here," another nurse says.

"Oh, yes. Here." He opens a cupboard and hands her the bucket.

I take that opportunity to end this conversation until later. "I should grab Leighton and get going. I'm sure you have other patients to see."

He steps in front of me. "Tonight?"

I tilt my head toward the chart sitting on the counter. "My number is in there. Give me a call. I'll be ready, say, around six?"

He smiles a genuine smile that eases my anxiety about the moment. "Six it is."

I walk out of the room with my heart pounding and my breath taken away. For the past years, I wondered if I'd made him up in my head to be this great guy that he really wasn't. I thought maybe he was more handsome in the bar light than in real life.

I was wrong.

He's exactly what I remembered, but I'm not sure if my heart can take losing him now that I know what I thought was real.

CHAPTER EIGHT

I DIDN'T TELL MY PARENTS WHY I NEEDED THEM TO WATCH LEIGHTON tonight. I need to process what is going on before I let anyone else know. They've been a great help with raising him, but sometimes, their opinions are a little much, and I need to remind them that I'm Leighton's parent, not them.

I dropped him off an hour ago, and now, I'm pacing my place, wondering if I'm going to be sick as I wait for Travis's arrival.

When there's a knock at the door, my chest tightens, and I feel like I'm in quicksand, sinking to the unknown. Once I hear him knock for the second time, I shake myself out of whatever fear is going on inside my head and open the door.

He's dressed casually in a pair of shorts and a black polo. When my eyes meet his, I can't help but smile. Every emotion from that night comes rushing back, just by seeing his face.

He has a welcoming spirit that's contagious, and I just want to curl up in his arms like I did all those years ago and feel that level of comfort again.

"Hi," he says, snapping me out of my trip down memory lane.

I close my eyes and take a deep breath in before smiling sweetly and opening the door wide for him. "Hi. Please, come in."

He enters, and I close the door behind him, falling against it as I try to gain my composure because, really, what do you say to the man who impregnated you years ago and you haven't seen since?

That's when I notice he's carrying a bag. "What do you have there?" I ask.

He holds it up for me to see. "I thought we'd eat here, if that's okay." He shakes his head from side to side in a wishy-washy way. "I figure we have some pretty personal things to discuss, and doing so in a public place just feels weird, I guess."

"Oh, yes. Okay, that makes sense. Here." I walk toward the kitchen and grab some plates. "What did you bring?"

"Italian. I'm hoping you're good with ravioli and salad. Sorry I didn't call ahead to ask what you wanted. My staff places my dinner order when I have late patients and having them call you to ask didn't feel right. I told them to double my order saying I'll have it for lunch tomorrow as well."

"Yes, thank you for not having them call me." I laugh as I place the plates down on the table. "That might have been a little awkward, seeing as how I just met you today." Our eyes meet, and I add, "I mean, again."

His lips tilt up slightly at my mishap and how funny it is. This is only my second time seeing him today, yet I carried a part of him with me for nine months and have stared at his mini me every day since.

We dish our plates and sit down. The silence quickly sets in, and I hop up when it gets to be too much.

"Would you like some wine?" I ask, almost knocking over my chair.

I turn my back, so I don't see his reaction and grab a bottle I have sitting on the rack in my kitchen. When I spin around to hold it up for him to see, he's standing right there.

"I don't want you to be nervous," he says with so much sincerity that I want to melt right here.

I grin as I stop what I'm doing and give in. "I'm sorry. Why does this feel so weird?"

"Well, let's see. We met one night. Had an amazing time together, even more incredible sex, and then I woke up to an empty apartment with not even a note saying good-bye."

I sigh, staring up at him through my lashes, ashamed. "Yeah. That. I'm sorry I left."

He places his hands on my hips. "And I'm sorry you've been a single parent ever since then. I feel horrible that I wasn't there for you. I want to change that. I hope you don't mind, but I really want to be a part of Leighton's life. Does he know anything about who his dad is?"

A sharp laugh escapes my lips, but I recover it quickly when I realize this isn't really a laughing matter. "He knows his middle name is your name. Thankfully, he's too young still to ask serious questions, so I haven't had to say more."

"You haven't told him anything about me?"

I try to hide my giggles. "I don't know anything about you. I didn't even know your last name until today."

His shoulders sag, and I can tell I hit a sore subject with him.

"Hey." I nudge his arm. "Don't be sorry. I'm the one who left, remember?"

"Yeah, but it's still not okay. You shouldn't have had to raise a child on your own. I should have made it easier for you to find me."

"Come on." I move his large frame to face him back to the table. "There's no way you could have known."

He sits down, and I can tell something is weighing very heavily on his mind.

"But I wondered if you could have gotten pregnant," he says under his breath before looking up to me as I pour our wine.

"Now, why would you have thought that?"

He places his hand over mine, stopping me to make sure I'm paying attention. "When I was cleaning up the next morning, I picked up the condom wrapper. That was when I noticed I'd grabbed the wrong one from my wallet. I'd had that one in there since I was fifteen. It was expired by a few years. I kept it in there as kind of a joke. I thought I had grabbed the newer one I had as my just-in-case backup. So, really, this is all my fault."

It's my turn to put him at ease. "Leighton is no one's fault. He's been a true blessing in my life. I should be thanking you for giving him to me."

His head tilts to the side, questioning if I'm telling the truth.

"I'm serious. I was really unhappy, and when—" I quickly stop myself, not ready to tell him everything about that aspect of why I was at the bar that night. That will have to come later. I sit down and take a sip of my wine to buy time. "Just know, I've never blamed you for anything."

He nods, obviously feeling better about the guilt he must have been holding on to since we first saw him this morning. "Tell me about him."

That's when it hits me. Here I was, worried about what this meant to me, seeing him again, but I didn't put myself in his shoes. He just found out he has a son that he knows nothing about. My heart aches when I think about how much he's missed.

"Here, let me get something for you." I stand and head toward my bookshelf that houses my photo albums. When I come back, I'm wearing a huge smile as I show him my favorite picture of Leighton as a baby.

He's mid-bite of his food, and he gasps, wiping his mouth and then reaching out to grab the frame I'm showing him.

"This is him?" he asks in awe.

I sit and watch as his eyes tear up at the cutest little boy you've ever seen.

My mom loved playing a game with him where she would ask, "How big is that baby?" She'd taught Leighton to raise his arms high above his head, and she would say, "So big!"

In the photo, he has his arms up high and the cheesiest grin, making his chubby cheeks look even bigger. I can't look at the photo without a glee of happiness washing over me.

Travis peels his sight from the picture and turns to me. "He really does have my eyes."

I grin. "I can tell you, not a day has gone by since he was born that I haven't thought about you when I see him."

He props the photo up on the table, so we can see it clearly.

"Was he a good baby?" he asks, taking another bite of his food.

"As long as he was being boob-fed, he was happy."

"That's my boy," Travis teases.

I pick up a napkin and throw it at him, which feels really good because he's right. Leighton is his boy, and for the first time since he was born, I'm not worried about having the conversation with him about who his dad is.

After dinner, we move to the couch, where we spend the rest of the night talking about Leighton and where we've been since he was born. Every memory I had of Travis comes rushing back. I learn quickly that I didn't just make him up to be something he wasn't.

He's better.

He's grown, as I have too. I can see the maturity of being out of college and being a doctor has done him well. He tells me he hasn't dated much, but by the looks of him, I find that hard to believe. When he mentions how he spends most of his days with married women and their kids, it makes a little more sense.

"What about you? Have you dated much?" he asks.

I'm nervous to tell him I haven't been with anyone since him, so I leave that part out and say, "The only dates I've had are with a little blue-eyed boy."

He takes my hand and stares into my eyes. "So, what about *this* blue-eyed boy?"

My heart stops, and I inhale a quick breath.

Thankfully, he continues, "I've thought about you often after that night. We definitely clicked. I'll never understand why you left, but none of that matters now. Seeing you again was a surprise—especially with Leighton—but I'm so glad to get a chance to be with you again."

I grin, knowing I feel the same way. All night, I've felt like we were back at the bar, getting to know each other all over again yet really for the first time.

We stare at each other, and I feel that pull, that drive that brought us together last time. It's more than magnetic, and it's bigger than the universe.

Right now, he's the only thing I want, and when he takes my hand in his, I feel his touch deep in my soul.

"I know we've already done this, but, Michelle, I really want to kiss you," he says, running his finger down my cheek.

I lick my lips, nodding my head and leaning into him.

When we meet, sparks fly, and electricity shoots through my body. It's here and now that I remember why I threw caution to the wind. When he touches me, I feel things I didn't know were possible. Last time we were here, I thought it was the pain Daniel had brought me as well as the loneliness our marriage had caused me. Now, I know it was none of that.

It's him.

If there's anything such as soul mates, Travis is absolutely mine. There's no doubt in my mind now. The universe brought us together twice and gave us Leighton in the process because it knew we were meant to be together, just in due time.

When he pulls away from me, he takes my hand and places it against his chest, so I can feel his heart pound.

"Do you feel that?" he asks, keeping my palm against him.

I nod and take his hand, holding it against my own beating heart. "I feel it here too."

He stands and takes me in his arms, walking me down the hall to my bedroom. When he steps past Leighton's room, he stops, taking in where his son sleeps every night. The way his face lights up is the sexiest thing ever.

He wants this. He wants me just as much as he wants Leighton.

There's not a single hesitation in his stride as he enters my room and places me down on my bed.

Slowly, he removes my flats and kicks off his own shoes.

When he leans down, his lips meet with mine. With his strong arms holding him above me, I run my palms down his torso, feeling each line of his abs through his shirt underneath my fingertips.

I want more of him, so I take the next step and move his shirt up. When my hands touch the softness of his skin, a tiny moan escapes my lips. It's been so long since I've been with a man, but no man is like him.

Travis puts my body on pins and needles of lust and need. I become a woman I don't even know when I yank his shirt over his head, taking it completely off.

Once his is on the floor, I don't wait for him to reach for mine, removing it myself. He can tell I'm greedy to take it to the next level, and he wastes no time as he crashes his lips against mine.

We rush our hands to each other's pants and pull them down as fast as we can. Without any thought, my panties are off, and his boxers are on the floor.

As he slides into me, I scream in ecstasy.

I've spent many a nights dreaming of having a man next to me, with me, making love to me, yet even in my dreams, I didn't imagine this.

He fills me to the brim, and I'm so wet and turned on that it sends the most intense sensations through my core to fill my entire body.

I don't know whether to scream or moan or lie here in absolute shock from the way he makes my body feel.

It's intense.

It's almost too much.

Yet, when he slides in and out of me, it's like the feelings double, and I quickly lose control.

I grip his ass, needing to hold something before I float away. He grinds harder, and I scream louder.

When he holds my face, kissing me while slamming into me, I finally lose every part of my being and clench around him so hard that he pauses, enjoying the waves of me gripping around him.

As his body convulses and quakes inside me, my head falls back, and I take a deep breath, closing my eyes and not wanting to move a muscle, praying the sensations rushing through my body never go away.

He brings his lips to mine and kisses me senseless. I'm a puddle of sex and orgasm, and he's to blame. After a minute of getting lost in kisses, he pulls out of me, yanks me into his side, and cuddles against me.

I curl up willingly, holding his arm tightly.

He kisses my ear and whispers, "That was even better than the first time."

I nod. I couldn't agree more.

CHAPTER NINE

WAKING UP IN A MAN'S ARMS STARTLES ME. WHEN I REMEMBER IT'S TRAVIS and everything that happened last night though, I'm filled with joy.

He makes me feel so alive again, and now, knowing I have nothing standing in my way of actually being with him, I couldn't be happier.

I stir a little more, and he does the same. I roll off his chest and grab my pillow, curling on my side while I watch him wake up.

When his eyes meet mine, he smiles. "Morning," he whispers sleepily.

"Morning." I grin, gripping my pillow tighter as nerves suddenly wash over me.

This is the part I never got with him last time. I've never really had the morning-after talk with anyone like this. Even though we spent the night talking away, I still barely know him.

"Coffee?" I ask, giving me a reason to gather myself.

He reaches over and flips me around, pulling my back into his front. "Sure but not yet. I want to enjoy this a little bit longer."

I tug on his arm that's holding me. I've heard endorphins rush through your body after hugging someone for twenty seconds. With Travis, I don't need any time at all. One touch from him, and my body feels lighter, safer, as I'm wrapped in his arms.

We drift in and out of sleep until I hear my phone ring from the front room, reminding me that I didn't even put it on the charger last night.

With a sigh, I slide out of bed to retrieve it.

When I see it's my mom calling, I head to the kitchen to make coffee, hoping to not bother Travis.

"Morning," I say into the phone as I get the coffee grounds from the container on the counter.

"Mommy!" Leighton sings into the phone.

I smile big, loving the sound of his voice. "Hey, baby. Did you sleep good at Grandma and Grandpa's house?"

"I did! They even let Ming sleep on the bed with me!"

Ming is their little shih tzu and Leighton's absolute joy in life.

"That's fun. Where's your grandma?" I ask, pouring in the necessary amount of water.

"I'm right here," Mom calls from somewhere next to Leighton.

"What's your plan today?" I ask.

Yesterday, she wasn't sure if her Saturday morning tennis match with her friends was on or not.

"We're going to play, so I was thinking I'd drop Leighton off in about a half hour or so."

My eyes open wide as panic sets in.

I can't have them see Travis.

"Yeah. Okay." I purse my lips as I think of a tactful way to say, *You have to leave, so my son—your son—doesn't see you here.*

"Okay, Mommy. Grandma's making me pan-ee-cakes, so I'm going to go now. See you soon. Love you!"

I smile, loving our nickname for pancakes and the way he says it. "Sounds good. I'll see you shortly."

He hangs up, and I press the coffee button before rushing back to my room.

As I enter, I see Travis propped up by some pillows with his hand behind his back. He slipped on his boxer briefs, but his bare chest is on full display, seriously making my mouth water.

I shake my head, remembering I need to get him to go home. I grip my hands in front of my body, ripping off the Band-Aid. "I'm sorry, but I'm going to have to ask you to leave."

A sharp laugh escapes his lips. "It's like that, huh?"

I rush to his side. "No. I'm sorry. It's just ... my mom is bringing Leighton back in a half hour, and I don't want them to see you here."

He tilts his head to the side and raises his finger to tuck my hair behind my ear. "I understand, but I'd like to see you guys again today."

I rub my lips together, not realizing how fast we were going to jump into this. "You want to see us? Or just me?"

"I'd like to see Leighton. Actually, I'd like to see him as much as I can from this day forward."

I know I should be thrilled, but all of this is happening so fast, and nothing has really sunk in yet. I pull back slightly. "We can arrange that."

His lips tilt to the side. "Arrange that? You make it sound like you're not sure."

My shoulders fall forward. "You have to remember, this time yesterday, I had no idea I would ever see you again."

"Yes, and this time yesterday, I had no idea I was a father, let alone to a five-year-old little boy. I get the enormity of the situation, but I also want to make up for all the time I've lost."

I nod, reaching for his hands to grasp in mine. "Yes, I know. Let's just take things slow. Between us and you with Leighton."

He inhales, and I can see his wheels turning. "How slow?" he finally asks. "I want him to know I'm his father."

I close my eyes, my chest suddenly tight. "It's just ..." I open them and stare into his gorgeous blues that match the ones I've treasured for the last five years. "I'm just afraid. I can't have you coming into our lives and saying you're his dad and then not staying around."

Travis snaps the covers back. "You need to understand, I'm not going anywhere. Don't forget who left me that night." He stands, and I feel the dagger he just threw at me.

"That's harsh." I face him.

He stops and takes a deep breath, letting us both calm down from the sudden rush of emotions filling the room.

He places his hand on my face, and I instantly fall into it. "Look, I don't know what will happen between us. I'd like to see us make this work and be together. That night, I thought I'd met *the one*. Last night, I had that same feeling. I know it will take time. But no matter what, I will not leave my son. I'm in his life from here on out. That, I can absolutely and without a doubt promise you from the bottom of my heart."

I nod, and he leans in to kiss my lips.

As he pulls back, he grins. "Can I at least get that coffee you promised before you kick me out?"

I laugh and love the way he changes the tension between us so easily. No one could ever be prepared for the situation we're in, but knowing he's levelheaded and in it for the long haul definitely helps.

CHAPTER TEN

I WATCH AS TRAVIS PULLS ON HIS PANTS AND SLIPS HIS SHIRT OVER HIS HEAD. When he turns around and catches me staring, he pulls me in his arms and kisses me so senseless that I forget I'm a mom who needs to get him out of here. I wish he could stay, so we could have round two, but I know that can't happen.

He steps away, and I want to pout until my son's face pops in my head. I do a little turn and start to pull him out of the room.

Of course, I make him a cup of coffee first, which makes me feel slightly better about kicking him out. The only to-go cup I have is one that says *Wonder Mom* with the Wonder Woman logo.

He picks it up, smiling at me. "Cute cup."

"Leighton picked it out for Mother's Day last year."

"Good man. He chose right."

We walk to the door, and Travis takes me into his arms again. My knees go weak when his lips meet mine. Even though it takes me a few seconds, I get my wits about me and place my hand on his chest, stopping our kiss and opening the front door.

That's when I hear, "Mommy!"

Travis jumps to the right as Leighton rushes to my side and hugs me as tight as he can.

"Hey, buddy. I didn't expect you here so fast," I say, picking him up and hugging him properly.

"Obviously," Mom says as she enters my place, checking Travis up and down. "I'm Judy, Michelle's mom. And you are?" She holds her hand out to Travis and smiles like he was caught with his hand in the cookie jar. "Hmm." She glances at me and then back to Travis. "Your eyes are stunning, just like my—"

"Dr. Rivers!" Leighton says, thankfully interrupting my mom's thought process. "Why are you here? Did my mom need a doctor?" He places his hand to my forehead, like I do when he says he has a tummy ache. "Are you feeling sick, Mommy?"

Mom laughs, and I eye her to stop.

"I'm okay, baby. Dr. Rivers was just bringing me a paper I forgot to sign."

"So, Dr. Rivers"—Mom sashays over to him, wrapping her arm around his and bringing him back into my living room—"are you Leighton's new pediatrician?"

"Yes, ma'am. I sure am," Travis says, looking over to me to make sure this is okay.

I shrug and shut the door, knowing she'll keep him here so there's no need to try to fight it.

She walks to the kitchen, where she pours herself a cup of coffee.

"So, Mom, I thought you guys were making pancakes?" I ask, widening my eyes at her.

"We were, but Susie called and asked that I come earlier, so we only made the two he ate, and I put the rest of the batter in the fridge for later."

"Then, don't you have to leave? Is she waiting for you?" I motion toward the door.

"Oh, no worries. She'll understand why I'm late when I tell her who I met." The way her grin shines through over her coffee mug makes Travis chuckle into his cup. "So, did you two just meet yesterday?" she asks.

Travis looks at me, and I jump in, making sure she doesn't know just how long I've known him. "Yes, just yesterday really." As soon as the words slip from my mouth, I want to slap my own forehead when I realize just how bad that sounded.

"Well, I sure am glad to meet you and see you here, bright and early like this. I keep on telling Michelle she needs to date. I don't think she's been on one since she split with that horrible husband of hers."

Travis turns to me with a questioning expression. "Husband?"

My heart beats so hard in my chest that I feel like it might explode. "Oh dear, look at me. Telling her story. I'm sorry. There's nothing to know though. We like to think of him as the sperm donor since he bailed as soon as Michelle found out she was pregnant."

I close my eyes, not wanting to see Travis's expression after my mom so nonchalantly just dropped the bomb. When I finally open them, he's staring daggers at me.

He holds out his hand to my mom. "Judy, it was nice meeting you, but I think I should be going." He holds his palm up to Leighton. "Give me five, little man."

Leighton jumps up to slap his hand, and Travis smiles big as he looks at his son. When his eyes meet mine though, that smile is gone.

"Walk me out?" he asks.

I turn on my heel and lead the way, needing the fresh air to calm the waterfall of emotions rushing through me. I make sure we're clearly away from my front door before I turn to face him.

He wastes no time. "Please tell me what I think happened didn't."

"Let me explain." I place my hand on his chest, and he tosses it away.

"Were you married the night we met?"

"Yes, but I didn't mean for that to happen," I plead.

He steps back. "No. No. I remember checking multiple times for a ring because I was shocked you weren't married. You weren't wearing one."

I drop my head to my chest. "It's because I threw it at him when I left that night."

He narrows his eyes at me. "That's why you were so upset? Because you'd had a fight with *your husband*?"

"Yes, but you have to understand, he was a horrible man, and our marriage was not okay. I didn't see just how unhappy I was until I met you. You showed me that night what it meant to feel normal again."

"Yeah, normal for one night. God!" He throws his hands up in the air and starts to pace. "That's why you bailed. Because you had to get back home to your husband! How could I have been so stupid?"

I grab his arm. "Don't say that. You said you thought I was *the one* that night. I felt the same way. I'd never felt that way with him."

He shakes his head. "Really? Is that why you stayed with him? Is that why you never once came back to find me until you found out you were pregnant?" He leans away from me, and I can see the wheels turning in his head. "Wait. How do you even know Leighton's mine? Why would you not think he was your husband's?"

I take a deep breath. "I told you, he was a horrible man, who was lying to me. He treated me terribly and was a workaholic. The fight we had that night was over his dinner not being perfectly hot when he walked in the door two hours late. That's when I threw the ring at him and walked out, heading to that bar. Then, when he found out I was pregnant, seven weeks after we were together, he informed me he'd had a vasectomy a year earlier and never told me." I drop my head in shame of the memory of standing on the street that day.

"So, he knew you'd cheated on him …"

I glance up, my eyes filling with tears, and nod.

He takes a deep inhale, crossing his arms and staring at me. When he reaches for his keys in his pocket, my heart sinks.

"Look, I meant what I said. I *will be* in Leighton's life. But this … this I need to work my way through. Knowing that you made me the other man doesn't sit well with me. I believe in the sanctity of marriage. Learning you threw that away one night with someone else…"

He stops, and my shoulders sag.

He steps past me and heads toward his car, leaving me helpless.

I reach for him. "Please, don't leave like this."

"Just"—he holds up his hands, making sure I don't touch him—"give me some time. I need to process all of this. I want to see Leighton though. I'd like for him to know I'm his father sooner than later. I've already missed so much." He glares at me, making me feel even guiltier about the situation. "I'll call you later."

Tears fall down my face as I watch him get in his car without looking back at me.

Leaving him years ago was easy, but watching him drive away now is the most painful thing I've ever felt.

CHAPTER ELEVEN

WHEN TRAVIS TEXTED ME LATER IN THE DAY, MY MOOD LIFTED. WHEN I SAW it was just about Leighton, that moment of excitement flew away just as quickly as it had come. I tried to text about us, but he shut that down real quick. As I read his words, saying it would take time, I couldn't help but feel the pang in my chest.

He's taking us to dinner tonight. I'm hoping he's not going to bust out and tell Leighton he's his father, but since we left on such bad terms, I wouldn't be surprised if he did.

We decided to meet at the pizza place, so we'd be on neutral ground. I can't help but think if this morning had ended differently, then we would have driven together. It's something I've been obsessing about all day, and now that it's time to leave, my fears are getting the best of me.

On our way there, I look in the rearview mirror at Leighton. "So, baby, you remember Dr. Rivers, right?"

"Yeah, Mommy. Why?"

"He's going to join us for dinner tonight. Is that okay with you?"

"Will he play games with me?"

I laugh. "Not sure. You can ask him though."

"Okay. I hope he does."

Me too, baby. Me too.

We pull up to the restaurant and see he's already inside, seated at a booth in the window.

Leighton unhooks his own straps on the car seat and hops out of the car before I can get to his side. I follow behind him as he runs to the front, swinging the glass door open. I hold it, so it doesn't fall on his small frame.

When my eyes meet with Travis, a mixture of excitement, fear, and nervousness courses through me, but I tamp it down and head toward him with a smile on my face.

"Hey, little man. High five," Travis says, holding up his hand to Leighton.

Leighton slaps it and then starts in on his question. "Will you play games with me?"

Travis chuckles as he stands up, holding his arm out to Leighton. "Only if you'll play the basketball one."

"Of course, duh," Leighton says, grabbing his hand and leading him to the playroom.

Travis turns to me as Leighton yanks him away. "I already ordered pizza, and the cups there are for you guys."

"Okay, thank you." I smile and wave.

He looks at Leighton and then back to me. "No, thank you."

I sit back and watch through the windows that line the playroom as Leighton and Travis play so many rounds of the game that I'm sure Travis has spent over twenty dollars by now.

Seeing them together makes my eyes tear up. Pretty soon, I'll be the crazy woman, bawling while sitting alone. I wondered if Leighton would ever have a father figure in his life. Never in a million years did I think I'd find *his* father.

Our pizza arrives, and I wipe my eyes for the tenth time before standing to get Travis's attention. He brings Leighton back to the table after they headed to the restroom first to wash their hands.

Leighton dives into the cheese pizza Travis bought just for him. His eyes are definitely bigger than his stomach, and though he's excited, I know he'll only finish two slices, maybe three max.

"Cheers," Travis says, holding up his slice to Leighton.

They bump their food together before each taking a bite.

"Mom, you should have seen Dr. Rivers. He was making so many shots!"

Travis laughs as he wipes his mouth with a napkin. "You can call me Travis, buddy. Or …" His eyes meet mine, and my expression must match the emotions that just raced through me. *Please don't just blurt it out loud like this.*

Thankfully, Travis takes a bite and doesn't finish that sentence.

"Dr. Rivers, hello," a woman says as she walks by our table with her daughter. She takes one look at Leighton, and a grin spreads across her face. "I had no idea you had a son of your own! I'm surprised I've never seen pictures at your office. Man, he is your twin for sure!"

Travis covers his mouth with his napkin as he finishes his bite. He raises his eyebrows to me, and I close my eyes as I take a deep breath.

"Megan, this is Leighton and his mother, Michelle," he says, dodging the ball for sure.

"It's so nice to meet you. We sure do love Dr. Rivers here. My poor baby hasn't had the best of luck health-wise, and he's been a dream to work with."

I smile sweetly. "I'm glad to hear he's helped you so much."

"Well, I'll let you guys get back to your dinner. It's nice to meet you, Michelle."

"Nice to meet you too." I wave as I prepare my next bite.

"It's pretty cool that you and I look so much alike," Travis says to Leighton, making my heart pound harder.

Leighton nods nonchalantly, paying more attention to his food than the words being said.

"I think that means we're supposed to be friends. Are you okay with that?" Travis asks.

Leighton nods his tiny head. "Will you take me to play real basketball?"

I laugh, realizing how easy life is to a five-year-old. He doesn't fully understand the situation. He doesn't understand what having his father in his life will be like.

I sit back and let out a breath that feels like a huge weight being lifted. Yes, we haven't told him yet, but if it's as simple as playing basketball, maybe I'm thinking too much into this.

"Have you never played for real?" Travis asks.

Leighton glares over at me. "She only lets me play here."

I laugh out loud and hold up my hands. "Hey, don't look at me like that. The hoops at the park are really tall, and there are always people playing. I don't want you to get trampled."

"You know, your mom has a good point." Travis points his pizza at me. "It's a good thing I have a basketball hoop at my house."

"You do?" Leighton bounces in his seat.

"Do you want to come over tomorrow to play?" Travis asks.

"Can we, Mom? Can we? Can we? Please?" He holds his hands under his chin, sticking out his bottom lip.

Travis chokes on his food as he laughs. "Yeah, Mom. Please?" He mimics Leighton's pose.

I shake my head, smiling at the two twins staring back at me with the same expression. "Yeah, we can do that."

"Yes!" They high-five over the table before diving back into the food.

After dinner, Travis walks us to my car. I buckle Leighton in and step back for Travis to say good-bye.

"You and me tomorrow, okay?" Travis asks and then leans in. "I guess we'll invite your mom, too, but I bet she plays like a girl."

"Hey, I heard that," I shout over his shoulder.

"Nah, my mom's probably pretty good. She can throw a baseball at least," Leighton replies.

"Aw, thanks, kiddo," I say with a grin.

"See you tomorrow." Travis stands and shuts the door. We walk to the trunk of the car and stop. "So, you play catch with him?"

"Of course I do. The boy loves every ball he can find."

Travis leans against the car, crossing his arms. "You've done a good job with him."

I shrug, nerves taking over. "He's my son. I'd do anything for him."

Travis nods. "And it shows."

I take the plunge. "So, listen, I'm sorry you had to find out the way you did about Daniel."

He holds up his hand to stop me. "Daniel?" He lets out a breath. "I take it, he's the husband." Travis's entire demeanor changes, and he stands straighter.

"Ex-husband," I point out.

"Yeah, because I—"

"Stop right there." I repeat his same gesture. "You need to understand, we were already having problems. I was there that night, contemplating leaving him."

Travis steps closer to me. "Then, why didn't you? Why did you leave my bed and go back to him, never even giving me a chance?"

I drop my head down. "For the same reasons you said earlier. I believed in my vows. I was a married woman, and I needed to make our marriage work." I place my palm on his chest. "I promise you though, at that point in our marriage, he was not the same man I'd married. We had grown apart, and I wasn't happy. Leaving you was the hardest thing I'd ever done. I was so confused. Being with you felt right, but that didn't make sense to me because I was married. I can tell you this though … that one night with you was better than my entire marriage. And I'm not just talking about the sex. It was just spending time with you. I didn't realize how much I'd settled for what I'd thought I wanted. For who I'd thought he was."

Travis places his hand over mine that's still on his chest and removes it. My eyes meet his, and he nods.

"Okay. I hear you. I still …" He takes a deep breath. "This is all just a lot to take in at one time. Let me get to know Leighton, and then we can focus on *if* there will be an us to go along with that."

I blink away the tears that sting my eyes. "Okay." I step toward my side of the car.

He rushes to open the door for me and holds on to it, standing firmly with the door in between us, which I take as a solid sign that he meant what he said.

"Thank you for meeting me tonight," he says.

"Thank you for dinner."

"Come over around ten tomorrow? We'll play, and then I'll grill us some cheeseburgers."

I smile and nod. "Okay, we'll be there."

"I'll text you the address. Night."

I wave. "Night."

I get in the car and want to bang my head on the steering wheel, but I am reminded very quickly that Leighton is still sitting behind me.

"You guys took forever!" he whines.

"Sorry, baby. We're heading home right now."

Lord knows, I need to put him to bed and pour myself a glass of wine!

CHAPTER TWELVE

THE NEXT DAY, WE ARRIVE AT TRAVIS'S PLACE, WHICH IS THE CUTEST HOME ever. I can only imagine he makes good money, being a doctor, but his modest two-bedroom bungalow with a small porch doesn't scream money. It screams home.

A long driveway on the side leads back to a detached garage, and I see a basketball hoop set up on the side.

We walk up the steps to his porch and ring the doorbell.

When Travis opens the door, he has a dish towel flung over his shoulder. "Hey, glad you guys found it okay. Come on in."

Leighton runs in without a care in the world, but I stop and take my time. When I entered his apartment all those years ago, I didn't look around to get a glimpse of who he was. Now, I want to see if I can understand him more by being in his personal surroundings.

His living room is not full bachelor pad but not full designer either. His black leather couches and sleek coffee table are counteracted with a homemade quilt flung across the back of the chair.

"Can I go out back to play?" Leighton asks, standing at the back door.

Travis slings the towel off his shoulder, placing it on the counter. "Sure! Here, let me get the basketball for you." Travis opens the door, and the two head outside.

I lean against the frame, crossing my arms, as I watch them take a few shots. Leighton can barely get the ball high enough to reach the basket, so Travis holds him up, allowing him to make the shot.

"Yay!" Leighton says, holding his arms up in celebration and bouncing around once Travis puts him on the ground.

"Nice shot, buddy!" I cheer from my spot on the deck.

Travis turns my way, and the grin that's covering his face is amazing. I know my dad looks at him like a grandpa, but seeing someone look at him like a father puts the biggest smile on my face. Travis should be proud of the little boy he created. Leighton has been such a special addition to my life, and I have Travis to thank.

They play for an hour more while I swing in the hammock he has set up on his back deck.

I so could get used to this …

I'm drifting away when I hear them laughing and walking toward me. When they notice my eyes are shut, I hear Travis whisper, "Shh. I think your mom fell asleep."

"Should we tickle her?" Leighton asks.

"Well, duh," Travis responds. "On three. One. Two. Three."

They both charge me, and I let them, loving this moment and never wanting it to end. We are all giggles as I pick Leighton up and hug him tightly. To my surprise, Travis wraps his arms around both of us.

It feels good.

It feels right.

I turn to Travis. "We should tell him."

Travis shoots up. "Seriously?" He doesn't hide his surprise one bit.

I smile and nod, taking Leighton and sitting him up straight so we're all swinging together.

"So, Leighton, how would you feel if you got to see Travis more often?"

"And play more basketball?" Leighton's face lights up.

Travis and I laugh.

"Yes, and we can play more basketball, whenever you want," Travis says.

"Yes!" Leighton celebrates.

I glance to Travis and grin, feeling so happy to be able to tell Leighton who Travis really is. "So, you like Travis?"

Leighton nods. "Of course I do. Did you see him pick me up for a basket?"

Travis holds out his hand to high-five Leighton.

"How would you feel if he were your daddy?"

Leighton's eyes narrow slightly as he takes in what I just said. He holds his hand to his chest. "But I don't have a daddy," he says shyly.

Hearing him say that breaks my heart, but it heals when Travis grips my hand.

"You do now, son," Travis says, his voice cracking. "Can I be your daddy?"

Leighton jumps off my lap and crawls up onto Travis's. "Seriously?" he says, his voice laced with that of Christmas-morning excitement.

"Seriously," I say as tears fill my eyes.

"Would you be okay with that?" Travis asks.

"Yes!" He wraps his arms around Travis's neck. When he pulls away, he turns back to me. "Does this mean we get to move here? Shouldn't I live with you *and* my daddy?"

My chest tightens at his question. "Well, sweetie—"

Travis grips my hand again. "I can imagine we can make that happen very soon."

The tears I was holding back start to fall instantly.

"Just give your mommy and I some time to sort things out, and we'll make sure your room is ready and fit for a king when you do move in."

I wipe the tears from my eyes and lean in to kiss Leighton's cheek.

He snuggles between Travis and me, placing his hands on each of our legs. "How cool! I get to sit here with both my mom and my dad!"

Travis leans over and kisses my lips. "Yeah, it is pretty cool."

EPILOGUE
THREE YEARS LATER

"HOLD ON! I HAVE TO GET MY SHIRT!" LEIGHTON YELLS AS HE RUNS DOWN the hall.

I grip my stomach in pain, trying not to get upset with my son.

Travis leans over, kissing the top of my head. "Breathe, baby. Don't forget to breathe."

I follow his lead as I take a deep inhale and then exhale as he does it with me.

"Got it!" Leighton comes running to the living room, wearing his *I'm the big brother* shirt that we bought him when we told him I was pregnant.

He's been so excited ever since he found out. I know we agreed it was okay for him to come to the hospital with us, but as we sit here, waiting on him, I'm getting nervous about how this is going to go. Since Travis knows everyone at the hospital, they promised they'd watch him when the delivery actually happened if my parents or his mom hadn't arrived yet.

We're so lucky to have both of our families here in town to help us raise our kids.

I can't believe it—our kids.

When I gave birth to Leighton, I only had my mother by my side. Yes, she was supportive and excited to be there, but it wasn't the same. I remember thinking about Travis as the doctor laid Leighton on my chest. I wished he were there, celebrating the miracle we'd created. I tried not to have the thought ruin my own happiness, but I'd be lying if I said it wasn't in the back of my mind.

I can't believe I'm getting a second chance.

I can't wait to see his face as he sees his daughter for the first time.

That's right. His daughter. We're having a baby girl.

I've seen the way he is with Leighton, and I can tell you now that this little girl is going to have him wrapped around her finger. She already does. He painted her entire room pink and decorated it with every princess decor he could find, saying she was his little princess.

"Okay, let's go have a baby!" Travis shouts as he leads me toward the door.

I've seen movies where the dads freak out and act crazy, but that's not Travis at all. He's as calm as a cucumber as he walks me down the stairs of our home.

Leighton and I moved in only a few months after I first ran into Travis again. We'd tried to take it slow, but just like that first night we'd met, we had known we were destined to be together.

People always told me that when you found *the one*, you just knew. I thought they were crazy. That was, until I met Travis. I kick myself for even marrying Daniel and staying with him for so long in such a horrible marriage, yet I have to thank him as well. He led me on our broken path, which gave me Travis.

If not for Daniel, I would never have met Travis, and I would never have had Leighton. God knew we were meant to be together, and that was why we met up again the way we did.

We were married a year after our reunion in a ceremony that included Leighton since we'd also changed his last name to Rivers.

And now, He's blessed us again.

I walk down the driveway as Leighton rushes past me and jumps in the backseat. I slowly sit down just as a contraction grips hold of me. I grab for the handle and squish my eyes in pain.

"Breathe, baby. Breathe," Travis says as he wraps his arm around me.

As the contraction calms, I nod my head, letting him know I'm okay and that he can shut the door.

"You'll be okay, Mommy," Leighton says as he rubs my shoulder from the backseat.

I glance behind me, smile at him, and place my hand over his. "Thank you, baby."

"That's the last time you can call me that, you know. I'm not the baby anymore." He sits up taller.

I laugh. "I don't care how old you are; you'll always be my baby."

Travis gets on the road, and thankfully, I only have two contractions on the way to the hospital. When we pull up, a nurse is there with a wheelchair for me.

Travis and Leighton follow behind as they rush me to the room they have ready for us. Leighton waits outside as they get me set up in a bed.

Once he's in my room, he stakes his claim in the chair to my right as Travis stands to my left.

We talk as I try to relax during the calm times, and they each hold one of my hands as contractions rip through my body. Both of our families arrive shortly after we do, and excitement for our newest delivery fills the room.

An hour after I arrived, the doctor checks me again and says it's time to push. Everyone takes Leighton outside, leaving Travis and me to have our special time alone.

When the doctor tells me to push, I scream with the burning pain, but I feel secure with the help of the man by my side. He leans in and kisses my forehead when I inhale a quick breath and push even harder.

As I drop my head back, he whispers, "You're doing great. I'm so proud of you."

Our eyes meet, and I see the tears falling freely down his face. Having him here gives me so much courage and keeps me calm as I inhale a deep breath and push again when the next contraction hits.

I push for a few minutes more. Just when I think I can't take it anymore, I feel the release, and the scream of a baby girl fills the room.

I fall back, letting my head drop as well, exhausted yet relieved that I did it. I gave birth to our baby girl.

Within seconds, the doctor sets her on my chest as Travis screams, "She's here!"

Tears of joy stream down his face as he places his hand on her back, taking in the moment of seeing his daughter for the first time. "I'm your daddy," he says with a huge smile on his face.

Hearing him say this makes me burst into tears. I couldn't be happier with the life I live and the family I have. I've been blessed in so many ways, and the birth of our daughter just adds to that.

"Is she here?" I hear my mom, Judy, ask from the door. She peeks her head in with Christine, Travis's mom, right behind her.

"Yes, come see!" Travis says, and they all shout out cheers.

Leighton runs in first and straight to my side. "Hi," he says. "I'm your big brother." Everyone laughs as he leans back, holding his shirt out for her to see.

"What's her name?" my mom asks.

My eyes meet with Travis as we both grin with our choice. We wanted to keep it a secret, and when he nods, I smile big as I say, "Justine," a blend of our mothers' names.

"Oh!" Christine bursts out in even more tears.

"I love it!" my mom says as she wraps her arm around my father, giving him a hug.

As I glance at our family surrounding my bed, I can't help but close my eyes and take in the moment.

Our moment.

Our family.

THE END

EVERY OTHER MEMORY
BY KAYLEE RYAN

CHAPTER ONE

CADENCE

THE BEAT OF THE MUSIC POUNDS THROUGH THE SPEAKERS. IT'S SO LOUD I can feel the vibration in my chest. Then again, maybe that's the alcohol or possibly the fact that I'm done. After four long, grueling years, I've graduated from college. Not only am I a college graduate, but I got my results back today. I passed my boards. I am officially an occupational therapist. It's time for me to enter the world of adulting, and I'm ready. I am so ready. I've busted my ass for this.

"Drink!" my best friend, Shelby, screams over the music. I nod my agreement, link hands with her, and follow her through the throng of people on the dance floor. "This place is on fire tonight," she says once we reach the bar.

"That it is," I agree.

"Two waters." She holds up two fingers when the bartender finally reaches us.

"I can't believe I convinced you to come out with me," she states, pulling me into a sweaty hug, making me laugh.

"You act like I never go out." She gives me a look that says "you never go out," and she's right.

"You were the most dedicated student I know."

I nod. She's not wrong. I put everything into studying—no time for partying or skipping class. I needed to know that I was on the right track to a career where I would always be able to take care of myself financially. Luckily, my nose-to-the-grindstone determination in high school landed me scholarships. Add in my part-time job at the coffee shop, and I'm not only a college graduate, but I'm also debt-free. That's almost unheard of—especially someone with my background. Hell, few in the foster care system make it to college. At least not the ones that I know. I, however, was determined. I *am* determined to make something of myself and my life.

"Now, if I could just convince you to find you a hottie to go home with, I'd call this night a success." She wiggles her eyebrows, handing me a bottle of water.

"You know casual isn't my thing."

"You don't have a thing," she counters. "Besides, look around you, Cadence. You can have your pick. You've got the eye of every man in this room."

"Uh, that would be you, my friend. Guilty by association." Shelby is what most men, even most women, refer to as a blonde bombshell. She and I are the same height at five foot six, but my hair is dark to her light. Her eyes are an exotic brown, with gold hues, and her skin flawless. Whereas my eyes are a light blue, and my complexion fair.

"Don't even," she warns me. A slow smile crosses her face, and it's one of mischief. I know it all too well. We've been roommates since our freshman year of college, and that look, that smile tells me she's up to no good.

"Excuse me." She places her manicured hand on the shoulder of the guy next to her. "I was hoping you could help me with something," she coos. Yes, coos. The sound of her voice alone could have him eating out of the palm of her hand. "My friend here, she's just gone through a bad breakup." Lies. "He told her, well, let's just say she's feeling down about herself. What do you think? She's beautiful, right?" she asks him.

His eyes rake over me from head to toe, stopping a little longer at my chest, making me regret the spaghetti strap form-fitting tank top I decided to wear tonight. I knew this place would be packed, and if Shelby and I agree on anything, it's hitting the dance floor.

"She's a fucking knockout," the guy slurs.

"Thanks, sugar." She winks at him, drops her hand, and focuses her attention on me. "Told you."

"He's drunk."

"Drunk or sober, I'd take you home with me," he chimes in, still listening to our conversation.

I give him a kind smile, grab Shelby's arm, and pull her away from the bar, and to a small table that surprisingly is vacant next to the dance floor. "So, where's Matt?"

"Who knows." She rolls her eyes.

"Are you guys broken up again?" Shelby and Matt have a long history of on-again, off-again. It started our freshman year, and they're still doing… whatever it is they do. One day they're happy and moving forward. The next, they hate each other, and it's over. I live with her, and I have a hard time keeping up.

Her shoulders slump, and the look in her eyes is defeated. "I don't know, Cadence. I love him, but we're toxic for one another. I want us to work, but I just don't know if we're able to get through all the bullshit and make it happen."

"Maybe letting him go, I mean, really walking away for longer than a few days is what you guys need?"

"Maybe." She shrugs. "I wish I had the answer. I know he's struggling with football being over, and he's not going on to the pros like a few of his friends on the team. That was never his plan, but it's a huge part of his life that he's going to miss."

"Yeah, I get that. However, what about the last four years? He's always put you second. That's still going on now. There always seems to be something or some kind of excuse."

"I know. Now that we're graduated, I don't know where we're going."

Reaching over the table, I place my hand over hers. "You two will figure it out. Just don't hold out too long. I want to see you happy. Sometimes letting go is what it takes to make that happen."

"Yeah," she agrees when a shadow falls over our table.

Glancing up, Matt is standing there, hands shoved in his pockets, and a look more serious than I've ever seen from him on his face. "Hi." His eyes are locked on Shelby. From the look of surprise on her face, she had no idea that he was going to be here.

"Hi." The DJ slows things down a bit, and when he reaches his hand out to her, I know what he's asking. From the way her eyes soften, she does too. Matt never dances with her. Never. She loves it, and it's not something he ever takes part in.

"Will you dance with me?" he asks, his voice so soft I can barely hear him.

I watch as tears well in my best friend's eyes and nods her agreement. She takes his hand and stands before turning to me. "Cad—" she starts, but I smile and shake my head.

"Go. I'll be fine right here. This might be your moment," I tell her. The smile she gives me lights up her face before she turns and allows the love of her life to lead her out on the dance floor. Regardless of how distant he's always been, she loves him. Deep down I know he loves her too. I wish more than anything that they could get it figured out and be happy.

Not wanting to look like the loser sitting at a table all alone, I pull out my phone and begin to scroll through my emails. Shelby and I are moving to a new apartment, a bigger, better apartment, and we're waiting for our move-in date. After scrolling as long as I can, I head back to the bar for a drink, this time of the alcoholic variety. I am celebrating after all.

Moving up to the bar, I raise my hand half a dozen times and still get ignored by the bartender. Shelby never has that problem.

"Allow me," a deep husky voice says from behind me. Turning to look over my shoulder, I see a man with the most gorgeous hazel eyes I've ever seen. "What are you drinking?"

"Beer is fine, anything," I tell him.

He nods before leaning in and placing one hand on the small of my back while raising the other to get the bartender's attention. His touch is like a jolt of electricity to my system, and even though my back is the only place he's touching me, I feel him everywhere.

"Two beers," he says, placing our order. "So, you come here often?" he asks with a smile as he slides onto the now vacant stool beside me.

"Does that line work for you?" I ask, not even trying to hide my smile.

"I'm not sure. This is my first time. How am I doing?"

"Meh." I tilt the bottle of beer to my lips, trying not to smile.

"Okay. All right." He chuckles. "I admit I need to step up my game. It would help if I spent less time working and more time doing… this." His eyes roam around the bar.

"You're not the only one," I confess. "This is the first time I've been out in, well… I don't really know how long. Too long, let's just leave it at that."

"Special occasion?"

"Kind of. I passed my state boards, so I am officially a licensed occupational therapist." It's the first time I've said those words aloud to anyone other than Shelby. I can't believe college is over, and I did it. I graduated, and I made something of myself. For me, life is just beginning, and for the first time in a very long time, I'm excited for what's to come next.

"That's incredible." He leans in and gives me a hug. His scent's something woodsy, mixed with the alcohol on his breath. It's intoxicating. "Congrats."

The hug surprises me, but I find myself accepting his arms wrapped around me and hugging him back. "Thank you. It was a long four years, but I'm done and ready to start my new career."

"So what's next?" he asks.

"I have a job lined up. It's local. I did my internship with them, so I already know most of the staff."

He nods. "I know you said you don't do this scene often, but what do you like to do for fun?"

"Well…" I can feel my face start to heat as embarrassment coats my cheeks. "I'm not much for spontaneity. If I wasn't in class or studying, I was working or sleeping."

"Ah, so this really is a celebration for you."

"Pretty much. I know I'm probably the most boring human on the planet, but my life… it's not been the easiest, and I was determined to make something of myself." I have no idea why I just told him all of that, but it's too late to take the words back now.

"Drink up," he says, taking a long pull from his bottle of beer. "We have some celebrating to do."

"Do we now?" I smile at him, and he winks. This isn't me. I'm not the girl who flirts at the club. My life has been hyper focused on graduation and my career. Now that I have all of that, I'm left feeling… unsettled, which is not how I thought I would feel at this stage in my life. Although I'm not much of a flirter, the easy banter with this handsome stranger seems to come naturally.

No harm in enjoying his company, right?

"Hell, yes, we do. You can't just sit at the bar all night. You need the full experience, and I'm going to give it to you. You and I are going out there." He points to the dance floor.

"I don't even know your name." It's my lame attempt at stalling. This man is too gorgeous and too damn tempting. My experience with men is limited at best. My first and only priority was to graduate from college. Now that I've done that, I'm not exactly sure what to do with myself.

Maybe this handsome stranger is a good place to start.

A slow, sexy grin pulls at his lips as he slides off his stool and steps in close to me. He's so close I can see the flecks of green, gold, and brown in his eyes. Maybe even a small amount of blue. They are the most mesmerizing eyes I've ever seen. Add in his dark hair, the five o'clock shadow, and the obviously toned body under that tight black T-shirt, and he's absolutely mouthwatering. "We're working on your spontaneity here, gorgeous." He smirks. "Come on. Time's a-wasting."

I don't know what the night holds, but I'm suddenly eager to find out. I quickly finish my beer and hold the bottle out for him. He takes both of our now empty bottles and places them on the bar, lacing his fingers through mine and leading us through the throngs of people to the center of the dance floor. It's a bold move, one that I'm not opposed to. He seems to have that effect on me.

We stop in the middle of the floor, and he moves to step in behind me. His hands grip my hips, and together we begin to move. I'm hesitant at first, which is odd because I love to dance, but this sexy stranger, he's got me off-kilter. It's not until Shelby and Matt appear in front of us, and she smiles, giving me a thumbs-up, that I start to loosen up.

"Feel the music. Feel me," his deep voice whispers into my ear. My eyes dart to Shelby, and she's swaying her hips against Matt as they stand in our same position. I mimic her movements. Closing my eyes, I let the beat of the music flow through my veins and just feel.

The beat.

His hands.

His hard chest.

Desire.

"That's it, beautiful. Let go for me." His voice is husky, and from the bulge in his pants, he's just as affected by me as I am by him.

I lose track of time as our bodies grind together on the dance floor. We're both sweaty, but we don't let that stop us from our hands roaming over each other. I've never been this turned on in my entire life. I can't believe I'm here with this Adonis of a man, and he's into me. Me, Cadence Wade, has all of his attention, and it's a heady feeling.

Across from me, Shelby motions for me to come closer. "We're going to go. You going to come with us?" she asks.

I'm not ready to leave yet and to be honest, I'm tired of being the third wheel on nights like tonight. "No." I turn to look over my shoulder to find smoldering hazel eyes. "I'm going to stay for a while."

"I don't want to leave you here on your own."

"She's not alone. She has me. I can promise you that I'll get her home safely," my sexy hazel-eyed stranger speaks up.

"No offense, but we don't know you," Shelby challenges him.

"I'm a man of my word." There is something about the conviction in his voice that makes me believe him. He's just one of those people that you can read, and I know that he's not going to hurt me or force me into anything. My gut tells me that this is okay. I can't explain it, and I'm not sure I'd want to if I could. There's something to this being spontaneous. Then again, it's all him. The man standing behind me with his arms wrapped around my waist, holding our sweaty bodies tethered to one another. He's the spontaneity, and yeah, I'm not ready to give that up.

"I'll call you when we leave," I tell my best friend.

She surprises me when she pulls out her phone and snaps a picture of us, then points her phone at my companion. "I've got this as proof as to who she was with. Take care of her."

"Without question," he replies.

Shelby studies him for a few moments before nodding. "Call me," she says, and I nod. I wait until they are out of sight before turning in his arms and locking my hands behind his neck. I don't say anything as we stare into each other's eyes. I allow myself to not think about what's next. Instead, I live in the moment, the feel of his tight grip on my waist, and when his head lowers and his lips hover over mine, I, Cadence Wade, do something I've never done.

I initiate a kiss.

Without reservations, my lips press against his, committing the feel of them to memory.

CHAPTER TWO
TREVIN

HER LIPS ARE FIRE. SOFT AND SWEET LIKE CANDY AS THEY PRESS AGAINST mine. I need her closer. Sliding my hand behind her neck, I deepen the kiss. She opens, willingly allowing me to explore her mouth with my tongue. Gripping her hip, I hold her body close to mine. I don't give a fuck that we're in the middle of a club, damn near in the center of the dance floor. All I care about is this pleasant surprise of a woman in my arms and having every inch of her body pressed against mine.

When I came here tonight, I was just trying to get out of the house. I'm in town visiting my sister, who is recently married. The newlyweds kept making eyes at one another, and nobody wants to see all that. So I left. I told them I was meeting a friend and ran from their apartment like my ass was on fire. The reality of my situation is that I wasn't meeting anyone. I've been working my ass off for the last year, and I've lost touch with most of my friends, well, except for my best friend, who married my sister—the same one who was making eyes at her, and the reason I had to flee. I walked around town and ended up here. I told myself I was coming in for a quick drink, and then I'd head back. However, the minute I saw her sitting at the bar, I knew I had to say hello. I couldn't explain it if I tried.

Something pulled me toward her.

Now, here we are, her in my arms, our mouths devouring each other, and I want more. I can't seem to get her close enough. I can't seem to kiss her deep enough. My heart is beating in my chest, and my palms, I'm sure, are sweaty, but I refuse to let go of her to find out.

She's intoxicating.

When the song changes to Keith Sweat's "Nobody," I grind my hips into hers as we move like a well-oiled machine to the beat. I can't stop my hands from roaming over her body. My pulse pounds in my ears when she turns and places her back to my front, rubbing her ass over my hard cock. Bending over, she sways, her hips causing me to bite down on my bottom lip. It's been a long damn time since I've been this turned on. In fact, I don't know that I've ever been this worked up.

We find our rhythm with the slow, sexy grind of the song. We might as well be in this crowded club all alone because there is no one I see but her—just this gorgeous, enchanting stranger who's making me feel reckless and out of control.

And horny as fuck.

As the beat of the song transitions to another, my lips find her ear. "Come home with me." It's not so much as a question as a demand. I'd never force her, but I don't really want her to take the chance to refuse either. I have to have her. I need to be inside her. It's a need deep in my gut that I can't explain, but it's there, nagging at me, telling me that no amount of time spent with her would ever be a regret.

"Spontaneity," she mumbles, pressing her lips to mine.

"Spontaneity, need, desire, want, I don't care what you label it. I just know that being inside you is as much a necessity as breathing." Trailing my lips down her neck, I'm hit with the reminder that I'm staying with my sister. We'll have to get a room, which honestly, is better. I can take my time with her.

"I don't do this kind of thing," she tells me, chewing on her lip. I start to speak, to say anything that will make her change her mind, but she beats me to it. "But I want to with you. I don't know—" She shakes her head as if clearing the fog. "I don't have an explanation other than I don't want this night to end."

"Music to my ears, dream girl." With my arm around her waist, holding her as close as I can get her without carrying her out of here, I lead us out of the club.

"Dream girl?" she asks once we're outside on the sidewalk.

Turning, so her back hits the side of the building, I cage her in with my hands braced over her head against the wall. "You're my every fantasy come true." I give her no other explanation as I fuse my lips with hers. I let my body do the talking as I move in close, pressing my hard cock against her belly. Showing her precisely what she does to me.

Her nails dig into my biceps as I slow the kiss, resting my forehead against hers. "I want you."

Her chest heaves for breath. "I want you too."

"I'm in town visiting family. Hotel room?" I pull my forehead from hers so that I can gauge her reaction.

"I— Yes."

Sweeping her hair from her eyes, I make sure I have her attention before saying, "We don't have to. There's no pressure. I can see you home if that's what you want." While I say the words, my cock throbs at the idea of never being inside her.

"No. I-I want to. This is just a first for me," she replies, looking down at the ground.

"Hey." With my index finger under her chin, I move her eyes to mine. "It's been over a year for me, and I promise you that you're safe with me."

"I believe you." She gives me a shy smile. "I don't know why. You're a complete stranger, but I believe you."

I feel ten feet tall and bulletproof from her admission. I don't deserve her trust as a complete stranger, but the fact that I have it has me wanting to show her she made the right choice. "We'll get a room, and we can just talk or kiss." I run the pad of my thumb across her bottom lip. "More kissing isn't a bad thing," I say, wanting to feel her lips against mine more than anything else in the world.

I watch as her fingers fly across the screen of her cell phone. I assume texting her friend, letting her know where she is. That's smart, and I'm glad. No matter how much she trusts me, she needs to be safe. Sliding her phone into her purse, she laces her fingers with mine and nods. I don't say anything. I'm afraid my words could make her change her mind, and that would be a tragedy. My heart thunders in my chest as we walk two blocks to the closest hotel. Silence lingers between us, but the electricity sparks as if we both could ignite in flames at any second.

It doesn't take long before we're checked in and I'm sliding the card into our newly rented room. I push open the door and motion for her to walk in ahead of me, with me following her, making sure to push the door closed and twist the lock, tossing the keycard on the dresser.

My eyes follow her as she walks toward the window, pulling back the curtains to peer outside. "Nice view," she says, her voice shaking.

"The best," I agree.

She turns to look at me over her shoulder. "You can't even see it." Her lips tilt in a shy smile. She knows exactly what I'm referring to.

Her.

"I can see everything I need to." I stand still, hands shoved in my pockets when all I want to do is rush to her, rip her clothes off, and devour every sexy fucking inch of her. But something holds me back. It's more than the fact that I told her she set the pace. It's— I'm not ready for my time with her to end, and I'm afraid that once I'm inside her, once our bodies have come together, she's going to leave, and yeah, I'm not ready for that to happen.

Not yet.

"I don't know how to do this." Her words are a whispered confession that pulls at something deep in my chest.

"We don't have to do anything."

"I want to." She looks down at the floor. My eyes follow her stare, and I watch as she steps out of her heels. It's on the tip of my tongue to tell her to leave them, but this is her show. I'm just the extra. The man who is desperate for time with her, to feel her skin against mine, to feel her heat wrapped around me. "I'm just going to need some help."

I look up to find those big blue eyes of hers watching me intently. My legs move on their own as they carry me to her. With my eyes roaming over her body, I take her in, memorizing that little black dress. There is nothing special about it—I've seen the same version on hundreds of women in my lifetime—but on her, on my dream girl, it's the sexiest fucking thing I've ever seen.

When we're toe to toe, I reach for the hem of my shirt, pulling it over my head and dropping it to the floor. Her breath hitches. The sound is blaring through the silence of the room. I repeat the process with my jeans, tugging them over my thighs and kicking them to the side. That leaves me standing before her in nothing but my boxer briefs that do nothing to hide my desire for her.

"My turn?" she asks. There's a wobble in her voice, but the firm set of her shoulders tells me that although she's nervous, she's in this. We're in this. Here. Together.

"I want to see you."

She nods and turns, giving me her back, moving her long dark locks to hang over one shoulder. "Unzip me?"

"My pleasure," I say. My voice is confident, but the tremble in my hands as I grasp her zipper and slowly pull until it reaches the small of her back tells another story.

I stand still as I watch her pull the dress from one shoulder then the other. She shimmies her hips and lets it fall to the floor, pooling at her feet. Black lace is all that's left covering her, and my cock twitches. With my index finger, I trace from one shoulder to the other, feeling her soft skin.

With a shudder, she slowly turns to face me. Blue eyes full of desire find mine. I cradle her face with my hands, staring at her intently, hoping she can see into the depths of my soul how much I want her. I don't mask the need that I have for her or the surprise that it's there. I've never in my life felt like this.

"Can I kiss you?"

"You better," she replies, and if she was going to say anything else, it's too late because my lips are on hers.

Her hands wrap around my waist, and I drop my hands, doing the same, needing her closer. My tongue strokes against hers, the taste of her exploding on my tongue. "So sweet," I murmur. I've never kissed someone as sweet as her, and her skin, it's so damn soft. I softly trace her back until I reach her bra strap. "May I?" I ask against her lips.

"Hurry," she says breathlessly.

And that's all the go-ahead I need.

I make quick work of the clasp and step back, pulling the small scrap of lace from her body. Her tits, more than a handful, are staring at me, her hard nipples, begging for my mouth. Not able to wait, I bend my head, sucking one into my mouth, making her moan from somewhere deep in her throat. As her nails dig into my shoulders, I take my time going from one breast to the other, lavishing them with equal attention, before dropping to my knees.

I kiss her belly and down until I reach the waistband of her thong. Gripping the material on one side, I tug, the sound of ripping fabric fills the room, and an audible gasp comes from the beauty standing before me. "Fuck," I murmur as I lean in and trace my tongue between her folds.

"Oh," she gasps, her hands finding their way to my hair.

When her legs start to tremble, I know it's time to move this to the bed. It's a struggle to pull myself to my feet. "Bed," I say huskily.

She moves to take a step and stumbles. I don't hesitate to bend and lift her into my arms. She yelps out her surprise but wraps her arms around my neck. In a few long strides, I'm laying her gently on the bed, stripping out of my boxer briefs, and reaching for my jeans. I fumble with them until I find my wallet and pull out my one and only condom. One. "Fuck," I mutter. Once will never be enough with her.

"My purse," she murmurs, her voice thick. "I have some in my purse."

"Thank fuck," I mutter, scanning the room for her purse. Once I'm in that bed with her, I don't want to leave.

Ever.

I can already feel it deep in my bones. She's got a hold on me.

"My best friend, she always insists we're prepared, but I-I've never needed them before." Her confession is soft, almost shy, and I find my chest swelling with pride that I'm the man she needs them for that this breathtaking woman has chosen me to give her pleasure.

Finding her purse, I hand it to her and watch as she pulls back the zipper and retrieves three condoms, handing them to me. "She was a girl scout," she says, shrugging.

"Thank her for me," I say with a cocky grin.

Placing the four condoms on the bed beside her head, I climb over the top of her. Her legs automatically open, allowing me to settle between her thighs where I belong. At least that's what this moment feels like. It's as if I'm finally home, and I don't understand it, and right now, I don't want to. I just want to be with her. I want to slide inside her and feel her heat. I want her nails digging into my back and her legs wrapped around my waist.

My lips find hers. I kiss her slow and deep, trying to calm my racing heart. Her legs wrap around my waist, just as I imagined, and with her feet locked, she's squeezing, drawing me in closer, my hard cock resting against her wet pussy. "Fuck," I swear, pulling out of the kiss. "You sure you want this?"

"I've never been more sure of anything." She reaches up and rests her hand on my cheek. "I can't explain this connection that I feel toward you. It's like I've known you forever, and I know I want it to be you. I have zero doubts. No reservations that you are who I want."

Who am I to argue? Instead, I reach for a condom and sit back on my legs, covering my cock, before aligning myself at her entrance. My lips seek out hers, and as my tongue slides past her lips, I push forward on one long stroke. I'm inside of her tight, wet heat. Her gasp and soft whimper have me pulling out of the kiss to stare down at her. The moonlight shows that her face is pained, and my mind slowly connects the dots.

"You okay?" I ask, my voice thick.

"Yes." Her eyes open slowly, and she smiles up at me. "Just needed a minute."

I swallow hard. "Is this…?" My voice trails off. I can't seem to find the words to ask her if this is her first time. That's impossible. She's in her early twenties if I had to guess and a fucking knockout. Shit, I should have asked how old she was. She's a college graduate, so I know she's legal. Fuck me. I don't even know her name.

Something stirs with the idea that I could be the only man to ever feel her like this. I've never been with a virgin, and never wanted to, but with this woman beneath me, big blue eyes shining up at me, I feel… possessive. I want to claim her as mine. Not just for tonight, but for as long as I can convince her to be mine.

What. The. Fuck?

"I wanted it to be you," she whispers her confession. "Spontaneity," she whispers.

"I don't even know your name." I give voice to my earlier thoughts.

"You're just passing through town. We both know this is a one-night thing. Can we just… finish what we started so that we can maybe do it again?" She smiles. She turns to look at the three condoms she pulled from her purse. "Maybe three more times?"

"You'll be sore."

"So worth it," she counters. "Please."

I've known her a few hours, and already I could never tell her no. Not that I want to. "I should have gone slow. Taken my time."

"I wanted it to be real. I wanted to feel the need that seems to be tethering us together. It was perfect. Spontaneous."

Leaning my forehead against hers, I take in a deep breath. "You tell me if I hurt you. If there is something you don't like, you tell me, and I stop. It's that simple."

"I won't tell you to stop." She lifts her hips, causing me to slide just a fraction deeper, something I didn't think was possible. "You feel too good."

"Fuck," I curse. My lips find hers as I pull out and slowly push back in. Our tongues battle as my hips thrust to a rhythm that has us both gasping for air.

"That… right there," she pants. Her legs tighten, just like her pussy as it grips my cock.

Resting my weight on one arm, I slide my hand between us, finding her clit, and with my thumb, I rub small circles. She's squeezing me like a vise, and I don't know how much longer I can hold on.

"Y-Yes!" she screams, and her body convulses around me. I feel the shudder run through her body, and that does it. I can't hold on any longer as I release inside her, in what will go down in the books at the best fucking orgasm of my life.

After we've both caught our breath, I kiss her softly before pulling out of her and climbing out of bed. I take care of the condom and wet a cloth from the bathroom to clean her up. Her eyes pop open in surprise, but otherwise, she says nothing, letting me take care of her. Tossing the cloth through the bathroom door, I climb into bed and pull her into my arms. As we lie in the darkness, nothing but our breathing between us, she has me questioning everything I've ever thought about myself. She's making me reconsider taking a job that will give me roots just to be next to her.

Over the next several hours, even with my protest that she's too sore, we manage to go through the three remaining condoms, and each time is better than the one before. As I finally drift off to sleep in the early morning hours, I know that I want to see her again. I've never felt this kind of connection, and I'm willing to do whatever it takes to keep her and the feeling of her in my arms and in my life.

However, when I wake just a few short hours later and reach for her, the bed is cold. Sitting up, I look around the room, and there is no sign of her, except for the condom wrappers on the floor and her torn panties that are lying under the chair. She must have missed them. Plopping back on the bed, I curse myself for not insisting on getting her name. My dream girl gave me the best sex of my life and snuck out like a thief in the night.

All I have left is a memory.

CHAPTER THREE
CADENCE
NINE MONTHS LATER

I'M SOBBING UNCONTROLLABLY, MY FACE IS COVERED IN SWEAT, AND I'M utterly exhausted, but that doesn't stop my smile when the nurse lays my little girl on my chest after her first bath. My hand rests against her back, holding her close to me, and my lips press to the top of her tiny little head. She's bound up like a tiny pink burrito, and my heart is full.

I'm a mother. I have a family.

Sure, it's small, just the two of us, but we will always have each other. I will never let a day go by that she doesn't know that she is my greatest accomplishment, my greatest gift in this life.

"Mommy loves you," I whisper to my daughter.

I have a daughter.

I'm a mommy.

Sadness washes over me as I think about her father. The man who gave me this incredible gift, yet he has no idea. I never knew it was possible to be in the happiest moment of your life, but also feel sadness and regret.

I left like a coward that night because of what he made me feel. I was embarrassed to do the walk of shame and if I'm being honest, I had already fallen hard for him. It took one night, and I knew my heart couldn't take the rejection, so I left like a scaredy-cat. I tried to convince the hotel to give me his information, even offered up cash that I didn't really have to spend on my journey to single motherhood, but it was useless. They refused.

I've cursed myself more times than I can count for not paying attention when he booked our room. I was so wrapped up in our "spontaneity" that I stepped away. That's just another regret to add to my growing list from that night.

"We'll give you a few minutes, then we need you to try nursing her," a nurse tells me, bringing me out of my thoughts.

"Okay." I nod as more tears well in my eyes.

When I found out I was pregnant, I was surprisingly calm. It's not how I'd planned to have a baby. I wanted to meet a man, fall in love, get married, and then start a family—a family I never really had growing up. When I was nine, I was placed with my foster family. After jumping from one placement to another, the Gardners stuck.

The Gardners are decent people. They made sure I had a roof over my head and three hot meals a day. I always had clothes that fit and the supplies I needed for school, but there were no hugs. No declarations of a job well done when I placed first in the spelling bee. No, "we're proud of you" when I graduated high school at the top of my class. They were detached. And while I still keep in touch with them—I send them Christmas and birthday cards every year—there are never any in return or invitations to join them for celebrations or the holidays.

The day I graduated, they told me I could stay until I left for college in the fall, and I haven't been back. That's not my home. But I was lucky and found that at college. Shelby and I were roommates freshman year, and we hit it off. We've been thick as thieves ever since. She's been my only family and listened to me as I obsessed over grades and my life plan.

However, life often has other ideas, though I'll never regret the night that resulted in me being a mother. Not just because this little angel was created, but because of him. Hazel Eyes as I've taken to calling him. He was my every fantasy come true. He told me the same thing, that I was his. He made me… feel, and I knew the score. It was a one-night thing, so when he fell asleep, I snuck out. I forced myself to walk away to avoid the awkwardness that was sure to be there when the sun came up.

When I found out I was pregnant, that wasn't the first time that I regretted running out that night. It wasn't the first time I wished I was still back in that hotel room, laying in his arms, feeling whole for the first time in my life.

As I lie here holding my daughter, who's not even an hour into this world, I worry about how I'll tell her about her father. I don't know his name, but I know deep in my soul that if I did—if I had a name and if he knew about her—he would have accepted her.

Don't ask me how I know, but it's a feeling, one that I will stand behind when my daughter is old enough for me to tell her about the man with hazel eyes who gave me the greatest gift in the world.

Her.

"You doing okay, Momma?" my best friend asks from the chair beside my bed.

"I'm good," I assure her. "Thank you for being here with me today."

"Are you kidding? There's no way I was missing this."

"You've done so much," I tell her, tears beginning to form again.

"Stop. You would have done the same thing for me. That's what best friends are for. Besides, as this little angel's aunt, I deserve the right to be here," Shelby says, giving me a watery grin. "Now—" She clears her throat, sitting up straighter in her chair. "Can you finally tell me what you're naming her?"

I look down at my chest to my sleeping daughter and smile softly. The moment I found out I was having a girl, I knew what I was naming her. However, I kept it to myself. I told Shelby that I needed to see her first, something I've heard other mothers say—at least from what I've read on the blogs I follow.

"Hazel. Her name is Hazel Marie." My voice cracks and my heart swells with love.

"Hazel Eyes." Shelby nods in understanding.

"Yeah. I took her father from her, and I want her to have a piece of him. That's all I know about him to give her, and Marie, as you know, is my middle name. She has a piece of both of us."

"I love it." She reaches across the bed and gives my arm a gentle squeeze. "For the record, you didn't take her father from her. You don't know what would have happened that next morning. You also had no idea that this little sweetie was created that night. You're doing the best that you can. Don't be so hard on yourself."

I nod. I don't agree with her because I will forever live with the regret of walking away. I was a coward. I was inexperienced, and the feelings that he awoke in me that night, they had my mind racing and my heart aching to never let go. I knew that wasn't what our night was, so I fled. I regret leaving, but I will never regret my night with him and my daughter. She's my everything.

"You sure you don't need me to stay with you for a while?" Shelby asks.

"No, but thank you. You need to keep living your life, and I need to learn how to live mine as a single mother."

"It's okay to ask for help."

"Oh, trust me, I will." I chuckle. "You're going to wish that you lived in a different apartment building."

"Never. I don't care what time it is. If you need me, you call me."

I nod. "Thank you, Shelby. I don't think I could have done this without you."

She swallows hard and nods. "So, is the plan still that Thea is going to watch her for you?"

"Yes. She's excited to bring in some extra income since Scott is the only one working. He insists that she raise Clint, and they not put him in daycare."

"Phew." Shelby fans herself. "That man of hers is intense, and finnneee." She drags out the word.

"That he is," I agree. "Thea's going to have her hands full with Clint and this little one, but she assures me she can handle it, and I trust her."

"I do too. She's good people. They both are."

"I agree. However, Clint will be four months by the time I go back to work, and Hazel six weeks, so she's definitely going to be exhausted at the end of the day."

"You sure you don't want to take more time?"

"I do, but I don't have the time to take. I'd barely started when I told them I was pregnant. I'm lucky they didn't fire me. My only saving grace is that they do offer up to six weeks paid leave, so I'm not going without money."

"That's going to be a hard day."

"Yeah," I agree, my heart already breaking just a little at the thought of leaving my little girl when I go back to work.

"Knock, knock," the nurse says. "Time to see if we can get this little one to eat."

"I'm going to take a walk. I'll be back." Shelby stands and leans in for a hug, placing a kiss on Hazel's head. "Love you," she says softly before standing and leaving the room.

With the help of the nurse, Hazel latches on right away, and as I watch her, I can't help but wonder if there is another way I can find him. Maybe I could hire a private investigator. Not that I have the money to do that. Sure, I make a good living, but I'm doing it all on my own, and babies are expensive. Maybe I'll start saving, and when I have enough, I'll try to find him. I owe that to both of them.

I want my daughter, *our* daughter, to have more than just my memories of her father. I just hope if I do find him, that my gut is right, and he accepts her in his life. I know what it's like not to have loving parents, and I don't want that for my little girl.

CHAPTER FOUR

TREVIN
THREE MONTHS LATER

IT'S BEEN OVER A YEAR SINCE I'VE BEEN HOME TO SEE MY PARENTS AND MY sister. Twelve long months since I've stepped foot in this town. When I accepted the job as plant manager for the Lexington branch of Riggins Enterprises, I knew it would take me away from my family, but the pay and the opportunity were too good to pass up. When I visited a year ago, I was missing home and was ready to ask for a transfer or give it all up. After I woke up in the hotel room alone, I couldn't leave this town and the ghost of her memory fast enough.

That night still haunts me. Every other memory is her, my dream girl, who seems more and more like a figment of my imagination as time passes by. The memory of that night hasn't faded over the last year, which is what has kept me away. However, I can't hide forever, as my sister, so eloquently reminded me when she handed me my ass for not coming to visit my nephew. He was born around Christmas, and the family came to my place in Lexington. That was five months ago, and I've been summoned. I miss my family, so it's time to face my memories and stop being a coward.

The reality is, she was a woman I knew for a matter of hours. I shouldn't be letting her keep me from the people I love.

"You all packed?" Mom asks, standing in the doorway of my childhood bedroom.

"Yeah. You know your daughter, she insisted I stay with them for a couple of days."

"She's always been strong-willed that one," Mom says wistfully.

"That she has. I'm heading home when I leave her place."

"Well, try not to make it so long between visits. It's a three-hour drive from Lexington to Indianapolis." She gives me a pointed look.

"I know. I'm sorry. I let myself get lost in work. I'll do better. I promise."

"Good. Now you better get moving. Your sister is going to be calling and tracking you down, and it's about an hour to get to her place from here."

"I have a feeling you and Dad have been taking that drive a lot the past five months."

"Not as much as I'd like. We're actually considering moving closer."

"Really?" I ask, surprised.

"Yes. We want to be closer to our grandson. You know it would be nice if you moved home and gave us more grandkids."

"Mom," I sigh. "I'm not sure that's in the cards for me." A year ago, I would have shut her down, but one night—no, not just one night, the hottest night of my life with my dream girl—has me wishing for things I know I'll never have. Not without her. How she managed to ruin me in the small span of a few hours is beyond me, but she succeeded.

"I'll back off." She grins. "Just know I'm thinking it." She winks, wrapping her arms around me in a hug. "Love you, son."

"I love you too. Tell Dad I'm sorry I missed him."

"Will do. He wanted to cancel his fishing trip, but I wouldn't let him."

"I'm glad. He deserves a break. He's only been retired for what, two months, and he's just now getting out of the house?"

"Exactly!" she exclaims. "I get the place to myself. Now, shoo," she says with tears in her eyes.

"I'll come home more. Promise."

"Good. Love you. Give your sister and her family a hug from me. I'll be there to see them next weekend."

"I'll tell them." With a final wave, I'm in my truck and headed to the other side of town to see my sister and her family. It's long overdue. On the drive, I get lost in my memories of that night, the feel of the mystery woman's soft skin beneath my fingertips, the taste of her on my tongue, the way it felt to be inside her, and the knowledge that back then, I was the only man to ever have her.

I bang my hand against the steering wheel. I should have got her name. I should have insisted on knowing every little detail about her.

My dream girl.

WHEN MY SISTER OPENS HER DOOR, I'M HIT WITH THE SOUND OF CRYING. Not just from my nephew, who is in her arms, but from somewhere else in the house. "Come in," she says. I reach for my nephew to help her out, but he vomits all over her before I have a chance to take him.

"Shit," she mutters. "The second time today."

"What can I do?"

"He woke her up. Can you try and calm her down while I get him changed? I already called her mom at work. She's on her way." My sister is already headed down the hall toward her bedroom before the words are out of her mouth. Not that I can blame her.

Closing the door, I find my way to the Pack 'n Play next to the couch. Peering down, I see a tiny little bundle of pink, her arms and legs waving in tune to her cries. I've not had much experience with kids. It's limited to the visit from my family over Christmas when my nephew was still a tiny infant and didn't do much but eat, shit, and sleep. The cries intensify, and I know I've got to fight back the panic of not knowing what the fuck I'm doing and pick her up.

"Hey," I coo as I carefully lift her into my arms. Placing her on my shoulder, I begin to rub her back as I pace the room. That's what they do in the movies, right? "Shh, it's okay. He didn't mean to. Little man isn't feeling well," I tell her, and her cries turn to a soft whimper. "There you go," I tell her softly. "All better," I say as she shudders a tiny breath, which I feel against my neck, and her tiny body relaxes into my hold.

Something in my chest tightens at the realization that I was able to calm her down, and give her the comfort that she needs. Eyeing the rocking chair in the corner of the room, I take a seat and begin to rock her, continuing to rub her back. "Feeling better?" I ask her just as there's a knock at the door.

"I'll get it," Thea says as she walks back into the room with my nephew, Clint, and them both in clean clothes. "Hey, Cadence, I'm sorry I didn't know what else to do. I hate that you had to leave work."

"It's fine. I had a light afternoon anyway. Can I do anything?"

That voice. My body is frozen as my night with her comes rushing back. I'd know that voice anywhere. I've heard it every fucking day over the last year. In my dreams, walking down the street, in a restaurant, you name it, and my mind has made me think that it's her when it's never been quite right, not until right now at this moment. My memories and my present are colliding, and I know it's her before I even see her.

"Luckily, my brother Trevin showed up just in time for the second round of vomiting. I hope you don't mind. Clint woke her up, and I asked Trevin to help."

"It's fine. I'll gather her things and get out of your way. Is there anything I can do while I'm here?"

"No. I've already started my second load of laundry for the day, and Trevin's here if I need anything. Come on in, and I'll introduce you."

I know that in a matter of seconds, I'm going to see her again. My heart is racing, and my palms are sweating. As if the little angel in my arms knows I'm nervous, her tiny hand rests against my cheek, and my heart trips over in my chest.

"Cadence, this is my brother, Trevin. Trev, this is Cadence, and that's her little girl you're holding," Thea introduces.

Cadence, also known as my dream girl, the one who has consumed my every other memory for over a year is standing before me. My breath stalls in my chest as her eyes widen. She looks from me to her daughter and back again.

My wheels start to turn. Her daughter. I look down at the tiny human in my arms, and that tight feeling in my chest intensifies. "H-How old is she?" I ask, my eyes laser-focused on Cadence.

"Three months," she whispers.

I nod as I count the time in my mind. It's been exactly thirteen months tomorrow from the night we shared together. A night I'll never for the rest of my life forget. "What's her name?" I ask. My voice is gritty like I've swallowed sandpaper.

"H-Hazel." She clears her throat. "Her name is Hazel."

"Hazel," I repeat softly. My lips find the top of my daughter's head as I close my eyes and breathe her in.

My daughter.

There isn't a single doubt in my mind that she's mine. The look in her mother's eyes tells me all that I need to know.

I'm a father.

"Um, what's going on here?"

"Thea," Cadence says, her voice breaking. "He's, I mean Trevin, your brother, he's Hazel Eyes," she says, her voice barely audible over the thunderous beat of my heart.

"Oh my God," Thea murmurs.

"I didn't know your name. I didn't know how to find you. I'm sorry. I'm so sorry," Cadence says as tears begin to race down her cheeks.

Carefully, I stand with *our* daughter in my arms. I don't stop until I'm close enough to snake my arm around her waist and pull her into me. A sob breaks free from her chest, and I find myself fighting back the emotions of the moment. She's here in my arms, and she's not alone. I have a daughter. *We* have a daughter.

Clint lets out a whimper that has me lifting my head to catch my sister's eye. She's smiling and crying as she tries to soothe her son. I never told a single soul about that night. No one except for Scott, my best friend, and I know from the look on my sister's face, he told his wife.

"Can we go somewhere and talk?" I ask Cadence. Such a beautiful name. It suits her. I also need to know everything. I want to hold her, hold both of them, and just… hell, I don't even know. I'm mad that she ran out on me that night, but I'm also mad at myself for spouting all that spontaneity bullshit. I'd known the minute I got my hands on her she was different. That was confirmed when I pushed inside her for the first time. I should have told her then that I wanted more than just one night with her. I should have insisted I get her name. There are so many could haves… should haves. But she's here. They're here, and we need to figure this out.

"I-I live across the hall," she tells me, reaching for Hazel.

"Can I? I'm not ready to let her go yet." Fuck me, but I don't know that I'll ever be able to let her go. This tiny little angel is a part of me. How do I walk away from that?

"O-Okay. Let me just grab her bag." She tugs out of my arms, and I miss her warmth. I want nothing more than to pull her back into my arms and kiss the hell out of her, but there are things that need to be said.

"Trev?" Thea says. I turn to look at her. "You good?" There are tears in her eyes, and a smile on her lips. Her husband, my best friend, definitely cannot keep a secret.

I nod because I don't really know what I am. I'm angry. So damn angry that I missed too much time with my daughter. With Cadence. With my family. There is so much swirling in my mind right now, I can't really determine which is stronger—anger for what I've missed. Hurt for the memories we've lost. Relief that she's here, that Cadence is within my reach, something I never thought would be a possibility. Disbelief that she's been living next door to my sister, for I don't know how long.

I've heard Thea talk about her friend next door who was unexpectedly a single mom, and she was helping her out, and it gave her some extra spending money. All this time, it was my dream girl and my daughter. My dumbass let fear keep me away when I could have been with them.

"Thea, do you need me? Need anything?" Cadence asks. There's a tremble in her voice.

"No. You two go ahead. But call me later." Thea gives no room for argument in her response.

"Will do," Cadence says before turning her gaze to me. "Ready?"

"Love you, sis," I say, not taking my eyes off Cadence.

"Love you too, big brother," she says softly.

I follow Cadence out the door and to the one directly across the hall. As I hold our daughter in my arms and follow her into her apartment, I can't help but think that this is my family. They're my family.

My mind is a jumbled mess. I hope Cadence didn't have plans tonight because we have a lot to talk about, I think, as I shut the door behind us.

CHAPTER FIVE
CADENCE

FUMBLING WITH THE KEYS, MY HANDS SHAKE AS I TRY TO UNLOCK MY apartment door. The weight of his presence behind me is a reminder of what we're about to face. What I'm about to face. The mistake of my past, not Hazel, and not him, but leaving him, is about to catch up with me.

"Take a deep breath," he instructs as he places his hand on the small of my back. The heat from his skin seeping through my shirt isn't at all unwelcome. After all this time, my body remembers his touch. The shiver that rolls over me is all the reminder I need.

Closing my eyes, I pull in a slow, deep breath and exhale in the same manner. Steeling my resolve, I open my eyes and manage to get the key in the door and turn the lock. Stepping inside, I hold the door open, allowing Hazel Eyes, who I now know as Trevin, to enter.

After shutting the door, I place Hazel's diaper bag on the floor next to the couch. "I can take her," I offer.

"No." His voice is clipped, and Hazel whimpers in his arms. "I'm sorry, baby girl," he whispers, placing his lips on her head. "Daddy's sorry." His tone's feather-soft as he speaks to our daughter.

My heart is thundering in my chest and feels as though it might explode at any moment. "I'm sorry," I croak out my apology. I don't know what else to say.

Standing in my small living room, I watch as he settles his tall frame on the couch, expertly holding our baby girl as if he's done it a million times in her short life. Shuffling so that she's lying in the crook of his arm, his eyes rake over her, almost as if he's committing everything about her to memory.

I don't move. My body is statue-still as I watch them together. It's not until he glances up at me that I move to sit for fear my knees will give out, and I'll end up a pile in the middle of the floor.

"Cadence," he murmurs my name. "Why did you leave?"

There it is. The question I knew that I'd one day have to face. I just imagined it being our daughter asking, not her father.

"I—" I open my mouth to tell him I was saving him the trouble and decide he deserves my honesty. "I was scared." I swallow hard, collecting my thoughts. Wiping my sweaty palms on my dress pants, I push forward. "You made me feel too much, too soon, and we were strangers. I told myself it was to save you time in the morning. We went into the night with our eyes wide open. I knew it was a fling. But with each passing minute, it felt less like a fling and more like… everything," I confess.

"If you would have stayed—" He shakes his head, and I can hear not only the disappointment but the sadness in his voice. "I missed this," he says, staring down at Hazel in his arms. "I missed you." His voice is so soft I almost miss his confession. Lifting his head, his hazel eyes bore into mine. "I'm angry. I'm so fucking angry," he says in a hushed tone. "But you're not the only one to blame. I'll own my part in this. I didn't offer my name or get yours, even though I wanted to. In fact, I had planned to. The next day."

"Oh, no." I cover my mouth with my hand to prevent my sob from falling from my lips. Not that it matters. My shoulders shake on their own accord from my cries, and there is no hiding it.

"What's her full name?" he asks.

"Hazel Marie Wade."

"Cadence Wade," he mumbles. I'm not even sure he realizes he's said it. "I want her to have my last name."

"Okay."

His head pops up. "Just like that?"

"You're her father."

"I'm her father," he agrees with a nod.

"Trevin, I'm sorry. I tried to get the hotel to give me your information, but they refused. It didn't matter how much I begged and pleaded or how many tears I cried. They wouldn't budge. I didn't know what else to do. It was just the two of us that night. There was no one I could ask about who you were. My only choice was to move on."

"What about her? What about Hazel? Were you going to tell her about me?"

I nod. "Yeah. My life growing up was… not one a child ever dreams of. I made a vow the day I found out about her that she would know what I knew about you."

"What's that? What do you know about me?" His tone is soft, and his eyes are full of intrigue.

"That you were a handsome man, who gave me not only the best night of my life but my greatest gift. Her." I hold his stare. I promised myself and my daughter that if I ever crossed paths with him again, I'd tell him what that night meant to me. I'd tell him what *he* meant to me. It was one night, but my heart didn't seem to care.

"Tell me everything. Were you sick? I mean, women who are pregnant get sick, right? When is her birthday? How much did she weigh? I've missed so much. I didn't get to watch her grow inside you."

"How much time do you have?" I ask, wiping the tears from my cheeks.

"I'm here all weekend."

"I know you came to see Thea, Scott, and Clint."

"They'll understand."

I nod. "It's time for her to eat."

"Can I do it?" he asks softly.

"Yeah," I reply, just as soft. I stand and go to the kitchen to warm up a bottle and take it back to the living room. "She might not take it if she can see me. She's used to being breastfed when I'm around. I'm going to step out of the room so that she'll eat for you."

"You can do it if she needs…." His voice trails off.

"No. This is breast milk." I feel my cheeks pink from embarrassment. This man has had his mouth and hands on every inch of my body. We created a beautiful little girl together. I should be beyond embarrassment.

His heated gaze trails over my chest. My eyes zero in on his throat as he swallows hard. "If it's better for her to, you know." He nods toward my boobs.

"It's the same thing, but it's our bonding time. It's fine. You need this time with her."

"I don't really know what I'm doing."

"Here's a burp cloth. When she's about halfway through, you have to stop and burp her. Make sure this is on your shoulder. She sometimes spits up. She also might grumble and fuss because she's a little piglet like that." I smile at my baby girl, who has her eyes on me just from the familiar sound of my voice.

"How do I burp her?"

"I'll be right here," I assure him. "All you have to do is take the bottle from her and place her on your shoulder. Then you rub or pat her back softly until she burps."

"Okay. I got this. We can do this, right, Hazel? You can help Daddy?" he asks, his voice raising an octave when he refers to himself as Daddy.

"I'm just going to step away, so she doesn't see me." I place the burp cloth over his shoulder and then hand him the bottle, quickly stepping out of Hazel's line of sight.

"Mommy says this is a piece of cake. Take it easy on me, yeah?" he asks, placing the bottle to her lips.

Our little girl is a champ, and enjoys her bottle and goes to town. I'm far enough to the side that she can't see me, but I have a clear view of the magnificent smile that lights up Trevin's face as he feeds our daughter for the first time. As quietly as I can, I move to my purse that I placed on the floor near the diaper bag and dig out my phone before taking my place across the room. I snap picture after picture of the two of them, all while wiping tears that are silently racing down my cheeks.

"Mommy thinks she's a photographer." He chuckles. "You're going to send me those, right?" he asks, not taking his eyes off our daughter.

"How did you know?" I ask.

"I can feel you. Don't ask me to explain it because I can't."

I wasn't going to ask, because I don't need an explanation. I have the same intuition when it comes to him, just like when Thea opened the door for me earlier. I knew something big was about to happen. I could feel it. I just didn't know what it was.

Never in my wildest dreams would I have imagined that my new friend, one who has been there for me since the day I moved in, would be my hazel eyes' sister. It just goes to show you how small the world really is. Or maybe it's fate? The universe's way of telling us that we were meant to be together? That's probably wishful thinking on my part, but I have to be honest with myself. He's been my one and only since that night.

"You're good with her."

"She's beautiful, Cadence. Her name. Is there a meaning behind it?"

I know he heard my hazel eyes comment when I was talking to Thea earlier. That's all it took was telling her that her brother was Hazel Eyes, and she was caught up to speed as to what was happening between her brother and me.

"Marie is my middle name."

"And Hazel?" From the tone of his voice, he's fishing, but that's okay. I'll tell him what he wants to hear.

"Your eyes, they follow me in my dreams every night. I wanted her to have a piece of both of us, and well, that's really all I had to go on that was appropriate to name a little girl." I smile, and he chuckles.

"I like it."

"What comes next?" I hate the wobble in my voice.

"Next?" He shrugs. "I don't know, Cadence. What I do know is that she's mine, I have no doubts, and I want to be in her life."

"Just hers?" The question is out before I can think better of it. My already racing heart seems to kick it up a notch as I wait for his reply.

"You are her mother."

"You know what I mean, Trevin."

He nods. "I do, and honestly, I don't know if I can think about that right now."

"Please don't take her from me," I plead, my voice cracking.

"What?" The look on his face mixed with the tone of his voice tells me he's appalled at the mere mention of him keeping her from me. "Do you think that's the kind of man that I am? That I would keep my daughter from her mother?"

"I kept her from you."

"That wasn't your fault."

"I left."

"I'm just as much to blame. I didn't tell you what was in my head. What was growing in my heart. Instead, I curled up with you in my arms and figured we could figure out in the morning."

"And I was gone."

"The past is the past. I promise you I won't take her from you. I don't… I don't know what the future holds for us. I don't live here. Decisions need to be made."

The worry that's been sitting on my chest eases just a fraction. He doesn't want to take her from me, but what does that mean? We have decision to make? Does he want me to move? I've worked hard to build a life for Hazel and myself. This is the first true home I've ever had. I don't want to leave. Taking a deep breath, I decide I have to trust his word, and trust that we will work it out together. "Would you like to stay for dinner?"

"Try getting me to leave your apartment before I have to. Unless she's with me, I'm not going anywhere."

His words cause my panic to rise again, but he promised he wouldn't take her from me. The way that Thea talks about her brother, he's good people. My gut tells me the same—the same exact way it did the night I followed him out of the club and to the nearby hotel. Fate brought him back to us. I have to have hope that everything will work out the way that it's supposed to.

"Come keep me company while I make dinner. I have some photo albums you can look through." I made it a point to catalog her life. One, because I don't have any pictures from when I was her age, and two, I had always hoped the two of us would find our way back to each other, and he would want to see them.

With Hazel snuggled in his arms, Trevin follows me into the small kitchen and sits at the table looking through pictures of me when I was pregnant and every milestone our baby girl has surpassed in her short three months in the outside world. We eat dinner together, and Trevin helps me give her a bath, insisting on feeding her a bottle and rocking her to sleep. I hate losing that time with her, but I've had her for the last three months. It's his turn. He deserves this time with her as well. I just hope that when he needs to go back to work, we can figure this out. Being that far from her would kill me.

I send up a silent prayer that Trevin Hubbard is the man I thought he was over a year ago. I also pray that he remains a part of my daughter's life, and I might have maybe asked for him to be a part of mine as well as more than just my baby daddy.

CHAPTER SIX

TREVIN

THE SOUND OF A CRYING BABY JOLTS ME FROM SLEEP. SITTING UP ON THE couch, I lift my arms over my head, stretching out the kinks. A quick glance around the room in my sleepy haze, it takes me a minute to remember where I am.

Cadence.

Hazel.

My girls.

Crying. Something's wrong.

On my feet, I rush down the small hall and peek into her room. Her crib is empty but what I see just about brings me to my knees. Cadence is sitting in the white rocking chair in the corner of the room, Hazel in her arms. It's not the two of them together, sitting in that chair, that's affecting me, well it is, but not as much as the short shorts and sheer tank that Cadence is wearing. Or the fact that her full breast is bared as she feeds our daughter.

I don't know if there are protocols for this kind of thing, but I need to be close to them. Both of them. My feet carry me quietly into the room, and I don't stop until I'm standing beside the chair. I lower myself to the floor and reach out, offering Hazel my finger. My little girl looks at me through sleepy eyes, but her grip on my digit is tight. Not just my finger, but my heart. If you told me a week ago that this little girl would steal my heart in a matter of seconds, I would have told you that you were fucking crazy. Now, as I sit here on my daughter's bedroom floor with her tiny hand wrapped around my finger and my heart, watching her eat from her mother's breast, I know better.

This is love.

Is it possible for my heart to be too big for my chest? I feel as though it could explode at any second as I watch the two of them together. "She's hungry," I say, my voice thick.

"Yeah. We're still working on the sleeping through the night thing," Cadence replies, her voice soft. "She's done it a few times, but this little stinker loves to eat."

"I should have let you feed her," I say, as the guilt washes over me.

"What? No, she would have done this if I would have breastfed her. She's a little piglet." There's nothing but love in her eyes as she glances down at our daughter. "You'll get it figured out, won't you, baby girl?" she asks Hazel, with a small grin tilting her lips.

The room is lit with a faint glow of a small pink teddy bear lamp sitting on the dresser. It's just enough for me to make out the features of the mother of my child. She's beautiful. More beautiful than my memories painted her to be. Right here, in her tiny pajamas, her hair a mess, her eyes tired, and her breast bared as she gives our daughter the nutrients she needs to thrive, she's never looked more beautiful. I know that in this lifetime, there will never be a moment that I will think that she looks better than she does right here. Right now.

I need to touch her.

Reaching out with my hand that's not occupied by our daughter, I rest my palm on her bare thigh, tracing small circles with my thumb. Our eyes meet, and that same electric current ignites between us. The same one that was there that night in the club. The same current that led us to a hotel room for a night of passion that changed me.

No words are exchanged, but none are needed. I can see it in her eyes. They're hooded, and the sleep is replaced with desire, and if I'm not mistaken, need. I see it in the way she shifts her position in the chair. She wants me.

I want her.

It's as simple as that. I can't explain it, and I don't want to. Never in my life have I met a woman who affects me as Cadence does. I don't know what it means, and tonight, right now, I don't care. All I can think about is tucking our daughter safe into her crib and getting my hands and mouth on Cadence.

All. Over. Her.

I don't have to wonder if she wants the same thing because when my eyes meet hers, her breath hitches. My cock stirs as the memories of our time together replay in my mind. This is nothing new for me. I'm not ashamed to admit that I've taken matters into my own hands, literally, at the memory of that night. Now, here she is sitting before me with a piece of the two of us in her arms.

With each passing minute, the anger fades, and something else takes its place. That something causes a flutter in my chest. I'm as much to blame as she is. "We used protection," I say out loud. "That night, we used protection."

"We did. Every time."

"Then how did we get this little angel?" I ask, nodding toward Hazel, whose eyes are growing heavy as her belly gets full.

"Condoms are not 100 percent effective."

"Were you not on the pill?" I realize as I ask the question that we should have had this conversation that night, but I was too wrapped up in her and the indescribable connection to worry about the specifics. I suited up. I thought we were good. "Sorry," I say when I realize how my question sounded. "I'm just thinking out loud. I don't blame you, Cadence." Her name rolls off my tongue like a caress.

"No. I'm not on the pill," she answers. "I wasn't sleeping with anyone. I hadn't," she adds, and I kid you not, my cock aches at the memory of knowing that I'm the only man who's ever been inside of her. Well, I was the first.

"And now?"

"No. I'm not— I mean, Hazel is my priority."

"Has there been anyone since me?" I toss the question out there. Partly because I'm curious, and the other part knows that not knowing will eat me alive until I have the answer.

"No." Her voice is barely audible, but in the silence of the room, I hear her loud and clear. "W-What about you?"

"No. However, that's not from my lack of trying. I tried random hookups a few times and never made it past a kiss or two. They didn't taste like you," I say, leaning in and pressing my lips to her bare thigh. "They didn't smell like you. You've ruined me." There hasn't been a woman in my life who could compare to her since that night. Hell, there has never in my life been a woman who has compared to her, and I know as I sit here looking up at her, that there never will.

"I need to lay her down," she says. Her voice is soft, but I still hear the vulnerability as she speaks. We're both on a road less traveled. We've made it to the fork in the road, and we need to decide our path.

I watch as she stands with our daughter in her arms and carries her to her crib. She places her back on the small mattress and quickly covers herself, much to my dismay. My eyes are glued to Cadence as I watch her kiss the tips of her index and middle fingers and place them on our daughter's forehead.

"Mommy and Daddy love you," she whispers, and my heart stops.

"C-Cadence?" She turns to look at me. "Do—" I swallow hard. "Do you tell her that every night?"

"Tell her what?" She tilts her head to the side, and I want nothing more than to trace the slender column of her neck with my lips, but I need to hear her answer first.

"That Mommy and Daddy love her."

"Oh." She places her hand over her mouth, and tears well in her eyes. "I'm sorry. It's a habit, and I know you can tell her now on your own, but I wanted her to know that she was loved, and I knew… something in my gut told me that if you knew about her, you would be in her life, and well, I didn't have the best childhood. I never wanted her to wonder if she was loved." She opens her mouth to say something else, but I'm faster. My hand slides behind her neck, and I pull her lips to mine. I kiss her hard as the emotions of her confession wash over me.

At this moment, with our lips pressed together, there is no time between us. No missed moments. It's just the two of us and the passion that we can't deny. It doesn't matter that she left, and it doesn't matter that I should have told her that it meant more to me than just a night of fun. We've both made mistakes, but I don't want to live in the past. I want to live in the present, with a future that involves the two of us and our baby girl. It's as if no time has passed as our tongues collide.

"I want you," I whisper against her lips.

"Bedroom."

Not needing any further invitation, I lift her in my arms and carry her across the hall to her bedroom. As soon as her feet hit the floor, she's raising her arms in the air. I waste no time pulling the small tank over her head, allowing her full breasts to spill out. My mouth waters needing them in my mouth. Bending my head, I suck one hard nipple gently into my mouth. Cadence moans, burying her hands in my hair. With the pad of my thumb, I trace the other, giving it equal attention.

"That's good," she moans. "So sensitive."

"Am I hurting you?" I pull back just far enough to ask.

"No. No. No, don't stop," she says, panicked.

"Don't worry, baby. I'm just getting started," I assure her, before dropping to my knees and helping her out of the tiny boy shorts she's wearing.

"Trevin." There's something in her voice that has me looking up at her, giving her my full attention. "I'm not— I mean my body. It's different now," she says with a wobble of worry in her voice. From the glow of the bedside lamp, I can see the rosy color of embarrassment on her cheeks. Then again, that might be desire. I can't be sure.

My lips kiss just above her pelvic bone over the pale red stretch mark. "You mean the body that grew and created our daughter? The body that gave her life and still nurtures her. Your body is different, Cadence, but it's sexy as fuck. I wish I could have seen you.

I wish I could have cradled Hazel when she rested here." My hand roams over her belly. "I wish I could have seen your body grow and change with our daughter." Resting my forehead against her belly, I wrap my arms around Cadence and hold her tight. The enormity of what I've missed catches up to me. Those are memories I'll never have.

I won't let the same mistake happen twice. We were both responsible for our pasts, but we are the ones who decide our future. I'm determined never to miss another chance for a memory with either of them. I feel her hands in my hair, and when I peer up at her, I see the silent tears rolling down her cheeks. The sight breaks my heart open. I need her to know, need her to understand that I'm in this. That I'm not going anywhere, and if I do, they're coming with me.

Standing, I cradle her face in the palm of my hands. "I'm here, Cadence. I'm here, and this is exactly where I want to be. I'm not leaving you. I'm not leaving her. I don't know what that looks like. There are so many things that we're going to have to work out, but I want you." I stare deep into her eyes, willing her to believe me. "I want both of you."

Moving to stand on the tip of her toes, she presses her lips to mine. I can taste the saltiness of her tears, but that doesn't stop me from tracing her lips with my tongue. I could kiss her like this every day for the rest of my life, and it wouldn't be enough. No amount of time with her will ever be enough. When we finally come up for air, I grip her hips and toss her on the bed. She bounces a few times as the sound of her laughter fills the room.

"Is she a light sleeper?" I ask.

"Not at all. I read a book that said to keep doing normal household chores so that the baby will be used to sleeping through noises. We won't wake her up."

"Don't move a muscle. I'll be right back." Rushing out of the room and down the hall, I grab my wallet from the coffee table and pull out the single condom that has been there for months. Not wasting time, I head back to her room and hold it up. "It's been in my wallet for a few months." I walk toward the lamp so that I can see the expiration date. "But it's still good."

Cadence shrugs. "It didn't work out so well for us the first time."

"What are you saying?"

"Just that they're not 100 percent."

"You telling me I can go bare?" I ask, my voice thick at the mere thought.

"Hazel isn't ready for a sibling just yet."

"But if it fails?"

She shrugs. "Then, she gets to be a big sister sooner than later."

I nod. What I don't say is that I would be perfectly fine with another baby. Fuck me. I want a house full of tiny humans that we create. I'm not a man who's said he's never getting married and didn't want kids. I've just never found a woman I wanted to spend every day of forever with.

Until now.

Now I have two ladies in my life that I'm going to hold onto with everything I have and never let go. After ripping open the condom, I slide it over my length and climb onto the bed, settling where I belong—between her thighs. "We only have one. Unless...." I let the unfinished question hang between us.

"Then we're going to have to make it count," she says, draping her arms over my shoulders.

"We are definitely going to make it count." My lips press to hers, and I do exactly that.

CHAPTER SEVEN
CADENCE

A CRASH FROM SOMEWHERE IN THE APARTMENT WAKES ME UP. I STILL AND listen but hear nothing. Glancing at the clock, I see it's after eight, and I never sleep this late. Hazel never sleeps this late. *Shit. Hazel.* I jump out of bed and race to her room. She's not there. A deep throaty voice comes from the living room, and I follow the sound. Last night comes rushing back to me. Trevin "Hazel Eyes" is here. I tug at the hem of his T-shirt that I'm wearing, and the memory of him moving inside me causes my body to heat.

My racing heart slows as my mind realizes that it's Trevin in my apartment with our daughter. Peeking around the corner, I see him sitting on the couch with Hazel in his arms. He's shirtless, wearing nothing but his boxer briefs, with a burp cloth tossed over his toned shoulder.

"Daddy's not too good at this yet, pumpkin. You need to bear with me. I promise I'll learn how to take care of you. I watched Mommy do this yesterday and I think I've got it." He tests a small drop of the bottle on his wrist. "I read this online last night that I should test the temperature here. I guess if Mommy was feeding you, we wouldn't have to worry about that."

He offers Hazel her bottle, and she takes it without issue. I can hear her gulps from here. Trevin smiles down at her, and there is nothing but love in his eyes.

"Morning, beautiful," he says, looking up at me. "You going to come and join us?" He nods to the empty cushion next to them on the couch.

I don't waste any time walking further into the room to take the offered seat. "Hey, sweet girl." I lean over and kiss my daughter on the forehead. I expect her to want me, but she just grins around her bottle and goes back to eating.

"I think she likes me." Trevin smiles.

"I'd say she more than likes you. You're her daddy. I think she knows that."

"Really?" The insecurity in that one single word has me reassuring him.

"Absolutely. Babies are smart, and it helps that you treat her like she's your world."

"She is." He looks over at me. "You both are."

"Trev—" I start, but he stops me.

"No. Let me finish. That night, I wanted to wake up with you the next day and tell you I wanted to see you again. I knew that the one night was never enough. I didn't know how we were going to make it happen, just that I wanted to. Sitting here with the two of you… the last twenty-four hours have been more than I could have hoped for. I want you in my life. I want to be in her life and in yours. I know it's soon, but I feel it deep."

"Sounds like a fairy tale."

"It is, baby. It's our fairy tale. I want to live it out with you." He looks down at Hazel. "Regardless of what happens between us, I have some changes I need to make. I need to find a job and put my place on the market, find a new place here."

"What? You're just uprooting your life?"

"You're here. She's here. My family is here."

"But your job, your life is in Lexington."

"That's where you're wrong. My life is in the apartment. My girls." He leans over and places a kiss on my temple. My heart skips a beat as I will his words to be true.

Before I can reply, there's a knock at the door. Standing, I go to answer it. "Hey," I greet Thea. I'm nervous standing before my best friend. How will my relationship with her brother affect our friendship? How will she react to actually being Hazel's aunt, not just an honorary title we've given her?

She looks at Trevin's shirt I'm wearing, that thankfully comes to just above my knees. "I see things went well," she states.

"We're a work in progress," I tell her. That's not exactly true, but this is his sister, and I don't know what he wants her to know and not know. It's difficult because she's become one of my closest friends.

"We're a family," Trevin says from behind me.

I turn to look at him, and he's standing with Hazel pressed against his chest and shoulder, rubbing her back.

"Come on, Trev, I don't need to see all that." Thea pretends to gag and shield her eyes from her brother. However, I didn't miss the soft expression in her eyes at seeing him holding his daughter. Our daughter.

"Then don't come knocking on my girl's door first thing in the morning," he fires back.

"Your girl, huh?" she asks, amused.

"My girls," he corrects. He steps closer to me, and slides the arm not holding Hazel around my waist. I step into his embrace, loving the feel of being in his arms. Loving that we're his girls.

"What are the two of you doing later? I thought we could maybe take the kids to the aquarium."

"Babe?" Trevin looks to me.

"Um… yeah, if you want."

"What time?" Trevin asks his sister.

"Around noon? That will be after morning naps, and both kids will have full bellies," she comments.

"Good point," I agree with her.

"We'll meet you there," Trevin says. "Now, let me get back to my family, and you need to get back to yours."

"You do remember that I'm your sister, right?"

"Yes. And I love you, but I just got them, Thea."

Tears well in Thea's eyes. "I love you." She leans in for a hug. "And you," she says, turning to look at me once she's released him. "How have I gone all this time and not realized it was my big brother?"

I too have tears in my eyes. "Because I didn't have a name. I didn't know where he was from, just that he was visiting."

"But Hazel Eyes. I should have connected the dots."

"Why would you? There are millions of men with hazel eyes."

"Yeah," she concedes. "You good?" From the soft tone of her voice, I know she's not asking as my daughter's aunt, but as my friend.

"We're good."

She turns and points at her brother. "Don't be late."

"Then leave so I can finish feeding my daughter and work on feeding her mother." He wags his eyebrows, and Thea, although laughing, pretends to gag.

"I could have gone without that," she says, opening the door and stepping into the hall.

"Love you, little sister," Trevin says, closing the door. "I have to give her hell because she's my little sister, but I'm so fucking glad that she was the one watching Hazel."

"She's amazing, and she's been a huge help to me with Hazel. She was there for me while I was pregnant and during and after delivery. She and my best friend, Shelby. I couldn't have done any of this without them."

"I doubt that. You're an amazing mother."

"You don't know that."

"Bullshit. I see how happy Hazel is. She's healthy, and you came right away yesterday. You're the best momma this little angel could ask for. Her daddy too."

"You got her?" I ask, changing the subject. I still feel a mound of guilt resting on my shoulders, that due to my actions, Hazel lost time with her daddy. Sure, she'll never remember, but one day she's going to ask why he was never in any of my pregnancy photos, or photos of her the first three months of her life. I'm going to have to answer for that. "I'm going to make us some breakfast."

"I wanted to have you for breakfast." He smirks.

"No condoms," I remind him.

"Don't need them for what I have planned." The devilish smile tilting his lips tells me exactly what that is.

A shiver of anticipation races down my spine. "Real food first, and then we'll see."

Snaking an arm around my waist, he pulls me into him and presses his lips to mine. "It's going to happen, baby. I promise you that." He smacks my ass and struts back to the living room to finish giving Hazel the rest of her breakfast. I can't help but wonder how this is my life.

* * *

IT TURNS OUT I HAD A HARD TIME PULLING TREVIN AWAY FROM HAZEL. HE insisted he hold her while we ate our own breakfast. He played with her until she was too fussy to keep going. She was a handful as he tried to get her to sleep, but he insisted that he could do it. My mom instincts told me to just take her from him, but then I reminded myself that he is her father. More importantly, he's here and wants to help take care of her. He wants to learn our routine, what she likes, and what she doesn't. How do I get in the way of that?

"I have to admit," Trevin says, coming back to the living after laying Hazel in her crib. "I wasn't sure I was going to be successful at getting her to sleep."

"She fights it sometimes. My guess is that she was having too much fun playing with you, and she didn't want to miss it."

"Yeah?" His eyes light up.

"Yes."

"I love her, Cadence." He shakes his head, and the look on his face tells me that he's in disbelief. "I never thought—" He smiles. "She's perfect."

"She is. She's such a good baby."

"You've done an incredible job with her. Thank you. I know it was hard for you to do it all on your own. I'm sorry I wasn't here for both of you."

"It was unavoidable. The past is behind us."

"Moving forward," he says, offering me his hand. "I believe I made you a promise."

"I'm not going to hold you to that. We really need to get ready."

"We have time," he says, not bothering to glance at the clock. His phone rings, and he grins when he looks at the screen. "Hey, Mom."

I freeze when I hear the word "Mom" come out of his mouth. My attention is focused on him as I wait to see what's going to happen. Will he tell her about Hazel? About me? My hands grip the hem of his T-shirt that I'm still wearing to keep from wringing them together. Will they hate me? Will they accept her? There are so many questions filtering through my mind.

"Oh, she did, did she?" He grins. "Yeah, I do have some news. Hold on, let me switch to video, and I'll show you."

I shriek and take off, running down the hall. His laughter follows me. "That was Cadence," he explains. "She's special." I hear him tell his mother.

I'm in my bedroom with my ear pressed to the door. I'm not ashamed to be listening to his conversation. I would have remained out in the living room, but the last thing his mom needs to see when she meets me for the first time, via video or in person, is me in her son's T-shirt sans bra, and my hair a mess from our lovemaking the night before.

That's a hard pass for me.

I'm sure it's going to be a hard-enough battle when she finds out I kept Hazel from him, even though it was beyond my control. I'm glad Thea understands the entire story. She knows how the night went down. I hate that she has the intimate details of my time with her brother, but at least she knew the story before he appeared back into my life.

"Mom, I need you to remain calm and not scream or cry. You have to be quiet when I show you what I'm about to show you," he says. I hear Hazel's bedroom door open. His voice trails off, and that won't do. I need to hear her response.

As quietly as possible, I open the bedroom door and sneak out into the hall and stand just outside Hazel's door.

"Mom, I'd like for you to meet your granddaughter. Her name is Hazel."

The sound of a female gasp hits my ears. "Trevin, explain that gorgeous little girl to me," his mom says, her voice cracking.

"Cadence, that's her mom. She and I met over a year ago. It was a night I'll never forget, and it gave us Hazel."

"Your dream girl?" she asks. My eyes widen at his mother's knowledge of our night together.

"That's her."

"How did you find her? Does she know that you looked for her? Oh, honey," his mom murmurs.

"I'm moving home, Ma," he says. "I need to be here for my girls." Butterflies take flight, and emotion clogs my throat. It's as if it's real now that he's telling his mother.

"What about your job?"

"I'm going to call Grant Riggins on Monday and tell him. Maybe they have a spot here for me at the Indy location? I'm not sure, and right now, I can't find it in me to care. I can't walk away from them. I won't." There's conviction in his voice that threatens to take my breath away.

I wipe the tears from my eyes and slide to the floor, burying my face in my hands. It's too much. Too many emotions are running through me. Regret that I ran scared, happiness for my daughter who has a father who loves her and is willing to uproot his life to be with her, and then there is this flutter in my chest that's always there when I think about him. The him from my past, and the him from the present. I feel this deep-rooted connection with him that scares the hell out of me. I've never had someone who stuck around. No one except for Shelby, and well, Thea if you count the last year.

My head jerks up when I feel his hand on my shoulder. Trevin is crouching in front of me, a look of worry on his handsome face. "Baby, what's wrong?"

"Nothing." I smile, wiping at my cheeks.

"It's something."

"You're really moving here?"

"Of course, I am. I told you that."

"I know, but I—" I stop speaking. He doesn't need me to lay my shit life on him right now.

"Come on." He stands and offers me his hand. I take it and let him pull me to my feet. He leads us into my bedroom and motions for me to climb into bed. Too exhausted to argue, I do as he asks. "Now, tell me. Don't hold back with me, Cadence. We know what happens when we do that. Nothing but truth between us from here on out. Tell me what's on your mind."

"I lost my parents when I was young. Well, my mom. I guess my dad was never around, at least that's what I've read in my file. My mom was addicted to drugs. She overdosed when I was six. I went into the foster care system, and was bounced around from home to home. When I was about nine I landed with a family that stuck. They were good to me, but not overly loving. They made sure I had food, clean clothes that fit, and everything I needed, they were just emotionally detached. When I turned eighteen, they allowed me to stay with them until I could move into my college dorm and that was it. Shelby, my best friend, was my roommate my freshman year and we've been close ever since. She's been my person until I met Thea when I moved here about a year ago."

"I'm sorry," he says softly.

"I don't want you to be sorry for me. I just— To hear you say you're staying and then tell your mom the same thing, it just kind of hit me that Hazel is going to have both parents. That you're a man of your word, and that she's not going to grow up like I did. She's going to have two parents who love her, an aunt who she already adores, and grandparents," I say, choking on the word. "She's going to have a real family. Something I never had."

"It's not just her, Cadence. It's you too. You're her mother. My family is your family. *You're* my family." He leans in close and kisses the corner of my mouth. "I'm not letting you leave me again," he says, pulling me into his arms.

We lie together, holding onto one another as his words filter through my mind. I know we need to start getting ready for the day, but I never want to leave his arms, or this

apartment where, for the time being, he's not just a memory, he's all mine.

All ours.

CHAPTER EIGHT

TREVIN

IT'S SUNDAY NIGHT AT SIX, AND I'M STILL IN INDIANAPOLIS. I HAVE A LONG three hours' drive back to Lexington, but I can't seem to make moves to go. I hate the thought of leaving here, leaving them. It's pulling at my heart, and I hate it.

"Don't you need to get on the road?" Scott asks.

"Yeah," I agree, not taking my eyes off Cadence and Hazel, where they sit on the couch with my sister and nephew, Clint.

"I can't believe Cadence is your dream girl." He smiles. "It's a small world. At least now I know it wasn't just some drunken dream," he comments.

"Hey." I turn to face him.

"There he is. Now I have your attention."

"I don't want to leave them here."

"They're going to be just fine. I'm next door, and I've been watching out for her since the moment my wife declared Cadence as her new bestie."

"It's my job," I say, irritated and thankful at the same time that my best friend has been looking out for my family.

My family.

"Maybe I can convince her to come with me?"

"Nah, she's got a good job, which she never misses unless it's for Hazel. She saves all of her time off for that little girl."

"She's a good mom."

"She is."

"I'm in love with her." I see him nod from the corner of my eye.

"Figured as much."

"It's crazy, right? One night, and then this weekend, and my heart feels as though it could explode from how much I feel for her."

"Is it maybe just because she's the mother of your daughter? And by the way, no paternity test?"

"No. She's mine. I feel it."

"She looks like you. I don't know how Thea and I didn't put it together before now. Well, I do. I knew about your dream girl, and so did Thea."

"Yeah, thanks for that," I say to him, but he keeps going.

"She also knew about Cadence's situation. I'm shocked she didn't put two and two together."

"She probably would have, but I never told you where I was when I met her. I didn't tell you it was my last visit."

"That's probably it. You know my wife, if she even suspected, she would have been all over that like a rat on a Cheeto."

"I do know *my* sister, and you're right. She would have been," I agree. Cadence and I both have regrets from that night. We both have to live with them, and move forward.

That's exactly what I plan to do. Move forward as a family. Leaving him, I go to my girls, lowering myself to the floor to sit next to them. I offer Hazel my finger, which she latches onto immediately.

"Are you ready to go?" Cadence asks.

"No."

"You have a three-hour drive," Thea reminds me.

"I know. I'm not going."

"What do you mean you're not going?" my sister asks.

I ignore her and look to Cadence. "I can't make myself leave the two of you." I hear my sister say "aww," but I continue to ignore her. "Do you think you can take a day or two off and come with me?"

"I don't know. I save that time in case Hazel gets sick."

"You're not doing it all on your own anymore, Cadence. You have me, and I promise you I'll be there for every minute. Please?" I'm aware of the pleading in my voice, and I'm not the least bit ashamed, not when it comes to my girls. I'll do what it takes.

"Babe, have you seen my phone? I need to record this. Trevin Hubbard is begging." Scott chuckles.

Raising my hand in the air, I flip him off, making him laugh. Hazel turns to look at me, and I move to take her from Cadence. "Hey, baby girl," I say softly. "Tell Momma you want to take a road trip with Daddy," I tell my daughter. She just smiles and coos. "See, babe. She wants to go."

"I can't just call in, Trevin."

"How much time do you need?"

She's quiet so long I think she's going to flat out turn me down. I'm surprised when she pulls out her phone and taps the screen before putting it to her ear. "Hi, Debbie, this is Cadence. Something has come up, and I was hoping to take a few days off. I know I have patients scheduled, but—" She stops and listens. "Really? Are you sure? Thank you so much, Debbie. I'll be back on Monday." She hangs up and looks at me. "That was my boss. It turns out she was going to offer me some time off this week. There's a new therapist starting, and she wants her to take my schedule for the week, while Debbie works with her to show her the ropes."

"Why not just have you train her?" Thea asks.

"Debbie likes to get firsthand knowledge of how her new hires are with patients. She always trains herself. The last time she did this, I got caught up on charting and did some continuing education classes."

"You said Monday."

"Yeah, I'm free this entire week." I don't even try to hide my smile. My girls are coming home with me, which means I don't have to be without them. I've already missed so much time, the thought of leaving them even temporarily was tearing me in two.

"Come here." I motion for her to lean closer. As soon as her lips are close enough, I kiss her, not giving a damn that we have an audience. "You're coming home with me?"

"For a few days."

"That's all I need. Come on." I manage to stand, still holding Hazel. "We need to pack what she's going to need for the week. I read that it's best to travel when babies are sleeping to not interrupt their routine. If we leave here around eight, we can make it to my place at eleven, feed her, and maybe she'll sleep for the rest of the night."

"You read? Why have you been reading about babies?" Scott asks.

"Because I'm a father."

"When?" Thea asks.

"While my girls were sleeping the past two nights."

"Trevin," Cadence whispers. I can see the wonder in her eyes, and the disbelief. I don't care how long it takes, I'm going to prove to her that I'm in this. That she and our daughter are my world. I know it's fast, but when you know, you know, and I am certain that she is who I want. I want us to raise our daughter together, and have more babies that I'll be there for every step of the way.

"I needed to know what to expect, how to take care of Hazel, and help you. You've had the entire pregnancy and the first three months of her life to get up to speed. I had some catching up to do. I still have some catching up to do."

Cadence nods, leaning in and pressing her lips to mine. "You're one of a kind, Trevin Hubbard. I'm so glad we found our way back."

"Me too, baby. Me too." My voice is thick, and I'm man enough to admit I'm choked up. I went from wondering if I had imagined her and our night together, to having a family. I'll take the latter every damn time.

"You better get moving," Thea says. I can hear the tears in her voice, and sure enough, when I glance at my sister, she's wiping at her cheeks as Scott takes their son into his arms.

"Hear that, baby girl?" I ask Hazel. "You get to come home with Daddy for a few days." I'm already imagining them in my space. Sure it's not where we're going to be living, but having them in my home, it's going to make this all that much more real.

"Call me when you get there," Thea says.

"We will," Cadence assures her.

I stand with Hazel in my arms, offering Cadence my hand. We say a quick goodbye before heading across the hall to pack.

"FOR SUCH A TINY THING, SHE SURE NEEDS A LOT," I SAY AS I CARRY IN THE final bag.

"Well, she needed the Pack 'n Play to have a safe place to sleep. Bottles, diapers, formula, clothes, blankets, toys." Cadence stops and begins to laugh. "She does have a lot. I've never gone anywhere except to Thea's or to visit Shelby for a few hours or to the doctor's office. This is a first for me."

"Well, we're going to need to find a bigger place. She's already overrunning your apartment, and when we have more, it's going to get worse. Besides, there are only two bedrooms."

"We? A bigger house?" she asks.

"Yeah, we're doing this, right? You, me, and Hazel?" I study her hard and see the tears well in her eyes.

Slowly, she nods. "Y-Yes. We're doing this."

"Good. Now, let me figure out how to set this thing up in my room, and we'll get her fed and changed and back into bed."

"Let's just set up the Pack 'n Play and try to lay her down. She might sleep a little longer."

"Okay. Well, here goes nothing."

"You watch her, and I'll put it up."

"I need to learn how to do it," I tell her.

"It's easy. It just pops open. Show me where to set it up."

Picking up Hazel's car seat which she's snoozing in, I lead Cadence to my bedroom. "In the corner, maybe?"

"That should be fine." Cadence wastes no time getting to work setting up the Pack 'n Play, and I watch, making sure I see how she does it. I don't want to be the dad who never does a damn thing for his kid. We made her together. We're going to take care of her together. That's how my parents raised Thea and me, and that's how I plan for us to raise Hazel.

Together.

"You want to try, or do you want me to?" Cadence points to our sleeping daughter.

"I'll do it." I set the seat on the bed and slowly unclasp the straps. Well, I try to. "What is this, some kind of torture device?" I ask Cadence, making her laugh.

"Let me show you." She moves in close, and I step back, letting her do her thing. My hands rest on her hips. She's standing in front of me, with me looking over her shoulder, watching her as she expertly unclasps the straps and lifts our sleeping daughter. Hazel's little body stretches, but she doesn't wake up, not even when Cadence lays her back down. "She'll sleep for a few more hours."

"Okay. Well, let's make sure we have everything we might need unpacked for when she does, and we can lie down and try to get some sleep too."

"Everything we should need is going to be in the diaper bag. I made sure it was well packed before we left."

"Perfect. T-shirts are in the top drawer. I'm going to go lock up. Need anything?"

"No." She shakes her head.

"I'll be right back." With a quick kiss to her lips, I leave my room to lock up the house. I find myself checking all the doors twice, and even the windows. I have two ladies to protect, and I take that shit seriously. Satisfied that the house is secure, I grab two bottles of water from the fridge and, in the dark, make my way to my room.

"Is this okay?" she asks, looking down at the old concert T-shirt of mine that's covering what I know is the sexiest body I'll ever lay eyes on.

"You're perfect." I place one of the bottles of water on the nightstand next to where she's standing and walk around the bed, peeking in on Hazel before stripping down to my underwear. I take a drink of water and turn to Cadence. "Do we need to keep the lamp on for her?"

"No, she'll be fine in the dark."

"What about you?"

"You're here to protect me, right?" she teases.

"Always." I switch off the lamp and crawl under the covers. The bed dips when she does the same, and I waste no time moving over and pulling her into my arms. "Night, baby."

"Night, Trevin."

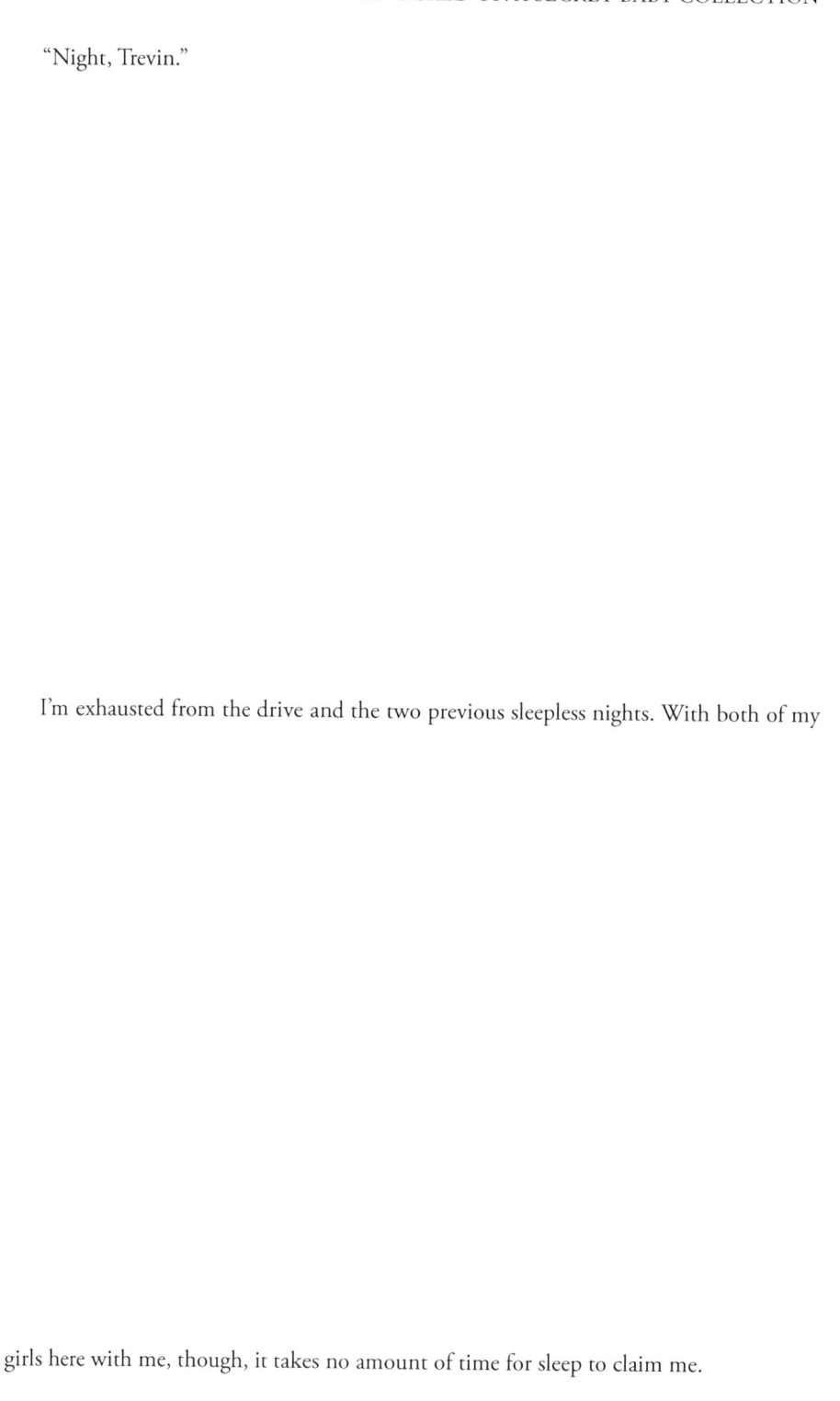

I'm exhausted from the drive and the two previous sleepless nights. With both of my girls here with me, though, it takes no amount of time for sleep to claim me.

CHAPTER NINE
CADENCE

WE'VE BEEN AT TREVIN'S PLACE IN LEXINGTON FOR FOUR DAYS, AND THE time has been nothing short of amazing. He's had to go into the office each day while Hazel and I hang out at the house. He brought boxes home the first day and asked me if I minded helping him pack. That's when it hits me that this is really happening. He's moving back to Indianapolis. He's going to be a constant in our lives.

"Honey, I'm home," Trevin calls out. I don't bother to hide my smile when he walks into the living room where Hazel and I are spread out on a blanket on the living room floor. "I missed you." He settles on the other side of Hazel, leaning over her to kiss me, then dropping a kiss to her forehead. "What did my girls do today?"

"The kitchen is packed, and it wore us out, huh, Hazel?" I ask like my daughter is actually going to respond.

"Thank you for doing that. I know it's a lot to ask of you when you're also taking care of her."

"It's no problem. I did most of it while she was napping. How was work?"

"Well, we got it all figured out. I'll be transferring to the Indy plant. I'm going to be the new assistant plant manager. It's a small pay cut, but that's okay. It gets me home with my family, and I love working for Riggins Enterprises. It's the best of both worlds. Not to mention, Harold, the current plant manager, is talking about retiring next year. I had a meeting with Royce and Grant today, and they've assured me that the position is mine when that happens."

"Are you sure this is what you want?" I know I sound like a broken record. I've asked him this same question every day since we've been here. This is all happening so fast. I just want to make sure this is truly what he wants.

"Positive. I was prepared to leave Riggins Enterprises all together. Luckily, I don't have to. They're a great company to work for, and they've been good to me. I get my girls, I get to move closer to my parents and my sister, and I get to keep working for them. I couldn't think of a better scenario."

There's an ease in my shoulders, as though a weight has been lifted. "I know this is a lot for you, but I'm so grateful you're going to be in her life."

"It's not just her, Cadence. It's you too. I want a life with you. I want us to be a family." He pauses, letting his words sink in. "I know we've not really talked about us, we've kept it all about me moving to be closer to Hazel, but, babe, it's not just her I want to be closer to. It's you too."

Tears burn my eyes as they threaten to fall. I open my mouth to speak, but no words come, so instead, I give him a watery smile and nod. "O-kay." I manage to push the words out after swallowing back the lump in my throat.

"Although I think we're going to need a bigger place. I don't see all of my stuff fitting in your small apartment."

"You're probably right," I say with a smile.

"I'll start looking for houses. We'll need to research the schools and surroundings areas. It's going to take us some time. Plus, we want it to be a convenient distance to both of our jobs."

"You're buying a house?" My heart stammers in my chest. Is this really happening? Every dream I've ever had for Hazel and me, to find him one day, is finally happening.

"No. *We're* buying a house," he corrects me. "It's going to be our home, Cadence. All three of us."

The words *I love you* burn on the tip of my tongue. It's crazy to even think about saying that to him, but he gave me Hazel. He gave me the most incredible gift in this life and a night that I know I will never forget. He's handing me my dreams—for me and my daughter—on a silver platter, and my heart is full. Each night after we put Hazel to bed, he makes love to me. I feel our connection in my bones, and he's so tender, so gentle, it couldn't be described as anything else.

"Since the kitchen is packed, how about we go out to eat?" he suggests.

"Order in?" I motion to my short shorts and an old T-shirt. "I'm not really dressed to go out."

"Whatever you want." He leans over and kisses me. His tongue slides past my lips as he deepens the kiss. I lean in too, wanting more of him, but tiny hands tugging at my hair have me pulling back and yelping in pain.

"No, no, sweet girl," Trevin coos. "That hurts Mommy. We don't pull hair," he tells her. "You good?"

"I'm fine. Not the first time, and I'm sure not the last." I tap Hazel's nose with my index finger. "This one has an iron grip."

"Any preference for dinner?"

"Nope. Surprise me. I'm going to take this little one and give her a bath."

"I'm going to order, and I'll be up to help." He bends to give Hazel a kiss on her cheek, and then a little further pressing his lips to mine.

"All right, little lady. It's time for your bath." Before I can lift her off the floor, Trevin is on his feet and taking her with him.

"Did you grow today while Daddy was gone?" He lifts her into the air over his head, and she babbles like she always does when she's the center of her daddy's attention. He blows a raspberry on her belly, where her shirt has ridden up, and her tiny hands fist his hair, making him laugh. "All right, baby girl. We need to work on that," he tells her with a smile. "Go to Momma so I can order us some food." He kisses her cheek once more and places her in my arms. "I'll be right there," he says, kissing me too.

I stand still and watch him walk toward the kitchen. I can't believe this is my life, that everything I ever dreamed of is coming true.

I have a family.

"We love Daddy, don't we, Hazel?" I whisper to my daughter as I turn and head to the bathroom to give her a bath.

I've barely gotten her undressed when Trevin appears beside me. "I ordered Mexican. It will be here in about thirty minutes."

"Perfect. That gives us enough time to get her bathed and into some pajamas." I place her in the small bathtub that we had to buy because, of course, I forgot to pack it. Together we sit on the floor beside the tub that holds her baby tub and give our daughter a bath.

This has become our routine. I tell him he doesn't have to help, but he claims he doesn't want to miss another moment of her life. I melt into a puddle every time he says things like that, which is pretty much any time he's talking.

"Trev?"

"Yeah?" he asks, lifting Hazel from the tub and wrapping her in a towel.

"I'm glad it was you. I'm glad you were my first, and that this situation—" I motion between the three of us. "I wouldn't want it to be anyone else."

His eyes soften. "Hazel, Mommy's making Daddy soft." My eyes dart to his crotch, and he is most definitely not soft. "In here." He taps his free hand that's not holding our daughter over his heart. "There will never be an issue with soft there." He looks down at his crotch and back up to me. "Not where you're concerned." Those hazel eyes of his show me that he means what he says.

The doorbell rings, and he smirks. "That's dinner." He stands, our daughter wrapped up in a thick towel and heads to the door. "Oh, Cadence?"

"Y-Yeah?" I reply.

"You're dessert." With that, he leaves me kneeling next to the tub on the bathroom floor, aching for him. I love my daughter, but I can't help but hope she goes to sleep with ease this evening. Her daddy promised me dessert.

CHAPTER TEN

TREVIN

IT'S BEEN A MONTH SINCE I MOVED BACK HOME TO INDY, AND THERE HAS not been a single day that I've regretted my decision. I get to fall asleep with Cadence in my arms and wake up the same way. I get to hold my daughter, give her baths, and read her stories while her momma feeds her at night. I get to hold both of my girls in my arms, and there is nothing more in this world I could ask for.

Well, maybe one thing. A bigger house. This two-bedroom is cramped with the three of us. I have most of my things in storage. We've been looking at houses, but nothing has jumped out at us as being the one. Not to mention, we still have my house in Lexington on the market. As soon as we get that sold, we'll have more flexibility with what we can purchase. I want a home. I want the big yard and plenty of space for our growing family. I want Hazel to feel settled, safe, and secure, just like Thea and I were as kids.

Not just Hazel, but Cadence too. There is a pain in my chest anytime I let myself think about how she grew up. I want her to have everything she's missed out on, everything she's ever dreamed of. I won't stop until I do. That's what you do when you love someone.

And I love her.

Not just because she's the mother of my child, I love her spirit. I love coming home to her, and I love knowing that we're a team. I could sit here for hours and list off items that make me love her and fall harder every day. However, I don't need to. I know it's her. It's who she is as a person.

Raising my hand to knock on my sister's door, it opens before I get the chance. "Hey," Scott greets me. "You're home early."

"So are you."

"Yeah." He grins.

"What's going on?"

He looks over his shoulder and pulls the door shut. "Nothing, I came home early, that's all."

"You do remember we've been best friends since kindergarten, right?"

"Fuck. You can't tell her I told you," he says. There's a smile on his face, and he runs his hands through his hair. A sign he's excited or nervous.

"Spill it."

"We're pregnant." I swear I've only ever seen him smile like he is now when it comes to my baby sister.

"Congrats, man." I give him a half hug.

"Thanks. We weren't trying, but fuck, man, I'm stoked."

"Spare me the details of how my nieces and nephews get here," I joke.

"We need a bigger place."

"I know that feeling. We've been looking," I say as my phone rings. "Hello."

"Mr. Hubbard, this is Alice from Lexington Realty. I wanted to let you know I sent an offer to your email. Full asking," she says excitedly.

"Perfect. I'm picking up my daughter now. I'll log in as soon as I can and sign it."

"That sounds like a plan. I'll be in touch."

"Thanks, Alice."

"Good news?"

"Yeah. I sold my place in Lexington. Full asking."

"Congrats, man."

"Thanks. I'm going to get Hazel, and you and my sister can celebrate. You want me to take Clint to our place?"

"Nah. I want him close."

I nod because I know how he feels. No matter how much time I spend with my girls, it's never enough. "If you change your mind, let me know."

"Thanks, man." He opens the door, and I follow him inside their apartment.

"Hey, you're early," Thea says from her spot on the couch. She has Hazel in her arms and Clint sitting next to her. Both kids are sound asleep.

"Looks like Aunt Thea has the magic touch."

Her eyes flash to Scott. "Something like that."

My sister is glowing, much like my best friend. "I'll take her." I gently lift Hazel from her lap and cuddle her in my arms, pulling in her baby scent. If you would have told me a year ago I'd be sniffing babies and finding comfort in that, I would have told you that you've lost your damn mind. Now? Now, it's what I crave.

"Everything okay? You're never home this early."

"Yeah, it's all good. Cadence works late tonight. I decided to come home and get this little one bathed and in her jammies and have dinner ready when she gets home. That way, we can have our family time before Hazel has to go to sleep."

"Aww," Thea says, her eyes welling with tears. "I love the way you love them."

"Nothing in life is worth doing halfway." I wink at Thea, give Scott a nod, and gather Hazel's things. "Thanks, sis."

"You're welcome."

"Hey, we're looking to move. We want you to keep watching her if you're interested."

"Definitely."

"We're looking too," Scott adds.

I nod. "Well, maybe we should discuss locations. We can maybe buy in the same area for convenience."

"Good schools are a must," Thea says.

"We agree with that. Nothing has to be decided now. I just wanted you to know we're looking but want you to continue to watch her. The thought of a stranger keeping her doesn't sit well with me."

"We feel the same way."

"Thanks. We'll see you in the morning." I wave to them and head across the hall to our apartment. Since Hazel is still sleeping soundly, I pick up the living room, unload the dishwasher, and start a load of laundry. Thankfully this apartment complex offers a small closet in each unit for a laundry room. I'm just finishing tossing the first load into the dryer and starting a second when Hazel wakes up. We go through the routine of giving her a bottle and reading a couple of books. She's so still in my arms as I read to her.

"It's time to start on dinner," I tell her. "We're going to set you up in your swing while

Daddy gets lasagna in the oven." I chatter to Hazel the entire time I'm cooking, and she babbles right back. I love every second of my time with her.

"Now that that's done, it's time for you, Miss Stinky Butt, to get a bath." I pick her up and fly her through the house like an airplane, and she laughs. Her little baby giggles are the best sound on this earth. Bath time is fun. The older she gets, the more splashing and playing she does.

I'm zipping up her pajamas when I hear Cadence's keys in the front door. "Mommy's home," I tell Hazel, lifting her from the changing table into my arms.

"What's going on?" Cadence asks.

"Dinner is almost ready, and this one just got her bath."

"How did you manage to do all of this? I'm only, what, an hour later than usual?"

"I left the office early. I know you've had a long week with your patient load, and I wanted to take some of this off your plate. I know you've been missing your snuggle time with dinner and bath each night getting home later, so we did it all before you got here." I step toward her and slide my arm around her waist, pulling her into me and kissing her softly. "Sit. I'll make you a plate." Hazel is already reaching for her mom, so we make the switch, and I turn to walk away.

"Trev?" she calls out. There's a quiver in her voice.

"Yeah?"

"I love you."

The room stills, but my heart keeps on beating like a bass drum in my chest. In two long strides, I'm standing in front of her. Cradling her face in the palm of my hands, I stare into her eyes. "I love you. So fucking much," I say, kissing her.

I take my time tasting her, showing her with my kiss how much she means to me. Pulling out of the kiss, I press my forehead against hers. We both laugh when Hazel mimics us. "I love you too," I tell our daughter.

I've been waiting for the perfect time to tell her, and this moment, it's another one to add to my long list of unforgettable. That's how it should be. Every other memory is them. My girls and I wouldn't want it any other way.

EPILOGUE
FIVE YEARS LATER
CADENCE

"COME HERE, YOU LITTLE BUGGER." I RUN AFTER MY DAUGHTER, WHO IS crawling all over the place, and scoop her into my arms.

"She likes the extra space." Trevin laughs.

"This is overkill, Trevin. Why do we need a five-bedroom house?"

"For the kids?"

"We have one kid."

"But we're going to have more. Trust me. We've been practicing. I think the odds are in our favor." He smirks.

He's not wrong. It's been six months since the day I walked into Thea and Scott's apartment and saw him holding our daughter. Six months of happiness and love. So much love. We've been living in my two-bedroom apartment until today, when Trevin and I signed the loan papers to purchase our first house. We have been looking for a while, and nothing screamed home to us. Not until we found this place. It just so happens to be only two miles from the house that Scott and Thea moved into two months ago. They wasted no time purchasing a bigger place when they learned they would be adding to their family. He wanted a house. Hell, he wanted to buy one as soon as he moved back to town. It was my insistence that we take some time before jumping into anything that kept him from it. As soon as his house in Lexington sold, he was a man on a mission. We looked at maybe a couple of dozen before deciding on this one. I thought it was too big. Trev said it was perfect. I admit it's gorgeous, but it's huge compared to our apartment.

"Just wait until she starts walking. Scott was telling me how Clint is into everything these days. They found him on the bathroom sink covered in shaving cream the other day." Trevin laughs.

"Stop," I tell him, barely containing my own laughter. "You're going to jinx us."

"No way, not our angel," he says, taking Hazel from my arms. He blows on her belly, making her cackle with laughter.

"Where do we start?" I ask, looking around at all the boxes.

"One box at a time. We're both off this week, and Thea said she would keep Hazel even though we're not working, so we can bust it all out. However, right now, I want to show you something."

He holds his hand out for me and leads me down the hall toward the first-floor master suite. Pushing open the door, he motions for me to walk in first. When I step into the room, I gasp at what I see. There are hundreds if not thousands of rose petals spread out on the gray hardwood floor. Candles, which appear to be operating on batteries instead of actual flames, are placed around the room as well.

I turn to look at him and find him kneeling on the floor, Hazel still on his hip. "Mommy, we love you," he says, glancing down at Hazel. "You take care of us and have given us, given *me* my reason for living. I can't imagine my life without either of my girls.

What do you say we make this forever thing official? We want you to be a Hubbard with us," he says, as he offers an open tiny blue box, with a diamond ring sparkling at me.

I don't need to think about it. "Yes." I walk to where they are and kneel with them. He places Hazel on the floor, and she crawls away.

"That's why I chose the battery candles." He shakes his head, watching our daughter before turning those hazel eyes on me. His lips capture mine, and time seems to stand still as I process the fact that this man just asked me to marry him.

"We're getting married," I murmur against his lips.

The smile he gives me lights up his face. Pulling the ring out of the box, he slides it on my finger. "I love you, future Mrs. Hubbard."

"I love you too."

He looks around me to check on Hazel. "No, baby girl. We don't eat flowers," he says, standing to grab her and take the rose petal she was trying to shove into her mouth.

I smile at them and look back at my ring.

A lifetime of this is exactly what I want. Trevin is no longer a memory; he's my heart, and he's my future.

TREVIN

AS I SIT HERE ON THE BACK DECK, NURSING A BEER HOLDING MY SON, I CAN'T help but reflect on my life. A chance meeting at a club. An attraction that was undeniable led me here to where I am today. Hazel cackles with laughter as Cadence chases after her, our middle daughter Violet doing her best to catch up with them.

Cadence drops to her knees in a pile of leaves, our daughters doing the same and their laughter of my girls fills my heart. Connor stretches his little arms and legs, but stays resting against my chest. He'll be three weeks old tomorrow. I missed all the pregnancy moments with Hazel, so when we found out we were pregnant with Violet, I made sure I didn't miss a single second. Nothing changed when we found out we were pregnant with our little man. There is nothing better in this life than watching the woman you love grow with a child that the two of you created out of the love that you share.

Nothing better.

The fall leaves blow through the air, and as the sun begins to set, I know I need to get Connor inside. Standing, I grab my half-empty bottle of beer to do just that, but the Hubbard girls race to the back deck, and two sets of little arms are wrapping around my legs.

"Hey, handsome." Cadence rises on her toes and kisses me. "I see he's still snoozing."

"He is." She places her hand over mine that's resting on Connor's back.

"Daddy, can we have a piggyback ride? Please?" Hazel asks.

"Pwease?" Violet, at three, mocks her older sister.

"Hand him over, Hubbard. You know you can't resist them."

"It's not just them I can't resist." I bend down and kiss her again. No matter how many times my lips are pressed against hers, it will never be enough. Not in this lifetime, and not the next. I crave her.

"Eww, Daddy, stop kissing Mommy." Hazel pulls on my jeans.

"Oh, I think someone needs the tickle monster after that." The words barely leave my mouth before my daughters are screeching with pure joy and racing into the house to hide.

"I love you, Trevin Hubbard."

"I love you too, Mrs. Hubbard."

THE END

BETWEEN THE LINES
BY MICAELA SMELTZER

CHAPTER ONE
ALBA

THE CHEERY CHIME SIGNALING MY ENTRANCE IS AN ODD CONTRAST TO THE tattoo shop I've walked into.

My tattoo shop, I remind myself like every time I step inside.

I worked hard to purchase the shop and put my personal touch on it like the black walls with silver glitter in them, the shiny red leather couches, the art—skulls made out of roses—, and all the mirrors and chrome accents.

I used to spend more time here than at home and I wanted this to be a place I felt comfortable.

Lowering the leather bag slung over my shoulder to the ground, I don't have a chance to straighten up when one of my employees, and now a really good friend, shrieks and comes running toward me with grabby hands.

At only four-foot-nine, Astrid is a tiny pixie next to me at my height and chubby body. Her maroon-colored hair is cut bluntly at her chin with bangs straight across her forehead. The silver ring in her left nostril reflects in the light and her tank top highlights her full sleeve of flower and butterfly tattoos on each arm.

"Give me that baby."

She doesn't give me a chance to answer before she snatches the baby from my arms.

My daughter, Dahlia, starts to cry at first but when she sees who it is she instantly quiets. At only four months old I swear there's more intelligence in her eyes than most adults. The blue-gray shade of those eyes is all her father, a constant reminder of the man I haven't seen in over a year now.

Travis Alexander left town as quickly as he rolled into it. Suddenly and without a word.

Peeking out the window, his tattoo parlor stands right across the street. A constant reminder of not only what a pain in the ass he was, but the fact that he has a child he doesn't know about.

When he first left town the day after we hooked up, I didn't let it bother me. We all have our secrets after all, but when my period didn't show I eventually took a pregnancy test and did try to contact him.

I sent numerous texts telling him to get back to me, that it was important.

All went unanswered.

In the end, I couldn't bring myself to care. He was my rival—not only in business but in art too. I could hate his guts all I wanted but the guy was a talented tattoo artist.

I'm better, though.

My eyes widen at the old black Harley Davidson sportster parked out front.

It wasn't there when I walked in, but the owner is gone now.

"There's no way," I mutter more to myself than for anyone else to hear.

"What?" Astrid strides over and glances out the window. Her mouth parts and she looks at me with wide panicked eyes, ones that I'm certain mirror my own.

"Alba," she gasps my name, "that's his bike."

"I know." I wet my lips and turn away from the window. Maybe if I don't look at it the motorcycle will disappear.

"What are you going to do?" She has to nearly jog to keep up with me, Dahlia giggling in her arms as she bounces up and down.

Walking behind the desk and looking at the sticky notes scrawled on with things for me to go over before the day starts, I wait a moment before I answer her. "Nothing."

"Nothing?" she repeats, taking a seat on one of the couches. "But … but … I mean … he's her dad."

Astrid is the only person besides my mother who knows who Dahlia's father is. Not that I'm ashamed of Travis, because I'm certainly not. At least when he left town he was a good-looking, successful guy. Who knows what he might have gotten into now?

I look up from one of the notes telling me to call back a Linda with no explanation as to why I'm calling her. "Yeah, and I'm sure he'll disappear again by the end of the day."

Astrid blinks at me, uttering a quiet, "What if he doesn't?"

I give the smallest shrug of my shoulders. "Then I'll figure it out."

The thing about keeping a secret like this is the longer you keep quiet the harder it becomes to say anything.

Sorting through the mail, I try to ignore Astrid standing up and looking out the window searching for a peek at Travis.

"Don't you wonder why he disappeared?"

"No."

Yes.

Of course I do. I'm human. We're curious by nature. Anyone that says they're not is a liar.

Astrid makes a sound that I know means she thinks I'm full of shit.

She'd be correct.

"Oh, ew!" She exclaims suddenly. "Someone made a stinky and that's mom duty not fun auntie's job." She scurries over to me and holds the baby out. "Take her."

I shake my head and scoop my daughter up, who does smell like literal shit.

When I found out I was pregnant I made a space for her in my office—a changing area, crib, and even a small space where she can sit and play as she gets bigger.

I didn't plan on ever becoming a mom. It wasn't something I felt I wanted and I was content to never have children. Life had other plans for me. I wouldn't take Dahlia back for anything. She's the best thing that's ever happened to me and it might be silly, but even when I'm tired and exhausted from dealing with a cranky baby I still crawl into bed at night and say thank you that the universe realized I needed her when I didn't know it.

"Is someone smelly?" I kiss her round pink cheek and she giggles, reaching for my hair. "Nice try missy." I grab the dyed black strand before she can and toss it over my shoulder. I'm not fond of the hair pulling stage and I'm dreading the day she tries to get ahold of my nose ring.

In my office I lay her down on the changing mat and clean her up, tossing the diaper in the trash. Snapping her plain white onesie back into place I smother her in more kisses, repeating over and over how much I love her and that she's the prettiest girl in all the land. The way she giggles I take to mean she approves of the sentiments.

I settle her into her crib for her morning nap. Almost immediately her tiny mouth seeks out her thumb and her lids grow heavy. Thank God she's finally sleeping well. The first three months were tough with tummy issues that usually resulted in screaming throughout the whole day and an inability to go to sleep. Luckily my mom was there to help out during those months and my doctor gave me advice on how to help her with her gas.

Easing the door closed behind me, I walk back out to the front. "Astrid, can you give me those notes off the counter? I'm going to start making some calls." Silence. "Astrid?"

I round the corner and stop dead in my tracks.

Travis Alexander stands at the counter, leaning casually against it. Despite the summer heat he wears a leather jacket over a white wife-beater. Black jeans hug his long lean legs, ripped at the knees, with his black boots rounding out the look. Straightening to his full height, he smirks at me. Those sinfully full lips turning up at the corners. The tattoos on his neck beg my eyes to take a peek, but I remind myself I spent an intimate night tracing the shape of them.

"Alba." My name is a purr on his tongue.

I straighten, tugging my t-shirt down to hide the shaking in my hands. "Travis."

He walks toward me but stops with at least four feet separating us.

Across the room Astrid is making all kinds of faces and eyes where he can't see, silently urging me to just blurt out to him that his child is sleeping a few feet from here.

After I never heard back from him, I fully expected he was out of my life for good. His shop stayed open, but I assumed he sold it to someone else.

Stupid assumption now I see.

Silence fills the space and I curse myself for not at least turning on my playlist because I hate quiet like this. It's the kind of quiet that's so loud it hurts.

Tilting his head to the side, he wets his lips. "I'm back."

I blink. Blink again. *I'm back.* That's all he has to say after over thirteen months.

"I see that."

"Thought you should know."

Turning, he swipes a pen off the counter. My *favorite* pen. The one that's black with red lips on it. He tucks it behind his ear and looks back at me before opening the door. He doesn't say anything, only winks like the annoying bastard he is.

"Give me my pen back," I demand.

"Nah. I like playing games with you too much."

He pushes the door open, checks for traffic, and strides back across the street to Timeless Ink.

"Wow," Astrid gasps. "The chemistry. The sexual tension." She pretends to shiver. "If that's what it's like when you guys have clothes on *please* let me watch the next time you guys have sex."

My mouth drops open and she giggles. "There's not going to be next time, and if there was, the answer is hell no."

She laughs, shaking her head. "Oh, hun, if you witnessed what I just did—" she flicks her finger where I am and Travis was mere seconds ago "—you'd know there's not just going to be a next time, but a lot more times. Like a whole lifetime's worth."

"You're delusional." I grab the notes I need from the counter, shaking my head in disbelief. My freaking pen. I want it back.

"No, babe," she calls after me as I head for my office, "you are."

CHAPTER TWO
TRAVIS

I TWIST THE PEN BACK AND FORTH BETWEEN MY FINGERS, AGAIN AND AGAIN, my eyes memorizing the shape of the red lips decorating the glossy black surface. Red lips that remind me so much of the color and shape of Alba's. I can see why she likes this pen so much. Aesthetically, it's her.

It's pathetic how much the dark-haired beauty has been on my mind since I first moved to town and how she stayed there, rooted deep, even when I had to leave.

Even now, I'm sitting here thinking about *her* when I should be focused on reacquainting myself with my business and calling old clients to let them know I'm back. Sure, as the owner I have plenty of other responsibilities as well, like bills and bookkeeping, and monotonous things that drive me up a wall. All I really care about is the art, but I started my own shop so I could do things my way.

"You know, it's no good having you back if all you're going to do is sit there and look like a decoration." Jessie, the manager, flicks my forehead as she passes by me where I sit on a stool in the breakroom. She bends down and grabs a bottle of water from the minifridge. "I know you have a lot on your mind but go home and think about it. You don't have to come back here yet."

Sympathy drips from her words and fills her expression. I hate it and wish it wasn't there. I don't want her, or anyone else's sympathy. When I got the call and dropped everything, my whole life, to travel back home to California from Virginia to take care of my sick younger brother—dying of a nasty brain tumor—I knew his death was inevitable just like he did. Sympathy feels like a filler emotion when death is unavoidable.

"I'm ready to be back." I took three months after his passing to drive along the coast of California and then back home on my motorcycle. I've taken all the time I need. What I want now is to get back to normal. To tattoo again, feel the buzzing of the gun between my fingers, and to mess with the curvy gorgeous woman across the street.

Jessie gives a shrug and caps the water bottle. "All I'm saying is we understand, and I'll keep this place running as long as you need me to."

I level her with a look and tuck the pen into the pocket of my jeans so I'll stop playing with it. "I'm here, Jess. I'm not going anywhere so get used to the boss being back."

She laughs, tossing her teal-colored hair over her shoulder. "Now that's the Travis I know."

She leaves me to my thoughts, heading back to the main floor to work on her client.

Swiping an energy drink from the fridge, I shut myself in my office. Popping the top, I take a swig of the liquid cringing at the fake grape taste and immediately drop it into the trash, questioning how anyone drinks that stuff.

Picking up a stack of papers, I look through them and find that, at least in my quick perusal, Jessie has done a solid job keeping track of everything. I knew she would, but I guess a part of me hoped to find some flaw in the way she handled things in my absence just so I would feel useful.

There's a piece of paper with names and numbers of clients who specifically wanted to wait until I returned for more ink, so with nothing else to do, I start making calls.

THE DOOR TO MY APARTMENT CREAKS OPEN AND I FLICK THE LIGHT SWITCH on, bathing the entry in light. There's something incredibly lonely about coming back to the same place, day in and day out, with no one there to greet you. No one who cares about you. No one who loves you.

Kicking the door closed with my boot, I lock it and secure the latch.

The apartment is small, and all I have to do is take two steps to my right to walk into my bedroom and the attached bathroom. Immediately, I remove my boots and then shuck my shirt to the floor. My pants next. Less than a minute after I walked into the apartment, I'm in the shower. The plumbing is shotty, so the water pressure sucks and sometimes the water changes from hot to ice cold back to scalding, but it's mine. I could afford something nicer if I wanted, but since it's just me and I've always been a workaholic as long as I have a place to crash that's all that matters.

I spend way longer than necessary in the shower, but when I get out I feel halfway human so that has to count for something.

Yanking on a pair of shorts, I don't bother with a shirt as I head across the hall to the tiny galley kitchen. There's a half-eaten sandwich in the fridge from earlier. Not the most ideal dinner, but it'll do until I can pick up groceries tomorrow. Grabbing a drink, I settle onto the loveseat that serves as my couch and turn on the TV. There's no cable so I connect to Netflix and pick a show at random that should distract me for a while. Something about horrible bakers—and man, they are *terrible*. Not that I could do much better.

Kicking my legs up on the coffee table I stifle a yawn.

It's been a long day. An even longer year. But I'm ready to return to a relatively normal life. I know the ache in my chest from the loss of my brother will never fully go away. I never imagined living a life without him in it, but I guess the universe had different plans.

I don't regret dropping my entire life to go back home to take care of him. When my mom called and explained the situation, I knew she couldn't do it alone. I was even more horrified that Colin didn't want me to know at all—not because he felt I wasn't worth knowing, but because he knew I'd do exactly what I did and rush to his side.

I would've been absolutely livid and hurt if I hadn't gotten to spend his last few months by his side.

Still, even while I was gone, Alba was always in the back of my mind.

I don't understand what is about the woman that I can't get out of my head. From the moment I laid eyes on her I've been enamored. She's wicked smart with a sharp tongue and undeniable wit that I find extremely attractive. I thought one night with her would be enough to quench my thirst, but I was wrong. I'm sure after the way I completely left town the last thing she'll ever want is a repeat.

All I can hope is given enough time, I can convince her I'm worth the risk.

CHAPTER THREE

ALBA

"WHO'S THE PRETTIEST BABY IN ALL THE LAND?" DAHLIA GURGLES AS I WIPE the warm cloth beneath her double chin during her nightly bath. Bubbles float through the air along with the calming scent of lavender. Her chubby legs kick and splash at the water. "You are." I tap her nose and she lets out the most adorable laugh that lights my whole world. She reaches for my finger, wrapping her fist around it and squeezing tight. "Look at you my strong girl."

Plucking my finger from her grasp I finish wiping her down and pull her from the bath, wrapping her in a towel. She gives a little cry, sad to be leaving the water, but quiets once I start rubbing lotion into her skin.

"If someone gave me a full body massage like this every night, I'd be a happy camper too." I smile down at her and she grins back, reaching up to try to grab my hair.

Finally, I stuff her squirming limbs into her pajamas and sit down on my bed with her in my arms, grabbing the book I always leave on the nightstand and start reading to her.

Her eyes grow heavy and I set the book aside, rocking her in my arms until she's fully asleep. Slowly, making sure to keep rocking her, I settle her into the crib down the hall in her nursery. She stirs a little, letting out a tiny cry when my arms are no longer holding her. I hesitate, waiting to see if she'll drift back to sleep and when she does, I breathe out a sigh of relief.

Climbing into bed, I turn the TV on—I always keep the volume low so I don't have to worry about it waking her—and flip through the channels, settling on a ghost hunting show.

With that playing in the background I grab my sketchpad and pencil from the side table. I always try to spend a little time every night sketching something for my own pleasure and not anything commissioned for a client. I never want my art to feel like *work*.

Slowly, the drawing comes into shape. The flowers and vines curling around each other.

Dahlia makes a noise in her sleep through the monitor and I freeze, glancing over to see if she's going to wake up. She gives a wiggle of her nose, but her eyes stay closed.

Stifling a yawn, I set the sketchpad aside and get comfy beneath the covers. I think I only stare at the TV for five minutes before I'm fast asleep.

* * *

"She woke me up four times last night." I pass off the baby to an eager Astrid who takes her excitedly, along with the diaper bag. "I *have* to run and get coffee before I keel over."

"Make sure you get a muffin too," she warns, twirling in a circle to make Dahlia giggle. "I have a feeling you didn't eat breakfast and you're a monster when you're hungry."

"Shut up," I grumble, digging my wallet out of my bag.

"See," she says in her baby voice to Dahlia, "mommy is mean when she's hungry."

"I hope she throws up on you."

"My princess would never," she calls after me as I leave through the front door.

Striding down the street, I walk into the local coffee shop that's a town favorite. Having Griffin's within walking distance of my shop has been a godsend on days like today when I need an IV full of caffeine.

While waiting in line I start digging through my bag for my wallet so I'll be ready to pay when it's my turn and things can keep moving.

"I've got this, babe."

Disgust crawls up my spine as I cease plundering through my purse and turn to find Travis standing beside me in line. His dyed black hair is pushed away from his face and he's dressed head to toe in the dark color as well. His neck tattoos seem to glow from the lighting in the shop but I know that's not true. It's just me who's helpless to take my eyes off the ink.

"Got what?" I bite out.

"Our order."

I don't miss his use of the word *our* like we planned to meet here or that we're something other than acquaintances.

"I can get my own."

"I'm perfectly aware of your capabilities of ordering and paying by yourself, I like that about you, but today it's on me."

I narrow my eyes at him. He looks right back, his blue-gray eyes threatening to make me feel guilty. Not over the coffee, but the baby only a few stores down who he doesn't even know about.

I tried to tell him, I remind myself. *For months I contacted him and heard nothing. I didn't keep her a secret on purpose, but now ... I don't know how to tell him and what's to say he won't leave town in a blink again? I won't let Dahlia deal with an absentee father. I can be all she needs.*

"Why?" My tone is suspicious because when it comes to Travis, I've learned that he always seems to have some ulterior motive.

"No reason." His smirk tells me those two little words are complete bullshit.

"What do you want?"

"Sit with me and have breakfast."

"No, I have to get back to work. We're opening in twenty minutes."

And I have our child to check on.

"Give me fifteen then."

"I don't understand you." We move forward in line and if I wasn't so desperate for coffee and food—because Astrid's right, I need to eat—then I would turn tail and leave so I didn't have to deal with him.

"I don't understand you either and it's one of the things I like most about you."

"You're not allowed to do that," I snap, my words holding more bite than I intend.

"Do what?" He arches a brow. "Compliment you?"

"Exactly."

There's only one person left in front of us to order.

"Why not?"

I squirm. "You're just ... not."

Turning, I look in the opposite direction at the bustling café so he can't see the hurt on my face. Travis is nothing. He means *nothing*. So why can't my heart get the memo? Sure, we had a flirtation despite our non-stop bickering, and the one night we shared together might've been the best sex I ever had, but it all means zilch now. He left. Life moved on.

When I finally grow brave enough to look back in his direction *of course* he's staring at me with an amused smirk. What a jerk face.

The lady in front of us moves over to wait for her order, which means it's my turn to give mine. Travis swings his hand dramatically for me to step forward and I glare at him and have to use all my self-control to not roll my eyes.

"Hi, Emory," I flash a smile at Griffin's grandson, "I'll take the vanilla iced latte and one of the lemon blueberry muffins."

"Anything else?"

Travis bumps my hip with his, effectively shoving me out of the way. His long slender tattooed fingers are already plucking his credit card from his wallet. "Yeah, I'm going to have a cold brew with coconut milk and one of the chocolate croissants."

Emory rings everything up, oblivious to the daggers I'm glaring at Travis.

Taking his receipt, Travis places a gentle hand on my spine, guiding me to a table.

"I'm not eating breakfast with you." *And your hand definitely doesn't feel pleasant at all.*

"We're not eating breakfast."

"What do you call this then?" I reluctantly pull out a chair at the table he picks and plop in the seat with a disgruntled breath.

"Coffee and a snack."

Crossing my arms over my chest, I lean forward. "I don't understand what you think you're going to accomplish?" His eyes drop to my breasts, which have grown annoyingly larger since I got pregnant. "Stop looking at my boobs."

He clears his throat. "Sorry." His apology is slightly sheepish and at least feels genuine. "I can't help it. You have nice tits."

"Travis," I bite out.

"I'm a guy." He gives a shrug like this is all the explanation I need which I guess it is. Our order is called out and he narrows his eyes on me. "I'm going to grab that. Don't leave."

"I won't. Only because I want my coffee," I gripe.

His lips twitch as he fights not to smile. Sliding from the table he rises to his full height and I have to bite my lip to hold back a sigh. He might irritate me to no end, but there's no denying he's one of the sexiest men I've ever laid eyes on.

Returning with our order he passes me my muffin and iced coffee. I narrow my eyes with suspicion since he's stolen my order in the past.

"Why are you looking at me like that?" He takes a bite of the end of his croissant, chewing carefully like he's afraid I might make him choke on it or something equally nefarious.

"Because I don't trust you."

He winces, pressing a hand to his firm chest. "You wound me, Alba."

"I'm sure you're bleeding out and dying on the inside."

He grins. "You have no idea."

"Start talking. You have less than five minutes until I eat this whole muffin and then I'm gone."

"Can't we catch up like old friends?"

"We're not old. Nor friends."

He laughs, running his fingers through his hair. "This is why I like you."

I arch a brow. "Because I hate you?"

He bites his lip in a gesture that I know he doesn't intend to be sexual but oozes in sex appeal. "Oh, babe, we both know you don't hate me."

I take a sip of my coffee and set the cup down on the table. "I don't?"

He leans in, dropping his voice to a whisper. "Haven't you ever been told the line between love and hate is thin? You think you're on the side of hate, but I know better."

I narrow my eyes. "That so?"

"Mhmm," he hums.

"So cocky."

"Confident, not cocky—there's a difference, babe."

Stirring my drink with the straw, I hesitantly ask him, "How long are you back in town for?"

"Permanently."

"Why'd you leave?"

He plucks a marker from his pocket and starts doodling on his cup, not quite meeting my eyes. Pursing his lips, he finally says, "Because I had to."

"That's not an answer."

Something shadows his face. "I know."

My stomach drops. What if he has a wife and children somewhere else? I mean, I doubt it, but you never know and he's acting weird.

His tongue sticks out slightly between his pouty lips as he works on whatever he's drawing on his cup.

"For someone who wanted to have breakfast you're sure being quiet."

He looks up, flicking his hair out of his eyes. "You're the one who said we couldn't have breakfast and I need a lot longer than five minutes to talk to you." Standing, he smiles but it doesn't quite reach his eyes. "I'll see you later."

Before I can reply, he switches our drinks in a blink of an eye, striding out the door before I can even offer a retort.

Picking up the cup, I study the roses and thorny vines he drew easily in only a minute. Spinning the cup, I find them wrapped around a number. His number. It's different than the one I tried so many times to get ahold of him on. Looking out the window of the coffee shop I watch him disappear from sight and into his shop.

My stomach rolls, because if Travis is indeed back permanently there's definitely no hiding the tiny human that's half his who's currently only a matter of feet from him and he doesn't even know it.

Fuck. I'm so screwed.

CHAPTER FOUR

ALBA

LOCKING THE SHOP DOOR BEHIND ME I STIFLE A YAWN. IT'S BEEN A LONG day and I'm exhausted after working on a four-hour piece, but at least I'm not in pain like the client. It was worth it. The intricate dragon is one of the most detailed pieces I've had the pleasure of doing. Thankfully, my mom picked up Dahlia after she was done with her work, so I didn't have to worry about the baby.

"You're just finishing up too?"

"Ahh!" I shriek, throwing my heavy purse—I swear my entire life is in that thing—at the perpetrator.

"Jesus Christ!" The breath gets knocked out of Travis as my purse collides with his stomach. "What is that?"

"Don't sneak up on people!" I shriek, causing more than a few heads to turn in our direction. Dropping to my knees I grab my bag, stuffing the few things that fell out back inside. Thankfully none of them are baby items.

"I didn't sneak," he defends, swiping a tube of lipstick and passing it to me. "You're just oblivious."

I narrow my eyes on his ridiculously handsome face. "Do you want me to punch you in the face?" I wiggle my fist menacingly but the way he laughs I must not look ferocious at all, which makes me frown. Here I am trying to look menacing and I probably look like a yapping puppy.

"You can try." He rubs his jaw. "Could you even reach my face?"

"I'd find a way," I grumble under my breath, walking around the building toward the parking lot a block away. "Why are you walking with me?"

He gives a shrug, shoving his hands in his pockets. "Thought I'd walk you home."

My steps falter, panic rising, but then I remember he thinks I still live downtown. "I moved."

He arches a brow. "Moved? Where?"

"Across town."

My townhouse is nothing extravagant, but it's definitely better for Dahlia and me compared to the old apartment I lived in.

"Why?"

"Why'd I move?" I repeat in confusion. "Because I can. Because I wanted to. What's it to you?" I realize I probably sound way too defensive and wince, closing my eyes.

"You're with someone now." I don't know how or why he draws this conclusion and I swear I detect the barest hint of hurt in his tone.

I don't correct him even though I should. "Yeah." I tuck a piece of hair behind my ear to hide the shaking in my fingers over the lie. "I am."

He rubs his lips together, bowing his head. "That's that then, I guess?"

"Mhmm." I know better than to open my mouth because I suck at lying.

He clears his throat and looks away. "Let me at least walk you to your car. It's dark."

I nod, because this part of town can be sketchy at this hour. "Okay."

It only takes us three minutes to make it to the parking lot and my waiting car. Thank God it's too dark for him to see the baby seat in my car—my mom has her own when she has Dahlia.

I open up my car door and he stands a few feet away. He digs in his pocket and pulls out a pack of cigarettes. He taps the bottom of the carton against his palm a few times before opening the new box. He slides out two white cylinders, offering one to me since I used to smoke.

"No, thanks. I quit." After I got pregnant I knew I had to quit cold turkey. It was hell, but I don't regret it. I had been trying to quit for years and nothing ever worked, but I wasn't willing to harm my unborn baby.

He chuckles, putting one away and placing the other between his lips. "A lot's changed, huh?"

More than he knows. "Life goes on."

He lights up and inhales a lungful, letting it go slowly as he looks toward one of the streetlights. "That is does," he murmurs. His eyes meet mine in the dark and in them I see regret and something that looks almost like longing. "Be safe."

He taps the hood of my car as he walks past and I slip inside, starting the engine.

Blowing out a breath I didn't know I was holding, I finally put the car in reverse and go to pick up my daughter.

CHAPTER FIVE
TRAVIS

I'VE BEEN HOME A WEEK AND LIVING OFF TAKEOUT, SO THAT MEANS A TRIP to the grocery store is necessary. Grabbing a cart, I stroll over to the fruits and vegetables first. More than a few eyes stray my way, zeroing in on the tats covering both my arms and wrapped around my neck. I can see the judgment, feel it too, but it doesn't bother me. I've always found it amusing how people want to base someone's worth on whether or not their skin is naked or covered in ink. Last I checked, a tattoo doesn't make someone asshole—that's all personality. But apparently there's this old school thought that if you're tatted, you're a thug.

I smile at a little old lady as I pick up a bag of apples dropping them into my cart.

"Oh!" She clutches the collar of her pink shirt, looking away in embarrassment.

Yeah, I caught you staring.

Pushing the cart through the store I collect everything I need and drop way more money than I planned on spending but at least it's cheaper than what I've spent on restaurant and fast food this week.

Since I have so much stuff, I choose to go through the line instead of self-checkout like I'd normally do.

Of course, there's only one lane open and everyone apparently decided to come to the grocery store tonight. I feel irritation crawl up my spine, but really, it's not the cashier or anyone else's fault. It's mine. I've been prickly all week since I found out Alba has a boyfriend. It shouldn't matter that she's in a relationship. There are plenty of other women in the world and I've never wanted to settle down with any of them. But the fact that she's officially off-limits grates on me in a way I've never had before. It's not this need of wanting her because I can't have her, it's the gnawing realization that I've lost something that has the potential to be really great—all because I was too dumb to see it before it was too late.

The line moves up the smallest bit and I feel bad for the cashier. It's nearing closing time and I'm sure the last thing she wants to deal with is a string of people cramming up the line.

A tap on my shoulder has me looking behind me, but the guy I see is too far back to have touched me.

"Down here, Giant."

Dropping my head I take in the tiny woman standing behind me with a bottle of wine in one hand a gallon of ice cream in the other. I recognize her immediately as Alba's right-hand woman and friend.

"Astrid, right?"

"Yep. So, are you back for good now?"

My brow wrinkles at her question, wondering why it's important to her. "Um, yeah. I had some family stuff to deal with, but I'm back. Why don't you go in front of me? I have a lot more than you."

"Oh," she smiles gratefully, "thank you." She wiggles her body between my cart and the shelf of candy bars. She tugs her bottom lip between her teeth and lets it go. I can see the nerves vibrating off of her. "This isn't my place," she looks around like someone might overhear, "but be careful with her."

"With who?"

"Alba." She rolls her eyes like I'm so dumb for not realizing who she was referring. "She's a good person and she cares a lot about the people in her life. She deserves everything and I know she likes you even if she won't admit it. So, be careful with her. If you're not interested in her in that way then stay away from her but you need to be there for—" She squeezes her eyes shut. "Shut up, Astrid, it's not yours to tell," she mutters to herself. "Anyway, just be careful."

"I am." Now she's the one looking confused. "Interested in her, I mean. But she told me she has a boyfriend."

Astrid lets out a pig-like snort. "Trust me, Alba doesn't have a boyfriend. The closest she's come in years is the weird little flirtation you two have." She wiggles her fingers at me, nearly dropping her wine bottle in the process.

"She doesn't?"

Why is hope filling my chest? It shouldn't matter. *She* shouldn't matter. But here I am.

"Nope." Astrid places her two items on the conveyer belt as we finally get close to being able to checkout. "She's as single as a pringle—extra crisp too because she needs to get *laid*." She deepens her tone on the word laid and does a dramatic fanfare with her hands. "Trust me, she'd be a lot easier to deal with."

I crack a smile, amused by the tiny woman in front of me and her antics.

She doesn't say anything else to me as the cashier finishes with the man in front of her and rings up her two items. Astrid pays and grabs her bags, but doesn't leave immediately, turning to me where I work on getting the last of my shit out of the cart.

"Don't be mad at her when you find out."

I narrow my eyes. "Huh?"

"Just remember what I said."

She hurries toward the exit and disappears. I know by the time I get checked out and to the parking lot she'll be long gone and I won't be able to question what she means.

That doesn't mean it'll stop me from puzzling it over all night long.

DRINKING MY COFFEE, I STARE ACROSS THE STREET AT ALBA'S SHOP. THE crimson red script spells out Between the Lines. Thoughts swim through my head, all centering around the curvy dark-haired beauty and wondering why she'd lie about a boyfriend. More so, I wish understood Astrid's cryptic statement to not be mad when I find out. Find out what? Astrid told me the boyfriend thing was a lie so what else could she be referring to?

"Whatcha thinking about man?" Harry, one of the artists that works in my shop, steps up beside me, following my eyes out the window. He chuckles, running his fingers through his ice blond hair. "Still hung up on that chick after all this time?"

"I'm looking out a window," I deadpan.

He rolls his neck back and forth cracking it. "I'm not dumb. You had a thing for her before. If you asked me, she always liked you too. Fiery that one. You should go for it."

Was it that obvious to everyone but Alba and me?

I blink at Harry. He's not someone I know all that well, he works at the shop and we've been to the bar together a few times, but we've never talked much and definitely not about Alba.

"Hey," he says when I don't say anything, tossing his hands in the air, "who am I to tell you what to do?"

I allow my eyes to linger across the street a few seconds longer before tearing them away and getting my station ready for my first client.

I've been lucky that in the short time I've been back several past clients have been eager to book me for new work. Already I have the next three weeks fully booked and since I need the money I'm not complaining.

When my first client shows up for a simple quote on her inner forearm I sit down and get to work. The feel of the gun buzzing between my fingers is a familiar reminder that life goes on. My brother's life ended but mine hasn't and that means I have to get out there and do something about it.

Two clients later and it's already time to break for lunch. Heading out, I grab a cigarette and stick it between my lips. I don't light it. Not because I don't want to, but because I owe it to my brother to try to quit. He always used to gripe about them giving me cancer. Little did we know that it'd be my health nut baby brother who got sick instead.

Nothing in life is guaranteed—particularly life itself.

Tossing the unused cigarette into a trashcan I pull open the door for the local ice cream shop. There are only a few people in line so I take a look at the menu deciding what kind of sandwich and ice cream I want. I've always had a terrible sweet tooth, another bad habit I should try to kick, but today's not that day.

"Oh, you've got to be kidding me." I know the voice, only because I think about it way too often. Peeking over my shoulder I meet the fuming eyes of Alba. "How are you always everywhere?"

"Magic."

"Ugh," she rolls her eyes, "I can't escape you."

"Are you trying to escape me? Because last I checked I was here first, you could always leave?"

"Don't spew your weird man logic at me." She speaks to my back since I'm facing forward. "I'm craving ice cream and I'm going to have ice cream."

"I just so happen to want ice cream too. Seems we're at an impasse."

She becomes silent behind me and I'd think she'd decided to leave if it weren't for the heat searing into my back from her stare.

It's my turn to place my order and I smile at the girl working the register. "Hi, I'll have the turkey, apple, and brie sandwich with fries and two scoops of the peach ice cream."

She rings me up and I pass her enough cash to more than cover my order and whatever Alba gets. "This is for her order too," I whisper low enough for Alba not to hear.

The girl peeks over my shoulder and smiles. "That's sweet," she whispers back. She dips out my ice cream into a cup and passes it across the counter to me. "Your sandwich and fries will be out soon if you want to take a seat."

I grab a plastic spoon and take a seat at one of the booths tucked into the corner. I've only taken two bites of ice cream—I couldn't resist—when Alba storms over simmering with barely controlled rage. Her hackles are raised and she looks like some sort of avenging warrior. My treacherous dick starts to get hard. I'm way too attracted to this woman for my own good.

"You took the last of the peach ice cream!" Her shriek draws looks from the other patrons.

"Uh … I didn't know?" For some reason it comes out as a question. "You want some?" I hold out the cup of ice cream to her.

"I don't want *your* ice cream." Her hands go to her hips as she glowers at me. The glasses she sometimes wears slide down her nose, but she doesn't bother pushing them up. "I want my own."

"But … they're out according to you. Should I go in the back and churn more?"

Do you even churn ice cream or is that butter?

She throws her hands up. "I just don't understand what it is with you and messing with my life all the time. Now that you're back you've already stolen my pen, my coffee, and my ice cream."

I point my spoon at her. "I didn't intentionally steal your ice cream so there's a difference."

"You didn't have to pay for my order either," she continues to rant, "I am a smart, independent woman and I don't need a man's help for anything. I'm fine on my own."

I quirk a brow. "I apologize if I offended you or any way implied you're incapable of taking care of yourself. I was just trying to be nice."

"Well, stop!" she cries, desperation on her face. I swear even her eyes look a little glassy. "I don't need you. I never needed you. I can handle things just fine on my own."

I sit in stunned silence as she tucks tail and runs out the door.

The girl that had been working the register brings my sandwich and looks from me out the window to Alba's retreating figure. "Why is she running away?"

"Honestly?" I let out a quiet, humorless laugh. "I have no idea. Did she get lunch?"

"Mhmm."

"Can you bring it to me? I'll drop it off for her."

"Sure thing."

I throw my ice cream away, not able to stomach it anymore after that encounter. Normally our banter excites me, but today it's left me with a heavy feeling in my stomach.

It isn't long before the girl is passing Alba's lunch to me. I had planned to eat here, but there's no point now.

Stopping in front of the door for Between the Lines I take a deep breath, not sure what wrath I might be facing this time. But when I open the door Alba isn't in the main area. Astrid sits at the front counter and there's a guy at a station with a client.

Astrid arches a brow at me, fighting a smile as she flicks a gossip magazine closed.

"To what do we owe this pleasure?" She flicks her hair over her shoulder, glance darting to the back where Alba must be.

I hold up the bag of food that's hers. "She forgot this."

Astrid's brow furrows. "Did you guys get lunch together?"

I shake my head. "Accidentally."

She throws her head back and laughs. "The fates are playing a cruel joke on my lovely boss." She holds her hand out for the bag and I pass it over. "I'll give this to her."

I hesitate for a second, rocking on my feet. "She's okay, right?"

My brother's tumor and death is still a fresh wound for me and it makes me feel particularly uneasy about the people around me. I never used to be paranoid, but when you see someone in their early twenties cut down so quickly it's a hard pill to swallow.

"Yeah, I'm sure she's a little overwhelmed with ... everything." I linger for a second and she smiles like she senses my worry and hesitation. "I'll check on her, go on back to work."

Clearing my throat, I utter a barely audible, "Thanks."

Back across the street the door hasn't even closed behind me when Jess eyes the sack of food in my hands. "I thought you said you were eating there?"

I walk past her, heading toward my office. "I don't want to talk about it."

Dropping the bag on my desk I collapse in the chair, my head falling to my hands. Confusion rages through me, all because of the crazy woman across the street and I have no idea what I'm going to do about it. I've always been able to let things roll off my back and not be bothered about what people think of me, but when it comes to Alba, I find myself wanting her to like me and I can't shake the feeling there's something I don't understand.

CHAPTER SIX

ALBA

"KNOCK, KNOCK."

"You know, most people would actually knock." I look up from the desktop computer to find Astrid standing in the doorway. My eyes zero in on the brown paper bag in her hands with a fox logo. "Where did you get that?"

She strides further into my office and sticks her arm out, the bag swaying. "Lover boy dropped it off. Did you run out on your secret lunch date?"

Snatching the bag from her I peek inside and find my sandwich and bag of chips. "There was no secret lunch date. It was coincidence that we were there at the same time and as you can see, I left because of it."

She perches her butt on the end of my desk. I've never been a physically angry person before, but I find myself wishing I could shove her off.

"Stop being so immature, Alba. You're nearly thirty. You're a business owner. You have a good head on your shoulders." She ticks everything off on her fingers. "Travis is back for good. You have to tell him." Her eyes stray to the playpen in the corner of the room where Dahlia snoozes peacefully, milk drunk from the bottle I fed her before I went to get my own lunch.

My shoulders slump with the weight of the guilt I've been carrying around. "I know." I bury my face in my hands. Letting them drop I face her with tears in my eyes. "I tried, remember? When I found out I was pregnant I tried to tell him."

Sympathy floods her face, and she covers my hand with hers. "I know you did, babe, but he obviously never got them, and he has a right to know about her. I know it's scary, but you have to tell him."

I wet my lips, damming back the tears so desperate to fall. "I will. I'll do it."

She squeezes my hand in reassurance. "Don't overthink it."

* * *

Staring at the number I put in my phone against my better judgment I pace back and forth down the upstairs hallway of my townhome.

I'm being pathetic. A total and complete wimp. My mom didn't raise me to be like this.

Straightening my shoulders, I click on the contact and bring up a new message.

Me: Travis?

Almost immediately a response comes through.

Travis: Who is this?

Me: Do you frequently write your number on your coffee and then steal the other person's coffee?

We're only three texts into this conversation and I'm already starting to sweat. Bending over I take off my socks and ball them up, tossing them into my bedroom.

Travis: I didn't think you'd use my number.

Me: I didn't plan on it.

Exhaling a deep breath, I pinch the bridge of my nose.
What the hell are you doing Alba?
What has to be done.

Travis: Why are you using it then?

Me: Because I have to.

Travis: That's not cryptic at all.

Me: There's something I have to tell you in person. Can you come over tonight?

I send him my address, my eyes widening in panic with realization.

Me: This is NOT a booty call. I repeat, this is not a booty call. Do not get your hopes up. Your dick is going nowhere near my vagina.

Travis: You sure? This sounds like a booty call.

Me: I hate you. Can you come over or not? This is important.

Travis: Yeah, give me a few.

My anxiety mounts with the realization that this moment is finally here in front of me, unavoidable. Going forward Travis will know about Dahlia and he'll be a permanent fixture in my life—*her* life.

My palms dampen with perspiration. I wipe them on my sweatpants, giving myself a mental pep talk.

I shoot texts to my mom and Astrid, letting them know I'm telling him. They both respond with *finally*. Well, Astrid's says *fucking finally*.

Tiptoeing downstairs I light a candle, filling the home with the scent of freshly baked cookies. Hopefully he doesn't think I've actually baked cookies. God knows I burn everything I attempt to make.

I sit down on the couch, but my butt has barely touched the cushions before I'm up and moving again because *oh my God I have to tell Travis he's a father.*

Not only do I feel nervous, but I'm ashamed. Astrid was right, I should've told him as soon as I realized he'd come back to town for good. I think my anger overshadowed rationality, because I had to go through my entire pregnancy, delivery, and now the first few months of her life without him. Sure, we weren't a couple, but he should've been there at least for her sake.

And, well, if I tell him and he decides to bounce again I know I can be all my daughter will ever need. I'll make sure of it.

Just then a fussy cry rings out from the upstairs nursery. Pinching my eyes shut I curse my luck. Of course she'd wake up now for a bottle when she's not due for another hour. I was hoping to be able to tell Travis first, not just shove a baby in his face, but I guess the fates have decided for me.

Climbing the stairs, I push open the door to the nursery. It's painted a calming green and then I painstakingly painted a mural over top of frolicking forest animals and trees. The white noise machine in the corner irritates my ears, but it helps Dahlia sleep more soundly, so I tolerate the thing. Stars twinkle on the ceilings from the nightlight my stubborn baby girl won't go to sleep without.

My bare feet sink into the large fluffy gray rug I put down on the floor to help hide the old, stained carpet beneath. One day I'll be able to afford a beautiful home for her, but for now this does the job.

Leaning over the crib I find Dahlia squealing, her tiny arms and legs kicking violently, her small face contorted with rage and blooming a bright red.

"Come here, little one." I scoop her into my arms, and she quiets somewhat. A horrible smell hits my nose and I gag. "Oh, Dahlia you smell nasty."

Placing her on the changing table I wrangle her small squirming form out of her sleeper and get to work cleaning her up, all the while choking on the smell that has somehow turned into a bitter taste on my tongue. No one warned me that infants have poops so bad that you not only smell them, but you can taste them too. It's a circle of hell I never thought I would visit.

Once she's clean, I cradle her in my arms and carry her downstairs, warming a bottle. I've barely pressed the nipple to her mouth when there's a knock on the door.

The heavy weight on my chest only grows harder to bear. "That'll be your daddy."

One foot.

Another.

I take each step until I stand in front of the door. My eyes take in the peeling paint, the crack at the bottom, stalling for more time. He knocks again.

Hand on the door.

Turn the knob.

Swing it open.

Blue-gray eyes wait for me. He starts to smile but then he sees the baby in my arms. His lips turn into a surprised O, shock bleeding into his eyes.

I utter one word, it's all I'm capable of and pathetically inadequate.

"Hi."

CHAPTER SEVEN
TRAVIS

"HI."

My eyes flicker from Alba to the baby in her arms and back again.

"You're holding a baby."

She sighs, holding the door open wider so I can step through. "That's typically what one does when they've had a baby and said baby is hungry."

I step through the threshold and she shuts and locks the door behind me, good thinking since the neighborhood looks sketchy as hell.

"Y-You have a baby," I stutter, feeling awkward and completely out of place. I slide my hands into the pockets of my sweats, rocking back on my heels. When Alba asked me to come over this was the last thing I was expecting. Even though she said it wasn't a booty call I stupidly thought she was lying.

Now her behavior since I returned is starting to make sense. I guess she couldn't find a way to tell me she'd had a baby. At least according to Astrid there's no guy in the picture, but Alba … she's a mom now and that makes things different. With a kid to take care of she doesn't have time for my juvenile bullshit.

"You're taking this surprisingly well." She lets out a breath of relief. "I thought you were going to be mad I didn't tell you."

I raise a brow. "Why would I be mad about that? I mean, you don't owe me an explanation on having a child. That's your business and you have the right to share it with who you want."

She pales and if I'm not mistaken, she looks a little sick. "No, you're not getting it." She shakes her head rapidly, tearing her eyes from me to gaze at the little baby girl in her arms. Well, I'm assuming it's a girl since she's in hot pink pajamas with clouds on them. She nibbles on her bottom lip, her eyes darting around the room and not landing on one single thing.

"What am I not getting?" I prompt, cocking my head to the side, pure confusion etched into the lines of my face.

Her face squishes, her eyes flooded with tears. She almost looks like she's in pain.

"Are you okay?" I ask, touching her elbow. My eyes briefly dart to the child in her arms, half-afraid she might drop the infant in her current state. "Are you dizzy? Light-headed? Should you sit down? You don't look so good."

She exhales a mighty breath and blurts, "You're the dad."

I touch the back of my hand to her forehead. "I think you have a fever. I'm not *the* dad. I'm *the* man."

"Stop." She pushes my hand off her. "Listen to me," she pleads brokenly, nearly bowing in half. "You're the dad," she repeats, slower this time. When I still give her a blank look she huffs out an irritated breath. Looking down at the baby in her arms she smiles at the infant and looks back at me, waiting for me to connect the dots.

Connect.

The.

Dots.

"Holy fucking shit." I slap my hand over my mouth, appalled I just used such bad language in front of a baby.

Not just a baby … my …

"My baby?"

She nods, her lower lip trembling either with potential tears or nerves. My eyes drop to the little one cradled in her arms. The baby's eyes are at half-mast and she's curled around Alba, clearly feeling safe and protected in her mother's arms. Dark hair covers her tiny head and her cheeks are plump and rosy. Her tiny pink mouth moves like she's sucking a binky even though she's not. Her lashes are long and curled against her cheeks. Tiny chubby hands lay over her chest.

An ache I've never felt before, a *desire* I never once had to be a parent, settles inside me as I can't take my eyes off the infant—my *daughter*.

My heart picks up speed with a combination of nerves, excitement, fear, and even anger.

"My daughter?" I know it's a variation of the same question I asked before, but I can't stop the words from blurting out.

"Your daughter," she confirms. She gives a tiny shrug. "It certainly took me by surprise, but I can't imagine how you feel."

My eyes move to Alba from the baby. "You didn't tell me," I accuse, my tone hurt and harsh. She nods her head towards the couch for us to sit. "I don't want to fucking sit right now, Alba."

She winces at my tone. "Okay," her voice is soft, hesitant like she's handling a bomb about to go off at any moment. "I did try to tell you. Repeatedly. I texted you. Begged you to call me. I felt more and more pathetic with each attempt so finally I just … stopped." She gives a tiny shrug and turns away from me, placing the baby in a rocker.

The little one gives a tiny cry but quiets when the bouncer or whatever it is starts moving.

"I broke my phone and ended up switching carriers so my number changed."

She nods, blowing out a breath. "I figured it was something like that. I wasn't going to continue to hunt you down. It wasn't worth it. I already figured I'd be going this alone." She wraps her arms around her frame, her eyes straying to the baby.

My brows furrow and I shake my head. "Go it alone? You didn't think I'd want to be involved?" There's an incredulous note to my voice, because sure, I've never been the settling down type but I'm not a complete prick. Does she really think so little of me that I'd just walk away from my child if I'd known about her?

She gives another shrug. It seems to be just about the only thing she's capable of at the moment. "I wasn't going to pressure you to be a present parent, Travis. It's not like either of us expected me to get pregnant."

The organ trapped behind my rib cage pounds relentlessly like it's looking for any weak points it might escape through.

Swallowing past the lump lodged in my throat, I nearly whisper to her, "I'm sorry." Clearing my throat and gaining more of a voice I repeat, "I'm sorry." I tug on the ends of my hair, my eyes going back and forth between Alba and the baby. "I would've been there for you. For all of it."

She gives a weak smile. "Sure."

Sure. *Sure.* I've never hated a word more. The doubt behind it aggravates me.

My hands shake at my sides from nerves and the unexpectedness of all of this. "What's her name?" I realize how dumb I've been to not even ask what my daughter's name is.

"Dahlia," she replies, absentmindedly rubbing her fingers against the same flower tattooed on her arm. I know that tattoo was there before so it must have some significance to her. Before I can say anything though, she quickly adds, "It was my grandmother's name and I loved her a lot. It felt fitting to name Dahlia after her." Her voice holds a tone that's almost begging me to argue or tell her the name's a horrible choice.

"It's a beautiful name and I'm sure it'll mean a lot to her when she gets older to know you named her after someone who meant so much to you."

Alba gives me a thin-lipped smile. "You're taking this surprisingly well."

"I'll freak out later." I give a small laugh, letting her know it's a joke, but I guess really, it's not. Right now, I'm still processing the shock of this. Later, I'll realize how big of a deal this is.

I'm a dad. A father. I'm responsible for the livelihood of another human being. It's my job to teach her right from wrong, to be there for her through every milestone and heartbreak.

Alba moves to the couch, sitting down, but I can tell she's far from comfortable. "I just want you to know that I understand this is all very sudden for you and I won't be mad if you choose to walk away from us—from *her*," she corrects. "If you want a paternity test, we can do that too, but I promise, she's yours. Before that night I hadn't been with anyone in a long time and not after either."

"Can you stop fucking saying stuff like that? I'm not walking away, and I believe you, okay? I never said I didn't." Even now, gazing at the infant who's fast asleep I can see tiny pieces of myself in her features. "I've never been around babies, so I don't exactly know what I'm doing here. This is going to be a learning curve."

"It's going to be one for me too." Her eyes meet mine hesitantly. "I have my life, my routine, everything all built around her and now I have to accommodate you."

I blow out a breath, hands on my hips. As much as I try to maintain eye contact with Alba, I can't stop looking at the sleeping baby.

Dahlia.

The name is perfect for her. Delicate and strong. Uniquely beautiful.

"I can't believe she's mine," I find myself whispering, not in doubt that she's my daughter but in wonder.

Looking at her, it's like something inside of me has shifted already, prepared to be the dad I never thought I wanted to be.

"She's amazing, isn't she?" She stands and tucks a piece of hair behind her ear. "You can stay for a while if you want. She'll wake up and you can hold her."

Panic freezes my blood. *Hold her?* She expects me to hold something to small and fragile like it's no big deal?

"I have to get going," I lie, overcome with fear at actually holding her. "I'll uh see you tomorrow." I rub the back of my head awkwardly, already treading slowly backwards toward the door.

Alba narrows her eyes, seeing straight through my bullshit. "Okay."

She doesn't argue with me, just sees me to the door.

It closes quietly behind me, the lock clicking into place. I find myself immobile on the tiny front porch, trying to process everything that's happened since I got here, but my brain can't seem to handle it. In a haze I walk back to my motorcycle and drive home, the enormity of everything crashing down on me.

My life's never going to be the same.

CHAPTER EIGHT

TRAVIS

"I HAVE A KID." THE FOUR WORDS BLURT OUT OF MY MOUTH, THE FIRST thing I've uttered all day since walking into my shop.

Jessie looks up from the design she's sketching, arching a brow. "No shit. I'm not surprised considering your dick really gets around."

I scrub my hands over my unshaven jaw. I was too shaken to bothering shaving it this morning. "I'm being serious."

She erases a line on the intricate lace rose she's working on. "So am I."

"Jessie." I kick her stool. "Seriously. I need to talk about this."

She drops her pencil and exhales a heavy breath like it's killing her to deal with my bullshit. "What do you need to talk about?"

"The fact I have a kid I didn't know about. I'm a dad."

Her eyes widen. "Oh, you were serious?"

"Yes!" I snap, tugging on the ends of my hair.

"Wow, what are you going to do with a kid? And who's the lucky lady?"

I don't answer the first question, because frankly I have no clue. "Alba."

Jessie rears back, pointing her pencil toward the front windows. "Stick up her ass, thinks you're scum, Alba? The Alba you constantly fuck with? *That* Alba?"

I clap my hands together. "Yup."

"That's … something."

"What's that supposed to mean?" I don't exactly like her tone.

She looks at me like I'm crazy for taking offense. "It's just … you act like a boy on the playground with her—you know taunting her pathetically for attention, and she seems to hate you, so how are you two going to co-parent? Honestly, how did the two of you end up doing the deed at all?"

"Have *you* never enjoyed a little hate sex?"

That shuts her up, her lips pursed. "Now that you have baby daddy status what exactly does that mean for you?"

My brows furrow. "That I'm a dad."

She rolls her eyes. "Travis," she tosses her pencil onto the table, "be serious."

"I am."

She blinks at me and slowly shakes her head. I swear she mutters, "Men are idiots," under her breath. "What I mean is, like are you going to be involved with the kid? What about Alba? Are you two a couple now? Are you just going to pay child support? What's your game plan?"

"Fuck, Jessie, I only found out last night. You can't expect a guy to have all the answers that fast."

"Are you even *thinking* about answers to those questions? Because seriously, get on it."

I rub my face with both worry and frustration. "This is a lot."

"Duh, Dipshit. It's a baby—a child—that's a whole *life* to care for and not fuck up.

This is why I'm *never* having kids."

"Christian would've been a great uncle. He would've been so happy," I choke out around the lump suddenly stuck in my throat at the thought of my brother.

Jessie's eyes fill with sympathy. "I know—and you'll be a great dad, don't overthink it. Just be there."

I blow out a breath, but it does little to ease the tension in my body.

"Just be there," I repeat, my eyes drifting to the shop across the street.

It sounds entirely too easy, but maybe it's just that simple.

CHAPTER NINE
ALBA

I'M NOT AT ALL SURPRISED WHEN TRAVIS STROLLS INTO MY SHOP JUST BEFORE closing. I pause in my process of cleaning the floors and flick a piece of hair out of my eyes. "Hi," I say, awkwardness coating my words. "Dahlia isn't here. She's with my mom."

He gives a single nod, hands shoved into the pockets of his raggedy black jeans. His eyes dart around my shop, taking in all the details like he hasn't been here before.

Leaning against the mop handle I blow out a breath. "Why'd you stop by?"

He shrugs, his leather jacket crinkling with the movement. "Thought we should talk."

"But you haven't said a word," I point out, arching a brow in wait.

He walks over to one of the paintings hung on the wall. It's simple, a swipe of black paint of a white canvas, abstract and left to the viewers interpretation. For me, I've always seen the curve of a woman's body, the sensuality that's carefully leashed because of society's standards.

"This is nice." He waves his fingers lazily toward the painting and turns around. "Do you have any plans tonight?"

"N-No," I stutter. "But I have to get Dahlia when I leave here."

He smiles. "That's cool. I'll pick up pizza and meet you at your place."

"Wha—I—" He doesn't give me a chance to say yes or no. He makes the statement and walks straight out the door.

I toss my hands up in the air, rolling my eyes. This is what I get for involving myself with Travis of all people.

AS PROMISED TRAVIS IS SITTING ON THE FRONT STEPS OF MY PLACE, A LARGE pizza box in his lap.

I shake my head as I park the car and shut it off. Climbing out, I nearly scream when I come face to face with him. My hand flies to my chest and I blink at him, no sound coming out of my mouth.

How does he move so fast? He's like a ninja.

"Can I get her out?"

I look at Dahlia, kicking happily in her carrier while making cooing sounds.

"Um, sure."

He gives a hesitant, nervous smile. I step back, giving him space to open the back passenger door. He fumbles with the straps, but I don't want to sound overbearing so I let him figure it out and scoop her up. He cradles her awkwardly, but he's got a steady hold on her so I don't worry. Dahlia squishes her face as she looks up at the unfamiliar person holding her. I know she's probably two seconds away from crying, but she's going to have to get used to him if he's going to be in the picture.

She gives a small cry as we walk up to the front door. I stiffen, prepared to take her if he can't handle it, but he shocks me when he starts bouncing her up and down, a quiet hum rumbling in his chest. She quiets, bottom lip still trembling but content for now.

I unlock the door and scoop up the pizza box from the porch, letting Travis head in first with the baby.

I wish I could say it wasn't sexy as hell seeing tattooed, muscled Travis holding a baby, but *damn* I'm glad he already got me pregnant or I might just ask him to do the deed right now.

"Where should I put her?"

"Just hold onto her for now." I walk past him into the kitchen, setting the pizza box on the table and taking off my purse, draping the strap over the chair. "I need to change her diaper."

"Can I change it?"

I whip around, staring at him in shock. "You want to change a dirty diaper?"

"Well, yeah? Shouldn't I? I have to learn somehow."

I blink at him, half expecting him to disappear like some sort of mirage.

"Okay, then." I lead him over to the downstairs playpen with an attached changing station.

He lays Dahlia on it while I grab a diaper, wipes, and ointment from the side compartment.

"First, you have to take off her pants and undo her onesie snaps." He gives me an apprehensive look but follows those steps. "This is a pee diaper, so you're getting off easy this time. She might not be a boy, but she has peed on me before so don't be surprised if that happens."

His eyes widen with panic. "Babies *pee* on you?"

I giggle and he gives me a large smile in return. "They can't exactly control it."

He shudders. "Okay, what do I do once the diaper is off?"

"I always fold it under her so none of the nasty gets on her, wipe her, and switch out the dirty for the clean."

"I can do this," he says more to himself than me.

I finish talking him through the process. It takes him twice the time that it would me, but I don't complain, I'm just happy he's trying.

"Good job." I give him a literal pat on the back because I'm a giant dork and he grins, amused by my awkwardness. "I'll take her." I hold my hands out for her, but he shakes his head.

"No, I've got her." He saunters past me into the kitchen. "Where are your plates?" He starts opening cabinets with one hand, holding onto Dahlia tightly with the other.

"Just make yourself at home," I mutter sarcastically, greeted with a cocky grin in return. "It's that one." I point to the cabinet on the right of the sink.

"Aha!" He chimes like he's the one who found it. He pulls down two plates and I open up the pizza box, giving us each two slices to start. Something tells me I'll need more than two to deal with Travis this evening.

"Are you going to hold her while you eat?" I pull out a chair and sit down, trying not to let out a sigh at how good it feels to rest.

He looks down at our baby and back at me. "I want to hold her for as long as I can. I have to make up all the time I've lost." He glides his tattooed finger over her plump cheek, a mystified expression on his face. "How is it possible that I already love her? I don't even know her."

I shrug, biting into a slice. "That's how kids work. It's darn annoying. You pop them out and it's insta love."

He settles in the chair across from me. "Were you scared when you found out?"

I let out a humorless laugh, shaking my head. "Terrified." Rubbing my lips together, I hesitate on whether to say more or not, but then the words just start coming out. "I never saw myself as a mother, but as soon as the I saw the positive test I knew I had to step up to the plate. I was never *not* going to have her. Personally, that wasn't a thought in my brain when I missed my period. I figured if I was pregnant then this was life steering me onto a path I hadn't thought was for me, but apparently needed. Now, I don't know what I'd do without her." I let out a breath, staring at the veggie and meat pizza instead of him. "Life gives us unexpected miracles and she's the biggest and best one that's ever been sent my way."

God, I sound insane. Like a total nutcase, but it's how I feel. The universe knew I needed Dahlia when I didn't. She's changed my life for the better and I wouldn't take anything back.

Silence falls, both of us eating our pizza with only the quiet whir of the fridge as background noise.

Travis wipes his fingers on a napkin, clearing his throat. Dahlia is passed out asleep in his arms. Her easy acceptance of him surprises me. She's never done well with strangers. I can't understand how, but maybe on some level she knows he's her dad.

"You've never asked me why I left."

I blink at him, surprised he brought this up. "I don't care."

"You don't?" His brows furrow, at a complete loss.

"I did to start with, I was pissed that we … that we …"

"Fucked? Slept together? Did the dirty?"

"Shut up," I grumble, blushing. Yes, I'm a grown woman blushing, but after so long without sex when I'm not utterly exhausted, I'm hornier than I've ever been in my entire life. Any topic of sex now makes me ache in a way I never understood before. "Anyway, I was mad to start with since you literally disappeared like you never existed, but I got over it. We're adults. Your business is yours."

I take the last bite of my pizza, dropping the crust onto the plate.

"My brother needed me," he murmurs quietly, rocking Dahlia.

"Hmm."

"He got cancer." His voice thickens with emotion. "Terminal. I…I dropped everything to be with him. He didn't want me too, but Christian was my little brother, my best friend, and I couldn't *not* be there for him. I wanted all the time I could get with him because I knew it was limited. I wasn't going to look back and regret not going."

"I'm really sorry."

I swear tears swim in his eyes, and he gives Dahlia a small smile. "He would've loved her and being an uncle. I know he would've spoiled her silly."

I don't know what makes me do it, but I reach over and put my hands on his forearm. He jolts like I've electrocuted him. "She has him as a guardian angel now and you'll make sure she knows all about him."

"I will," he vows.

IT'S MORE THAN AN HOUR LATER WHEN I COME DOWN FROM PUTTING Dahlia to bed. Travis helped me give her a bath, but I insisted on handling getting her settled for the night. We have our routine and I didn't want his presence to affect that.

A shadow moves and my hand flies to my chest. "Oh my God!" I flick on the light, finding Travis sitting on the couch. "You're still here."

It's such an obvious statement. He's right in front of me. But when he descended the stairs after her bath, I expected him to let himself out.

"Is that okay?" The elegant slope of his brow arches.

He unfolds that long lean body from my small couch, towering above me. My heart beats faster, the throbbing impossible to ignore.

"Huh?" I blurt, losing all sense.

The light I turned on isn't bright, the room still muted, and in the tiny space his scent permeates every square inch of air and even though he's not touching me it *feels* like he is. I don't want him to touch me. I don't, I don't, *I don't*.

This feels all too similar to that night.

The one that led to a tangle of limbs amidst sheets. His skin pressed to mine. Lips biting and nipping. Fingers clasped.

It was never supposed to happen again. We agreed on that. A one and done deal.

I hated him.

I *still* hate him.

He steals my coffee and my pens and does everything he can to irritate the shit out of me.

But now with Dahlia I can't erase Travis from my life. He's a permanent fixture, one I can't get rid of as much as I may wish.

With him taking one step closer to me I'm actually contemplating what it would be like to be touched by him again. Would it feel as good? The passion still as intense? Would it make me lose all sense of control?

He cocks his head, pausing right in front of me. Close enough that his breath caresses the edge of my lips when he speaks, "I asked if that was okay, that I'm still here?"

My tongue slides out of its volition, wetting the suddenly dry, desert like surface. "Y-Yes, but why are you?"

He grins, blue orbs flashing to my lips. "Do I make you nervous?"

"No," I scoff. The very idea that *he* makes *me* nervous is the dumbest thing I've ever heard.

"Then why are you shaking?"

I didn't realize I was, but suddenly he's scooping up my hands, cradling them between his and the tremble is unmistakable.

Damn him.

I look away from his too penetrating gaze. Travis Alexander has always been able to see right through me. It's like some superpower of his, being able to strip me bare with a single glance. It's almost unfair how well he seems to know me.

"Cold," I finally reply.

"Mhmm," he hums, eyes sparkling. He doesn't believe me at all. I didn't expect him to, but the lie makes me feel better, nonetheless. "Then come here."

I don't have a moment to question him before he tugs me over to the couch and down beside me. He grabs the blanket folded neatly on the arm and drapes it over the two of us. For once, I'm shocked to silence. He picks up the remote, turning the TV on and flicking through the channels.

"I didn't know you lived here," I grumble, wiggling to get comfortable which somehow pushes me even further into his body. In my defense my couch is closer to the size of a love seat.

"Shh," he hushes me, giving me a cocky smile, "we both know you like my company. You don't have to pretend to hate me all the time, you know? Especially when no one's watching."

"I don't ... I don't *hate* you."

"But you don't like me either."

"It's complicated," I sigh.

He stops on the Travel Channel, some ghost hunting show, not the typical one I watch, is playing and a guy is screaming in an empty room. "I'll make it even more complicated. *I* like *you*."

I snort. "You don't even know me."

"I know you better than you think I do."

"Try me," I challenge, sitting up straighter. The blanket pools on my lap and I rub my fingers on a worn piece of fringe.

He grins at the challenge. Scooting back, he drapes his right arm along the back of the couch, crossing his left leg over top the right.

"For starters, I know you live off vanilla iced coffee."

I roll my eyes. "That's only because you *always* steal my fucking coffee." I push at his knee but it barely moves. "Try again."

"Your favorite color is red. There are hints of it in your tattoo shop and even here." He flicks his fingers down to the red blanket draped over my legs. "You're closed off, but not because you hate people. You're trying to protect yourself because you've been hurt before." I look away. How does he see and know so much? It's not fair. I'm not nearly as observant when it comes to him. "You smile when you talk about your mom. She's your best friend I'd wager to guess." My lips press together, color flooding my cheeks as he rattles on. "You have a sweet tooth but wish you didn't. I've seen you buy so many of those nasty grain muffins at Griffin's only to throw them away and turn around and buy the chocolate croissant you really wanted instead. I know your art is beautiful, both the ones on you and what you create." Goosebumps pimple my skin from his touch as he traces a vine snaking along my arm. His voice drops, "And I know that I unintentionally hurt you with my absence and you don't want to believe I'm sorry, it's easier to be mad at me, and that's okay. I'll be the bad guy for a little while longer. Being a villain isn't all bad."

"Why is that?" I muster up the words, my voice softer than normal. He's barreling through every wall I've ever put up around myself faster than I can repair them and it's not fair. I'm a smart, independent woman. I don't *need* a man. But God, I hate to admit it he's one I *want,* and I'm not prepared for that realization at all.

"Because villains get the best redemption stories." He stands then, my eyes following as he unfolds that large thin body from the couch. He shocks me when he bends, placing a gentle kiss on my cheek, dangerously close to my mouth.

Without another word, he lets himself out, and I'm left haunted with the feeling that this whole time I thought I hated Travis it was an entirely different emotion forming instead.

CHAPTER TEN
TRAVIS

ALBA DOESN'T LOOK AT ALL SURPRISED WHEN I STROLL INTO BETWEEN THE Lines. We've fallen into a routine over the last week and she no longer gives me a skeptical look when I arrive.

"I'm not making dinner tonight," she announces, sipping a glass of water. "Are you good with Thai?"

"Always." I pull out a stool and sit down. "Do you want me to pick it up while you get Dahlia?"

Dahlia—fuck, I love the name of my daughter on my lips. In such a short time it doesn't feel foreign at all. For someone so small, that doesn't even talk, only coos, she's stolen my heart.

"Actually, my mom's dropping her off any minute." Alba flicks a page in the magazine she's looking at. "I thought we could eat at the restaurant."

I arch a brow, unconsciously wringing my hands together. "So, I'm going to meet your mom?"

"Is that a problem?" she challenges, her tone almost implying she hopes it is.

"Nope." We're silent for a few minutes before I ask, "What does she know about me?"

Alba closes the magazine, resting her elbow on the counter and her head in her hand. Her lips twitch with the threat of either a smile or laughter, I'm not sure which. "Just that you knocked me up."

I let out a snort of indignation. "She hates my guts then."

"No," she says seriously. "She loves Dahlia, and sees how much I love being a mom, she would never hate you for giving me that."

"But?" There's totally a but, it's stinking up the air.

"But, you left," she finishes, moving the magazine to the side to busy her hands. "You had good reasons, sure, and *I* understand them, but she's my mom. She's allowed to be mad at you for hurting her daughter. I know I'd feel the same if it was Dahlia." She traces her finger idly on the black quartz countertop dotted with specks of silver. "She'll get over it one day if…" She trails off, dark brows narrowing together.

"If?" I prompt, not letting her off the hook.

She sighs, straightening her shoulders. "If you don't leave again."

"I'm not leaving you again."

"Me or her?" she voices so quietly I don't think she intends to be heard. There's a tiny flinch after she says it and I know then she really didn't mean to say it.

"Both."

Her eyes spark to mine, but quickly look away flitting across the room and not settling on one thing in particular.

I know she's doubtful and doesn't want to trust me. Can't say I blame her, but when I left I had no way of knowing she was pregnant. It was a complete fluke that I broke my phone. Still, I don't regret being there for my brother. I'd do it all again. But that doesn't mean I don't want to try my damn hardest to make it up to her. Alba deserves that.

That back door bangs open and Alba hops up before I have a chance to blink, hurrying to help her mom.

I quickly follow, taking Dahlia in her carrier while Alba gets the diaper bag from her mom's shoulder.

Her mom follows the two of us to the front of the studio. She watches us both closely, like she's taking notes and detailing every nuance. She leans casually against the wall as I set Dahlia's carrier down. She coos, already reaching for me as I bend down to snap her out of the carrier.

"How's my beautiful girl?" I grin at her, lifting her into my arms. I never knew babies had a specific smell, but I do now. I think it's my favorite scent in the world besides the hint of rose and vanilla that always lingers around Alba. Coming up from kissing each of Dahlia's cheeks I find both women watching me closely. "What?" I ask hesitantly, hoping I haven't done something horribly wrong. "I'm holding her head the right way, aren't I?" I panic, ready to adjust my hold.

"No, you're fine," her mom assures.

"Then what is it?"

Alba clears her throat and starts rearranging things on the counter she had already straightened before I even walked into the shop.

Her mom bends to pick up the carrier—it's hers so that she doesn't always have to swap with Alba—and gives me a curious look. "You're not what I expected."

"Oh." I eye the tattoos covering every inch of my arms. I can't see the ones on my neck but I'm sure those are cause for concern too.

Her mom laughs, shaking her head. "Not your tattoos. I'm well-used to those and don't judge anyone based on them." She cocks her head toward her daughter. "I just … I guess I expected you to just be here out of some weird sense of obligation. Not because you want to be."

Dahlia touches my cheek with her chubby hand. When I reach out to take it she wraps her fist around and holds on with more strength than something so small should possess.

Clearing my throat, I look her mother in the eyes. "I don't do anything I don't want to do." Then my gaze swings to Alba, silently trying to express to her that that night was more than just a whim or trying to get off. In the moment I might've tried to make myself believe that, but it was a lie.

"Hmm," her mom hums, giving Alba a little smirk. "Interesting. You two have fun," she tosses the last part over her shoulder as she leaves out the back.

It's silent for a solid thirty seconds between us before Alba claps her hands together. "So, food, yeah?"

THE THAI RESTAURANT IS PACKED. IT'S A FAVORITE AMONG LOCALS. HELL, I've heard of people driving all the way from D.C. just for this food. It's *that* good. Dahlia sits in the carrier Alba had me grab from her car so we could eat without one of us holding her. A few people eyed us warily when we came in with the infant. Terrified I guess that she might start screaming and disturb their meal. But Dahlia is a princess and would never scream like a banshee, I'm sure of it.

Alba rocks the baby carrier absentmindedly, nibbling on her bottom lip. Her dark brows are drawn, and you wouldn't have to know her well to sense her obvious tension and worry.

I've never been much good at the whole *talking* aspect when it comes to women, but with Alba I find myself wanting to delve further into her mind and learn everything I can.

"What's bothering you?" I prompt, wiping condensation off my glass.

"Nothing," she responds in a voice that tells me something is definitely bothering her. I'm a guy, but I'm not an idiot.

"Alba, come on. Talk to me. Whether you like it or not we're in each other's lives. Communication is kind of part of that deal."

She pushes noodles around her plate, clearly thinking about what she wants to say.

"What's your end game here, Travis?"

My brow furrows and I lace my fingers together, resting them on the table.

"My end game?" I repeat. "What do you mean?"

She exhales a breath, her eyes drifting over to the snoozing infant. Dahlia sucks on her binky, her lashes fluttering against her pink cheeks, lost in a blissful dream world.

Slowly, Alba brings her dark eyes to mine. "We're not a couple. We're not … anything. Not to each other anyway. So why are you here? You must have some idea of what you're doing but I'm clueless." She wiggles her fingers between the two of us. "Forgive me for wanting some clarity on the situation."

Rubbing a hand over my jaw I try to think of the best way to respond. "We're parents," I finally say. "This was all a bit unexpected for me." Understatement of the century. "But I'm trying, Alba. To be here for you. For her."

"But *why?*" she practically cries. Confusion is written plainly on her face. I wish I could erase it, but frankly I don't know how, not when I'm as lost as she is.

Wetting my lips, I admit, "I don't know."

She winces, that answer apparently not being what she wants to hear.

"I want to go."

"Go?"

"Yeah." She pulls her dark hair into a ponytail. "I'm not very hungry anymore."

"Oh." Something heavy sinks into the pit of my stomach. "Okay. I'll get the bill."

Standing up, I go in search of our waiter so I can pay, but when I get back both her and Dahlia are gone.

CHAPTER ELEVEN
ALBA

I HATE MYSELF.

I hate myself for being confused over Travis.

For not wanting anything from him but then wanting everything.

I hate myself for wishing he'd go away, but I hate myself more for wishing he was here.

I'm a fucking mess and I can't tell up from down anymore and that's all that cocky bastard's fault.

Wiping down the kitchen counter I do a quick turnaround, making sure everything is clean and in place before I head up for the night.

Starting up the stairs I hear a knock on the door and freeze. A knock at this time of night is never a good thing and can only spell bad news. Ignoring it, I finish my trek upstairs to get ready for bed.

My phone vibrates and I yank it from my pocket with a disgruntled breath.

Travis: Open the door.

My breath catches in my throat. Turning around, I head downstairs and swing the front door open, finding his tall, commanding presence filling the doorway. The front porch light seems to make his neck tattoos glow from where they stick out from the collar of his shirt and jacket.

He stands there, just staring at me with those blue-gray eyes I wish I could hate but never could, not just because he gave them to our daughter, but because if I'm honest with myself I've been falling for Travis Alexander since the moment I met him.

"What are you doing here?" The words come out barely a whisper.

He blinks down at me, Adam's apple bobbing. Clearing his throat, he holds out a small cylindrical object.

"I came to return this."

"Return … this?" I repeat, my eyes finally lowering. "My pen?"

He steps inside, closing the door behind him. "Yeah," his voice is low and gravelly. "But don't make me go."

"Huh?"

"I realized something after I turned around and you two were gone."

"W-What's that?" I stutter, trying to ignore the flutter in my belly when he watches my lips.

"That I don't like it when I'm not with you. I don't know when or how it happened, but fuck, Alba. You were under my skin before I even left town and now that I'm back, I'm never letting you go."

"Wha—"

He silences me with the sudden pressure of his lips, his hands cupping my cheeks. I'm enveloped completely in him. His touch. His scent. His taste. He's everywhere and I'm drowning.

The logical part of my brain shouts at me to push him away.

That this is wrong.

It's *Travis* of all people.

But my heart. My heart says *it's him. He's the one I want.*

I'm helpless to deny that silly organ even if it would be the smarter thing to do.

He backs me against the wall. Moving one hand beside my head he uses the other to tilt my chin up, angling my lips closer to him. He lets out a tiny hum and I revel in that sound.

I push at his jacket, desperate to free him of the garment and shirt underneath. He pulls away only long enough to get rid of both before he's back on me, licking, nipping, and sucking at me like he's starved for the feel of my skin and the taste of my lips.

"Travis," I murmur, my fingers delving into his thick strands of black hair.

"Mmm," he hums back, and I'm lost once more in the kiss.

I let out a tiny yelp when he picks me up. My arms automatically go around his neck to hold on. In the back of my mind I worry about my weight being too much for him, but he doesn't hesitate and walks up easily, kissing me all the while.

"Which room?" He growls out when he reaches the top of the stairs.

"Back left," I answer.

I don't have a chance to catch my breath before his mouth is on mine again and he's carrying me through the doorway. A moment later the soft touch of my mattress hits my back.

"You have no fucking idea how much I've wanted to see you like this again. I had dreams about it when I was gone and still didn't want to admit it to myself."

"Admit what?" I blink up at him, my tone a little breathless.

"How fucking much you mean to me."

He captures my lips between his, sucking and nibbling like his life depends on it. His movements feel both fast and slow somehow. Like he's desperate for my taste but he wants to savor it.

His fingers inch beneath my shirt, slowly guiding up my sides.

Once again, insecurity rears its ugly head because my body looks different since having Dahlia. *I* don't hate my new body but that doesn't mean he might judge it. There's extra skin there now and stretch marks that haven't yet faded.

Almost as if he can sense my train of thought, he murmurs into the skin of my neck, "You're beautiful. You're the most beautiful woman I've ever seen."

My heart warms at his words and I tug him closer by the back of his neck, forcing him to look into my eyes. "Do you mean this?" I'm not referring to whether he thinks I'm beautiful or not.

"More than you know."

With that declaration I decide to trust him with something I've never let anyone else have.

My heart.

His fingers find the button of my jeans. He pops it open deftly, sliding the zipper down. A shiver runs down my spine. "I've got you, baby," he murmurs. "Don't be nervous."

I want to tell him I'm not nervous, but it would be a lie.

With my jeans loosened his hand skims down my belly past the band of my panties.

Further. *Further.* I gasp at the first touch of his fingers against my core.

"*Fuck,*" he rasps against my ear, "how are you so wet already?"

He doesn't give me a chance to answer. It seems he can't stay away from my lips for long.

Slowly, because he keeps pausing to kiss every inch of exposed skin, he undresses me before doing away with his own clothes.

He grabs a condom from his jeans, smirking at me. "I came prepared." He tosses the foil packet on the bed beside my head.

"You intended for this to happen?"

His eyes sober, his tongue sliding out to moisten his bottom lip. "I hoped."

He moves down my body and my back arches at the first swipe of his tongue against my most sensitive spot. It's been so long since I've been touched my body responds with a desperation I didn't expect.

I wiggle and he clamps his hands around my thighs to hold me in place, a tiny whimper breaking through my lips. Slapping a hand over my mouth I try to quiet my mewling. The last thing I want to do is wake the baby up.

He swirls his tongue around my clit with an expertise ninety-nine percent of men are missing. He takes his time too, unbothered by the fact that despite how turned on I am it's taking me a little while to get there.

When I finally do, the orgasm rattles my entire body. I bite down on my fist but that still doesn't completely silence the noises coming from me.

Travis swipes the condom from the bed and rips open the foil packet, rolling the rubber down his length, his eyes on mine the entire time.

He pulls me to the end of the bed and grabs the base of his cock, lining up with my entrance. I watch with bated breath as he sinks into me, both of us moaning in unison.

"*Fuuuuck,*" he growls out in a strangled voice. "You feel too fucking good. It's better than I remember."

Lowering his head his hair brushes my forehead and then he's kissing me. His tongue pulsing into my mouth in time with his cock. It's sexy as hell.

"Harder," I plead against his lips. "Fuck me like you mean it."

He rises up, blue-gray eyes twinkling. "Is that a challenge?"

He doesn't give me a chance to respond. He slides out and I mewl in protest, but then he's turning me over and back inside before I can feel too bad about it.

"Don't make me leave," he begs. My sex delirious brain thinks for a moment that he means not to make him leave my pussy, but then he continues. "I want to stay. I want to give us a try. I want to be a father. Don't make me leave."

I grip the sheets, struggling to find words from the pleasure. I'm on the cusp of another orgasm when his cock disappears. A second later there's a sharp smack against my ass.

"Answer me," he demands. "Don't make me leave."

I look back at him, my eyes lazy. "I won't."

A look of relief washes over his face and then he's fucking me relentlessly until we're both sated and spent. Somehow, I find myself curled beneath the covers—my body coiled around his as I drift off into one of the most restful sleeps I've had in months.

CHAPTER TWELVE

ALBA

I WAKE UP SOMETIME IN THE VERY EARLY MORNING TO COOL SHEETS. Blinking my heavy eyes open I find the spot beside me now empty of Travis's body. With a groan, I sit up. Before disappointment can settle too far into my chest, I hear murmurings from down the hall. I heave my body from the bed, pulling on a sleep shirt since I didn't bother with pajamas after I returned to bed from using the bathroom.

Down the small hall I pause, peeking into the nursery.

My heart clenches in the most delicious way when I see Travis in the nursery. He dances around the room with Dahlia in his arms, singing softly to her while feeding her a bottle. I watch for a few minutes before he looks up and notices me in the doorway.

"Hey," he says in a sleep-thick voice. "I heard her over the monitor in your room so I thought I'd tend to her and let you sleep."

"The bed got cold," I say in reply.

"Is that your way of saying you missed me?"

I give a small laugh, stepping further into the nursery. "Maybe."

Travis stops dancing as I come to his side. We both peer down at Dahlia in awe as she sucks at her bottle, already half-asleep once more.

"How did we make something so perfect?" he asks me. I'm not sure he even means to say it aloud.

"I don't know," I reply anyway. "But I'm thankful every day for her."

Clearing his throat, he murmurs, "I'm glad I finally found my way back here. To both of you."

There's a nervous glint in his eyes but it disappears when I say, "Me too."

I'm fiercely independent. To a fault. I can admit it, but I've always had trouble pushing past it. Now I can accept that I like spending time with Travis. I enjoy his company and miss when he's gone.

I want him to have his time with Dahlia and since I trust him with her now, I turn around and go back to bed.

It's maybe thirty minutes later and I've barely dozed back asleep when the mattress dips with his added weight.

"Are you awake?" he whispers softly into the darkened room.

"Mhmm," I hum sleepily. His body scoots closer, a second later his arm wraps around my body. "Are ... are you *spooning* me?"

"Shut up," he growls against my neck, "I want to hold you."

"Did she give you too much trouble?"

"No. She's always an angel. She gets that from me."

I smile sleepily. "You wish."

WHEN I WAKE UP TRAVIS IS MISSING YET AGAIN. SLIPPING FROM THE BED, I quickly use the bathroom and pull on some leggings and a t-shirt. Down the hall I poke my head into Dahlia's room but I'm not at all surprised when I find it empty.

As I start down the stairs, I hear Travis in the kitchen and he's definitely talking to her.

"Who's the prettiest girl I've ever seen? You. Mommy's a close second but you knocked her out of first place." There's some banging of pots and pans and then he says, "Daddy loves you so much. I didn't know I could love like this."

I pause on the stairs, my eyes falling closed. This is what he was missing out on by keeping her a secret. More so, this is what I was keeping from our daughter. True, she's an infant, she won't remember him not being here initially, but *I* will and it's my fault. I could've tried harder to get ahold him. I could've…

"Are you sleeping on the stairs standing up?"

My eyes pop wide open to find Travis standing at the bottom of the stairs, a mug of coffee halfway to his lips. I have to admit my *Gilmore Girls* mug looks strange in his hands, but even stranger it doesn't make me mad.

"No, just needed a moment," I mutter, coming down the rest of the stairs.

In the kitchen I find Dahlia kicking happily in her vibrating bouncer. She's freshly changed and dressed for the day. He even put one of her headbands on her.

"I made eggs and bacon for breakfast. Hope that's okay."

"It's great." I give him a hesitant smile and his eyes narrow a bit. "What?"

He touches his thumb and forefinger to my chin. "Don't get shy on me. Not after everything we shared last night."

"I'm sorry." I feel my cheeks heat. "This is … just weird for me. Relationships are … not something I'm good at or have much experience with."

I look away from him because it feels almost shameful to admit that I prefer my own company over others, but it's true. I've never met someone worth giving up my time for. But Travis … it seems he's worth giving up all my previous notions.

Travis shrugs like it's no big deal. "I don't either. We'll learn together." Then like some English gentleman out of a Jane Austen novel he grabs my hand and places a tender kiss on my knuckles. "There's no way to know how things will go or turn out. You just have to trust the process."

"Trust the process?" I try not to smile.

He grins. "Trust *me*." He rubs the back of his head. "More like we have to trust each other."

I give a small nod because he has a good point. I could hurt him as easily as he could me.

"What happened to my pen?" I ask belatedly, spooning some scrambled eggs onto my plate.

"Oh, you remember that now, huh?" He laughs a little. "You'll get that back when you've earned it."

"Earned it? It's *my* pen," I scoff, both of us sitting down at the table. Dahlia flails her hands, an excited giggle bubbling out of her.

"Yeah." He cocks his head. "You have to earn it back."

"When?" I ask incredulously. This man has to be kidding me. *He* stole *my* pen.

He gives me a smug smile. "I don't know yet. But I will."

CHAPTER THIRTEEN

TRAVIS

"YOU'RE SMILING AND IT'S FREAKING ME OUT."

I arch a brow at Jessie. "Do I never smile?"

She waves a hand at my face, her own pulled into an expression like she's tasted something sour. "Not like this. Like … ooey and gooey." Her pinched lips fall into a frown. "Oh my God you're in love."

"Love? I don't think so."

But as soon as she says it something in my chest tells me she's right. I've never felt like this before. Light and almost giddy. I find myself thinking about Alba more than almost anything and wondering how I can spend even more time with her. It's been a week since I showed up at her townhome and we had sex. In these seven days it's happened five more times and I'm not complaining.

Jessie snorts, rolling her eyes at me as she cleans her station. "You're fucking whipped."

I roll my tongue around my mouth. Normally the sound of the word *whipped* would grate on me and send me running, but for some reason I don't mind it this time. If bearing that label means I get to feel this happen then I'll wear it as a badge of honor.

"Are you finished for the day?"

She adjusts her hair and picks up the water bottle from the table beside her. "Yeah, I'll head out in a few." She rubs her lips together, a thoughtful look on her face. "You know, it's dumb, but at one point I thought maybe you'd open your eyes and see *me* and we'd end up together."

I rear back in surprise. "Us?" I don't mean for my tone to sound offended, but no doubt it does. I've never pictured Jessie as anything other than an employee and a pain in my ass. She's great at her job with a work ethic even *I* envy. It's why I trusted my shop in her hands.

She gives a self-deprecating laugh. "You and me, what a joke right?"

"That's not what I meant, Jess. I just…" I shake my head. I'm not good with words. "I guess I never thought about it."

"Like I said. It was dumb. But…" She toys with her bottom lip between her teeth like she's not sure she wants to say what comes next. "Just make sure she treats you right. You deserve that."

My brows furrow surprised by the genuineness in what she says. My eyes drift across the street to Between the Lines. "Don't worry about that."

She gives a forced smile, heading to the back. It's only a few minutes later when I hear the back door close with her exit.

It isn't long until my next client comes in and I'm more than glad to allow myself to get lost in my art. I have one more appointment after that and then I close up shop early.

Standing out back, I find myself pulling the cigarette pack from my pocket. I've been going longer between needing them, but right now I'm desperate. Maybe it's the conversation with Jessie or maybe it's the realization that Alba means even more to me than I originally thought. Whatever it is, I find myself sucking down another right after the first. Chain smoking has never been my thing, but right now I need the nicotine more than I need just about anything.

Toeing the cigarette out, I grab my shit and head over to Between the Lines.

Alba immediately swivels around in the stool behind the front desk, beaming as soon as she notices me.

Her smile falls a tiny bit when she sees my stormy expression.

"Tra—"

I don't give her a chance to finish saying my name. I grab her face in my hands, pulling her up to meet me in a kiss that's not exactly gentle. I'm wild, mad, desperate to brand her.

Mine. She's mine. My mind chants over and over. *Claim her. She's yours.*

Her body is stiff with surprise at first but relaxes in my hold. Then she's kissing me back just as desperately.

"Please tell me you're done for today."

"Yes," she pants.

"Thank fuck."

I pick her up and her legs automatically wind around my waist. As much as I'd like to fuck her right here and right now I don't want everyone on the walking mall to get a show, so I carry her back to the office.

Placing her down on the desk I strip us bare faster than should be humanly possible. Ripping the condom open I stroke my fingers over her pussy and nearly shutter with relief that she's ready for me. I'm not sure I have it in me to wait.

"Hurry up," she pleads and must be having similar thoughts as I roll the condom on. "Travis, plea—" The word ends with a moan as I enter her in one hard thrust.

Her nails rake against my back, grappling to hold on as I pound into her relentlessly. It's like something has been unleashed inside me and I can't stop. I have to fuck her as hard as I can. Make sure she knows she's mine. I can't let her ever forget me. Forget *us* and the magic between we create.

She leans back on the desk, arms above her head and her black hair fans out around her. Her breasts are full, even bigger since the baby, and I lean down taking one pert nipple in my mouth. I swirl my tongue around the sensitive bud and then give the other the same treatment.

Straightening, I grab her hips, my fingers digging in hard enough to bruise. "Please tell me you're close," I beg, rubbing her clit with my thumb. "I'm gonna come, baby, and I want you to come too."

"Almost." Sweat beads on her forehead. "Don't stop. Whatever you do don't stop."

I grit my teeth, my head falling back as I pound into her. Her pussy clamps even tighter around my cock and I growl as my release sends a shiver down my spine. Mewling sounds pass through her lips. I bend over her, stealing a kiss because I want to swallow those sounds.

Mine.

I lay over her, both of us struggling to get enough oxygen. Gently her fingers comb through my hair in a soothing gesture.

It takes me a moment, but I rest my hands on the table by either side of her head and peer down into her brown eyes. They're glazed with lust, but blink back at me with understanding.

Not a word passes through our lips but both of us understand.

There's no going back.

We're done for.

Endgame.

Finally, I pull out of her body and dispose of the condom. We both go about redressing and she goes to use the bathroom.

When she exits, she finds me leaning against the wall twirling her pen through my fingers.

She eyes the pen, her lips pinched but she doesn't comment on it this time. I think I've fucked all the words out of her for once.

Tucking the pen back in my pocket, I step away from the wall. "I was thinking ... I know you're closed and all, but there's some ink I want, and I have a feeling you're the girl to do it."

She arches a brow. "That so? What makes you think I'm up for the job?"

"Oh, I know you're perfect for this."

"Hmm," she hums. "Can you afford it?"

I know she doesn't mean it in a monetary way. "I hope so."

"Then right this way." She sweeps her hand toward the front and I follow, taking the chair she indicates. "Where do you want it?"

Hooking my thumbs in the back of my shirt I yank it off and drop it to the floor.

"Right here." I place my hand over the left center part of my chest, over my heart, where I've been leaving a blank spot. In my mind I knew whatever I put here had to be close to my heart, both literally and figuratively.

She eyes the spot and nods. "And what exactly do you want?"

"A dahlia." Her eyes widen and I'd swear even begin to fill with tears. "And right beside it a pair of lips. Bright red."

Her tongue slides out at those words, rubbing right over where there's the barest hint of red stain from the lipstick I kissed away.

"Are you sure?" She's staring at me in awe. Both of us are covered in ink, and despite my sometimes less than stellar choices—like the anchor on my ankle—we both know putting something permanently on your body is a big deal, especially when it's a very obvious declaration like this is.

"Never been surer."

She still looks hesitant but goes about getting everything ready. "What color for the dahlia?" She's bent over, and when she looks over her shoulder at me her hair falls forward and for a moment I'm breathless.

How is it possible that this beautiful ethereal creature likes me?

"Purple," I answer. "Like this." I quickly bring up an image on my phone, showing her the exact shade.

She nods and mutters to herself as she finishes gathering everything she needs.

While her tattoos are mostly black and red ink, I've gone for a more hodge podge—or I guess you could call it eclectic—look for mine, with all different colors depending on what I wanted for the design.

Once she starts, I can't help but watch her in awe. I've never seen Alba in action. She's focused, I don't think anything could distract her right now and as much as I want to try I won't, and there's a spark in her eyes I've never seen before, one that tells me she's in the zone.

I don't pay attention to the time that goes by, too engrossed in studying her nuances, but suddenly she's standing up and telling me to go take a look in the mirror.

My body groans with stiffness from sitting for so long, but it's worth it when I see the finished product. The dahlia looks almost 3D and the layers of colored ink seem to make it glow. The red lips beside it are a perfect match for Alba's.

"What do you think?" she asks shyly when I turn around.

I cross the space between us until we're toe to toe. My worn boots against her black Converse. "It's perfect."

"Really?" She sounds surprised, which is insane because her art is beautiful.

"I wouldn't lie to you, Alba."

"You wouldn't?" She arches a brow in challenge.

"Babe, I'm many things but a liar isn't one of them." I let her cover the tattoo and help her clean up before we go. Taking her hand, I kiss her knuckles. "Let's go get our girl."

She smiles, her eyes crinkling at the corners.

Fuck.

I want this. Her. Dahlia. A family—*my* family.

CHAPTER FOURTEEN

ALBA

IT'S QUITE STRANGE HOW QUICKLY YOU CAN GET USED TO A NEW NORMAL.

I'm not at all surprised when I head downstairs and find Travis in the kitchen making pancakes, singing to Dahlia who swings back and forth in the new baby swing he bought for her because he thought she'd love it. He was right too. She's obsessed. She grabs at her sock covered feet, cooing like she's trying to sing along with him.

The man can't sing, but I give him an A for effort.

"Do you need any help?"

"No, I'm almost done. Just sit down."

"You know," I draw out the words, "this would be ten times hotter if you were wearing an apron."

He scoffs like the idea is offensive, but then purses his lips in thought. "Next time."

I cackle, amused by the soft side of him I never appreciated before. It's like I decided to hate him from the get-go, when really he's … well, he's kind of my perfect match.

He slides a plate with pancakes in front of me, already buttered and drenched in syrup. Just the way I like them.

"So," I hedge, wiggling in the chair, "I've been thinking about something."

"And what's that?" he asks around a mouthful.

"Well, it's just … you've been staying here exclusively the last month."

He arches a brow. "You telling me to leave?"

"No, no." I shake my head rapidly despite the humor in his tone. I rub my lips together, nervous because Travis and I have yet to put a label on what we are. All I know is things have moved quickly since he returned to town, but sometimes you can't put a timeline on these sorts of things. "I was thinking that maybe if you want … you could … move in?"

His eyes widen and he's speechless. I don't think I've ever seen Travis at a loss for words.

"You want me to move in? Permanently?" He blinks, blinks again, like he's trying to make sure he's not dreaming.

"I mean, only if you want to. That might be something you don't want," I ramble, realizing I'm basically repeating myself. "But you spend so much time here anyway, you're taking over my dresser drawers, not to mention the sink, and—"

One second he's across from me and the next he has my face cradled in hands, his lips silencing mine. "Shut up already and let me answer." I stare, waiting for him to finish. "Yes." He sits back down and goes back to eating his stupid pancakes like we didn't just agree to something monumental.

A sigh rattles my chest. "Travis?"

"Mhmm?"

"What are we?"

"Well, you're a female and I'm a male, we're both homo sapiens—"

"That's not what I meant, and you know it. You living here is a big deal but we've never discussed us."

"I didn't know we needed to." He shrugs. "You're my girl and that's that."

He says it so simply. So easily. Like it's no big deal at all.

"Ugh!" I groan, throwing my hands in the air. "I love you!" I blurt out, my cheeks heating at my sudden outburst. "What do I mean to you?"

His lips part, syrup drying in the corner of his mouth. Then a huge smile takes over his whole face, eyes crinkling at the corners. "I thought you'd never admit it."

"Admit what?" I ask stupidly even though I know exactly what he's going to say.

"That you love me." He gets up and holds out his hand for me. Hesitantly I slide my hand into his open palm and let him pull me up. "For the record, I love you too. I don't know when it happened. It's like it was slowly and then all at one. Like an avalanche gathering speed," he rambles. "One second it was innocent flirting and fuckery."

"Yeah, yeah, you like stealing my shit, I get it."

"Shush." He presses a finger to my mouth. "Let me finish."

I mime zipping my lips and throwing away the key.

"The next I don't know how exactly it happened, but for one night you were mine, and we created the most beautiful perfect little girl together. You know that saying everything happens for a reason? That's us Alba. Everything happened for a reason to lead us together, to each other, to this moment, to her." We both turn to look at Dahlia, drool dripping down her chin as she giggles at the jungle animals hanging above the swing. "So yeah, crazy girl, I love you too."

He kisses me again, the kind of kiss you feel all the way down to your toes. The kind of kiss that has fireworks going off in the background. The kind of kiss that is a beginning to the greatest adventure of your life.

Things happen in life that we don't understand, but Travis is right, everything does happen for a reason. Life, death, even accidents that turn out to be the best thing that ever happened.

Pulling back slightly he places a small kiss on the end of my nose. He slides his hand into his pocket, pulling out my pen he stole from my shop only a couple of months ago.

"Say it again," he pleads.

"What?"

"You know what."

"I love you."

He grins and holds out my pen. "I told you I'd know the moment you earned it."

I take my pen back from him and toss it behind me before I wrap my arms around his shoulders, lost in his kiss once more.

It was never about a prank, or stolen coffees, and swiped pens.

It was about two people who fell in love slowly, accidentally, but perfectly.

THE END

MEANT TO BE
BY JENIKA SNOW

CHAPTER ONE
LIA

"I FEEL LIKE I OVERDID IT WITH THE BOOZE," I SAID AS I LOOKED AT THE bottles lined up on the counter. I glanced over at Jameson, watching as he reached up and opened the door to the cabinet to grab us a couple shot glasses.

He stared at me for a second over his shoulders, then glanced at the bottles and shrugged. "We're in for one hell of a night though, right?" He gave me a wink and I laughed softly, but had to look away quickly because the sight of his big, muscular body stretched out like that was doing all kinds of very inappropriate things to me.

Not to mention that wink... that had parts of my body heating unbearably.

I opened my mouth as if I were actually going to tell my best friend—finally—how I felt about him. But I snapped my jaw closed and shook my head to myself.

"Oh yeah, so I'm actually in love with you, Jameson. I know it's weird since we've always just been friends and I never said a damn thing, but I can't see myself with anyone but you."

Yeah... I didn't see that going over very well.

The reality—and not what my fantasy was about—would be me saying that to him and he'd blink a few times, clear his throat, then tell me that... no, we were just friends. Then I'd have successfully put this weird wedge between us, which was the last thing I wanted to do.

I internally grimaced and then sighed in exasperation.

But I was in love with him. That was the absolute truth. I wanted to tell Jameson that I saw him as a hell of a lot more than a best friend, and had for quite some time. I'd actually played it all out in my head so many times, a part of me had convinced myself that maybe—just maybe—things could work out.

I'd known Jameson for years and years, both of us going to the same middle school, then high school. We'd gone different directions as far as college went, with him getting into a prestigious one and me heading off to the local community one. But we'd still seen each other, still kept in contact. And I'd never been happier for that in my life.

He was all I had, and he told me the same thing. I knew that was the truth. With his family life shit, his ultra-rich parents cutting him off because he'd refused to go into the family business and wanted to become a doctor. Apparently, that hadn't been good enough for his folks. But fuck them. They could leave him, but I never was.

My life wasn't as shitty as that, but I certainly didn't have some kind of happily ever after story either. My mother had been a single parent, working two jobs while I grew up so I didn't see much of her. My father was unknown and she refused to give me a name because she said he hadn't wanted anything to do with her or me. And although I knew my mother loved me, because she was so busy worrying and trying to keep a roof over our heads and food in our bellies, she was... absent, distant, and didn't have enough time or energy for me.

And it was fine. It was what it was. Life and all that.

Then life, fate, hell, bad luck that seemed to hang around my mother, took her from me in the form of her being somewhere at the wrong place, wrong time, drunk driver hitting her kind of thing.

And I'd been alone, an adult by then, but still now… alone.

If not for Jameson, I truly would have been in a dark, deep hole with no one to help pull me out.

I scolded myself for even going down that depressing road, but sometimes shit just popped in your head and refused to leave. Kind of like having a wound so deep that you forgot about it at times, but then every once in a while it poked its ugly, infected head up and said, "Peekaboo… Miss me, bitch?"

I shook my head at where my thoughts had led, and said "fuck you" right back to them, burying them deep again and focusing on this one moment in time.

Jameson was leaving for a year. A. Year. Tonight was about celebrating, and then I'd count down those twelve months until he returned… until I felt whole once more.

Jameson looked over at me with a furrowed brow, as if I'd spoken all that out loud, or maybe he just knew me well enough he sensed it.

The present. Stay in the present.

I cleared my throat and looked at the alcohol bottles again. He came over with the shot glasses and started mumbling to himself what to make. I trusted him to either mix us some drinks, or decide what nastiness I'd be consuming. He'd tended bar for a couple years while he went to school. I, on the other hand, had worked at the local diner. So unless he wanted Shirley's secret apple dumpling recipe, I was no help with this.

I watched him silently, which I shamelessly did a lot. A lot.

God, I wished I would have told him how I felt so long ago. At least I would have had more time to fix things if it would have caused problems. Yet with life, it always seemed like the timing wasn't right, like there were just more important things that I needed to be focused on. Then of course the whole "don't cross any lines".

But now it was clear I'd run out of time, at least for the next twelve months.

Jameson had become an M.D. four years ago. After his residency at the local hospital, then focusing on wanting to do the whole Doctors Without Borders, he decided that's what he wanted to focus on… being a healer in every sense of the word.

I couldn't actually pinpoint when it happened—when I realized that I was in love with him. I just knew that one day I looked at Jameson and something had sparked, surged, opened up, then caved in.

I felt like these emotions had always been buried deep down, and they'd stayed that way as some kind of defense mechanism. Protection, maybe?

But there was no ignoring them.

I breathed out as I remembered that day I fully realized what I felt for Jameson, and that it consumed me.

I stared into his blue eyes, ones that reminded me of the Caribbean. I couldn't breathe all of the sudden.

"Are you okay?"

I blinked a few times, Jameson's deep voice breaking through my shock. I rubbed my hands up and down my thighs, then transferred one of them to my chest, rubbing slow circles over my heart. I tried to gather my self-control, but was pretty sure I failed. I could feel him watching me, practically felt his curiosity and concern reaching out to me.

I felt like the world had just opened up and nearly swallowed me whole because of what I knew was the absolute truth in my heart.

That I was in love with him.

I was in love with my best friend.

That realization would've knocked me on my ass if I wasn't already sitting down.

"I'm fine," I murmured, waving off the situation because I was so damn confused and shocked and... woke, that I couldn't form any more words than that.

Please don't let him press. Please don't let Jameson figure it out because the result could be disastrous.

I was pulled back to the present, realizing I must've been standing here thinking about that moment in time for a while because Jameson was grabbing the last two bottles on the kitchen counter and facing me, this expectant look on his face.

"Thought I lost you in thought there for a minute."

I gave him a smile but I knew it probably looked forced as hell. "What, ugh, what's going on with the bottles?" I gestured to the two in his hands.

He lifted them up. "I figured we might as well put them out in the living room, since that's where we'll be drinking. I don't want to have to be coming in and out to do a refill, especially if I am good and drunk." He gave me a grin, then gestured toward the tiny living room for me to follow. And I did, on shaky legs and knees that threatened to buckle under me.

But I managed to follow him out, and prayed—prayed like hell—that tonight could just be normal. Because my fear was getting a little too loose in the lips and spilling my deepest secret that I was in love with him.

CHAPTER TWO
JAMESON

I KNEW I SHOULD HAVE TAKEN IT EASY TONIGHT, BUT IN MY HEAD THIS HAD all sounded like a good idea.

Get drunk with Lia.

Don't worry about the fact I was leaving for the next twelve months.

Don't let the thoughts that I couldn't even contact her because I would be moving around so much, and in areas so impoverished there was hardly any food to go around let alone medical intervention.

But as I tossed back another shot despite being pretty drunk, it was really fucking clear this was a bad idea.

All around.

There was a movie playing on the TV, but I couldn't tell anyone what the fuck it was about. I was too focused on Lia, staring at her profile, memorizing it over and over again because it would be what would get me through the next year. Yeah, this had been my choice to go across the ocean to help those in need, to heal and protect, to try and make the world a little better for someone, but it was all because of the goal to come full-circle and be the male Lia deserved.

I wanted to be wholly good, wanted to have this moment in time under my belt so that when I came back home I could start my own business, do non-profit work, and donate my time, show Lia that I was the perfect man for her.

But with the thought of leaving in less than forty-eight hours looming over me, leaving Lia sounded like the worst fucking idea imaginable, and now drinking just made my emotions for her even that more intense.

I lifted my hand and ran it over my jaw, trying to look at Lia inconspicuously.

I'd first felt a tingling of awareness about my feelings for her back in high school, but I pushed them away, burying them deep because our personal lives had been so up in the air. Both of us had been struggling in different ways—what with her mother hardly home because she worked so much, and the relationship between me and my parents becoming unbearable.

I hadn't wanted to add more confusion and conflict to the mixture.

But then as the years passed, I felt those feelings start to push their way to the surface once more, becoming stronger. I grew jealous of any attention a guy gave her. It was when I saw guys look at her, I became enraged if they thought they had the right to speak to her. It was a good thing she never dated—at least not that I ever knew about—because the jealousy would've been so monumental it would have sucked the life right out of me. That, and I would have hurt the bastards.

And that's when I knew that what I felt for her wasn't fleeting. It was so deep inside of me, another entity so strong that it rivaled my own consciousness. There was no going away from it, no dodging it, no trying to push it back down. It just kept growing until it consumed me, until the only thing I could think about was making a life for myself because then I could show Lia what I had to offer her.

Keeping my focus on her, I watched as she brought the shot glass to her lips and tossed it back, a drop of amber colored liquor sliding down her bottom lip. I felt my eyelids lower as heat cooked deep in my body. She dragged that perfect pink tongue out and ran it over the droplet, and I heard this low growl leave me. Thank fuck whatever scene was playing drowned out the primal noise.

She reached across the table and grabbed a length of red licorice, and fuck me I couldn't tear my eyes away from the sight of her eating it. She was so engrossed in the movie that it made watching her easy because I didn't have to even try to hide my reaction.

Increased breathing.

Body tight.

Muscles clenched.

Cock so fucking hard the length ached something fierce.

I was vaguely aware of parting my lips, the image of Lia having her lips wrapped around something else that was long and hard. Another groan ripped from me, and this time the movie didn't muffle the sound. She glanced at me and lowered her brows, the red licorice still in her mouth. She slowly slid it out, her lips perfectly formed around it.

Jesus Christ.

I was pretty sure I came a little in my jeans at the sight alone.

"You okay?" Her brows were still low as a look of concern crossed her face. "You getting sick? Is that why you made that sound?"

I opened my mouth but nothing came out. I was buzzed really hardcore, and I knew even if I stopped drinking right now, the amount of booze I'd consumed would keep rising in my bloodstream until I was slurring like an asshole.

And all I could do was stare at Lia during this whole inner monologue, knowing that I was about to open my mouth and insert my foot right in there.

CHAPTER THREE

LIA

I FELT HIS EYES ON ME, HAD FOR A WHILE NOW, BUT I'D KEPT STUFFING MY face with licorice--the red kind cause the black kind tasted like medicinal shit to me--and trying to act like I was watching the movie plastered across the TV screen. But I didn't want to look over at him because I was feeling loosey-goosey, you know, the kind that was caused by alcohol. It was the kind that made you think that "hey, why not just tell your best friend you're in love with him", 'cause now seemed like the perfect time. Not to mention I was hot, that being this close to him had me very aware that he was all male and I was all female.

I swallowed and promptly started to choke on a piece of licorice, my eyes watering. I reached for the drink closest to me, which wasn't water, but more alcohol… and that in turn had me coughing even more.

Once I had my composure, I wiped the tears under my eyes and exhaled. Then I went back to *trying* to act like he wasn't *still* staring at me. I grabbed a piece of licorice and slipped it between my lips, tasting the artificial cherry flavor and idly thinking who came up with creating these fake flavors and trying to pass them off as cherry, strawberry, or even grape. Not to mention the blue raspberry flavor.

I focused on the TV even harder, all the while sucking on that licorice.

And then I heard him make a sound. At first I wondered if a wild animal was right beside me, the noise gruff and harsh, more of a growl than anything else. I looked at Jameson.

My breath caught.

My heart stuttered.

And the world faded away.

All because of the way he looked at me.

It was the way I'd always wanted him to see me… with longing in his eyes because he wanted me.

God, he really was looking at me like he… wanted me.

"You okay?" I felt my brows lower as I stared at him, concern coming up thick in me. "You getting sick? Is that why you made that sound." I had pulled the latter out of my ass because the way he looked at me told me he was feeling just fine. "Jameson?" Was that my voice, all thready and thin, all breathy and filled with desire? Yeah. Yeah it was, and it was all because of the combination of the alcohol and the way he watched me.

He had yet to respond, but the hooded look in his eyes had my breath catching all over again. Although I could smell the liquor we'd consumed bouncing through the air between us, the strongest scent of all was Jameson and whatever cologne he wore. It had deep and dark notes laced in a very masculine aroma. And it made me uncomfortably wet.

"I always wanted to see what it would be like to kiss you," he murmured, his voice slightly slurred, his eyes locked on my mouth.

Yeah… we'd just totally gone down this rabbit hole.

I didn't know how long I sat there, just letting his words really sink in. I inhaled, wondering if I'd been holding my breath this entire time.

Okay, so I was drunk. Not so trashed that I was seeing double or couldn't walk a straight line. Well, the latter was debateable, but the point was I was with it enough that I could see the way Jameson stared at me, and most certainly heard him clearly enough.

I replayed what Jameson had said so many times in these past few moments that nothing else was penetrating by brain.

"I always wanted to see what it would be like to kiss you."

He had? Or was he just drunk that he thought he did, or this sounded like the best thing to say at the moment?

Either way, I really didn't care because my body was humming and singing and doing a little jig.

"You have?" I finally said after what seemed like far too long of us sitting here in silence. He was still looking at my lips, but after I spoke he slowly lifted his eyes from my mouth and looked directly at me.

"I've thought about kissing you so many fucking times it's become this obsession."

Well. Okay then.

His brows were pulled down low, his focus on my lips for only a second before he looked back in my eyes. I should have said something, anything, but I was struck silent by his words... ones I'd longed to hear for so long.

And the longer we stared at each other, the more I felt that electric heat bounce between us.

"Jameson?" I whispered his name, wondering if he'd heard me or if I'd spoken that word in my head only.

He glanced away, breaking the spell, only to run a hand over his jaw and glance back at me right away. It was so damn hot in here. Why was it so hot?

His eyes lowered back to my lips and I forced myself not to lick them.

A part of me said this was a bad idea--whatever *this* was. But a way bigger part of me... the part that wanted Jameson and only him, told that other voice to back the hell off and sit down.

I was drunk.

He was drunk.

He admitted to wanting to kiss me.

And I wouldn't stop him.

But had anything ever felt righter than this very moment? No, no I didn't think so.

I didn't know how long we stared at each other, but I felt the arousal heighten, and knew my pulse was pounding rapidly in my wrists, at the base of my throat. I could feel it.

The way he looked at me was full of heat, need, the booze making everything in the peripheral seem hazy, distorted, as if I could almost imagine this wasn't real life.

Maybe I'd passed out and I was dreaming, having this wonderful fantasy where I finally got the one person I'd always wanted.

God, could something happen between us right now in this moment?

I watched as Jameson lifted his hand, and a second later he was cupping my cheek, his fingers big and masculine against my skin, his flesh like fire on me.

"Lia," he whispered, still staring at my lips, his cheeks tinged pink, his pupils fully dilated. And then he leaned in close, so close I felt how warm his breath was, smelled the whiskey he'd been taking shots of all night.

I should stop this. *But I won't.*

He hovered so close yet so far away, maybe rethinking this, maybe trying to talk himself out of it.

Kiss me.

And then as if I'd screamed those two words out loud, Jameson growled and slammed his lips on mine. He kissed me hard, feverishly, as if this feral animal had broken free, had been unleashed inside of him. He gave me it all, and I accepted him with open arms and a greedy body.

He pulled me against him almost frantically, but I willingly leaned in more, shifting so I was now straddling him, both of us on the floor, his back to the couch, mine to the TV. He had his arms wrapped around me, my breasts to his chest, my knees elevating me slightly so I wasn't pressed fully down on him.

I rectified that right away, this surge of power claiming me because I was buzzed and feeling oh so good, and didn't want this to ever end with Jameson.

I sank down fully on him, our clothes a barrier I desperately wanted gone. But God did I feel every hard inch of him, especially the stiff length tenting his jeans and pressed right up against my extremely wet sex.

He groaned harshly and I felt him lift his hip, and if he couldn't help himself. He ground that massive erection into me and I gasped, then kissed him with more fervor.

"Lia," he grunted against my mouth. "I've wanted you like this for so long."

It's just the booze making him say these things. It's just the passion and being in the heat of the moment.

I gasped at how good this all felt. Hearing his groan, knowing he felt good because of this, because of me, was like an auditory orgasm all on its own.

"You feel that?" His words were murmured against my mouth, and before I could answer he was kissing me even harder at the same time he lifted his hips again and ground that massive erection against the most sensitive spot on my body. "You feel what you do to me?"

God. Yes.

"I am so fucking hard for you, baby."

The way he said those words, so crudely, so very brutally, were nothing I'd never envisioned coming out of Jameson's mouth. He seemed so very masculine in this moment, desire and the primal need to join us overriding everything else.

God, I was so ready for him, for this.

The alcohol had most definitely helped my reservations leave. They'd packed their bags and said, *"Bye bitch. You're on your own."*

"Tell me you want this just as much as I do, just as much as I have." He had his mouth at my throat, his tongue flicking, licking, his teeth nipping. "Lie to me if you have to."

God, I wouldn't have to lie. Not about this. Not about him.

"I want this, Jameson." I felt drunker than I was, the feeling of floating, of being high, as if this were an out of body experience, moving through me like a derailed train.

He swallowed, the sound amplified in the room, and then was moving his hands between our bodies and going for the button and fly of his jeans all the while kissing me like he was drowning and I was his life raft.

The kiss was sloppy, hectic, filled with passion, but I didn't care how uncoordinated we both were as we started tearing at our clothing. I just wanted this moment with Jameson no matter what. My heart was in my throat, sweat beading between my breasts, and my anticipation and nervousness was so strong I felt dizzy from it all.

"I need you--"

"I want you--"

He groaned at my words. I moaned at his. And the way we were continuing to get the clothes out of the way that separated us.

I pulled back so I could get my shirt up and over my head. My gaze was locked on him as he did the same. Then my bra. I stood and shucked off my pants and underwear; Jameson doing the same, my mouth drying when the thick, long length of him was revealed.

Oh. God. He's huge.

My nipples were so hard they ached.

He was masculine with hard lines, sharp edges, and defined muscle.

I opened my mouth to say something--anything--maybe beg for this, or sputter out unintelligible words. But before a word could leave my lips, he was on the couch and pulling me back down on his lap. I straddled him once more, his hand sliding up my chest, over my collarbone, and then he was curling his fingers around the side of my throat, keeping me in place as he kissed me hard and possessively.

His body was so hard where mine was soft, his groans deep where mine were feminine.

But we were both so damn aroused, the same intensity in our touches and kissing.

"Maybe we should slow down," I found myself saying, then cursed because that was the last thing I wanted to do.

He pulled back, panting, his great, wide chest heaving. It was clear it took a hell of a lot of strength on his part to pull away. His eyes were on my mouth, his lips parted, his eyes hooded.

"Is that what you want?" he asked softly, his voice husky.

I shook my head. "Figured one of us should probably say it, you know, the voice of reason and all that."

"Fuck reason," he groaned, and slammed his mouth back down on mine.

Maybe this was a bad idea, but it didn't feel wrong. It felt right and perfect and way overdue. I'd fantasized about doing just this with Jameson for so long that it almost seemed like I was dreaming, still locked in that fantasy.

I moaned at Jameson's flavor, and just like his namesake, he was spicy and warm, filling me with a buzz that had my muscles aching and my pussy growing impossibly wetter.

He started gently lifting his hips up, grinding that massive length that stood straight up and proud against me, letting me know where he really wanted it.

"I never want you to stop," I cried out as a shockwave of pleasure moved through me.

He purred.

There was no stopping this, but I didn't want it to end. In fact, I wanted it to go even further, as far and as wide as humanly possible.

"Touch me," he groaned against my mouth, the sound guttural, harsh, a demand like it was the only thing that would ease his pain. "*Please,* Lia. *Christ,* please touch me."

My nipples tingled and my pussy clenched at how he said those words, begged and pleaded for me to ease his suffering. The ache I felt was something only Jameson could ease. I wanted him deep inside me, stretching me, taking my virginity, making the pain and pleasure coalesce as one.

Moving his mouth from my lips, along my cheek, and finally stopping by my ear, I listened to the harsh sound of his breath leaving him and bathing my ultra-sensitive skin. "I *need* your hands on me, baby."

My eyes closed on their own and a shiver wracked my body, my emotions having me writhe against him. And then I found myself reaching between us, as if my hand had a mind of its own.

"*Yes*," he hissed. "Fuck… *yes*. Do it. Touch me."

I felt renewed power as I gripped that massive length between his thighs. Every part of me went tight then stilled when I felt his cock jerk in my hold.

"God," he groaned and rested his head back on the cushion, his eyes nothing but mere slits of teal light. He kept watching me, his lips parted slightly as he breathed harshly. "I'm doing everything in my power not to come right now."

I breathed out roughly as all I could feel was Jameson.

All I could smell, feel, hear, experience was this man right here in front of me.

All I wanted was Jameson. Now and always.

He moved a hand down my hip, along my lower back, and stopped when his fingertips brushed along the crease of my ass. I swore he held his breath. I know I did.

"I'm barely hanging on as it is, Lia." His voice was so gruff, so deep. "I could get off by just holding you close, but coupled with your hand on my cock…." he groaned again.

I let the air leave me harshly, not able to hold it in.

My body was on fire, my pussy so saturated from my heat that I felt all that wetness sliding down my inner thighs.

And then I did wrap my hand around his erection, a gasp leaving me at finally holding him in my hand, the sheer size of him, his length, girth… the whole package so startling even though I'd seen it with my own eyes.

I may be inexperienced, but even I knew his size was well above average. Soooo above average.

"Yes," he hissed when I tentatively stroked my hand up his length. "I've never had anyone touch me, Lia. Never done anything like this."

My heart was thundering at his words. Could he mean what I thought? Was he saying he was---

"I've never been with anyone," he finished my inner thoughts as if I'd spoken them out loud.

That had me stilling, my hand no longer moving up and down his length, my eyes opening wide, my heart momentarily stopping.

"Mood killer?" He grimaced and shifted on the couch, but a flush stole over me, heat settling into my core even more.

"I've never been with anyone either." Those words spilled from me on a rush and he closed his eyes, clenched his jaw, and I heard this rumble leave his chest. "So no… not a mood killer. In fact, knowing you haven't been with anyone either turns me on."

He leaned forward and crushed me to him even more, his mouth back on my neck. I was starting to realize Jameson was a throat man for sure. He licked and sucked at my neck at the same time I started moving my palm up and down his length again.

"*Fuck*." He groaned against my neck. His mouth was back on mine in an instant, his hands on my ass as he squeezed the mounds as if he couldn't control himself.

And then in a move so fast I didn't even have time to prepare for it, Jameson was off the couch with me in his arms. Instinctively I wrapped my legs around his waist, my arms around his shoulders. He didn't tell me where he was going, but it didn't take a genius to know he was taking us to the bedroom.

And I'd never anticipated anything more.

Once in the room I was vaguely aware of Jameson shutting the door with his foot, the slam of that wood sealing us in seeming to barely pierce the fog of arousal drowning me in the best way.

"I want you. I *need* you so fucking bad."

"Yes," I found myself murmuring against his lips, then tilted my head and deepened the kiss, needing more… so much more. I wanted to be flat on the bed, wanted Jameson over me, his much bigger body covering me, pressing me down on that mattress. My mind was pleasantly fuzzy from the liquor, but even more so because of my desire.

I stroked my tongue along his, tasting the alcohol he'd also consumed, a little voice in the back of my head telling me I needed to think this through more.

I shut that inner door just as hard as Jameson had shut his bedroom door.

We were both pleasantly, vertically naked, and the feel of all his hot, hard flesh pressed against mine, of the wet slickness of his cockhead against my belly, his pre-cum smearing into my flesh, had me moaning.

"Mine," he groaned, but the word was so low I wondered if I'd imagined it.

"I'm burning alive," I found myself saying.

"We can both go up in flames then, baby," he responded and kissed me with more fervor.

And then my back met the mattress and Jameson was right on top of me, splitting my thighs wide, settling between them, and letting me feel that hard length that would soon be buried deep in my body.

CHAPTER FOUR

LIA

"JAMESON," I GROANED HIS NAME, MY MOUTH AT THE CROOK OF HIS NECK, both of us breathing so hard.

"I want this to last." His voice was muffled, his warm, humid breath skating along my body and sending shivers up and down my arms. "But I'm so far over the edge I'm afraid this'll be over with before we really begin."

The fact he was that worked up turned me on even more. I found myself lifting my hips a bit more, my slick sex rubbing against his rigid cock. He hissed and turned his head so he could kiss me, and for long, drugging seconds that's all we did.

I wrapped my arms around his neck, steadying myself for what was about to come, for what I really wanted to happen. I was done waiting. I'd felt like I'd been holding my breath for this experience for so long that I'd die if it didn't happen now.

Jameson broke away and lifted his head up slightly, only enough that I could see his eyes were closed, his jaw was set tight, and he bit his lower lip and he pressed his hips further into the cradle of mine. The simple motion brought the very male part of him to the very female part of me, and now it was my turn to hiss at the contact.

"God, Lia." He swallowed as if he couldn't get the rest of the words out. "You're so wet for me."

I could only nod. I was soaked, my wetness coating my inner thighs embarrassingly so.

He moved his fingers on the outside of my thigh, curled the digits under my knee, then pulled my leg out at the same time he moved back a little more. I held my breath as I watched him lower his eyes to the spot he spread wide, and he revealed my pussy in the dim lighting of the room.

The air left him almost violently. "God. Fuck… Lia." He snapped his eyes back to my face. "You're perfect." Those last two words were so low I almost couldn't make them out.

Jameson sat back on his knees, still holding me open. I braced my other foot on the bed, splitting my thighs open even wider, to which he groaned and closed his eyes for a second. I watched his nostrils flare slightly as he inhaled, then this rumble left him.

"You smell incredible."

"Kiss me," I begged and he growled right before he pressed his chest to mine again and our mouths crashed together in a tangle of lips and teeth.

He ground his cock against me. I writhed underneath him.

"Be with me." I didn't care if I sounded desperate.

I shifted and as if our bodies were magnets and hungry for this just as much as we were, his cockhead aligned perfectly with my opening. He stilled and gnashed his teeth together. His eyes grew hooded as he stared at me, and the blue color of his irises seemed to glow.

"You feel so… big, and you're not even in me yet." I don't know why I'd said those words, but I saw this absolutely primal expression cover his face after I spoke them.

He leaned in and rested his forehead against mine, and we gasped against each other's mouths. "You sure you're ready?"

I wrapped my arms around his shoulders again, and did the same with my legs around his waist. "I've never been surer, Jameson."

"I love you," he said against my cheek. "I love you, Lia."

I closed my eyes, not reading into it. Loving someone and being *in* love with someone were two very different things.

"I love you, too," I said, the truth in those words so real I teared up.

And then he started to push inside of me, stretching me, thrusting those thick inches into my virgin body, giving himself to me just as I was doing the same to him.

I let my head fall back against the mattress and closed my eyes, pushing past the discomfort, noting he moved slowly, giving me time to really feel him and get used to the sensations. It felt like I was burning alive, stretched in two, so fully penetrated I couldn't even catch my breath.

And then Jameson was buried to the hilt inside of me, his cock so thick and long, so hard and filling me up completely. For long moments he didn't move, just stayed there, his cock twitching, my inner muscles clamping down.

"You doing okay?" he asked right by my ear, and I nodded, not trusting my voice.

In and out. Slow. Steady. Jameson moved within me like he thought I'd break. I wanted to tell him I wanted it all, fast and hard, completing me and consuming me.

"Oh, Lia. *Christ*." He grunted. "You feel so fucking good wrapped around me." He pulled back, his arms straight on either side of my head, his skin tight. Seeing all of that hard muscle flexing under golden flesh had a shiver working through me.

He felt so deep inside of me.

"More," I whispered and Jameson made this low sound in the back of his throat before he pulled almost all the way out, the head poised at my entrance, then slammed back into me.

I arched my back, tipped my head, and closed my eyes as that discomfort started being pushed away and pleasure took control.

His movements became fluid. Steady. Even.

The sound of wet skin slapping together, of sex meeting sex, of grunts and groans filled my head.

Thrusting in. Pulling out. Pushing in deep, retreating until just the head was lodged in me.

Jameson had his eyes closed, a fine sheen of sweat all over his body. He clenched his jaw and relaxed it. Clenched and relaxed. He was the perfect male specimen. Strong and virile, masculine and powerful.

I felt a climax climbing.

"Lia," he moaned and rested his chest back on mine, went back to kissing me while never stopping his even thrusting. "That's it." His voice was tight. "God… fuck, yeah." His words were clipped and heated, his pleasure evident. He slammed into me once, twice, and on the third time stilled, pulling back and staring into my eyes, making me *feel* every last hard, big inch of him. "Tell me this is as perfect for you as it is for me."

I swallowed hard and nodded.

He shook his head. "Say it. Say the words."

"It's more than I could have ever dreamed of." And god wasn't that the truth. This would hurt in the morning, and not in a physical sense. I knew this was a once in a lifetime thing between us.

Jameson started thrusting in and out of me again, his motions faster, harder as if he were losing control. "Come on, Lia. Give me another one. Let go for me again."

His words were my undoing.

I felt myself falling over the edge once more, and climaxed long and hard, moaning softly as pleasure slammed into me. He kept up the thrusting until I sagged back on the bed, spent and exhausted, my body singing in pleasure.

The heavy weight of his muscles pressed to every single inch of me, having my pussy clench around him in need, causing my blood to catch on fire all over again. He buried his face in the crook of my neck, the sound of him inhaling deeply an auditory orgasm.

"Mine, Lia. God… so mine." He ran his tongue up the side of my neck and I arched up against him, moaning at the feel, loving how he started moving once more, still so hard in me, not yet finished.

I was helpless to try and grasp what was happening, to comprehend what I was doing, what *we* were doing *together*. I was lightheaded from the way he made me feel, from the rush of the alcohol moving through my veins, from the fire surrounding us.

"Yes," I breathed out. "So good, Jameson. More."

Jameson groaned, the vibrations ringing all over my body like an electrical current.

I wanted him everywhere, his hands on me, his cock nestled between my thighs. I always wanted this. As if he read my mind, he slid his hand down my chest and cupped my breast.

The room spun, my body feeling like it was disconnecting in the best way.

A low rumble left him, and he flattened his tongue at the base of my throat, dragging it up slowly, licking me like an animal marking my flesh. When he pulled back he looked down the length of my body. He pushed back inside of me and I cried out.

"That's it," he seemed to murmur to himself. "I can't explain what you do to me. I can't explain how you make me feel." He pushed back in and pulled out. "You make me so hard. I'm so ready to fill you up." He started thrusting a little faster, my pussy hugging his length, stretched around his girth. He cupped one bared breast, rolled the nipple between his thumb and index finger, and moved to the next. I was mindless with need.

He shifted positions, spread my legs wider, and he slid in deeper.

"Fuck," he barked out that obscenity. "So tight. So good. Better than I imagined." He said those things in rapid succession.

And then he started pushing into me and pulling out, swinging his hips and making me take all of him, giving me every single part of him, even the parts that weren't connected.

He fucked me.

Made love to me.

Owned me.

I moved up and down on the bed, and he gripped my hip, keeping me in place as he fucked me. A gasp of pain and pleasure left me, filled me.

His expression was one of pure ecstasy. Droplets of sweat coated both of us, and the way our bodies moved together, that slickness adding sensuality to the motion, had me perilously close to another orgasm.

"So. Good. So good. Sogoodsogoodsogood." He was saying that over and over again like a mantra, his square jaw tight, his focus trained on me. The drugged look he wore had my inner muscles clenching around his length, which caused him to groan deep in his throat. He pushed into me harder than before and I opened my mouth in a silent cry of pleasure. "I'll never get enough." I swore it was like he snarled those words. "You're mine." He closed his eyes and groaned in a very male way.

And then he became a wild man, uninhibited, intense... free in his passion as he gave me all of it.

"Jameson," I cried out as he sank in deep.

"Fuck, I'm sorry. I need to be gentle--"

"No," I moaned and bit my lip again. "Fuck me."

He closed his eyes and groaned. "You feel so fucking good, Lia."

My breasts shook from the force of his thrusts, and I felt that feeling of intensity coil within me about to explode.

"Oh god. Yes. Yes... fuck yes." He slid in and out of me, and when he pushed back in hard, burying his dick so far into me, I cried out as I came instantly. "*Jesus Christ*." He filled me, his balls pressed to my ass, his entire body wracking above me.

He pumped his seed into me over and over again, filling me up, giving me the very essence of him as if he marked me from the inside out.

I felt like I was now his, even though I knew that wasn't the case, not in the most elemental sense.

Before long we were both sated and he was pulling out of me and falling to the side. My head was dizzy from the pleasure and alcohol still thumping through my veins.

Before I could wonder what happens next, Jameson shifted to the side, curled his arm around my waist, and brought me close to him, chest to back.

I was drunk, not from the booze, but from the pleasure and the knowledge I'd just given myself to Jameson and he did the same in return.

Maybe tomorrow would be weird. Maybe we'd just built this wall up between us.

Or maybe--just maybe--things would still be okay in the morning.

I didn't know the answers to those questions, but right now I couldn't care because I had Jameson curled right up against me and nothing had felt better.

CHAPTER FIVE

JAMESON
TWO DAYS LATER: THE GOODBYE

IT WOULD HAVE BEEN EASY ENOUGH TO LET THE OTHER NIGHT THAT I shared with Lia consume me, make this moment awkward, ruin this goodbye. I refused to, though. And as I stared into her eyes, ones that would haunt me in my dreams for the next twelve months, I told myself I had to act like I was strong. I had to act like I had my shit together and leaving her wasn't the single worst experience I had ever had in my life.

She wasn't holding it together as well as I was. Or maybe I just thought I was keeping myself in check. As it was, every part of me hurt--my heart especially.

"It'll be okay," I found myself saying and reaching for her hand, taking her much smaller one, giving it a reassuring squeeze even though I felt like I was being a fraud in acting like I wasn't breaking in two.

"It won't, though," she whispered, staring down at the floor, and then at where our hands were conjoined. "It's such a long time."

God, it really was. So fucking long.

She lifted her head and stared at me in the eyes, her mouth parting as if she wanted to say something. And I knew what it was. She wanted to bring up the drunken night where I'd taken her virginity and given her mine.

I slowly shook my head and gave her a genuine smile. "It's okay," I murmured. "What we shared was special, even if we were both drunker than hell." Her cheeks turned pink but she smiled. "I'll never regret being with you. I'll never let it get between us. I love you more than anything or anyone else, Lia." *I'm in love with you.* I wanted to say those words out loud, but now wasn't the time, not when I was heading to a foreign country and would be so far away from her. When I told her those five words--*I'm in love with you*--I'd be here for good and be able to talk to her about it, hold her, let her know I was never going anywhere.

"I'll wait for you. I'll miss you. I hate this." Those three sentences were a rush of words and I heard all the emotion laced in them.

I didn't stop myself from pulling her into my much larger body. She barely reached my chest, and as I placed a hand on the back of her head, keeping her close to me, wanting her even closer, I closed my eyes and just absorbed this feeling. I let my fingers tangle in her hair, the strands dark and soft, causing memories of our intimate time together to slam into my brain on repeat.

Pulling back was a hard fucking feat, but I bent at the knees and lowered my upper body so I could look Lia in the eyes fully. I cupped each side of her face, knowing my expression was pretty severe by the way she gasped. She lifted her hands and placed them over mine, her breath stalling, tears making those gorgeous irises of hers sparkle.

"I'm coming back to you. You're my girl." *In more ways than you know.* "And before you know it, these next twelve months are gonna be behind us and we can get back to the way things were." I leaned in and kissed her right on the lips. I shouldn't have done it, but

I hadn't been able to stop myself, not when she looked at me with so much heartbreaking beauty or when she held my hands to her... and certainly not when my love for her was consuming me whole.

I heard another gasp leave her as our lips met. I felt the warm breath leave her from the contact. And I did everything in my power not to groan at how good it felt to be with her like this. Maybe she didn't know that this kiss meant so much more to me than a goodbye. It meant everything.

She meant everything.

LIA

I DIDN'T THINK I'D EVER FELT THIS KIND OF PAIN, ONE THAT SETTLED RIGHT in the center of my chest. It had me dizzy, nauseous, and feeling like if I hadn't already been sitting down my knees would have absolutely given out and I would have crumbled to the ground.

I'd been sitting at the airport for the last hour at least. Jameson's plane had already departed, yet I hadn't been able to leave, hadn't been able to work up the courage to get up and go home. I felt like doing so would have made this all so very real.

I closed my eyes, still aware of all the people coming and going from all over the country--the world--moving around me. Yet I felt like I was in this globe, this thick glass all around me, preventing me from really experiencing reality. And I knew I wouldn't feel right, wouldn't feel normal again until Jameson was back.

I lifted my hand and started rubbing the center of my chest as I opened my eyes and looked around. Was anyone else experiencing something similar to me? Had their heart been ripped out of their chest and held away from their body? Was that vital organ traveling half-way across the world right now?

I moved my hand on my chest to my mouth, feeling my lips tingle as I closed my eyes once more and remembered the kiss Jameson had given me. I should have felt shocked with that kiss. But I hadn't. It had been--felt--so incredibly perfect and right. Aside from the other night when we'd gotten drunk and been together sexually, he'd never kissed me on the mouth. And although that goodbye hadn't been anything erotic, it was hard not to want more, crave more... want the world with Jameson.

A year was a lifetime away.

Twelve months away from the man I was in love with would be the most painful time in my life.

But I'd wait for him. I'd wait a lifetime--eternity--for him. He may not know that, but it was the truth, and when he came back, I was telling him everything.

I was going to bare my soul.

CHAPTER SIX
LIA
SIX WEEKS LATER

THE SAME THOUGHT HAD BEEN RUNNING AROUND IN MY HEAD FOR HOURS upon hours. The thought had first struck me in the shower, then refused to leave. For what felt like the tenth time, I did the mental math, even lifting my hand and counting off. I felt my brows lower, and sat up, running a hand over my no doubt wild, dark and damp strands, pushing them out of my face, and trying in vain to not freak out.

My period was late.

I checked the clock, realizing I hadn't slept at all, but now it was late enough something would be open. Hell, I probably could have driven all the way out to the next town over and gone to one of the open-all-night stores, but I'd been trying to talk myself down from this proverbial ledge of fear.

I got up, got dressed, did the whole brushing my teeth and hair and getting ready for the day, but I felt like I was under water, wading through thick sludge, my mind not my own right now.

Was I pregnant?

I placed a hand on my otherwise flat belly, looking down, wondering if there was a little person growing in there, a little piece of me and Jameson.

I felt sick at that moment, knowing that if I was pregnant I had no way to contact Jameson and tell him. And it wasn't like I could contact his family. They hadn't had anything to do with him for so long they weren't even a blip on his radar anymore. And I had no family, no real friends to talk to about this aside from Jameson.

I braced my hands on the bathroom counter and just breathed.

What if. What if. What if.

AN HOUR LATER AND I WAS RIGHT BACK IN MY BATHROOM, THE OUTDATED interior especially a nuisance in this moment. The linoleum was a nasty yellow color, the counters this cheap Formica that had the edges peeling up from the glue coming undone. There were these golden veins running through it, as if they tried to make it look fancier than it ever could.

I straightened and breathed out slowly, refusing to look at that pregnancy test that sat on the counter just to my right.

I'd done the whole pee on it about two minutes ago, and as I picked up the insert, re-read the instructions for the fifth time, I knew I had about another minute to wait for the little digital readout to tell me my fate.

I turned my back to the mirror, not wanting to look at myself, not wanting to see how scared shitless I was. I tapped my foot, crossed my arms and uncrossed them, bit my lower lip, and only when I knew it was well past the three-minute mark did I turn around with closed eyes, my head downcast toward the stick, and told myself it would be okay.

It will... right?

PREGNANT

I didn't know if I was reading that, well, that wasn't true. I read it just fine, but my brain couldn't comprehend what I was looking at.

Pregnant. With a baby. Jameson's child.

Knocked up by my best friend who had no idea how in love I was with him.

I closed my eyes and felt tears start to threaten. It wasn't even the fear of having a baby. A part of me felt warm at the thought of carrying Jameson's child. No, I was terrified because I had no way to tell Jameson any of this. I had no family to lean on, no friends to talk to. I was truly alone, at least for the next year, until Jameson came back and I dropped this life-altering bomb in his lap.

I looked at myself in the mirror now, the woman staring back at me having a too pale face, wide eyes, and bags under them because sleep had been nonexistent last night. "I can do this," I whispered to my reflection just as a tear slid down my cheek. I angrily wiped it away. "It'll be okay," I said with a little more strength, or I thought I did.

I placed my hand on my belly and looked down at my flat stomach, this amazement and wonder breaking through the uncertainty and fear.

A baby. Inside of me.

And amidst all the fear that consumed me, I felt a glimmer of happiness, a light at the end of a very long and dark tunnel. Jameson would be shocked, just like me, but I knew him as well as I knew myself. He'd stand by my side even if he wasn't in love with me. He wouldn't leave me. Never.

I knew that with just as much certainty that I couldn't hold my breath forever.

I knew that because he'd said it enough times that there was no doubt in my mind that he'd be there for me and this baby. Forever.

CHAPTER SEVEN
LIA
SIX MONTHS LATER

I ADJUSTED MYSELF ON THE BED, PROPPING UP A FEW PILLOWS BEHIND ME, but still I couldn't get comfortable. The large belly I carried made it almost impossible these days, but I couldn't help but smile as I looked down, my stomach tenting my shirt, a silly grin on my face.

I ran my hands over the basketball shaped roundness under the cotton shirt, a little kick here, another jab there bumping up against my palms as if the little guy nestled safely inside was saying hello.

I focused on the mattress in front of me, papers spread out, pictures a scattered mess. All these months I'd been documenting the pregnancy, every day, every kick, every ache and pain. I'd been writing down my experience, collecting any and all images--even taking one every month to show the progress of my swelling belly. And now it was time to organize what I had.

I'd started doing this from the very first doctor appointment. Hell, I'd even taken a picture of the positive pregnancy stick with my cell phone and printed it off—the very first proof of what was going to change our lives.

Mine.

Jameson's.

And our son I carried.

I picked up the first ultrasound picture that had ever been taken, the little bean shape in the center of the black-and-white image nothing like how a baby looked as you held it in your arms, or even a profile picture that you got when you had the anatomy scan.

I'd been seven weeks pregnant for that image.

I set it down and picked up the next image, this one a couple weeks after that first ultrasound. Because I'd been spotting here and there, the doctor had been overly cautious, much to my relief. Besides, I would take as many images of the little baby inside of me as I could, things that I could show Jameson so he didn't feel like he missed out on anything.

I looked over every printout I'd gotten from my doctor appointments that showed my weight gain, the size of my belly, the growth of the baby. I started making a journal, writing down a page or two every single night before I went to bed, nothing really of much importance in most of the entries, but a look back so that if Jameson wanted to, he could read about how many times the baby kicked that day.

And despite the fact I really had no friends therefore there was no baby shower, no surprise gathering thrown in celebration, I was fine with that. I was used to taking care of myself, or supporting myself in all ways.

Over these last months, I'd scrapped and saved every single penny, buying everything myself, stocking up on wipes and diapers early on. I'd read every magazine I could, the *What to Expect When You're Expecting* book from front to back so many times the pages were dog-eared.

I was doing the best I could with what I had.

And I wished most of all Jameson was here to experience it all firsthand.

I leaned back again, crossed my legs at the ankles, and stared at the picture that sat on my dresser across from me. I couldn't see it very clearly because of the distance, but I didn't have to to know what the image was. It was seared in my brain. I'd memorized every single line, every single color, every facial expression.

Everything.

It was a picture of Jameson and I years ago, our graduation, one of the first milestones we'd experienced together. In the image I was staring off at the camera, a huge grin on my face. Jameson was looking down at me, a little smile curving his.

God, I couldn't wait until he was back home. I couldn't wait until I could share this new milestone with him. I just hoped things worked out. I just really hoped they did.

CHAPTER EIGHT

JAMESON
THE REUNION: TEN MONTHS LATER AFTER JAMESON LEFT

THE SPORADIC LETTERS LIA AND I HAD EXCHANGED DURING ALL THESE months hadn't been enough. Not seeing her face or hearing her voice had been the worst kind of fucking pain. Yeah, I left so I could gain knowledge and experience, to help those who needed it the most. But leaving Lia behind had been fucking awful.

Not telling her how I felt for longer than was even acceptable, I knew that all of that had to change. This wasn't even about both of us sleeping together ten months prior. This wasn't about me being in love with her well before that. This wasn't even about me realizing that I'd been nothing but a coward as I lay in bed alone across the fucking ocean wishing I'd been more of a man and just confessed how I felt before I'd left.

But I was a coward. The very idea that if I'd told her how I felt, and she didn't reciprocate those feelings, I would be gone and I couldn't have done anything to try and make things right. The time would pass, distance would make that absence even worse, and things would be so much worse than I could ever imagine.

That's what had gone through my mind as I kept my fucking mouth shut while in her presence, and had said nothing in the sparse letters we'd shared.

But I was back now, having come home a little earlier than projected, and all I wanted to do was surprise the only woman who had ever meant anything to me.

I pulled the SUV next to the curb in front of Lia's one bedroom duplex. The house was old, with white siding, black decorative shutters on either side of the windows, and a seventies aesthetic feel inside.

I sat there for several minutes, just staring at the front door, wondering if I should have called her and let her know of my arrival. That would have been the right thing to do, but I'd been so damn excited.

I didn't want to shock Lia, didn't want to just show up unannounced like an asshole, but I'd been unable to stop myself from just coming straight here, anticipating this reunion for so long that all I'd wanted to do was act.

Lia was my life. My everything. She wasn't just my best friend, but also my family. With parents that couldn't care less about me because I hadn't wanted to follow in my father's footsteps, parents that had cut me off when I'd told them of my medical aspirations, Lia had been the only one to stick by me through it all.

I exhaled, my heart racing, my chest tight, and my stomach in knots.

Running a hand over my mouth, I felt the day-old scruff make an appearance on my cheeks and jaw. I should have shaved. I should have changed out of the clothes I'd worn on that long ass flight across the ocean.

Go in there. See her. Talk to her. Hold her and tell Lia how much you love her.

I forced myself out of the vehicle and headed to the front door. The sun was just starting to set, my flight having come in just a couple of hours ago. I'd gotten my bags and headed straight to Lia's, not stopping anywhere because the only important thing to me was her.

Always her.

Once on the front porch I just stood there and stared at the door, hearing muffled sound on the other side. Her neighbor wasn't home, which I was thankful for, because I wanted this moment just for us, without any background noise from someone on the other side of the wall.

I wanted this to be about her and me.

In my head I'd thought about this moment for so long that now that I finally stood here, I was scared shitless. My pulse was racing, my throat was tight and dry. I felt dizzy, my face flushed, my breathing coming out in rapid pants.

I braced a hand on the door jam and closed my eyes for a minute, exhaling slowly, trying to gather my thoughts and just focus. This shouldn't have been as nerve wracking as it was, but when you were about to reunite with the one person who meant everything to you, when you were finally going to admit your feelings, things went upside down in your head and body.

Before I could stop myself, I brought my knuckles up and rapped three times on the door. And then I took a step back, my heart in my throat, sweat starting to form on my forehead. Only seconds had passed, but it felt like a lifetime as I waited there for her to open the door. Then I heard the lock disengage. The door swung open. And my breath caught as the world faded and I stared at Lia.

Her eyes widened as she took me in, and I let myself have the luxury of looking at her, starting with the top of her head and traveling down to the tips of her toes.

The long dark strands of her hair were piled high in a messy bun on the top of her head, pieces falling from the knot and framing her face. Her eyes seemed so big, like large saucers—a deer caught in headlights. I noticed the dark circles under them, as if she hadn't been getting sleep. I frowned, the part of me that worried about her and wanted to take care of Lia rising up viciously.

She had a small blue towel draped over her shoulder, or maybe it was a blanket. It was tiny, but looked soft, like fleece, not terrycloth. The white T-shirt she wore looked like she'd spilled water all down the front, damp spots showing tiny bits of her peachy flesh underneath. I kept looking her over, not sexually—although she was by far the most gorgeous woman I'd ever seen—but because a part of me wanted to make sure she was whole, that these last several months hadn't taken anything away from her.

She wore a pair of black yoga pants, ones that molded to her legs perfectly. She looked the same, yet didn't. She was curvier than I remembered, her breasts seeming larger. That last part had me imagining a moment in time from ten months ago--when we'd been drunk and she'd been writhing under me, her beautiful naked breasts shaking back and forth slightly as I slid in and out of her.

Oh God. Now was not the time to get aroused.

I cleared my throat, shifted on my feet, scrubbed a hand over the back of my neck. I was twitchy and nervous, and I felt her staring at me so intently it was like she touched me.

"You're back," she whispered, her voice sounded weird… thin, as if she stared at a ghost, or a stranger. "Early."

Fuck.

"I mean… I didn't mean for that to sound tense… dammit this is weird."

I glanced up and she still had that tight look on her face, her eyes still wide.

"I'm really happy you're back." And she smiled, one that was genuine and warm and sweet and made my heart skip a beat.

She stepped aside and let me in, and when I went over the threshold I smelled cookies in the air, then noticed the candle sitting on the counter in the kitchen.

I didn't even wait—couldn't, if I were being totally honest. I pulled Lia in, had a hand on the back of her head so she was pressed to my chest, then buried my nose in her hair, just inhaling deeply.

"God, I missed you," I murmured, feeling like I was finally home. I. Was. Home. She held me back just as tightly, her body melting into mine, this little sob coming from her, but I knew it was happiness that shook her much smaller body.

"I missed you, too," she whispered, and tightened her arms around me.

Fuck, that felt incredible.

I didn't know how long I held her, but it would never be enough. Never. I did pull away then, smiling down at her, pushing some of those errant strands of hair from her face, and letting my fingers linger along her ultra-smooth cheeks.

"I missed you so much." My heart started beating again for the first time in almost a year the moment she'd opened that door and I saw her again after all this time.

The smile she gave me lit me up from the inside out. I forced myself to let my arms drop away from her, not wanting to make this weird. We had a lot to talk about, especially where I stood on how she made me feel. I did give myself a moment to look around, reminiscing about her place since it seemed like a lifetime since I'd been here.

The duplex was a tiny little thing, with the living room and kitchen one room with only a breakfast counter style partition separating the door. There was a door that led off from the kitchen and into a large laundry room, and another door there that led out back.

Attached to the living room was an even tinier hallway, a bathroom off of that reminiscent of the seventies with a yellow and brown accented counter and linoleum floor.

The living room looked the same—the navy couch with tiny peach colored dots scattered over it that Lia had found at a yard sale. The black faux wood "entertainment center" that held her TV, DVD player, and an array of movies on the shelf. The rug in front of the couch was the same—cream with these darker cream accented swirls throughout.

Also off the hallway was the lone bedroom, nearly as large as the living room, which wasn't saying much since they were both tiny as hell.

The best part of the duplex set-up—and the reason it had sealed the deal for Lia renting the place—not counting the free water and heat—was the backyard.

The structure was situated on a hundred acres owned by the landlord, an elderly couple who farmed corn and soybeans. The backyard was fields and fields as far as the eye could see, and there was even a wood area that had a creek running through it.

As I stood here thinking about all of that, taking in her place, which I already knew by heart, but wanted to memorize all over again, I started noticing things that I hadn't picked up on right away. Things that most certainly had never belonged here before.

A baby swing butting up against the wall.

A woven basket beside the couch that held diapers, wipes, washcloths, and an array of other baby paraphernalia.

I snapped my focus to the kitchen and looked at the sink. A bottle rack sat on the counter, bottles situated upside down on it as they clearly dried.

Baby stuff. Everywhere.

I felt dizzy, so lightheaded I reached out and braced a hand on the wall beside me, hung my head, and closed my eyes. I breathed in and out. In and out.

A baby. There was a baby here. *Lia has a baby.*

Those words went through my head back and forth, on repeat, taking up reality.

The next thing that moved through my shock was pure jealousy, followed by a murderous rage to hunt down whoever had gotten her pregnant and tear their balls from their body before I fed them to him.

When I lifted my head and stared at Lia, I saw she'd taken that little blue blanket—which I now assumed might be a burp cloth of some kind—and started to wring it in her hands. She was watching me with a guarded expression, her teeth pulling at her bottom lip, her chest rising and falling as she breathed in and out hard.

I opened my mouth and closed it, not sure what to say, but it didn't matter because no words came out.

Then the sound of a tiny little human came through from the bedroom. My heart jerked in my chest and my throat tightened. She glanced over her shoulder at the bedroom, then back at me, the wailing tapering off before picking up again even harder.

"I have to get him. I'll be right back and we can… talk."

I found my way stumbling over to the couch, my body falling down onto it, my foot bumping into that little woven basket with the baby stuff in it. I reached down and ran my finger over the tops of the diapers and along the soft blankets, then straightened.

My hands shook and I curled them into themselves to try and stop it.

And then Lia stepped back out into the living room and as I stared at her holding that tiny little baby in her arms, I swore the world opened up and swallowed me whole.

CHAPTER NINE
LIA

THIS CERTAINLY WASN'T HOW I SAW TELLING JAMESON ABOUT THE BABY situation. But life really did like to give you surprises, and as I looked down at my son, truer words had never been spoken.

The only place for me to sit was on the couch, but I left a cushion between us, thinking maybe he needed a little bit of room, some space to this bomb I just dropped.

I knew I would have if the roles had been reversed.

The way he looked at me before glancing down at the baby, then back at me, told me all sorts of conclusions were popping up in his head. I wanted to just come out and tell him the truth, open myself up bare, let the chips fall where they may, but I was tongue-tied, scared of the fallout, afraid he'd be upset with me.

I exhaled slowly and adjusted the baby in my arms. I glanced down again at my son, seeing a tiny Jameson reflected back at me. He looked so much like the man I loved it was shocking. When I lifted my head to stare at Jameson once more, I cleared my throat, figuring I might as well just open this wound and bleed dry.

"You have a baby, Lia," Jameson said before I could get any words out.

I had your baby.

Of course I kept that to myself at this very moment.

I cleared my throat again and nodded slowly. "He's... he's a couple of weeks old." I felt myself smile in genuine love and happiness. I remembered everything that had transpired from the time I'd given myself to Jameson that night all those months ago to this exact moment now where he was back in my life and there was this tiny human that we'd created together in my arms. "His name is Caleb." I let those words hang between us as I looked into Jameson's so very blue eyes, hoping he would understand the significance of that.

Jameson blinked a few times and stared down at Caleb, maybe not processing what I said fully yet. The blanket obstructed little Caleb's face, and I pulled it down more, letting Jameson see the dark tuft of hair that covered his head. I shifted on the couch so that Jameson could get a better look at the baby.

His son.

"His name is Caleb?" The way he spoke was low, as if he said the words almost to himself.

I nodded again, so much emotion clogging my body that I couldn't think clearly, couldn't focus on anything. Everything was running through my mind at hyper-speed; nervousness and anticipation, excitement and hesitation all waging war inside of me.

"That's my middle name, Lia." He looked at me now with wide, shocked eyes.

I ran my free palm up and down my thigh, my hand shaking before I lifted it back up and cupped the baby's bottom.

"I... I named him..." *God, get the words out.* But I was all but shaking, and it was only when I felt Jameson place a hand on my knee, easing me, calming me further, that

I took a deep breath and just finished saying what needed to be said. "I named him after his father."

The silence that bounced between us was heavy and thick, the shock coalescing between us, moving back-and-forth, faster and harder until Jameson snatched his hand away, curled his fingers into his palms and made a fist. He started breathing harder as if he couldn't get enough oxygen into his lungs, and I watched as he gripped the arm of the couch, his nails digging into the fabric and making a soft scratching sound.

It was as if he were using it as leverage, as if he were afraid if he didn't hold on he'd crumble to the ground.

"The father?" Jameson wheezed out then shifted on the cushion so he was looking straight ahead, breathing harshly as if he couldn't catch his breath. And then his body went ramrod straight, his head turning toward me, his focus clear as water. "That night... that night we got drunk and..."

I nodded when it was clear he couldn't finish speaking. "Yeah." My voice was thick and husky. "I didn't have any way to tell you, and that broke me." I sniffed, cleared my throat, then started blinking a lot.

Don't cry. Don't cry. Don't cry.

"You were all alone," Jameson said with such a deep voice it was clear his emotions were just as high as mine were. "I left you all alone to deal with a pregnancy and a baby and... I'm so sorry."

I shook my head and brushed away the tears that fell, hating that I couldn't be stronger. "It's not your fault. No apologies. It's no one's fault. It is just something that happened, and here we are with this perfect little boy." Just then Caleb roused, his eyes blinking open, his body stretching in that way newborns did. His little mouth opened, his pink, adorable toothless gums coming into view.

"Can I... Can I hold him?"

I snapped my eyes up to Jameson and felt my heart race even more. I nodded slowly and moved closer toward him, watching as his shaky hands lifted up.

"I don't know what I'm doing." His voice was so soft.

I didn't speak as I placed the tiny bundle in his arms. "Just support his head." Jameson placed a big hand on the back of Caleb's head, and then he leaned back, resting against the cushions, his focus completely transfixed on the baby.

"Lia," Jameson groaned and closed his eyes before opening them and blinking rapidly. "He looks just like me."

I covered my mouth with my hands and nodded, then realized he couldn't see me because he was still staring at the baby. "I know. It's crazy, right?" Caleb's eyes were fully open now, and my heart broke in the best way as my son stared up raptly at his father. "I'm pretty sure his eyes will be the same shade as yours."

Jameson nodded and smiled, his thumb gently moving back and forth, stroking Caleb's downy soft hair. "Yeah," he finally said, then cleared his throat.

"I'd seen this visit going so differently," he murmured, his voice low and deep, as if he was trying to hold in all his emotion.

I was right there along with him, feeling like I'd been transported to some alternate dimension, knowing that life had turned itself upside down, and although he seemed so very accepting of the situation—of baby Caleb—I still worried about what was going to happen between him and I.

I was in love with him, still hadn't told him that, and I was afraid. I was terrified to alter this moment in time, where we were in this perfect little bubble.

"I'd pictured our reunion so many times over the last year." He looked at me then.

I felt my heart jump into my throat before plummeting into the pit of my stomach. But I said nothing. I didn't even move. I knew he had more to say. I could see that written across his face.

"This last year has been hell for me... because I was away from you." He swallowed. "God, it's been hell being away from you, and even more so now because I know what you had to go through alone." He closed his eyes, squeezed them shut for just a second before he opened them again and looked at me with those Caribbean blue irises. "I love you so much, Lia."

I smiled, feeling my emotions choke me up all over again. "I love you too, Jameson," I responded easily, so very truthfully. So much more truthfully than he'd ever know.

No, that wasn't true. He was going to know today. At this moment.

Right now.

"I'm in love with you—"

"I'm in love with you—"

We both spoke at the same time, the words war between us, hanging in the air, so thick you could cut them with a knife. I felt my eyes widen. I watched as his did the same.

It was Jameson who spoke first, his voice seeming even deeper. "W-What…" His eyes were so wide. "Say that again," he said the latter so softly I almost didn't hear.

I smoothed my hands up and down my thighs, trying to calm down, trying to look like I wasn't about to jump out of my own skin. "I'm in love with you, Jameson." I swallowed down the bile that rose up in my throat, my uncertainty of the situation so consuming that if I wasn't sitting down I surely would have fainted.

"I've been in love with you for so long, but too afraid to speak the words aloud, too terrified that things would be ruined between us." I looked down at my feet, ones that were covered in plain white cotton socks that didn't keep out the chill in the air whatsoever. "You're all I have, Jameson. You're my family, my best friend… my everything." I looked at him then and his eyes were red-rimmed, his jaw tight. I didn't know what emotions were playing across his expression. I couldn't read him at that moment.

His big body shook as if he couldn't control the action. "You're all I have too, Lia." He looked like he was going to cry, but after a moment of silence, as if he were trying to gather himself, he looked back down at Caleb. "You're my everything." His words were low, loving. "Both of you are now my everything."

I had my hand placed right over my heart, not realizing I'd done the act until after the fact.

"I am so in love with you." He looked back at me and I felt the stupidest smile cover my face. "For longer than I want to admit." He laughed softly. "And yeah, I was afraid of everything I'd lose if I admitted it and you weren't on the same page as me." He shook his head slowly. "I should have been a man and told you, not wasting time, not wasting what we could have had, no matter what could have happened." He looked at Caleb and I swore it seemed like Jameson was going to cry. "And you gave me this, him, a baby, Lia." He coughed as if he was choked up. I quickly wiped my falling tears of happiness away.

"You made me a father." He lifted Caleb up and kissed his little head, closing his eyes as he did the act.

I made a sound deep in my throat, one of happiness and relief and everything that I'd ever hoped and dreamed happening for our reunion.

"I recorded everything that happened while you were away, during the pregnancy. I have pictures and videos, journal entries, too." He snapped his head up to me, surprise on his face. I shrugged. "I figured you might want to see all that, but if not—"

"Come here," he murmured to me softly, and I shifted closer to him so we were thigh to thigh, Jameson's big body pressed to my much smaller one. "Thank you. I want to see it all. I want to feel like I didn't miss out on a single moment." He wrapped an arm around my shoulder and pulled me against him even more. "My little family," he said in this deliriously happy voice, a smile spreading over his face. "All mine."

I closed my eyes and rested my head against his bicep, never realizing how much I'd wanted this to be my reality until I was experiencing it. I'd only ever dreamed of it. I'd only ever wondered what this would be like.

But here I was. Here we were. Making our very own future.

EPILOGUE ONE
JAMESON
ONE YEAR LATER

I SIGHED IN CONTENTMENT AS I PULLED LIA IN CLOSER--IMPOSSIBLY CLOSER if I was being honest. She was already pressed right to me, but fuck, I wanted her closer. I closed my eyes and buried my face in her hair, inhaling deeply, the scent of the rose shampoo she always used causing fire to stir within me. I'd just made love to her good and hard, long and slow, yet I was ready to go again.

The baby monitor on the bedside table showed little Caleb was still fast asleep, and although we'd hoped he'd be sleeping through the night by now, there were times--stretches even--that he didn't. But no matter how tired I was, I wouldn't change this for anything.

I smoothed my hand over her arm, grabbed her wrist gently, and lifted her hand up and out of the blankets so I could look at the wedding ring she wore. I'd asked her to marry me as soon as I'd gotten back home, and knew that's what I wanted to do even before I knew about baby Caleb.

I'd just wanted Lia in my life, and I would have done anything to make that a reality.

The last year had gone by in a blur of tears and laughs, smiles and stress. And yeah, it was fucking hard being a parent and a husband, and making sure I didn't screw things up. I worked a lot because of my medical background, and Lia talked about going back to school, which made the stress on her even greater. And at the base of my core I just wanted to make things okay for her. I wanted things to be easy for us, always happy, and where we weren't wanting to pull our hair out because Caleb got into the flour and decided to use it in the kitchen like we needed a remodel.

But once again… I wouldn't change it all for the world.

We only had this one moment in time, this slice of life that would never happen again.

I'd never see my son at this exact same age. I'd never hold my wife in this way ever again. And I never wanted to take it for granted.

"If I could marry you all over again, I would, Lia," I found myself saying before I even knew the words were out in the open. She slept soundly, not even me lifting her arm waking her. And I couldn't deny I liked the fact she felt so utterly safe and protected in my arms, that she could be this deep in sleep.

I wrapped my arm around her again and buried my nose in her hair, inhaling once more.

"I love you more each and every day," I whispered into the strands. "Thank you for being my best friend, for being my wife, and for giving me Caleb. Thank you for making me a husband and a father." My arm tightened around her reflexively. "It's always been you." I leaned down to kiss the soft skin on her shoulder. "And there will never be anyone else for me for as long as I live." Truer words had never been spoken in the history of mankind.

EPILOGUE TWO
JAMESON
TEN YEARS LATER

THIS NEVER GOT OLD… NEVER GOT ANY LESS INCREDIBLE.

Not to me. Not ever.

I sat in what I knew was one hell of an uncomfortable hospital chair, but I was so deliriously happy that I could have had my ass on barbed wire and I wouldn't have felt anything but joy.

The little bundle cradled in one of my arms was so tiny, so light, it was almost like I held nothing at all. I stared down at my son, Abel, who had a head full of dark hair like Lia, and who, when I'd seen his eyes open, had looked at blue as mine, just like his older brother's. I loved him so much already. A tiny shift in my other arm had me looking at our daughter, Cellie, who, just like her older twin brother, had a head of dark hair, but eyes that looked like they'd be Lia's shade.

She already had me wrapped around her little finger.

The twins had been a surprise, the pregnancy not planned, but they were the best kind of shock, the kind that made you feel whole in every single way.

God, I didn't think my heart could have gotten fuller after finally making Lia mine and starting a family with her with Caleb, but here we were, all these years later and everything feeling like it was absolutely the way it should be.

I lifted my head and stared at Lia. She wasn't just my wife, my soulmate, my best friend, or the mother of my three children. She was my absolute, without fault, everything.

My everything.

And as I stared at her holding our oldest, Caleb, both of them snuggled together as they slept, Caleb so big already that he would soon tower over his mother in the next couple of years, I felt myself smile. He might be the oldest, but he was, and would forever be, a mama's boy, and didn't that just make me smile even more.

I looked back down at Abel and Cellie, the twins sleeping soundly, at least until they roused because they were hungry; but right now, in this moment, with the stillness and quiet surrounding them, I could just let myself go and know that everything would be okay.

Because these four people in the room with me were my world and I'd do everything in my power to make sure they were always safe and protected.

They'd never doubt how loved they were.

SNAPSHOT
BY MARLEY VALENTINE

CHAPTER ONE

BLAKE
BEFORE

"JUST CLOSE YOUR EYES," THE PHOTOGRAPHER, LIZA, INSTRUCTS. "I DON'T want to put a blindfold over your eyes and ruin your makeup, but the element of surprise is something I most definitely want to capture."

"It's fine," I respond as she takes hold of my elbow and guides me to whichever end of the penthouse the photo shoot is taking place. "Just don't let me fall, these heels are ridiculously high."

Together we walk in complete silence, and I feel my anxiety ratchet up a notch at the prospect of being intimate with a complete stranger.

When the ad to sign up for a photo shoot with a stranger featured on my Instagram Stories, I couldn't help but be intrigued by the whole concept. My friends have been using apps like Tinder and Bumble to try and date and hook up for ages, so it's not like the idea is completely foreign. It's just not something *I've* ever done before.

"Okay, we're here," Liza announces. "Keep those eyes closed, and I'm going to bring in your mystery man."

"I'll be here waiting," I joke, because we both know I'm not planning on walking around wearing a blindfold.

Alone, with my eyes closed, all my other senses work overtime as I prepare for the imminent arrival of my shoot partner. My pulse races at what feels like an unnatural speed while the beat of my heart tries and fails to regulate. To say I'm inexperienced when it comes to spontaneity is an understatement.

I'm the girl who wrote her yearly goals out on a yellow legal pad, and had been since I was seven years old. As each year passed me by, I became more and more determined to have every goal crossed out by the time the new year rolled around.

And now I'm a thirty-year-old woman who gets excited by to-do lists, spreadsheets, daily planners, and conversations about her ten-year plan.

Correction

I *was* that woman. Now… now, I'm not sure who I am.

The sound of loud footsteps coming closer forces me to stop thinking about all the things that brought me here and actually focus on the moment itself.

"Now, you stand here," Liza says, and I feel a wall of solid muscle press up against my back. "I'm going to get into position and then I'll get you two to turn around and meet each other, okay?"

"Okay," we both say, the stranger's voice a deep, rich baritone that strangely eases my anxiety almost instantly. Paired with my imagination, I've now conjured up a man in my mind who is nothing less than a masterpiece of sculpted perfection.

"Are you ready?" Liza's voice is unmistakably giddy, and I can't help but feel the same. "Three. Two. One. Blake, I want you to turn around and meet Rosario."

Inhaling long and loud, I carefully turn on my heels in Rosario's direction and keep my eyes closed for a few beats too long. When I finally gain the courage to open my eyes, I'm hit with a smile that could light up the darkest night and honey-colored eyes that I know with absolute certainty I've stared into a million times before.

But how?

"There you are." His voice wraps around me like a warm blanket, but the recognition in his tone and his words makes me feel like I'm living in an alternate universe.

"Do I know you?" I ask, almost hoping he can somehow explain the familiarity buzzing between us.

Without an invitation, he slips his large calloused hand in mine, his touch warm and inviting, and then brings it up to his lips. Eyes locked on mine, he presses a soft, tender kiss to my skin before answering, "I don't know, do you?"

Unsure of what to do next, I release a shaky breath and turn to look at Liza. "Is this okay?"

Her smile matches Rosario's, and I relax a little bit more. "This is perfect. Just keep talking. Just be, and when I call out a pose, just naturally, if you can, fall into it."

"Tell me about yourself," Rosario says, steering my attention back to him.

My eyes drop to his shoes and leisurely travel up the length of his body, taking in every aspect of his appearance. Just as Liza instructed us prior to the session, he's dressed up. Pressed black pants, a black button down, and a black blazer that fits him like a glove. The whole outfit accentuates the breadth of his shoulders, hinting at the cut body hiding underneath the layers, making it absolutely impossible to question or doubt his masculine perfection.

He's undeniably gorgeous. A head turner. That one man who's every woman's type.

"What do you want to know?" I ask, surprised by the flirty lilt to my voice.

"Anything." Smiling, he shakes his head emphatically. "Everything."

We both stare at each other, the connection irrefutable, even as the sound of Liza furiously clicking her camera reminds us we're not alone.

"Rosario," Liza calls out. "Place your hands on Blake's waist. Bring her close to you."

He's barely touched me and I'm already stepping toward him, my arms wrapping themselves around his neck like that's exactly where they belong.

"So, Rosario," I enunciate, enjoying the way his name sounds out of my mouth. "How'd you get a name like that?"

"It's my grandfather's," he tells me. "Rosario Alessio Ricci, but my friends call me Rio."

I raise an eyebrow. "Are we friends?"

"It's a good start."

"Are you Italian?" I ask, continuing my inquisition.

"What gave it away?" He smirks. "The name or my strapping good looks?"

Biting the inside of my cheek, I try to hide my smile. "Even if you were good looking, I wouldn't tell you."

"Okay, guys," Liza interrupts. "Rosario, I want you up in her space, like you're about to tell her a secret, or whisper sweet nothings in her ear."

In one soft move, he sweeps my hair off my shoulder, and the anticipation of our closeness has my stomach doing somersaults. He lowers his mouth to my ear, and the warmth of his breath causes an eruption of goose bumps along my skin. "You don't have to tell me I'm good looking," he whispers. "Your eyes and your body do all the important talking anyway."

My pulse quickens, and he presses his mouth to my neck.

"Told you," he says smugly.

"Now turn Blake around in your arms," Liza advises. "And just continue as you are. I'm loving how comfortable you are with one another."

We do as Liza asks, and before I know it, I'm completely engulfed by him. He circles his arms around my waist and buries his head in my hair. He's all muscles and man, and I'm stunned at how easy it is to relax in his hold.

I place my arms on his and tilt my head back to rest on his shoulder.

"You feel good in my arms," he says, voicing my thoughts.

"I bet you say that to all the girls." It's supposed to come out as a flirty quip, but an unwarranted hint of disappointment and resignation slips through.

"One girl," he corrects. "But she broke my heart."

The raw timbre of his voice seeps into the huge cracks of my own battered heart. Each word said with a sadness and resignation that only one who has experienced such loss could really understand.

Unknowingly, his revelation feels like solidarity.

"Okay, now I'm going to ask you to pose for a few shots," Liza says. "A bit more staged, a bit more direction from me."

Rosario clears his throat, and I inwardly curse at the timing of Liza's interruption. I have no idea what I was going to say, but finding out about his broken heart suddenly makes its way to the top of my priority list.

We go through the motions, with Liza ordering us every which way, but the mood is now different. The sexual tension is still there. Palpable almost. But now it's not just the lust that's the driving force between us, but the curiosity to know more. To know it all.

A cell phone rings, and Liza stops taking photos. "Sorry, guys. Normally, I don't have my phone on me, but my sister is so close to her due date, and I'm on hospital duty."

Instead of caring about Liza and her phone call, my gaze stays locked on Rosario's. We're now situated on a chair, his legs spread wide and I'm sitting on his lap. My legs are crossed, and the material of my floor-length dress has fallen to the sides, exposing the top of my thigh. As if they belong there, his fingers are tracing circles on my skin, and my arms are wrapped around his neck.

"Tell me about the girl," I say.

"Are you going to tell me about the guy?"

"How do you know there's a guy?"

Looking up at me, he raises his hand and tucks the loose strands of my hair behind my ear. "There's only one reason a woman like you is here in my arms and not at home in somebody else's."

I raise a questioning eyebrow. "A woman like me?"

"You're gorgeous, Blake," he says with such conviction. "I can't be the only person to tell you that."

He isn't, but for some reason, coming out of his mouth, it feels like the first time I've actually believed someone.

"And you got that from all of this." I wave my hand around the room.

"No," he says with a chuckle. "I got *that* from all of *this*."

He waves his hand up and down my body.

When I don't answer, he slips his hand through mine and brings it to his lips, incessantly peppering soft kisses on my skin. "How about we go out after this and I show you just how beautiful I think you are."

"Oh, really," I sass. "So, a man calls me beautiful and I'm just supposed to jump into bed with him?"

He smiles sheepishly. "Who said anything about bed?"

"My bad," I tease, dropping my hands from his neck. "I thought you wanted to sleep with me."

Gripping my wrists, he places my arms back around him. "Oh, baby. You have absolutely no idea what I *want* to do with you."

"Are you guys ready for a bed?" Liza's voice cuts in on our banter as she returns, and we both look at her, confused. *Was she listening to our conversation?* "A bed," she repeats. "For the photos?"

"Oh." I shake my head. "Yeah, of course."

I hop off Rosario's lap, trying to play it cool, and he's hot on my heels as the three of us silently make our way to the other end of the penthouse.

"Do you guys need to head to the bathroom to get dressed? Or undressed?" Liza asks.

Looking over my shoulder, I watch Rosario watching me and think of how I would usually be so nervous to undress in front of a stranger. But like a gift from God himself, this man looks at me like there isn't a single thing of interest around him but me. And I don't want to lose that.

I don't want to forget what it's like to be so enchanted by lust.

I don't care if he's a stranger who feels more like a long-lost part of me. I don't care that everything about this is unconventional and unexplainable.

I came here for spontaneity and recklessness, and no matter what, I never do anything half-assed.

"That's fine," I say, eventually answering Liza. "I'll undress here."

"Perfect," Liza muses. "Rosario, just unbutton your shirt for now. We'll see how it goes, and if you're comfortable, maybe I'll have you unbuckle your belt and unbutton your pants."

A barrage of images flash through my mind at the mere mention of him and I together, partially clothed. My breathing turns shallow and ragged, my blood pulses hard through my veins.

I can't remember a time in my life where I so blatantly wanted a man with such fervent need. I'm the woman who falls in love with a personality first; a typical friends to lovers scenario almost every time.

The physical connection is always the last piece of the puzzle.

But not this time.

Not with him.

Standing on either side of this California King, Rosario and I are facing one another, our eyes daring one another to make the first move.

He touches the first button on his shirt, and I mirror his urgency, reaching for the hidden clasp on the side of my dress. His fingers deftly move to undo the second one, and I begin dragging down my zipper.

By the time his shirt is open, I've slipped the straps of my dress down my arms, and we're both watching the material slide down my body and land in a heap at my feet.

Swallowing hard, I nervously raise my head, and my gaze meets his. His golden-brown eyes are blazing, and my breath hitches at the possibility of being wrapped in his heat.

He shakes his head slowly, almost in disbelief, and in a measured breath his words set me alight. "God, you're beautiful."

CHAPTER TWO
ROSARIO

I THOUGHT WATCHING THE WAY THE MATERIAL SLID DOWN HER BODY LIKE water would be my undoing, but I was wrong. There was no way I could anticipate what lay underneath, waiting for me.

AND IT WAS, WAITING FOR ME.

Blake herself was waiting for me, the exact same way I've been waiting for her. I didn't know it till the moment she turned around, but the second I laid eyes on her, every part of me shifted.

The woman was breathtaking. There's no denying that. Natural copper locks of hair framed her heart-shaped face and fell down in layers to the middle of her back. Her eyes were pools of chocolate I was desperate to drown in.

And her skin…

My gaze appreciatively peruses her body and all the creamy white skin that's on display. The most intriguing parts of her are still covered by an emerald green, lace bodysuit that clings to her every curve. She looks like porcelain wrapped up in the prettiest paper, and my fingers itch to unwrap her. To touch her. Too feel her.

I've spent years of listening to my family members spout bullshit about finding the "one". The Ricci's were known for their rash decisions that had forever-like consequences. We were led by our hearts, the occasionally untrustworthy organ almost always responsible for our choices. My grandparents' and parents' short courtships and long marriages proof of the way it *could* work. And my recent divorce a painful reminder of all the ways it didn't.

But this… I've never felt *this* with anyone.

So in tune and familiar at first sight. Like we'd met before. Like once upon a time, I *knew* her.

"God, you two are killing me with these looks," Liza says, her commentary the constant reminder of where we are, what we're doing, and that we're not alone. "I'm in photo heaven right now. I can't wait for you both to see these shots.

"Rosario, do you want to sit on the bed? And Blake, if you're comfortable, you could crawl to him? Maybe straddle his legs?"

The words alone have my dick stirring to life, and I find myself inhaling a lungful of air in anticipation.

"Do you want me to take my shoes off?" I ask Liza.

"I'll probably cut them out anyway," she responds. "So do whatever works for you."

Kicking off my shoes, I climb up onto the bed and maneuver myself till the headboard sits at my back, my eyes are on Blake, and my legs are spread wide in invitation.

Holding my gaze, she awaits no instruction from Liza, slowly slipping off her heels and stalking toward me. She crawls across the bed with a predatory gleam in her eyes, and I'm impressed. The shyness that I anticipated from her is nowhere to be found, and quite honestly, it has no business here. Not when I feel so connected to her.

Rising to her knees, she hooks a leg over my body, and I watch her slowly descend till the apex of her thighs is resting atop my semi-hard cock, her arms around my neck, and the smirk on her face showing she's not even a little bit surprised at my arousal.

"Now you guys do your thing," Liza calls out while taking photos. "Pretend I'm not here and let the chemistry unfold."

Like magnets, my hands gravitate to her hips, and it takes all my willpower not to slide them down to cup her ass. I drag my gaze off Blake and look at Liza. "I don't think you want to watch me fuck her."

"Rosario," Blake hisses, admonishing me while Liza bellows out a laugh.

"Oh, man," she continues, chuckling. "You're right, I don't want to see that, but if my instincts are correct, you're going to have to work a little harder for it. And *that* is something I do want to see."

She raises the camera, snapping some candid shots of us while we're both looking in her direction.

"When you two are married with a million kids and celebrating your sixty-fifth wedding anniversary, don't forget to send me a thank you card, yeah?"

"So you're that sure," I ask, smiling.

Her face turns serious, and she stops the incessant clicking. "If you two here today isn't fate, then I don't know what is."

I want to scoff. Disagree. Ridicule her observation. But none of that happens. I flick my eyes up to Blake. "What do you think? Do you believe in fate?"

"Not enough to let you in my pants."

"I could buy you a drink, though," I suggest. "After this?"

Her body relaxes ever so slightly into mine. "Will you tell me about the girl?"

"Why? So you can tell me about the guy?" I retort. I hold her tighter and shift her closer, my arms wrapping around her middle, pressing her breasts right up against my chest. "Wouldn't you rather forget they ever existed instead?"

"You up for the challenge?"

"Come here," I murmur. Lightly, I rest my palm on the curve of her neck and raise my head till my lips are in line with hers, my intention to kiss her very clear.

Wordlessly, I give her the opportunity to say no. To look away. But when her eyes continue to hold my stare, and her tongue peeks out to lick her lipstick-coated bottom lip, the small distance between us becomes too much.

Guiding her to me, I gently press my lips to hers and enjoy the feel of someone's mouth against mine for the first time in over a year. It's a soft and delicate union that echoes none of the fervent need that's coursing through my body right now. But it's perfect. For this moment. For this woman. Because as the kiss naturally deepens, I realize the last thing I want her to think is that this is just about her body and me wanting to be inside of her.

Surprisingly, it's only a small part of whatever this is. It's the part I know with certainty that will come easy to us. But everything else, I want to enjoy finding out. I want to peel back all the layers and find out what it is about this woman that has me inside out just by looking at her.

We pull apart, both of us teetering on the edge of more and holding back, because this isn't really the time or the place.

I watch her eyes flutter open and fall in lust with the red blush that's currently decorating her cheeks. *I did that.*

"What's his name?" I ask smugly.

"What?" she asks in a daze.

"Told you I could make you forget about him."

Her lips split into the widest grin, and I've never felt such satisfaction in being the one to make someone smile.

Tilting my head to kiss her again, I'm reminded that Liza is just a few feet away when her phone rings.

"Shit, guys, we may have to reschedule this," she says while putting her cell phone to her ear. "Hello."

Wanting to be ready for my next move, I look back at Blake. "Get a drink with me."

I don't say the words as a question, or a demand, but it's more like the only option I'm giving us, because more hours in her presence is all I want.

"Yeah?" She puts out there shyly.

"Yeah," I answer with conviction. "Please."

Nodding, she surprises me when she leans forward and presses a kiss to the corner of my mouth. "Let's get out of here anyway."

"You don't want to finish the photo shoot?"

She shakes her head. "I think I got what I came for."

Me too.

Just as we've decided to move on, Liza comes back in the room looking frazzled. "Sorry, guys, my sister's water broke and I've got to go."

"That's okay," Blake says. "We decided we'd end it here now anyway."

"What? Why?" She narrows her eyebrows at us. "You're leaving together, right?"

Chuckling, I hold on to Blake tighter. "Yeah, definitely together."

Liza slides a hand in her back pocket and flicks a card onto the bed. "Why don't you two stay here. I was staying here overnight because I had another shoot in the morning, and something tells me you guys will have a lot more fun here than I was going to."

"We couldn't," Blake argues, but Liza isn't listening. She's haphazardly packing up her stuff, desperate to get to her sister.

"Here," I start. "Let me help you pack all your stuff up to say thank you."

Blake looks at me quizzically, and I kiss the tip of her nose. "Just wait for me here, okay?"

Like the gentleman my mama raised me to be, I hop off the bed, put my shirt and shoes back on and wait for Liza to zip up her collection of camera bags.

Without a second thought, I hike the multiple straps over both my shoulders. "Lead the way," I say.

"Thanks for this." She sighs. "I will contact you both in a few days, and if you're up for it, we can reschedule. You guys have paid and there's no way I want you to walk away with a less-than-stellar experience."

"It's okay," Blake soothes. "Worry about your sister, we can work whatever's easier out when your niece or nephew is born."

Her kind words don't shock me, but rather, they add one more thing to the list of reasons it'll be very hard to walk away from this woman.

When we finally make it to the lobby, Liza turns to me and reaches for her bags. "I've got it from here," she states. "I really appreciate you helping me."

"Of course."

"I'm really sorry I had to cancel," she reiterates while walking to the concierge. "But something tells me today hasn't been a total bust."

When she pulls out a credit card, I place my hand on her shoulder and stop her. "I'll pay for the room."

"No." She shakes her head. "That's completely unnecessary."

"Seriously." I drag out my wallet from my back pocket. "I think you may have just changed my whole world. I owe you."

"You know, I do these shoots often, and each time my romantic heart plots out a happy ever after for each couple. It almost always eventuates into nothing. But this, with you and Blake, this could be *it*."

"So it wasn't all in my head?" I ask, confiding in a complete stranger.

"Oh my God," she exclaims, placing her hand over her heart. "Definitely not. Just wait till you see the photos, because trust me when I say a picture really is worth a thousand words."

Liza's honesty, as well as her understanding, fills me up with hope that I can trust myself and the way I'm feeling. That maybe after a horrible marriage, and a shitty year, I can make the leap and Blake could catch me.

Finally, it's our turn at the reception desk, and Liza explains the situation to hotel staff. Without too much hassle, they switch over the credit card details on file to mine so it can be charged upon checkout.

Once we've signed off on everything and said our goodbyes, I race back to the room, desperate to get back to Blake.

I rush in as soon as the door unlocks, taking big, purposeful strides to the main bedroom.

"What are you doing?" I ask, a flutter of panic settling in my bones as I lean on the door jamb. I watch her meticulously step back into her dress and slide it up her body before zipping it up. "Where are you going?"

"I can't do this," she breathes out, her voice full of indecision. "I just don't do things like this. On a whim, you know? That isn't me."

Pushing off the wall, I stalk toward her. "I know we just met, and this is an impossible ask, but please, please, don't walk out that door."

Looking pensive, she chews on her bottom lip, and I take the fact that she's still standing before me as a sign that there's a chance she might stay.

"We can keep our clothes on," I state. "And I can sit on the opposite end of the room if it makes you feel better. But, please, Blake." Needing even the simplest of touches, I step forward and grab her hand, lacing my fingers with hers. "Please don't leave me wondering," I beg. "If you leave right now, every part of me knows I could be missing out on potentially the best thing that's ever walked into my life."

CHAPTER THREE

BLAKE

I SHOULD BE RUNNING FOR DEAR LIFE. AND BEFORE HE WALKED BACK IN here, that's exactly what I was going to do. Any sane woman would walk right out of this room and away from this man. But I can't.

LOGICALLY, I KNOW THE THINGS COMING OUT OF HIS MOUTH ARE impossible. They're too much, too soon. Too… *everything*.

But my heart… my soul. They feel electrified at Rosario's insistence. Everything about him is inviting and welcoming, and everything about that should scare me.

Strangers don't feel this way about one another.

Not this quickly, and possibly not ever.

His hold on my hand tightens. "What do you say?"

"I'll stay," I say, trying to sound way more put out than I feel. "But can we move whatever this is to the living area? Take the pressure off and keep it light?"

I don't know why I expect his mood to change, as if taking the possibility of sex off the table would turn him into a grumpy, unsatisfied prick, but he remains unfazed by my decision to keep my legs closed.

"Of course. We'll order room service and find something to stream."

"And no sex," I repeat.

"Oh, Blake. Baby," he croons, pulling my hand and moving me closer to him. "Tonight is just the beginning."

I raise a questioning eyebrow. "The beginning of what?"

"Of us."

The words roll off his tongue without hesitation or preamble. The expression on his face and the sincerity in his voice add to the honesty of the statement.

In truth, the words are perfect. They're promising. They're words I would've expected and accepted from the man I devoted three years of my life to.

But from this stranger?

From this stranger, they should be comical. Absurd. One hundred percent unbelievable. But even as my mind tries to talk me out of this unrivaled connection, my heart starts to beat to a new rhythm. One made up of two words and a stream of endless possibilities.

Bringing my hand up to his cheek, I lean into his mouth and softly kiss his lips. "You have one night," I tell him. "One night to make me want and see and feel what you do."

Mirroring my actions, it's his turn to kiss me, except his lips linger, and his hands wander, and I almost forget all the reasons why we were already not doing a rough and tumble in the sheets together.

As if he can read my mind, he drags his mouth away from mine.

"Let's eat first," he suggests breathlessly. "Food would be a nice distraction right now. Are you hungry?"

Knowing we need to put the brakes on the physical touch, I find myself leading us out of the bedroom and away from temptation. "I don't know if I could stomach anything right now," I tell him honestly.

"You're not one of those people, are you?" he asks, stopping mid-stride, a hint of worry in his tone.

I straighten my back in defense. "What people?"

"Someone who doesn't eat in front of someone they're attracted to."

I want to dismiss his assumption and level out his cockiness, but who am I trying to lie to? I'm very much attracted to him, but the nervousness… that's new. I'm usually confident in my own skin, doing what I want, when I want. But right now, this isn't me.

This electric current running through me isn't familiar. I've never felt such a kaleidoscope of emotions for another person, in such a short period of time. Especially not for a man.

"Blake." He says my name with such seriousness, it shocks me. "I'm Italian."

"And?" I ask, confused.

"The act of consuming food is no joke," he deadpans. "It's our love language."

There's something about the genuineness in his voice that leaves me speechless. Like the presence of a love language between us isn't odd, or uncharted territory.

Not wanting to argue, I nod softly and tug on his arm, leading him to the sectional sofa. Releasing my hold on him, I lower myself onto the couch and tuck my legs underneath my body. Fiddling with the material of my dress, I spend a little too much time trying to make sure I'm not exposing too much skin.

Noticing the room is a little too quiet, I look up to catch Rosario watching me.

"What?" I ask, self-consciously.

"Don't cover up on my account."

I roll my eyes at him, and he hands me a room service menu before casually lounging on the opposite side. "Is there anything particular you want to eat?"

My eyes gloss over the words staring back at me, my mind finding it very difficult to concentrate on one single thing.

My silence must clue Rosario in to my inability to make a decision, and he leans forward and plucks the menu out of my grasp.

"How about I pick for us?"

Without waiting for me to answer, he reaches behind him for the sleek hotel handset. He presses a button to connect him to the hotel kitchen and then raises it to his ear.

"Hi, could I please put in an order?" he asks the person on the other end of the line. "Yes, a twenty-minute wait time is perfect." He places a hand over the speaker. "Are you allergic to anything?"

I shake my head at him, curious about what he's going to pick.

He smirks at me and winks as he relays a long and extensive list of delicious sounding dishes, without even looking at the menu. It's clear his eyes are bigger than his stomach, because as he continues to rattle off more items, my mind can't comprehend how he thinks we'll fit it all in.

There's currently a flurry of butterflies causing a ruckus in my stomach. Being in Rosario's presence and anticipating the way the night will unfold, I'll be lucky to even manage a salad.

"So, is this how you woo all the girls?" I ask, a little more relaxed as he places the receiver back down, ending the call.

"With food?"

"Yeah."

"It's usually a solid start," he answers smugly.

"You're so sure of yourself." The words are intended to be a slight insult, but the smile that involuntary spreads across my face reveals I have absolutely no problem with Rosario's cockiness.

"You don't seem to mind," he says with a matching grin.

Shrugging, I feign nonchalance. "It's somewhat impressive."

"Oh, really?" He scoots across the length of the couch and grabs my feet, dragging my legs from under my body. "Just somewhat, huh?"

"I thought we were taking it slow," I squeal.

"Your clothes are still on." He drapes my legs over his and slips his hands underneath my dress, his fingertips ghosting along my skin. "That's the definition of slow."

My breath catches at his touch, a delicious shiver racing through me that doesn't go unnoticed. "Tell me what you'd do," I say boldly, completely disregarding the distance I was so eager to put between us only moments ago. "If we were moving at your pace, what would you do first?"

"Blake," he warns. "You're playing with fire."

"Tell me," I repeat, my voice thick with need.

His hands slide farther up my dress, gripping my hips. "You're too far away from me for this conversation to happen."

Effortlessly, he maneuvers me onto his lap, till my thighs are straddling his, and my dress is falling around us, hiding the way my lace-covered center grazes the length of the thickening bulge in his pants.

He hisses at the contact, and it takes everything in me not to shamelessly rub myself against him. Rosario's eyes bore into mine, and he swallows hard, the effort of his self-control noticeable in all his features.

"If we weren't going slow, you'd be sitting on me, naked" he starts, his voice low and gravelly. "I'd start by kissing you." He raises a hand to my face, his palm on my cheek, his thumb tracing the shape of my mouth. "I would start off slow," he teases. "Light, soft pecks. Over and over," he continues. "Then I'd deepen the kiss. Slide my tongue between these beautiful, plush lips."

I swallow hard, and his eyes drop to my neck. He brushes his knuckles down the column of my throat and across my collarbone while continuing with his verbal foreplay.

"I'd kiss every inch of your skin," he tells me. "Down the valley of your tits." His fingers dip in the exact place he's just mentioned, and my skin pebbles in goose bumps. "Then I'd spend a decent amount of time licking your nipples."

His gaze flicks back up to mine as he brings his hands to my covered breasts and cups them gently. His thumbs draw whisper-soft circles over my nipples, and even through the padded layers, I can feel them harden under his light touch.

Holding his stare, I exhale loudly while my body shamelessly shudders in arousal. My hips shift involuntarily, and I'm dragging myself along Rosario's obvious erection, desperate for some kind of friction.

"You're imagining it aren't you," he breathes, his eyes still locked on mine, his hands now finding purchase underneath my dress.

"I wouldn't stop," he admits, gripping my thighs. "My mouth would be all over you while my fingers… fuck." My breathing quickens when his hands still at the apex of my thighs. Splayed against my heated skin, he feels so close, but just not close enough. "I'd drive you fucking crazy with my fingers, sliding them inside of you," he says huskily.

His words are dipped in sex, and every part of me struggles to remain still and unaffected. The salacious smirk on Rosario's face tells me he knows he's got me right where he wants me. And there's no one else to blame but myself. I said I wanted to take it slow, but when he threw the bait, there wasn't any other option in my mind but to take it.

Who was I kidding? I needed to feel this man. Feel him soon. Feel his large, capable hands on me and in me.

"Do you want to know what comes next?" he asks, his fingers teasing the edge of my panties, his mouth now right by my ear. "Do you want to hear about how I would kiss my way down your stomach?" I feel the tip of his thumb gently slide up and down the fabric covering my center. "Do you want me to tell you about how I'd move down your body till my tongue met my fingers and I fuck your pussy with both?"

"Rio," I pant, letting my head fall back in resignation and my body slowly rub against his, wanting more. "Please."

The plea slips past my lips and past my remaining defenses. It's been so long since I've felt this turned on.

A long time since I felt so wanted.

A long time since I felt so irresistible

A long time since I felt so *alive*.

"Please what, Blake?" he asks, leaning back and looking at me knowingly

"Fuck me," I blurt out, my eyes stuck on his. "Please."

His mouth descends on mine, dropping a punishing kiss before murmuring, "All you had to do was ask."

We rise up off the couch, my legs wrapped around his waist, and his arms securing me close. We're two steps in when there's a quick knock on the door, followed by a muffled voice calling out, "Room service."

"Fuck" he grits out. Still holding me in his arms, he changes direction and heads for the door.

"Oh my God, Rio, what are you doing?" I squeal as he swings the door open.

The waiter is a young man no older than twenty. His eyes widen as he takes us in; me holding on to this man like a monkey, our intentions very much evident.

"Uh, you ordered room service?" he questions, probably wondering why we ordered food if we had no plans to eat it.

"Yeah," Rio confirms, stepping us out of the doorway. "Just leave it in the middle of the room." The waiter pushes the large trolley past us, the mixed smell of hot, cooked food wafting behind and permeating the air.

He offers a soft nod as he heads back to the door.

"Shit," I whisper into Rio's ear. "He needs a tip."

Not as quiet as I thought I was, the young man looks over his shoulder like he's heard me. "It's okay. You guys just get back to whatever it is you were doing."

Embarrassed, I bury my head in the crook of Rio's neck, desperate to hear the sound of the door closing behind the waiter. When the lock clicks, I chance looking back up at

Rio and try to untangle myself from him, expecting to have lost him to the interruption, but his grip on me tightens; his eyes still with me. Still blazing with desire.

"You still want this, don't you?"

There's something reassuring about a man who takes the time to check in. About a man who can push his needs aside to make sure I'm okay. To make sure we're still on the same page.

Moved by his gesture, I nod. Because I do want this. I don't care if it's fast or weird or unexplainable. I want to feel it.

All of it.

As soon as I give him my consent, he squeezes me to him and takes us both back to the bedroom. When we reach the edge of the bed, he raises his knee to the mattress, and as if I weigh nothing, deposits me gently in the middle.

Determined not to waste a single second, his hands leave my body and reach for the buttons on his shirt. My eyes zero in on his movements, the way he expertly undresses himself. And with each sliver of skin he exposes, the more I know I've made the right decision.

I want this man, and I'm not wasting any more time in my own head trying to tell myself otherwise.

Rising to my knees, I have the desperate urge to meet him halfway. Like I want to do my part, so we can get to the touching and kissing quicker.

Hooking a finger underneath the strap of my dress, I slide it off my shoulder, letting it fall down my arm. At the sound of the sharp intake of his breath, I do the same thing to the other side and raise my eyes to meet his.

He's shirtless now, the extent of his strength as plain as day. He's all dips and definition, and I want nothing more than to run my hands all over him. But surprisingly, it's not his body that pushes me over the edge. No. It's his eyes that make me want to take the leap. Brown pools of hunger and need encourage me. Goad me. Make me feel bold.

"Watch me," I say, sliding the dress down my body. "Watch me strip for you."

CHAPTER FOUR
ROSARIO

THE TABLES ARE TURNED, HER WORDS MORE OF A DEMAND THAN A REQUEST, but it doesn't matter because she couldn't get me to look away even if she tried.

Standing in front of her, I'm at her mercy, my eyes taking in every expanse of skin she slowly gifts me. My eyes take in her lingerie, the second time still leaving me speechless.

Unable to restrain myself, I drag the heel of my palm up and down my stiff cock.

I ache at how undeniable her beauty is. I ache to touch her, to feel her. To get lost in a body that I know I'll never forget for as long as I live.

Her gaze follows my hand, her eyes hungry, her tongue peeking out to lick her lips. She likes it.

"You want to watch me now?" I ask.

"Let me," she says, reaching for the belt buckle of my pants.

"Please do." I cup one of her lace-covered breasts, running my thumb over the visible creamy swell. A loud groan leaves my mouth when she expertly slips her hand into my briefs and wraps her delicate fingers around my length.

Hooking a finger into the cup of the built-in bra, I tug at it, watching her bountiful breast spill out. Desperate to taste her, I lower my head to her nipple, capturing the stiff peak with my mouth, licking and sucking just as her hand begins to glide up and down my dick.

She lets out the softest whimper, and I mirror my actions on the other breast, wanting to be the reason for her every sound.

She continues to stroke me, her hands moving faster. "Slow it down, baby," I murmur against her skin. "I have so much more I want to do to you before this ends."

I reluctantly drag my mouth away from her breasts and move up her body. Trailing my tongue past her collarbone and up the length of her neck. When I finally press my lips to hers, it's nothing like the soft, introductory-like kisses we've shared before.

This kiss lacks the reservation from earlier. Blake's no longer shy, and I'm no longer scared my eagerness will chase her away. Our tongues move to a familiar rhythm, leading and following. Giving and taking. Talking and listening. I kiss her with worry and want, and she kisses me back with reassurance and desperation.

Raising a knee to the mattress, I wrap an arm around her and lower us both gently till her back hits the bed and my body is hovering over hers.

Her hands move from my pants and up my torso. She rests them on my shoulders before moving down my arms and back up again, her touch reverent and exploratory.

I take my time kissing her while she takes her time touching me, neither of us wanting to rush this moment. We're in sync, and the pounding beat of my heart tells me it's more than just our bodies.

Together, we deepen the kiss, and her legs wrap around my waist, wanting me closer. Using all my strength, I scoop her into my arms and move us farther up the bed. I lower myself onto her, her breasts pressing into my chest, my hard cock straining against her center.

Slowly, I grind into her, a delicious torture that has me wanting to devour and savor her all at the same time. The fear of never having this with her again taunts my subconscious, driving my every touch, my every kiss.

I move my lips down the length of her body, pressing open-mouthed kisses along every inch of her skin. Just like I promised, I lick down the valley of her breasts while my thumbs strum her nipples. My tongue joins my fingers, and she moans softly, writhing beneath me. Having her unravel at my touch, mixed with the anticipation of what's to come, hardens my cock to an unbearable stretch. I can't wait to be inside her.

"I want you," she pants, reading my mind, and those three words send me into overdrive.

She wants this.

She wants me.

And I *need* her.

I need this, and I'm desperate to sear every moment I have with her into my memory, because while I know I feel something more, I also know that I have a life outside these walls that doesn't care about lust and chemistry and connection.

Right now, we're two people with complicated pasts, who owe one another nothing more than this moment. It's a dangerous combination that urges me to take and take and take, because there's a very good chance the world will get in our way of ever doing this again.

My hands eagerly find the rest of her corset and drag it down her body, hungrily watching her pussy come into full view.

My breath catches at the sight of her naked, splayed out before me, and I take a long moment just to stare at her.

"You're goddamned beautiful," I rasp.

I watch her chest rise and fall, followed by a pink blush that spreads beautifully across her body, leading my eyes to her slick center. From her eyes, to her skin, to the way she breathes, her arousal is evident, and my dick throbs knowing that it's all for me.

I tear my gaze away from her pussy and meet her lust-filled eyes.

"Touch yourself," I demand gruffly.

A flicker of hesitation crosses her face before she slowly slides her hand down her body and presses two fingers to her clit. Moaning, she gracefully arches off the bed as she caresses herself.

It's heady.

Being this close and giving her all the power.

Watching her inhibitions slip away as she takes what she wants and gives in to the pleasure. Every part of me knows this isn't something she does all the time. She wasn't one to indulge. She wasn't one to let loose. But for me, she was doing it, and I was staring at her, torn between wanting to watch her fall over the edge, or for me to be the one to lead her there.

Unable to keep my distance, I spread her legs farther apart and kiss my way up one of her thighs. Her body shudders the closer I get to where she's touching, but instead of taking what I want, I turn my focus to her other thigh and drag my tongue over the expanse of her pebbled skin.

When I reach the dip in her leg, her movements slow down. I look up at her and she's eyeing me curiously.

"What?" I ask innocently.

Wordlessly, I move her hand and slip her wet, slick fingers between my lips. She tastes like eagerness and excitement, and I want to drown in it. She drags her two digits from my mouth, and I lower my head to her pussy before she gets a chance to touch herself again.

A surprised gasp leaves her mouth when my tongue connects with her clit, her body coiling with anticipation at the contact. Wanting nothing more than to drive her wild, I let myself get lost in the taste and feel of her against my mouth.

Hands glide through my hair, gripping and pulling at the strands, as her hips buck up against me. Brazenly, she begs, "Please, Rio, I need to come."

"Not yet, baby," I taunt as I slowly push a finger into her tight heat. "I'm not done yet."

Like an addict, my mouth returns to her pussy, needing more, sucking and licking the swollen nub. Adding another digit, I flick my wrist and shamelessly pump into her, ready for her to explode all over my fingers and tongue.

Her legs quiver around me as the slide in and out of her becomes frantic and full of purpose.

"Rio," she cries out, tugging at my hair. "Rio. Rio. Rio."

With my name falling from her lips like a chant, echoing around us, I feel her whole body tightening one last time before she cries out in pleasure, coming and pulsating on my mouth and around my fingers.

"Oh my God," she expels, trying to catch her breath. "Oh my God."

Untangling myself from the lower half of her body, I try to ignore the almost painful throb of my own arousal and crawl up and over her. Resting on all fours, I look down at her, and she throws an arm over her face in embarrassment.

"Hey," I say with a chuckle, moving her arm and bringing her face back into view. "You okay?"

Disregarding my question, Blake's eyes roam down my body, stopping at my hard-on and then making her way back up to meet my gaze.

"Are you okay?" I repeat.

"Are you?" she asks, extending her arm and palming my cock.

Even though I want nothing more than for her to touch me, I place my hand over hers and stop her. "I need inside you."

It's probably the most truthful thing I've ever said, because I do *need* inside her. Not only because I'm desperate to fuck her, but because I need to carve my own little spot inside her, so she remembers me just the way I'll be sure to remember her.

A look of understanding washes over her as she drops her hand. The mood shifting to something a little more tense. A little more palpable. A lot more necessary.

Raising herself up on her elbows, she lifts her mouth and presses her lips to mine.

"Condom?"

Still kissing her, I reach for my wallet, dragging it out of my back pocket and throwing it on the bed beside her. Like we've done this a million times before, our lips are still locked as Blake finds the condom in my wallet.

When I hear the familiar tear of the foil, I pull away and stand to my full height. Naked, Blake scoots to the edge of the bed, just as I let my dress pants and boxers fall to the floor. Enamored, I watch her gaze take me in. She wraps her fingers around my stiff cock, and I feel myself jolt in her grasp. Her thumb circles the wet head of my dick, smearing my pre-come, and it takes everything in me not to stop her. Gazing up at me, she gives me a mischievous wink before teasing my crown with her tongue.

"Blake," I growl in warning.

"Okay. Okay." Laughing softly, she stops and tips her chin up at me. "Taste yourself."

Greedily, I do, just as she so delicately rolls the condom down my length. Ready, I feel her falling back onto the bed, and my lips and my body chase her.

With my mouth melded to hers, I settle between her legs and gently sink myself inside her.

"God, Blake," I breathe out. "I knew you'd feel good, but… fuck."

Good was an understatement. Being inside Blake was phenomenal. It was no short of life-changing. And I didn't care that I couldn't explain why it felt so right; all I cared about was making it last.

Making it memorable.

Making her mine.

Not knowing what to do with the unexplainable need to have this woman, I bury my head in her neck and let myself get lost in her warmth instead. While my hips rock back and forth into her, I kiss and taste every stretch of skin within reach, my lips refusing to break the connection and my body begging to make it last.

Wordlessly, Blake hooks her legs around my waist, and we fall into a wordless rhythm of push and pull, our bodies tangled in a web of longing and lust that I feel in the echo of every stroke.

"Rio," she pants. "It's never…"

Her voice trails off, the words turning into a breathy moan, and I don't need her to finish the sentence to know exactly how she feels. Because I'm right there with her, having this out-of-body experience where I can hardly recognize myself and the tidal wave of unexplained emotions coursing through me.

Our eyes connect as I pick up my pace, thrusting inside of her, long and deep. I refuse to look away, and from the way she's staring back at me, she doesn't want me to either. I piston my hips almost aggressively, panic and greed consuming me.

As if she can sense my frantic energy, she places a palm in the middle of my chest, as if to soothe me. And like magic, it does.

She calms my racing heart and we move in unison, our bodies rocking in a deliciously slow grind that has me wanting to make promises and declarations that have no business between us. Instead, I lower my mouth to her skin, licking her neck, nipping on her collarbone. I let my hand caress her plump breast and tease her hard nipple while my body tries desperately to climb inside hers.

"More," she cries out, her hands gripping my biceps. "Fuck, Rio. More."

"Show me what you want," I tell her, reluctantly sliding out of her and rolling onto my back. "Ride me, baby. Take everything you want."

Effortlessly, she straddles me, one hand around my sheathed cock, eagerly guiding me into her, and the other pressing into my chest. I groan as her wet heat envelops me while the shock that everything I feel for this woman rises at a rapid rate, causing me to grip her hips and thrust into her relentlessly.

With her tits bouncing in my face and her copper-colored hair dancing around her, I'm certain I've only got a handful of minutes before my body explodes.

She's a vision.

She's everything I didn't know I would want in one sweet, delectable package.

A familiar tingle starts to spread in my veins as Blake rises and falls on my cock. Together, our bodies are making memories, carving out this one moment, and writing this single chapter in the story of our lives.

"Fuck, Blake, I'm going to come," I tell her.

I slide my hand between us, finding her clit and expertly rolling it between my fingers, determined to bring us both to orgasm at the same time.

"Please don't stop," she cries out. Closing her eyes, she tips her head back and begins to vigorously rock against me.

"Couldn't if I tried," I growl out. "Couldn't if I fucking tried."

Blake's thighs clench around me, the telltale sign her orgasm is approaching, as I let myself give in to the inferno of heat that's curling around the base of my spine. In a frenzy, her mouth descends onto mine, all tongues and teeth, granting us both the permission we're so desperately seeking.

Our bodies detonate; unrivaled pleasure and ecstasy exploding like fireworks and live wires.

Blake drops her body to mine in a clammy sated heap, and my arms don't hesitate to wrap themselves around her. I want her close. I want her near.

I want very much to do that all over again.

"Oh my God," she says breathlessly. "I can't believe I just did that."

I maneuver my head to get a better view of her. "Was it that bad?"

"So bad." She shakes her head. "So bad, I want to do it again and again and again."

I laugh in relief, grateful we're somewhat on the same page. "Doesn't sound like a bad idea," I muse. "I mean, I'm down if you are?" I look at her, hopefully, watching a myriad of thoughts and emotions cross her face. "Just tell me," I urge. "Whatever it is you're thinking, tell me."

Getting comfortable, she rests her head on my chest, and my fingers trail up and down the knobs of her spine. "It's weird to want more, isn't it?"

"Depends what more is." I respond cautiously, not wanting to get my hopes up.

"Like, maybe, you'd want to go out on a date sometime?"

Taking hold of her chin, I tip her face up, so her gaze meets mine. "Are you saying I convinced you?" She shrugs nonchalantly. "Admit it," I insist. "You want to see where this goes too?"

She presses her lips to mine. "Don't get ahead of yourself. You just have a really nice dick."

CHAPTER FIVE
BLAKE
AFTER

UNLATCHING THE CLIP ON MY MATERNITY BRA, I REST MY BODY ON THE millions of throw pillows supporting my back and rest Alessia on the feeding cushion. She searches for my breast, and I can't help but watch as her head lolls from side to side and her mouth widens desperately, trying to find my nipple.

"Here you go," I coo. "Mommy's got the goods."

Cradling the back of her head, I guide her to me and, like a pro, her mouth expertly latches on to me. Sighing with relief, I lay my head back on the headboard and close my eyes, grateful for the moment of extended silence.

We're almost three months into the mommy/daughter thing and I think we've finally found our groove. No more cracked nipples, no more colicky baby, no more excessive screaming. For now, she just eats and sleeps enough that I can manage to function.

My phone vibrates on the nightstand beside me and I reluctantly open my eyes and maneuver my arms underneath Alessia so I can stretch and reach for it.

It's Chad.

I'll be over in twenty minutes with groceries. See you soon. Love you. xx

Love you?

If I had the energy, I would throw my phone across the room in frustration. Ever since Chad found out I was pregnant, he's been by my side.

The man who, after three years together, broke my heart and told me he was in love with my ex-best friend, came running to try and win me back.

And while I haven't taken him back, I haven't exactly told him to leave me alone either.

The thing that makes this all worse is the only person I miss when I see him is my best friend.

When he came back into my life, I realized I didn't feel a thing for him except sadness. And not because he and I were over, but because he stole my best friend. He ruined everything I shared with her. Tainted my past. My memories.

And while I'm very aware that she too played a huge role in my betrayal, when I held Alessia for the first time, none of that mattered.

Since Rosario wasn't there, she was the one single other person I wanted to share that moment with.

Instead, I have an ex-boyfriend crowding my space and a heavy conversation I'm not ready to have weighing on my shoulders. I cringe every time he's around.

At him. At myself. At *all* of this.

It's a complicated mess of epic proportions, and I'm just too focused on Alessia to deal with it.

My phone vibrates again and I see my sister's name flash, and I feel my lips tip up in a small smile. This is a phone call I'm always more than happy to answer.

"Hello," I greet.

"Hey," she responds cheerfully. "How are you doing?"

"I'm doing really well."

A soft chuckle fills my ears. "The word *really* wasn't necessary, Blake. You only brought more attention to the lie."

I'm not surprised she noticed. My sister Evie spent years hiding and pretending and lying to herself after her first husband passed away. She could spot that type of behavior from miles away.

"How's Lior?" I ask, trying to distract her from me and my problems.

"Good. As Always. Being married to your sister looks good on him."

Even though she can't see me, I roll my eyes and shake my head at her antics. Love looks so good on my sister. It wasn't always easy for Evie. She's lost so much in her life, but hearing and seeing how happy Lior makes her proves that the heartache is sometimes worth it.

I think of Chad.

Nope. Not going there again.

"Talk to me," Evie persists, bringing me back to the conversation. "Lior and I want to come and spend time with you."

"No," I argue, knowing what they really want to do is check on me, and I don't need them to see me and my million moods. Or for Lior to see Chad. "I'm doing fine. And," I add, "I've got Mom and Ray visiting any chance they get."

"Blake." Her tone is all-knowing and laced with concern. Since our father left us when we were younger, Evie and I have always been thick as thieves—a bond not even distance could dampen. While it's hard not having her around, it's also the exact same reason I'm glad she isn't.

I don't need her coming to my rescue.

I really don't need anybody to come to my rescue.

Contrary to popular belief, a woman can take care of a child on her own, especially when she went ahead with the pregnancy knowing being a single parent was very much what was in the cards for her.

I don't have any regrets about Alessia. I have regrets about Chad, and I have regrets about lying to Evie.

But not about my daughter.

"Fine, I'll let it go," Evie concedes. "How's my favorite niece?"

"You mean your only niece," I correct.

"Whatever. Is she awake? Can we FaceTime?"

"She's on my boob," I tell her. "Let me finish feeding her and I'll call you back."

"I don't care about seeing your boob," she protests.

"Just give me a second."

She huffs, and it's the cutest sound. For reasons of their own, Evie and Lior don't have kids and don't plan on having any, but that doesn't mean they don't know how to be the best aunt and uncle that ever lived. They're obsessed. And since they left New York and moved to Colorado to be closer to Lior's family, they're constantly asking for updates and sending her stuff in the mail.

They were here for a week after I gave birth, and I won't be surprised if they come back again under the guise of checking on me, just like Evie implied.

It takes just under forty minutes for me to finish up feeding, burping, and changing Alessia. I lay her down in the middle of the mattress and I lie beside her. Extending my arm, I raise my phone above our heads and FaceTime Evie.

Surprising me, both Evie and Lior's faces appear on my screen, and my lips split into a grin.

"Oh my God, look how much she's grown," Evie squeals. "She's even trying to find where the voices are coming from."

I move the screen closer to her, moving me out of the view while they "ooh and ahh" and murmur between themselves about how they just want to squish her cheeks or smell her skin.

They're ridiculously adorable.

"B," Evie calls me. "Move the phone so we can see your face."

"Give me a sec."

Maneuvering around Alessia, I stretch out and build a wall of pillows around the empty side of the bed and place one underneath my head, getting comfortable.

"Hey, Lior," I greet, realizing I didn't give him a proper hello earlier. "How are you doing?"

A mischievous smile plays on his lips. "I'm really good. Just waiting for my sister-in-law to move to Colorado. You know how it is."

A laugh bubbles out of my mouth. "You two don't really think that's going to happen, do you? I don't know anybody there."

"Mom and Ray would move too," Evie tells me, her voice a lot more serious now. "She said if you moved, they would come too."

"What?" Shocked, I straighten up, causing Alessia to whine. I turn to face her and lower my lips to her forehead. "Sorry, little one."

I look back at my sister and her husband. "Can you two just stop beating around the bush and tell me what it is you're getting at?"

"You don't want to talk about Alessia's dad or tell him about her, so I don't understand why you can't come here and we can all be a support system for you."

"I'm totally capable of taking care of her by myself," I snap.

"That's not what I meant and you know it. Is it such a bad thing if we all live close by and I can see her anytime and she'll grow up around a tight-knit family?"

I know what she means, and I know her intentions come from a good place, but my own insecurities of not being able to do this rear their ugly heads, making me wonder if everyone else can see my failings too.

"Tell me about her dad," she presses. We seem to have this conversation almost every week. And the truth is, it isn't an elaborate story.

I ran out of that hotel room that night faster than I've ever run from anywhere, because he scared me. I woke up and he was just lying there, asleep, and I saw our whole lives mapped out.

The kids. The house. The happy ever after.

And it terrified me.

Rosario is the most passionate man I've ever had the pleasure of being with. The way he spoke, the way he touched.

The way he fucked.

I feel my face heat up at the memory alone, and I have to look away from my sister's gaze.

Swallowing hard, I recall that overwhelming fear that engulfed me when I imagined our life together, knowing just like my relationship with Chad, whatever Rosario and I had could end too.

And I knew without a shadow of a doubt that I wouldn't survive it the same way I did with Chad.

And then I found out I was pregnant and I couldn't find him.

I tried. I asked Liza for his contact details, and when I called, nobody answered, and when I emailed, nobody responded.

What else am I supposed to do? Troll the internet and hope I stumble on someone who knows him?

"Like I've told you a hundred times," I start. "There's nothing to tell. He was a one-night stand, and despite my efforts, I haven't been able to get in touch with him."

I watch Evie give Lior a side look that clearly says, *"I don't believe a word she's telling me,"* but thankfully, he gives his head a little shake, telling her to just let it go.

And, reluctantly, she does, but not before adding, "I could get you a job here when you're ready to go back to work." I open my mouth to object, but she just raises her hand, silencing me. "At least think about it."

I give her a small nod at the same time Alessia begins to fuss. "I've got to put her to sleep, and I might try to catch some z's with her. I'll speak to you guys soon?"

"You know it," they say in unison.

We say our goodbyes, and I switch out my phone for Alessia, checking her diaper and getting her all bundled up for a nap.

Placing her in her bassinet, I press the button that allows it to sway, knowing it will eventually lull her to sleep.

Sitting on the edge of the bed, I watch her in awe and think of Rosario, my earlier conversation with Evie returning him to the front of my mind.

I don't know how other single parents have felt, but it's moments like this when I feel so lonely. I mean, parenting is hard, but that's to be expected and it doesn't impact or effect the way I feel about her.

What it does do, though, is make me wish I could share these moments with someone.

No.

Not someone.

With *him*.

The whole experience has made me irrationally pine for Rosario. Both as my lover and as her father.

The loss aches a little more knowing that he would probably be an amazing dad. He would dote on her and love her the way she deserves.

And then there's Chad. He showed up just as I passed the twelve-week mark and my baby bump was clearly visible. He didn't even hiccup at the fact that I was pregnant with another man's baby, which really should be applauded, but honestly, it just made me hate him even more.

I know he's got a list of transgressions a mile long, but he was almost ambivalent about it all, and maybe it was because he had more difficulty connecting with a baby that was not physically in our arms yet. But something told me he had been kicked to the curb, and he's now scared to be alone.

Or maybe he's trying to pay penance for good Karma. Either way, I'm not here for it. He buys groceries, helps me clean up, but I don't let him go anywhere near Alessia.

He doesn't touch her, bottle feed her, or put her to bed. She is one hundred and ten percent my responsibility, and something in the back of my mind tells me that Rosario wouldn't appreciate another man attending to his child before he'd even been given a chance to meet her. Or even after that. And for an unexplainable reason, I want to respect what I think Rosario's wishes would be.

It makes no difference to my rationalizing that he doesn't even know about Alessia. Because my gut tells me one day he will. It might not be today, or tomorrow, or even next week.

But if the universe could align once, I truly believe it could do it again.

Feeling brave, I wait for Alessia's eyes to close, and with my cell in my hand, I walk out of the room and pull up the number I managed to wrangle off Liza.

I wait for the ring, but like all the other times I've tried, it never comes; however, instead of the recording letting me know the phone is off and the mailbox is full, the recording now informs me that this number is completely out of operation.

Crestfallen and a little defeated, I sigh into an empty house.

I didn't really anticipate ever being a single mom, or having a one-night stand in the first place. And while I don't necessarily have regrets about Alessia, I realize with that last phone call, I probably should have done things differently.

I probably shouldn't have run at the crack of dawn.

Maybe I should have run but still left him my number.

Maybe we should've made actual plans before falling asleep, or I at least should've waited for him to wake up.

I should've given him the opportunity to have a say.

I should've and I could've and I would've.

So many things that I should've done, but now it all feels too late.

Now I have this beautiful little girl, who is nothing short of perfect with her ten fingers and ten toes and rosy red cheeks, and I don't know how to get to him.

It's this moment that Chad walks through the door, and the sight of him turns my stomach.

What am I doing?

My daughter has a father. *Correction. Our* daughter has a father, and she *needs* her father.

Not this man. Not a replacement. Not a half-assed version of the dad I know Rosario could be.

"Hey," Chad greets me cautiously "Are you okay?"

I shake my head at him. "We need to talk."

CHAPTER SIX
ROSARIO

WHEN YOU'RE ALWAYS ON THE MOVE, YOU DON'T THINK YOU NEED ANYTHING extravagant to survive. You teach yourself how to sleep anywhere and know that everyone around you couldn't care less when the last time you showered was.

But as I wake up after a full night's sleep for the sixth week in a row in my own bed, I know it's one of the many lies we tell ourselves to survive that lonely military life.

It's been a long and agonizing ten months. Originally, I was only supposed to be gone for six, but an operation gone wrong added another four months that I wasn't mentally prepared for.

Being a Marine wasn't something I ever had second thoughts about. I had felt the need to serve my country for as long as I could remember, and when I was old enough to do so, there was absolutely nothing that could stop me.

What I didn't anticipate was all the things I would have to choose between and all the things I would lose along the way.

Including my marriage.

While in hindsight I can see my military life wasn't the sole reason it ended, it still played a very big part. Lately, I found myself both resenting it and loving the very thing that defined me. Hating the way it had stolen my wife, but grateful when it became my only consistent companion after she was gone.

The vibration of my phone against my wooden nightstand interrupts my thoughts. Reaching for it, I bring the screen closer to my face, not recognizing the number in front of me. Thanks to an accident overseas, I spent the majority of my time there without a cell phone and only able to contact my family through email.

It wasn't too much of a hassle considering there's usually no service for your cell anyway, and the cost to call home is only worth it in an emergency. When on base, we often get allocated Wi-Fi hours, and thankfully that allowed me to tell my parents and siblings that I was safe for the majority of the time.

But since being back home, my usual struggle with being readily available for people to contact me all the time has been amplified by the need for a new phone and distribution of my new number. The longer I'm away, the harder I always find it to connect back to my life at home. It's something civilians have a hard time understanding, namely my family.

The phone keeps ringing, so I swipe at the screen and bring it to my ear.

"Hello," I answer groggily.

"You're still asleep?" Thankfully, I recognize my mother's voice immediately and don't have to play any guessing games about who's on the other side of the line. "I was hoping you could come over for dinner this weekend. The whole family is coming."

I'll forever wonder why my mother calls to "invite" me, when the only option I have unless I'm away is to attend.

"Yeah, Ma. It should be fine."

"What do you mean? Is it a yes or a no, Rio?"

"No," I tease.

"So, I'll see you Sunday for lunch then?"

A sleep infused chuckle leaves my mouth. "Yeah. I'll be there."

"Okay, good. Now tell me how you're doing. What's new?"

I indulge my mother in conversation, talking about what's been going on while I've been gone while she babbles on about setting me up with some good Italian girls.

"I'm not interested, Mom," I argue, while simultaneously putting my mother on speakerphone and tapping away at my phone till I open the file I'm looking for.

I scroll through the photos that have graced my inbox for the last ten months and stare at the only woman I've been interested in since my ex-wife.

Flicking through the photos Liza sent me of Blake and me for the millionth time and wondering why the fuck she fled from the room before either of us had the chance to talk. Before we even had the chance to entertain the idea of making plans.

It's pathetic and borderline obsessive, but that night, and the memory of being inside her, was one of the only things I clung to when I was away. I haven't been able to shake off how strong the connection was between us.

I've toyed with the idea of possibly looking for her, but doubt is a motherfucker, reminding me she left for a reason, and I still have a whole host of baggage I need to deal with before I pursue something with Blake.

She doesn't know I'm in the military, and a small niggling voice in the back of my head worries that she changed her mind and she looked for me, only to come up empty-handed. Another reason how being a Marine has failed me.

My mind returns to my mother's voice, leaving behind the pros and cons list I seem to always spend too much time making when it comes to Blake.

The sobering truth is that she probably walked out of that room and didn't even give what we shared a second thought.

You know that's not true.

Ignoring the thought, I wrap up the call with my mom, telling her I'll be there on Sunday with bells on.

I continue to fuck around on my phone after she's gone, deleting the majority of emails that accumulated while I was asleep and filing others away for another time. My eyes catch on an email from Liza, the subject reading "Alessia." Since the photo shoot, Liza has kept my email on her database, constantly sending specials and any exciting news she thinks is relevant to her clientele.

Call me crazy, but I've never had the heart to unsubscribe. It takes me back to that moment, just confirming that it wasn't a figment of my imagination.

But something about the subject of this email hits a little differently. It's basically a variation of my middle name. *Did she mean to send it to me?*

Clicking on it, my eyes scan the email, and I feel my whole world tilt on its axis.

Is this for real?

Blake,

Here are the newborn photos of Alessia, tell me which ones you want to keep, and I'll bundle them up in a digital package for you, with one large print.

Thanks for letting me photograph her, she's gorgeous.

Liza.

I read the email again and again, before it registers that there are *actual* photos attached to the email. My hand freezes, hovering over the screen, wanting to scroll down but scared to see. And suddenly I feel like I can't breathe. Like my skin is on fire and my lungs are so full they're going to explode.

Blake had a baby? And named her Alessia? After me?

Overwhelmed by a plethora of unanswered questions, I toss my phone onto the mattress and pace around my room, wearing a hole in the carpet. I close my eyes and try to count my breaths before I send myself into a panic attack. Thoughtfully, I count to one hundred and then try to count backward. Working on inhaling and exhaling slowly.

How did this happen?

"Okay. You can do this. You *need* to do this," I tell the empty room. "You're a Marine for fuck's sake. Get your fucking shit together."

Reaching my bed, I stretch for my cell, grabbing it and going straight back into the email. I sit down, and my leg bounces in anticipation. Scrolling, I press on one of the attachments and wait for the first photo to load.

I don't know what I expected, but a baby that is so obviously mine wasn't it. I cover my mouth with my hand and stifle the strained sob threatening to escape. She's a replica of every baby photo I've ever seen of myself, with her olive coloring and full head of brown hair that's decorated with an adorable looking headband. She's wrapped in a waffle blanket and sleeping so peacefully in what looks like a tin wash bucket.

She's everything.

Sliding my finger across the screen, I get lost in the hoard of photos Liza has sent, my heart aching from how much I feel from just simply looking at her. Tears born of fear and anxiety stream down my face.

I say a prayer to myself. Over and over, hoping this is going to be as simple as me finding them and the three of us just being a family.

Because that's all I want. Everything else will work itself out.

It has to, because she's it for me.

They both are.

THE SURPRISING THING ABOUT TRYING TO LOCATE BLAKE WAS REALIZING we'd been under one another's noses the whole time. Living less than forty minutes away, it's no time at all to mentally try and prepare myself for every possible scenario between us.

I've been sitting on this information, wanting to discuss everything with her before I tell a single soul, and it's been eating me alive not being able to tell anyone about Alessia.

I've cleared my schedule, and I found a little motel close by that I can crash at if I need to.

While there's no denying I want to spend every moment with them, I don't want to overwhelm them with my presence to the point that Blake then feels the need to push me away.

I'm still a stranger, after all.

Once I'd processed that Blake and I had a daughter, I called Liza and reminded her who I was. Surprisingly, she said she never forgot about Blake and me and was sad to see we hadn't reconnected.

When I told her she sent me Alessia's photos, she blanched. Cursing and apologizing for the mistake, unknowingly confirming that the baby photos were in fact of *my* daughter.

I didn't tiptoe around the bullshit and flat out asked her for Blake's number.

Initially, she hesitated, but something eventually made her give it to me and I'd never been more grateful in my entire life.

Instead of calling, I gave the number to a friend of mine who was able to locate her exact address. This wasn't a conversation I wanted to have over the phone, and I didn't want to risk being stood up, especially after what happened the night we were together.

I didn't know her headspace then, and I was certain I didn't know it now. But I didn't know what else to do. I don't want to trap her, but I also don't want her to run.

When I reach her block of apartments, it takes me a while to find street parking. When the car is parked and turned off, I just sit there like a weirdo, second guessing everything I've done up until this point.

Rubbing my hands together, I tug the sun visor down and take a quick look at myself in the mirror. Not really sure what I'm expecting, I give myself a little shrug, flip it back up, and exit the car.

It's now or never.

I open up the notes app on my phone and make sure I have the right place. When I'm on the third floor, I head for her door and quickly knock before I lose my nerve. A whole minute passes, and I can feel the panic rising up in my chest.

Feeling antsy, I make the decision to stay for one more minute before returning to my car. I look down at my watch, and just as the digital number changes, the door finally opens.

I raise my head, and I'm met with a very different, but equally distracting, version of the woman I met all those months ago.

She looks freshly showered with her rosy cheeks and wet hair. She's wearing a loose button-up shirt that swallows her delectable frame and leggings that are like a second skin covering her shapely legs. Even dressed down, Blake is breathtaking.

"Hey," I say cautiously.

Her eyes widen, and I prepare myself for some kind of backlash, but when she throws herself at me, I don't even hide the relief that washes over me as I wrap my arms around her, bringing her close to me.

With her head buried in my chest, her body shudders against mine in one huge sob, and there isn't a single part of me that doesn't want to make whatever it is better.

"Shhh," I soothe, running my fingers through her damp hair. "It's okay. Whatever it is, you're okay."

Not wanting to stand in the middle of the public hallway, I bend at the knees and lift her up in my arms, carrying her in a fireman's hold into her apartment.

Finding the nearest couch, I gently place her down, then go back and close the apartment door.

As soon as the lock clicks, a loud wail fills the room. Blake's body stiffens and worry is written all over her face as she watches for my reaction.

I don't give anything away, even though every fiber of my being is being pulled toward the sound. I stare at her, waiting to see what she does or what she's going to say.

Instead, she rises to her feet and leaves me alone in the middle of the room. The way the hum of her voice immediately soothes the crying baby has me following her footsteps, no longer willing to just be a spectator. I walk toward the sound and step into a beautifully decorated nursery.

My heart tugs two ways, grateful that there's nothing my daughter doesn't have, but pained that I wasn't the one to provide for her.

Blake turns to face me, Alessia over her shoulder while she comfortably rubs at her back.

"You know, don't you," she deadpans. "What took you so long?"

I nod, my eyes darting between the two people who, in a matter of days, have become the most important people in my life.

"What took you so long?" she asks again.

My face scrunches up in confusion. *Excuse me?* "What do you mean what took me so long? I only found out three days ago."

She cocks her head to the side. "So you didn't get my email?"

A little irritated that we can't seem to find common ground, I step closer. "Can we talk about this later?" My gaze moves down to Alessia. "Can I hold her?"

Blake's face softens, and the mood between us shifts. She glances down at the calm baby and then back at me. "Yes. Of course."

With her hand supporting the back of Alessia's neck, she lifts her off her shoulder and cradles her in her arms. I mirror the action and she places her across my forearms.

Emotion clogs my throat while my heart grows infinitely bigger for the small baby in my arms.

"Rosario," Blake whispers. "I'd like you to meet Alessia Rosario."

My head snaps up at her full name, my eyes filling with tears. "You named her after me?"

A beautiful, blinding smile spreads across Blake's face. "Of course. She's yours."

CHAPTER SEVEN
BLAKE

I DON'T KNOW WHAT BROUGHT HIM TO MY FRONT DOOR, OR HOW HE found out about Alessia, but watching him as he reverently watches his daughter for the first time irrevocably changes me.

He might be holding her, but there's no doubt that right now he's at her mercy.

I notice as a single tear falls down his face, and I don't even think twice when I raise my palm to his cheek and let my thumb swipe the corner of his eye.

He raises his gaze to mine, his voice nothing more than an emotion-filled whisper. "She's beautiful."

"Come and sit down," I suggest, placing my arm on his shoulder and guiding him to the rocking chair that sits in the corner of the room.

He's a complete natural, holding her with such fierce protection. When he sits down, Alessia opens her eyes, and I wait for her to fuss at Rio for sitting down, the way she does with me, but it never comes.

Traitor.

Not wanting to be apart from them, I kneel on the floor beside them, and Rio's eyes follow my movements, still somehow managing to peruse my body in a way that makes me light up inside.

Surprising me, he bends his body, careful not to wake Alessia, and kisses me on the top of the head. "I'm so happy to see you."

My tears from earlier return, the relief at seeing him in my doorway unable to be contained.

There's no doubt that he and I have *a lot* to talk about, but right now, I want to indulge in his presence. In this overwhelming sense of security that I didn't realize I was craving.

Seeing him again only confirms I was an absolute idiot for running out on him that day, and not because of the events that followed. But because whatever he and I have was never fleeting. It wasn't a single moment; it was an introduction for the life we could have together.

I can see that now, even if I should've seen it then.

I'm grateful for the small cry that slips from Alessia's mouth, allowing me to focus on something else, instead of all the time Rio and I could've been together if I hadn't run.

"Is she okay?" Rio asks nervously.

"She's fine," I reassure him. Considering the time and the heaviness of my breasts, I know it's time for her to eat. "It's just feeding time."

"Oh."

I can't help but laugh at the disappointment in his voice. "I promise you'll get to hold her after. Let's go sit out in the living room."

Standing up, I put my arms out for Alessia, who's crying has now gotten significantly louder. Carefully, he hands her to me, and we both walk out of the room and settle on the large, suede three-seater.

I begin to unbutton my shirt when Rio clears his throat. "Do you want me to leave?"

"What?" I ask, completely oblivious to his question.

"So you can…" He uses his hands to gesture to my breasts. "So you can feed her?"

Amused, I raise an eyebrow at him. "Does breastfeeding make you feel uncomfortable?"

He shakes his head vehemently. "No, not at all. I just want to make sure you're not uncomfortable with me in your space."

"I'm glad you're here," I admit honestly. "Am I allowed to say that?"

"You should always say exactly how you're feeling." Nervously, he rubs a hand across the back of his neck. "Does that mean I can ask why you didn't tell me? About Alessia?"

Continuing to undress, I keep myself busy while trying to find the right words to say. Pulling the front of my maternity bra down, I angle Alessia's head till she effortlessly latches onto my nipple and then look back up at Rio.

When our eyes meet, he swallows hard, as if he's trying to push down his emotions, except there's no use, they're written all over his face.

Fear. Worry. Adoration. Love.

"I tried to contact you. Got your number and email address off Liza but…" I give him a shrug, trying to rid myself of the guilt that maybe I should've tried harder. "Your phone was never on. I couldn't leave a message. I texted and emailed, and I never got a response." My voice waivers as those horrible feelings of rejection return. "Time moves so fast, and before I knew it, she was here and I kinda didn't have time to find you."

Sighing, he scoots closer to me, grabbing my free hand and squeezing it. "If you hadn't run from the hotel, I could've told you I'm a Marine."

"Like in the military?" I interrupt.

He chuckles. "Yeah. Is there another type of Marine?"

"Sorry, that's just not what I was expecting you to say."

"Normally, I have my phone with me when I'm deployed, and when I get cell service or Wi-Fi, I can use it, but there was an incident and the phone was a casualty and it wasn't a priority to get a new one," he explains. "And I never received an email from you," he says with such certainty. "Had I known there was someone trying to get in contact with me, I would've made more of an effort. If you gave me even a sliver of hope that we had a chance, I would've never fucked that up."

Not ready to pick apart all the reasons why I left and all the ways technology actually made this situation harder, I focus on the other details. The ones that will impact my daughter in years to come.

"So, you were deployed?"

"Not straight away. I wasn't scheduled to leave for another four weeks, and I got carried away that night. I don't have any regrets on how we chose to spend our time, but I foolishly thought we'd be able to talk about whether we wanted to see one another again in the morning; when leaving one another was more of a reality."

"And by the time I was ready to get in touch, you had already left," I continue, the puzzle pieces slowly starting to fit together. "I set up a meeting with a PI last week."

He smiles at this new piece of information. "You did?"

"Why are you smiling?"

"Because it means you didn't give up."

"I wanted to," I confess, looking down at Alessia and then back up at him. "I refused to send another email because I told myself that you'd already read it and you didn't want anything to do with us."

His face falls, and it's the reassurance I need to know I was right. In the end, after I got over myself and came to my senses, I was right. Because there's no way a man like Rio would ever intentionally miss being in his daughter's life.

From the moment we met, I knew there wasn't a single thing in this man's life that he didn't give one hundred percent to, and that included, if given the opportunity, being a father.

"Where's your phone," he blurts out.

"Huh?"

"I have a new phone and number. Have since I got back" he explains, lifting his backside off the couch so he can pull his cell out and hand it to me "Put your number in."

Caught off guard, I save my number and return the cell. He looks down at the screen, his face screwed up in concentration. When my own phone pings from somewhere in the house, a look of satisfaction washes over him.

"Now you've got my number. And, please…"

He reaches over and runs a hand over Alessia's head. "Please use it, Blake. Anytime and I'll answer. I'll be wherever you need me to be."

"Okay." Nodding, I realize I never asked the most important question. "Hold on. How did you find me?"

"I got your phone number from Liza."

"But that still doesn't explain how you're here." I wave a hand around the apartment.

"So, she swears it was an accident." Without any further explanation, he's back tapping at the screen of his cell again. When he's found what he's looking for, he hands it to me.

"Wait," I say, raising a hand to stop him. "I just need to burp her and switch boobs."

"Now that's something you don't hear every day."

I can't help but laugh, remembering how foreign it all seemed to me not that long ago. "You'll get used to it soon enough," I tell him.

His eyes bore into mine, with nothing but truth and honesty. "I really hope so."

Butterflies I haven't felt since the day we met begin to make themselves known in my stomach. Tucking my breast back in my bra, I hand Alessia to Rio. "Put her over your shoulder and rub her back."

He drops the phone and follows my instructions. "Like this?"

His movements are slow and careful. His hands so big and protective on her back. *God, she suits him.* "Exactly like that."

Once he gets into a rhythm, he tips his head at his cell, bringing us both back to the conversation. "Pick it up. The code is two, six, two, six."

Doing as he says, I'm surprised to see a photo from Alessia's studio shoot on the screen. My head snaps up, annoyance in my tone. "How did you get these? Liza said it was an accident?"

"That's what she said." As if the thought just dawns on him, he stops mid-back rub, his eyes narrowed at me. "What? You don't think she did it on purpose, do you? So, she knew Alessia was mine?"

"Of course she did. She looks exactly like you. Never mind she practically had a front row seat to her conception," I huff. "I'm of the mind to call her and tell her off for sending these photos. It's one thing to give you my number, but this…" I look back down at the photo. "This feels like a whole different level of unprofessional."

"Just calm down for a second, and read the email thread," he instructs. "She said she wasn't meant to send it to me at all."

My eyes fly across the screen, reading an exact replica of the email I received with Alessia's photos, followed up by an explanation that doesn't seem all that plausible, if you ask me. "So she's claiming it was an accident? And her address book confused Alessia's name for the Alessio in your email address?"

"That's what she said," he supplies. I want to be mad he's not as enraged as I am, but watching how enamored he is with the simple act of burping his daughter, it's easy to understand why he doesn't really care that Liza's intentions aren't all that transparent. "If it's any consolation, when I called to question her, she knew she'd fucked up and was extremely apologetic."

A loud belch, far too big for the little body it came out of, interrupts our conversation, and Rio looks over at me, his face morphing from disbelief to pride. "Holy shit. That was so good." He lowers her to his forearm so he can look down at her. "Huh, *Picolina*? That was a good one, wasn't it? Do you feel better?" he coos. "Are you ready for more milk? Are you ready for more milk from your mama?"

Touched by the way he interacts with her, emotion wells in my eyes and swells in my heart. This is what I wanted for her. This is what I wanted for *us*.

When he raises his head, his eyes catch mine, vulnerable and earnest. "I'm sorry you're mad, but I don't care how we got here. The details don't matter. You contacting me on your own didn't work, so yes, I'm going to be grateful for Liza's mistake. Intentional or not. I'm here now, and I'm not going *anywhere*. I'm not turning my back on her."

The words "what about me?" almost slip out of my mouth, but I control myself.

This isn't about us. Not yet, anyway. It's just about Alessia having the family and love she deserves, whether it be conventional or not.

She begins to fuss in his arms, the constant reminder that there's always three of us in every conversation, and no matter how small she is, her needs and wants will always be the most important.

I take her out of his arms and quickly undo my bra and guide her to my breast. The ease of being able to feed and comfort her sitting or standing absolutely anywhere is my favorite thing about breastfeeding.

"I don't think that's ever going to get old," he says. "Watching you with her."

Knowing exactly how he feels, my heart squeezes and I smile. "So, you're not freaked out by any of this?"

"I should be, but…" He shrugs. "I mean it's different, but I don't think I would say I'm freaking out."

"What would you say then?"

He runs his hands over his face and exhales loudly. "There's so much I want to say, but I don't know if I should."

"You can tell me anything," I encourage. "Whenever you're ready. There's no rush on my end, I'm just so glad you're here and that you want her." My voice cracks on the last few words, because the thought of anyone not wanting her cuts me to the core. "She's your daughter, and the doors for a relationship with her are open. Always."

"And what about you?" He surprises me when he steps closer, his eyes wholly focused on my face, completely unfazed by the baby sucking at my nipple. "What about a relationship with you?"

CHAPTER EIGHT
ROSARIO

THERE'S NOTHING BUT SILENCE AFTER MY QUESTION, AND UNEASE BEGINS to bubble at the pit of my stomach.

Was I too forward? Am I coming on too strong? This probably isn't the best time to ask such a thing anyway.

"Sorry, that was stupid," I say, trying to retreat. "You don't have to answer that."

She raises an eyebrow. "Which part was stupid? The question or the timing?"

"I want to know the answer," I tell her honestly. "But maybe I'm a little off with the timing."

"Let me finish up with this and put Alessia down first." She catches my gaze. "I want to answer that question, I just want the conversation to have all my attention."

Grateful that she, too, is aware of the importance, I feel less uncomfortable by the whole exchange.

"Come on," she says. "This boob seems to have less milk, so it only takes half the time."

Clueless, I just look at her and shake my head. "You know none of that makes any sense to me."

Blake laughs. "I figured. But there's time to teach you, right?"

My chest tightens at what she's really asking, loving the clues that hint at her wanting me around. "Of course."

Eventually, after a bit of small talk about breast milk and milk flow—things I didn't even know would fascinate me—Blake heads to her bedroom with Alessia in hand and me quick on her heels.

Fed, burped, and changed, Alessia is a new baby. It's crazy how quickly the time passes before she's ready to sleep again. There're so many details that go into her routine, and Blake does it all effortlessly, but it doesn't take a blind man to see the toll it's taking on her, doing it all by herself.

She's exhausted.

"Do you want me to hold her? Put her to sleep?" I ask, wanting to show how much assistance I can provide, whilst simultaneously wanting to devour every second available to me with Alessia.

"Do you think you can manage?" she smarts.

"I'm a quick learner."

"You know I'm not judging you on how good of a dad you are?" she asks more seriously. "Especially not when this is your first time with her."

"I know, but I have nieces and nephews," I counter, trying to sound confident and sure, yet still feeling completely out of my element. "I know the basics."

"Okay, Mr. Hotshot," she sasses. "Show me what you got."

Blake hands me Alessia and then eagerly sits on the edge of the bed. I look down at my daughter, placing a soft kiss on her forehead and letting the fresh smell of new life overwhelm my senses.

"It helps if you tap her bottom," Blake advises. "The constant rhythm lulls her into sleep."

"And then you just put her into the bassinet?" I confirm.

"Yeah. All the books say not to let her get too dependent on falling asleep in my arms. But sometimes I just like holding her, you know?"

Instead of answering, I offer Blake a knowing smile. Of course I know what she means, because while this is all new, my attachment to my daughter is immediate. And I didn't even need to hold her in my arms to feel that way. All I know is that if Alessia wants to sleep in my arms, I'm going to damn well hold her until she doesn't fit anymore. Because one day, she won't. She'll be all grown up and these small moments will be nothing but a memory.

Without a care or worry for the time, I get caught up, rocking and singing to her. Eventually, she yawns a few times and her blinks become longer, her body relaxing in my hold. When she seems to have fallen asleep, I look up to Blake to check in, but she's curled up on the bed, fast asleep.

My gaze lazily shifts between the two, my heart and soul feeling more content than they have in almost forever.

Wanting Alessia to be comfortable, I chance putting her down, and pray she doesn't wake up.

Thankfully, the gods are on my side and Alessia doesn't even flinch when I place her in the middle of the bassinet. Looking back at Blake, a rush of pride runs through me that I was able to hold down the fort and let Blake rest too. She needs it, that much is obvious.

Not wanting to leave, but not wanting to invade their space, I consider seeing if there's anything around the house I can clean or wash or fix.

And because I can't help it, in quick succession, I lower my mouth to Alessia's forehead, kissing her softly and then move across the room, doing the same to Blake.

"Stay," she whispers.

"I'm not going anywhere."

"Lie down next to me," she asks, her eyes still closed.

"Are you sure?"

"Please, Rio." She opens her eyes and meets my stare. "Hold me."

She doesn't need to ask me twice. I kick off my shoes and climb onto the mattress. Lying down beside her, I wrap my arms around her waist and bring her close to me. Because I can't help myself, I nuzzle into the space between her neck and her shoulder and breathe her in.

Loving the way she fits in my arms and how she feels against me, the request tumbles out of my mouth before I even have a chance to stop it. "Tell me why you ran."

She turns in my arms and looks up at me. "Because of this." She brushes her fingers down the side of my face. "It's so easy between us. Almost too easy," she says wistfully. "That night was perfect, and I was too scared of what the new day would bring. I don't know if I was more scared that it would only ever be a one-night stand, or scared of the fact that we could have been more."

"I wish you'd waited to speak to me," I say honestly. "I wish you'd let me tell you that I wanted to try." My voice thickens, the hint of sadness in my tone unmistakable. "I wish I were there when you found out you were pregnant. Helped you out during those nine months, read those books with you. I wish I were there for her birth."

With regret in her eyes, she whispers, "I wish you were too."

"I want to be here now," I say boldly. "With you and Alessia."

"I'm scared," she confesses.

"Of?"

"Scared we don't live up to the expectation. Scared that you're only saying you want me because you don't want to lose her." She shakes her head. "For the record, I would never keep her from you. Not intentionally."

I don't say anything. I don't reassure her with empty words and promises, because the truth is we don't know what the future holds. But I do know me, and I know how I've felt every day since meeting her. I know how much I've thought of her.

How much I want her.

How much I've missed her.

"You know those photos we took?" My fingers skate up and down her arm, wanting to touch her but not wanting to overwhelm her. "The one's Liza ended up sending, even though we didn't finish the shoot."

She nods.

"Every chance I get, I look at them. When I was away, it was the first thing I did when I logged on to a computer. And now, finally having a phone, I find myself pulling them up a few times a day and getting lost in those memories." Softly, I press my lips to her forehead before looking back down at her. "You're allowed to be worried about what the future holds, because you're right, so much has happened in such a short time, and we don't really know one another. But I want you to know this. Every time I looked at those photos, I thought about you. I thought about you in past tense. I think about you in the present tense. I think about you in my future. For almost twelve months, without even knowing about Alessia, you have been the only thing I think about."

I press a palm to her cheek and continue, unable to stop this onslaught of emotion brewing inside of me. Words continue to fall from my lips, every part of me wanting to make sure that there are no doubts in Blake's mind that I. Want. Her.

"I know life got in the way, and maybe you not having to endure my deployment worked out in our favor, but I have no doubts in my mind that on both the day we met and today, I am exactly where I'm meant to be."

She swallows hard, her eyes welling up, her face flittering with a plethora of unnamed emotions.

"Talk to me," I plead, desperately wanting to know where she stands.

"It's stupid," she mumbles.

"Try me."

"It's just… it just hit me. That Marine thing. I know it's your job, but I just realized you leaving is a thing."

On instinct, I stiffen at her words, my head remembering the last time I had this conversation with someone and my heart beating in fear at how much more I have to lose this time.

"I don't have to reenlist." The words surprise me, because in all my time in the military, leaving has never been an option. Not even to save my marriage. "I'm finishing up my sixth year and I don't have to—"

Blake places a hand over my mouth, silencing me. "I would never ask you to do that. Not for me and not for Alessia. I know how important your job would be to you, and what kind of person chooses to serve their country. I'm not asking you to make any changes. Please don't think that." She moves her hand to cup my cheek. "What I meant to say was that Alessia and I would worry about you." Her voice is laced with vulnerability when she adds, "We would miss you."

Not that I've ever loved hearing that people are worried about me, nor is it the first time someone has said they'll miss me, but when Blake says it, it feels like hope. Her determination to make sure I know I don't have to choose, is a stark difference to so many other people in my life.

It all feels like the beginnings of a promise, a start of a commitment between the three of us that could continue to blossom.

"I'd miss you both too."

With a small smile, Blake stretches her neck ever so slightly, bringing her lips to mine. It's a soft peck, but it's all I need as an invitation. My body hums as I press my mouth to hers, the distance of the last twelve months closing with every movement.

She relaxes into me and I deepen the kiss, reacquainting myself with her tongue. With her taste. I drag her closer to me, her body now flush against mine. Just like I remember, we're the perfect fit.

"I thought it was all in my head," Blake breathes out. "But it's even better then I remember."

My cock stirs, and my thoughts become a jumbled mess, knowing I should take it slow, but finding it very hard to do so.

I roll her onto her back and settle between her legs. "What's the protocol for fooling around while our daughter's in the room?"

A breathtaking smile takes over her flushed face. She grabs my cheeks and pulls me to her.

"Say it again," she murmurs.

"What?" I go over my words and smile in understanding when it hits me. "That's what she is isn't she? Our daughter," I repeat.

We both turn to look at her, and I find myself absolutely perplexed by my body's ability to still be ridiculously turned on while my mind is completely focused on my daughter.

Welcome to fatherhood.

When I look back at Blake, I catch her covering her mouth, trying to stifle a yawn.

"Hey." I swat her hand away. "Don't try to hide how tired you are from me."

"I'm okay," she lies, wrapping her arms around me, holding me close to her. "Honestly."

"I'm not going anywhere," I reassure her. I kiss the tip of her nose. "Why don't you sleep now while Alessia is sleeping, and I promise to be here when you wake up."

I can see the indecision on her face, so I roll off her to try and make it easier. "Come on, baby. Get some sleep. I'll find something around the apartment to keep me busy."

Her hand finds my forearm, stopping me from moving off the bed. "Stay. Hold me."

IT'S NOT TILL I HEAR THE SOUND OF A DOORBELL RINGING THAT I REALIZE I, too, fell asleep.

When the sound echoes throughout the apartment a second time, I panic that the person on the other side of the door is going to wake either or both of my girls up.

Slowly disentangling myself from Blake and rising off the bed, I quietly but quickly make it to the front door.

When I open it, I'm shocked to see a man standing opposite me. He's a little shorter than me, and of a smaller build, looking more like a lanky frat boy than a man who is close to my age.

The surprised look on his face makes me feel uneasy, and on instinct, I begin clenching my fists.

"Can I help you?" I ask him.

"Um, is Blake home?" He looks at his watch and then back up at me. "I usually stop by after work."

What. The. Fuck.

"Chad." Blake's voice sounds behind me.

I look over my shoulder and the sliver of guilt that crosses her face makes my blood boil.

"What are you doing here?"

Straightening his shoulders, he looks between us. "Is this Alessia's father?"

Not giving Blake a chance to answer, I step toward him. "Who the fuck's asking?"

CHAPTER NINE
BLAKE

SHIT.

If I don't jump in between them right now, I'm almost certain Rio is going to lose his ever-loving mind.

Rushing over to the front door, I purposefully stand in front of Rio, putting some distance between the two men but letting my back rest on Rio's front, hoping he knows there is absolutely no competition here.

"Chad, what are you doing here?" I ask.

When I told him we needed to talk, I took responsibility for potentially leading him on and I told him he needed to move on. He seemed to have taken it well and understood where I was coming from, or so I thought.

"I've been here almost your whole pregnancy, helping with Alessia, and you're going to just act like seeing me is some big inconvenience?"

"Get my daughter's name out of your fucking mouth," Rio seethes.

"So he is the father. This the guy you fucked me off for?"

I balk at his twisted version of events. "Excuse me?" He just looks at me blankly, and suddenly I'm even more irate than Rio. "How fucking dare you come in here acting like you've been wronged? And to come here insinuating that in the last year you and I were ever a thing." I shrug and shake my head. "I'll ask you again, what are you doing here?"

His shoulders sag, seeming to lose some of his earlier bravado. "I thought I'd give you some space, and I did, but I'm not ready to walk away from us."

When I take a few seconds too long to answer, Rio beats me to the punch. "Listen, Chad. Can you give us a minute, please?"

Without waiting for an answer, he steps around me, holds on to the door and pushes Chad out of the entryway, closing the door in his face. When his eyes are back on mine, I feel my pulse quicken.

I can't tell if he wants to fight or he wants to fuck, but there's no denying the tension in the room.

"Listen, Rio, I can explain," I start.

He grabs my face in between his large calloused hands. "I don't want to hear it. Just answer me this. Do you want him?"

"No." I've barely uttered the word when Rio smashes his mouth to mine.

"Good," he growls. "Because in case I didn't make myself clear earlier, we are doing this. I'm not competing with your past. As far as I'm concerned, *he* doesn't fucking exist."

His lips capture mine, possession and desperation in his kiss. Every single thought flitters from my mind, any argument or insecurity I had for why this wouldn't work between us has completely disappeared.

"You. Are. Mine."

Without a care in the world, I throw my arms around his neck, and he lifts me up off the ground. He pushes me up against the wooden door and I wrap my legs around his waist, my usually dormant desire escalating to unbearable heights.

We've fused together. On the same page in every way possible. Body. Heart. Mind.

He drops his hold on my legs, and I put all my weight against the door, while his mouth moves across my jaw and down my neck.

His lips briefly skate past my covered breasts. "I can't wait to have these again."

He raises my tank top, peppering kisses across my now soft stomach. "I love this," he says in awe. "I love that you carried our baby. I love that you sacrificed your body to keep her safe."

My eyes begin to water, a heady mix of lust and love swimming through me.

"You're so fucking beautiful."

Without preamble, he's on his knees, tugging down my yoga pants, followed by my underwear.

"Outside," I pant. "Chad's outside."

His thumb circles my clit. "Wrong name, baby."

He continues to tease the nub, rolling and pinching, driving me insane. "Rio," I cry out.

"That's it," he coaxes, his voice full of pride. "I want him to hear you."

Rio swipes at my center, and I feel myself shudder at the contact. It's sick and depraved on so many levels, but just the thought of having the man who broke my heart on the other side of this door versus having the man who unknowingly put me back together worshipping me on every single level, is enough to have my whole body coiled in a knot, desperate for release.

He devours me.

Just like he did the first time; new body be damned.

His lips. His tongue. They can't get enough. In and out. Licking and sucking.

When he thrusts two fingers inside me, I know I'm teetering on the edge and there's no turning back.

"Rio," I breathe out, gripping his hair and pushing his mouth toward me. "Fuck, Rio, I'm going to come."

With all the precision and dedication of a man on a mission, he feasts on me until my legs quake around his head and my arousal fills his mouth.

I sag against the door, my chest rising and falling in sated exhaustion. He sits back on his haunches, his wet mouth turned up in a cheeky smirk. "How was that?"

The words don't work, laughter bubbling up and out of my mouth instead.

"Do you think he's still outside?" I ask.

"I fucking hope so."

Bending at the waist, I reach for his shirt and drag him to me till our mouths meet. I taste myself on his tongue, loving every single thing about this moment.

Right on cue, Alessia's little cries drift through the apartment. "Pass me my pants, please," I murmur against his lips.

He hands me my underwear. "I think these will suffice. The yoga pants just cover up your beautiful ass, and that is a fucking crime."

"So fucking smooth," I sass. I tug the pants out of his reach and begin untangling them till they're no longer inside out.

"I'm going to check on Alessia," he says while rising to his feet. He tips his chin in the direction of the door. "You can check to see if fuckwit is still outside. But if he's got any sense of self-preservation, I'm going to assume he fled the second we slammed the door in his face."

Rio disappears back into my bedroom, and I slowly thread my legs inside my leggings and pull them up over my waist.

When I finally open the door, I'm relieved to find Chad is no longer on the other side. But there is a piece of paper sitting in the middle of my welcome mat.

Message received. Chad.

I pick it up and head back into the apartment. Closing the door, I lean on it, just as Rio walks out with a sheepish smile on his face and a baby that should still be asleep in his arms.

I hold out the note. "Chad said, 'Message received.'"

"That's right," Rio says, looking down at Alessia. His eyes drift to me and he winks. "Nobody but me takes care of my girls."

CHAPTER TEN
ROSARIO
NOW

"Are you ready yet?" I call out. "Because I don't really want to be late to this thing."

"Oh my God," Blake shouts back. "Don't rush me. I don't want to fuck this up."

Shaking my head, I glance at Alessia, who's sitting comfortably in my arms. "Your mother is going to kill me," I tell her.

Heading for the bedroom, I walk through the room and peek my head into the en suite where Blake is currently changing into yet another outfit.

"What are you doing?" I ask, a little exasperated.

She looks around at the hurricane she's created. "I'm getting dressed."

"For the fifth time?"

She huffs as she slips her body into a tight pair of skinny-leg jeans. "I can't show up to your parents' place looking anything less than perfect," she explains.

"And who said you were going to look anything less than perfect?"

"I'm just trying to make sure I pull off more of the 'mother of your granddaughter' look rather than the 'harlot that had a one-night stand with your son and got pregnant.'"

I smile. "You're certifiable, you know that?"

"Shut up," she whines. "Now help me pick a top."

"Can you please hold Alessia?"

"Rio, I don't have time. *We* don't have time."

"Just humor me." I hand her Alessia and she places her on her hip. I then turn us so we're all facing the bathroom mirror.

"What do you see?" I ask.

When she doesn't answer, I prod again. "Come on. We can get out of here faster if you tell me what you see."

Her eyes roam across our reflection thoughtfully.

"My family," she answers.

I place a kiss on the back of her head. "Exactly. That's all she's going to see. That's all they're all going to see. *Our* family."

Blake runs a hand over Alessia's hair. "I just want it to be perfect."

Looking at our daughter, I mirror her action. "It will be," I promise. "Everything about us is perfect."

※ ※ ※

IT TAKES ANOTHER HALF AN HOUR BEFORE WE'RE FINALLY IN MY CAR AND on our way to my mother's for Sunday lunch.

My family has been dying to meet Blake and Alessia, but since there was so much that she and I needed to do and catch up on after reconnecting, this introduction—much to my mother's disappointment—is taking place six weeks later.

To say my mother was thrilled at the prospect of being a grandmother again is an understatement. Despite Blake's worries, there is no disapproval or judgement from my mother or the rest of my family on how Alessia came to be or that we were taking things slow.

The only thing my mother insisted on was that I show up for my daughter. "I didn't raise a deadbeat father," she'd told me. "I raised a brilliant, dedicated man."

And I did show up.

Every day.

If I wasn't at work or on base, I was at Blake's apartment, learning everything there was to know about my daughter and undoubtedly, slowly but surely, falling in love with her mother.

I hadn't told Blake yet, but there's no denying that's what I was feeling. She is everything I want and love in a woman and then some.

It didn't hurt that she'd mothered our child. The way she was with her made my heart double in size.

The universe couldn't have picked a better mother for my daughter.

We spent all our time getting to know one another, filling each other in on the lives we led outside the four walls of Blake's apartment. The lives we led before.

She eventually told me about Chad, and I told her about my marriage and divorce. It was hard for both of us to dredge up the past, but the truth of the matter is, without it all we wouldn't be here, together, today.

We also managed to tackle the big question of how did Blake actually get pregnant, because I was sure we used a condom and I don't remember it breaking.

Turns out there's a little warning on the packet that lets you know a condom is in fact not one hundred percent effective. Two out of a hundred people will become pregnant every year even though a condom was used.

If I didn't believe in instant love and fate before Blake and Alessia, I sure did now.

I finally understood that all consuming passion that my family was always ranting and raving about, and I had no plans to let her go.

"And we're here," I inform Blake as I turn into my parents' driveway.

Looking over at the woman who's stolen my heart, I notice she's nervously chewing on the corner of her lip. I reach over and tug it out from between her teeth. "You okay?"

"I'm so nervous," she breathes out.

Stretching over the center console, I press my lips to her cheek. "It's going to be fine, and if it's not, we'll leave."

"I'm not going to make you leave your mother's house. Alessia and I can just Uber home. Or I can get my mother to come out. She's got a seat in her car too."

And this was another thing Blake seemed to be obsessed with. Giving me an out. I don't know if it's because she's used to being alone when it comes to Alessia—which I hate—or that she's worried if things are a hassle I won't stick around.

It's our biggest point of contention, and when I narrow my eyes at her, she knows she's put her foot in it again.

"I'm sorry," she says quickly. "I'm being ridiculous. Your mom is going to love us."

"And if you feel uncomfortable?"

"We'll just go home," she answers.

"See, that wasn't so hard." I guide her face toward me and meld my mouth to hers. Kissing always grounds us. Reminds us what we have, what we share, and just how right this is.

We get lost in one another, enjoying the unusual silence from Alessia, when there's a succession of knocks on my driver side window.

Blake looks past me and then drops her chin to her shoulder, hiding her face. "I'm pretty sure that's your mom waiting for us," she says quietly.

Turning, I find my mother with a shit-eating grin on her face, looking at us expectantly.

"You guys can continue making out, but can I please see my granddaughter now?"

Quickly looking back at Blake, I check in before we get out of the car. "If you need *anything* just tell me."

She nods and I lean over and give her another quick kiss, hoping it's all the reassurance she needs.

When I finally climb out of the car, my mother doesn't even bother with pleasantries. "Hurry up, Rio, I've already gotten a dozen new gray hairs waiting for you to introduce me to my granddaughter."

Opening the back door, I unbuckle Alessia from her seat. She's wide eyed and smiling, kicking the air, itching to be held.

The rapid pace in which she grows scares the shit out of me, but it's been an absolute pleasure to watch her find her feet and thrive.

I pick her up and turn to my mother. "Ma, I'd like you to meet our daughter."

She opens her arms excitedly, and I hand her Alessia. "This is Alessia Rosario Ricci."

My mother's face beams with happiness as she takes hold of my daughter, and I know she's remembering the conversation we had when I told her Blake agreed to change Alessia's last name to mine.

Raising her head, her gaze flickers between Blake and me, her smile never wavering. "Now all you have to do is change Blake's last name and the three of you are good to go."

Without a care in the world for our reactions, my mother walks away with Alessia perched on her hip and heads to the house.

I finally manage to look at Blake who's just staring at my mother, her eyes wide and cheeks red.

When she opens her mouth and then closes it again, I almost feel bad at how shocked she is.

But that's the keyword here, almost.

"What? Did something about what she said surprise you?"

"You're not proposing, are you?" she asks, almost panicked

"Not today."

"Wait." She scrunches up her nose. "But you're proposing one day?"

I hadn't thought that far ahead. In fact, my only goal for today was to convince Blake that she and Alessia should move in with me. You know, one step at a time. But here we were, and I wasn't going to shy away from how I felt.

I hadn't the first moment I laid eyes on her, and I wasn't about to start now.

Closing the car doors, I walk around the hood of the car to Blake's side and take her hands in mine.

"If you think we are anything less than a proposal and a life together, then I'm afraid

I've been doing this all wrong."

"Rio." She manages to say my name with both hope and warning in her voice. "You don't have to. I mean, you don't need to."

I silence her with my mouth, wanting to devour all her fears and insecurities and give her nothing but my unconditional love.

"I don't have to," I murmur against her lips. "I don't need to either. But I want to." I rest my forehead against hers. "In case you haven't figured it out, I'm in love with you. I think I loved you the moment I laid eyes on you. But I knew I loved you when you introduced me to our daughter. Naming her after me, and giving me a place in her life before I even knew about her. And these last six weeks." I take a sharp breath, trying to control my emotions. "They've been perfect, but I want more."

"More?" she says with a shaky breath.

"Move in with me? Or we can buy a brand-new house together. I don't care which it is, but I want you and Alessia to be with me always. I'm already committed to time away from you two because of work and I don't want to be constantly missing you two unless I have to."

"Okay," Blake says, surprising me. "You're right."

"I am? I thought for sure I was going to have to work harder than that."

She laughs while sliding her hands up my arms to rest on my shoulders. "You're always right."

"Hey, a man could get used to hearing that."

"Well, don't," she sasses before her face morphs into an expression a little more serious. "I love you, Rio. Alessia and I both love you. So much. You are a man women would kill to have and a father that rivals any expectation I had of you. You're it for us, and I don't want us to be unnecessarily away from you either."

"I love you," I reply on an exhale, not realizing how much I needed to hear that. "Thank you."

"Don't thank me, just marry me."

"What?" I rear my head back to look at her. "Did you just ask me to marry you?"

"Well," she starts, her smile sheepish. "And I quote, 'If you think this is anything less than a marriage proposal and life together, then I'm afraid I've been doing it all wrong.'"

THE END

DOCTOR DADDY
BY MISTY WALKER

PROLOGUE

LANCE

MY FEET DRAG ALONG THE TIGHTLY WOVEN CARPET AS I WALK DOWN THE hall to my apartment. I'd like to say something poetic like, no part of me wants to do what I'm about to do except my heart. But it's not true. My heart is an organ whose only function is to pump blood through my organs so I don't die.

No, this has absolutely nothing to do with my heart. It's something else inside me that medical school didn't teach us. Something that can't be examined. Something intangible.

Whatever it is, it's ruining my life. Now I have to walk inside my apartment and ruin someone else's life. Someone who has loved me, supported me, and been with me for ten years. To say she deserves more is an understatement. But in order to give her more, I have to let her go. I can't be the person she needs, and there's nothing that would show up in my autopsy to make her understand.

After some time, she'll realize I'm right and she'll realize this didn't come out of the blue. It's easy to ignore the blaring red flag above my head when every other aspect of our relationship is perfect. From the time we wake up until the time we go to bed, we talk, laugh, and connect. But the second the lights go out and we're lying next to each other, it's glaringly obvious we don't fit. And it's even more obvious the issue is with me.

I type the code into the door and listen as the bolt disengages. I rest my hand on the knob, and my forehead on the door. It would be so easy to go through with this if I had anything bad to say about Maisy. But I don't. She's successful, beautiful, and kind. There isn't one person in this world who would look at what I'm doing and understand.

Not even me.

Not really.

I take one last breath, turn the knob, and enter. Our apartment is artfully decorated. Modern, yet warm. Maisy calls it transitional. We purchased it for our one-year wedding anniversary. I'm going to miss it, and the twenty-minute walk to New York Presbyterian Hospital where I've been a hospitalist for five years.

"Is that you?" Maisy's sweet and bubbly voice calls from the kitchen.

A delicious aroma fills my nostrils. She's an amazing cook, and it's yet another reason I am an absolute idiot for wanting to leave her.

"Yeah." I toe off my shoes and hang my coat.

"I'm making piccata. Hope you're hungry."

I walk down the hallway into the open concept kitchen and living space. My wife is dressed only in one of my button-down shirts. Her blond, short, curly hair is messy and wild. She's beautiful as she dances around the kitchen without a care in the world. She won't have a problem replacing me. At least not in theory. Unfortunately, I know she loves me with all her heart and it's not conceited to say she won't move on easily.

"We need to talk," I blurt out before I lose the nerve like I've done so many times before.

"'Bout what, buttercup?" She saunters up to me and reaches to her tiptoes, throwing her arms around my neck.

"Maybe we could chat over dinner." I kiss the tip of her nose affectionately. I don't want to be married to her, but I do love her.

"O-okay." Her smile falls and she releases me. "Well, it's ready now."

She serves us our dinner while I pour her wine and myself an IPA. Wordlessly, we seat ourselves at the dining room table. I stare into my food, pushing the chicken around on my plate. I don't have an appetite. If I tried to take a bite, I'm certain my stomach would revolt.

"What is it, Lance?"

I look up to see Maisy staring at me with furrowed brows. I want to reach over the table and smooth the wrinkles out. I want to change my mind and come up with some other reason for my behavior in order to save her the heartache. But it's not fair to either of us, so I push my glasses up the bridge of my nose and steeple my hands.

"I want a divorce." The words come out as though I'm stating how cold it is outside. I've been reciting the words in my head for months, maybe even years, so they hold no meaning to me.

Her shoulders slump and her eyes become glassy. She covers her face and whimpers into her hands. I jump up and rush over, pulling her chair from the table and turning her to face me. She's a slight woman, so it takes zero effort. I collapse onto my knees in front of her and gently draw her hands down.

"Why?" she asks in a small, shaky voice. "Is it because I can't have babies? I'll go back to the fertility doctor, I just needed a break—"

"That's not it." I stop her downward spiral. We've been trying for children for a year now. Secretly, I was happy when it didn't happen. "I wish I could explain it. I wish I could tell you I've found someone else, that I'm a cheating bastard. I wish I could tell you I've developed a drug habit or taken up gambling. I wish I could say anything that would make sense. But it's nothing like that."

"Then what is it?" she pleads.

"I'm not in love with you. Not in the way a husband should love his wife."

She nods sadly and quietly sniffles. "Maybe you're stressed. We could take a vacation. We could go back to Bali. Pretend we're on our honeymoon."

"If you remember, we had a terrible honeymoon," I remind her.

We waited until we were married to have sex and when I couldn't step up to the plate, it caused a rift. At the time, I was certain it was due to nerves or performance anxiety. But that's a lie because we've never been very good in the bedroom. The last five years, we've only made love a handful of times.

"Are you not attracted to me? Is that it? I know I've gained weight. I got comfortable after we married." She ignores my comment the way she's ignores my inability to please her.

"Maiz, you're beautiful. There's absolutely nothing wrong with you. I don't know what's missing between us, but it's something. If it were only me I was concerned with, I'd stay married to you forever. But I don't want to hear you cry in the bathroom when you think I've left for work. Or see the disappointment in your eyes every time I'm unable to satisfy you."

"I know we've had issues," she says in her shy voice that's reserved for when we attempt to talk about sex. "But I can change. I can read books or we can see a therapist."

"You're not hearing me. I don't know what's wrong with me. Maybe I'm asexual or something. Whatever it is, it has nothing to do with your attractiveness. It's not only you I'm not attracted to, it's every woman. I'm broken, and I'm so sorry I didn't realize this before we were married. I'm an asshole who doesn't deserve you."

I've probably said too much, but Maisy has an uncanny ability to overlook the obvious, so I don't panic.

"You're not any of those things." She shakes her head adamantly.

"Perhaps not." I don't press the issue. We had similar childhoods and had very conservative views pressed upon us. For me to open up about my real theory on why my dick doesn't respond to her would throw her very delicately balanced reality off its hinges.

She dries her eyes with the palms of her hands. "We don't need to have sex. We can keep everything the same. We're more than physical urges. You're my best friend."

"You're my best friend too. But you're entitled to a fulfilling marriage. I can't give that to you."

"This is just perfect," she hisses, her attitude changing from sad to angry in the blink of an eye. She pushes away my hands from where they rest on her legs and raises to her full height. "My parents are going to give me so much crap about this. I can hear my mother's voice telling me she told me so."

She grabs our plates and storms into the kitchen. I hear the clank of the china being tossed into the sink, causing me to flinch. I knew her rarely expressed temper would make an appearance and honestly, it's better than her despondency. At least with anger, she'll yell and say horrible things about me. I deserve to be punished.

"I'm sorry. I really am. I wish I were a better man."

She returns to the dining room, bottle of wine in hand. She picks up her wine glass from the table and stomps toward the bedroom. "Fuck you, Lance. You wasted the best years of my life."

She slams the bedroom door behind her. I stand frozen for a long time, listening to her sobs. She'll thank me for this someday. She'll find someone who can't keep their hands off her. They'll make her feel beautiful and cherished. I won't be jealous. I'll be grateful that I was strong enough to give her a gift she didn't know she wanted.

I make my way to the kitchen and clean up. I've ruined her dinner, she shouldn't have to clean up as well. Then, I go to my office and convert the sofa into a bed. I quickly shower and climb under the covers. With the lights out, I lie in bed, staring at the sunburst pattern in the plaster of the ceiling.

I'm going to miss this apartment.

I'm going to miss New York.

Maisy doesn't know it yet, but I've accepted a new job at a hospital in a small town in Maine. A colleague of mine, Shawn, told me his father was retiring and had begged him to move and take over. But Shawn loves the city and couldn't imagine leaving. He was surprised when I approached him the next day, asking if he could give me a referral. Turns out, I didn't need one. Beacon Island Hospital hired me with few questions asked. They were growing desperate.

My salary will be cut in half and the hospital is so small, I'll be the only full-time hospitalist. But it'll get me far away from a life I shouldn't have created. Far away from my mistakes and lapses in judgement.

Hours pass while my mind wanders. I have so much to do and not much time to do it. I'll leave all of our acquired material possessions to Maisy. She can sell it all, smash it in to a million pieces, or keep everything as is. I don't care, but I don't want any of it. I need a fresh start.

Around three a.m., I hear the creak of the door opening. Maisy pads into the room and crawls under the covers. I open my arms to her and she snuggles into my chest.

"You're right. I know you are. But it hurts," she whispers.

I knew if she took the time to really think things through, she would see this is for the best. She would uncover all the signs from over the years and then know how much better things could be for her. She's an intelligent woman, both emotionally and logically. It's one of the reasons I wanted to spend my life with her.

Unfortunately, love isn't enough.

I sigh. "I know. I wish I could take away the pain, but the growing pains are necessary."

She climbs on top of me and rests her forehead to mine. "Will you please make love to me?"

I begin to push her off, so good at rejecting her, it's an impulse. But then I stop. If there's one thing I can give her, it's this. I've changed the entire trajectory of her life. Surely, I can give her the one thing she's always wanted from me. Intimacy.

So instead, I trick my body into responding the way I've done more than once. I kiss her and worship her. I make her come once with my tongue and then again on my dick. I orgasm too, but it's weak and fills me with no satisfaction. For me, sex is like peeing or burping. Something my body tells me I need to do, but I don't feel any particular way about it. It's a bodily function, plain and simple.

When I wake in the morning, she's gone. While I'm making coffee and preparing to leave for work, I find a note.

> Lance,
> Thank you for last night. I spent so long falsely romanticizing our relationship and making it into something it's not. Last night showed me the truth. I paid attention to the way you reluctantly touch me and the way you robotically went through the motions, as though making love to me was a task.
> You're right. I do deserve someone who wants every part of me.
> I've gone to my parents' house for the week. I ask that when I get home, you're not here. I don't know what your plans are or where you're going, and I don't want to. At least not right away. For now, the only contact I want is through our lawyers. I hope you understand.
> I love you and I hope you're able to find happiness.
> Maisy

CHAPTER ONE
LANCE
TEN MONTHS LATER

"DR. MILLER, MRS. PORTER IS REQUESTING YOUR PRESENCE."

I remove my reading glasses, set them on my desk, and look up from my computer to see Boaz, a nurse at Beacon Island Hospital, standing in the doorway. He's a beautiful man. Statuesque, full of hard lines and soft curves. Like the way his sharp jawline meets his tender neck. Or his delicate caregiving hands meet his veiny and muscled forearms. Past me would shy away from recognizing these things about a man, but current me has come to some realizations about myself. Mainly that I'm gay. Not asexual or bisexual. Flaming gay.

"What now?" I ask, digging my fingers into my tired eyes.

"She thinks she's having a heart attack. I showed her that the monitor would alert us, but according to her"—he air quotes—"only a doctor would know for sure."

"That woman is going to be the death of me. Can't we release her already?"

"Sorry, doc. That woman refuses to pass gas, or at least admit to it." He strolls further into the room and plops down on the couch I keep for the nights I'm too swamped to go home. "But if you sign off on it—"

"Fuck that. Can you imagine if she developed a POI? We'd be stuck with her for weeks."

His chuckle is deep and throaty. "Yeah, you're right. I'd have to plan a vacation to get out of being her little bitch again."

Boaz leans back, resting his arms behind his head on the back cushion and throwing his long legs open wide. He has a casual and relaxed air around him. It's what attracts me most to him. He's the polar opposite of myself.

I know he's gay. I've heard him talking to other nurses. If I were further along on my self-discovery and we didn't work so closely together, I might ask him out. It's a recurring fantasy I have that will stay firmly in the illusory section of my mind, but it's fun to pretend sometimes. Especially when you're a lonely man in a new city.

"Tired?" I ask.

"Yeah, man. My brother had an algebra test today and I was up all night teaching him linear equations"

"If he's related to you, he must be smart," I compliment.

"Apparently, I got all the smarts in the family. That idiot's brain is fried from too many video games." He sits upright and meets my gaze with his light brown eyes that are kind and soulful.

"Your parents couldn't help him? Your job is life or death, after all."

He jumps up abruptly and holds his hands out defensively. "My home life would never get in the way of my job, doc."

"I didn't mean it like that. You're the epitome of professional and prepared. I'm sorry." I close my mouth and shake my head to stop my word vomit. Then I try again. "I only meant you seem to take on a lot of responsibility."

"Yeah, well, my dad works long hours as a mechanic. It's a taxing job for a man in his sixties, so by the time he gets home, he's not good for much."

"And your mom?" I pry. I've worked with him for a year, but we aren't friends. What I do know about him is said in passing.

"She died giving birth to Elijah. I was a seventeen at the time and stepped in to help raise him." He lifts his chin in pride.

"That's commendable." I put my glasses back on and stand. "Better go see to Mrs. Porter. If we're both in here, there's only one person she could be bothering right now."

Boaz's eyes widen. "I'm never going to hear the end of this."

We both rush down the hallway. Sidney, the other nurse working today, is nothing short of a bitch. She's very good at what she does, but she has no people skills. If she's left alone with a patient, I'll no doubt be hearing from the hospital administration about her cussing out yet another patient.

***

I COLLAPSE ONTO MY BED, EXHAUSTED AFTER ANOTHER LONG DAY. I DON'T regret moving here, I'm more settled than I've ever been in my life. But the job is exhausting and I'm becoming a shut-in. My time is spent at the hospital or at home in bed. I haven't made friends and my social life is nil.

Despite all that, I'm happier than I've ever been. It was scary to dig deep and admit my truths to myself. I get panicky and sweaty thinking about the day I admit them to someone else, but there's also a twinge of excitement. I want to explore the side of me I've ignored for so long.

After I packed my meager belongings and filed for divorce, I spent two weeks road tripping from New York to my new home. I took the time coming to peace with my decision and forgiving myself for all the hurt I caused. I can't change who I am, and if I'd stayed, I would've prevented myself from the living the life I was meant to have.

After arriving in Brigs Ferry Bay, I purchased a penthouse in the Wolffish Luxury Condos. I love it almost as much as the one I had in New York. It's smaller and isn't decorated as immaculately, but it's brand new and modern with a gorgeous view of Wolffish Bay. The real estate here is dirt cheap and it barely made a dent in my savings.

I'm still a short walk from the hospital, but everything here is a short walk. The townspeople are nosy and gossip, but since I'm a recluse, there isn't much for them to say.

Eventually, I'll get out and meet people. If I have it my way, a second hospitalist will be joining the team soon. The blossoming developments have increased the population, making the job too big for one person. I found the money in the budget and wrote up a proposal I'll present to the board next week.

My cell phone rings from where I left it in the kitchen. I groan. It must be the hospital. I was hoping for a much deserved and necessary night off. Every bone in my body is screaming for a full eight hours of sleep. It was wishful thinking.

The ringing stops abruptly, then immediately resumes.

"I'm coming. I'm coming." I hoist myself up and amble back to the kitchen, answering without looking at the caller I.D. "Hello?"

"Is this Lance Miller?" an unfamiliar voice asks in a professional tone.

"This is."

"Hi, Mr. Miller. My name is Claire Fremont. I'm your ex-wife's attorney."

It's been a while since I've thought about Maisy. I respected her wishes and haven't contacted her since I left the city. At first, it was difficult. We went from speaking daily to radio silence. It was an adjustment I struggled my way through. Occasionally, she pops into my mind and I spend a moment or two hoping she's doing well, but mostly I've tucked her and everyone else from my previous life into a neat folder in the back of my mind.

"How can I help you?"

"I'm hoping you can come to my office so we can talk in person."

"That's not possible. I moved to Maine."

"I see that here in my notes. Brigs Ferry Bay. Is that correct?"

"Yeah. Listen, if you need tax forms or something, I can give you the name of my lawyer. He can help you."

"Mr. Miller, you have a daughter," she blurts out.

My vision tunnels and I feel light-headed. It's not possible. If I had a daughter, I'd know. Maisy is the only one I've had sex with and she's infertile. Not to mention, it's been quite some time since we had sex. I slump down onto the floor.

"You have the wrong person. Maisy and I haven't been together in a year."

"There's one more thing I need to tell you."

"What?"

"Maisy has passed. Unfortunately, she died in childbirth," she says easily, as though she didn't completely turn my world upside down.

"She's dead?" I ask, disbelieving. I feel like I've been punched in the gut. I divorced her because I loved her. I wanted her to experience a full life, and now she's gone.

"Yes. She suffered an amniotic fluid embolism during childbirth. It was sudden."

"No. It can't be." I picture the happy and healthy ball of energy I left behind. I can't reconcile that image with one of a deceased woman.

"I'm sorry for your loss. But you can see why it's important for you to return to New York. Mr. Miller, you have a daughter who doesn't have her mother. She needs you."

"Okay. It'll take some time. I need to book a flight and a hotel." I remove my glasses, set them next to me, and pinch the bridge of my nose. A headache is fast approaching and thinking is becoming a challenge. "A daughter? Are you sure?"

"Yes. Maisy was prepared. She has an ironclad will and your name listed on the birth certificate." Then she adds in a snippy tone, "Much to her parents dismay."

"Her parents?"

"Lane was placed in their custody until you could be reached. I get the impression they'd like to keep it that way."

"Lane?"

"Your daughter, Mr. Miller. Her name is Lane."

"She always said if we had a daughter, she would want to name her Lane after me," I say.

"Looks like she got her wish. Can I expect you tomorrow?" Claire's growing impatient with me. I don't blame her. I'm not handling this well.

"Yes. I'll make arrangements now."

"Sounds good," she says. "Oh, and Mr. Miller?"

"Yeah?"

"Be prepared for a fight. It seems your ex-wife's parents have more money than sense, and very large mouths. I don't think they'll be giving up the baby easily."

The line goes dead and I set it on the ground next to me. I have a daughter. Maisy's dead. I'm devastated at the loss of someone who was once the most important person in my life, while also curious about the baby we created.

I'm a father. I'm the least qualified person in the world for such a job. Maybe Maisy's parents are the better choice. I quickly dismiss that idea. Maisy loved her parents, but didn't have many good things to say about her childhood. She was ridiculed often for being quirky and not the silent princess they had wanted. The thought of my daughter experiencing the same, drives nails down my spine.

Sitting here on the ground isn't going to help anything. I pick myself up and go to my office. I flip on my computer and start making preparations.

I need to get back to New York.

CHAPTER TWO
BOAZ

IT'S BEEN A FULL WEEK OF CHAOS. LANCE HAS GONE MISSING AND, IN HIS place, Dr. Old Balls is back. Not his real name, obviously, but true all the same. Beacon Island Hospital was better off the day he retired with his ancient view on medicine and his sleepy vibe. Hand to God, I caught him dozing off while I was updating him on the status of a patient today.

The best thing to happen to Brigs Ferry Bay was the day we got a new doctor. He stepped right in, modernized the hospital, and in turn, made my life so much easier. Definitely doesn't hurt he's easy on the eyes. He has this hair that's longer on top and shorter on the sides. He tries to keep it tame with products, but after a few hours, he's run his hands through it so many times it spikes up all over the damn place. He keeps his facial hair to a sanitary stubble, same as me. And the man is fit. His scrubs pull taught across his biceps and thighs.

I'd kill to feel all those hard muscles pressed against me.

I'm not sure he's queer. I send hints, both subtle and otherwise. Most of the time he gets flustered and shies away. But then there are the times he watches me a minute too long, or goes out of his way to continue our conversation and keep me in his company. He's either friendly, oblivious, or straight. I'm leaning toward oblivious.

Sometimes I hype myself up to make a move. Or at least be a little more overt with my flirtations, but I chicken out every time. It's a small town and an even smaller hospital. If things go badly, it'll make for an awkward work environment.

Either way, he needs to get his ass back to work. Dr. Old Balls tried to send a little girl home today when she clearly had appendicitis. Good thing I caught her before she left and called in our surgeon.

That's why, after a particularly grueling day, I find myself walking to the ritzy part of town to knock on the good doctor's door and find out why the hell he thinks it's okay to abandon us. There's one good thing about living in this tiny ass town, no privacy. It only took asking a few colleagues to find out where he lives. It's a hot summer day and I'm sweating my balls off by the time I reach his place.

The Wolffish Luxury Condos are nicer than anywhere I've lived. I grew up on the old side of town, where the houses aren't shit, but they aren't like this. The house I live in with Dad and Elijah hasn't been updated since the nineties, but the bones are good. The appliances work, and I force Elijah to keep the grass cut and bushes trimmed. Much to that little jerk's dismay.

I walk into the lobby and see an elevator to my left. A fucking elevator. I guess rich folks can't be bothered to take stairs. I ride up to the top floor and knock on the first door I come to. I didn't get his apartment number, but there's only two on this level, so if I'm wrong, I'll just move down the hall.

I knock and wait. No answer. I knock again and am met with the howling cry of a baby. I know I've got the wrong place now. I start down the hallway, hoping to be gone by the time the mom answers and cusses me out for waking her newborn. I remember those days with Elijah. I woulda knocked someone's head off their shoulders if they'd woken him up.

"Boaz?" I hear someone call my name.

I flip around and see Lance standing outside the door I just knocked on. He's in a pair of athletic shorts and is shirtless. It's the most skin I've seen on him and my mouth goes dry. But it's the baby in his arms that throws me hardcore. I walk back over, taking in how frantic and stressed he looks.

"You have a baby?" I ask dumbly.

"New development. Why are you here? How did you know where I live?"

"I asked around. How's a baby a new development? Don't they have to cook for nine months?"

The baby lets out an almost painful screech and Lance winces. He bounces up and down in an effort to calm, what I'm assuming is a girl, based on the Pepto Bismol pink onesie she's sporting.

"Why don't you come in? My neighbors already hate me without letting her cries echo through the hallway." He holds the door open for me and I step inside.

It's a fucking disaster in here. There are bottles sitting mostly empty on every flat surface. There's a portable crib in the living room, along with a swing, bouncy seat, and changing table. The sink is full of dishes and the trash is overflowing with diapers. Dude is drowning.

"Where did you get the baby?" I ask.

"Well, Boaz. When a man and a woman—"

"You know what I mean. Do you have a wife I don't know about?" I shout over the baby's trill cries.

"Divorced." He resumes his bouncing.

"Let me take her." I reach for the little bundle.

His eyes shift back and forth from me to the baby, looking hesitant. I thrust my hands out again and the baby cries so hard not even a sound comes out. He finally caves, handing her over.

"Hello, miss sass. Got some air bubbles? Let me hook you up." I cradle her in my arms and walk over to the couch covered in pink clothes. I shove them off and take a seat, laying her down on the cushion.

"I have a blanket around here somewhere." He runs a hand through his hair, scanning the area.

"She's not gonna die from lying on the couch for a second." I take her skinny legs in my hands and pump them up and down. After the second pump, she releases a very unladylike toot. "There we go."

The crying stops immediately and I lift her back up onto my shoulder.

"How did you do that? She's been like that for hours."

"She had some gas. That's all."

"Thank you," he says with way too much emotion. Under his eyes are bruised and there's spit up crusted on his shoulder. Dude must be exhausted.

"So, what's up with the baby?" I ask.

"I was married before I moved here. My ex-wife, she got pregnant before I left, I guess."

I got the call a week ago. She died giving birth and now here we are."

I guess that answers the question about the doc being gay. Disappointment churns in my gut. Not that I stood a chance with a man like him, but I'm still bummed out.

"Did you know she was knocked up?" I ask.

"Um, no. It was a shock."

"And they let you walk away with a whole ass baby you have no idea how to take care of?"

"Yes." He swallows hard.

"What's her name?"

"Lane." A small smile creeps onto his full lips. He's smitten.

I spot a blanket draped over the arm of the couch and spread it flat across my lap. I swaddle the sleeping infant up tight, the way I used to with Elijah. "And there we go. A Lane burrito. She's kinda cute for a white baby."

"Ha-ha."

"This is why you haven't been at work?"

"Yep." He reaches over and drags a finger gently down her cheek affectionately. Something about this clueless man being so sweet makes my heart pound in my chest.

"You want me to stick around for a while so you can get this place picked up? No offense, but she's going to contract a bacterial infection with all this filth."

His eyes widen and his mouth drops open.

He's completely forgotten he's a capable doctor who knows how bacterial infections are contracted. Babies make even the smartest men dumb.

"Bro, I'm kidding. But for real, this place is a dump. I'll snuggle the drama queen and you clean up." I chuckle.

"Really? That would be helpful. Those diapers smell. I haven't even had time for a shower in a week, let alone take out the trash."

I lean in, getting close enough to sniff. "Oh my God. I take it back. Go shower, I'll clean."

"But what about…" he gestures to the bundle in my arms.

"She's out cold. I'll put her in the swing." I get up and gently ease her into the contraption. I turn the knob and it starts swaying. "See? She's fine. Go."

"Thank you. Really, you don't have to do this."

"I know." I shrug.

He gives me a tight-lipped smile and disappears behind a door that must be his bedroom. I look around, seeing disaster in every corner. No better place to start than the stinkiest. I dig through the cupboards until I find a box of garbage bags. For the next twenty-minutes I power clean. I've gotten good at it over the years, though I've never tried with this big of a pigsty.

After twenty more minutes, every surface has been wiped down with disinfectant wipes. Lance doesn't come out of his room. I get a little nervous. We're on the top floor, so I don't think he could escape, but maybe there's a fire ladder or something. Who knows? He looked crazed enough to try some shit.

I turn the handle on the door he went into and open it just a little. I peek an eye through the gap and see the end of a bed and bare feet dangling over the edge. I open the door more and see Lance passed out, face down. I stifle a laugh and shut the door. He deserves some rest and I'm free for the rest of the night.

Lane starts to fuss and I scoop her up, knowing she must be getting hungry. I'm assuming she's about a week old, so her feedings must be closely spaced. I take her in the kitchen and make a bottle one handed. This rich fucker has a bottle warmer, which it easier than the water boiling method I had to use with Eli.

I sit down and bring the bottle to Lane's lips. She opens for me right away and latches on. Her eyes open and she stares up at me with icy blue eyes.

"You've got your daddy's eyes."

She makes little noises that sound like moans of pleasure as she sucks down her dinner.

"I feel the same way when I eat," I coo. "When you're old enough and grow some teeth, I'll take you for a steak. You'll wonder how you were ever satisfied with this formula nonsense."

After she finishes, I prop her up for a burp. She belches so loudly, I'm certain she'll wake up her sleeping daddy, but the room stays silent.

For the next hour, we hang out. I show her the joy of Tiktok, and hand to God, she smiles at a cheesy video of a dog who wants to be appreciated. I flip over to my camera and snap a picture. That's probably pretty creepy considering she isn't my baby, but she's adorable and I can't help myself.

"She likes you," Lance says from the doorway of his room, looking almost human again. He has on a different pair of athletic shorts and his torso is covered by a T-shirt now, but his hair is still a mess.

"I like her too." I kiss the top of her head. I feel a little self-conscious, like maybe kissing random babies is not a good idea, but Lance beams at me.

"Sorry I passed out. I only meant to close my eyes for a minute." He holds out his arms and I transfer Lane over to him. I don't want to, I've grown attached to the squirt. But he's her dad and it'd be weird for me to argue.

"It's cool. We were just bonding."

"I don't know how I'll ever thank you. This place looks immaculate." He scans the open concept kitchen and living room.

"Don't worry about it."

"I never did find out why you came by." He takes a seat on the couch next to me. I get a whiff of his aftershave. It's clean and crisp, like the ocean on a cold morning.

"Dr. Old Balls was giving me problems, so I came to chew your ass out." I laugh.

"Sorry about that. I'll be back next week. I needed time to get things settled."

"I see why. You find a daycare?"

"No. I thought about it, but I didn't want Lane to catch something since she's so young."

I nod. "Understandable."

"I found a babysitter instead. I'll have to cut back on hours at the hospital, but I talked the board into hiring a second doctor who starts next week too. Should make things easier for everyone."

"That's good news, doc." I stand up. "I guess I should go."

"You don't have to." He shrugs and then laughs. "Never mind. Go. You don't want to stick around with an old man and a baby."

"You're not that much older than I am."

"I'm forty-one," he says. I already knew that. I asked around.

"I'm thirty-five."

"Really? You look much younger."

"It's my melanin magic. I don't age." I sit back down. "If you're paying for the pizza, I'll stay and help you eat it."

"Deal."

CHAPTER THREE

LANCE

I PASS LANE BACK OVER TO HIM WHILE I FIND MY CELL PHONE AND WALLET. Boaz must've found them first while he was cleaning, because they're sitting on the kitchen island, and I know they weren't there before.

He surprised me by showing up today, but that's not new. He impresses me with his dedication and competence. I'm drawn to his personality and charm. And it's not because he cleaned my apartment and milked gas bubbles from my baby's belly. I've felt this way toward him since I started working at the hospital. He turns me into a bumbling idiot, but he also puts me at ease about my awkwardness.

One night, when I first started working at the hospital, I stepped into the small locker room to change into a fresh pair of scrubs after spending the night in my office. I was met by a nearly naked Boaz. The only article of clothing he had on was a pair of white briefs. Every other inch of his perfect, silky dark skin was on display. I was dumbfounded. Frozen in place. He could've made a big deal of my obvious perusal, but instead he cracked a joke about how close we had become in the span of three seconds and went back to changing, as though it was no big deal.

I shake away the memory and call the local pizza place to make an order for delivery. When I come back, he has Lane stretched out along one of his long, muscular forearms and is talking softly to her. I'm a man who's not immune to the appeal of a man with a baby.

I've only known my daughter for a week, but I'm already wrapped around her finger. She's small, even for her age, apparently getting her height from her mom. But she has my blue eyes and dark hair.

The last seven days haven't been easy. I've never been around a baby before, let alone taken care of one. Google is my bible. Nothing makes feel more incompetent than using a search engine to figure out how to snap up infant pajamas. I don't know what genius decided to put eighty-seven snaps on those things, but if I knew, I'd punch him in the balls because it was definitely a man.

Lane makes a noise at something Boaz says. He lifts her little fist up and bumps it with his. I smile at the adorableness and it strikes me my adoration isn't limited to Lane. It's partially because of the long and fit man who has me off my game, as well.

I don't know what to make of it and it's not the first time he's caused… fuck, I can't put a name to it. Sometimes, he'll be joking around in a way that could be flirting. Maybe he is, I don't know.

Realizing I'm gay is too new for me. I'm the equivalent of a middle schooler, uncomfortable and self-conscious. I'm a fucking doctor. I save lives for a living. Yet here I am, fretting if a man is into me or just being kind.

"Hope meat lovers is okay." I resume my place on the couch. There's an armchair on the other side of the room I could sit at, but I don't want to. I want to be close to both of them.

"There's a joke somewhere in there." He snickers.

"Joke?" I ask, confused.

"I'm a gay man and you just offered me meat lovers."

"You're gay?" I fake surprise.

"Yeah. You didn't know?"

"I don't know a lot about you," I note.

"It's not like it matters. Especially for a guy like you." He peers over at me through a curtain of long, dark lashes.

"What do you mean?"

"I mean, you're straight. You were married. I don't tend to blab my sexuality unless it's relevant."

"Oh, right." Except it is relevant.

"Sorry about your ex, by the way. Even if you weren't together, it must've been tough news."

I sink back into the couch. I haven't had free time or brain space to deal with Maisy's death. Back in New York, I was busy in meetings with lawyers when it became clear Maisy's parents weren't going to give Lane up. A judge ruled, at an emergency hearing, that between Maisy's will and the DNA match, I could take her home.

Although I was the one fighting for custody, I wasn't sure the judge had made the right choice. But now that I've met Lane and we've bonded, there's no doubt in my mind I want her. I need her. She's part of me.

"I don't know how to feel about her passing. She was my best friend for a lot of years. We hadn't spoken since I left New York, but I still cared about her. I'm also a little angry she didn't tell me she was pregnant with Lane. I wonder if she ever would've told me. I'll never know now."

I have mixed feelings that will go unresolved. Perhaps she was waiting until Lane was born to tell me. Perhaps she would've kept her a secret her whole life and I wouldn't have known until she turned eighteen and was searching for her father.

"That's pretty fucked." He slaps a hand over his mouth. "Sorry."

"It's okay. I doubt she can repeat your words yet."

"I've never been good at cutting out the swearing. One of Eli's first words was shit. My dad was so pissed at me." He laughs at the memory. "If I hadn't been nineteen when it happened, he would've whooped my ass."

"I'm sorry you lost your mom when you were so young."

"It was hard back then, but it's easier now. She had an undiagnosed heart condition that caused complications during childbirth. At first, I blamed Eli. Then he came home from the hospital looking like a chubby alien and I couldn't hold it against him."

"Newborns do look like chubby aliens."

Boaz turns his attention to Lane. "Don't listen to him. You're a pretty princess."

"She's a loud, pretty princess." I chuckle. He's so sweet with my daughter, it makes me want to know more about him. "Did you grow up around here?"

"Sure did. My parents moved here after they were married. They thought it'd be a good place to raise a family."

"Was it?"

"Yeah, I love BFB. I want to see the world someday, but if I ever have a family, this is where I want to raise my kids."

"You want kids one day?"

"I think so." He smiles wide and my attention is drawn to his bright white teeth framed by plump, kissable lips. I'm transfixed. "You okay?"

"Huh?" I look away and shake my head, embarrassed to have been caught staring. "Sorry. I'm more tired than I thought."

"It's all good. How about you? Did you grow up in New York?"

"Yes. Well, a suburb of New York."

"Your parents must be proud of you, being a doctor and all."

Lane drifts asleep in his arms and he lifts her to his chest. She sighs, but doesn't wake.

"My future was well planned and laid out for me. I was to become a doctor, like my dad. Although he's a heart surgeon, making me a disappointment for only becoming a hospitalist. My mom stayed home, but not to take care of me. Mostly to volunteer and keep up appearances. It was made clear someday I was to have a wife who'd do the same." I reach over to flick away dried milk from the corner of Lane's mouth, but really it just gives me an excuse to be close to Boaz for a moment.

"They must've been pissed when you got divorced."

"My parents loved Maisy until they found out we couldn't have kids. Then they tried to talk me into leaving her. It's what drove a rift between us and them. I don't ever call unless it's a holiday or one of their birthdays. They don't know about the divorce or even that I moved. They don't know about her either." I tap Lane's nose. "They don't deserve to know."

They'd be especially miffed if they saw me right now, looking at a man and thinking he's the sexiest person I've ever seen. But I keep that part to myself.

"Why did you get a divorce?" he asks.

I blow out a breath. He doesn't know how loaded this question is.

"A few reasons. I'd been hiding who I really was, even from myself. Unfortunately, my moment of actualization happened after I was deep into a life I didn't want." It's vague, but the truth. I can't decide if I want him to meddle. I need a reason to force honesty with someone other than myself, but it's scary as fuck.

"That sounds ominous." He chuckles. "I'm not one to pry… no, fuck that. I am one to pry. What the hell does all that mumbo-jumbo mean?"

"You have to remember I grew up in a very conservative home. Certain things weren't talked about or accepted. People with alternative lifestyles were shunned and publicly demeaned."

"You into some 50 Shades shit, doc?" he asks in a serious tone, but a smirk plays on his lips.

"No, nothing like that. I'm, uh. I'm like you." My mouth goes dry and I feel a bead of sweat trickle down my back. I don't dare look over to see his reaction.

"A black nurse?" He chuckles in that deep throaty way I love, and it's the ice breaker I need to peer over at him. His eyes are glimmering with amusement, taking my nervousness down a small notch.

"No." I chortle. "I'm uh, gay."

His mouth drops open and his eyes widen comically, but none of it is genuine. "I had my suspicions, not gonna lie."

"Really?"

"Yeah. The baby threw me off for minute, though." He gestures to Lane.

"Join the club." Suddenly the fifty-pound weight I've been carrying on my chest lifts. When I admitted the truth to myself, it was astounding. Like my world became clearer and everything made so much more sense, but admitting it to someone else feels like validation. Boaz was a safe choice to be the first, but he was an important choice too.

"Does anyone else know?"

"You're the first," I admit.

"I'm honored. Really." He rests a hand on my knee and gives it a gentle squeeze. "That's huge and I'm grateful you trusted me with it."

"I'm glad it was you too." The room suddenly becomes quiet and heavy as we share in the moment. I'm proud of myself, and his reaction gives me confidence to not hide my sexuality. No matter how anyone else reacts, I know I at least have one person on my side.

The doorbell rings and I startle. Boaz pulls his hand away and I jump up to grab the pizza. We don't mention my sexuality or talk about anything heavy for the rest of the night. We joke and get to know each other better. It's friendly, fun, and exactly what I needed after the heaviness of our earlier conversations.

At some point Lane begins to fuss, demanding her dinner.

"I'm gonna head out. Let you get the little princess fed. Hopefully she'll let you sleep tonight." Boaz walks over to the door and toes his shoes on.

"Thanks again. I've spent the last week drowning. You showing up was exactly what I needed to feel human again," I say.

"This is going to sound weird, but do you want my number? You know, in case you need help again? Or even just to talk."

"Sure. Yeah. It takes a village, right?" It's a platonic offer, but my inner middle schooler is stupid and flutters to life.

"Where's your phone?" He holds his hand out and I dig it out of my pocket. He taps a few buttons and I hear his own phone chirp. "There. Call or text anytime. I mean it."

"Thanks, Boaz."

"My friends call me Bo."

"You never told me that before."

"We weren't really friends before." His chin tips down and he smirks. If I didn't know any better, I'd think it was a flirtatious move.

Then he's gone, closing the door quietly behind him. I expel a loud breath and smile to myself. Tonight was remarkable. I meant it when I told him I'd been drowning. Between coming to terms with the loss of Maisy and becoming an overnight father, life had quickly become chaotic. And not in a good way. Boaz showing up was the mental break I needed.

CHAPTER FOUR
BOAZ

HE HAS A BABY.

He's a dad.

He's gay.

I process it all on the walk home. It's dark now and the breeze coming off Wolffish Bay feels damn good. It's quiet out, peaceful. It's the time of night where everyone in town has made it home to their families. Dad and Eli are probably home and I hope they've scrounged up dinner. I don't feel much like doing anymore domestic shit tonight.

The walk takes a half hour, and I'm no closer to wrapping my head around Lance Miller when I get there. It was a fun fantasy to think about getting it on with the hot doc, but that man has more proverbial and literal baggage than I know what to do with. If I'm overwhelmed at the amount, he must be next level freaked out.

I open my front door and am met with the sound of a blaring TV. I find Dad passed out in his old, worn out recliner. He's got the remote in his hand and he's snoring. The man works harder than anyone I've ever met. I pry the clicker from his hand and turn the TV off. I shake his shoulder until he startles awake.

"What time is it?" he asks.

"Almost nine."

"Where have you been?" He uses the lever on the side of the recliner to lower his feet to the ground.

"A friend's house." I plop down on the sofa.

"What friend?"

"Pops, I'm thirty-five years old and you still treat me like I'm a teenager."

"No matter how grown you are, you'll always be my kid."

"Speaking of teenagers, where's ours?"

"In his room doing homework. Can't you hear?"

I listen and hear the tell-tale sound of loud music. I stand up. "I'm going to see how his English test went today and then head to bed. Need anything?"

"I'm good. You're really not going to tell me who you were with?"

"Nope," I call over my shoulder as I walk down the hallway. Coming out to Dad at twenty was hard and he didn't accept it at first. He didn't want me to have to deal with any more discrimination I was already going to face as a black man. Even if we live in a gay friendly town. Brigs Ferry Bay has become a mecca for gay men.

Eventually Dad came around, but only in a very abstract way. He knows I'm gay, but he doesn't want to talk about it or acknowledge it. It's a very *don't ask, don't tell* relationship.

It's not an issue since I don't see myself ever settling down. I haven't found anyone I want to be with for longer than a week, let alone a lifetime. While it would be nice to not feel like I have to check my sexual orientation at the door, I can deal with it. I have a good life. I have friends, my job, my family, and occasionally I find someone to fuck. Not nearly as often as I'd like, but that's on living in a small town.

I knock twice and open Eli's door. He doesn't hear any of it, because the damn music is too loud. I walk over to his Bluetooth speaker and press the power button. His head flips around and he scowls from where he's sitting in front of his laptop.

"What the fuck?" he snarls.

"Watch your mouth. You're too young to talk like that."

"Whatever." His teenage angst is comical.

"How'd your test go?" I ask.

"Fine." He clicks a few buttons and pulls up his grades.

"A B is more than fine. Proud of you, E." I give his shoulder a squeeze.

"Thanks. It wasn't as hard as I thought it was going to be."

"No, you were prepared. There's a difference."

"I guess." He shrugs.

"Need anything before I go to bed?"

"Nah. I'm good."

I take a quick shower and climb under the covers. It was a long ass day and I'm beat. I wonder how Lance's night is going. It's that thought that has me snagging my phone from the nightstand and shooting a text to him.

Me: Little miss go to bed?

I click on his contact info and program his name into my phone. On impulse, I assign him the name of Dr. Daddy.

Dr. Daddy: Apparently, she's a night owl.

Me: Shitty.

Dr. Daddy: Thankfully a friend stopped by and let me take a power nap.

Me: That's a real good friend.

Dr. Daddy: He is.

Me: I could come over tomorrow after my shift to help you out again.

Dr. Daddy: You don't need to do that. I'm sure you have much better things to do on a Saturday night.

Me: Would I sound like a loser if I said no?

Dr. Daddy: Not to me. The only fun I've had in over a week is earlier when I took a piss without a baby in my arms.

Me: You win. That's just sad.

Dr. Daddy: To be honest, I wasn't much more fun before Lane came.

Me: Well, let's change that. I'll bring over dinner tomorrow and if the babe cooperates, we can play Xbox. I saw your Series X earlier.

Dr. Daddy: It's a plan.

I grin at my phone. I have no business fucking with a man who hasn't come out to anyone except me and is a new father, but I push aside all rational thoughts. This is innocent enough. Just a couple guys hanging out.

AFTER WORK, I PICK UP MY FAVORITE FRIED CLAMS AND A COUPLE LOBSTER rolls from Martha Joy's seafood restaurant. I drove to work today so the food didn't get cold on the walk to Lance's place. After I park, I text to let him know I'm here. If Lane's sleeping, I don't want to knock and wake her up. He tells me the door's unlocked.

I take the elevator up and am happy when I don't hear crying from the other side of his door. I walk in and am surprised to see the place is still clean.

"Hey," Lance whispers from where he's spread out on the sofa. Never in my life has the image of a half-naked man with a sleeping baby on his chest been a turn on. But seeing Lance shirtless with Lane on his chest does something to me.

"Hey." I set the bags of food on the counter. Lance slowly gets up and disappears into his room. He returns seconds later empty handed.

"She go down okay?" I ask.

"Yeah. She's been up most of the day, so I'm hoping for a couple hours before she wakes for her next feeding." He shakes his head. "Fuck it's weird hearing myself say things like that."

"I'll bet."

"Oh my God. Did you get Martha Joy's?" He opens one of the bags and inhales deeply.

"Hope it's okay. Didn't ask if you had a fish allergy."

"I don't, and this is my favorite. Thank you." He beams at me and my fucking heart skips a beat. I've spent a year lusting after this man and here I am, in his house, with him standing inches from me with no shirt on. "Mind if we eat in the living room?"

"Nope."

I close the gap between us and we stand shoulder to shoulder, divvying up the food. When we each have what we want, we take our places on his couch. I could sit in one of the high back chairs, but fuck that. I want to be close to him.

"This is so fucking good," he says around a mouthful of lobster roll. The way he wraps his lips around it, has my horny brain making the leap to other things I want to see his lips wrapped around. I should've jacked off last night.

"I think you're just sick of Chinese and pizza. I'm assuming that's all you've had in a week since they're the only two places that deliver."

"True," he agrees, shoving more food into his sexy as sin mouth. "But it really is my favorite."

"You've got a little…" I reach over and brush some breadcrumbs from the corner of his mouth. I realize my mistake the second I touch his skin. It's too tempting to be this close to his lips. Our eyes meet as my thumb sweeps along his entire lower lip. His pupils dilate and his breathing slows. Hot doc is into me. There's no doubt. And because I'm a cocky bastard, I drop my hand and turn back to my food, shoving a fried clam in my mouth. He lets out a small groan. "You okay?"

"Fine," he croaks and pushes away his Styrofoam container.

"Full?"

"Stuffed," he breathes out.

"Then you won't mind if I…" I reach over to snag a hunk of lobster off his roll and eat it. "You know they use lobster caught right here in Brigs Ferry Bay?"

"Makes sense."

"Remember that patient we had a while ago, Archer? The one who fell off the lobster boat?"

"Yeah, I remember."

"He told me. We've gotten to be friends. He's with Kian now. You know the cute guy who was there with him?" I carry on as though we didn't just have a heated moment.

"He is pretty cute. But I think Archer is more my type," he says hesitantly. This conversation is difficult for him. I remember when I first started surrounding myself with gay men. I'd been keeping my sexuality private for so long, being around people who were open and unapologetic was both eye opening and uncomfortable.

I quirk a brow. "What's your type?"

"Muscular. At least my height. Confident. Secure."

Check, check, check, and check. I'm hot doc's type.

"I can get behind all that."

"What's your type?" he asks.

I quickly run through my options. I don't want to scare him away and be too abrupt, but I also really like the guy and it's not in my nature to filter myself.

"You're my type, for starters." I close the lid on my food and lean back onto the couch.

"I am?"

"Hell yeah. You're in shape, you're successful, and have those blue eyes." I extend my arm along the back of the couch in his direction. Not close enough to touch him, but almost.

"That's flattering," he murmurs.

"Look, Lance. I know things are crazy for you, so I'm not going to make it more difficult. But you should know that the second you're ready, I'm pursuing you."

"Pursuing?" he repeats.

"Going on dates, hanging out, and everything that comes with it," I say.

"Like what?" He leans slightly into me and it's exactly enough that my fingertips graze his bare shoulder.

"Come here. Let me show you." I turn to face him and beckon him closer.

His tongue peeks out to wet his lower lip and he inches nearer. I eat up the distance between us and kiss him, moaning at the contact. It's everything I'd ever fantasized it being. He scoots closer and grips the back of my neck. It surprises me and excites me all at the same time. I rest one hand on his hip and the other strokes his stubbly cheek.

I want to push him down and climb on top of him. Let him feel the heat of my arousal. But some things are best savored and I want every drop of this man to last, so I pull away. His chest heaves and he's not hiding anything under those basketball shorts. It makes it even more difficult not to maul him.

"Did I do something wrong?" he asks.

"No, doc. Not at all. I just don't want to do too much, too fast."

"That was my first kiss with a man, but I assure you, I'm not a virgin."

I chuckle. "I figured that out by the baby in the other room."

"Lane." He smacks a hand to his forehead. "Is it bad I forgot I had a baby for a minute?"

"No." I laugh harder. "I think all the blood rushed south for both of us."

"Truth." He scrubs a hand through his hair. "I now know what I was missing all those years."

"What do you mean?"

"When I kissed girls, even my wife, there was something missing. It was fine. I wasn't grossed out or anything. But it didn't make me excited. And what happened with us a minute ago? That had me very excited."

"It's only the beginning."

Lane chooses this moment to fuss from the other room.

"I better make her a bottle." He stands up, and I do too.

"I think I'm going to go."

"Why? I thought we were going to play Xbox?"

"If I stick around any longer, we won't be playing Xbox. I'll have you naked and under me, and I don't think you're ready for that quite yet." His mouth makes an O. "I don't work tomorrow. You want to hang out again? Don't feel like we have to, but I like you and I want to spend more time getting to know the real you."

"I want that."

"Okay. I'll text you in the morning." I lean in for one more quick kiss. His lips fit perfectly with mine. Every part of me wants to stay and do more of this, but I know it's a bad idea. "Bye, doc."

"Bye."

CHAPTER FIVE
LANCE

THE NEXT FEW WEEKS ARE BLISSFULLY EXHAUSTING. I GO BACK TO WORK, despite the apprehension I feel leaving Lane with the nanny, Liz. I text and call her too often, but she's a good sport and puts up with my neurosis.

Lane and I develop a routine. My confidence as a parent grows and I think she can feel me relax, because she sleeps a bit longer each night, helping with my constant fatigue.

What doesn't help are the late nights I spend with Bo. He comes over after work most nights for dinner and to hang out. Each time we're together, we spend more time making out and less time talking.

It's exciting and new. I've been in a holding pattern my whole life. I was alive and functioning, but I wasn't going anywhere. Bo has shown me how to soar, and I don't ever want to come down.

The thing about flying though, is that eventually gravity takes hold and what goes up must come down. The crash happens abruptly one Tuesday evening. I arrive home after work and stop to grab my mail before heading upstairs to relieve Liz.

I grab the stack of letters and notice a pink slip for certified mail that the leasing department signed for. I make a pit stop and pick it up before getting on the elevator. The return address is in New York. Without opening it, I know what it is. Maisy's parents warned me the fight for custody wasn't over, so I knew this day would come.

I send Liz home and bathe Lane. I'm making her a bottle when Bo arrives. He had his brother's basketball game after work to attend, so he's later than usual. He sets a bag of groceries on the kitchen counter before coming to greet me. The man can cook, and it's a good thing because I'm absolutely useless in the kitchen.

Between living in New York where you can have takeout delivered easier than you can get to a grocery store and Maisy being an excellent cook, I never learned. My mom definitely didn't teach me since we had a personal chef growing up.

"Hey, doc. How are you?" He leans down and kisses first my daughter's forehead, then me. It makes my chest ache at how easily he's come to care about both of us.

"Fine."

"You don't sound fine. What's up?" He plops down next to us on the couch and gently caresses Lane's head while she noisily sucks down her bottle.

"I got a letter in the mail today."

"Who from?"

"I haven't opened it, but I think it's from Maisy's parents. Or their lawyers, most likely." I want to vomit thinking about what it says. I know refusing to open it won't make it disappear, but reading it will make it real.

"Why would you be getting a letter from them?" he asks, but he already knows. He jumps up and finds the letter in question on the island before returning to me. "You need to open it."

"I can't. I've been trying for an hour."

"Doc, we need to see what it says so we can come up with a game plan."

"We?"

"This guy," he says to the heavens, like he's praying for patience. "My ass has been here almost every night. I've cooked for you, cleaned for you, helped take care of your baby, and you're still confused."

I open my mouth to say something and then shut it. He's right. We've gotten to know each other so well in a few short weeks. I don't know how it happened, but I think he might be my boyfriend.

"Wipe that confused look off your face." He grips my chin between his thumb and forefinger. "I'm in this with you. Your fight is my fight."

"Okay," I deadpan.

"So, can I open it?"

I nod and he plants a chaste kiss on my lips. He then rips the letter open and unfolds the documents. He reads for what feels like an hour. I finally lose my patience.

"What does it say?" Lane finishes her bottle and I set it on the coffee table before lifting her to my shoulder for a burp.

"It says you have a court date. Maisy's parents are suing for custody."

I chew on the inside of my mouth, trying not cry. I haven't cried since I don't remember when, but with the threat of my daughter being taken away from me, my vision blurs with unshed tears.

"When is it?"

"Two weeks. You have a family lawyer, right?"

"I hired one when I was told Lane was born and Maisy had died."

"I think it's time to give them a call." He refolds the papers and sets them down before reaching over and lifting Lane from my arms. "I'm going to lay her down. I'll be right back."

I stare at the wall, so overwhelmed I can't move. Even thinking about saying goodbye to Lane is too much to bear. She's made my life exponentially more difficult, but she's my whole world. Even the most difficult challenges have become the most rewarding and seeing her grow and change every day is the biggest honor I've ever experienced.

"You're scaring me," Bo says. He maneuvers me so we're lying down face to face on the oversized sofa. It's our favorite position to take every night after Lane is asleep and before he has to go home. "Talk to me."

"I don't know what to say. I can't lose her."

"You won't. I promise. You're her dad. You've been taking care of her this whole time. They don't have a leg to stand on."

"Except that I'm a single man who works long hours in a demanding job."

"You have a capable nanny and you spend every possible second with her. I haven't even been able to convince you to hire a sitter for an evening out."

"She's still so small."

"I know." He rubs circles on my back.

"What if they win?"

"They won't—"

"But what—"

He covers my lips with his hand. "They won't, but *if* they do, we'll handle it. You're not in this alone."

"Thank you," I say, but it's muffled by his palm. He lowers his hand, resting it at the base of my throat.

"I want to make you forget about all of this for a while."

"That's not possible."

He gives me a sly smile and crashes his lips to mine. He devours me and second by second, I give into to kiss. Our tongues duel and our lips lock. It's the most intense kiss we've ever shared. His hand reaches under my shirt and his fingers dance along every inch of skin he can reach. His thumb swipes over the flat disk of my nipple, sending shutters down my spine.

He climbs on top of me, his weight pressing me into the couch. I feel his rock-hard erection as he grinds it against my own. We've never moved past this level of intimacy. He's always quick to stop, telling me I'm not ready. I pray he doesn't this time. I need him.

He must know what I'm feeling, because he lifts my shirt up and over my head. He kisses his way down my neck and across the spans of my shoulders. Then he moves lower, flicking his tongue against my nipples. He continues his way down my abdomen, only stopping to tug my basketball shorts down. God, how I've wanted this. He's teased me for weeks, getting me worked up and then leaving. I've had to finish myself off in the shower each time, but it wasn't satisfying. Not like this is.

My hard cock springs free, slapping against my abdomen. I watch as he grips around the base and drags his tongue along the tip, lapping at the pre-cum.

"Fucking hell, doc. You taste so good." He wraps his lips around me and sucks. My hips jerk up at the sensation.

Maisy tried to give me head once, but her touch was too light and her lips were too soft. It felt all wrong. But Bo's tight fist, his firm mouth, and strong suction are fucking perfect.

"Bo," I moan. "Your mouth feels amazing."

His other hand goes lower to my balls and he rolls them in his palm. I'm not going to last. I never worried about such a thing with Maisy. I only wanted it over with. But Bo's a man too, and I worry he'll judge me on my stamina. That thought has my dick softening ever so slightly.

"Stop it. Whatever you're thinking. Stop it. Be here with me. I want you to come in my mouth. I want to be the one to get this experience with you. Please give it to me." His gaze bores into me and I'm instantly at ease. He takes me down his throat and it's all it takes to get me back in the moment.

My fists clench at my side and my eyes squeeze shut. He bobs up and down, saliva and pre-cum spilling down my cock and onto my balls. A tingle spreads from the base of my spine and a pleasure like I've never felt overtakes my body. I don't just come. I explode. Or at least that what's it feels like. I bite my fist to stop myself from screaming his name and waking the baby.

Bo takes it all, swallowing over and over to drink all of me down. He waits until my body stills to release me. He kisses the tip of my dick sweetly, before releasing me and climbing back up my body, dragging my shorts and underwear up as he goes. His lips press onto mine and his tongue thrusts into my mouth, allowing me to taste myself. It's nothing I thought I'd enjoy, but with Bo, I doubt there's anything he could do I wouldn't find pleasure in.

I want to discover how he tastes too. I want to make him feel as good as he just made me feel. I slide out from underneath him and slink to my knees on the area rug. I drop one of his feet to the ground and crawl between his legs. He shifts so he's sitting up and studies me carefully.

"I don't expect this from you," he murmurs, running a hand through my hair.

"I want to. So badly."

He lifts his hips up so I can tug down his shorts. His dick is massive, the same color as his skin except for a slightly pink and swollen mushroom head. Clear pre-cum glistens between the slit, and my tongue darts out to lick without thought. It's heady, salty, and delicious.

"Fuuuuuuck," he draws out under his breath. It fills me with the much needed confidence to continue. I take him into my mouth as far as I can go, which isn't far. A brief thought about how this will fit inside me during sex flutters through my mind, but I push it away. That's putting the cart before the horse.

I bob up and down at my leisure, getting used to the motion and depth most comfortable for me. Bo's patient, letting me explore and cluing me in on what feels best through his grunts and groans. I release him with pop and lick down the underside of his impressive length. I want to taste all of him, so I move down to his weighty sack. I suck one into my mouth before releasing it and moving to the next, all while jacking him off. Bo lets out a sigh of pleasure, so I do it again.

"I'm going to come. You decide where it goes." His voice is thick and breathy.

"I want to feel you come in my mouth," I admit and go back to sucking on his cock. His hand rests on the back of my head but he doesn't put any weight on it.

It only takes a minute longer before his breath catches and his cock jerks. Thick, hot, semen spills into my mouth. My throat wants to reject it, but my mind doesn't. I swallow each spurt as he ejaculates, making soft sounds of pleasure.

"Get up here." He pulls his shorts and underwear back over himself and then tugs me up his body, turning so we're once again lying side by side. He kisses my forehead, my cheeks, and my nose before giving me another heart stopping kiss on my lips.

"Was I okay?" I ask, and I hate myself for it. I want to have the same confidence with sex that I have with my patients. At work, I'm knowledgeable and self-assured. But here, like this, I'm a novice at best. I know the mechanics, I've seen it done in porn, but it's not enough to prepare me for the reality.

"Better than. That was the best blow job I've ever had," he swears. I narrow my eyes at him and he chuckles, the sound rumbling through his body. "Hand to God, it was."

"I'm going to choose to believe you because the alternative is mortifying."

That makes him laugh even harder. "You're too much, doc."

We lie there for long, quiet minutes before I ask the question I've been too nervous to ask. "Do you plan on sticking that thing up my ass?"

He roars his laughter this time and I slap a hand over his mouth. We both freeze, expecting a cry to come from the bedroom, and then let out a collective sigh when it remains silent.

"If that's what you want," he says.

"What do you mean? Isn't that how this works?"

"Everyone has their own preferences and it works differently for each couple."

"What if that's what I want?"

"Then that's what we'll do. I've bottomed a couple times, mostly to see what it feels like, but I'm a top." He takes my hand in his and rests it over his heart. The steady *thump thump thump* calms me.

"When I think about sex, I picture myself being on the receiving end."

"Looks like we're a perfect match then."

"Looks like," I agree. And isn't it the damn truth. He came into my life at the peak of chaos. Anyone else would've turned tail and ran. But not Bo. He embraced the mayhem.

"Are you hungry? I brought stuff to make carbonara."

My stomach rumbles and he takes that as his answer. We untangle ourselves from each other and he gets up. I watch as he walks into the kitchen. I bite my lower lip, wondering what I did to get so lucky.

CHAPTER SIX
BOAZ

"ARE YOU GOING TO TELL ME WHERE YOU'VE BEEN GOING EVERY NIGHT?" Dad grumbles from his chair while I unload groceries.

"I told you, with a friend." I roll my eyes.

He's been pressing me for information the last couple weeks, but I'm not ready to tell him about Lance. If I could keep him a secret for however long we're together, I would. But lately, however long feels more like forever and hiding someone I want to spend my life with seems implausible.

"There ain't no friend good enough for me to want to hang out every night of the week."

"Then you don't have the right kind of friend," I say under my breath.

"What's that?"

"Nothing, Pops." I put away the milk, turn to grab the cheese, and am startled to see Dad standing in my way.

"I know you've met someone," he says.

"We don't need to go there."

"I think we do because if you're spending this much time with… someone," he says carefully. "Then they must be important. I'll remind you that I'm tolerant of a lot of things, but you need to keep that shit private."

"Jesus, do you even hear yourself? You're tolerant, but only if it's not in front of your face."

"Your mother and I raised you to be God fearing. When you told me you're… the way you are, I didn't say nothing. Your brother needed you and I didn't want to take that away from him."

"More like you needed me to take care of him and were willing to accept me if it benefitted you. Am I right?" This conversation grates on my nerves and has my blood boiling.

I knew he wasn't thrilled when I came out to him, but he didn't shun me. I took it as a good sign. But after hearing what he's saying now, I realize he needed the free childcare. Plain and simple.

"I don't care what you do when you're away from this house. But I don't want you to get twisted and think I'm okay with it. Your brother is young and impressionable—"

"Afraid he's going to catch homosexuality, Pops? Is that it?" I rub my hands up and down his arms. "Oh no. You're gay now."

It's petty and immature, but I don't care. He can say a lot of things about me, but calling me a bad influence because of who I choose to love has pushed me off the edge of sanity.

"I'm not an idiot. I know it's not contagious, but Eli looks up to you. When he finds out, he might think it's the cool thing to do. Is this the life you want for him?"

My jaw drops in disbelief. When we silently agreed my private life would remain private, I had no idea how different our views were. I thought he needed time to adjust and come to terms. I didn't know this entire time, he'd been waiting to drop this bomb when I finally met someone I cared about.

"That's not how sexuality works. You either are or aren't. And even if he is, you should be so lucky that he'll have someone in his life to support him, because clearly he won't be able to rely on you."

"You're selfish and juvenile."

"No. I'm happy, Pops. More than I've been in a long ass time. Don't you want that for me?" I plead.

"I hope whoever he is, that he's worth giving up your family."

"His name is Lance. He's a doctor at the hospital. He's smart and successful. He also has a beautiful daughter that might someday be your granddaughter if you'd pull your head out of your ass."

"You two are getting an innocent child mixed up in your debauchery?"

I snap. It's one thing to insult me and my life, but it's another to insinuate Lance is doing something wrong by being a gay parent.

"I swear to God, if you don't get out of my face, I'll drop you to the floor, old man. You've pushed this too far because that man is the very best father I've ever seen. And that's including your sorry ass." I shove past him and down the hall to change so I can meet Lance at his place.

"I want you out. Take your shit and go," he shouts after me.

I flip around and face him. "Oh right, and suddenly you're going to step up and be a dad to Eli? You gonna help him with his homework? Make him dinner every night? Go grocery shopping? Pay the bills? Because last I checked, it was me doing all those things."

"I don't need you. I let you do all that because you wanted to."

"You think at seventeen-years-old I wanted to get up in the middle of the night to feed my newborn brother? You think I wanted to put myself through nursing school and make sure my kid brother makes it to basketball practice? All while you came home and sat your ass in that recliner? I did it because the day Mom died, you gave up on life." I ball my fists at my sides.

I didn't realize how much anger and resentment had built up over the years. I convinced myself he was working too hard to do everything. When I had it all wrong. He wasn't man enough to take on his own responsibilities. He let a kid do it instead.

"Don't you ever talk to me like that about your mom. She'd be embarrassed of the man you've become," he spits out.

With every ounce of self-control I have, I leave him in the hall and go inside my room, slamming the door behind me. He wants me gone? He thinks he can do everything I've been taking care of for over half my life? Well, fuck him. He can try.

I find a couple duffle bags at the bottom of my closet and toss some clothes inside. I storm to the bathroom and gather my toiletries, throwing them inside a bag too. I don't have time or space to pack everything, so I only take what's necessary for a few days. I don't know where I'll stay, but I know it won't be here. I'm sure Lance will let me crash at his place for a few days until I can figure my life out.

I should've done this a long time ago, but I wanted to get Eli to college or on the path to whatever he wants to do with his life. He graduates in six months. That's close enough.

I'm glad when I leave my room and Dad isn't in the hallway. As angry as I am, I worry my temper would get the best of me and I don't want to do something I'll regret.

I load up my car and speed away from my childhood home and everything I've ever known. I'll call Eli from Lance's house to let him know what's going on. He's going to be upset, but I hope by promising him nothing will change between us, it'll soften the blow.

Five minutes later, I'm parking and heading up the elevator. I don't bother knocking when I get to his door. Lance made it clear I can skip that step when he gave me a key to the condo just in case I ever needed it. We might be moving fast, but it feels right. I haven't had one moment of hesitation when it comes to him and Lane. We just fit. And fuck whoever has a problem with it.

"Doc?" I call out when I don't immediately see him.

"Bathroom," he calls from inside his room. It has an ensuite with a bathtub, unlike the hall bathroom that only has a shower.

I drop my bags and seek him out. I stand in the doorway and take in the most adorable sight. Lane's in the bathtub, resting on some kind of soft sponge in the shape of a giant teddy bear. She's wide awake and her gaze is fixed on the floating bubbles Lance is blowing over her. Her hands and legs pump up and down in time, and is that a—

"Is she smiling?" I ask inching further into the room and kneeling next to Lance.

"Yeah. Can you believe it? The nanny said she smiled at her today and I didn't believe her. I told her it was probably a gas bubble. Then I put her in the tub and she smiled up at me like she's been doing it her whole life."

I wrap an arm around his waist and lean my head on his shoulder. We watch as she kicks and smiles toothlessly. It's almost enough to make me forget what happened back at the house. Almost.

"How are you? You feel tense." Lance blows another round of bubbles.

"Need a roommate? At least for a week or two?"

He screws the lid on the soapy mixture and his face scrunches in concern. "What happened?"

"My dad kicked me out. We didn't talk about me being gay after I came out to him, but he never said he was against it per se. I guess it was wishful thinking that he was cool with it. He figured the reason I was spending time away from home was because I met someone and he spelled things out for me. He's okay with me being gay as long as he doesn't ever have to meet my partner or see us together."

"Were you thinking of introducing us?"

"Yes. No. I don't know. Of course I want to share the people in my life who are important, but I wasn't planning on taking that step yet. I wanted to talk it over with you. But he assumed things were getting serious since I wasn't coming home except to sleep," I explain.

"Babe, you wanted me to meet your family. I love that," he coos.

"Are you even listening to the words coming out of my mouth?"

"I am, but I'm choosing to ignore the blatant homophobia and skip to the part where Lane and I mean so much to you that you want us to meet your dad."

"You're so fucking weird." I give him a quick kiss so he doesn't take his eyes off Lane for too long.

I'm instantly cheered up. I don't know how he managed to get me from a level ten nuclear meltdown back to happy, but it's part of the reason I care so deeply for him.

"I know and I'm sorry things went so badly. I don't mean to make light of it."

"It's okay. But is it cool if I stay until I can find my own place?"

"Of course. However long you need." He squeezes my hand reassuringly. "All right, little Lane. Time for a bottle and bed."

I hold a towel wide and he hands me the wet baby who cries when the cold air hits her skin. I bundle her up tight and walk out to the changing table while Lance cleans up the tub. I secure a diaper on her and rub lotion into her baby soft skin. She watches me with curious blue eyes, like she's only now realizing there's a person attached to the voice she's been hearing. And maybe she is because until recently, she was more asleep than awake. I put her pajamas on and play a game of patty cake with her feet.

Then it happens. Her lips spread wide and she beams up at me, letting out a coo. My eyes well with emotion I can't put a name on. Pride or something. It's in this moment I realize I've fallen in love with this tiny human. It didn't take long, but how could it since she was only a week old when we met? Parents fall in love with their babies when they first lay eyes on them, I'm not saying I'm anything close to her dad, but I'm something.

"She's so happy and alert tonight." Lance appears at my side and wraps an arm around my middle.

"She is."

"I should probably feed her before that changes."

"Let me," I say.

He looks up at me, and whatever he reads from my expression must please him because he grips the back of my neck and pulls me in for kiss. It's sweet and comfortable. And so fucking perfect.

"Sounds good. I'll go make it."

I scoop Lane up in my arms and get comfortable on the couch. He brings me a bottle and I cradle her while she eats. So much is fucked up in our lives right now, but being in this moment with her makes everything perfect. I can only pray we get to keep her.

I can lose Pops and it would suck, hard. But losing Lane is unfathomable.

"I think I'm going to see if Lane will sleep in the nursery tonight," Lance says nonchalantly. A week ago, I helped him put together her room. He spent way too much money on a beautiful crib and soft pink and gold decor. At the time, he complained about how hard it would be to have her away from him.

"Oh yeah?" I ask.

"Yeah. We might need the privacy." He rests a hand on my thigh.

"Will we?"

"You don't think so?" I hear the edge to his voice. He's nervous. We've been taking things further and further each time we're together. I've been taking care to stretch him with my fingers every night, preparing him for when I can finally sink into his body.

"You know I want that," I say, knowing we're not talking about being alone. We're talking about sex. "But I don't want you to feel pressured to kick this one from your room."

"I set up the video monitor over her crib and the SIDS detector. I think she'll be fine." He traces down her cheek that's growing more and more chubby each day.

"Then I think it's bedtime." I smirk.

CHAPTER SEVEN
LANCE

I WRAP LANE IN HER SWADDLE BLANKET, MY PALMS GROWING SWEATY AND excitement building in my belly. I haven't been this nervous in my life. Not even my first night with Lane. I lay her down and double check the monitoring systems I purchased are working.

She fell asleep while Bo was feeding her, so she doesn't fuss when I flip the light out and close the door. I don't find Bo in the living room. I lock everything up and head to the bedroom. It's only nine, but we're not planning on sleeping.

I find him on the bed, lying on his side with a cocky smirk on his face. He pats the space in front of him. I crawl across the bed and straddle his hips.

"Did she go down okay?" he asks with his hands on my thighs.

"Yep." I run my hands up and down his torso. "I'm excited for a sleepover."

"Me too."

He removes my glasses and sets them on the nightstand before fisting my T-shirt and tugging me down for a kiss. His lips are plump and delicious. Right away, his tongue demands entry. Our kiss is heated and full of intensity as he sits up with me astride on his lap. His arms wrap around me tight and I feel his erection against my ass. He's as excited as I am for tonight.

Part of me wants to rush through it so I can finally know what it'll feel like, but the other part wants to savor every second because I'll never have another first time. It feels ridiculous to be my age and only now be experiencing my first real sexual encounter. I don't count the heterosexual sex I've had. It wasn't really me and it meant little. This, however, means everything.

He breaks from our kiss and rolls us so I'm on my back before he steps off the bed.

"Clothes off," he orders, and we both scramble to disrobe.

He takes me in, while I do the same to him. I don't have the wherewithal to be concerned with what he sees, because I'm too busy gaping in awe at him. He's fucking gorgeous with the light reflecting off his dark skin, making him glow in an ethereal way. He's a masterpiece. Like someone took extra time on him, making sure he's perfectly symmetrical, and each ripple of muscle is ideally defined.

He climbs back onto the bed in all his nude glory. He parts my knees and settles between them, leaning over to kiss me again. He's rougher this time, more urgent. His lips envelope mine and his tongue explores my mouth. His cock weighs heavy on my stomach, turning me on more than I've ever been before.

"I'm going to make this so good for you." He sits up and reaches over to the nightstand where a row of supplies I didn't see before now are lined up.

He grabs the lube first and squirts a line down my rigid erection. He interlinks his fingers and closes his hands around my rigid length. He pumps up and down slowly, his thumbs exploring every ridge. It's euphoria. One hand releases me and moves lower. He rubs slow circles against my hole, building the anticipation.

"God, you're so responsive. I love that about you," he says, pressing into me. I squirm with need. He starts with one finger, hooking it to rub against my prostate. He then moves to two, all while stroking my cock almost lovingly. When he gets to three fingers, I worry I'm going to explode.

"Had enough?" he asks, reading my mind.

"I want to come with you inside me."

"Me too."

I miss the contact immediately when he lets go, but I know what's to come will be even better. He grabs a condom and tears it open.

"We don't need that," I say.

"Don't we?"

"We're both clean." Weeks ago, we both got tested, knowing eventually we would be here.

"I didn't want to assume."

"I want it to be you I feel. And only you."

He tosses the condom and drizzles a line of slick down his cock. He repositions himself and grips the base of his dick. His brows furrow in concentration as he presses against my hole. I relax my body, knowing it's going to burn, but wanting it more than anything.

"If you need me to stop, tell me. I don't want to hurt you." He glances up and I nod.

With slow precision he pushes in. He fills me completely. It's so much more profound than I thought it would be. Not only do our bodies join, but so does everything else. Our breaths, our heartbeats, our desires.

"Bo," I say through a gasp.

"I know." He reaches over to briefly stroke my cheek comfortingly. When he's fully seated, his hands go to my knees and he groans. "You're so tight. I never want to come so this never has to end."

He picks my dick back up and strokes me in time with each thrust. His movements are deliberate and careful, keeping his eyes trained on me. I know he's worried about this, but I'm not. I'll greedily take whatever he gives me.

Then he shifts positions so that he's driving into my prostate, and I see stars. I blow my load without warning. Thick ropes of cum jet from my dick and land on my stomach and chest.

"That's it, doc. Come for me. You're so fucking sexy." He bites his lower lip, his eyes fixed on me as I orgasm.

It's not long after I'm coming down, that his thrusts become erratic. He uses my knees as leverage to fuck me harder. I've only just come, but seeing him this out of control has me wishing I could do it all over again.

"Give it all to me. I want to see you," I say, squeezing around him intentionally.

"Jesus fuck," he roars. He doesn't have to tell me he's coming, the warmth I feel deep inside and the sudden wet noises from where we're joined alerts me.

He pulls out, collapses on top of me, and I wrap my arms around him. I'm aware of the mess we've made between us, but I don't care.

"That was incredible," I say, trailing my fingers up and down his back.

"I'm in love with your ass," he murmurs, and I smack him.

"Is that all you're in love with?" I joke before realizing what I said. His head pops off my chest and gives me a wide-eyed look. "That's not what I meant."

God, I'm mortified. Despite how often that thought has been popping into my head, I never meant to say it out loud. It's too soon and there's still so much I need to deal with in my life before I can give a relationship my full focus.

Doesn't change a goddamn thing, though. Boaz Dixon showed up at my door at the exact moment I needed someone the most. He gave me his time, his energy, and his heart. I couldn't ask for more from a partner.

"It's okay if you did." He runs a hand through my hair. "Because I am in love with you."

"You are?"

"Of course I am." He shakes his head in disbelief. "If you would've told me a year ago, I'd be in love with a single dad who happens to be the new doctor at the hospital, I wouldn't have believed it. You crushed every expectation I had for my life and gave me something I want to deserve. You and Lane are it for me."

"You mean it?"

"Of course. Beats the hell of living the life of a fuck boy."

I smack him again. "Glad I could save you from a life of depravity."

"Whoa, whoa, whoa. I didn't say all that. But I want all that depravity to be with only you. There's a difference."

"That's better."

"You got nothing to say to me?" he asks, his voice pitching high.

"I love you," I blurt out.

"Mmm. Like music to my ears."

"I didn't think the person I met after my divorce would be the person I want to spend my life with, but here we are."

"You say that like it's a bad thing."

"Definitely not a bad thing. I'm lucky." I lift my head off the pillow and kiss him. "And messy. Let's go shower."

"Deal."

We shower and change the sheets before climbing back into bed. He wraps his warm, hard body around mine, holding on tight. It doesn't last long since Lane wakes up for a feeding before I can even close my eyes. But it's not me who gets out of bed, it's Bo. I listen over the monitor as he gives her a bottle from the new rocking chair I bought for the nursery and sings her nursery rhymes he's made up his own lyrics for.

"Hush little baby, don't you cry, your daddy's gonna buy you an apple pie. If that apple pie is gross, your daddy's gonna buy you overnight oats. If those overnight oats are dry, your daddy's gonna buy you the earth and sky."

I laugh as his song continues to barely make sense. I should use this time to catch up on sleep, but I'm too engrossed in how irresistibly sexy Bo is with my baby. He burps her, changes her diaper, and somehow manages to get her back to sleep. It's something I rarely accomplish.

I feel the bed shift when he climbs back in, and I turn to face him.

"You're amazing. You know that?" Lane chooses that moment to make a noise in her sleep, exposing my eavesdropping.

"You heard everything that went on in there?"

"I did."

"Well, I guess you now know I'm an amazing singer. I didn't want to say nothing about it because I knew you might be intimidated," he says smugly.

"I am. Especially with your songwriting skills. It must be hard to have so much talent and keep it all inside."

"It is. It is. But we all have a cross to bear."

I hook a hand around the back of his neck and pull him in for a kiss. The happiness that fills me is indescribable. As though I'm standing on top of a mountain, the hurt and pain from my life swimming at the bottom, but I'm too high for it to touch me. All it took was an eight-pound baby and full-grown man.

I know there are storm clouds coming, but in this moment, it's blue skies, sunshine, and a warm breeze.

CHAPTER EIGHT
BOAZ

I WALK OUT OF THE HIGH SCHOOL GYM, CONFUSED. ELI HAD A GAME tonight, but he wasn't there. I pull out my phone and dial his cell.

"Hello," Eli answers his phone.

"Hey, bro. What's goin' on? I came to watch you play and Coach said you never showed."

He sighs loudly. "Pops told me I couldn't go."

"Why?" My temper flares. Eli works hard to keep his grades up so he can play. School isn't easy for him, but basketball is. The only way to keep that kid in check, is to hold the game over his head.

"He was too tired to drive me, and he wouldn't let me walk."

"Why didn't you call me? I would've picked you up. I still can so you'll be here for the third quarter."

"Don't bother," he grinds out.

"What do you mean?"

"He won't let you drive me. Why did you have to bring up your sexuality? You knew how he felt. You fucked everything up. It's all your fault." His voice shakes and it stabs me through the heart. He only shows his tough guy persona. It's rare he shows anyone his emotions.

"We talked about this. I met someone important to me. I shouldn't have to pretend like he doesn't exist."

"You couldn't wait until I finished school? You're so selfish."

"Eli. That's not fair."

"You know what's not fair? That I'm missing the game and won't be able to play in the next one because I was a no-show tonight. That's not fair."

I open my mouth to explain, but the line goes dead.

Fuck.

I jump in my car and drive to my childhood home. It's a bad idea. I feel it in my gut, but I'm spittin' mad and I need to make this right. I pull up two minutes later and walk inside.

"No. You're not welcome here," Pops shouts, pointing at the door I just came in.

"I only want to talk. Hear me out."

"There's nothing you can say I want to hear. Now go before I call Sheriff Bell."

"And tell him what?" I bite out. "That I came by to talk you out of being an asshole to your youngest son?"

"You're trespassing. I kicked your ass out of this house."

I ignore him. I doubt he'll call the sheriff and if he does, the worst he'll do is ask me to leave.

"Listen. You can hate me all you want. I don't give a shit anymore. But that boy in there needs you. You don't get to be too tired anymore. You made the choice to kick me out, now you have to deal with the consequences." I point a finger in his direction.

"Guys, it's okay. I'm fine," Eli says from where he's listening in the hallway. He hasn't looked like a little boy in a long time, but with his shoulders hunched and his head lowered, he looks younger than his seventeen years.

"Go to your room and stay out of it," Dad yells, and Eli drags his feet back down the hall.

"Don't yell at him. He's not the issue," I say.

"That's right. He's not. It's you. Now I'm going to tell you one more time,"—he stomps toward me and shoves me in the chest—"get your ass out my house."

I feel everything all at once. Resentment for what should've been my most fun years. Anger for being judged on something I can't fucking control. Bitterness for having my own father treat me like scum. All of it. I shove him back. His nostrils flare, his eyes widen, and he breathes out heavily from his mouth. He charges at me, throwing his shoulder into my gut. We land on the ground, him on top of me. He throws a punch that makes perfect contact with my cheekbone. I feel a gush of warmth stream down my face.

I don't want to hurt the old man, but I'm not going to lie here and take it either. I block his swings and roll to my side, hoping he'll be forced off me, but he's not. I'm stronger than he is, but he's got at least seventy pounds on me, making him hard to move. We wrestle around, each of us trying to get the upper hand.

"You're not my kid," he grits out, throwing another punch that lands on my ear. Pain explodes from inside my head and all I can do is try to block his attack. Apparently, I'm not the only one who has pent up emotion.

I sock him in the gut, knocking the air from him, but it does nothing to remove his formidable weight from on top of me. He drives his fist into my jaw and I cross my arms over my face to block future hits. I don't want to hurt the old man, but he's giving me little choice.

The next thing I hear are sirens and the front door being thrown open. Someone drags Pops off me. It's the sheriff, Jaxson. Pops tries to throw a punch at him, but Jax backs up and holds his hands out, clearly surprised.

"Mr. Dixon, this is not a road you want to go down," he says.

Realization hits Pops and his body slumps, his face falling, and the fight visibly leaving him.

"I-I'm sorry, Sheriff," he mutters.

"It's okay. Why don't you go have a seat in the living room, and I'll be there in a minute." Jax pats Pops' shoulder. As soon as he's out of sight, he approaches me. "You need an ambulance?"

"No, I'm good. Just a little blood." I lift the hem of my shirt up and wipe away the stream of blood. "I have a first aid kit in my car."

"Let me go grab it. Trunk?"

I nod and he walks out the front door. My adrenaline crashes, and I realize the extent of what just happened. This is Jerry Springer shit. I never in a million years thought I'd be in a physical altercation with my own dad. I'd gone so long making excuses for his behavior, and I realize now that it was self-preservation. I think I knew in the back of my mind this is how things would go if my sexuality wasn't an idea any longer, but a reality.

"I'm sorry. I didn't know what else to do." Eli's small voice comes from the darkened hallway. He must be the reason for the cops.

"Come here." I manage to pull myself off the ground and stand just in time for Eli to tackle me, hugging me around the middle. I pat his back and tell him it's okay.

"Bo, I got your kit." Jax holds a plastic red tote out to me.

"Thanks, man."

"You want to tell me what happened here tonight?" Jax looks uncomfortable.

"Just a little spat. It's fine," I say.

"It wasn't a spat. Pops attacked you," Eli defends.

"What were you fighting over?"

"Well, I'm gay and Pops doesn't seem to like that fact." I speak freely because the sheriff is gay too. He came out not that long ago and is living with some developer.

"Shit." Jax rubs at the back of his neck. "Do you want to press charges?"

"Technically, I don't live here anymore. He told me to leave, but I wanted to have a conversation. Does that make it my fault?" I pry myself away from Eli and crack open the tote. I pull out some gauze and apply it to my cheekbone.

"A judge would be the one to decide that. But I can take him in to put some distance between you two."

"No. I'll go, and that'll solve everything," I say.

"Can I come with you?" Eli asks.

"I don't think so. You're only seventeen." I rub his head affectionately.

"What if he comes after me too?" Fear shines in his eyes. I don't blame him. That was heavy shit for a kid.

"He won't. It's me he has a problem with."

"Tell you what," Jax interjects. "If I get your dad to agree to let Eli go with you for the night, do you have somewhere he can stay?"

I think about Lance's condo and wonder how he'd feel about me showing up with a teenager. Even if he doesn't want us there, I'd rent a room at the B&B before I said no to Eli.

"Yeah. I got a place."

Jax looks curious, but doesn't interfere. "Okay. I'll go see what I can do."

After he's gone, I turn to my kid brother. "I'm sorry. I should've left when he asked me to. This is my fault."

"It's not your fault. You're the only one who has been there for me. I can't be here without you."

"That's not necessarily something I can control. Maybe in a few months when you turn eighteen."

His face falls.

"All right, guys. Eli, you're free to go with Bo tonight," Jax says. "Just make sure you're at school tomorrow."

Eli nods and darts to his room, presumably to pack.

"I'm sorry you got mixed up in this."

"Don't worry about me." Jax opens the front door. "Coming from someone who lived a lot of years hiding who he is for the sake of his parents, don't do it anymore. Be yourself. Love whoever the hell you want to. Fuck 'em."

"I'm trying. I really am."

"And the guy is worth it?" he asks, and I chuckle. At least he tried not to pry.
"He is. You know Dr. Miller, I'm guessing."
"I do."

I smile and nod. Jax returns my grin and walks out. Seconds later, Eli is at my side. We load his backpack and the first aid kit and drive away. I should call Lance and warn him, but something tells me he'll be okay with it.

"Where are we going?" Eli asks.
"My boyfriend's house."

CHAPTER NINE
LANCE

I HEAR THE FRONT DOOR OPEN AND I PEEK AROUND THE CORNER FROM THE kitchen where I've been attempting to make dinner. I've got Lane strapped to my chest in some kind of harness and she's sound asleep. Thank God.

What I see sucks the air from my lungs. A bloody and swollen-faced Bo looks back at me, and at his side is a scrawny teenager who looks like a younger version of his big brother.

"What the hell happened?" I rush toward him and cup his face in my hands, inspecting his injuries. He twists out of my hold, brushing me off.

"Pops happened," the kid says.

"Lance, this is Eli. Eli, Lance."

"Nice to finally meet you." I give him a warm smile I don't feel, because on the inside I'm freaking out.

"I would say the same, but I didn't know about you until five minutes ago," Eli sasses, glaring at Bo.

"Can we talk for a second?" Bo asks.

"Yeah, sure." I turn to Eli. "Make yourself at home. The remote is on the coffee table."

"Thanks."

Bo grabs my hand, tugs me toward the master bedroom, and then into the ensuite. He's wired, I feel it coming off of him in waves. He rifles through the medicine cabinet and brings out something I don't recognize. He opens the white box up to reveal a first aid kit.

"I didn't know I had one of those."

"You didn't." He smirks. "But with little Lane there, you needed it."

"Good call. I didn't even think about that." I place a hand on his shoulder. "Are you okay?"

"I'm fine. Pissed off, but fine."

"What happened?" I ask his reflection in the mirror.

"I showed up to Eli's game and he wasn't there. Found out it was because my dad was too lazy to take him and too stubborn to let me." He cringes as he rubs his face with an alcohol wipe.

"Let me." I take the wipe and blot the wound. "Probably could use a stitch."

"I'm fine. Put a butterfly on it."

We have a stare-down, but eventually I give in. He's had enough shit tonight. He doesn't need it from me. I take out a butterfly bandage and get the wound closed the best I can.

"I went to go talk to my old man, but the stubborn bastard didn't want to talk," he says.

"Jesus. He did this to you?"

"He's a brute."

"And Eli?" I ask hesitantly.

"He didn't want to stay. Sheriff Bell got Pops to agree to let him leave with me, and since this is my home right now, here we are." He shrugs. "But say the word. We'll go stay at the B&B. I don't want to put you in a bad spot."

"No. Of course he'll stay here. I have a pull-out sofa in my office."

He turns around and leans against the vanity, folding his arms. "I lost it. He started spewing all this bullshit about how I'm not his kid and how I should leave and never come back."

"Oh, babe. I'm so sorry." I pull his arms apart and settle between his legs the best I can with a sleeping baby between us.

"I didn't even say hello to my princess." He ducks down and kisses the top of her head. "How's she been tonight?"

"Good. Happy. I tried to keep her awake, but she conked out on me twenty minutes ago."

"Aww. Couldn't hang tonight, huh?" He settles his hands on my hips. "Are you sure about Eli?"

"Of course. He's your family and well, you're my family, so that makes him mine too."

He leans in and kisses me. "I love you."

"I love you too."

I PULL MY WHITE LAB COAT ON AND TAKE A SEAT BEHIND MY DESK, BRINGING my computer to life to check emails before starting my shift. It's been a rough morning already, and I'm hoping the day will improve.

As hard as Eli tried to talk his dad into letting him stay through the weekend, he had to go home the next day. Bo was hesitant to send him back, but our hands are tied.

It was fun seeing the brothers together. They bickered, but they also joked around and laughed a lot. I've gotten a glimpse of the nurturing side of Bo seeing him with Lane, but he's much more paternal with Eli. He made him eat his vegetables and brush his teeth. I never had any doubts of what kind of dad he would be, but my suspicions were confirmed seeing him with Eli.

I scroll through endless emails I don't feel like responding to, when one from my family attorney catches my eye. I've been pushing thoughts of next week's hearing to the back of mind, knowing that stressing out about it won't solve any of my problems.

I quickly read through it, and my jaw drops. How in the hell did they find out about…? I pick my cellphone up from my desk, go to my favorites, and click on Bo.

"Hey, I'm just pulling into the parking lot right now."

"How would Maisy's parents find out about your altercation with your dad?" I blurt out.

"What?"

"My attorney sent me an email this morning telling me that Maisy's parents filed an emergency petition to get Lane removed from my custody because I have a violent man staying with me."

"Excuse me?"

"Shit. I have to go. I need to call him back and figure this out."

"Wait. Lance," he says, but I hang up.

I dial my attorney's cell and it rings three times before he answers.

"Lance, I was hoping you'd get my message sooner rather than later," his rich baritone comes over the line.

"I don't understand what this means. Tell me I'm not losing my daughter." My leg bounces uncontrollably and I already have my glasses off, digging at my eyes.

"Not if I can help it, but I need more information. What happened last night?"

"My boyfriend got into an argument with his dad. But they weren't at my house. Lane was nowhere near them."

"An argument or a physical fight?" he asks calmly.

"A fight. But his dad attacked him. He had nothing to do with it, he barely defended himself."

He sighs heavily. "Will his dad sign a testimony saying that?"

My stomach sinks. "Probably not."

"Then it's a moot point. Does your boyfriend have a violent past?"

"No."

"Is he living with you?"

I hesitate. "He's staying with me, but he hasn't moved in." I don't tell him I planned on asking him to move in as soon as this case is settled. Now that I've had him in my bed, I never want him to leave.

"That's going to be a problem. If I were you, I'd put some distance between you and him."

I shake my head even though he can't see. "Until the case is over?"

"Until forever. I've been practicing law for a long time and I've rarely seen anyone as motivated to get custody as Mr. and Mrs. Smith are."

My stomach feels like it's fallen out of my body and splattered all over the ground. I finally found happiness with someone I can be myself with. Someone who knows everything about me and loves me anyway. The choice will always be Lane, but that doesn't make it easy.

"How did they find out about what happened?"

"Private detective would be my guess. They have unlimited resources and no common sense." He has the decency to sound affronted.

"Is there any other way?" I ask without really wanting to know the answer.

"Afraid not. Of course we can always argue your case and hope the judge sees it your way, but you run an even higher risk of losing your daughter."

"I can't chance it."

"I hoped you would say that. I'll get the emergency petition thrown out since no police report was filed. They'll still bring it up in court, but it's too soon for them to have enough proof."

"Thank you," I say and mean it. He's costing me a pretty penny, but he's worth it.

"You're welcome. Talk soon."

I've no sooner set my phone down, when my office door is flung open and Bo rushes in.

"You hung up on me. What's going on?"

I hold a hand to my forehead, my mind racing. "Maisy's parents had a private detective watching me. And you too, apparently. He must've been following you last night and somehow found out about the fight with your dad. They're trying to get Lane removed from my custody."

"Fuck." He sinks onto the couch. "I'm sorry, Lance. Jesus Christ. I fucked up."

"You didn't. You were trying to do right by your brother. I can't hold that against you."

"Why do I feel a but coming?"

"But I have to protect Lane. This isn't what I want. I hope you know that."

"What are you saying?" His eyes narrow.

"I have two options. Get a sworn statement from your dad saying he attacked you—"

"Or kick me out of your life," he finishes for me, and I nod sadly.

"I'm guessing your dad won't admit to that."

"Not in a million years." He rubs a hand over his nearly bald head.

"I didn't think so."

He stands up and tucks his hands in his pockets. "I'll have my stuff out before you get off shift. I'll go explain to the manager on duty that I can't work today."

"Bo," I say, but nothing else comes out. What else is there to say?

"I know. I'm so fucking sorry, doc." His voice breaks and I eat the distance between us. I wrap him in my arms like it's the last time this will ever happen. Probably because it *is* the last time this will ever happen. I commit the way he feels and the way he smells to my memory. Then I kiss him so I can commit his taste to my memory too.

He will always be my happy. It fucking sucks he couldn't be my forever.

"I love you," I say against his lips, my eyes burning with unshed tears.

"I love you too." He gently extricates himself from me. He cradles my cheek in his hand, brushing a thumb over the drop of sadness that fell. "Take care of our princess."

"I will."

He walks out and I sink to the floor. It was only a few months ago I was in the same position learning my ex-wife was dead. When shit hits the fan, I hit the floor.

I get the sudden urge to hold my baby. She got me through Maisy's death, I can only hope she'll get me through this.

THE NEXT WEEK PASSES BY IN A SERIES OF DEVASTATING MOMENTS. FIRST when I got home after learning Bo and I can no longer share a life, to find an empty home. It's not like he had moved in any more than a couple of duffle bags, but it wasn't the material possessions that left me feeling empty. It was him not being there to share all the moments. The blow-out diapers, the cuddling on the couch, the quiet love making. I missed all of it.

Then it was the awkward and sad encounters at work. He looked so depressed and lost. He'd start to ask how Lane and I were, only to stop himself and walk away like it was too painful to know. I was almost relieved because I didn't want to lie to him. I didn't want to tell him I'd been absolutely miserable without him.

And now, I'm getting on a plane with Lane and my nanny to New York. Without him. We had planned for him to come along. He had me convinced everything would be okay and after I was awarded permanent custody, I'd show him and Lane around the city. We were going to stay a few days and make a vacation out of it.

But instead of Bo sitting next to me on the plane, it's a twenty-three-year-old girl who loves my daughter, but not in the way Bo does. Not like Lane belongs to her.

After we land, we check into the hotel and I say goodnight to Liz, telling her what time to be at my suite tomorrow morning. I shorted the trip and will be going home the day after tomorrow. Hopefully with Lane.

Not only is my heart eviscerated from losing Bo, there's at least a fifty percent chance I'll lose my daughter.

Lane and I spend a somber night together. I order myself room service and feed her a bottle. I put on my bathing suit and get into the jetted tub with her for bath time. I don't bother laying her down in the portable crib the hotel delivered to me. Instead, I keep her snuggled on my chest all night. I know it's not the safest place for her, but I can't bear to have her away from me. Besides, I only manage to get sleep in ten-minute increments before I remember my dire situation and my mind would race once again.

The next morning, I dress in an expensive suit and kiss Lane before walking out the door. When I come back, I'll either be the dad who gets the honor of raising her, or a stranger who gets to see her on holidays and over the summer. If I'm lucky. Who knows what kind of visitation Maisy's parents will agree to should I lose.

My hand feels empty as I walk up the stairs to the courthouse. I wish, more than anything, Bo was here to give me the support I desperately need.

I almost hear his voice yelling, "Doc!" over the crowd. I shake my head. I'm such an idiot. This isn't the movies and that's not the way things happen.

"Doc! Wait!" I hear again, only this time it sounds real.

I flip around and see a tall, gorgeous, sexy as hell, black man running toward me. He's dressed in wrinkled, sea foam green scrubs. Holy fuck. It is him. It's Bo.

CHAPTER TEN

BOAZ
TWELVE HOURS EARLIER

I GET OFF SHIFT AND DRIVE IN THE DIRECTION OF THE B&B TO SPEND another night alone. I haven't been eating or sleeping. It's irresponsible since I work in life-or-death situations, but I can't bring myself to care. Especially since this is Brigs Ferry Bay, and not too many true emergencies walk through our door.

I walk in the door of the swanky B&B, ready to bury myself under the covers and wallow. But I don't get that far because I spot Eli sitting on a sofa right inside the entrance. He spots me and jumps to his feet. I've texted with him every day to make sure he's safe, but things have quieted down at home. Pops hasn't been an attentive dad or anything, but he did drive Eli to practice the last few days with minimal bitching.

"What are you doing here?" I ask, giving him a bro hug with a slap on his back.

"I did something," he says, holding out a manilla envelope.

"Uh oh. Why does that scare me?"

"I think you'll like it."

"Come on. Let's go to my room."

I lead him where I've been staying and we take a seat on the bed. I open the manilla folder and pull out some documents. My eyes catch on the wording on top. *Brigs Ferry Bay Police Department Witness Report.*

"What is this?" I ask.

"I felt bad you lost Lance and Lane because you wanted to make things right for me. I knew Pops wouldn't admit he was the one who attacked you, but I go to school with Sheriff Bell's brother, Zak, and I told him about what happened. He talked to the sheriff—"

"Eli."

"Just listen. He said I could fill out a witness statement. Yeah, I'm a minor, but apparently kids don't lie as often as adults do, so the judge might actually believe me." He shrugs and shows me another form. "Plus Sheriff Bell filled out a report saying what he found. That Pops didn't have any injuries, but you did. A judge will have to believe a cop."

"I don't think this will change anything." Even with reports, it's best I stay clear from the whole situation.

"I'm not doing this for you and Lance. You guys might not be able to be together even with proof you aren't a violent person. I'm doing this for Lane. To show the judge that Lance didn't have her around a dangerous person. She deserves to have a good dad and not grow up thinking she wasn't wanted by her parents." He sniffles and wipes his nose with the back of his hand. It hits me why he's so adamant about this.

"You have always been wanted."

"Not by Pops."

"It's complicated." I don't want to defend the man when I'm still so fucking angry, but I don't want Eli to have the same bitterness toward him that I do. "He loves you but he lost his way when Mom died. It wasn't your fault and he knows that."

"Maybe. It doesn't matter." He stabs a finger into the papers. "Are you going to give this to him?"

"He wasn't at work today. I think he's already gone."

"Then go to him. You have to try. He's a good person. Lane should get to stay with him."

I toss it around in my head. He's right. I don't know if it will matter, but it definitely won't hurt.

"Fine. I'll make some calls." I unlock my phone and pull up the browser.

"I need to get home. Text me and let me know how it goes."

"Thanks, Eli. I love you."

He rolls his eyes at me, but he smiles. It's the same thing as an *I love you too* in teenager speak. Then he leaves and I make plans.

"DOC! WAIT!" I CALL OVER THE BUSTLING CROWD IN FRONT OF THE courthouse. I've never seen him in a suit, and it's probably a good thing because I would demand it from him every day. Fuck gray sweatpants, doc in a gray three-piece suit with a royal blue tie is the sexiest thing I've ever seen.

He freezes in place and slowly turns. I catch up to him, out of breath and my heart racing. The only flight I could catch left me with no time to change or pack. I had to jump in my car and speed to the airport. There was a four-hour layover in Charlotte, North Carolina, which makes no sense at all, but it was the only flight with an open seat.

"What are you doing here?" His eyes shift nervously, obviously hoping Maisy's parents don't see us together.

"I have something that might help your case." I hand him the folder, feeling proud of my brother.

Lance pulls the papers out and flips through them, his brows knit together and his eyes move back and forth quickly across the words.

"Eli?" he asks.

"Yeah."

"He did this for me?"

"For Lane. He told me Lane deserves a dad like you."

"I don't know what to say. I'm touched." He holds the documents to his chest.

"Do you think it could help?"

"I don't know, but I'm going to give it to my attorney. I'm meeting with him in…" he looks at his watch, "…four minutes."

"Go." I motion toward the entrance of the courthouse.

He turns, but then faces me again. "What about you?"

"I have to get back to the airport and see when I can get a return flight."

"This was really amazing of you." His hand brushes mine. My heart skips a beat at the brief contact. I've been craving his touch for so long, it wasn't enough, but I know it's all I'm going to get.

"No problem. Good luck in there." I tip my chin up.

He purses his lips together, appearing to be thinking about something. Then says, "Lane is in my suite with Liz at the Four Seasons. You should go there and wait for me. I'll text her and tell her you're coming."

"Are you sure? I don't want to fuck anything up for you."

"I'm either going to walk out of here knowing I have to turn my daughter over to two people who don't love her, or I'll walk out knowing she's mine forever. Either way, I need you there."

"Okay. I'll see you soon. Good luck, doc. Go get your girl."

He nods and disappears into the crowd and I hop into a cab. My stomach is twisted and I do something I haven't done in a long time. I close my eyes and beg for God's help. If there is any mercy left in the world, He will see to the little princess staying with her daddy.

CHAPTER ELEVEN
LANCE

I RIDE THE ELEVATOR UP TO MY SUITE. IT'S BEEN A LONG AND EXHAUSTING day. I don't know how to feel. I'm in a state of shock, I guess. I'm emotionally drained and could easily go right to sleep.

I won't, though. I have one last night in New York with my girl, and I plan to show her the sights. Not to mention Bo is waiting for me too. I hope he'll want to join us.

Inside, I find Lane tucked into Bo's side on the couch. There's a basketball game on the TV and he's softly explaining the game to her.

They're adorable.

Both of them.

"Hey," I say, and slump onto the couch next to them.

"Hey? That's what you're going with? You better have a whole lot more to say because we're dying here."

I scoop Lane into my arms and hold her tight. Tears I didn't know I'd been fighting off spill down my cheeks and my breath catches. Before I realize it, I'm choking on a sob.

"Doc?" he asks, scooting closer and wrapping an arm around me. I sag into him. "You've got to tell me what's going on. You're freaking me out."

"She's mine," I cry out. "I won."

"Jesus Christ. You scared the shit out of me." He rests his head on top of mine. "I love you both so much."

"We love you too," I say through my tears.

I know he's dying to ask questions, but he knows what I need right now, and it's not to talk. I need a minute to catch my breath. To absorb everything that happened in the courthouse. Nothing about it was easy, but it was all worth it because Lane won't be going anywhere. Bo holds me through long minutes of pent-up stress, frustration, and anxiety. He doesn't push or ask questions. He gives me his quiet strength, and it means everything to me.

After I collect myself, I say, "The judge basically threw the case out. She said there is no reason why I shouldn't have sole custody since I'm the biological father and I only didn't know about her birth because Maisy kept it from me."

"Wow."

"She also disregarded their claim that I was living with a violent man. Mostly because of Eli and Sheriff Bell's statements. I don't even know how to thank them, and you, for bringing them."

"Eli's head is going to grow even bigger when he hears that." His chest rumbles with laughter, deep and comforting.

"He deserves it. That was brave and thoughtful."

"Yeah, he gets it from me."

I slap his hard chest. "The Smiths requested it be temporary custody and that we revisit it in six months. I was ready to agree, because at least I would have six months to prove

I'm a good father. But the judge declined. She said they should be working with me, and not against me, if they wanted to see their granddaughter."

"Smart judge."

"I didn't think they would, but after I left the courtroom, they caught up to me. We went and had coffee."

"You did what?" he gasps.

"I know. I wanted to tell them to fuck off and that they'd never see Lane again. But they're her grandparents. They're all Lane has left of her mother, and I couldn't take that away from her." I think back to the conversation we had at the diner. "They told me they were sad about losing their own daughter and it was terrifying to think about losing Lane too. Especially since I don't live in New York."

"They know Maine isn't that far away, right?"

"I told them they're free to visit and I can try and get time off to visit the city more often. I think we all left feeling like we were getting what we wanted."

"Sounds like the best-case scenario for everyone."

"It really was."

"What does this mean for us?" he asks in a nervous tone. I sit up so he can see me fully.

"I want us to be together. To be a family. I'm sorry I walked away instead of fighting for us. I let the doubts in and I was scared."

"Doc, you don't ever have to apologize for putting the princess first. I'm a grown ass man and can take care of myself. But she needs someone on her side and I'd be disappointed in you if you chose any differently." His eyes sharpen and his words are clear and meaningful.

"I love you."

"I love you too. And there's nothing more I want, than to be part of your family."

"Fucking hell." My eyes water again, and Bo's there to brush the tears from my cheeks. "I'm not a crier."

"Even if you were, it'd be all right. You must be exhausted. Why don't I start you a bath in that big ass tub and order us some food?" His plump lips fall onto mine in a kiss.

"I thought we could go out. Show Lane the lights from Times Square."

He looks down at the snoozing baby. "You think she cares about blinking lights?"

"I guess not."

"I think we need a quiet night. Just the three of us." He raises to his full height. "I'll start that bath. You go lay Lane down."

"You're the best. You know that, right?"

"Yeah, I do." His chest puffs.

He disappears into the bathroom and I rock my daughter, having a hard time putting her down into the portable crib I'm so glad I get the chance to use. I sniff her head, getting a boost of serotonin. Months ago, I never would've guessed this would be my life. At best, I thought maybe I'd have a date or two. Dip my toes in the water of sexuality.

I skipped right over testing the water and jumped in head first, and with a baby in tow. And I wouldn't have wanted it any other way.

I kiss her chubby cheek and set her down. I grab the baby monitor and follow the scent of French lavender to the bathroom. Bo's down to his scrub pants and is running his hands through the water as it fills, to mix the bath oil.

I remove my clothes, tossing them into a heap in the corner. I hope I don't have a reason to put it on for a long time to come. Bo's eyes catch on me and his lips part. I pad over to him, unable to help my growing erection. I haven't so much as masturbated since we parted ways, and seeing his sexy torso is doing things to me.

"What's up, doc?" he asks in a low and throaty tone.

"Will you get in with me?"

"I can do that." He pulls on the string to release his pants and they fall to the ground. I hook my thumbs in his boxer briefs and drag them down, sinking to my knees as I go. "Doc. It's been a stressful day. I want to take care of you."

"Please let me do this. I've missed your dick so much. It's all I could think of when I was alone in bed at night." I wrap my hand around his girth, loving the way it twitches at my touch.

"I'm a man. I'll never turn away your warm mouth on my cock." He reaches over and shuts off the faucet. "Bath time will have to wait."

I wrap my lips around his tip and suck, stroking him long and languidly. I don't rush through the blow job I give him, teasing every ounce of pleasure I can get from him. He grunts and groans through it all, until he's spurting down my throat. I'm much better at swallowing now. Practice makes perfect.

When I'm done, I step into the tub, leaving room behind me. Bo climbs in, settling me between his legs. The hot water seeps into my stressed-out muscles and he uses the lavender scented oil to massage my shoulders. My mind tranquil and my body relaxed.

"Lean back," he says, and I do, resting my head on his chest and closing my eyes. I feel a hand cup me from under the water. He rolls my balls around in his palm, occasionally pressing a teasing finger against my hole.

"That feels so good," I murmur.

"It's about to feel even better." He strokes me from under the water. His hands are soft, but his grip is firm. "That's it. You're getting hard for me."

I bite down on my tongue, not wanting to wake the baby. His other hand rubs up and down my chest, flicking over the flat disks of my nipples. Whoever said nipple play was only for women has no clue it can be just as good for a man.

"Let's move this to the shower," he whispers gruffly, and releases me so he can step out of the tub. He flips on the steam shower and I amble after him, dripping puddles of water along the way.

He guides me to the bench and motions for me to sit, which I do while admiring his naked form. I don't know how I repressed my desire for men my whole life, because seeing his chiseled abs and semi-hard cock is the biggest turn on of my life. I'm an idiot for thinking I could be asexual.

I am, in no way, indifferent to the male form.

He kneels before me and swallows my dick whole. The way his throat constricts around me has me hissing and my hips bucking. He rubs the muscles of my thighs, as his mouth works me over.

Every sense is on overload. The calming lavender scent, the sucking and slurping sounds he's making, seeing him peer up at me through his light brown eyes, feeling his warm mouth around me, and tasting his cum on my tongue from earlier. It's too much. Within minutes an orgasm hits me, sending my semen shooting down his throat.

"I need to fuck you now. Turn around and kneel on the bench." He leaves me for a minute. I look over my shoulder to see when he returns, he has a small bottle of lube.

"Where did that come from?" I ask.

"I stopped at the gift shop earlier. I wanted to be ready for our celebratory fuck."

"How did you know it would be good news?"

He wraps his arms around me from behind and kisses my neck. "Because you're the kindest, most honest, caring man I've ever met, and I knew the judge would see that."

"Oh."

His lips find mine, and we kiss. I'll never tire of the way his larger lips envelope mine. His tongue laps at mine, sending shivers down my spine. He moves down my neck and then down even further. He spreads my cheeks and tongues my hole. My eyes roll back in my head as he barely breaches the ring of muscle.

"Spread wide for me." He smacks my outer thigh.

I part my knees and listen as he pops the cap of the lube. Then his dick is between my ass cheeks, begging for entry. I relax my muscles, as he slowly invades my hole. He fills me so completely, in every way. I rest my forehead against the tile and surrender myself to the way he stimulates from deep inside. I came not ten minutes ago, but he's milking my prostate and I know I'm going to come again.

"This ass is mine forever, you know that, right?" he grunts.

"Yes," I hiss.

"I'm going to fill you up. You want that?"

"Do it. Please."

"Touch yourself for me. Show me how hard you can get," he whispers in a seductive voice.

I stroke myself while he pounds into me, driving into my prostate. We come together in a series of gasps and groans. He pulls me up and tenderly washes me. It's a good thing because I'm completely boneless.

"I'm going to marry you," he announces while drying me off.

"I'm sorry, what?" I choke on my own saliva.

"You said we were a family. Did you mean it?"

"Yes. Every word."

"Then I'm going to marry you. Make it legal and shit." He wraps his own towel around his waist. "And I want to adopt Lane."

"You do?"

"Yeah, babe. I do." He chuckles.

"Then we're yours."

Boaz Dixon is a sneaky one. He snuck into my life, into my heart, and now into my future. I wonder what else he's going to surprise me with.

"And I think we need at least two more kids."

There it is. Always shock and awe with this guy. Big moments and calm in-betweens. Finally, I'm where I'm supposed to be.

THE END

MISS B BY K WEBSTER
A Taboo Treat & Brigs Ferry Bay Crossover

CHAPTER ONE
KERRY

YOU EMBARRASSED ME.

Daddy's words keep replaying in my head over and over again.

Anything that impacts his public image is embarrassing. In this case, it was a failed date with one of his politician buddies. The guy was a sleazeball and I couldn't get away from him fast enough. When he got handsy, I smacked him. The jerk tattled on me to my father.

And now I'm trying desperately to dry my tears before my after-school appointment shows up. Of all the people to see me cry, it can't be *him*.

Zane Mullins.

School's bad boy who spends more time in the principal's office than anyone else who attends Brown High.

Zane sniffs out weakness and preys on it. I've seen him zero in on it time and time again with different teachers. With me, he knows his shameless flirting gets under my skin, so he turns on his charm during our forced Monday meetings.

It wouldn't be so annoying except he's incredibly good-looking. His muscular frame towers over mine and his deep voice never ceases to vibrate me to my core. He flusters me and I think he knows it.

That's another reason why these dates don't work that Daddy keeps setting me up on. I'm harboring a shameful crush on a student at the school I work at. It doesn't matter that he's eighteen and very much a man in all the ways it counts.

He's. My. Student.

It's my job to guide him and counsel him in regard to his grades, his behavior, and his future. Our school's principal, Adam Renner, tasked me with making sure he gets on the right track. If I let my guard down for a second, Zane will pounce. I'm afraid if he pounces, I might like it.

Now *that* would embarrass Daddy.

I can only imagine what a scandal that would be. It gives me hives just thinking about having my name splashed all over the news and social media, everyone seeing me as some sexual predator or something.

It's times like these, I miss my twin brother, Keith. He's not dead or anything, but because he doesn't conform to Daddy's strict rules, he's pretty much been excommunicated from the family. When we all moved out of Brigs Ferry Bay to this town so Daddy could grow his law firm, Keith stayed back with Grandma. I speak to him on his birthday and on Christmas, but mostly we catch up via texts. I don't dare go visit him in case Daddy finds out, and Keith certainly doesn't come out this way. If I had my other half here, I could loosen up a bit, not always worrying about the rug being pulled out from under my feet.

The school bell rings, signaling the end of the day and the start of my meeting with

Zane. A flush creeps up my neck as I wonder how I'll thwart his advances today. Outside my office, I can hear Zane and his friend, Elma, laughing about something. Those two would be better suited for each other, but no matter how hard Adam tries to hide it, I know he's sleeping with her.

There's been a few times I've heard…stuff…in his office. Giggles. Smacking. Moans. I shift in my seat, suddenly too warm. Adam has PTSD, and most recently after fireworks going off in the auditorium, he had a panic attack. Elma was able to calm him down by kissing him. I was shocked to say the least and disappointed that the principal whom I admired was obviously in an intimate relationship with a student. I'd expected outrage from Coach Long, since he was the other witness to the event, but he didn't seem surprised, nor did he seem to care. So, I never breathed a word of it to anyone.

Elma giggles once more, but not from whatever it is she and Adam get up to in his office. No, her laughter is from Zane. Again. For some reason, it's grating on my nerves today.

It's not her fault, though.

Because Daddy chewed me out over the phone earlier, I've been overly anxious and upset. That explains the tears and bitchiness, not Elma.

"Looking extra fine today, Miss B," a deep voice rumbles. "I like when you wear white because I can totally see your bra."

And just like that, I'm bright red.

As though he has a magnetic pull I'm helpless to fight against, my eyes greedily land on him. He closes the door behind him, a satisfied smirk on his handsome face as I blatantly check him out. His black hair is messy today, but it's as though he fixed it that way on purpose. Bright green eyes blaze with amusement and his lips twitch like he wants to smile. Today he's wearing a too-tight black T-shirt that shows off his impressive physique and jeans with more holes than is allowable for the dress code.

Stop looking.

As though he can hear inside my head, his grin spreads across his face in that wicked way I sometimes fantasize about. I straighten in my chair, pursing my lips, hoping like hell he can't see how much he affects me.

"Stop the nonsense, Mr. Mullins."

"You know I prefer it when you call me Daddy Z." He waggles his brows at me as he crosses the room, wafting his manly scent my way. He drops his body into the chair across from me, sprawling out as though he's royalty and I'm here to serve him. "Besides, Mr. Mullins is my dad and I'd prefer not to be anything like him if I can help it."

His words are said in jest, but I don't miss the clipped way in which he says them. Zane is tightlipped most of the time about his father, but I know he doesn't get along with him.

"How did training with Coach Long go last week?" I ask, ignoring his attempts to fluster me.

"Did you see me limping when I came in?" he asks, his green eyes brightening.

No, I was too busy staring at your kissable mouth.

"I did not." I clear my throat and smooth out the non-existent wrinkles on my skirt. "I take it he's helping you work through your injury?"

His features grow stormy and he nods. "Coach is such a dick, but he knows his shit."

"Don't curse," I grumble.

"Oh, sorry," he amends, "I forgot you have virgin ears."

He licks along his bottom lip and dammit if I don't follow the action, completely enamored by the movement.

"I, uh, don't have virgin ears. It's just inappropriate for school." I lift my chin, hoping to assert some authority over him. "Can we discuss your plans for when you graduate next month?"

"Probably prison if we're being honest." He shrugs and then chuckles. "Don't look so surprised, Miss B. We both know it's inevitable."

I'm about to chide him when my phone buzzes with another call from Daddy. Probably to apologize for being so cruel earlier. I try to ignore it, but as soon as it hits voicemail, he tries again. He wouldn't continue to call unless it were an emergency.

"Answer it," Zane says, gesturing to my phone. "I can tell it's driving you crazy not to."

"I just need to make sure nothing's wrong." I swipe a finger over my screen to take the call. "Hello?"

"For heaven's sake, sweetheart, you know I hate when you don't answer the first time," Daddy chides in greeting.

"I'm in a meeting," I mutter back. "What's the emergency?"

"No emergency," he assures me. "I just have someone new for you to have dinner with. Someone I think you'll be more compatible with. Sean Gentry is also an attorney at our firm, but he's younger than Carl. I think you'll like him."

A flash of annoyance bursts through me. He's so hot and cold. One minute he's calling me a disgrace to our family and now he's pretending as though that conversation didn't happen. He's back to auctioning his daughter to the highest bidder.

"Daddy," I clip out, "I have a student in my office. You know Mondays I have this weekly career meeting. Can we discuss this another time?"

The line goes silent. All irritation fades as my anxiety spikes. I don't like upsetting my father, but sometimes he's too overbearing that even the good girl who's used to pleasing him loses her cool.

"Just meet Sean for dinner at five. I'll text you the details," Daddy says in a curt tone. "We can discuss your disrespectful attitude over Mom's roast on Sunday. Goodbye, sweetheart."

And just like that, the stinging tears are back.

I swallow down the giant ball of emotion forming in my throat. Now's not the time to analyze why no matter what I do, it'll never seem to be enough for my father. Keith had the right idea. He chose himself. His happiness. His needs. My brother knew he'd never measure up to Daddy's impossible standards, so he didn't even try. Keith's happy being a single, nearly thirty-year-old playboy bartender.

"I'm sorry," I mutter, unable to look at Zane as I set my phone down on the desk. "I shouldn't have answered that. Where were we?"

When he doesn't reply, I lift my eyes to meet his intense stare. He jokes around a lot, but on occasion, I catch him staring at me as though he has private access inside my mind. Like he knows secrets about me no one else does.

"Your dad sounds like he's just as much of a dick as mine is," he says, his brows furling. "Want to talk about it?"

I chew on my bottom lip. No matter how much I try and force him to talk about his future, it's pointless. He doesn't budge. Yes, his grades have improved and he seems to enjoy training with Coach Long, but as far as his plans beyond graduation next month, we haven't made any progress. So, straying from the usual argument we have, I decide on a different tactic. Maybe if he can trust me a little as a friend, I can get him to open up.

"He's not a…" I fight a smile. "Dick."

Zane laughs. "There's my girl."

My heart does a flutter inside my chest. I feel like an idiot for letting him get to me, but I can't help it. His forward nature these past three months is wearing me down.

"He's just overbearing," I admit with a sigh. "I'm the good girl. The twin who followed the rules and got a respectable job within the community. He's used to me obeying and when I don't, I think it reminds him of my brother."

Zane crosses his arms over his chest, which makes his biceps bulge. Not that I notice or anything. His scrutinizing gaze has me squirming in my seat.

"What?" I mutter, suddenly self-conscious.

"I'm just trying to imagine another version of you. I bet he has no problems getting laid."

I curl my lip up. "No one wants to imagine their brother getting laid."

"You have a point there." His lips quirk up on one side. "You never have the urge to disobey *Daddy*?"

My face flames hot at the breathy way he says the word Daddy. "No," I hiss. "I don't like disobeying him…"

"But? Come on, Miss B. Don't hold out on me now."

"But sometimes I wish he'd stop trying to set me up on dates. There. You happy?"

His features darken and his jaw clenches. "Am I happy that your dad is trying to pimp you out to old douchebags? Fuck no."

Warmth pools in my belly. "I, uh, think we should discuss college now."

"Why?" he probes, his gaze dropping to my chest. "Is the conversation getting *inappropriate*?"

The room goes silent and then we hear it.

Soft, breathy moans in the office next door.

My eyes widen and Zane stands, shaking his head.

"Just let them be," he grits out, a fierce expression on his face. "Please."

"I…holy crap."

This is so awkward. And wrong. I should tell someone, right? The principal of our school is not just kissing a student like I witnessed recently, but is most definitely fucking her, clearly unbothered by the fact others can hear. I can't live in denial when I'm witnessing it firsthand and with another student no less. I need to report this, right? But I'm no better because I have far too many late-night secret fantasies where the man, who's now rounding the side of my desk, warms my bed. I wouldn't act on them, though.

Liar.

The idea of Adam losing his job because of me makes my stomach clench violently. Someone else will have to report him. I don't want that guilt on my hands.

Zane grabs the arms of my chair and turns it so I'm facing him. With him in my space and so close, I can't form words or think or breathe for that matter. All I can do is stare up at his perfect, handsome face and inhale his masculine, soapy scent.

"It can be our secret," he rumbles, green eyes boring into me. "Say okay, Miss B."

I open my mouth as if to argue, but no words come out.

"How about I tell you what I really want out of life?" He squats down in front of me. "Do we have a deal?"

When I nod, trading my silence for his words, I realize I've just made a deal with the devil.

His evil grin confirms he knows this too.

CHAPTER TWO
ZANE

FUCKING FINALLY.

I've hit on this woman every day for months and she won't open up. Sure, she's cracked a little here and there, letting me see past her stiff, prissy exterior but always closes back up before I have a chance to slip inside to see the real her. The vulnerable woman who aches to be loved and adored.

I want to be the man who gets in.

Not just in the physical sense.

I'd be lying if I said I don't dream of stripping her bare and pinning her beneath my hard body, fucking her like a madman. But it's more than that with Kerry Bowden. Everything about her is so soft and refined and fucking perfect. It calls to the dark, baser parts of me that want to ruffle those parts of her. She's someone trapped in this veneer package. Someone broken and sad. Someone like me. I just need to save her from herself.

"Tell me," she murmurs, a blond tendril falling from her tight bun. "Please."

Always so sweet and well-mannered.

"Take your hair down." I rise to my feet. "And join me on the sofa."

Her blue eyes narrow as she studies me with suspicion. "Why?"

"Because I need you to relax." I hold my hand out to her. "When you relax, I relax. How are we to become friends, Miss B, if you don't let me inside you?"

She gasps, her plump pink lips parting. "Mr. Mullins!"

"Relax," I say again, winking at her. "Come on."

To my surprise, she takes my hand. It's so small and soft. I'm not eager to let it go, so I don't.

"Shoes," I say, giving her hand a squeeze.

She rolls her eyes, taking years off her age, and she kicks out of her heels. I like how just like that she becomes a short, tiny thing.

Mine.

She's *my* short, tiny thing.

"Now the hair." I raise an eyebrow, waiting for her to comply.

Averting her gaze, she reaches up to tug at the hair tie. Golden waves tumble out over her shoulder and she gives her head a shake. Her floral scent becomes stronger with her hair now down. I crave to take a handful of it in my fist and bury my nose in it.

"That feels so much better," she says, a smile teasing her sexy lips.

I'm unable to tear my gaze from her pretty features. With her hair down, she seems younger. After stalking her lame-ass social media accounts, I learned she'll be thirty in November. I've never dated a woman twelve years my senior, but I'd make an exception for her, because something tells me dating her would be better than any shallow relationship I've ever been in.

"You can let go of my hand now." Her voice quivers and based on the way she peers shyly at me from beneath her lashes, I'd say she doesn't actually want me to. She's just saying what she thinks is the right thing. That daddy of hers has tried his damnedest to turn her into a compliant, rule following robot. Since my dad is no different, I understand this probably better than anyone ever could. It also makes me want to drag her out from under his influence, because unlike me, she's still trapped.

I don't release her hand, and instead tug at it for her to follow me over to the sofa in her office. Once we sit, our thighs touching, I drag her hand into my lap. I expect her to try and pull free, but she doesn't. Her blue eyes probe me in an expectant sort of way, as though she wants me to lead the way for us.

Don't worry, Miss B, I'll take care of you.

"Dad doesn't care what I do so long as I don't interfere with his campaign," I mutter, the words bitter on my tongue. "I don't want to go to college."

"But—"

I cut her off with a frown. "I thought you were going to listen."

She purses her lips together and nods.

"I like math," I tell her even though she already knows. "Coach Long likes to bust my balls in the classroom too, not just on the track, but unlike on the track, I can answer every damn one of his questions."

"There are lots of careers that involve math," she blurts out and then her cheeks turn pink. "Sorry. I'm trying."

I flash her a wide grin. "I forgive you, beautiful."

This time, her lips curl up into a shy smile that makes my dick twitch in my jeans.

"When I was ten, my dad and I built a treehouse in our backyard," I explain, my voice dropping to a husky drawl as I remember the past. "It was one of the last times we did something together. Back when he liked me."

"Your dad likes you," she exclaims in vehemence. "Tell me you know that."

"I'm not a liar. He doesn't. Not anymore." I rub my thumb over the back of her hand. "Anyway, so this treehouse was awesome. Dad let me design it. It had real windows and cabinets and tile floors. I spent more time sleeping in my treehouse than in my real house."

Her blue eyes are wide as she intently listens to my story. I take a moment to study her pretty face up close. Cute little nose. Long, dark mascara-painted lashes. Pouty mouth. So fucking beautiful.

"For four years, I loved that thing. But, as Dad got more and more bogged down with work, he came out to see it less and less." I grimace as I think about how many nights I spent yearning for my dad to care about me more than his job. "It wasn't until I broke my leg freshman year that I too stopped going to the treehouse."

Because I couldn't climb.

By the time I could again, I was too angry at the world. The last thing I gave a shit about was a stupid treehouse I built with my dad.

"The thing I missed about it wasn't so much the space but the love and hard work that went into it. We built it. From nothing." I lean into her, unable to blatantly inhale her delicious scent. "That, too, seemed like a pipe dream after my injury, but I don't know, after the past few months working with Coach Long and working past the pain in my leg, I think maybe it's possible. That maybe I could do something with my hands. Design, build, create. The idea of making something from nothing excites me."

The idea of having my own business and not having to answer to anyone is enticing.

Some people aren't made to work for the man. I think I'm one of those people.

A smile graces her lips. "I can see your passion."

"Can you?" My voice is a guttural growl as I reach up with my free hand to toy with a strand of her hair. "See my passion, that is?"

She sucks in a sharp breath. "Maybe we should cut this meeting short."

"But we're just getting started, Miss B."

Her eyes flutter closed as I dip closer to her face, unable to resist the pull she has over me. I'm desperate to capture her lips with mine and kiss the hell out of her. Testing my luck, I slide my hand into her hair, gripping just hard enough for her to understand I'm in charge here.

Not her daddy.

Not Renner next door.

Not her inner moral code or the ethical code of conduct she signed.

Me.

I tighten my grip, tilting her head back and exposing her creamy neck. With a gentleness I didn't know I even possessed, I kiss the pulsating vein on her neck. A brush of my lips and a swipe of my tongue. Her whimper sings to my fucking soul, drawing me in closer to her hot flame. I don't even care if I get burned. I kiss her neck again, this time nipping at her flesh with my teeth. I can burn too.

The doorknob twisting has me releasing Kerry and sitting back as though I wasn't about to bruise her neck with my mouth. As the door swings open, I stand up, drawing the attention of our intruder and giving her a moment to collect herself. If I know my girl, she's mentally freaking the fuck out.

"Principal Renner," I greet, giving him my most antagonistic grin. I like Renner, even if he does bust my balls about as much as Coach Long does. He's a good guy. "Miss me, man?"

He rolls his eyes. "I came to check in before I left to make sure you guys were making any progress."

"Oh, we're progressing." I wink at him. "Did Elma get into trouble again? I could have sworn I heard her getting punished."

He gives nothing away aside from a tick in his jaw. Good. I may like the guy, but I don't need him reading into how flustered Kerry is or the fact she's shoeless and her hair is down. Or the fact her neck is wet from my mouth. No, I'll turn the tables and run him the hell out of here.

I know what you did in there with my friend, Renner.

As I knew he would, he tenses and begins his retreat.

"Miss Bowden," Renner grunts, "just email me an update. I need to get going."

She squeaks out a goodbye as he closes the door. By the time I turn to look at her, she's pulled her hair back into a bun and is sliding her shoes back on. The moment is lost, which fucking sucks, but I'm no quitter. Not with her at least.

"Mr. Mullins," she chokes out, frantic eyes meeting mine. "That was…it shouldn't have…"

I stalk up to her, crowding her space. She bumps her ass against the edge of the desk. Now that I've trapped her, I take my time devouring her nervous expression. Blue eyes flicker with worry and she chews on her bottom lip. I reach up and run my thumb along her skin that's still damp from my mouth.

"It did," I whisper, "and I believe it'll happen again. That and so much more."

"What have I done?"

"You didn't do anything," I croon, sliding my hand to her jaw. "Look at me."

She squeezes her eyes shut, the little brat. My fingers are firm as I press them into her skin, angling her head up to face me. Since she refuses to look at me, I give her what we both want, though only one of us will admit it. I brush my lips over hers in a whisper of a kiss before nipping at her bottom lip. She gasps, parting her lips, and I make my move. My tongue plunges into her mouth, eagerly seeking her sweet one. The sounds coming from her are pure honey and I could get drunk from them. I don't give her a chance to kiss me back. I simply own her with my kiss. She's afraid to step out into the unknown with me, so I'll just make her my unwilling victim, dragging her with me. That way, she can blame me rather than herself.

hands find my chest, pressing against me, but not hard enough that I take her seriously. Especially not when her tongue teases me back, almost unsure, but definitely there taking part in the kiss. I don't take advantage of the moment and pull back all too soon, my eyes searching her clear blue depths.

"You okay?" I ask, studying her for signs of distress.

She swallows and tears well in her pretty blues. "Not really, no."

"You will be," I assure her. "You have me to take care of you."

Her mask slips and for a brief moment, she looks at me as though it's exactly what she wants. For me to take care of her.

Consider it done, Miss B.

"Y-You should go," she stammers. "I need to leave. I have to meet someone for dinner."

I step back, irritation burning in my gut. "You're still going on that date with a douchebag your daddy set you up with?"

Guilt has her flinching and unable to look at me. "I have to."

"No, Kerry, you don't," I growl, my words dripping with anger. "Not now."

Teary eyes finally meet mine. "What happened here can't happen again, Mr. Mullins."

Mr. Fucking Mullins.

"You know I won't agree to that." I yank my phone from my pocket and open it. "What's your number? At least let me check in on you later."

To my surprise, she recites her number and then she sighs. "I'll be fine."

"No, you're willingly going on a date with someone your dad has chosen. He's essentially arranging your marriage for you. Is that what you want, Miss B? To be forced into a relationship you didn't choose?"

"None of this is your business," she exclaims, her voice going shrill and her face turning red.

"You're wrong, beautiful," I grind out. "It became my business the second you let me touch you. You're mine, even if you refuse to admit it yet."

She turns away from me, gripping the edge of the desk. "Just go. Please."

Stepping behind her, I run my fingertip down her spine over her silky white shirt. "I'll go, but I'm calling you later so you can tell me all about your date. Promise me you'll answer and then I'll leave."

"Yes," she breathes. "I'll answer."

"Good girl." I give her sexy ass a playful smack. "I can't wait."

CHAPTER THREE
KERRY

I PACE THE FOYER OF THE ITALIAN RESTAURANT, WAITING ON MY DATE TO arrive, a bundle of nerves. Not because of the date. Because of him.

Zane.

We kissed.

Oh, God, we kissed.

And, rather than hating it, I loved it. Ache for more. Yearn for him to hold me in his arms. Everything in me craved to throw in the towel and just give in. Give in to the feelings he evokes when around me. To, for once, ignore the rules in front of me and make my own.

Instead, I pushed him away.

Hardest thing I've ever done, too.

I glance at the clock. Fifteen after five. Maybe Sean will be a no-show and I can leave. My fingers itch to text Zane. I already told him what happened can't happen again, but he's not the type to listen. I should try anyway. Pulling my phone out from my purse, I glance over the text from Daddy saying Sean was running late and find Zane in my phone. I expect a nickname for himself or something silly, but all it's listed under is Z.

Me: You shouldn't worry about me.

His response is immediate.

Z: I do a lot of things I shouldn't.

My heart flutters at his words. Kissing and touching me are definitely at the top of the list, but he did it anyway.

Me: Perhaps you should turn over a new leaf. Try being good for a change.

Z: How's that working out for you, Miss B?

Me: Fabulous.

Z: I can hear your sarcasm from a mile away.

Me: A mile? Where are you?

Z: It's a joke. Where did the douchebag take you anyway? Obviously not anywhere good if you're sneaking in texts to me.

Me: The new Italian place downtown. It smells good, but my date is late.

Z: Need a fill in? I'm actually three miles away, but I could be there in five.

The thought of him sharing a meal with me thrills me. However, that cannot happen. Not while he's a student at Brown High.

Me: He'll be here soon. No need to worry about me.

Z: Just get shitfaced. That'll get you through the boring date. You can sneak off to the bathroom and call me if you need entertaining.

Me: I don't drink. I'll have to endure the boredom without any aides.

Z: That doesn't surprise me. You really are a good girl. Don't forget to call me later, beautiful, so I don't worry.

My chest tightens at his words. Had I met Zane anywhere aside from school, I know we would've hit it off right off the bat. I wouldn't even mind the age gap if he were just a few years older and if seeing him didn't affect my employment. Life never works out the way it's supposed to.

As if on cue, a handsome man in an expensive suit struts in. He has the same air of superiority my father does. Smug. Arrogant. Untouchable. His gait is no-nonsense as he approaches me, as if doing me a favor by showing up finally.

"You must be Kerry," he says, a forced smile on his face. "Sorry about my tardiness. I'm working on a big case that's stolen nearly all of my free time. Forgive me, sweetheart."

I cringe because it's the same endearment Daddy uses, not to mention spoken in the same condescending tone.

"It's fine. Sean, is it?"

"Excuse my manners. Sean Gentry." He shakes my hand and then glances at my phone still in the grip of my other one. "I hope I'll have your attention tonight and not that."

Heat burns up my neck, settling on my cheeks. I feel like I've been chastised for being impolite and I haven't even done anything wrong. Like the dutiful girl I am, I mutter out an apology before shoving my phone into my purse.

"Thank you." He flashes me a shark-like grin, revealing all his white, shiny teeth. "Now let's get you a drink."

Me: Save me.

Z: Really?

Me: No, I'm kidding. But you were right. Lamest date ever. He wasn't thrilled when I declined wine and asked for sweet tea instead.

Z: There's my good girl.

MY HEART PATTERS IN MY CHEST AT HIS WORDS. I SHOULDN'T BE TEXTING him, but compared to the kiss we shared, it feels far more innocent. Besides, I promised I'd check in.

Me: I should get back out there. If I waste any more time hiding in the bathroom, he might suspect I'm avoiding him and texting. I already got in trouble once for having my phone.

Z: You? In trouble? Sorry, I can't imagine it.

Me: Oh, I was in trouble. It would have made you proud.

Z: Did you take your hair down for him?

On a whim, I take a selfie.

Me: No, I only do that for you.

Rather than waiting for his reply, I shove my phone down into my purse and take a calming breath before exiting the bathroom. I'm on a date with a man my daddy wants me to be with and I'm ruining it by texting with my hot student. It's horrible, but I don't feel guilty. I didn't want to go on this date in the first place. If Daddy would stop to consider what I want for once, he'd know this.

When I reach the table, our food is sitting there. Sean hasn't touched his and his expression is cool. I guess I spent more time in the bathroom than I thought.

"This looks amazing," I say, unable to keep the nervous quiver from my voice. "Thank you for waiting on me."

"Of course, sweetheart."

The meal is extra salty. I want to complain to the waiter and have them remake it, but based on the disapproving glare Sean is giving me, I don't think it's wise. I gulp down my sweet tea, hoping to wash it down instead. The waiter refills my tea and disappears again.

"You see that guy over there," he says, pointing behind me. "He works at the firm with your father and me."

I twist in my seat to see who he's pointing at. The room spins, immediately making me nauseous. Squeezing my eyes shut, I will the woozy feeling to disappear. Slowly, I reopen my eyes and turn back to Sean. There's a glint in his eyes I don't trust.

"Feeling okay, sweetheart?"

"I'm not sure the food is sitting right," I admit. "It was a little salty."

"You should have told me," he challenges, his eyes darkening. "We could have returned it."

"It's fine," I say, picking up my tea glass. I'm bringing it to my lips when I notice white residue on top.

"Is there a problem?"

"I, uh, no. I think I might throw up. If you'll excuse me, I'll be right back."

"Let me grab the check," he says, faux concern in his voice. "I'll run you home too, since you don't seem to be feeling so well."

It takes everything in me to keep from wobbling or puking on my way to the restroom. Once inside, I lock myself in a stall and fish my phone out. Everything is spinning too much to text, so I dial Zane.

"Must have been lame if—"

"Zane," I croak out. "I think…I think I've been drugged."

"What?" The furious growl has me bursting into tears. "Hey, beautiful," he says, his voice softening, "talk to me. Explain what happened."

"I went to the…I went to the bathroom. When I came back, the…the food was there and…I…it was salty." I lean my head against the metal stall wall. "I drank my tea. He, uh, distracted me. When I looked in my glass…I can't be sure, but…Zane, I don't feel so good."

"I'm on my way, Kerry, okay? Don't worry. I'm coming to get you."

I swipe at the tears on my cheek. "He says he's going to take me home."

"You're not going anywhere with that douchebag. Stay put. Promise me."

"I promise," I whisper. "Hurry."

We hang up and I place my phone back into my purse. Bile crawls up my throat, forcing me to my knees in a quick scramble to reach the toilet on time. I puke up the contents of my stomach, sobbing the whole time. When I've purged my system of the horrible dinner, and what I believe to be the drugs I ingested, I finally climb to my feet. I'm just washing my mouth out and splashing water on my face when Sean enters the bathroom.

"You look terrible," Sean says, frowning. "Want me to call your father? Do you need to go to the hospital?"

I want to scream in his face.

You know what you did!

My lips refuse to move. Tears well and spill out of their own accord. He rushes over to me, wrapping an arm around me. I'm disgusted by his touch.

"Let's get you out of here. Don't worry, I already spoke to management that you'd clearly eaten undercooked food or something. They comped our meal, but it doesn't feel like enough. I'll be filing a formal complaint later."

He guides me out of the restaurant, past all the curious onlookers. As soon as we make it outdoors, I start dragging my feet.

"You can, uh, just go. I have a ride," I murmur, unable to meet his hard stare.

"Your father?"

"No, my—"

"Brother," a deep, familiar voice growls. "Keith Bowden."

I snap my head up, locking into Zane's intense green ones. "There you are. See, Sean, my brother is here."

Sean releases me, his jaw clenching. "I could have gotten you home, sweetheart. You didn't need to call your brother."

"It's fine. I know you have your important case you're working on. Thanks for dinner." I force a smile. "Good night, Sean."

His eyes flicker with barely contained rage. Finally, he bites back whatever he was going to say, leaning in to kiss my cheek. "We'll have to do it again sometime soon. I cook one helluva steak. Next time, we can dine at my place."

He stalks off, climbs into his Porsche parked out front, and then zooms away. Zane pounces on me, drawing me into his arms and hugging me tight.

"It's okay," he croons. "I'm here now. I've got you."

I cling to him, my tears soaking his shirt. "I don't feel so good."

"I know, beautiful. I'm going to take you to the ER."

"N-No. Just take me home."

He pulls back to look at me, his palms sliding to my cheeks. "I can't do that. Not until I know you're going to be okay. Once I know you're not going to die on me, I'll take you home. Trust me?"

"Y-Yes."

The softness in his stare cuts me deep, burrowing its way into my heart. I don't know how or why I chose Zane Mullins of all people to connect with, but it's happening and I'm powerless to stop it.

I feel like whatever's been brewing between us for months has finally been tapped into. When he touched and kissed me in my office, we crossed a line we can't come back from. I'm terrified for what could happen, but I'm also relieved. The fantasy come to life feels realer than anything I've ever known.

CHAPTER FOUR
ZANE

"AGAIN," DR. MORRIS SAYS, FROWNING AT KERRY, "IF YOU THINK YOU WERE drugged, you really ought to let me call Sheriff McMahon."

She stubbornly shakes her head, glowering at me. "Like I told you already. It was the food. I think it's just a simple case of food poisoning."

"Your brother disagrees," Dr. Morris challenges. "Right, Keith?"

Her eyes roll, but she doesn't correct him. We may have fudged a bit on our relationship so I could come back with her.

"Maybe I'm just too overprotective," I grumble. "If that's what she wants to believe, who are we to change that?"

Dr. Morris crosses his arms over his chest, studying her for a beat before glancing my way again. "I trust you won't let her eat there ever again."

And with *him*.

"Never," I growl, understanding his unspoken words.

Relief floods through him. "Good. The fluids should have flushed any toxins out and since your vitals are good, I feel comfortable discharging you now, Miss Bowden, but make sure you take tomorrow off to rest up."

It takes forever, but eventually, we're back in my car and headed to her place. She's quiet as she motions the directions leading up to her apartment. As soon as we park, she tries to hurry away, but I catch up to her, not willing to let her make the trek alone.

"You rescued me. I'm safe now," she mutters. "You can go."

"Nah, beautiful, I'm not done taking care of you yet."

She doesn't resist me when I tuck her into my side as we walk. The elevator ride two floors up is uneventful. We make it inside her apartment a few moments later. The floral scent is stronger here and I love it. It's thick in the air, and like a creep, I inhale it.

"Why don't you shower and wash up?" I suggest. "I'll make some tea."

Rather than arguing, she nods and disappears. I flip the lock on the apartment door and make my way into her kitchen. Everything is neat and orderly. The apartment lacks personality. It makes me wonder what it is Kerry Bowden likes besides pleasing people like her father. I rummage around until I find a kettle. My nanny, Peg, used to make tea for me when I was little and would sob over missing my mother. When Mom left my dad, she left me too. As though I was just as guilty as him for his affair. I was three at the time, so I didn't understand, and by the time I knew what an affair was, I couldn't be mad at Dad since he wasn't the one who left me. It was her.

I'm just filling a couple of teacups with the hot water when Kerry emerges from her room and walks into the kitchen. Stopping to let the teabags steep, I turn to look at her. Long blond hair is wet and combed through. Her face is free of makeup and slightly red around her eyes, which makes me think she cried some more in the shower. Contacts have been replaced by her nerdy black-rimmed librarian glasses that I secretly love when she wears. She's no longer in her glossy office clothes. No, she's fucking perfect in black yoga pants and an oversized hoodie that says, "Lost my Focus at Blur."

"You're almost too big for my kitchen," she mutters, shamelessly roaming her gaze up my front.

"Guess you'll need to move somewhere bigger so I'll fit."

She rolls her eyes but smiles as she grabs the milk from the refrigerator. After we fix up our tea, I follow her over to the sofa in the living room. She sits down on one end and doesn't balk when I plop down beside her.

"You're full of surprises, Mr. Mullins." She eyes me over her teacup, the steam fogging up her glasses. "You're chivalrous *and* make tea. Who knew?"

"It's Zane when we're alone, Kerry. I know what you taste like, remember?"

Color floods her cheeks and she breaks my stare to set her teacup down on the end table. I lean over and do the same. Then, I hug her to me. I'm thankful when she doesn't resist, instead settling against my side and clinging to my shirt.

"I still hate that you wouldn't call the police," I mutter, frustration evident in my gritty words.

A sigh pushes past her lips. "It's complicated. He works with my father."

"It doesn't give him a free pass. You lied to the doctor to protect that sonofabitch. I seriously doubt your father would be so approving of him now."

"Why would he drug me anyway?" Her voice is hoarse. "I don't understand."

"I don't understand either." I kiss the top of her head as I stroke my fingers through her damp hair. "You need to tell your dad, though, you're done with being set up."

She tenses. "That'll go over well."

"Who the hell cares? He's not exactly trying to hook you up with choice men here. That man was a predator and had the circumstances been different, he could have had you in his bed as we speak doing fuck knows what to you."

Her entire body trembles at my words. "I'll...I'll tell him what happened."

"Good girl."

"Thank you, Zane. And I'm sorry."

"For?"

"For misjudging you. You didn't deserve that."

"I didn't exactly make it easy for you," I say with a chuckle. "All these months I've just been trying to get you to confess your attraction to me. I'll admit my methods have been obnoxious."

She turns her head to peer up at me. "You drove me crazy."

"And now?"

"Still doing it."

"But..." I grin at her.

"But it worked. I'm attracted to you."

"That wasn't so hard now, was it?"

Her bottom lip gets tugged between her teeth as she frowns. "This...friendship... it's unethical and goes against my employment contract. And though I won't go to jail, I could certainly get fired."

"By Renner?" I snort. "He'd have to take his dick out of Elma long enough to grab a pink slip."

"Zane!"

I tickle her to remove the scowl from her face, which has the cutest giggle erupting from her. This goes on until I have her pinned beneath me on the couch, both of our chests heaving as we grin at each other.

My smile fades as I study her up close. Cute freckles I never noticed before are scattered over her cheeks and nose. Leaning forward, I kiss her lips. Just a peck. But then her fingers slide into my hair, pulling me closer. A small moan escapes her. I use the opportunity to kiss her deeply, noting how she tastes like mint from her toothpaste and a little like tea. We kiss until we're both panting and aching for more.

"I should go," I murmur, unable to keep my eyes off her swollen, pink lips. "If I stay, there's no telling what'll happen."

"Please stay." Her eyes water, vulnerability glimmering in them. "I'm…after tonight…"

"You don't want to be alone? He scared you?"

She nods, shame coating her flesh in crimson. "You think I'm weak?"

"No, beautiful, I think you're perfect. I'm the weak one. How the hell will I ever tell you no about anything? You hold power over me, woman."

"I don't want to be alone and I like spending time with you." She scratches her nails through my scalp. "Maybe you could stay over."

My dick throbs painfully as I consider her words. "You were drugged and went to the ER, Kerry. The last thing you need is getting fucked raw."

She laughs and smacks me on my shoulder. "No one said anything about sex."

"Nah, it's just a given. It'll happen and you'll love every second of it."

"But not tonight?"

"Tonight I'm just going to hold you."

"Tomorrow?"

"I can only promise to behave one day at a time," I tease and pull away from her. "Since you threw up your dinner and mine was interrupted, I'm going to make soup and grilled cheese. That okay with you?"

She grabs my hand. "Don't spoil me. I might get used to it."

"That's the plan, beautiful."

"THIS SHOW IS SO LAME," I SAY, SHAKING MY HEAD. "WHO ACTUALLY AGREES to marry someone they don't know?"

"It's called reality TV," she sasses back. "Be quiet."

"How about you watch the show and I'll find other ways to entertain myself?"

She ignores me, so I let my hands roam over her stomach, teasing a sliver of flesh above her waistline of her pants. A laugh escapes her as I bury my head under her hoodie. I inhale her sweet, fruity scent as I trail kisses up her bare stomach to her tits I often fantasize about. She's not wearing a bra underneath, which pleases me endlessly. While grabbing her right tit, I seek out the nipple of her left with my mouth. She groans, arching up as though she aches for more.

"Pay attention to your show," I tease and then bite her nipple.

"I can't," she breathes. "Oh, God, that feels good."

I suck on her nipple hard enough she cries out. Then I lick away the pain until she's squirming with need.

"I want you," she murmurs. "Please, Zane."

"As much as I want to give you what you want, beautiful, I don't think it's a good idea to fuck after the night you had." I bite her tit again. "But if you want me to get you off, that can be arranged."

"Y-Yes. I want that."

"That makes two of us."

I kiss my way down her stomach until I reach her belly button. My tongue fucks the shallow hole while I work her yoga pants and panties down her thighs. I sit up on my knees, yanking them the rest of the way off.

"Take off that hoodie," I command. "I want to see your tits when I worship your pussy."

She whimpers at my words and then peels it off her body. Kerry Bowden is a fucking vision in all her naked glory. I cannot wait until I can bury my dick deep inside her, claiming her forever. And it'll be forever. You don't have such intense feelings for someone like I have for her and it just be a random hookup. No, this is deeper than anything I've ever known.

"I want to see you too." Her tits jiggle when she sucks in a sharp breath. "It's only fair."

Chuckling, I rip off my T-shirt and toss it away. Her hungry stare devours the ink on my chest and my newly defined muscles thanks to Coach Long killing my ass after school several days a week.

"Pants too," she sasses.

"If the pants come off, I'm going to fuck you."

Her blue eyes flash with heat. "So?"

"We talked about this. Ain't happenin'."

"Leave your boxers on then," she rushes out. "I just want to see you."

I undo the button on my jeans and shove them down my thighs. Once they're gone, I grip her knees, crudely spreading her apart for me.

"Time for a lesson in pleasure, Miss B."

CHAPTER FIVE
KERRY

THIS IS SO WRONG.

So. Wrong.

Yet my body is quaking with need as Zane—my student!—places open-mouthed kisses all over my inner thighs, making me yearn for more. His muscular shoulders bunch and tighten with each movement. Everything about him is just so damn perfect.

He saved me.

I know it's bad that I was talking to him in the first place because of my position at the school, but had I not had that lifeline to him, I have no doubt I would've ended up in Sean's bed. It's repulsive and sickening that he'd go through the lengths of drugging me to get me into his bed. Is that all I'm seen as? A means to get to my father? And in this case, what was his play? To hurt Daddy or to get in good with him, knowing I'd never divulge to my father if I ended up sleeping with Sean?

My mind is reeling from earlier when I'm suddenly jerked to the here and now. I latch onto Zane's stare as he flattens his tongue against my pussy, licking along the seam, his green eyes flashing with wickedness. When the tip of his tongue reaches my clit, he teases it, barely brushing his tongue over it. I whimper, my breasts jiggling as I squirm beneath his ministrations.

"There's my girl. I want you out of your head and watching what I'm doing to you. You're getting your pretty pussy licked by me. And you can't deny your attraction to me anymore because I know it tastes like honey. So thick and sweet for me." His thumbs pull apart my opening, gaining him access inside. I gasp as his tongue slides into my body briefly before he pulls it back out. "Your lust for me is leaking out, Kerry. I'm going to clean it all out with my tongue. And when you feel better, I'm going to fuck this pretty hole until it's sore."

His words are a hot button inside me. I writhe with need, wanting him to touch me everywhere all at once. He latches his mouth on my pussy once more, sucking and licking and biting until black spots form in my vision. I crave for him to fuck me like he promises because I need more. So much more from him. I settle for rubbing at my nipples, aching for more touch.

"Good girl," he croons. "Twist those pink nipples until it hurts a little."

I'm so lost for this man.

Barely a man, but he is still a man.

There's nothing boyish about the seductive way he licks away my arousal and orders me to touch my body. I obey his command, pinching and tugging on my sensitive nipples. He smiles against my pussy, pleased, and then sets forth licking me right into an explosive orgasm. My entire body jolts as though lightning has struck me, a low, guttural moan escaping me. I'm too uptight for casual sex, so my encounters have been few and far between. The last good orgasm I had was when I'd had too much wine and got a little crazy with my vibrator.

Still, my toes didn't curl.

My voice didn't go raw from the moans.

And I didn't feel so utterly consumed.

He crawls up my body, leaving wet kisses along the way until his mouth meets mine. The taste of myself should be a turnoff, but it's not. I greedily devour him with a hungry kiss as he settles his cock against the part of me that still throbs. A thin layer of material separates us from what I really want.

Him.

All of him.

Every long, thick inch of this virile young man.

He finally pulls away, rolling onto his back, his eyes still locked on me. I'm instantly cold and I hate it. I want his heated touch. I need more.

"Zane—"

"I can't," he rumbles. "You're too fucking tempting and my self-control is hanging on by a thread."

I sit up and boldly straddle his hips. "We don't have to have sex, but you need to get off too." Seating myself over his dick, I shudder at how I can feel every vein and groove.

"You're a bad influence on me." His green eyes flash with a mixture of pleasure and devious intent. "I'm supposed to be the bad one." His large hands grip my hips and he squeezes.

I rest my palms on his solid chest and begin moving my hips, grinding along his thickness. His eyes flutter closed and his full lips part. I've never seen anyone so gorgeous in all my life. As his breathing intensifies, I go faster and faster.

"I'm going to come in my boxers," he croaks out. "Pull me out, baby."

I lift up, just enough to free his big dick from his underwear, before continuing my efforts of rubbing against him. It's bliss now that we're skin on skin. My pussy easily glides along his cock, bringing us both immense pleasure. I get lost in the sensation, quickly finding my way to another earth-shattering orgasm. As I moan, his fingers bite roughly into my hips and a grunt escapes him. His cum spurts out, landing on his lower stomach in thick, plentiful ropes. Lost in the moment, I run my fingers through it, smearing it along his cock and giving us more lubricant to work with. He hisses as I slide my throbbing pussy along his dick that still twitches as cum continues to leak out.

"Holy fuck," he mutters. "You're going to kill me."

I laugh because his expression is so serious. He smirks and then grabs my hips, drawing me off his dick onto the spent cum sitting on his stomach.

"Now you have to sit in the mess you made." His green eyes dance with humor.

"Not exactly a punishment," I tease, grinning at him.

He grabs a fistful of my hair, drawing me to his mouth where he ravishes me. One of his hands grabs my ass almost painfully as he thrusts his tongue into my mouth. We kiss hard and fervently until he's hard again, the tip of his dick poking at my asshole.

"Kerry," he bites out. "We're not fucking."

I know he's trying to be a gentleman because of what happened tonight with Sean. I'm desperate to have Zane, though. After denying myself for so long, it feels right and as though I deserve to have a sliver of happiness.

Can I find it with Zane Mullins?

"Okay," I grumble. "You win."

"I'll wreck your pretty pussy soon enough. Don't worry, Miss B."

I WAKE AS THE SUN RISES, MY BEDROOM SLOWLY BRIGHTENING WITH THE start of the day. Zane sleeps beside me on his stomach, his dark hair in disarray, with his pink lips barely parted. I'm amazed that this man would want me. Not that I have low self-esteem or anything, but he just seems so young and gorgeous and perfect. Like any beautiful girl would be lucky to have him, but he somehow got his sights set on me. I'm selfish because I want to keep him. I want this forbidden romance we've stumbled upon.

My job is at stake.

My reputation could be ruined.

My own father might disown me.

But none of it seems important with him in my bed.

I'm still naked and he's wearing his boxers. Maybe today he'll realize I'm fine and we can have sex. I ache to finish what we started last night. Zane has this intensity about him that calls to me. His good looks and charm are alluring, sure, but it's more than that. It's him. Something about the way he wants me and seems to care for me has me drawn to him in a way I can't come back from. I've never liked any guy as much as I do Zane.

It's a terrifying thought.

He's young and I'm his guidance counselor.

So much could go wrong. I read about such stories on the news and they always end badly. Most often, the woman is fired for being with her student, assuming he's old enough like Zane is, and escapes any jail time, but the articles posted are always shaming and embarrassing. If it gets out that I'm carrying on a romantic relationship with a student at Brown High, my career is over. Daddy's career could even take a hit from it.

It's so selfish because I still want him.

Yesterday and last night, we crossed the line and now that we've done it, I can't go back to the way things were. We've been intimate and now share secrets.

Bang. Bang. Bang.

I jolt upright in bed, my heart hammering in my chest. Zane's green eyes are wild and open now.

"Who is it?" he demands, his voice deep and gravelly with sleep.

"I, uh, don't know. Stay here."

I hurry out of bed and yank my silky robe off the back of the door. Quickly, I pull it on and tighten the ropes. The banging continues. I peek out the peephole and my stomach flops.

"Daddy?" I say through the door. "What are you doing here so early?"

"I came to check on you. I got a text this morning from Sean. He was worried about you."

I cringe but begin to unlock the door. I'm praying like hell Zane stays in the bedroom. As soon as I get the door open, Daddy runs his stare over me, assessing my appearance.

"You look terrible, sweetheart."

I clench my teeth, forcing a closed-lip smile as I gesture for him to come inside. "Thanks, Daddy."

He chuckles. "I wasn't being cruel. Do you think you've caught the flu?"

"No," I clip out.

His humor fades and he narrows his eyes at me. "What's going on with you?"

"Nothing. I'm fine."

"Everything go okay with Sean?"

I want to scream at him that Sean is a monster. But, right now, I just want him out of my house. If I get into a yelling match with Daddy, Zane might come out and I really don't need Daddy finding out about Zane this way.

"We're not compatible," I state in an icy tone.

Daddy frowns. "Your mother and I weren't either, but we grew to love each other. Sometimes relationships are more than just lust and love. Sometimes they're more practical if they have any luck of making it to the end."

"I don't like him." My voice rises a few octaves. "I don't want to see him again."

Annoyance flashes in his eyes that match mine. "You're being a child."

I gasp, blinking in shock. "Because I don't want to go out with the guy?"

"Because you're not even giving anyone a try. In case you didn't notice, Kerry, you're almost thirty. Your chances for finding a successful husband will decrease tenfold once you reach that hump."

Hot tears fill my eyes and I'm twelve again. Lectured to death by my father. Never quite measuring up or trying hard enough. Whenever I give him my tears, I know it only confirms what he feels.

"I think you should go," I croak out. "I think I'm going to be sick."

He purses his lips. "We're not done discussing this. Perhaps we can continue it for Sunday's dinner with your mother. Don't be late. In the meantime, put some effort into things with Sean."

I watch him leave, not having the guts to tell him what Sean did. I'm a weak idiot, just like my father alludes to. When I'm with Zane, he makes me feel like maybe I'm worth something. Funny how Daddy can crush it all in an instant.

The moment the door closes, warm, strong arms envelop me from behind. I sink against Zane's firm chest, allowing him to hold all the breaking pieces of me together.

"Your dad's an asshole."

"Yeah."

"Want me to make your day better?" He nips at my ear as his hands untie my robe. "I can make you so, so happy, beautiful."

I nod, my eyes rolling back as his fingers find my clit. He takes control of my mind—making all thoughts of him—as he rubs me right into a knee-buckling orgasm. Before I've even come down from my high, he twists me around and pushes me against the door. His mouth crashes to mine as he shoves his boxers down. As soon as he's free, he picks me up and my legs wrap around him. Like our bodies have always known the way, his cock presses against my opening and then glides right into me, stretching me to the point of pain as I take his large size.

Oh my God.

Zane Mullins is inside me.

I dig my heels into his ass and my fingernails into his shoulders. This spurs him into action. His fingers bite painfully into my ass cheek as he fucks me hard. My moans and his growls are the animalistic sounds coming from us as he tries to drive me through the door one thrust at a time. He's everywhere at once—his lips on mine, a hand on my ass and one on my breast, and deep inside of me. I shudder hard as an orgasm tears down my spine, lighting up every nerve ending in the process. The groan that rumbles through him is my only warning of his release. Heat surges into me—thick and potent. My body loves it because I clench around him as though to milk him for every drop.

"Oh, fuck," he murmurs against my mouth. "I probably shouldn't have done that."

Probably not.

But we've been doing everything we shouldn't, so why stop now?

Being reckless with him is exhilarating. I don't feel weak or small like usual. It's as though he's empowered me somehow. I feel strong and beautiful and worthy.

"Are you on birth control?"

I squeeze my eyes shut and bite on my bottom lip as hot tears burn the backs of my eyelids. Getting caught up in our little fantasy world is nice until reality smacks you in the face.

"Baby, shh," he croons, hugging me to him. "It's fine. I fucked up, not you. I was desperate to be inside you. It's okay."

I bury my face against his neck, the sobs finally escaping. He rubs my back and whispers assurances as I cry. His cock is still inside me, not completely soft, holding all of his cum inside. I know what a mistake this is and I still can't find it in me to want to undo it.

"It all makes me sick," I whisper. "In the past, I've been careful with condoms."

"I'm clean," he assures me. "As for the rest, if something happened, I would be there for you. You know that, right?"

This thing between us is quick and hot and crazy, but I know without a shadow of a doubt he would. He's a better man than anyone I've ever encountered.

"I do," I tell him. "Next time we'll be more careful."

He chuckles. "As long as there will be a lot more next times, I can live with that."

"Ready to shower so I can feed you?"

"Depends on what you're feeding me. I could eat right now, but you don't need to shower for that. In fact, I think I'd like to lick away the filth."

"Mr. Mullins!"

He laughs all the way to the shower, filling my heart and soul with something I never knew was missing until now.

Happiness.

CHAPTER SIX
ZANE

I'M AN IDIOT.

Somewhere along the way this year in my quest to wear Kerry down, I fell for her. And, since Renner forced those meetings on us back in January, I've developed feelings for her. It was slow and subtle, a gentle tug with each blush of her cheeks or smile. Though she refused to entertain my advances, I felt the pull on her end. The attraction and chemistry we have is undeniable. So, naturally, when we both dove into this thing together, we sank.

Deep.

Fast.

Hard.

It's been days since we first slept together. Every night is spent in her bed. Every morning we share breakfast and coffee and fantastic sex. When at school, our touches are behind closed doors. Each smile she gives me is in secret but loaded with promise. Now that we're finally saved by the weekend and she's ready to have Sunday dinner with her parents, I'm reluctant to let her go.

I'm addicted to her.

She curses from the bathroom and I bite back a chuckle. Since we've been intimate and spending time together, I get to see past the veneered façade of the perfect Miss Bowden and see the quirky, funny, adorable Kerry.

Sliding off the bed, I grab my jeans, pulling them up my thighs sans underwear. I zip them but don't fasten the button. When I reach the doorway, I grip the top of the doorframe, leaning in to watch her as she applies mascara.

Everything about her in this moment is flawless. A demure, floral print dress hugs her body. Her long blond hair has been straightened to sleek perfection. As she paints her naturally pretty face, she transforms into a glossy version of the woman who an hour ago was gagging on my cock, making a mess with slobber and tears.

"What?" she demands, her hand shaking badly enough she has to recap the mascara.

Frowning, I release the doorframe and step into the bathroom, wrapping my arms around her. Our stare meets in the mirror. "Are you nervous?"

"To have dinner with my parents?" She huffs. "Of course not."

"Then what's wrong?"

She gnaws on her plump bottom lip, her brows knitting together. "I don't know."

I sweep her hair to the side to expose her neck and press a soft kiss there. "If you don't want to tell him about Sean, don't. You've successfully avoided any more attempts by your father to set you up with him. Sean is a predator, but he's one we don't have to worry about anymore."

She turns in my arms, her palms cradling my cheeks. "How is it you're better than any man I've ever known?"

I chuckle. "You don't get out much. It's like you forgot I'm the town bad boy."

"You like to stir up trouble, but you're far from bad." She kisses my lips. "School will be out soon and we won't have to hide anymore. Then maybe you can meet my family one day. I could handle them better if I wasn't alone."

"Your parents are about as exciting as my dad. Your brother, on the other hand, I'd like to meet him. Sounds like he's my kind of guy."

She beams at me, her blue eyes twinkling. "Keith is great. I miss him."

"We could always get out of here this summer and go visit," I offer, stroking my fingers through her silky hair.

"I'd like that. Sometimes I wish I'd stayed back with him in Brigs Ferry Bay. It makes me wonder how my life would have turned out. I certainly wouldn't be going out on dates with sleazeballs to please my father."

"But then you'd never get to bang your student." I flash her an evil grin that earns me a smack to the arm. "Kidding sort of. On a serious note, I wouldn't have met you." Leaning forward, I kiss her forehead. "But, it's not too late to go back."

"What about you?"

"What about me?" I smirk at her. "I'm following your ass out there."

"Promise?"

"Sure do, Miss B. Now bend over that sink and let me fuck you nice and sweet to give you something to smile about over your dinner from hell."

She rolls her eyes at me, but obeys, turning and lifting her dress over her ass. I give it a playful smack.

"Good girl."

※※※

I STEP INTO THE CAVERNOUS FOYER OF MY HOME AND LISTEN FOR SOUNDS of my father. It's Sunday, which means since he can't be in the office working, he'll be in the one at home. I weave my way through the house until I reach his doorway. His voice is deep and commanding in his fierce Felix-Mullins-who-doesn't-take-shit tone as he puts someone—probably his poor assistant—in their place over the phone. With a frustrated growl, he ends the call.

My knuckles rap at the door three times before I push through, entering the imposing space. Dad is so career oriented and focused on his goals. His office always intimidated me growing up. I felt like he had plans for me that I'd never measure up to.

"What's wrong?" I ask, sauntering into his space and taking the seat in an armchair nearby.

Dad swivels in his desk chair to scowl at me. "What?"

"You're mad, and for once, it's not at me."

His expression softens slightly. "I'm not mad at you. In fact, your grades this term have been impressive. I see you're walking without a limp too."

I sit a little straighter in my seat. "Coach Long has been working with me. Reconditioning me. It's…nice."

"Have you thought about which college you're attending?" His sharp green eyes laser into me, making me squirm.

I seriously wish we could spend five minutes without discussing my future.

"I'm not sure, Dad," I mutter, a drastic change from my usual smartass response. "There are things I want to do, but nothing that college seems helpful for."

Rather than snapping at me, he frowns harder, as though he's trying to understand my inner workings. "Like what?"

I blink at him, confused. Since when does he consider anything but college?

"I'd have to tap into my trust fund," I state, pushing him because it's in my nature.

He doesn't bite this time.

"Sounds like an investment. Explain."

"You're busy—"

"It's Sunday, Son, and you've been absent all week. Excuse me if I'd like to ignore work to focus on my boy."

Since when?

His career is usually his pride and joy. However, lately, I must admit it doesn't seem to bring him the happiness it once did.

I arch a brow at him in shock. "You'll probably hate it."

"Probably. I still want to hear it."

Glancing over at the clock on the wall, I note that I still have time. Kerry won't be back at her apartment until closer to eight she guessed.

"Do you remember when I was in the sixth grade and I went through my skateboarding phase?"

Ever since Kerry and I got together, I really did some soul searching, because despite my resistance to commit to a career or college, it's weighed heavily on my mind.

His green eyes twinkle and he laughs. "Your hair was atrocious."

I playfully scoff. "It was awesome, Dad. Admit it."

"Hell no," he says, shaking his head. "I was so glad you got the hots for that cheerleader and cut it off to impress her."

"Yeah, yeah," I grumble. "Laugh it up, old man."

We're both smiling. It takes me a minute to realize we haven't done this in a while. I blamed my dad for a lot, but I wasn't exactly easy to get along with. After hearing stories upon stories from Kerry about her controlling, asshole father, it makes me appreciate mine a little more.

"So, let's hear it," he says, smoothing out his tie. "And then I want to hear about her."

I stiffen, my features hardening. "Who?"

"The girl. You're in love, Zane. I just wonder when I'll get to meet her."

There's no way in hell my dad will be cool with me sleeping with my guidance counselor.

"Her name's Kerry," I admit, leaving out her job title. "She's beautiful and funny and sweet."

"Careful," he warns. "You're young."

"Not every woman is like Mom." I pin him with a hard stare. "Kerry is different."

Guilt morphs his features. "It's not her fault. I'm the one who had the affair."

"She abandoned me, Dad. If we're comparing crimes, hers wins as the most heinous by a longshot."

He nods slowly, vulnerability shining in his gaze. Right now, I'm reminded of the man who singlehandedly was the tooth fairy, Santa Claus, birthday party coordinator, sports dad, and filled a million other roles. When I broke my leg playing basketball, I broke my spirit too. And I took it out on my father. He and I have butted heads ever since, but he's always been there for me. Always.

"Tell me about the skateboards," Dad urges, his voice going back to business mode.

I bite back a chuckle. "Not the skateboards, but the logos. Remember I designed the cool as hell skull wearing a halo and hand stamped it on everything I owned?"

"Skalo. Yes, I remember. Even the back window of my Porsche." He gives me an annoyed smirk. "It looked ridiculous."

"Yeah, on your lawyer dadmobile, but the logo itself was cool."

"It was eye-catching and you put it everywhere. All those damn kids at your school started buying your shit."

"Merch, Dad. It's called merch."

He rolls his eyes, reminding me of when I was a young boy. "Right. Merch. You were hustling for a while there until your principal shut that shit down."

"Mrs. Langford was such a bitch." I chuckle. "Anyway, I want to own my own shop one day. Design graphics for apparel and all sorts of cool shit. I know you think it's dumb—"

"I don't think it's dumb," Dad barks out. "In case you forgot, I funded every single one of your endeavors."

He did.

Guilt weighs heavily on me.

"It's going to require startup capital," Dad says, a frown marring his face. "Probably more than what you should access your trust fund for."

"But, Dad—"

"Which is why I'll allow you to take out half of what you need. You can borrow the rest from me." He crosses his arms over his chest. "If it's profitable and you're serious about it, we can renegotiate your loan and consider it a gift later."

I gape at him. "That's risky."

"Having kids is risky. You'll understand one day."

I glance at the clock again, fighting a smile. "You're for real? You'll let me do this?"

"You're eighteen years old, Zane. I believe my letting you do anything is irrelevant. We both know you'll do what you want. I'm just happy you're showing an interest in something. It's all I want for you."

"I'm sorry," I blurt out. "For being such a dick."

He grins, shaving years off his age. "Apology accepted. Do you have time to grab dinner with your pops?"

"I can make time."

For the first time in years, I feel like I have my dad back.

Based on the genuine smile on his face, maybe he feels the same way about having his son back too.

CHAPTER SEVEN

KERRY

I ALREADY MISS HIM.

My hands tremble as I stare up at my parents' stately home through my windshield. I do this every week. Why the sudden bout of nerves?

I know why, though.

I'm changing and Daddy hates change.

Ever since I took the leap to be with Zane, I have felt as though I could breathe. Like the woman inside me is stretching her limbs and realizing she has the freedom to not just move around, but to run free. It's both exhilarating and terrifying all at once. Daddy doesn't like for a woman to think for herself. I've witnessed that firsthand with Mom.

I'm not like Mom.

If I stand up to Dad, I never will be.

I know this means, eventually, I'll be forced to put some distance between myself and my parents. I can't tell him about Zane, at least not yet, because that's what he'll make it about. No, I need to tell him about Sean, that I want him to stay out of my dating life, and that I am a successful, worthy woman who's tired of him insinuating otherwise.

With a deep, calming breath, I attempt to silence the doubts running rampant through my mind. Once the air is exhaled, I climb out of my car and head toward the front door. With each step, the confidence to go against my father begins to rise like the swelling sea. Zane's handsome face is forefront in my mind—smiling, encouraging me, kissing me. I'm raising my hand to open the door when a car pulls into the driveway.

The front door opens as I try to peek at who the visitor could be. A familiar man steps out of the car as Daddy's strong hand clutches my shoulder, squeezing.

"So glad you made it, sweetheart. And look, our guest has arrived at the same time." Daddy chuckles when I suck in a sharp breath. "Don't worry. This isn't a date. He and I actually have business to attend to."

Sean's predatory smile reaches me as he joins us on the porch. Daddy releases his grasp on me to shake hands with the man who drugged me this week. I shoot daggers Sean's way. Rather than being put off, he flashes me a cocky grin and winks.

Asshole!

"Daddy, I—"

"Sweetheart, why don't you go on inside and say hello to your mother. I'm sure she's already opened the wine. You could use a drink." Daddy ushers Sean into his office, leaving me alone in the foyer, trembling.

I should leave.

Turn on my heel and go.

Fumbling for my purse, I grab my phone out to call Zane. I realize I've missed a text from him.

Z: I can't wait to tell you about tonight. Dad is being cool. We decided to grab dinner. Call me when you finish up and I'll meet you at your place.

He's having dinner with his dad.

The same dad who he's struggled with having a relationship with for years. This is important and fragile. The last thing he needs is me asking him to come play hero. My eyes burn with tears as I type out that I'm happy for him and can't wait to see him later.

Coward.

All I have to do is tell my parents what happened with Sean. So why does it seem like I'll never get the words out?

It's just one dinner.

All I have to do is make it through one dinner.

***

"MORE?" SEAN ASKS, HOLDING THE WINE BOTTLE UP LIKE AN OFFERING.

I shoot him an icy glare. "Nope."

"Kerry," Daddy admonishes. "Mind your manners."

Mom's face is plastered in the same fake, uncomfortable smile she gets sometimes when a situation gets awkward. I feel sorry for her. Did she ever have dreams before Daddy? Would Brigs Ferry Bay have been good to her if she'd met someone else? Who knows how her life would have turned out.

"Who wants dessert?" Mom asks, her voice shrill.

"That's a great idea, Darla," Daddy says. "Sean, do you mind helping her while I have a chat with Kerry?"

I wither at the stern expression on Daddy's face. I'm disappointing him again. It's the story of my life. I'll never be the poised, polished daughter he wants me to be. Mom and Sean leave the dining room so Daddy and I can have our private conversation.

"What the hell has gotten into you, Kerry? You're being a bitch to our guest," Daddy snarls.

I recoil at his words, gaping at him in horror as tears quickly form. "I…Daddy—"

"Quit your blubbering," he hisses. "Sean is well connected in this town. I need him for my campaign." He scowls at me. "All I ask is for you to be polite to our guest and you can't even do that. For the record, sweetheart, he's a catch you'd be lucky to have. The man comes from old money. You'd be set. Your children—"

"Stop," I choke out. "Just stop. He's…He's not the man you think he is."

Daddy's eyes narrow. "I've looked into him. His family is impeccable. You know how important it is to keep good company around me while campaigning. No blips or anything on his record."

"It's just—"

Daddy cuts me off with a wave of his hand when they reenter the dining room. "Enough. We'll discuss it later."

I'm dismissed as he begins chatting up Sean. I swallow down my emotion, fighting tears. All I need to do is get through the rest of this dinner. Then I can get back to the man who appreciates and cares for me.

I've just polished off my dessert when I feel it.

The slight twist of the world around me.

No.

Not again.

Gripping the table, I drag my stare over to Sean. His eyes flash in a wicked way, but his smile for my father never falters.

"I don't feel so well," I slur out, closing my eyes to keep the spinning at bay.

Sean is out of his seat in an instant, his hands on my shoulders rubbing. "Everything okay, Kerry? Are you sick again?"

I try to wriggle out of his grasp, but it makes the sensation worse. All I can do is keep my eyes clamped shut.

"Too much wine?" Mom asks, her voice tight.

I attempt to speak, but the bile in my throat won't let me.

"I didn't want to say anything," Sean murmurs. "But she drank a lot on our date, too. Is this a normal thing for her?"

Hot tears leak from my eyes, racing down my cheeks. Daddy stumbles all over his words, making excuses for me. I don't hear any of them. It isn't until I feel someone lifting me out of the chair that I open my eyes.

"Don't worry, sir, I'll make sure she gets home safely. You can check in on her in the morning."

I open my eyes long enough to lock my gaze onto Daddy. His face is red from embarrassment and his blue eyes flash with fury. At me. My hands feel as though they're weighed down by sand. I attempt to open my purse to locate my phone, but am unsuccessful. Daddy opens the passenger side door for Sean.

"We'll come by in the morning, sweetheart, with your car," Daddy says through gritted teeth. "Perhaps we can try this another day without the wine."

Sean chuckles, turning my blood to ice water. "Everyone has their down days, sir. She just needs a little guidance. I don't mind helping her."

"You're a saint," Daddy praises.

Once inside Sean's car that smells like him, I fall asleep. It isn't until he's carrying me again that my eyes crack open. I clutch onto my purse and hope like hell he leaves me in my apartment and goes home.

That's delusional.

He wouldn't drug me to leave me be unless this was some sort of power play.

Somehow, he finds my apartment without my having to tell him which one. It sends another quiver of nerves trembling through me. I never heard Daddy mention where I lived, which means he found out on his own.

He's a creep.

Probably a stalker too.

I need to get a hold of Zane.

Fresh tears form as I think of his gorgeous face. The intensity that always rolls off him in scorching waves. He's strong and smart and sweet. Zane is someone I always imagined myself to be happy with, not whatever horrible men Daddy has been scooping out of the filth for me like Sean.

I'm dazed as Sean unlocks my apartment. It's not my key ring. Did Daddy give him his keys? The room spins again, making me dry heave.

"Don't be getting sick on me, sweetheart," Sean says, his voice dripping with malice. "We have the whole night ahead of us."

"Wh-Wha d-di you giff to may." My words are slurred and make no sense.

He sets me down on my bed that still smells like Zane. "I call it the wife maker. Gave you a little more than last time, though, since it didn't quite do the trick then."

I dry heave again, and then again when he laughs.

"It'll make you compliant. You have all the right components, Kerry. Sexy, intelligent, successful. But you're just a bit too reckless for my liking. If I'm going to settle down, I expect it to be with a woman I can trust to behave as I've taught her."

"Water," I croak.

He studies me for a beat. "Sure, sweetheart. I'll get you some water. Let's get you out of these clothes first."

I whimper as he pushes my dress up my thighs. Disgust ripples through me when he grabs hold of my panties and peels them off my body, exposing me to him. His knuckle runs down my slit and he grins at me.

"Your father won't be pleased if I get you pregnant out of wedlock, but it'll ensure a quick wedding, which is for the best."

He's gentle as he removes my dress and bra. I'm useless to fight against him. Once I'm completely naked, he runs his nose between my breasts, inhaling me.

"You'll learn, sweetheart, that if you comply, you'll be rewarded." His lips twist into a vicious grin. "Understand?"

"W-Water," I croak again.

His lips purse together, a flash of annoyance crossing over his features. "Fine. I'll get you some water so you don't puke, but then you're going to behave and let the inevitable happen."

A tear leaks out of my eye, but I find the strength to nod. As soon as he storms from the room, I put all my energy into grabbing for my phone that's in my purse on the bed beside me. I manage to pull it from the bag and get it opened. I'm not sure I can type, so I hit the microphone button on the text.

"S-Sean. Partment. Drurgsh. Halp." It takes my finger two mashes before it sends.

Heavy footsteps thud my way. A tremble in my hand has me dropping the phone back into my purse.

Please, Zane, hurry.
I can't do this.
I need you.

CHAPTER EIGHT
ZANE

"SO?" DAD ASKS, A SMILE TUGGING AT HIS LIPS. "TELL ME MORE ABOUT THIS girl, Kerry."

Woman.

Not a girl.

"She's great." I shrug, unable to meet his eyes. "Really great."

"What is it? Is she underage?"

I nearly choke on my drink. "W-What? No, Dad. She's legal."

Relief floods through him. "But?"

"But it could get messy if the wrong people found out."

His eyes narrow. "Please tell me you're not fucking a married woman."

"Not that you have any room to judge, but no," I growl, pinning him with a hard stare. "She's single."

Dad, a damn good lawyer, starts connecting dots far too quickly for my liking. "What did you say Kerry's last name was?"

"I didn't," I clip out.

"Zane."

I lift my gaze, trying not to wither under Dad's furious one. "Bowden."

Confusion mars his features as he runs the name through his mind. I can tell the moment he realizes it because his eyes widen.

"As in Miss Bowden, your damn guidance counselor, at Brown High?"

My phone buzzes as the waitress delivers our check. He hands her some cash and tells her to keep the change, before turning his stern glare my way.

"We're both consenting adults," I challenge. "It's fine."

His nostrils flare as he leans toward me. "It's not fine, Zane. I know I didn't raise you to be a damn idiot."

"I can handle it," I growl.

"Can she?" he snaps back. "Can she handle being dragged through the mud? It's her reputation that will take the hit, not yours."

Guilt infects my every pore. "We're being discreet until the end of the year."

"If anyone finds out, they will turn it into a media circus sideshow. You're my son. Not some Joe Blow who doesn't matter. They will turn this into a nightmare for everyone involved."

I rise to my feet, anger bursting up inside me. "So sorry to embarrass you, Dad. Take me back home so I can get my car. I'm not going to do this with you. I'm a grown ass man who knows what he's doing."

He curses under his breath the whole walk out to his car. I pull out my phone to check the notification I missed. A voice message. As soon as Dad sits down in the car, I listen to the message.

"S-Sean. Partment. Drurgsh. Halp."

What the fuck?

Icy dread washes over me.

"Dad," I bark out, throwing myself into the passenger seat. "Drive me to Woodmeadow Apartments. Hurry!"

He doesn't question my alarm, but instead peels out, hauling ass out of the parking lot. I try to dial Kerry back to no avail.

"Fuck!" I roar, slamming my hand down on the dashboard. "He has her. That motherfucker has her."

"Who?" Dad demands.

"Sean. Some lawyer asshole Kerry's dad set her up with."

Dad curses. "Sean Gentry?"

"I don't know his last name. Greasy, weasel looking rich guy."

"He's bad news," Dad growls. "He's also loaded and well connected. When we get there, let me handle it."

I can't make that promise.

As soon as he puts the vehicle into park in front of the building, I fly out of the car. I don't wait for the elevator. Instead, I take the stairs two at a time. When I reach her floor, I fling the unlocked door open and charge into her bedroom.

The sight before me is disgusting and wrong.

Sean is shirtless, groping my naked woman.

My fucking girl.

Red fills my vision as I lose myself to rage. I grab his shoulders, slinging him off her into the floor. Turning, I tackle him, pummeling him with my fists. I slam my fists into his smarmy face over and over again, the world around me a blur. I'm vaguely aware of my hands in pain and a stern voice in my ear before I'm dragged away.

So much blood.

I stare at Sean's battered face, unblinking and unperturbed. Dad tells someone to hurry and then he tosses his phone down to grab my face.

"Listen to me, Son," Dad bites out. "We were walking by and heard the commotion. You stepped in to help the woman."

"But she's my—"

"No," Dad bellows. "She's not. Not as far as anyone knows. Trust me. If that gets out, all of this becomes worse. You have to trust me."

"Is she okay?" I croak out.

"She will be. Just sit tight and do whatever Sheriff McMahon asks you to."

All I want to do is take care of Kerry, but the severity in Dad's tone tells me we're walking a thin line here and one error could have everything blowing up in my face.

TWO DAYS LATER...

"MULLINS," SHERIFF MCMAHON GRUNTS. "YOUR DAD IS HERE. LET'S GET YOU to the interview room."

He unlocks the cell door and guides me to another room where my dad waits, dressed sharply in a three-piece suit. His expression is cool and unreadable. I know, from experience, it's for the benefit of the other person. It's clear he wants to keep his emotions in check until Sheriff leaves the room. As soon as Sheriff is gone, Dad sits down at the table in front of me.

"Kerry?" I ask, pain slicing through me.

"She's been thoroughly checked at the hospital and was released yesterday. I can't represent her, because I have you to think about, but I called a buddy of mine, Dane. He specializes in divorce law, but he can handle this case just fine."

"Is Sean going to jail too?"

"Dane and I are doing our best to make sure that happens."

"But?"

"But…" He sighs. "Kerry's father is representing him."

"What?" I snarl. "How could he do that to his own daughter?"

"He believes Sean is only guilty of taking care of his daughter who was inebriated. Sean is denying that he drugged her and that their sexual acts were consented upon. They did a rape kit at the hospital, but he hadn't had the opportunity to have sex with her yet, so it's a lot of he said she said at this point."

I pinch the bridge of my nose. "He drugged her, Dad."

"Toxicology proves she had traces of drugs in her system, yes," Dad agrees, "but there's no proof that he gave them to her. Currently, they have the story spun that Kerry is troubled and is lashing out at her father through Sean."

"Unbelievable."

"That's not the bad part."

My eyes lift to meet his. "How could it get much worse than that?"

"They know you weren't just passing by. Sean remembers seeing you with Kerry. He claims you were having a sexual relationship with her and are a jealous ex-boyfriend who wanted to hurt him for dating her."

"Fuck."

Dad nods, frowning. "And because you're my son, they're like wolves, ready to destroy me."

"What do we do?"

"If either of you admits you were in a relationship, then the story points back to Kerry. It'll become that she's a predator who lured her student into her bed. It'll prove their case that she's troubled and it'll be a slam dunk. I can get you out of the fire, but it's at her expense."

"What about Sean?"

"If the story turns on Kerry, he'll never get the justice he deserves."

"But if I quietly take my punishment, she remains the victim?"

"Yes," Dad says with a heavy sigh. "I will unearth every piece of evidence against Sean Gentry to put in her arsenal. By the time I'm done with him, he'll be doing hard time. Not just eight to fifteen months in County."

His words are a punch to the gut. "Eight to fifteen months?"

"I'm sorry," Dad mutters, "but you beat the shit out of Sean. It's assault and battery no matter how we twist it. At the end of the day, you fucked him up and they'll want to see you pay for it."

"This will ruin your political career," I state, unable to look at him. "Me doing time."

"Fuck my career," Dad snarls. "I care about you. And this woman, because you care about her, means I care too. I'm putting my family first for once. Hell, I should have done it years ago."

I sit up in my chair, pinning my dad with a firm stare. "Okay. I'll plead guilty and deny any relationship with Kerry if that's what it'll take to help her case against that motherfucker."

Dad pats my hand. Pride shines in his green eyes.

We can do this.

If it means I can protect Kerry and help her finally get out from under her father's paw, I'll do it. I can afford a year of my life. What I can't afford is hers being unfairly ruined. If she cares about me the way I care about her, she'll be waiting for me on the other side of it. And if not, it's still the right thing to do.

Sean will pay.

Even if it means I have to pay too.

CHAPTER NINE
KERRY
TWO MONTHS LATER

TEN MONTHS.

They sentenced Zane Mullins to ten months in County for trying to protect me. I'm going to be sick. It's unfair and disgusting. Sean Gentry wears a smug grin on his face as my own father congratulates him.

"We knew this would happen," Felix murmurs to me as the judge continues to speak. "It's the only way. We're lucky Judge Rowe was on the case. Any other judge would have let your father trample all over them. Rowe gave Zane the best sentence we could ask for."

I nod, swiping a rogue tear from my cheek. "They're so happy he's going to jail."

Felix pulls a handkerchief from his pocket, handing it to me. "For now. We'll get our day in court with Sean and your father, and when we do, I will destroy Gentry. His sentence will be much worse. Trust me?"

"Yes," I whisper. "I'm sorry about your son. It's all my fault."

Felix shakes his head. "My kid is tough. He can handle this. We'll be there for him when he gets out. This was the only solution. If not, your name would be all over every news headline from coast to coast. They would have shredded your life."

It feels selfish and wrong.

"How could Dad even defend that monster?" I glower at my father.

"They're the same, Kerry. It'll do you some good to break free from them."

I know he's right. It's the same thing Zane always says to me. The same thing my brother says when we speak on the phone.

"I don't want to leave Zane," I mutter. "I should stay here in case—"

The courtroom erupts into a dull roar of voices as we're dismissed. My eyes find Zane. He's wearing a suit that's a little snug on his muscular frame. His attorney, Dane, clasps his shoulder and nods at him. They share a small smile. Then, as though he can feel my stare on him, Zane's intense green eyes bore into me. Not long enough for me to get lost in, because we're still hiding our relationship, but enough that I feel him inside every vein and muscle.

"Go," he mouths.

To Brigs Ferry Bay.

We've only corresponded through letters passed through Felix, but I know what he means. He wants me to leave this hell hole town and go back to where my brother lives. Where it's safe. Where I can be free.

"I'll miss you," I mouth back.

He winks, heating my blood. It's the kind of wink that promises he'll come find me when he's able to. They usher him away seconds later. I stand and follow Felix out of the courtroom, leaving my heart with the selfless man who owns it anyway. My father starts my way, but Felix stands in front of me, rippling with authority.

"You're not allowed to speak with my client," Felix spits out. "And I suggest you tell your client to obey his restraining order."

Sean's face turns purple with anger and he storms away. Daddy's eyes narrow on me before he shakes his head in disgust, stalking off after Sean.

I thought I might feel pain from having my father choose Sean over me, but all I feel is relief. Zane helped me unload the weights my father put on my shoulders and encouraged me to run free. I'm not tied down anymore, so I can do just that.

But...

Another roil of sickness churns in my gut. I wanted to tell Zane about the positive pregnancy test, but I couldn't bear for him to have to live with that agony while locked away. It'll be his surprise when he gets out.

"Everything okay?" Felix asks.

"It will be. Just help me bring Sean down first."

SEVEN MONTHS LATER

IT'S RAINING CATS AND DOGS. A WINTER STORM WAS SUPPOSED TO HIT, BUT at the last moment, it turned before it hit Beacon Island and went south. We caught all the rain and some strong winds, but no snow yet.

I rub my palm over my swollen belly, a smile gracing my lips. "Three more months and Daddy will be here to see you."

My brother's new girlfriend, Brie Larsen, and Brigs Ferry Bay's deputy pokes her head into the kitchen dressed in a uniform for work. "Who are you talking to?"

"Emily." I smile at her. "You're up early. After all the noise you and Keith made, I was certain neither one of you would get up this morning."

Her face burns crimson, but then she grins at me. "Who said I ever went to sleep?"

"Gag," I tease.

She starts a pot of coffee and crosses her arms over her chest. "How are you feeling?"

"Big," I say with a laugh. "And melancholy."

Her features soften. "It won't be long now, Ker. Then you and your baby daddy will be reunited." She grimaces. "Are you sure you don't want to tell him about Emily? Prepare him a little?"

I think about all the heartfelt letters Zane has sent me. Ones that went from infatuation to full-on love. He's dedicated to me and our future. Telling him about Emily is cruel. I know Zane. He'll worry himself to death over it, letting the guilt turn him inside out. It's better this way. When he gets here, he'll get to meet her and fall instantly in love. I know it.

"Zane will understand. If I tell him now, it'll just make him worry. Keith is taking care of me and my new job at the library is great. Me and Ems have this. We'll be ready for Daddy when he gets here."

She pours a cup of coffee and joins me at the kitchen table. "Is Felix still coming to visit this weekend with the weather being a bitch?"

"He has to. We have some paperwork to go over and sign."

"How does he feel about being a grandpa?"

I groan. "He's just as bad as Zane. I swear if he buys one more outfit for Emily, I'll never have to do laundry. She can wear a new outfit each day until her eighteenth birthday."

"That's kind of sweet," Brie says, chuckling.

"Someone call for me?" Keith grunts, sauntering shirtless into the kitchen.

Brie seems to melt at the sight of him. I'm happy for them, even if they do gross me out a bit sometimes.

"You're not sweet," Brie sasses.

He steps behind her, wrapping his muscular arms around her and kissing the top of her head. "Not what you said three hours ago, baby."

"Anyway," I say in a shrill tone. "Enough of that."

Keith barks out a laugh. "I sure missed my prissy sister."

I flip him off, earning a giggle from Brie.

"You two gonna drop by and see me tonight on my shift? I'm working at Focus. Water for preggo over there and the best wine on Beacon Island for my girl."

Again, she melts at his words.

I let my gaze drift back to the window that faces the sea. With all the rain and gloom, you can barely see the ocean, but I know it's there. I feel such a sense of peace here at Brigs Ferry Bay. This will be our home. And after today when we make it official, Felix will join us.

I can hear the smacking and groaning of Keith and Brie making out. As much as I love their blossoming romance, it'll be nice to get my own place. Felix found the cutest apartment on Main Street that sits above some retail space for Zane and me. When Zane gets out, it'll be perfect for his shop and there's room for Felix to office as well. Everything is coming together.

The best part is, Sean is in prison.

It took a lot of work, but we managed to build a case against him. Once we went public with it, many other women stepped forward with stories of their own. With their testimonies and mine, we were able to stack the charges on him. When I told the authorities about him already knowing my apartment number and having a key, coupled with how other women were speaking out, they had enough to get the proper warrants to search his belongings and home. And what they found was damning. This time, Judge Rowe wasn't at all lenient on the charges. Sean Gentry will be spending the next fifteen years in prison. It would have been longer, but he admitted his guilt and motives in exchange for a lesser sentence. All he wanted was to marry into a wealthy, successful family since his own family's money had run dry.

A sharp pain lances through me, making me groan. They'd been happening off and on all morning, but I'd thought it was nerves. Emily isn't due for a couple more weeks. Before I can recover from that one, another one rips down my spine, wrapping a painful claw around my belly.

"Owww," I hiss. "I think—"

My words are cut off by the gush of warmth that floods out of me, soaking through my cotton pants.

"Keith," I cry out. "I think the baby is coming."

"YOU READY TO HAVE THIS BABY?" DR. MILLER ASKS, A SMILE ON HIS HANDSOME face.

He's not my doctor, though. Where is Dr. Hutchens?

"I can wait until my doctor gets here," I grit through clenched teeth.

Keith barks out a laugh. "Lance has delivered babies before," my brother assures me. "He's a hospitalist who does it all. Basically, a jack of all trades. Don't worry."

I am worried, though.

This hurts and I wish Zane were here.

My emotions win over me and I burst into tears.

"It's okay," Dr. Miller croons. "Don't cry. Right now I need you to be brave and start pushing. She's ready to come out."

"Where's Felix?" I hiss to my brother. "He should be here!"

"Something important came up," Keith says, his face splitting into a wide grin.

"More important than the birth of his grandchild?" I shriek. "Tell him to get in here now!"

"Can't, sis," Keith replies, a smirk on his face. "Only two family members at a time. I think dads trump grandpas."

I snap my head up to glower at him. "What?"

"It means, little momma, you're going to have to settle for having me in here."

Zane's voice soothes all the battered parts inside me, mending every painful moment away from him. Slowly, I turn my head to find the man I've ached for standing in the room, grinning at me. Somehow, in the course of several months, he's grown more handsome. Stronger, broader, wiser. Mine.

"I'm sorry I didn't tell you about her," I choke out, my hand stretching out for him.

He stalks over to me, cups my cheeks, and kisses me until I'm dizzy. Another jolt of pain hits me, ending the sweet reunion.

"Time to push, Kerry," Dr. Miller says. "No more stalling."

Zane grips my hand, grinning at me. "Come on, Miss B, you've got this. I'm ready to meet my baby girl."

The pushing goes on for what feels like hours, but when Dr. Miller finally deposits the beautiful, messy baby on my chest, the world blurs around the three of us.

"You got out early," I murmur as I admire the gorgeous infant that looks just like her father.

"Good behavior, baby." He brushes his thumb along her dark hair. "She's perfect."

Hot tears stream down my face as I press a kiss to her forehead. Then I turn and accept a kiss from Zane.

"I missed you so much," I choke out. "I know I told you in our letters, but I need you to hear it. I love you, Zane Mullins."

"Love you too, beautiful."

EPILOGUE

ZANE
LATE SUMMER

"MOMMY IS OBSESSED WITH THAT STORE," I TELL EMILY, HOLDING HER TO MY chest and pointing through the window of Granger Home Décor. "She's trying to make the dining room fancy now."

Emily smiles and drool runs down her chin. Fuck, this kid is so damn cute. I told Kerry we need to make ten just like her. She wasn't keen on the idea of having ten, but promised me more one day.

Addison Granger catches my stare from inside and waves me in. Emily and I step inside the shop. Kerry is at the register while Addison's sister, Adeline, bags her purchases.

"She's getting so big," Addison croons. "Pretty soon she'll be crawling all over the place!" Then she leans in and says, "How's Felix?"

I smirk at her. They think they're discreet, but Kerry and I busted them having dinner earlier this week.

"I think you would know more than me," I tease, enjoying the way her cheeks blush.

"Go away, rascal." She leans in and kisses Emily's head. "Take care of my girl."

I chuckle and leave her be as I make it over to Kerry. She looks fantastic this afternoon in a pair of white shorts and a pale blue halter top. Her legs are tanned and hot as fuck today. Thank God Dad has offered to babysit Emily tonight. I'm dying to have some alone time with my wife.

"Ready, Mrs. M?"

Kerry grins at me. "I am now."

She coos at Emily and our daughter giggles with delight. Kerry was made to be a mother. Since I didn't have my own mother around, I missed out on what a good mother would look like. Kerry is not just good, she's the best. Emily adores her.

"I booked us a room at Red Hake B&B," I tell her as we walk out of the shop. "I figured if I'm going to spend the night ravishing you and trying to make another baby, we should do it in style overlooking Wolffish Bay."

"Another baby already?" she teases. "You're certain we'll make one tonight?"

I grab a handful of her cute ass with my free hand. "I made Emily on the first shot."

She stops to look at me, a silly smile on her gorgeous face. Since we were married not a month after I got released and moved out here, I see those smiles all the time. It's incredible how much this woman has transformed from the scared, timid thing who was afraid to disappoint her father into this carefree, happy wife of mine. It pleases me to no end.

"You haven't worn a condom most of the times we've had sex, Zane," she sasses, her brow arching up.

"Those other times were just practice." I wink at her.

She shakes her head as she rummages around in her purse. When she pulls out a sack from Reyes Pharmacy, I frown at her. Inside is a pregnancy test. "I don't think you need to practice. You're that good."

I pull her to me for a hug, making Emily squawk between us. "You really think so?"

Kerry tilts her head up, her blue eyes shining with tears. "I don't know for sure, but I did miss my period a few days ago. I didn't want to take the test without you. This time, I want you to be there every step of the way, even if it turns out we're not pregnant again."

I capture her lips with mine. "I'll be beside you from now until the end, beautiful."

"You promise?"

"I promised you I'd take care of you, didn't I? After all we've been through, I'm still here. You're my wife and we run a pretty successful apparel shop together. Have I let you down yet?"

"Never," she whispers. "You're the best thing that's ever happened to me."

Emily whines in protest, making us both laugh.

"Will you settle for second best thing?" Kerry teases.

"Lose to this cutie? You bet, little momma." I kiss Emily's dark head and then point up Main Street to our storefront, Skalo. "Want to go see Grandpa, Emmers?"

She babbles and squirms. I'll take that as a yes.

"Let's get this little one dropped off to Grandpa and get checked into Red Hake B&B," I tell Kerry as I wrap my free arm over her shoulders and inhale her floral scent. "We'll do the pregnancy test in the morning. That way, beautiful, we can spend the entire night trying to make a baby." I nip at her ear. "I might even put it in your ass if you're a good girl."

"Mr. Mullins!" she shrieks, shooting me a wide-eyed stare as her cheeks burn bright pink.

I chuckle, letting my palm slide to her ass and giving it a hard squeeze. "Maybe tonight I'll let you be Miss B and I'll be your naughty student."

"You're horrible," she groans. "The absolute worst."

"And you love me. What does that make you?"

"Apparently that makes me yours."

"Damn straight."

THE END.

If you enjoyed this Taboo Treat, *Miss B*, you can check out Principal Renner's story in *Renner's Rules* and if you're curious about the small, seaside Maine town of Brigs Ferry Bay mentioned at the end, make sure to read *Sheriff's Secret*!

You'll get to read about Kerry's doctor, Lance Miller, in this anthology in Misty Walker's story called *Doctor Daddy*!

Made in the USA
Coppell, TX
12 June 2021